PUFFIN BOOKS

The Earthsea Quartet

Ursula Le Guin was born in 1929 in Berkeley, California, daughter of the anthropologist Alfred Kroeber and the writer Theodora Kroeber. After attending Radcliffe College and Columbia University, she married the historian Charles A. Le Guin in 1953; they have lived in Portland, Oregon since 1958.

Ursula Le Guin writes poetry and realistic fiction, science fiction, fantasy, young children's books, books for young adults, screenplays, essays, and voice-texts for performance. Among the honours her writing has received are a National Book Award, five Hugo and four Nebula Awards, the Kafka Award, a Pushcart Prize and a Newbery Honor Medal. She has taught writing in the United States, England, and Australia and holds several honorary doctorates.

Her most famous work of fantasy is the *Earthsea* quartet. The books have been translated into many languages around the world.

Ursula Le Guin

THE EARTHSEA QUARTET

PENGUIN BOOKS

PENGUIN BOOKS

Published by the Penguin Group
Penguin Books Ltd, 80 Strand, London WC2R 0RL, England
Penguin Putnam Inc., 375 Hudson Street, New York, New York 10014, USA
Penguin Books Australia Ltd, 250 Camberwell Road, Camberwell, Victoria 3124, Australia
Penguin Books Canada Ltd, 10 Alcorn Avenue, Toronto, Ontario, Canada M4V 3B2
Penguin Books India (P) Ltd, 11 Community Centre, Panchsheel Park, New Delhi – 110 017, India
Penguin Books (NZ) Ltd, Cnr Rosedale and Airborne Roads, Albany, Auckland, New Zealand
Penguin Books (South Africa) (Pty) Ltd, 24 Sturdee Avenue, Rosebank 2196, South Africa

Penguin Books Ltd, Registered Offices: 80 Strand, London WC2R 0RL, England

www.penguin.com

Contents

THE WHALE ILES

North Reach

CHEMISH

KOMOKOME
SORT

N. ENWAS

BERESWEK
S. ENWAS

THE ALLERNOTS

FERRINS

THE ANDRADES

N. TEETH

The Jaws
1 TEETH
ANDRAD
SORANDRAD

HUR-
AT-HUR

The Kargad Lands

PERREGAL

CARHIRIEN
CONT
The Albi
East Port
KAMEBER
Coat Port

ORANÉA
Gontish
Sea

EBÉA
SPEVY

ATNINI

KAREGO-AT

BARNISK
ATUAN

TORHEVEN

ESKEL

THE TORIKLES

Havnor
Great Port

THE HANDS

WAY
OTRAD

VEMISH
SATTINS
Mishoy

Kambersund

FELKWAY

VENWAY
YOR
SNEG

Felkway Bay

WAYMARSH
IFFISH

EN
PERILANE
Ismay

FAR TOLY

Ostoke
OUTER
ENNRAN
TOK
KOPPISH

LENC
BAIS OF UNY
INSMER

RY
HOLP

The Cloud
KORP
KOPP

UNY
APSO
SODERS

The East Reach

NAMIEN
ROLAMENY
CALE
PELIMER

DUNNEL
COSK

KORNAY

ASTOWELL

WASNY

A Scale of Miles

25 50   100 150 200   300

SOUTH SHOALS

THE ISLE
OF THE EAR

A WIZARD OF EARTHSEA

TO MY BROTHERS

CLIFTON, TED, KARL

Only in silence the word,
only in dark the light,
only in dying life :
bright the hawk's flight
on the empty sky.

— *The Creation of Éa*

1. Warriors in the Mist

THE island of Gont, a single mountain that lifts its peak a mile above the storm-racked Northeast Sea, is a land famous for wizards. From the towns in its high valleys and the ports on its dark narrow bays many a Gontishman has gone forth to serve the Lords of the Archipelago in their cities as wizard or mage, or, looking for adventure, to wander working magic from isle to isle of all Earthsea.

Of these some say the greatest, and surely the greatest voyager, was the man called Sparrowhawk, who in his day became both dragonlord and Archmage. His life is told of in the *Deed of Ged* and in many songs, but this is a tale of the time before his fame, before the songs were made.

He was born in a lonely village called Ten Alders, high on the mountain at the head of the Northward Vale. Below the village the pastures and ploughlands of the Vale slope downward level below level towards the sea, and other towns lie on the bends of the River Ar; above the village only forest rises ridge behind ridge to the stone and snow of the heights.

The name he bore as a child, Duny, was given him by his mother, and that and his life were all she could give him, for she died before he was a year old. His father, the bronze-smith of the village, was a grim unspeaking man, and since Duny's six brothers were older than he by many years and went one by one from home to farm the land or sail the sea or work as smith in other towns of the Northward Vale, there was no one to bring the child up in tenderness.

He grew wild, a thriving weed, a tall, quick boy, loud and proud and full of temper. With the few other children of the village he herded goats on the steep meadows above the river-springs; and when he was strong enough to push and pull the long bellows-sleeves, his father made him work as smith's boy, at a high cost in blows and whippings.

There was not much work to be got out of Duny. He was always off and away; roaming deep in the forest, swimming in the pools of the River Ar that like all Gontish rivers ran very quick and cold, or climbing by cliff and scarp to the heights above the forest, from which he could see the sea, that broad northern ocean where, past Perregal, no islands are.

A sister of his dead mother lived in the village. She had done what was needful for him as a baby, but she had business of her own and once he could look after himself at all she paid no more heed to him. But one day when the boy was seven years old, untaught and knowing nothing of the arts and powers that are in the world, he heard his aunt crying out words to a goat which had jumped up on to the thatch of a hut and would not come down : but it came jumping when she cried a certain rhyme to it.

Next day herding the longhaired goats on the meadows of High Fall, Duny shouted to them the words he had heard, not knowing their use or meaning or what kind of words they were:

> *Noth hierth malk man*
> *hiolk han merth han!*

He yelled the rhyme aloud, and the goats came to him. They came very quickly, all of them together, not making any sound. They looked at him out of the dark slot in their yellow eyes.

Duny laughed and shouted it out again, the rhyme that gave him power over the goats. They came closer, crowding and pushing round him.

All at once he felt afraid of their thick, ridged horns and their strange eyes and their strange silence. He tried to get free of them and to run away. The goats ran with him keeping in a knot around him, and so they came charging down into the village at last, all the goats going huddled together as if a rope were pulled tight round them, and the boy in the midst of them weeping and bellowing. Villagers ran from their houses to swear at the goats and laugh at the boy. Among them came the boy's aunt, who did not laugh. She said a word to the goats, and the beasts began to bleat and browse and wander, freed from the spell.

'Come with me,' she said to Duny.

She took him into her hut where she lived alone. She let no child enter there usually, and the children feared the place.

It was low and dusky, windowless, fragrant with herbs that hung drying from the crosspole of the roof, mint and moly and thyme, yarrow and rushwash and paramal, kingsfoil, clovenfoot, tansy and bay. There his aunt sat cross-legged by the firepit, and looking side-long at the boy through the tangles of her black hair she asked him what he had said to the goats, and if he knew what the rhyme was. When she found that he knew nothing, and yet had spellbound the goats to come to him and follow him, then she saw that he must have in him the makings of power.

As her sister's son he had been nothing to her, but now she looked at him with a new eye. She praised him, and told him she might teach him rhymes he would like better, such as the word that makes a snail look out of its shell, or the name that calls a falcon down from the sky.

'Aye, teach me that name!' he said, being clear over the fright the goats had given him, and puffed up with her praise of his cleverness.

The witch said to him, 'You will not ever tell that word to the other children, if I teach it to you.'

'I promise.'

She smiled at his ready ignorance. 'Well and good. But I will bind your promise. Your tongue will be stilled until I choose to unbind it, and even then, though you can speak, you will not be able to speak the word I teach you where another person can hear it. We must keep the secrets of our craft.'

'Good,' said the boy, for he had no wish to tell the secret to his playmates, liking to know and do what they knew not and could not.

He sat still while his aunt bound back her uncombed hair, and knotted the belt of her dress, and again sat cross-legged throwing handfuls of leaves into the firepit, so that a smoke spread and filled the darkness of the hut. She began to sing. Her voice changed some-times to low or high as if another voice sang through her, and the singing went on and on until the boy did not know if he waked or slept, and all the while the witch's old black dog that never barked sat by him with eyes red from the smoke. Then the witch spoke to Duny in a tongue he did not understand, and made him say with her certain rhymes and words until the enchantment came on him and held him still.

'Speak!' she said to test the spell.

The boy could not speak, but he laughed.

Then his aunt was a little afraid of his strength, for this was as strong a spell as she knew how to weave: she had tried not only to gain control of his speech and silence, but to bind him at the same time to her service in the craft of sorcery. Yet even as the spell bound him, he had laughed. She said nothing. She threw clear water on the fire till the smoke cleared away, and gave the boy water to drink, and when the air was clear and he could speak again she taught him the true name of the falcon, to which the falcon must come.

This was Duny's first step on the way he was to follow all his life, the way of magery, the way that led him at last to hunt a shadow over land and sea to the lightless coasts of death's kingdom. But in those first steps along the way, it seemed a broad, bright road.

When he found that the wild falcons stooped down to him from the wind when he summoned them by name, lighting with a thunder of wings on his wrist like the hunting-birds of a prince, then he hungered to know more such names and came to his aunt begging to learn the name of the sparrowhawk and the osprey and the eagle. To earn the words of power he did all the witch asked of him and learned of her all she taught, though not all of it was pleasant to do or know.

There is a saying on Gont, *Weak as woman's magic*, and there is another saying, *Wicked as woman's magic*. Now the witch of Ten Alders was no black sorceress, nor did she ever meddle with the high arts of traffic with Old Powers; but being an ignorant woman among ignorant folk, she often used her crafts to foolish and dubious ends. She knew nothing of the Balance and the Pattern which the true wizard knows and serves, and which keep him from using his spells unless real need demands. She had a spell for every circumstance, and was forever weaving charms. Much of her lore was mere rubbish and humbug, nor did she know the true spells from the false. She knew many curses, and was better at causing sickness, perhaps, than at curing it. Like any village witch she could brew up a love-potion, but there were other, uglier brews she made to serve men's jealousy and hate. Such practices, however, she kept from her young prentice, and as far as she was able she taught him honest craft.

At first all his pleasure in the art-magic was, childlike, the power it gave him over bird and beast, and the knowledge of these. And indeed that pleasure stayed with him all his life. Seeing him in the high pastures often with a bird of prey about him, the other children called him Sparrowhawk, and so he came by the name that he kept in later life as his use-name, when his true-name was not known.

As the witch kept talking of the glory and the riches and the great power over men that a sorcerer could gain, he set himself to learn more useful lore. He was very quick at it. The witch praised him and the children of the village began to fear him, and he himself was sure that very soon he would become great among men. So he went on from word to word and from spell to spell with the witch till he was twelve years old and had learned from her a great part of what she knew: not much, but enough for the witchwife of a small village, and more than enough for a boy of twelve. She had taught him all her lore in herbals and healing, and all she knew of the crafts of finding, binding, mending, unsealing and revealing. What she knew of chanters' tales and the great Deeds she had sung to him, and all the words of the True Speech that she had learned from the sorcerer that taught her, she taught again to Duny. And from weather-workers and wandering jugglers who went from town to town of the Northward Vale and the East Forest he had learned various tricks and pleasantries, spells of Illusion. It was with one of these light spells that he first proved the great power that was in him.

*

In those days the Kargad Empire was strong. Those are four great lands that lie between the Northern and the Eastern Reaches: Karego-At, Atuan, Hur-at-Hur, Atnini. The tongue they speak there is not like any spoken in the Archipelago or the other Reaches, and they are a savage people, white-skinned, yellow-haired, and fierce, liking the sight of blood and the smell of burning towns. Last year they had attacked the Torikles and the strong island Torheven, raiding in great force in fleets of red-sailed ships. News of this came north to Gont, but the Lords of Gont were busy with their piracy and paid small heed to the woes of other lands. Then Spevy fell to the Kargs and was looted and laid waste, its people taken as slaves, so that even now it is an isle of ruins. In lust of conquest the Kargs sailed next to Gont, coming in a host, thirty great longships, to East Port. They fought through that town, took it, burned it: leaving their ships under guard at the mouth of the River Ar they went up the Vale wrecking and looting, slaughtering cattle and men. As they went they split into bands, and each of these bands plundered where it chose. Fugitives brought warning to the villages of the heights. Soon the people of Ten Alders saw smoke darken the eastern sky, and that night those who climbed the High Fall looked down on the Vale all hazed and red-streaked with fires where fields ready for harvest had been set ablaze, and orchards burned, the fruit roasting on the blazing boughs, and barns and farmhouses smouldered in ruin.

Some of the villagers fled up the ravines and hid in the forest, and some made ready to fight for their lives, and some did neither but stood about lamenting. The witch was one who fled, hiding alone in a cave up on the Kapperding Scarp and sealing the cave-mouth with spells. Duny's father the bronze-smith was one who stayed, for he would not leave his smelting-pit and forge where he had worked for fifty years. All that night he laboured beating up what ready metal he had there into spearpoints, and others worked with him binding these to the handles of hoes and rakes, there being no time to make sockets and shaft them properly. There had been no weapons in the village but hunting bows and short knives, for the mountain folk of Gont are not warlike; it is not warriors they are famous for, but goat-thieves, sea-pirates, and wizards.

18

With sunrise came a thick white fog, as on many autumn mornings in the heights of the island. Among their huts and houses down the straggling street of Ten Alders the villagers stood waiting with their hunting bows and new-forged spears, not knowing whether the Kargs might be far off or very near, all silent, all peering into the fog that hid shapes and distances and dangers from their eyes.

With them was Duny. He had worked all night at the forge-bellows, pushing and pulling the two long sleeves of goathide that fed the fire with a blast of air. Now his arms so ached and trembled from that work that he could not hold out the spear he had chosen. He did not see how he could fight or be of any good to himself or the villagers. It rankled at his heart that he should die, spitted on a Kargish lance, while still a boy; that he should go into the dark land without ever having known his own name, his true name as a man. He looked down at his thin arms, wet with cold fogdew, and raged at his weakness, for he knew his strength. There was power in him, if he knew how to use it, and he sought among all the spells he knew for some device that might give him and his companions an advantage, or at least a chance. But need alone is not enough to set power free: there must be knowledge.

The fog was thinning now under the heat of the sun that shone bare above on the peak in a bright sky. As the mists moved and parted in great drifts and smoky wisps, the villagers saw a band of warriors coming up the mountain. They were armoured with bronze helmets and greaves and breast-plates of heavy leather and shields of wood and bronze, and armed with swords and the long Kargish lance. Winding up along the steep bank of the Ar they came in a plumed, clanking, straggling line, near enough already that their white faces could be seen, and the words of their jargon heard as they shouted to one another. In this band of the invading horde there were about a hundred men, which is not many; but in the village were only eighteen men and boys.

Now need called knowledge out: Duny, seeing the fog blow and thin across the path before the Kargs, saw a spell that might avail him. An old weatherworker of the Vale, seeking to win the boy as prentice, had taught him several charms. One of these tricks was called fogweaving, a binding-spell that gathers the mists together

19

for a while in one place; with it one skilled in illusion can shape the mist into fair ghostly seemings, which last a little and fade away. The boy had no such skill, but his intent was different, and he had the strength to turn the spell to his own ends. Rapidly and aloud he named the places and the boundaries of the village, and then spoke the fogweaving charm, but in among its words he enlaced the words of a spell of concealment, and last he cried the word that set the magic going.

Even as he did so his father coming up behind him struck him hard on the side of the head knocking him right down. 'Be still fool! keep your blattering mouth shut, and hide if you can't fight!'

Duny got to his feet. He could hear the Kargs now at the end of the village, as near as the great yew-tree by the tanner's yard. Their voices were clear, and the clink and creak of their harness and arms, but they could not be seen. The fog had closed and thickened all over the village, greying the light, blurring the world till a man could hardly see his own hands before him.

'I've hidden us all,' Duny said, sullenly, for his head hurt from his father's blow, and the working of the doubled incantation had drained his strength. 'I'll keep up this fog as long as I can. Get the others to lead them up to High Fall.'

The smith stared at his son who stood wraithlike in that weird, dank mist. It took him a minute to see Duny's meaning, but when he did he ran at once, noiselessly, knowing every fence and corner of the village, to find the others and tell them what to do. Now through the grey fog bloomed a blur of red, as the Kargs set fire to the thatch of a house. Still they did not come up into the village, but waited at the lower end till the mist should lift and lay bare their loot and prey.

The tanner, whose house it was that burned, sent a couple of boys skipping right under the Kargs' noses, taunting and yelling and vanishing again like smoke into smoke. Meantime the older men, creeping behind fences and running from house to house, came close on the other side and sent a volley of arrows and spears at the warriors, who stood all in a bunch. One Karg fell writhing with a spear, still warm from its forging, right through his body. Others were arrow-bitten, and all enraged. They charged forward then to hew down their puny attackers, but they found only the fog about them, full of voices. They followed the voices, stabbing ahead into the mist with their great, plumed, blood-stained lances. Up the length of the street they came shouting, and never knew they had run right through the village, as the empty huts and houses loomed and disappeared again in the writhing grey fog. The villagers ran scattering, most of them keeping well ahead since they knew the ground; but some, boys or old men, were slow. The Kargs stumbling on them drove their lances or hacked with their swords, yelling their war-cry, the names of the White God-brothers of Atuan:

'Wuluah! Atwah!'

Some of the band stopped when they felt the land grow rough underfoot, but others pressed right on, seeking the phantom village, following dim wavering shapes that fled just out of reach before them. All the mist had come alive with these fleeing forms, dodging, flickering, fading on every side. One group of the Kargs chased the wraiths straight to the High Fall, the cliff's edge above the springs of Ar, and the shapes they pursued ran out on to the air and there vanished in thinning mist, while the pursuers fell screaming through fog and sudden sunlight a hundred feet sheer to the shallow pools among the rocks. And those that came behind and did not fall stood at the cliff's edge, listening.

Now dread came into the Kargs' hearts and they began to seek one another, not the villagers, in the uncanny mist. They gathered on the hillside, and yet always there were wraiths and ghost-shapes among them, and other shapes that ran and stabbed from behind with spear or knife and vanished again. The Kargs began to run, all of them, downhill, stumbling, silent, until all at once they ran out from the grey blind mist and saw the river and the ravines below the village all bare and bright in morning sunlight. Then they stopped, gathering together, and looked back. A wall of wavering, writhing grey lay blank across the path, hiding all that lay behind it. Out from it burst two or three stragglers, lunging and stumbling along, their long lances rocking on their shoulders. Not one Karg looked back more than that once. All went down, in haste, away from the enchanted place.

Farther down the Northward Vale those warriors got their fill of fighting. The towns of East Forest, from Ovark to the coast, had gathered their men and sent them against the invaders of Gont. Band after band they came down from the hills, and that day and the next the Kargs were harried back down to the beaches above East Port, where they found their ships burnt; so they fought with their backs to the sea till every man of them was killed, and the sands of Armouth were brown with blood until the tide came in.

But on that morning in Ten Alders village and up on the High Fall, the dank grey fog had clung a while, and then suddenly it blew and drifted and melted away. This man and that stood up in the windy brightness of the morning, and looked about him wondering. Here lay a dead Karg with yellow hair long, loose, and bloody; there lay the village tanner, killed in battle like a king.

Down in the village the house that had been set afire still blazed. They ran to put the fire out, since their battle had been won. In the street, near the great yew, they found Duny the bronze-smith's son standing by himself, bearing no hurt, but speechless and stupid like one stunned. They were well aware of what he had done, and they led him into his father's house and went calling for the witch to come down out of her cave and heal the lad who had saved their lives and their property, all but four who were killed by the Kargs, and the one house that was burnt.

No weapon-hurt had come to the boy, but he would not speak nor eat nor sleep; he seemed not to hear what was said to him, not to see those who came to see him. There was none in those parts wizard enough to cure what ailed him. His aunt said, 'He has overspent his power,' but she had no art to help him.

While he lay thus dark and dumb, the story of the lad who wove the fog and scared off Kargish swordsmen with a mess of shadows was told all down the Northward Vale, and in the East Forest, and high on the mountain and over the mountain even in the Great Port of Gont. So it happened that on the fifth day after the slaughter at Armouth a stranger came into Ten Alders village, a man neither young nor old, who came cloaked and bareheaded lightly carrying a great staff of oak that was as tall as himself. He did not come up the course of the Ar like most people, but down, out of the forests of the higher mountainside. The village goodwives saw well that he was a wizard, and when he told them that he was a healall, they brought him straight to the smith's house. Sending away all but the boy's father and aunt the stranger stooped above the cot where Duny lay staring into the dark, and did no more than lay his hand on the boy's forehead and touch his lips once.

Duny sat up slowly looking about him. In a little while he spoke, and strength and hunger began to come back into him. They gave him a little to drink and eat, and he lay back again, always watching the stranger with dark wondering eyes.

The bronze-smith said to that stranger, 'You are no common man.'

'Nor will this boy be a common man,' the other answered. 'The tale of his deed with the fog has come to Re Albi, which is my home. I have come here to give him his name, if as they say he has not yet made his passage into manhood.'

The witch whispered to the smith, 'Brother, this must surely be the Mage of Re Albi, Ogion the Silent, that one who tamed the earthquake –'

'Sir,' said the bronze-smith who would not let a great name daunt him, 'my son will be thirteen this month coming, but we thought to hold his Passage at the feast of Sunreturn this winter.'

'Let him be named as soon as may be,' said the mage, 'for he needs his name. I have other business now, but I will come back here for the day you choose. If you see fit I will take him with me when I go thereafter. And if he prove apt I will keep him as prentice, or see to it that he is schooled as fits his gifts. For to keep dark the mind of the mageborn, that is a dangerous thing.'

Very gently Ogion spoke, but with certainty, and even the hard-headed smith assented to all he said.

On the day the boy was thirteen years old, a day in the early splendour of autumn while still the bright leaves are on the trees, Ogion returned to the village from his rovings over Gont Mountain, and the ceremony of Passage was held. The witch took from the boy his name Duny, the name his mother had given him as a baby. Nameless and naked he walked into the cold springs of the Ar where it rises among rocks under the high cliffs. As he entered the water clouds crossed the sun's face and great shadows slid and mingled over the water of the pool about him. He crossed to the far bank, shuddering with cold but walking slow and erect as he should through that icy, living water. As he came to the bank Ogion, waiting, reached out his hand and clasping the boy's arm whispered to him his true name : Ged.

Thus was he given his name by one very wise in the uses of power.

The feasting was far from over, and all the villagers were making merry with plenty to eat and beer to drink and a chanter from down the Vale singing the *Deed of the Dragonlords*, when the mage spoke in his quiet voice to Ged : 'Come, lad. Bid your people farewell and leave them feasting.'

Ged fetched what he had to carry, which was the good bronze knife his father had forged for him, and a leather coat the tanner's widow had cut down to his size, and an alder-stick his aunt had becharmed for him : that was all he owned beside his shirt and breeches. He said farewell to them, all the people he knew in all the world, and looked about once at the village that straggled and huddled there under the cliffs, over the river-springs. Then he set off with his new master through the steep slanting forests of the mountain isle, through the leaves and shadows of bright autumn.

2. The Shadow

GED had thought that as the prentice of a great mage he would enter at once into the mystery and mastery of power. He would understand the language of the beasts and the speech of the leaves of the forest, he thought, and sway the winds with his word, and learn to change himself into any shape he wished. Maybe he and his master would run together as stags, or fly to Re Albi over the mountain on the wings of eagles.

But it was not so at all. They wandered, first down into the Vale and then gradually south and westward around the mountain, given lodging in little villages or spending the night out in the wilderness, like poor journeyman-sorcerers, or tinkers, or beggars. They entered no mysterious domain. Nothing happened. The mage's oaken staff that Ged had watched at first with eager dread was nothing but a stout staff to walk with. Three days went by and four days went by and still Ogion had not spoken a single charm in Ged's hearing, and had not taught him a single name or rune or spell.

Though a very silent man he was so mild and calm that Ged soon lost his awe of him, and in a day or two more he was bold enough to ask his master, 'When will my apprenticeship begin, Sir?'

'It has begun,' said Ogion.

There was a silence, as if Ged was keeping back something he had to say. Then he said it: 'But I haven't learned anything yet!'

'Because you haven't found out what I am teaching,' replied the mage, going on at his steady, long-legged pace along their road, which was the high pass between Ovark and Wiss. He was a dark man, like most Gontishmen, dark copper-brown; grey-haired, lean and tough as a hound, tireless. He spoke seldom, ate little, slept less. His eyes and ears were very keen, and often there was a listening look on his face.

Ged did not answer him. It is not always easy to answer a mage.

'You want to work spells,' Ogion said presently, striding along. 'You've drawn too much water from that well. Wait. Manhood is patience. Mastery is nine times patience. What is that herb by the path?'

'Strawflower.'

'And that?'

'I don't know.'

'Fourfoil, they call it.' Ogion had halted, the copper-shod foot of his staff near the little weed, so Ged looked closely at the plant, and plucked a dry seedpod from it, and finally asked, since Ogion said nothing more, 'What is its use, Master?'

'None I know of.'

Ged kept the seedpod a while as they went on, then tossed it away.

'When you know the fourfoil in all its seasons root and leaf and flower, by sight and scent and seed, then you may learn its true name, knowing its being: which is more than its use. What, after all, is the use of you? or of myself? Is Gont Mountain useful, or the Open Sea?' Ogion went on a halfmile or so, and said at last, 'To hear, one must be silent.'

The boy frowned. He did not like to be made to feel a fool. He kept back his resentment and impatience, and tried to be obedient, so that Ogion would consent at last to teach him something. For he hungered to learn, to gain power. It began to seem to him, though, that he could have learned more walking with any herb-gatherer or village sorcerer, and as they went round the mountain westward into the lonely forests past Wiss he wondered more and more what was the greatness and the magic of this great Mage Ogion. For when it rained Ogion would not even say the spell that every weatherworker knows, to send the storm aside. In a land where sorcerers come thick, like Gont or the Enlades, you may see a rain-cloud blundering slowly from side to side and place to place as one spell shunts it on to the next, till at last it is buffeted out over the sea where it can rain in peace. But Ogion let the rain fall where it would. He found a thick fir-tree and lay down beneath it. Ged crouched among the dripping bushes wet and sullen, and wondered what was the good of having power if you were too wise to use it, and wished he had gone as prentice to that old weatherworker of the Vale, where at least he would have slept dry. He did not speak any of his thoughts aloud. He said not a word. His master smiled, and fell asleep in the rain.

Along towards Sunreturn when the first heavy snows began to fall in the heights of Gont they came to Re Albi, Ogion's home. It is a town on the edge of the high rocks of Overfell, and its name means Falcon's Nest. From it one can see far below the deep harbour and the towers of the Port of Gont, and the ships that go in and out the gate of the bay between the Armed Cliffs, and far to the west across the sea one may make out the blue hills of Oranéa, easternmost of the Inward Isles.

The mage's house, though large and soundly built of timber, with hearth and chimney rather than a firepit, was like the huts of Ten Alders village: all one room, with a goatshed built on to one side. There was a kind of alcove in the west wall of the room, where Ged slept. Over his pallet was a window that looked out on the sea, but most often the shutters must be closed against the great winds that blew all winter from the west and north. In the dark warmth of that house Ged spent the winter, hearing the rush of rain and wind outside or the silence of snowfall, learning to write and read the Six Hundred Runes of Hardic. Very glad he was to learn this lore, for without it no mere rote-learning of charms and spells will give a man true mastery. The Hardic tongue of the Archipelago, though it has no more magic power in it than any other tongue of men, has its roots in the Old Speech, that language in which things are named with their true names: and the way to the understanding of this speech starts with the Runes that were written when the islands of the world first were raised up from the sea.

Still no marvels and enchantments occurred. All winter there was nothing but the heavy pages of the Runebook turning, and the rain and the snow falling: and Ogion would come in from roaming the icy forests or from looking after his goats, and stamp the snow off his boots, and sit down in silence by the fire. And the mage's long, listening silence would fill the room, and fill Ged's mind, until sometimes it seemed he had forgotten what words sounded like: and when Ogion spoke at last it was as if he had, just then and for the first time, invented speech. Yet the words he spoke were no great matters but had to do only with simple things, bread and water and weather and sleep.

As the spring came on, quick and bright, Ogion often sent Ged forth to gather herbs on the meadows above Re Albi, and told him to take as long as he liked about it, giving him freedom to spend all day wandering by rainfilled streams and through the woods and over wet green fields in the sun. Ged went with delight each time, and stayed out till night; but he did not entirely forget the herbs. He kept an eye out for them, while he climbed and roamed and waded and explored, and always brought some home. He came on a meadow between two streams where the flower called white hallows grew thick, and as these blossoms are rare and prized by healers, he came back again next day. Someone else was there before him, a girl, whom he knew by sight as the daughter of the old Lord of Re Albi. He would not have spoken to her, but she came to him and greeted him pleasantly: 'I know you, you are the Sparrowhawk, our mage's adept. I wish you would tell me about sorcery!'

He looked down at the white flowers that brushed against her white skirt, and at first he was shy and glum and hardly answered. But she went on talking, in an open, careless, wilful way that little by little set him at ease. She was a tall girl of about his own age, very sallow, almost white-skinned; her mother, they said in the village, was from Osskil or some such foreign land. Her hair fell long and straight like a fall of black water. Ged thought her very ugly, but he had a desire to please her, to win her admiration, that grew on him as they talked. She made him tell all the story of his tricks with the mist that had defeated the Kargish warriors, and she listened as if she wondered and admired, but she spoke no praise. And soon she was off on another tack: 'Can you call the birds and beasts to you?' she asked.

'I can,' said Ged.

He knew there was a falcon's nest in the cliffs above the meadow, and he summoned the bird by its name. It came, but it would not light on his wrist, being put off no doubt by the girl's presence. It screamed and struck the air with broad barred wings, and rose up on the wind.

'What do you call that kind of charm, that made the falcon come?'

'A spell of Summoning.'

'Can you call the spirits of the dead to come to you, too?'

He thought she was mocking him with this question, because the falcon had not fully obeyed his summons. He would not let her mock him. 'I might if I chose,' he said in a calm voice.

'Is it not very difficult, very dangerous, to summon a spirit?'

'Difficult, yes. Dangerous?' He shrugged.

This time he was almost certain there was admiration in her eyes.

'Can you make a love-charm?'

'That is no mastery.'

'True,' says she, 'any village witch can do it. Can you do Changing spells? Can you change your own shape, as wizards do, they say?'

Again he was not quite sure that she did not ask the question mockingly, and so again he replied, 'I might if I chose.'

She began to beg him to transform himself into anything he wished – a hawk, a bull, a fire, a tree. He put her off with short secretive words such as his master used, but he did not know how to refuse flatly when she coaxed him; and besides he did not know whether he himself believed his boast, or not. He left her, saying that his master the mage expected him at home, and he did not come back to the meadow the next day. But the day after he came again, saying to himself that he should gather more of the flowers while they bloomed. She was there, and together they waded barefoot in the boggy grass, pulling the heavy white hallow-blooms. The sun of spring shone, and she talked with him as merrily as any goatherd lass of his own village. She asked him again about sorcery, and listened wide-eyed to all he told her, so that he fell to boasting again. Then she asked him if he would not work a Changing spell, and when he put her off, she looked at him, putting back the black hair from her face, and said, 'Are you afraid to do it?'

'No, I am not afraid.'

She smiled a little disdainfully and said, 'Maybe you are too young.'

That he would not endure. He did not say much, but he resolved that he would prove himself to her. He told her to come again to the meadow tomorrow, if she liked, and so took leave of her, and came back to the house while his master was still out. He went straight to the shelf and took down the two Lore-Books, which Ogion had never yet opened in his presence.

He looked for a spell of self-transformation, but being slow to read the runes yet and understanding little of what he read, he could not find out what he sought. These books were very ancient, Ogion having them from his own master Heleth Farseer, and Heleth from his master the Mage of Perregal, and so back into the times of myth. Small and strange was the writing, overwritten and inter-lined by many hands, and all those hands were dust now. Yet here and there Ged understood something of what he tried to read, and with the girl's questions and her mockery always in his mind, he stopped on a page that bore a spell of summoning up the spirits of the dead.

As he read it, puzzling out the runes and symbols one by one, a horror came over him. His eyes were fixed, and he could not lift them till he had finished reading all the spell.

Then raising his head he saw it was dark in the house. He had been reading without any light, in the darkness. He could not now make out the runes when he looked down at the book. Yet the horror grew in him, seeming to hold him bound in his chair. He was cold. Looking over his shoulder he saw that something was crouching beside the closed door, a shapeless clot of shadow darker than the darkness. It seemed to reach out towards him, and to whisper, and to call to him in a whisper: but he could not under-stand the words.

The door was flung wide. A man entered with a white light flaming about him, a great bright figure who spoke aloud, fiercely and suddenly. The darkness and the whispering ceased and were dispelled.

The horror went out of Ged, but still he was mortally afraid, for it was Ogion the Mage who stood there in the doorway with a brightness all about him, and the oaken staff in his hand burned with a white radiance.

Saying no word the mage came past Ged, and lighted the lamp, and put the books away on their shelf. Then he turned to the boy and said, 'You will never work that spell but in peril of your power and your life. Was it for that spell you opened the books?'

'No, Master,' the boy murmured, and shamefully he told Ogion what he had sought, and why.

'You do not remember what I told you, that that girl's mother, the Lord's wife, is an enchantress?'

Indeed Ogion had once said this, but Ged had not paid much attention, though he knew by now that Ogion never told him anything that he had not good reason to tell him.

'The girl herself is half a witch already. It may be the mother who sent the girl to talk to you. It may be she who opened the book to the page you read. The powers she serves are not the powers I serve: I do not know her will, but I know she does not will me well. Ged, listen to me now. Have you never thought how danger must surround power as shadow does light? This sorcery is not a game we play for pleasure or for praise. Think of this: that every word, every act of our Art is said and is done either for good, or for evil. Before you speak or do you must know the price that is to pay!'

Driven by his shame Ged cried, 'How am I to know these things, when you teach me nothing? Since I lived with you I have done nothing, seen nothing –'

'Now you have seen something,' said the mage. 'By the door, in the darkness, when I came in.'

Ged was silent.

Ogion knelt down and built the fire on the hearth and lit it, for the house was cold. Then still kneeling he said in his quiet voice, 'Ged, my young falcon, you are not bound to me or to my service.

You did not come to me, but I to you. You are very young to make this choice, but I cannot make it for you. If you wish, I will send you to Roke Island, where all high arts are taught. Any craft you undertake to learn you will learn, for your power is great. Greater even than your pride, I hope. I would keep you here with me, for what I have is what you lack, but I will not keep you against your will. Now choose between Re Albi and Roke.'

Ged stood dumb, his heart bewildered. He had come to love this man Ogion who had healed him with a touch, and who had no anger: he loved him, and had not known it until now. He looked at the oaken staff leaning in the chimney-corner, remembering the radiance of it that had burned out evil from the dark, and he yearned to stay with Ogion, to go wandering through the forests with him, long and far, learning how to be silent. Yet other cravings were in him that would not be stilled, the wish for glory, the will to act. Ogion's seemed a long road towards mastery, a slow bypath to follow, when he might go sailing before the seawinds straight to the Inmost Sea, to the Isle of the Wise, where the air was bright with enchantments and the Archmage walked amidst wonders.

'Master,' he said, 'I will go to Roke.'

So a few days later on a sunny morning of spring Ogion strode beside him down the steep road from the Overfell, fifteen miles to the Great Port of Gont. There at the landgate between carven dragons the guards of the City of Gont, seeing the mage, knelt with bared swords and welcomed him. They knew him and did him honour by the Prince's order and their own will, for ten years ago Ogion had saved the city from earthquake that would have shaken the towers of the rich down to the ground and closed the channel of the Armed Cliffs with avalanche. He had spoken to the Mountain of Gont, calming it, and had stilled the trembling precipices of the Overfell as one soothes a frightened beast. Ged had heard some talk of this, and now, wondering to see the armed guardsmen kneel to his quiet master, he remembered it. He glanced up almost in fear at this man who had stopped an earthquake; but Ogion's face was quiet as always.

They went down to the quays, where the Harbourmaster came

hastening to welcome Ogion and asked what service he might do. The mage told him, and at once he named a ship bound for the Inmost Sea aboard which Ged might go as passenger. 'Or they will take him as windbringer,' he said, 'if he has the craft. They have no weatherworker aboard.'

'He has some skill with mist and fog, but none with seawinds,' the mage said, putting his hand lightly on Ged's shoulder. 'Do not try any tricks with the sea and the winds of the sea, Sparrowhawk; you are a landsman still. Harbourmaster, what is the ship's name?'

'*Shadow*, from the Andrades, bound to Hort Town with furs and ivories. A good ship, Master Ogion.'

The mage's face darkened at the name of the ship, but he said, 'So be it. Give this writing to the Warder of the School on Roke, Sparrowhawk. Go with a fair wind. Farewell!'

That was all his parting. He turned away, and went striding up the street away from the quays. Ged stood forlorn and watched his master go.

'Come along, lad,' said the Harbourmaster, and took him down the waterfront to the pier where *Shadow* was making ready to sail.

It might seem strange that on an island fifty miles wide, in a village under cliffs that stare out forever on the sea, a child may grow to manhood never having stepped in a boat or dipped his finger in salt water, but so it is. Farmer, goatherd, cattleherd, hunter or artisan, the landsman looks at the ocean as at a salt unsteady realm that has nothing to do with him at all. The village two days' walk from his village is a foreign land, and the island a day's sail from his island is a mere rumour, misty hills seen across the water, not solid ground like that he walks on.

So to Ged who had never been down from the heights of the mountain, the Port of Gont was an awesome and marvellous place, the great houses and towers of cut stone and waterfront of piers and docks and basins and moorages, the seaport where half a hundred boats and galleys rocked at quayside or lay hauled up and overturned for repairs or stood out at anchor in the roadstead with furled sails and closed oarports, the sailors shouting in strange

33

dialects and the longshoremen running heavy-laden amongst barrels and boxes and coils of rope and stacks of oars, the bearded merchants in furred robes conversing quietly as they picked their way along the slimy stones above the water, the fishermen unloading their catch, coopers pounding and shipmakers hammering and clamsellers singing and shipmasters bellowing, and beyond all the silent, shining bay. With eyes and ears and mind bewildered he followed the Harbourmaster to the broad dock where *Shadow* was tied up, and the Harbourmaster brought him to the master of the ship.

With few words spoken the ship's master agreed to take Ged as passenger to Roke, since it was a mage that asked it; and the Harbourmaster left the boy with him. The master of the *Shadow* was a big man, and fat, in a red cloak trimmed with pellawi-fur such as Andradean merchants wear. He never looked at Ged but asked him in a mighty voice, 'Can you work weather, boy?'

'I can.'

'Can you bring the wind?'

He had to say he could not, and with that the master told him to find a place out of the way and stay in it.

The oarsmen were coming aboard now, for the ship was to go out into the roadstead before night fell, and sail with the ebb-tide near dawn. There was no place out of the way, but Ged climbed up as well as he could on to the bundled, lashed, and hide-covered cargo in the stern of the ship, and clinging there watched all that passed. The oarsmen came leaping aboard, sturdy men with great arms, while longshoremen rolled water barrels thundering out the dock and stowed them under the rowers' benches. The well-built ship rode low with her burden, yet danced a little on the lapping shore-waves, ready to be gone. Then the steersman took his place at the right of the sternpost, looking forward to the ship's master, who stood on a plank let in at the jointure of the keel with the stem, which was carved as the Old Serpent of Andrad. The master roared his orders hugely, and *Shadow* was untied and towed clear of the docks by two labouring rowboats. Then the master's roar was 'Open ports!' and the great oars shot rattling out, fifteen to a side. The rowers bent their strong backs while a lad up beside the master beat the stroke on a drum. Easy as a gull oared by her wings the ship went now, and the noise and hurlyburly of the City fell away suddenly behind. They came out in the silence of the waters of the bay, and over them rose the high peak of the Mountain, seeming to hang above the sea. In a shallow creek in the lee of the southern Armed Cliff the anchor was thrown over, and there they rode the night.

Of the seventy crewmen of the ship some were like Ged very young in years, though all had made their passage into manhood. These lads called him over to share food and drink with them, and were friendly though rough and full of jokes and jibes. They called him Goatherd, of course, because he was Gontish, but they did not go further than that. He was as tall and strong as the fifteen-year-olds, and quick to return either a good word or a jeer; so he made his way among them and even that first night began to live as one of them and learn their work. This suited the ship's officers, for there was no room aboard for idle passengers.

There was little enough room for the crew, and no comfort at all, in an undecked galley crowded with men and gear and cargo; but what was comfort to Ged? He lay that night among corded rolls of pelts from the northern isles and watched the stars of spring above the harbour waters and the little yellow lights of the City astern, and he slept and waked again full of delight. Before dawn the tide turned. They raised anchor and rowed softly out between the Armed Cliffs. As sunrise reddened the Mountain of Gont behind them they raised the high sail and ran south-westward over the Gontish Sea.

Between Barnisk and Torheven they sailed with a light wind, and on the second day came in sight of Havnor, the Great Island, heart and hearth of the Archipelago. For three days they were in sight of the green hills of Havnor as they worked along its eastern coast, but they did not come to shore. Not for many years did Ged set foot on that land or see the white towers of Havnor Great Port at the centre of the world.

They lay over one night at Kembermouth, the northern port of Way Island, and the next at a little town on the entrance of Felkway Bay, and the next day passed the northern cape of O and entered the Ebavnor Straits. There they dropped sail and rowed, always with land on either side and always within hail of other ships, great and small, merchants and traders, some bound in from the Outer Reaches with strange cargo after a voyage of years and others that hopped like sparrows from isle to isle of the Inmost Sea. Turning southward out of the crowded Straits they left Havnor astern and sailed between the two fair islands Ark and Ilien, towered and terraced with cities, and then through rain and rising wind began to beat their way across the Inmost Sea to Roke Island.

In the night as the wind freshened to a gale they took down both sail and mast, and the next day, all day, they rowed. The long ship lay steady on the waves and went gallantly, but the steersman at the long steering-sweep in the stern looked into the rain that beat the sea and saw nothing but the rain. They went southwest by the pointing of the magnet, knowing how they went, but not through what waters. Ged heard men speak of the shoal waters north of Roke, and of the Borilous Rocks to the east; others argued that they might be far out of course by now, in the empty waters south of Kamery. Still the wind grew stronger, tearing the edges of the great waves into flying tatters of foam, and still they rowed southwest with the wind behind them. The stints at the oars were shortened, for the labour was very hard; the younger lads were set two to an oar, and Ged took his turn with the others as he had since they left Gont. When they did not row they bailed, for the seas broke heavy on the ship. So they laboured among the waves that ran like smoking mountains under the wind, while the rain beat hard and cold on their backs, and the drum thumped through the noise of the storm like a heart thumping.

A man came to take Ged's place at the oar, sending him to the ship's master in the bow. Rainwater dripped from the hem of the master's cloak, but he stood stout as a winebarrel on his bit of decking and looking down at Ged he asked, 'Can you abate this wind, lad?'

'No, sir.'

'Have you craft with iron?'

He meant, could Ged make the compass-needle point their way to Roke making the magnet follow not its north but their need. That skill is a secret of the Seamasters, and again Ged must say no.

'Well then,' the master bellowed through the wind and rain, 'you must find some ship to take you back to Roke from Hort Town. Roke must be west of us now, and only wizardry could bring us there through this sea. We must keep south.'

Ged did not like this, for he had heard the sailors talk of Hort Town, how it was a lawless place, full of evil traffic, where men were often taken and sold into slavery in the South Reach. Returning to his labour at the oar he pulled away with his companion, a sturdy Andradean lad, and heard the drum beat the stroke and saw the lantern hung on the stern bob and flicker as the wind plucked it about, a tormented fleck of light in the rain-lashed dusk. He kept looking to westward, as often as he could in the heavy rhythm of pulling the oar. And as the ship rose on a high swell he saw for a moment over the dark smoking water a light between clouds, as it might be the last gleam of sunset: but this was a clear light, not red.

His oar-mate had not seen it, but he called it out. The steersman watched for it on each rise of the great waves, and saw it as Ged saw it again, but shouted back that it was only the setting sun. Then Ged called to one of the lads that was bailing to take his place on the bench a minute, and made his way forward again along the encumbered aisle between the benches, and catching hold of the carved prow to keep from being pitched overboard he shouted up to the master, 'Sir! that light to the west is Roke Island!'

'I saw no light,' the master roared, but even as he spoke Ged flung out his arm pointing, and all saw the light gleam clear in the west over the heaving scud and tumult of the sea.

Not for his passenger's sake, but to save his ship from the peril of the storm, the master shouted at once to the steersman to head westward toward the light. But he said to Ged, 'Boy, you speak like a Seamaster, but I tell you if you lead us wrong in this weather I will throw you over to swim to Roke!'

Now instead of running before the storm they must row across the wind's way, and it was hard; waves striking the ship abeam pushed her always south of their new course, and rolled her, and filled her with water so that bailing must be ceaseless, and the oarsmen must watch lest the ship rolling should lift their oars out of water as they pulled and so pitch them down among the benches. It was nearly dark under the stormclouds, but now and again they made out the light to the west, enough to set course by, and so struggled on. At last the wind dropped a little, and the light grew broad before them. They rowed on, and they came as it were through a curtain, between one oarstroke and the next running out of the storm into a clear air, where the light of after-sunset glowed in the sky and on the sea. Over the foam-crested waves they saw not far off a high, round, green hill, and beneath it a town built on a small bay where boats lay at anchor, all in peace.

The steersman leaning on his long sweep turned his head and called, 'Sir! is this true land or witchery?'

'Keep her as she goes, you witless woodenhead! Row, you spineless slave-sons! That's Thwil Bay and the Knoll of Roke, as any fool could see! Row!'

So to the beat of the drum they rowed wearily into the bay. There it was still, so that they could hear the voices of people up in the town, and a bell ringing, and only far off the hiss and roaring of the storm. Clouds hung dark to north and east and south a mile off all about the island. But over Roke stars were coming out one by one in a clear and quiet sky.

3. The School for Wizards

GED slept that night aboard *Shadow*, and early in the morning parted with those first sea-comrades of his, they shouting good wishes cheerily after him as he went up the docks. The town of Thwil is not large, its high houses huddling close over a few steep narrow streets. To Ged, however, it seemed a city, and not knowing where to go he asked the first townsman of Thwil he met where he would find the Warder of the School on Roke. The man looked at him sidelong a while, and said, 'The wise don't need to ask, the fool asks in vain,' and so went on along the street. Ged went uphill till he came out into a square, rimmed on three sides by the houses with their sharp slate roofs and on the fourth side by the wall of a great building whose few small windows were higher than the chimneytops of the houses: a fort or castle it seemed, built of mighty grey blocks of stone. In the square beneath it market-booths were set up and there was some coming and going of people. Ged asked his question of an old woman with a basket of mussels, and she replied, 'You cannot always find the Warder where he is, but sometimes you find him where he is not,' and went on crying her mussels to sell.

In the great building, near one corner, there was a mean little door of wood. Ged went to this and knocked loud. To the old man who opened the door he said, 'I bear a letter from the Mage Ogion of Gont to the Warder of the School on this island. I want to find the Warder, but I will not hear more riddles and scoffing!'

'This is the School,' the old man said mildly. 'I am the door-keeper. Enter if you can.'

Ged stepped forward. It seemed to him that he had passed through the doorway: yet he stood outside on the pavement where he had stood before.

Once more he stepped forward, and once more he remained stand-

39

ing outside the door. The doorkeeper, inside, watched him with mild eyes.

Ged was not so much baffled as angry, for this seemed like a further mockery to him. With voice and hand he made the Opening spell which his aunt had taught him long ago; it was the prize among all her stocks of spells, and he wove it well now. But it was only a witch's charm, and the power that held this doorway was not moved at all.

When that failed Ged stood a long while there on the pavement. At last he looked at the old man who waited inside. 'I cannot enter,' he said unwillingly, 'unless you help me.'

The doorkeeper answered, 'Say your name.'

Then again Ged stood still a while; for a man never speaks his own name aloud, until more than his life's safety is at stake.

'I am Ged,' he said aloud. Stepping forward then he entered the open doorway. Yet it seemed to him that though the light was behind him, a shadow followed him in at his heels.

He saw also as he turned that the doorway through which he had come was not plain wood as he had thought, but ivory without joint or seam; it was cut, as he knew later, from a tooth of the Great Dragon. The door that the old man closed behind him was of polished horn, through which the daylight shone dimly, and on its inner face was carved the Thousand-Leaved Tree.

'Welcome to this house, lad,' the doorkeeper said, and without saying more led him through halls and corridors to an open court far inside the walls of the building. The court was partly paved with stone, but was roofless, and on a grass-plot a fountain played under young trees in the sunlight. There Ged waited alone some while. He stood still, and his heart beat hard, for it seemed to him that he felt presences and powers at work unseen about him here, and he knew that this place was built not only of stone but of magic stronger than stone. He stood in the innermost room of the House of the Wise, and it was open to the sky. Then suddenly he was aware of a man clothed in white who watched him through the falling water of the fountain.

As their eyes met, a bird sang aloud in the branches of the tree.

In that moment Ged understood the singing of the bird, and the language of the water falling in the basin of the fountain, and the shape of the clouds, and the beginning and end of the wind that stirred the leaves: it seemed to him that he himself was a word spoken by the sunlight.

Then that moment passed, and he and the world were as before, or almost as before. He went forward to kneel before the Archmage, holding out to him the letter written by Ogion.

The Archmage Nemmerle, Warder of Roke, was an old man, older it was said than any man then living. His voice quavered like the bird's voice when he spoke, welcoming Ged kindly. His hair and beard and robe were white, and he seemed as if all darkness and heaviness had been leached out of him by the slow usage of the years, leaving him white and worn as driftwood that has been a century adrift. 'My eyes are old, I cannot read what your master writes,' he said in his quavering voice. 'Read me the letter, lad.'

So Ged made out and read aloud the writing, which was in Hardic runes, and said no more than this: *Lord Nemmerle! I send you one who will be greatest of the wizards of Gont, if the wind blow true.* This was signed, not with Ogion's true name which Ged had never learned, but with Ogion's rune, the Closed Mouth.

'He who holds the earthquake on a leash has sent you, for which be doubly welcome. Young Ogion was dear to me, when he came here from Gont. Now tell me of the seas and portents of your voyage, lad.'

'A fair passage, Lord, but for the storm yesterday.'

'What ship brought you here?'

'*Shadow*, trading from Andrades.'

'Whose will sent you here?'

'My own.'

The Archmage looked at Ged and looked away, and began to speak in a tongue that Ged did not understand, mumbling as will an old old man whose wits go wandering among the years and islands. Yet in among his mumbling there were words of what the bird had sung and what the water had said falling. He was not laying a spell and yet there was a power in his voice that moved Ged's mind so that the boy was bewildered, and for an instant seemed to behold himself standing in a strange vast desert place alone among shadows. Yet all along he was in the sunlit court, hearing the fountain fall.

A great black bird, a raven of Osskil, came walking over the stone terrace and the grass. It came to the hem of the Archmage's robe and stood there all black with its dagger beak and eyes like pebbles, staring sidelong at Ged. It pecked three times on the white staff Nemmerle leaned on, and the old wizard ceased his muttering, and smiled. 'Run and play, lad,' he said at last as to a little child. Ged knelt again on one knee to him. When he rose, the Archmage was gone. Only the raven stood eyeing him, its beak outstretched as if to peck the vanished staff.

It spoke, in what Ged guessed might be the speech of Osskil. 'Terrenon ussbuk!' it said croaking. 'Terrenon ussbuk orrek!' And it strutted off as it had come.

Ged turned to leave the courtyard, wondering where he should go. Under the archway he was met by a tall youth who greeted him very courteously, bowing his head, 'I am called Jasper, Enwit's son of the Domain of Eolg on Havnor Isle. I am at your service today, to show you about the Great House and answer your questions as I can. How shall I call you, Sir?'

Now it seemed to Ged, a mountain villager who had never been among the sons of rich merchants and noblemen, that this fellow was scoffing at him with his 'service' and his 'Sir' and his bowing and scraping. He answered shortly, 'Sparrowhawk, they call me.'

The other waited a moment as if expecting some more mannerly response, and getting none straightened up and turned a little aside. He was two or three years older than Ged, very tall, and he moved and carried himself with stiff grace, posing (Ged thought) like a dancer. He wore a grey cloak with hood thrown back. The first place he took Ged was the wardrobe room, where as a student of the school Ged might find himself another such cloak that fitted him, and any other clothing he might need. He put on the dark-grey cloak he had chosen, and Jasper said, 'Now you are one of us.'

Jasper had a way of smiling faintly as he spoke which made Ged look for a jeer hidden in his polite words. 'Do clothes make the mage?' he answered, sullen.

'No,' said the older boy. 'Though I have heard that manners make the man. – Where now?'

'Where you will. I do not know the house.'

Jasper took him down the corridors of the Great House showing him the open courts and the roofed halls, the Room of Shelves where the books of lore and rune-tomes were kept, the great Hearth Hall where all the school gathered on festival days, and upstairs, in the towers and under the roofs, the small cells where the students and Masters slept. Ged's was in the South Tower, with a window looking down over the steep roofs of Thwil town to the sea. Like the other sleeping-cells it had no furnishing but a straw-filled mattress in the corner. 'We live very plain here,' said Jasper. 'But I expect you won't mind that.'

'I'm used to it.' Presently, trying to show himself an equal of this polite disdainful youth, he added, 'I suppose you weren't, when you first came.'

Jasper looked at him, and his look said without words, 'What could you possibly know about what I, son of the Lord of the Domain of Eolg on the Isle of Havnor, am or am not used to?' What Jasper said aloud was simply, 'Come on this way.'

A gong had been rung while they were upstairs, and they came down to eat the noon meal at the Long Table of the refectory, along with a hundred or more boys and young men. Each waited on himself, joking with the cooks through the window-hatches of the kitchen that opened into the refectory, loading his plate from great bowls of food that steamed on the sills, sitting where he pleased at the Long Table. 'They say,' Jasper told Ged, 'that no matter how many sit at this table, there is always room.' Certainly there was room both for many noisy groups of boys talking and eating mightily, and for older fellows, their grey cloaks clasped with silver at the neck, who sat more quietly by pairs or alone, with grave, pondering faces, as if they had much to think about. Jasper took Ged to sit with a heavyset fellow called Vetch, who said nothing much but shovelled in his food with a will. He had the accent of the East

Reach, and was very dark of skin, not red-brown like Ged and Jasper and most folk of the Archipelago, but black-brown. He was plain, and his manners were not polished. He grumbled about the dinner when he had finished it, but then turning to Ged said, 'At least it's not illusion, like so much around here; it sticks to your ribs.' Ged did not know what he meant, but he felt a certain liking for him, and was glad when after the meal he stayed with them.

They went down into the town, that Ged might learn his way about it. Few and short as were the streets of Thwil, they turned and twisted curiously among the high-roofed houses, and the way was easy to lose. It was a strange town, and strange also its people, fishermen and workmen and artisans like any others, but so used to the sorcery that is ever at play on the Isle of the Wise that they seemed half sorcerers themselves. They talked (as Ged had learned) in riddles, and not one of them would blink to see a boy turn into a fish or a house fly up into the air, but knowing it for a schoolboy prank would go on cobbling shoes or cutting up mutton, unconcerned.

Coming up past the Back Door and around through the gardens of the Great House, the three boys crossed the clear-running Thwilburn on a wooden bridge and went on northward among woods and pastures. The path climbed and wound. They passed oak-groves where shadows lay thick for all the brightness of the sun. There was one grove not far away to the left that Ged could never quite see plainly. The path never reached it, though it always seemed to be about to. He could not even make out what kind of trees they were. Vetch, seeing him gazing, said softly, 'That is the Immanent Grove. We can't come there, yet ...'

In the hot sunlit pastures yellow flowers bloomed. 'Sparkweed,' said Jasper. 'They grow where the wind dropped the ashes of burning Ilien, when Erreth-Akbe defended the Inward Isles from the Firelord.' He blew on a withered flowerhead, and the seeds shaken loose went up on the wind like sparks of fire in the sun.

The path led them up and around the base of a great green hill, round and treeless, the hill that Ged had seen from the ship as they entered the charmed waters of Roke Island. On the hillside Jasper halted. 'At home in Havnor I heard much about Gontish wizardry, and always in praise, so that I've wanted for a long time to see the manner of it. Here now we have a Gontishman; and we stand on the slopes of Roke Knoll, whose roots go down to the centre of the earth. All spells are strong here. Play us a trick, Sparrowhawk. Show us your style.'

Ged, confused and taken aback, said nothing.

'Later on, Jasper,' Vetch said in his plain way. 'Let him be a while.'

'He has either skill or power, or the doorkeeper wouldn't have let him in. Why shouldn't he show it, now as well as later? Right, Sparrowhawk?'

'I have both skill and power,' Ged said. 'Show me what kind of thing you're talking about.'

'Illusions, of course – tricks, games of seeming. Like this!'

Pointing his finger Jasper spoke a few strange words, and where he pointed on the hillside among the green grasses a little thread of water trickled, and grew, and now a spring gushed out and the water went running down the hill. Ged put his hand in the stream and it felt wet, drank of it and it was cool. Yet for all that it would quench no thirst, being an illusion. Jasper with another word stopped the water and the grasses waved dry in the sunlight. 'Now you, Vetch,' he said with his cool smile.

Vetch scratched his head and looked glum, but he took up a bit of earth in his hand and began to sing tunelessly over it, moulding it with his dark fingers and shaping it, pressing it, stroking it: and suddenly it was a small creature like a bumblebee or furry fly, that flew humming off over Roke Knoll, and vanished.

Ged stood staring, crestfallen. What did he know but mere village witchery, spells to call goats, cure warts, move loads or mend pots?

'I do no such tricks as these,' he said. That was enough for Vetch, who was for going on; but Jasper said, 'Why don't you?'

'Sorcery is not a game. We Gontishmen do not play it for pleasure or praise,' Ged answered haughtily.

'What do you play it for,' Jasper inquired, '– money?'

'No!–' But he could not think of anything more to say that

would hide his ignorance and save his pride. Jasper laughed, not ill-humouredly, and went on, leading them on around Roke Knoll. And Ged followed, sullen and sore-hearted, knowing that he had behaved like a fool, and blaming Jasper for it.

That night as he lay wrapped in his cloak on the mattress in his cold unlit cell of stone, in the utter silence of the Great House of Roke, the strangeness of the place and the thought of all the spells and sorceries that had been worked there began to come over him heavily. Darkness surrounded him, dread filled him. He wished he were anywhere else but Roke. But Vetch came to the door, a little bluish ball of werelight nodding over his head to light the way, and asked if he could come in and talk a while. He asked Ged about Gont, and then spoke fondly of his own home isles of the East Reach, telling how the smoke of village hearthfires is blown across that quiet sea at evening between the small islands with funny names: Korp, Kopp, and Holp, Venway and Vemish, Iffish, Koppish, and Sneg. When he sketched the shapes of those lands on the stones of the floor with his finger to show Ged how they lay, the lines he drew shone dim as if drawn with a stick of silver for a while before they faded. Vetch had been three years at the School, and soon would be made Sorcerer; he thought no more of performing the lesser arts of magic than a bird thinks of flying. Yet a greater, unlearned skill he possessed, which was the art of kindness. That night, and always from then on, he offered and gave Ged friendship, a sure and open friendship which Ged could not help but return.

Yet Vetch was also friendly to Jasper, who had made Ged into a fool that first day on Roke Knoll. Ged would not forget this, nor, it seemed, would Jasper, who always spoke to him with a polite voice and a mocking smile. Ged's pride would not be slighted or condescended to. He swore to prove to Jasper, and to all the rest of them among whom Jasper was something of a leader, how great his power really was – some day. For none of them, for all their clever tricks, had saved a village by wizardry. Of none of them had Ogion written that he would be the greatest wizard of Gont.

So bolstering up his pride, he set his strong will on the work they gave him, the lessons and crafts and histories and skills taught by the grey-cloaked Masters of Roke, who were called the Nine.

Part of each day he studied with the Master Chanter, learning the Deeds of heroes and the Lays of wisdom, beginning with the oldest of all songs, the *Creation of Éa*. Then with a dozen other lads he would practise with the Master Windkey at arts of wind and weather. Whole bright days of spring and early summer they spent out in Roke Bay in light catboats, practising steering by word, and stilling waves, and speaking to the world's wind, and raising up the magewind. These are very intricate skills, and frequently Ged's head got whacked by the swinging boom as the boat jibed under a wind suddenly blowing backwards, or his boat and another collided though they had the whole bay to navigate in, or all three boys in his boat went swimming unexpectedly as the boat was swamped by a huge, unintended wave. There were quieter expeditions ashore, other days, with the Master Herbal who taught the ways and properties of things that grow; and the Master Hand taught sleight and jugglery and the lesser arts of Changing.

At all these studies Ged was apt, and within a month was bettering lads who had been a year at Roke before him. Especially the tricks of illusion came to him so easily that it seemed he had been born knowing them and needed only to be reminded. The Master Hand was a gentle and lighthearted old man, who had endless delight in the wit and beauty of the crafts he taught; Ged soon felt no awe of him, but asked him for this spell and that spell, and always the Master smiled and showed him what he wanted. But one day, having it in mind to put Jasper to shame at last, Ged said to the Master Hand in the Court of Seeming, 'Sir, all these charms are much the same; knowing one, you know them all. And as soon as the spell-weaving ceases, the illusion vanishes. Now if I make a pebble into a diamond – and he did so with a word and a flick of his wrist – 'what must I do to make that diamond remain diamond? How is the changing-spell locked, and made to last?'

The Master Hand looked at the jewel that glittered on Ged's palm, bright as the prize of a dragon's hoard. The old Master murmured one word, *'Tolk,'* and there lay the pebble, no jewel but a rough grey bit of rock. The Master took it and held it out on his own hand. 'This is a rock; *tolk* in the True Speech,' he said, looking mildly up at Ged now. 'A bit of the stone of which Roke Isle is made, a little bit of the dry land on which men live. It is itself. It is part of the world. By the Illusion-Change you can make it look like a diamond – or a flower or a fly or an eye or a flame –' The rock flickered from shape to shape as he named them, and returned to rock. 'But that is mere seeming. Illusion fools the beholder's senses; it makes him see and hear and feel that the thing is changed. But it does not change the thing. To change this rock into a jewel, you must change its true name. And to do that, my son, even to so small a scrap of the world, is to change the world. It can be done. Indeed it can be done. It is the art of the Master Changer, and you will learn it, when you are ready to learn it. But you must not change one thing, one pebble, one grain of sand, until you know what good and evil will follow on the act. The world is in balance, in Equilibrium. A wizard's power of Changing and of Summoning can shake the balance of the world. It is dangerous, that power. It is most perilous. It must follow knowledge, and serve need. To light a candle is to cast a shadow . . .'

He looked down at the pebble again. 'A rock is a good thing, too, you know,' he said, speaking less gravely. 'If the Isles of Earthsea were all made of diamond, we'd lead a hard life here. Enjoy illusions, lad, and let the rocks be rocks.' He smiled, but Ged left dissatisfied. Press a mage for his secrets and he would always talk, like Ogion, about balance, and danger, and the dark. But surely a wizard, one who had gone past these childish tricks of illusion to the true arts of Summoning and Change, was powerful enough to do what he pleased, and balance the world as seemed best to him, and drive back darkness with his own light.

In the corridor he met Jasper, who, since Ged's accomplishments began to be praised about the School, spoke to him in a way that seemed more friendly, but was more scoffing. 'You look gloomy, Sparrowhawk,' he said now, 'did your juggling-charms go wrong?'

Seeking as always to put himself on equal footing with Jasper, Ged answered the question ignoring its ironic tone. 'I'm sick of juggling,' he said, 'sick of these illusion-tricks, fit only to amuse idle lords in their castles and Domains. The only true magic they've taught me yet on Roke is making werelight, and some weatherworking. The rest is mere foolery.'

'Even foolery is dangerous,' said Jasper, 'in the hands of a fool.'

At that Ged turned as if he had been slapped, and took a step towards Jasper; but the older boy smiled as if he had not intended any insult, nodded his head in his stiff, graceful way, and went on.

Standing there with rage in his heart, looking after Jasper, Ged swore to himself to outdo his rival, and not in some mere illusion-match but in a test of power. He would prove himself, and humiliate Jasper. He would not let the fellow stand there looking down at him, graceful, disdainful, hateful.

Ged did not stop to think why Jasper might hate him. He only knew why he hated Jasper. The other prentices had soon learned they could seldom match themselves against Ged either in sport or in earnest, and they said of him, some in praise and some in spite, 'He's a wizard born, he'll never let you beat him.' Jasper alone neither praised him nor avoided him, but simply looked down at him, smiling slightly. And therefore Jasper stood alone as his rival, who must be put to shame.

He did not see, or would not see, that in this rivalry, which he clung to and fostered as part of his own pride, there was anything of the danger, the darkness, of which the Master Hand had mildly warned him.

When he was not moved by pure rage, he knew very well that he was as yet no match for Jasper, or any of the older boys, and so he kept at his work and went on as usual. At the end of summer the work was slackened somewhat, so there was more time for sport: spell-boat races down in the harbour, feats of illusion in the courts of the Great House, and in the long evenings, in the groves, wild games of hide-and-seek where hiders and seeker were both invisible and only voices moved laughing and calling among the trees, following and dodging the quick, faint werelights. Then as autumn came they set to their tasks afresh, practising new magic. So Ged's first months at Roke went by fast, full of passions and wonders.

In winter it was different. He was sent with seven other boys across Roke Island to the farthest northmost cape, where stands the Isolate Tower. There by himself lived the Master Namer, who was called by a name that had no meaning in any language, Kurremkarmerruk. No farm or dwelling lay within miles of the Tower. Grim it stood above the northern cliffs, grey were the clouds over the seas of winter, endless the lists and ranks and rounds of names that the Namer's eight pupils must learn. Amongst them in the Tower's high room Kurremkarmerruk sat on a high seat, writing down lists of names that must be learned before the ink faded at midnight leaving the parchment blank again. It was cold and half-dark and always silent there except for the scratching of the Master's pen and the sighing, maybe, of a student who must learn before midnight the name of every cape, point, bay, sound, inlet, channel, harbour, shallows, reef and rock of the shores of Lossow, a little islet of the Pelnish Sea. If the student complained the Master might say nothing, but lengthen the list; or he might say, 'He who would be Seamaster must know the true name of every drop of water in the sea.'

Ged sighed sometimes, but he did not complain. He saw that in this dusty and fathomless matter of learning the true name of each place, thing, and being, the power he wanted lay like a jewel at the bottom of a dry well. For magic consists in this, the true naming of a thing. So Kurremkarmerruk had said to them, once, their first night in the Tower; he never repeated it, but Ged did not forget his words. 'Many a mage of great power,' he had said, 'has spent his whole life to find out the name of one single thing – one single lost or hidden name. And still the lists are not finished. Nor will they be, till world's end. Listen, and you will see why. In the world under the sun, and in the other world that has no sun, there is much that has nothing to do with men and men's speech, and there are powers beyond our power. But magic, true magic, is worked only by those beings who speak the Hardic tongue of Earthsea, or the Old Speech from which it grew.

'That is the language dragons speak, and the language Segoy spoke who made the islands of the world, and the language of our lays and songs, spells, enchantments, and invocations. Its words lie hidden and changed among our Hardic words. We call the foam on waves *sukien*: that word is made from two words of the Old Speech, *suk*, feather, and *inien*, the sea. Feather of the sea, is foam. But you cannot charm the foam calling it *sukien*; you must use its own true name in the Old Speech, which is *essa*. Any witch knows a few of these words in the Old Speech, and a mage knows many. But there are many more, and some have been lost over the ages, and some have been hidden, and some are known only to dragons and to the Old Powers of Earth, and some are known to no living creature; and no man could learn them all. For there is no end to that language.

'Here is the reason. The sea's name is *inien*, well and good. But what we call the Inmost Sea has its own name also in the Old Speech. Since no thing can have two true names, *inien* can mean only 'all the sea except the Inmost Sea'. And of course it does not mean even that, for there are seas and bays and straits beyond counting that bear names of their own. So if some Mage-Seamaster were mad enough to try to lay a spell of storm or calm over all the ocean, his spell must say not only that word *inien*, but the name of every stretch and bit and part of the sea through all the Archipelago and all the Outer Reaches and beyond to where names cease. Thus, that which gives us power to work magic, sets the limits of that power. A mage can control only what is near him, what he can name exactly and wholly. And this is well. If it were not so, the wickedness of the powerful or the folly of the wise would long ago have sought to change what cannot be changed, and Equilibrium would fail. The unbalanced sea would overwhelm the islands where we perilously dwell, and in the old silence all voices and all names would be lost.'

Ged thought long on these words, and they went deep in his understanding. Yet the majesty of the task could not make the work of that long year in the Tower less hard and dry; and at the end of the year Kurremkarmerruk said to him, 'You have made a good beginning.' But no more. Wizards speak truth, and it was true that all the mastery of Names that Ged had toiled to win that year was the mere start of what he must go on learning all his life. He was let go from the Isolate Tower sooner than those who had come with him, for he had learned quicker; but that was all the praise he got.

He walked south across the islands alone in the early winter, along townless empty roads. As night came on it rained. He said no charm to keep the rain off him, for the weather of Roke was in the hands of the Master Windkey and might not be tampered with. He took shelter under a great pendicktree, and lying there wrapped in his cloak he thought of his old master Ogion, who might still be on his autumn wanderings over the heights of Gont, sleeping out with leafless branches for a roof and falling rain for house-walls. That made Ged smile, for he found the thought of Ogion always a comfort to him. He fell asleep with a peaceful heart, there in the cold darkness full of the whisper of water. At dawn waking he lifted his head; the rain had ceased; he saw, sheltered in the folds of his cloak, a little animal curled up asleep which had crept there for warmth. He wondered, seeing it, for it was a rare strange beast, an otak.

These creatures are found only on four southern isles of the Archipelago, Roke, Ensmer, Pody and Wathort. They are small and sleek, with broad faces, and fur dark brown or brindle, and great bright eyes. Their teeth are cruel and their temper fierce, so they are not made pets of. They have no call or cry or any voice. Ged stroked this one, and it woke and yawned, showing a small brown tongue and white teeth, but it was not afraid. 'Otak,' he said, and then remembering the thousand names of beasts he had learned in the Tower he called it by its true name in the Old Speech, 'Hoeg! Do you want to come with me?'

The otak sat itself down on his open hand, and began to wash its fur.

He put it up on his shoulder in the folds of his hood, and there it rode. Sometimes during the day it jumped down and darted off into the woods, but it always came back to him, once with a wood-mouse it had caught. He laughed and told it to eat the mouse, for he was fasting, this night being the Festival of Sunreturn. So he came in the wet dusk past Roke Knoll, and saw bright werelights playing in the rain over the roofs of the Great House, and he entered there and was welcomed by his Masters and companions in the firelit hall.

It was like a homecoming to Ged, who had no home to which he could ever return. He was happy to see so many faces he knew, and happiest to see Vetch come forward to greet him with a wide smile on his dark face. He had missed his friend this year more than he knew. Vetch had been made sorcerer this fall and was a prentice no more, but that set no barrier between them. They fell to talking at once, and it seemed to Ged that he said more to Vetch in that first hour than he had said during the whole long year at the Isolate Tower.

The otak still rode his shoulder, nestling in the fold of his hood as they sat at dinner at long tables set up for the festival in the Hearth Hall. Vetch marvelled at the little creature, and once put up his hand to stroke it, but the otak snapped its sharp teeth at him. He laughed. 'They say, Sparrowhawk, that a man favoured by a wild beast is a man to whom the Old Powers of stone and spring will speak in human voice.'

'They say Gontish wizards often keep familiars,' said Jasper, who sat on the other side of Vetch. 'Our Lord Nemmerle has his raven, and songs say the Red Mage of Ark led a wild boar on a gold chain. But I never heard of any sorcerer keeping a rat in his hood!'

At that they all laughed, and Ged laughed with them. It was a merry night, and he was joyful to be there in the warmth and merriment, keeping festival with his companions. But, like all Jasper ever said to him, the jest set his teeth on edge.

That night the Lord of O was a guest of the school, himself a sorcerer of renown. He had been a pupil of the Archmage, and returned sometimes to Roke for the Winter Festival or the Long Dance in summer. With him was his lady, slender and young, bright as new copper, her black hair crowned with opals. It was seldom that any woman sat in the halls of the Great House, and some of the old Masters looked at her sidelong, disapproving. But the young men looked at her with all their eyes.

'For such a one,' said Vetch to Ged, 'I could work vast enchantments . . .' He sighed, and laughed.

'She's only a woman,' Ged replied.

'The Princess Elfarran was only a woman,' said Vetch, 'and for her sake all Enlad was laid waste, and the Hero-Mage of Havnor died, and the island Soléa sank beneath the sea.'

'Old tales,' says Ged. But then he too began to look at the Lady of O, wondering if indeed this was such mortal beauty as the old tales told of.

The Master Chanter had sung the *Deed of the Young King*, and all together had sung the Winter Carol. Now when there was a little pause before they rose from the tables, Jasper got up and went to the table nearest the hearth, where the Archmage and the guests and Masters sat, and he spoke to the Lady of O. Jasper was no longer a boy but a young man, tall and comely, with his cloak clasped at the neck with silver; for he also had been made sorcerer this year, and the silver clasp was the token of it. The lady smiled at what he said and the opals shone in her black hair, radiant. Then, the Masters nodding benign consent, Jasper worked an illusion-charm for her. A white tree he made spring up from the stone floor. Its branches touched the high roofbeams of the hall, and on every twig of every branch a golden apple shone, each a sun, for it was the Year-Tree. A bird flew among the branches suddenly, all white with a tail like a fall of snow, and the golden apples dimming turned to seeds, each one a drop of crystal. These falling from the tree with a sound like rain, all at once there came a sweet fragrance, while the tree, swaying, put forth leaves of rosy fire and white flowers like stars. So the illusion faded. The Lady of O cried out with pleasure, and bent her shining head to the young sorcerer in praise of his mastery : 'Come with us, live with us in O-tokne – can he not come, my lord?' she asked, childlike, of her stern husband. But Jasper said only, 'When I have learned skills worthy of my Masters here and worthy of your praise, my lady, then I will gladly come, and serve you ever gladly.'

So he pleased all there, except Ged. Ged joined his voice to the praises, but not his heart. 'I could have done better,' he said to himself, in bitter envy; and all the joy of the evening was darkened for him, after that.

4. The Loosing of the Shadow

THAT spring Ged saw little of either Vetch or Jasper, for they being sorcerers studied now with the Master Patterner in the secrecy of the Immanent Grove, where no prentice might set foot. Ged stayed in the Great House, working with the Masters at all the skills practised by sorcerers, those who work magic but carry no staff; windbringing, weatherworking, finding and binding, and the arts of spellsmiths and spellwrights, tellers, chanters, healalls and herbalists. At night alone in his sleeping-cell, a little ball of werelight burning above the book in place of lamp or candle, he studied the Further Runes and the Runes of Éa, which are used in the Great Spells. All these crafts came easy to him and it was rumoured among the students that this Master or that had said that the Gontish lad was the quickest student that had ever been at Roke, and tales grew up concerning the otak, which was said to be a disguised spirit who whispered wisdom in Ged's ear, and it was even said that the Archmage's raven had hailed Ged at his arrival as 'Archmage to be'. Whether or not they believed such stories, and whether or not they liked Ged, most of his companions admired him, and were eager to follow him when the rare wild mood came over him and he joined them to lead their games on the lengthening evenings of spring. But for the most part he was all work and pride and temper, and held himself apart. Among them all, Vetch being absent, he had no friend, and never knew he wanted one.

He was fifteen, very young to learn any of the High Arts of wizard or mage, those who carry the staff; but he was so quick to learn all the arts of illusion that the Master Changer, himself a young man, soon began to teach him apart from the others, and to tell him about the true Spells of Shaping. He explained how, if a thing is really to be changed into another thing, it must be re-named for as long as the spell lasts, and he told how this affects the names and natures of things surrounding the transformed thing. He spoke of the perils of changing, above all when the wizard transforms his own shape and thus is liable to be caught in his own spell. Little by little, drawn on by the boy's sureness of understanding, the young Master began to do more than merely tell him of these mysteries. He taught him first one and then another of the Great Spells of Change, and he gave him the Book of Shaping to study. This he did without knowledge of the Archmage, and unwisely, yet he meant no harm.

Ged worked also with the Master Summoner now, but that Master was a stern man, aged and hardened by the deep and sombre wizardry he taught. He dealt with no illusion, only true magic, the summoning of such energies as light, and heat, and the force that draws the magnet, and those forces men perceive as weight, form, colour, sound: real powers, drawn from the immense fathomless energies of the universe, which no man's spells or uses could exhaust or unbalance. The weatherworker's and seamaster's calling upon wind and water were crafts already known to his pupils, but it was he who showed them why the true wizard uses such spells only at need, since to summon up such earthly forces is to change the earth of which they are a part. 'Rain on Roke may be drouth in Osskil,' he said, 'and a calm in the East Reach may be storm and ruin in the West, unless you know what you are about.'

As for calling of real things and living people, and the raising up of spirits of the dead, and the invocations of the Unseen, those spells which are the height of the Summoner's art and the mage's power, those he scarcely spoke of to them. Once or twice Ged tried to lead him to talk a little of such mysteries, but the Master was silent, looking at him long and grimly, till Ged grew uneasy and said no more.

Sometimes indeed he was uneasy working even such lesser spells as the Summoner taught him. There were certain runes on certain pages of the Lore-Book that seemed familiar to him, though he did not remember in what book he had ever seen them before. There were certain phrases that must be said in spells of Summoning that he did not like to say. They made him think, for an instant, of shadows in a dark room, of a shut door and shadows reaching out to him from the corner by the door. Hastily he put such thoughts or memories aside and went on. These moments of fear and darkness, he said to himself, were the shadows merely of his ignorance. The more he learned, the less he would have to fear, until finally in his full power as Wizard he need fear nothing in the world, nothing at all.

In the second month of that summer all the school gathered again at the Great House to celebrate the Moon's Night and the Long Dance, which that year fell together as one festival of two nights, which happens but once in fifty-two years. All the first night, the shortest night of full moon of the year, flutes played out in the fields, and the narrow streets of Thwil were full of drums and torches, and the sound of singing went out over the moonlit waters of Roke Bay. As the sun rose next morning the Chanters of Roke began to sing the long *Deed of Erreth-Akbe*, which tells how the white towers of Havnor were built, and of Erreth-Akbe's journeys from the Old Island, Éa, through all the Archipelago and the Reaches, until at last in the uttermost West Reach on the edge of the Open Sea he met the dragon Orm; and his bones in shattered armour lie among the dragon's bones on the shore of lonely Selidor, but his sword set atop the highest tower of Havnor still burns red in the sunset above the Inmost Sea. When the chant was finished the Long Dance began. Townsfolk and Masters and students and farmers all together, men and women, danced in the warm dust and dusk down all the roads of Roke to the sea-beaches, to the beat of drums and drone of pipes and flutes. Straight out into the sea they danced, under the moon one night past full, and the music was lost in the breakers' sound. As the east grew light they came back up the beaches and the roads, the drums silent and only the flutes playing soft and shrill. So it was done on every island of the Archipelago that night: one dance, one music binding together the sea-divided lands.

When the Long Dance was over most people slept the day away, and gathered again at evening to eat and drink. There was a group of young fellows, prentices and sorcerers, who had brought their

supper out from the refectory to hold private feast in a ⌐
of the Great House: Vetch, Jasper, and Ged were there, and
seven others, and some young lads released briefly from the Ison
Tower, for this festival had brought even Kurremkarmerruk out,
They were all eating and laughing and playing such tricks out of
pure frolic as might be the marvel of a king's court. One boy had
lighted the court with a hundred stars of werelight, coloured like
jewels, that swung in a slow netted procession between them and the
real stars; and a pair of boys were playing bowls with balls of green
flame and bowling-pins that leaped and hopped away as the ball
came near; and all the while Vetch sat cross-legged, eating roast
chicken, up in mid-air. One of the younger boys tried to pull him
down to earth, but Vetch merely drifted up a little higher, out of
reach, and sat calmly smiling on the air. Now and then he tossed
away a chicken bone, which turned to an owl and flew hooting
among the netted star-lights. Ged shot breadcrumb arrows after the
owls and brought them down, and when they touched the ground
there they lay, bone and crumb, all illusion gone. Ged also tried to
join Vetch up in the middle of the air, but lacking the key of the
spell he had to flap his arms to keep aloft, and they were all laughing at his flights and flaps and bumps. He kept up his foolishness
for the laughter's sake, laughing with them, for after those two
long nights of dance and moonlight and music and magery he was
in a fey and wild mood, ready for whatever might come.

He came lightly down on his feet just beside Jasper at last, and
Jasper, who never laughed aloud, moved away saying, 'The Sparrowhawk that can't fly ...'

'Is Jasper a precious stone?' Ged returned, grinning. 'O Jewel
among sorcerers, O Gem of Havnor, sparkle for us!'

The lad that had set the lights dancing sent one down to dance
and glitter about Jasper's head. Not quite as cool as usual, frowning,
Jasper brushed the light away and snuffed it out with one gesture.
'I am sick of boys and noise and foolishness,' he said.

'You're getting middle-aged, lad,' Vetch remarked from above.

'If silence and gloom is what you want,' put in one of the
younger boys, 'you could always try the Tower.'

Ged said to him, 'What is it you want, then, Jasper?'

'I want the company of my equals,' Jasper said. 'Come on, Vetch. Leave the prentices to their toys.'

Ged turned to face Jasper. 'What do sorcerers have that prentices lack?' he inquired. His voice was quiet, but all the other boys suddenly fell still, for in his tone as in Jasper's the spite between them now sounded plain and clear as steel coming out of a sheath.

'Power,' Jasper said.

'I'll match your power act for act.'

'You challenge me?'

'I challenge you.'

Vetch had dropped down to the ground, and now he came between them, grim of face. 'Duels in sorcery are forbidden to us, and well you know it. Let this cease!'

Both Ged and Jasper stood silent, for it was true they knew the law of Roke, and they also knew that Vetch was moved by love, and themselves by hate. Yet their anger was balked, not cooled. Presently, moving a little aside as if to be heard by Vetch alone, Jasper spoke, with his cool smile: 'I think you'd better remind your goatherd friend again of the law that protects him. He looks sulky. I wonder, did he really think I'd accept a challenge from him? A fellow who smells of goats, a prentice who doesn't know the First Change?'

'Jasper,' said Ged, 'what do you know of what I know?'

For an instant, with no word spoken that any heard, Ged vanished from their sight, and where he had stood a great falcon hovered, opening its hooked beak to scream: for one instant, and then Ged stood again in the flickering torchlight, his dark gaze on Jasper.

Jasper had taken a step backward, in astonishment; but now he shrugged and said one word: 'Illusion.'

The others muttered. Vetch said, 'This was not illusion. It was a true change. And enough, Jasper, listen –'

'Enough to prove that he sneaked a look in the Book of Shaping behind the Master's back: what then? Go on, Goatherd. I like this trap you're building for yourself. The more you try to prove yourself my equal, the more you show yourself for what you are.'

At that, Vetch turned from Jasper, and said very softly to Ged, 'Sparrowhawk, will you be a man and drop this now – come with me –'

Ged looked at his friend and smiled, but all he said was, 'Keep Hoeg for me a little while, will you?' He put into Vetch's hands the little otak, which as usual had been riding on his shoulder. It had never let any but Ged touch it, but it came to Vetch now, and climbing up his arm cowered on his shoulder, its great bright eyes always on its master.

'Now,' Ged said to Jasper, quietly as before, 'what are you going to do to prove yourself my superior, Jasper?'

'I don't have to do anything, Goatherd. Yet I will. I will give you a chance – an opportunity. Envy eats you like a worm in an apple. Let's let out the worm. Once by Roke Knoll you boasted that Gontish wizards don't play games. Come to Roke Knoll now and show us what it is they do instead. And afterward, maybe I will show you a little sorcery.'

'Yes, I should like to see that,' Ged answered. The younger boys, used to seeing his black temper break out at the least hint of slight or insult, watched him in wonder at his coolness now. Vetch watched him not in wonder, but with growing fear. He tried to intervene again, but Jasper said, 'Come, keep out of this, Vetch. What will you do with the chance I give you, Goatherd? Will you show us an illusion, a fireball, a charm to cure goats with the mange?'

'What would you like me to do, Jasper?'

The older lad shrugged. 'Summon up a spirit from the dead, for all I care!'

'I will.'

'You will not.' Jasper looked straight at him, rage suddenly flaming out over his disdain. 'You will not. You cannot. You brag and brag –'

'By my name, I will do it!'

They all stood utterly motionless for a moment.

Breaking away from Vetch who would have held him back by main force, Ged strode out of the courtyard, not looking back.

The dancing werelights overhead died out, sinking down. Jasper hesitated a second, then followed after Ged. And the rest came straggling behind, in silence, curious and afraid.

The slopes of Roke Knoll went up dark into the darkness of summer night before moonrise. The presence of that hill where many wonders had been worked was heavy, like a weight in the air about them. As they came on to the hillside they thought of how the roots of it were deep, deeper than the sea, reaching down even to the old, blind, secret fires at the world's core. They stopped on the east slope. Stars hung over the black grass above them on the hill's crest. No wind blew.

Ged went a few paces up the slope away from the others and turning said in a clear voice. 'Jasper! Whose spirit shall I call?'

'Call whom you like. None will listen to you.' Jasper's voice shook a little, with anger perhaps. Ged answered him softly, mockingly, 'Are you afraid?'

He did not even listen for Jasper's reply, if he made one. He no longer cared about Jasper. Now that they stood on Roke Knoll, hate and rage were gone, replaced by utter certainty. He need envy no one. He knew that his power, this night, on this dark enchanted ground, was greater than it had ever been, filling him till he trembled with the sense of strength barely kept in check. He knew now that Jasper was far beneath him, had been sent perhaps only to bring him here tonight, no rival but a mere servant of Ged's destiny. Under his feet he felt the hillroots going down and down into the dark, and over his head he saw the dry, far fires of the stars. Between, all things were to his order, to command. He stood at the centre of the world.

'Don't be afraid,' he said, smiling. 'I'll call a woman's spirit. You need not fear a woman. Elfarran I will call, the fair lady of the *Deed of Enlad*.'

'She died a thousand years ago, her bones lie afar under the Sea of Êa, and maybe there never was such a woman.'

'Do years and distances matter to the dead? Do the Songs lie?' Ged said with the same gentle mockery, and then saying, 'Watch the air between my hands,' he turned away from the others and stood still.

In a great slow gesture he stretched out his arms, the gesture of welcome that opens an invocation. He began to speak.

He had read the runes of this Spell of Summoning in Ogion's book, two years and more ago, and never since had seen them. In darkness he had read them then. Now in this darkness it was as if he read them again on the page open before him in the night. But now he understood what he read, speaking it aloud word after word, and he saw the markings of how the spell must be woven with the sound of the voice and the motion of body and hand.

The other boys stood watching, not speaking, not moving unless they shivered a little; for the great spell was beginning to work. Ged's voice was soft still, but changed, with a deep singing in it, and the words he spoke were not known to them. He fell silent. Suddenly the wind rose roaring in the grass. Ged dropped to his knees and called out aloud. Then he fell forward as if to embrace the earth with his outstretched arms, and when he rose he held something dark in his straining hands and arms, something so heavy that he shook with effort getting to his feet. The hot wind whined in the black tossing grasses on the hill. If the stars shone now none saw them.

The words of the enchantment hissed and mumbled on Ged's lips, and then he cried out aloud and clearly, 'Elfarran !'

Again he cried the name, 'Elfarran !'

And the third time, 'Elfarran !'

The shapeless mass of darkness he had lifted split apart. It sundered, and a pale spindle of light gleamed between his opened arms, a faint oval reaching from the ground up to the height of his raised hands. In the oval of light for a moment there moved a form, a human shape : a tall woman looking back over her shoulder. Her face was beautiful, and sorrowful, and full of fear.

Only for a moment did the spirit glimmer there. Then the sallow oval between Ged's arms grew bright. It widened and spread, a rent in the darkness of the earth and night, a ripping open of the fabric of the world. Through it blazed a terrible brightness. And through

63

the bright misshapen breach clambered something like a clot of black shadow, quick and hideous, and it leaped straight out at Ged's face.

Staggering back under the weight of the thing, Ged gave a short, hoarse scream. The little otak, watching from Vetch's shoulder, the animal that had no voice, screamed aloud also and leaped as if to attack.

Ged fell, struggling and writhing, while the bright rip in the world's darkness above him widened and sttretched. The boys that watched fled, and Jasper bent down to the ground hiding his eyes from the terrible light. Vetch alone ran forward to his friend. So only he saw the lump of shadow that clung to Ged, tearing at his flesh. It was like a black beast, the size of a young child, though it seemed to swell and shrink; and it had no head or face, only the four taloned paws with which it gripped and tore. Vetch sobbed with horror, yet he put out his hands to try to pull the thing away from Ged. Before he touched it, he was bound still, unable to move.

The intolerable brightness faded, and slowly the torn edges of the world closed together. Nearby a voice was speaking as softly as a tree whispers or a fountain plays.

Starlight began to shine again, and the grasses of the hillside were whitened with the light of the moon just rising. The night was healed. Restored and steady lay the balance of light and dark. The shadow-beast was gone. Ged lay sprawled on his back, his arms flung out as if they yet kept the wide gesture of welcome and invocation. His face was blackened with blood and there were great black stains on his shirt. The little otak cowered by his shoulder, quivering. And above him stood an old man whose cloak glimmered pale in the moonrise: the Archmage Nemmerle.

The end of Nemmerle's staff hovered silverly above Ged's breast. Once it gently touched him over the heart, once on the lips, while Nemmerle whispered. Ged stirred, and his lips parted gasping for breath. Then the old Archmage lifted the staff, and set it to earth, and leaned heavily on it with bowed head, as if he had scarcely strength to stand.

Vetch found himself free to move. Looking around, he saw that already others were there, the Masters Summoner and Changer. An act of great wizardry is not worked without arousing such men, and they had ways of coming very swiftly when need called, though none had been so swift as the Archmage. They now sent for help, and some who came went with the Archmage, while others, Vetch among them, carried Ged to the chambers of the Master Herbal.

All night long the Summoner stayed on Roke Knoll, keeping watch. Nothing stirred there on the hillside where the stuff of the world had been torn open. No shadow came crawling through moonlight seeking the rent through which it might clamber back into its own domain. It had fled from Nemmerle, and from the mighty spell-walls that surround and protect Roke Island, but it was in the world now. In the world, somewhere, it hid. If Ged had died that night it might have tried to find the doorway he had opened and follow him into death's realm, or slip back into whatever place it had come from; for this the Summoner waited on Roke Knoll. But Ged lived.

They had laid him abed in the healing-chamber, and the Master Herbal tended the wounds he had on his face and throat and shoulder. They were deep, ragged, and evil wounds. The black blood in them would not stanch, welling out even under the charms and the cobweb-wrapped perriot leaves laid upon them. Ged lay blind and dumb in fever like a stick in a slow fire, and there was no spell to cool what burned him.

Not far away, in the unroofed court where the fountain played, the Archmage lay also unmoving, but cold, very cold: only his eyes lived, watching the fall of moonlit water and the stir of moonlit leaves. Those with him said no spells and worked no healing. Quietly they spoke among themselves from time to time, and then turned again to watch their Lord. He lay still, hawk nose and high forehead and white hair bleached by moonlight all to the colour of bone. To check the ungoverned spell and drive off the shadow from Ged, Nemmerle had spent all his power, and with it his bodily strength was gone. He lay dying. But the death of a great mage, who has many times in his life walked on the dry steep hillsides of death's kingdom, is a strange matter: for the dying man goes not blindly, but surely, knowing the way. When Nemmerle looked up through the leaves of the tree, those with him did not know if he watched the stars of summer fading in daybreak, or those other stars, which never set above the hills that see no dawn.

The raven of Osskil that had been his pet for thirty years was gone. No one had seen where it went. 'It flies before him,' the Master Patterner said, as they kept vigil.

The day came warm and clear. The Great House and the streets of Thwil were hushed. No voice was raised, until along towards noon iron bells spoke out aloud in the Chanter's Tower, harshly tolling.

On the next day the Nine Masters of Roke gathered in a place somewhere under the dark trees of the Immanent Grove. Even there they set nine walls of silence about them, that no person or power might speak to them or hear them as they chose from amongst the mages of all Earthsea him who would be the new Archmage. Gensher of Way was chosen. A ship was sent forth at once across the Inmost Sea to Way Island to bring the Archmage back to Roke. The Master Windkey stood in the stern and raised up the magewind into the sail, and quickly the ship departed, and was gone.

Of these events Ged knew nothing. For four weeks of that hot summer he lay blind, and deaf, and mute, though at times he moaned and cried out like an animal. At last, as the patient crafts of the Master Herbal worked their healing, his wounds began to close and the fever left him. Little by little he seemed to hear again, though he never spoke. On a clear day of autumn the Master Herbal opened the shutters of the room where Ged lay. Since the darkness of that night on Roke Knoll he had known only darkness. Now he saw daylight, and the sun shining. He hid his scarred face in his hands and wept.

Still when winter came he could speak only with a stammering tongue, and the Master Herbal kept him there in the healing-chambers, trying to lead his body and mind gradually back to strength. It was early spring when at last the Master released him, sending him first to offer his fealty to the Archmage Gensher. For he had not been able to join all the others of the School in this duty when Gensher came to Roke.

None of his companions had been allowed to visit him in the months of his sickness and now as he passed some of them asked one another, 'Who is that?' He had been light and lithe and strong. Now lamed by pain, he went hesitantly, and did not raise his face, the left side of which was white with scars. He avoided those who knew him and those who did not, and made his way straight to the court of the Fountain. There where once he had awaited Nemmerle, Gensher awaited him.

Like the old Archmage the new one was cloaked in white; but like most men of Way and the East Reach Gensher was black-skinned, and his look was black, under thick brows.

Ged knelt and offered him fealty and obedience. Gensher was silent a while.

'I know what you did,' he said at last, 'but not what you are. I cannot accept your fealty.'

Ged stood up, and set his hand on the trunk of the young tree beside the fountain to steady himself. He was still very slow to find words. 'Am I to leave Roke, my lord?'

'Do you want to leave Roke?'

'No.'

'What do you want?'

'To stay. To learn. To undo ... the evil ...'

'Nemmerle himself could not do that. – No, I would not let you go from Roke. Nothing protects you but the power of the Masters here and the defences laid upon this island that keep the creatures of evil away. If you left now, the thing you loosed would find you at once, and enter into you, and possess you. You would be no man but a *gebbeth*, a puppet doing the will of that evil shadow which you raised up into the sunlight. You must stay here, until you gain strength and wisdom enough to defend yourself from it – if ever you do. Even now it waits for you. Assuredly it waits for you. Have you seen it since that night?'

'In dreams, lord.' After a while Ged went on, speaking with pain and shame, 'Lord Gensher, I do not know what it was – the thing that came out of the spell and cleaved to me –'

'Nor do I know. It has no name. You have great power inborn in you, and you used that power wrongly, to work a spell over which you have no control, not knowing how that spell affects the balance of light and dark, life and death, good and evil. And you were moved to do this by pride and by hate. Is it any wonder the result was ruin? You summoned a spirit from the dead, but with it came one of the Powers of unlife. Uncalled it came from a place where there are no names. Evil, it wills to work evil through you. The power you had to call it gives it power over you : you are connected. It is the shadow of your arrogance, the shadow of your ignorance, the shadow you cast. Has a shadow a name?'

Ged stood sick and haggard. He said at last, 'Better I had died.'

'Who are you to judge that, you for whom Nemmerle gave his life? – You are safe here. You will live here, and go on with your training. They tell me you were clever. Go on and do your work. Do it well. It is all you can do.'

So Gensher ended, and was suddenly gone, as is the way of mages. The fountain leaped in the sunlight, and Ged watched it a while and listened to its voice, thinking of Nemmerle. Once in that court he had felt himself to be a word spoken by the sunlight. Now the darkness also had spoken: a word that could not be unsaid.

He left the court, going to his old room in the South Tower, which they had kept empty for him. He stayed there alone. When the gong called to supper he went, but he would hardly speak to the other lads at the Long Table, or raise his face to them, even those who greeted him most gently. So after a day or two they all left him alone. To be alone was his desire, for he feared the evil he might do or say unwittingly.

Neither Vetch nor Jasper was there, and he did not ask about them. The boys he had led and lorded over were all ahead of him now, because of the months he had lost, and that spring and summer he studied with lads younger than himself. Nor did he shine among them, for the words of any spell, even the simplest illusion-charm, came halting from his tongue, and his hands faltered at their craft.

In autumn he was to go once again to the Isolate Tower to study with the Master Namer. This task which he had once dreaded now pleased him, for silence was what he sought, and long learning where no spells were wrought, and where that power which he knew was still in him would never be called upon to act.

The night before he left for the Tower a visitor came to his room, one wearing a brown travelling-cloak and carrying a staff of oak shod with iron. Ged stood up, at sight of the wizard's staff.

'Sparrowhawk –'

At the sound of the voice, Ged raised his eyes: it was Vetch standing there, solid and foursquare as ever, his black blunt face older but his smile unchanged. On his shoulder crouched a little beast, brindle-furred and bright-eyed.

'He stayed with me while you were sick, and now I'm sorry to part with him. And sorrier to part with you, Sparrowhawk. But I'm going home. Here, hoeg! go to your true master!' Vetch patted the otak and set it down on the floor. It went and sat on Ged's pallet, and began to wash its fur with a dry brown tongue like a little leaf. Vetch laughed, but Ged could not smile. He bent down to hide his face, stroking the otak.

'I thought you wouldn't come to me, Vetch,' he said.

He did not mean any reproach, but Vetch answered, 'I couldn't come to you. The Master Herbal forbade me; and since winter I've been with the Master in the Grove, locked up myself. I was not free, until I earned my staff. Listen: when you too are free, come to the East Reach. I will be waiting for you. There's good cheer in the little towns there, and wizards are well received.'

'Free . . .' Ged muttered, and shrugged a little, trying to smile.

Vetch looked at him, not quite as he had used to look, with no less love but more wizardry, perhaps. He said gently, 'You won't stay bound on Roke forever.'

'Well . . . I have thought, perhaps I may come to work with the Master in the Tower, to be one of those who seek among the books and the stars for lost names, and so ... so do no more harm, if not much good ...'

'Maybe,' said Vetch, 'I am no seer, but I see before you, not rooms and books, but far seas, and the fire of dragons, and the towers of cities, and all such things a hawk sees when he flies far and high.'

'And behind me – what do you see behind me?' Ged asked, and stood up as he spoke, so that the werelight that burned overhead between them sent his shadow back against the wall and floor. Then he turned his face aside and said, stammering, 'But tell me where you will go, what you will do.'

'I will go home, to see my brothers and the sister you have heard me speak of. I left her a little child and soon she'll be having her Naming – it's strange to think of! And so I'll find me a job of wizardry somewhere among the little isles. Oh, I would stay and talk with you, but I can't, my ship goes out tonight and the tide is turned already. Sparrowhawk, if ever your way lies East, come to me. And if you ever need me, send for me, call on me by my name: Estarriol.'

At that Ged lifted his scarred face, meeting his friend's eyes.

'Estarriol,' he said, 'my name is Ged.'

Then quietly they bade each other farewell and Vetch turned and went down the stone hallway, and left Roke.

Ged stood still a while, like one who has received great news, and must enlarge his spirit to receive it. It was a great gift that Vetch had given him, the knowledge of his true name.

No one knows a man's true name but himself and his namer. He may choose at length to tell it to his brother, or his wife, or his friend, yet even those few will never use it where any third person may hear it. In front of other people they will, like other people, call him by his use-name, his nickname – such a name as Sparrowhawk, and Vetch, and Ogion which means 'fir-cone'. If plain men hide their true name from all but a few they love and trust utterly, so much more must wizardly men, being more dangerous, and more endangered. Who knows a man's name, holds that man's life in his keeping. Thus to Ged who had lost faith in himself, Vetch had given that gift only a friend can give, the proof of unshaken, un-shakeable trust.

Ged sat down on his pallet and let the globe of werelight die, giving off as it faded a faint whiff of marsh-gas. He petted the otak, which stretched comfortably, and went to sleep on his knee as if it had never slept anywhere else. The Great House was silent. It came to Ged's mind that this was the eve of his own Passage, the day on which Ogion had given him his name. Four years were gone since then. He remembered the coldness of the mountain spring through which he had walked naked and unnamed. He fell to thinking of other bright pools in the River Ar, where he had used to swim; and of Ten Alders village under the great slanting forests of the mountain; of the shadows of morning across the dusty village street, the fire leaping under bellows-blast in the smith's smelting-pit on a winter afternoon, the witch's dark fragrant hut where the air was heavy with smoke and wreathing spells. He had not thought of these things for a long time. Now they came back to him, on the night he was seventeen years old. All the years and places of his brief broken life came within mind's reach and made a whole again. He knew once more, at last, after this long, bitter, wasted time, who he was and where he was.

But where he must go in the years to come, that he could not see; and he feared to see it.

Next morning he set out across the island, the otak riding on his shoulder as it had used to. This time it took him three days, not two, to walk to the Isolate Tower, and he was bone-weary when he came in sight of the Tower above the spitting, hissing seas of the northern cape. Inside, it was dark as he remembered, and cold as he remembered, and Kurremkarmerruk sat on his high seat writing down lists of names. He glanced at Ged and said without welcome, as if Ged had never been away. 'Go to bed; tired is stupid. Tomorrow you may open the Book of the Undertakings of the Makers, learning the names therein.'

At winter's end he returned to the Great House. He was made sorcerer then, and the Archmage Gensher accepted at that time his fealty. Thenceforth he studied the high arts and enchantments, passing beyond arts of illusion to the works of real magery, learning what he must know to earn his wizard's staff. The trouble he had had in speaking spells wore off over the months, and skill returned into his hands: yet he was never so quick to learn as he had been, having learned a long hard lesson from fear. Yet no ill portents or encounters followed on his working even of the Great Spells of Making and Shaping, which are most perilous. He came to wonder at times if the shadow he had loosed might have grown weak, or fled somehow out of the world, for it came no more into his dreams. But in his heart he knew such hope was folly.

From the Masters and from ancient lore-books Ged learned what he could about such beings as this shadow he had loosed; little was there to learn. No such creature was described or spoken of directly. There were at best hints here and there in the old books of things that might be like the shadow-beast. It was not a ghost of human man, nor was it a creature of the Old Powers of Earth, and yet it seemed it might have some link with these. In the *Matter of the Dragons*, which Ged read very closely, there was a tale of an ancient Dragonlord who had come under the sway of one of the Old Powers. a speaking stone that lay in a far northern land. 'At *the Stone's command*,' said the book, '*he did speak to raise up a dead spirit out of the realm of the dead, but his wizardry being bent awry by the Stone's will there came with the dead spirit also a thing not summoned, which did devour him out from within and in his shape walked, destroying men.*' But the book did not say what the thing was, nor did it tell the end of the tale. And the Masters did not know where such a shadow might come from: from unlife, the Archmage had said; from the wrong side of the world, said the Master Changer; and the Master Summoner said, 'I do not know.' The Summoner had come often to sit with Ged in his illness. He was grim and grave as ever, but Ged knew his compassion, and loved him well. 'I do not know. I know of the thing only this: that only a great power could have summoned up such a thing, and perhaps only one power – only one voice – your voice. But what in turn that means, I do not know. You will find out. You must find out, or die, and worse than die ...' He spoke softly and his eyes were sombre as he looked at Ged. 'You thought, as a boy, that a mage is one who can do anything. So I thought, once. So did we all. And the truth is that as a man's real power grows and his knowledge widens, ever the way he can follow grows narrower; until at last he chooses nothing, but does only and wholly what he *must* do ...'

The Archmage sent Ged, after his eighteenth birthday, to work with the Master Patterner. What is learned in the Immanent Grove is not much talked about elsewhere. It is said that no spells are worked there, and yet the place itself is an enchantment. Sometimes the trees of that Grove are seen, and sometimes they are not seen, and they are not always in the same place and part of Roke Island. It is said that the trees of the Grove themselves are wise. It is said that the Master Patterner learns his supreme magery there within the Grove, and if ever the trees should die so shall his wisdom die, and in those days the waters will rise and drown the islands of Earthsea which Segoy raised from the deeps in the time before myth, all the lands where men and dragons dwell.

But all this is hearsay; wizards will not speak of it.

The months went by, and at last on a day of spring Ged returned to the Great House, and he had no idea what would be asked of him next. At the door that gives on the path across the fields to Roke Knoll an old man met him, waiting for him in the doorway. At first Ged did not know him, and then putting his mind to it recalled him as the one who had let him into the School on the day of his coming, five years ago.

The old man smiled, greeting him by name, and asked, 'Do you know who I am?'

Now Ged had thought before of how it was always said, the Nine Masters of Roke, although he knew only eight: Windkey, Hand, Herbal, Chanter, Changer, Summoner, Namer, Patterner. It seemed that people spoke of the Archmage as the ninth. Yet when a new Archmage was chosen nine Masters met to choose him.

'I think you are the Master Doorkeeper,' said Ged.

'I am. Ged, you won entrance to Roke by saying your name. Now you may win your freedom of it by saying mine.' So said the old man smiling, and waited. Ged stood dumb.

He knew a thousand ways and crafts and means for finding out names of things and of men, of course; such craft was a part of everything he had learned at Roke, for without it there could be little useful magic done. But to find out the name of a Mage and Master was another matter. A mage's name is better hidden than a herring in the sea, better guarded than a dragon's den. A prying charm will be met with a stronger charm, subtle devices will fail, devious inquiries will be deviously thwarted, and force will be turned ruinously back upon itself.

'You keep a narrow door, Master,' said Ged at last. 'I must sit out in the fields here, I think, and fast till I grow thin enough to slip through.'

'As long as you like,' said the Doorkeeper, smiling.

So Ged went off a little way and sat down under an alder on the banks of the Thwilburn, letting his otak run down to play in the stream and hunt the muddy banks for creekcrabs. The sun went down, late and bright, for spring was well along. Lights of lantern and werelight gleamed in the windows of the Great House, and down the hill the streets of Thwil town filled with darkness. Owls hooted over the roofs and bats flitted in the dusk air above the stream, and still Ged sat thinking how he might, by force, ruse, or sorcery, learn the Doorkeeper's name. The more he pondered the less he saw, among all the arts of witchcraft he had learned in these five years on Roke, any one that would serve to wrest such a secret from such a mage.

He lay down in the field and slept under the stars, with the otak nestling in his pocket. After the sun was up he went, still fasting, to the door of the House and knocked. The Doorkeeper opened.

'Master,' said Ged, 'I cannot take your name from you, not being strong enough, and I cannot trick your name from you, not being wise enough. So I am content to stay here, and learn or serve, whatever you will: unless by chance you will answer a question I have.'

'Ask it.'

'What is your name?'

The Doorkeeper smiled, and said his name; and Ged, repeating it, entered for the last time into that House.

When he left it again he wore a heavy dark-blue cloak, the gift of the township of Low Torning, whereto he was bound, for they wanted a wizard there. He carried also a staff of his own height, carved of yew-wood, bronze-shod. The Doorkeeper bade him farewell opening the back door of the Great House for him, the door of horn and ivory, and he went down the streets of Thwil to a ship that waited for him on the bright water in the morning.

5. The Dragon of Pendor

WEST of Roke in a crowd between the two great lands Hosk and Ensmer lie the Ninety Isles. The nearest to Roke is Serd, and the farthest is Seppish, which lies almost in the Pelnish Sea; and whether the sum of them is ninety is a question never settled, for if you count only isles with freshwater springs you might have seventy, while if you count every rock you might have a hundred and still not be done; and then the tide would change. Narrow run the channels between the islets, and there the mild tides of the Inmost Sea, chafed and baffled, run high and fall low, so that where at high tide there might be three islands in one place, at low there might be one. Yet for all that danger of the tide, every child who can walk can paddle, and has his little rowboat; housewives row across the channel to take a cup of rushwash tea with the neighbour; peddlers call their wares in rhythm with the stroke of their oars. All roads there are salt water, blocked only by nets strung from house to house across the straits to catch the small fish called turbies, the oil of which is the wealth of the Ninety Isles. There are few bridges, and no great towns. Every islet is thick with farms and fishermen's houses, and these are gathered into townships each of ten or twenty islets. One such was Low Torning, the westernmost, looking not on the Inmost Sea but outward to empty ocean, that lonely corner of the Archipelago where only Pendor lies, the dragon-spoiled isle, and beyond it the waters of the West Reach, desolate.

A house was ready there for the township's new wizard. It stood on a hill among green fields of barley, sheltered from the west wind by a grove of pendick-trees that now were red with flowers. From the door one looked out on other thatched roofs and groves and gardens, and other islands with their roofs and fields and hills, and amongst them all the many bright winding channels of the sea. It was a poor house, windowless, with earthen floor, yet a better house than the one Ged had been born in. The Isle-Men of Low Torning, standing in awe of the wizard from Roke, asked pardon for its humbleness. 'We have no stone to build with,' said one, 'We are none of us rich, though none starve,' said another, and a third, 'It will be dry at least, for I saw to the thatching myself, Sir.' To Ged it was as good as any palace. He thanked the leaders of the township frankly, so that the eighteen of them went home, each in his own rowboat to his home isle, to tell the fishermen and housewives that the new wizard was a strange young grim fellow who spoke little, but he spoke fairly, and without pride.

There was little cause, perhaps, for pride in this first magistry of Ged's. Wizards trained on Roke went commonly to cities or castles, to serve high lords who held them in high house. These fishermen of Low Torning in the usual way of things would have had among them no more than a witch or a plain sorcerer, to charm the fishing-nets and sing over new boats and cure beasts and men of their ailments. But in late years the old Dragon of Pendor had spawned : nine dragons, it was said, now laired in the ruined towers of the Sealords of Pendor, dragging their scaled bellies up and down the marble stairs and through the broken doorways there. Wanting food on that dead isle, they would be flying forth some year when they were grown and hunger came upon them. Already a flight of four had been seen over the southwest shores of Hosk, not alighting but spying out the sheepfolds, barns, and villages. The hunger of a dragon is slow to wake, but hard to sate. So the Isle-Men of Low Torning had sent to Roke begging for a wizard to protect their folk from what boded over the western horizon, and the Archmage had judged their fear well founded.

'There is no comfort in this place,' the Archmage had said to Ged on the day he made him wizard, 'no fame, no wealth, maybe no risk. Will you go?'

'I will go,' Ged had replied, not from obedience only. Since the night on Roke Knoll his desire had turned as much against fame and display as once it had been set on them. Always now he doubted his strength and dreaded the trial of his power. Yet also the talk of dragons drew him with a great curiosity. In Gont there have been no dragons for many hundred years, and no dragon would ever fly within a scent or sight or spell of Roke, so that there also they are a matter of tales and songs only, things sung of but not seen. Ged had learned all he could of dragons at the School, but it is one thing to read about dragons and another to meet them. The chance lay bright before him, and heartily he answered, 'I will go.'

The Archmage Gensher had nodded his head, but his look was sombre. 'Tell me,' he said at last, 'do you fear to leave Roke? or are you eager to be gone?'

'Both, my lord.'

Again Gensher nodded. 'I do not know if I do right to send you from your safety here,' he said very low. 'I cannot see your way. It is all in darkness. And there is a power in the North, something that would destroy you, but what it is and where, whether in your past or on your forward way, I cannot tell: it is all shadowed. When the men from Low Torning came here, I thought at once of you, for it seemed a safe place and out of the way, where you might have time to gather your strength. But I do not know if any place is safe for you, or where your way goes. I do not want to send you out into the dark ...'

It seemed a bright enough place to Ged at first, the house under the flowering trees. There he lived, and watched the western sky often, and kept his wizard's ear tuned for the sound of scaly wings. But no dragon came. Ged fished from his jetty, and tended his garden-patch. He spent whole days pondering a page or a line or a word in the Lore-Books he had brought from Roke, sitting out in the summer air under the pendick-trees, while the otak slept beside him or went hunting mice in the forests of grass and daisies. And he served the people of Low Torning as healall and weatherworker whenever they asked him. It did not enter his head that a wizard might be shamed to perform such simple crafts, for he had been a witch-child among poorer folk than these. They, however, asked little of him, holding him in awe, partly because he was a wizard from the Isle of the Wise, and partly on account of his silence and his scarred face. There was that about him, young as he was, that made men uneasy with him.

Yet he found a friend, a boatmaker who dwelt on the next isle eastward. His name was Pechvarry. They had first met on his jetty, where Ged stopped to watch him stepping the mast of a little catboat. He had looked up at the wizard with a grin and said, 'Here's a month's work nearly finished. I guess you might have done it in a minute with a word, eh, Sir?'

'I might,' said Ged, 'but it would likely sink the next minute, unless I kept the spells up. But if you like ...' He stopped.

'Well, sir?'

'Well, that is a lovely little craft. She needs nothing. But if you like, I could set a binding-spell on her, to help keep her sound; or a finding-spell, to help bring her home from the sea.'

He spoke hesitantly, not wanting to offend the craftsman, but Pechvarry's face shone. 'The little boat's for my son, Sir, and if you would lay such charms on her, it would be a mighty kindness and a friendly act.' And he climbed up on to the jetty to take Ged's hand then and there and thank him.

After that they came to work together often, Ged interweaving his spellcrafts with Pechvarry's handwork on the boats he built or repaired, and in return learning from Pechvarry how a boat was built, and also how a boat was handled without aid of magic: for this skill of plain sailing had been somewhat sacred on Roke. Often Ged and Pechvarry and his little son Ioeth went out into the channels and lagoons, sailing or rowing one boat or another, till Ged was a fair sailor, and the friendship between him and Pechvarry was a settled thing.

Along in late autumn the boatmaker's son fell sick. The mother sent for the witchwoman of Tesk Isle, who was a good hand at healing, and all seemed well for a day or two. Then in the middle of a stormy night came Pechvarry hammering at Ged's door, begging him to come save the child. Ged ran down to the boat with him and they rowed in all haste through dark and rain to the boatmaker's house. There Ged saw the child on his pallet-bed, and the mother crouching silent beside him, and the witchwoman making a smoke of corly-root and singing the Nagian Chant, which was the best healing she had. But she whispered to Ged, 'Lord Wizard, I think this fever is the redfever, and the child will die of it tonight.'

When Ged knelt and put his hands on the child, he thought the same, and he drew back a moment. In the latter months of his own long sickness the Master Herbal had taught him much of the healer's lore, and the first lesson and the last of all that lore was this: Heal the wound and cure the illness, but let the dying spirit go.

The mother saw his movement and the meaning of it, and cried out aloud in despair. Pechvarry stooped down by her saying, 'The Lord Sparrowhawk will save him, wife. No need to cry! He's here now. He can do it.'

Hearing the mother's wail, and seeing the trust Pechvarry had in him, Ged did not know how he could disappoint them. He mistrusted his own judgement, and thought perhaps the child might be saved, if the fever could be brought down. He said, 'I'll do my best, Pechvarry.'

He set to bathing the little boy with cold rainwater that they brought new-fallen from out of doors, and he began to say one of the spells of feverstay. The spell took no hold and made no whole, and suddenly he thought the child was dying in his arms.

Summoning his power all at once and with no thought for himself, he sent his spirit out after the child's spirit, to bring it back home. He called the child's name, 'Ioeth!' Thinking some faint answer came in his inward hearing he pursued, calling once more. Then he saw the little boy running fast and far ahead of him down a dark slope, the side of some vast hill. There was no sound. The stars above the hill were no stars his eyes had ever seen. Yet he knew the constellations by name: the Sheaf, the Door, the One Who Turns, the Tree. They were those stars that do not set, that are not paled by the coming of any day. He had followed the dying child too far.

Knowing this he found himself alone on the dark hillside. It was hard to turn back, very hard.

He turned slowly. Slowly he set one foot forward to climb back up the hill, and then the other. Step by step he went, each step willed. And each step was harder than the last.

The stars did not move. No wind blew over the dry steep ground. In all the vast kingdom of the darkness only he moved, slowly, climbing. He came to the top of the hill, and saw the low wall of stones there. But across the wall, facing him, there was a shadow.

The shadow did not have the shape of man or beast. It was shapeless, scarcely to be seen, but it whispered at him, though there were no words in its whispering, and it reached out towards him. And it stood on the side of the living, and he on the side of the dead.

Either he must go down the hill into the desert lands and lightless cities of the dead, or he must step across the wall back into life, where the formless evil thing waited for him.

His spirit-staff was in his hand, and he raised it high. With that motion, strength came into him. As he made to leap the low wall of stones straight at the shadow, the staff burned suddenly white, a blinding light in that dim place. He leaped, felt himself fall, and saw no more.

Now what Pechvarry and his wife and the witch saw was this; the young wizard had stopped midway in his spell, and held the child a while motionless. Then he had laid little Ioeth gently down on the pallet, and had risen, and stood silent, staff in hand. All at once he raised the staff high and it blazed with white fire as if he held the lightning-bolt in his grip, and all the household things in the hut leaped out strange and vivid in that momentary fire. When their eyes were clear from the dazzlement they saw the young man lying huddled forward on the earthen floor, beside the pallet where the child lay dead.

To Pechvarry it seemed that the wizard also was dead. His wife wept, but he was utterly bewildered. But the witch had some hearsay knowledge concerning magery and the ways a true wizard may go, and she saw to it that Ged, cold and lifeless as he lay, was not treated as a dead man but as one sick or tranced. He was carried home, and an old woman was left to watch and see whether he slept to wake or slept for ever.

The little otak was hiding in the rafters of the house, as it did when strangers entered. There it stayed while the rain beat on the walls and the fire sank down and the night wearing slowly along left the old woman nodding beside the hearthpit. Then the otak crept down and came to Ged where he lay stretched stiff and still upon the bed. It began to lick his hands and wrists, long and patiently, with its dry leaf-brown tongue. Crouching beside his head it licked his temple, his scarred cheek, and softly his closed eyes. And very slowly under that soft touch Ged roused. He woke, not knowing where he had been or where he was or what was the faint grey light in the air about him, which was the light of dawn coming to the world. Then the otak curled up near his shoulder as usual, and went to sleep.

Later, when Ged thought back upon that night, he knew that had none touched him when he lay thus spirit-lost, had none called him back in some way, he might have been lost for good. It was only the dumb instinctive wisdom of the beast who licks his hurt companion to comfort him, and yet in that wisdom Ged saw something akin to his own power, something that went as deep as wizardry. From that time forth he believed that the wise man is one who never sets himself apart from other living things, whether they have speech or not, and in later years he strove long to learn what can be learned, in silence, from the eyes of animals, the flight of birds, the great slow gestures of trees.

He had now made unscathed, for the first time, that crossing-over and return which only a wizard can make with open eyes, and which not the greatest mage can make without risk. But he had returned to a grief and a fear. The grief was for his friend Pechvarry, the fear for himself. He knew now why the Archmage had feared to send him forth, and what had darkened and clouded even the mage's foreseeing of his future. For it was darkness itself that had awaited him, the unnamed thing, the being that did not belong in the world, the shadow he had loosed or made. In spirit, at the boundary wall between death and life, it had waited for him these long years. It had found him there at last. It would be on his track now, seeking to draw near to him, to take his strength into itself, and suck up his life, and clothe itself in his flesh.

Soon after, he dreamed of the thing like a bear with no head or face. He thought it went fumbling about the walls of the house, searching for the door. Such a dream he had not dreamed since the healing of the wounds the thing had given him. When he woke he was weak and cold, and the scars on his face and shoulder drew and ached.

Now began a bad time. When he dreamed of the shadow or so much as thought of it, he felt always the same cold dread: sense and power drained out of him, leaving him stupid and astray. He raged at his cowardice, but that did no good. He sought for some protection, but there was none; the thing was not flesh, not alive, not spirit, unnamed, having no being but what he himself had given it – a terrible power outside the laws of the sunlit world. All he knew of it was that it was drawn to him and would try to work its will through him, being his creature. But in what form it could come, having no real form of its own as yet, and how it would come, and when it would come, this he did not know.

He set up what barriers of sorcery he could about his house and about the isle where he lived. Such spell-walls must be ever renewed, and soon he saw that if he spent all his strength on these defences, he would be of no use to the islanders. What could he do, between two enemies, if a dragon came from Pendor?

Again he dreamed, but this time in the dream the shadow was inside his house, beside the door, reaching out to him through the darkness and whispering words he did not understand. He woke in terror, and sent the werelight flaming through the air, lighting every corner of the little house till he saw no shadow anywhere. Then he put wood on the coals of his firepit, and sat in the firelight hearing the autumn wind fingering at the thatch roof and whining in the great bare trees above; and he pondered long. An old anger had wakened in his heart. He would not suffer this helpless waiting, this sitting on a little island muttering useless spells of lock and ward. Yet he could not simply flee the trap: to do so would be to break his trust with the islanders and to leave them to the imminent dragon, undefended. There was but one way to take.

The next morning he went down among the fishermen in the principal moorage of Low Torning, and finding the Head Isle-Man there said to him, 'I must leave this place. I am in danger, and I put you in danger. I must go. Therefore I ask your leave to go out and do away with the dragons on Pendor, so that my task for you will be finished and I may leave freely. Or if I fail, I should fail also when they come here, and that is better known now than later.'

The Isle-Man stared at him all dropjawed. 'Lord Sparrowhawk,' he said, 'there are nine dragons out there !'

'Eight are still young, they say.'

'But the old one —'

'I tell you, I must go from here. I ask your leave to rid you of the dragon-peril first, if I can do so.'

'As you will, Sir,' the Isle-Man said gloomily. All that listened there thought this a folly or a crazy courage in their young wizard, and with sullen faces they saw him go, expecting no news of him again. Some hinted that he meant merely to sail back by Hosk to the Inmost Sea, leaving them in the lurch; others, among the Pechvarry, held that he had gone mad, and sought death.

For four generations of men all ships had set their course to keep far from the shores of Pendor Island. No mage had ever come to do combat with the dragon there, for the island was on no travelled sea-road, and its lords had been pirates, slave-takers, war-makers, hated by all that dwelt in the southwest parts of Earthsea. For this reason none had sought to revenge the Lord of Pendor, after the dragon came suddenly out of the west upon him and his men where they sat feasting in the tower, and smothered them with the flames of his mouth, and drove all the townsfolk screaming into the sea. Unavenged, Pendor had been left to the dragon, with all its bones, and towers, and jewels stolen from long-dead princes of the coasts of Paln and Hosk.

All this Ged knew well, and more, for ever since he came to Low Torning he had held in mind and pondered over all he had ever learned of dragons. As he guided his small boat westward — not rowing now nor using the seaman's skill Pechvarry had taught him, but sailing wizardly with the magewind in his sail and a spell set on prow and keel to keep them true – he watched to see the dead isle rise on the rim of the sea. Speed he wanted, and therefore used the magewind, for he feared what was behind him more than what was before him. But as the day passed, his impatience turned from fear to a kind of glad fierceness. At least he sought this danger of his own will; and the nearer he came to it the more sure he was that, for this time at least, for this hour perhaps before his death, he was free. The shadow dared not follow him into a dragon's jaws. The waves ran white-tipped on the grey sea, and grey clouds streamed overhead on the north wind. He went west with the quick magewind in his sail, and came in sight of the rocks of Pendor, the still streets of the town, and the gutted, falling towers.

At the entrance of the harbour, a shallow crescent bay, he let the windspell drop and stilled his little boat so it lay rocking on the waves. Then he summoned the dragon: 'Usurper of Pendor, come defend your hoard!'

His voice fell short in the sound of breakers beating on the ashen shores; but dragons have keen ears. Presently one flitted up from some roofless ruin of the town like a vast black bat, thin-winged and spiny-backed, and circling into the north wind came flying towards Ged. His heart swelled at the sight of the creature that was a myth to his people, and he laughed and shouted, 'Go tell the Old One to come, you wind-worm!'

For this was one of the young dragons, spawned there years ago by a she-dragon from the West Reach, who had set her clutch of great leathern eggs, as they say she-dragons will, in some sunny broken room of the tower and had flown away again, leaving the Old Dragon of Pendor to watch the young when they crawled like baneful lizards from the shell.

The young dragon made no answer. He was not large of his kind, maybe the length of a forty-oared ship, and was worm-thin for all the reach of his black membranous wings. He had not got his growth yet, nor his voice, nor any dragon-cunning. Straight at Ged in the small rocking boat he came, opening his long, toothed jaws as

85

he slid down arrowy from the air: so that all Ged had to do was bind his wings and limbs stiff with one sharp spell and send him thus hurtling aside into the sea like a stone falling. And the grey sea closed over him.

Two dragons like the first rose up from the base of the highest tower. Even as the first one they came driving straight at Ged, and even so he caught both, hurled both down, and drowned them; and he had not yet lifted up his wizard's staff.

Now after a little time there came three against him from the island. One of those was much greater, and fire spewed curling from its jaws. Two came flying at him rattling their wings, but the big one came circling from behind, very swift, to burn him and his boat with its breath of fire. No binding spell would catch all three, because two came from north and one from south. In the instant that he saw this, Ged worked a spell of Changing, and between one breath and the next flew up from his boat in dragon-form.

Spreading broad wings and reaching talons out, he met the two head on, withering them with fire, and then turned to the third, who was larger than he and armed also with fire. On the wind over the grey waves they doubled, snapped, swooped, lunged, till smoke roiled about them red-lit by the glare of their fiery mouths. Ged flew suddenly upward and the other pursued, below him. In midflight the dragon-Ged raised wings, stopped, and stooped as the hawk stoops, talons outstretched downwards, striking and bearing the other down by neck and flank. The black wings flurried and black dragon-blood dropped in thick drops into the sea. The Pendor dragon tore free and flew low and lamely to the island, where it hid, crawling into some well or cavern in the ruined town.

At once Ged took his form and place again on the boat, for it was most perilous to keep that dragon-shape longer than need demanded. His hands were black with the scalding wormblood, and he was scorched about the head with fire, but this was no matter now. He waited only till he had his breath back and then called, 'Six I have seen, five slain, nine are told of: come out, worms!'

No creature moved nor voice spoke for a long while on the island, but only the waves beat loudly on the shore. Then Ged was aware that the highest tower slowly changed its shape, bulging out on one side as if it grew an arm. He feared dragon-magic, for old dragons are very powerful and guileful in a sorcery like and unlike the sorcery of men : but a moment more and he saw this was no trick of the dragon, but of his own eyes. What he had taken for a part of the tower was the shoulder of the Dragon Pendor as he uncurled his bulk and lifted himself slowly up.

When he was all afoot his scaled head, spike-crowned and triple-tongued, rose higher than the broken tower's height, and his taloned forefeet rested on the rubble of the town below. His scales were grey-black, catching the daylight like broken stone. Lean as a hound he was and huge as a hill. Ged stared in awe. There was no song or tale could prepare the mind for this sight. Almost he stared into the dragon's eyes and was caught, for one cannot look into a dragon's eyes. He glanced away from the oily green gaze that watched him, and held up before him his staff, that looked now like a splinter, like a twig.

'Eight sons I had, little wizard,' said the great dry voice of the dragon. 'Five died, one dies : enough. You will not win my hoard by killing them.'

'I do not want your hoard.'

The yellow smoke hissed from the dragon's nostrils : that was his laughter.

'Would you not like to come ashore and look at it, little wizard? It is worth looking at.'

'No, dragon.' The kinship of dragons is with wind and fire, and they do not fight willingly over the sea. That had been Ged's advantage so far and he kept it; but the strip of seawater between him and the great grey talons did not seem much of an advantage, any more.

It was hard not to look into the green, watching eyes.

'You are a very young wizard,' the dragon said. 'I did not know men came so young into their power.' He spoke, as did Ged, in the Old Speech, for that is the tongue of dragons still. Although the use of the Old Speech binds a man to truth, this is not so with dragons. It is their own language, and they can lie in it, twisting the true words to false ends, catching the unwary hearer in a maze of mirror-words each of which reflects the truth and none of which leads anywhere. So Ged had been warned often, and when the dragon spoke he listened with an untrustful ear, all his doubts ready. But the words seemed plain and clear: 'Is it to ask my help that you have come here, little wizard?'

'No, dragon.'

'Yet I could help you. You will need help soon, against that which hunts you in the dark.'

Ged stood dumb.

'What is it that hunts you? Name it to me.'

'If I could name it –' Ged stopped himself.

Yellow smoke curled above the dragon's long head, from the nostrils that were two round pits of fire.

'If you could name it you could master it, maybe, little wizard. Maybe I could tell you its name, when I see it close by. And it will come close, if you wait about my isle. It will come wherever you come. If you do not want it to come close you must run, and run, and keep running from it. And yet it will follow you. Would you like to know its name?'

Ged stood silent again. How the dragon knew of the shadow he had loosed, he could not guess, nor how it might know the shadow's name. The Archmage had said that the shadow had no name. Yet dragons have their own wisdom; and they are an older race than man. Few men can guess what a dragon knows and how he knows it, and those few are the Dragonlords. To Ged, only one thing was sure: that, though the dragon might well be speaking truth, though he might indeed be able to tell Ged the nature and name of the shadow-thing and so give him power over it – even so, even if he spoke truth, he did so wholly for his own ends.

'It is very seldom,' the young man said at last, 'that dragons ask to do men favours.'

'But it is very common,' said the dragon, 'for cats to play with mice before they kill them.'

'But I did not come here to play, or to be played with. I came to strike a bargain with you.'

Like a sword in sharpness but five times the length of any sword, the point of the dragon's tail arched up scorpion-wise over his mailed back, above the tower. Dryly he spoke: 'I strike no bargain. I take. What have you to offer that I cannot take from you when I like?'

'Safety. Your safety. Swear that you will never fly eastward of Pendor, and I will swear to leave you unharmed.'

A grating sound came from the dragon's throat like the noise of an avalanche far off, stones falling among mountains. Fire danced along his three-forked tongue. He raised himself up higher, looming over the ruins. 'You offer me safety! You threaten me! With what?'

'With your name, Yevaud.'

Ged's voice shook as he spoke the name, yet he spoke it clear and loud. At the sound of it, the old dragon held still, utterly still. A minute went by, and another; and then Ged, standing there in his rocking chip of a boat, smiled. He had staked this venture and his life on a guess drawn from old histories of dragon-lore learned on Roke, a guess that this Dragon of Pendor was the same that had spoiled the west of Osskil in the days of Elfarran and Morred, and had been driven from Osskil by a wizard, Elt, wise in names. The guess had held.

'We are matched, Yevaud. You have your strength: I have your name. Will you bargain?'

Still the dragon made no reply.

Many years had the dragon sprawled on the island where golden breastplates and emeralds lay scattered among dust and bricks and bones; he had watched his black lizard-brood play among crumbling houses and try their wings from the cliffs; he had slept long in the sun, unwaked by voice or sail. He had grown old. It was hard now to stir, to face this magelad, this frail enemy, at the sight of whose staff Yevaud, the old dragon, winced.

'You may choose nine stones from my hoard,' he said at last, his voice hissing and whining in his long jaws. 'The best: take your choice. Then go!'

'I do not want your stones, Yevaud.'

'Where is men's greed gone? Men loved bright stones in the old days in the North ... I know what it is you want, wizard. I, too, can offer you safety, for I know what can save you. I know what alone can save you. There is a horror follows you. I will tell you its name.'

Ged's heart leaped in him, and he clutched his staff, standing as still as the dragon stood. He fought a moment with sudden, startling hope.

It was not his own life that he bargained for. One mastery, and only one, could he hold over the dragon. He set hope aside and did what he must do.

'That is not what I ask for, Yevaud.'

When he spoke the dragon's name it was as if he held the huge being on a fine, thin leash, tightening it on his throat. He could feel the ancient malice and experience of men in the dragon's gaze that rested on him, he could see the steel talons each as long as a man's forearm, and the stone-hard hide, and the withering fire that lurked in the dragon's throat: and yet always the leash tightened, tightened.

He spoke again: 'Yevaud! Swear by your name that you and your sons will never come to the Archipelago.'

Flames broke suddenly bright and loud from the dragon's jaws, and he said, 'I swear it by my name!'

Silence lay over the isle then, and Yevaud lowered his great head.

When he raised it again and looked, the wizard was gone, and the sail of the boat was a white fleck on the waves eastward, heading towards the fat bejewelled islands of the inner seas. Then in rage the old Dragon of Pendor rose up breaking the tower with the writhing of his body, and beating his wings that spanned the whole width of the ruined town. But his oath held him, and he did not fly, then or ever, to the Archipelago.

6. Hunted

As soon as Pendor had sunk under the sea-rim behind him, Ged looking eastward felt the fear of the shadow come into his heart again; and it was hard to turn from the bright danger of the dragon to that formless, hopeless horror. He let the magewind drop, and sailed on with the world's wind, for there was no desire for speed in him now. He had no clear plan even of what he should do. He must run, as the dragon had said: but where? To Roke, he thought, since there at least he was protected, and might find counsel among the wise.

First, however, he must come to Low Torning once more and tell his tale to the Isle-Men. When word went out that he had returned, five days from his setting forth, they and half the people of the township came rowing and running to gather round him, and stare at him, and listen. He told his tale, and one man said, 'But who saw this wonder of dragons slain and dragons baffled? What if he —'

'Be still!' the Head Isle-Man said roughly, for he knew, as did most of them, that a wizard may have subtle ways of telling the truth, and may keep the truth to himself, but that if he says a thing the thing is as he says. For that is his mastery. So they wondered and began to feel that their fear was lifted from them, and then they began to rejoice. They pressed round their young wizard and asked for the tale again. More islanders came, and asked for it again. By nightfall he no longer had to tell it. They could do it for him, better. Already the village chanters had fitted it to an old tune, and were singing the *Song of the Sparrowhawk*. Bonfires were burning not only on the isles of Low Torning but in townships to the south and east. Fishermen shouted the news from boat to boat, from isle to isle it went: Evil is averted, the dragons will never come from Pendor!

That night, that one night, was joyous for Ged. No shadow could come near him through the brightness of those fires of thanksgiving that burned on every hill and beach, through the circles of laughing dancers that ringed him about, singing his praise, swinging their torches in the gusty autumn night so that sparks rose thick and bright and brief upon the wind.

The next day he met with Pechvarry, who said, 'I did not know you were so mighty, my lord.' There was fear in that because he had dared make Ged his friend, but there was reproach in it also. Ged had not saved a little child, though he had slain dragons. After that, Ged felt afresh the unease and impatience that had driven him to Pendor, and drove him now from Low Torning. The next day, though they would have kept him gladly the rest of his life to praise and boast of, he left the house on the hill, with no baggage but his books, his staff, and the otak riding on his shoulder.

He went in a rowboat with a couple of young fishermen of Low Torning, who wanted the honour of being his boatmen. Always as they rowed on among the craft that crowd the eastern channels of the Ninety Isles, under the windows and balconies of houses that lean out over the water, past the wharves of Nesh, the rainy pastures of Dromgan, the malodorous oil-sheds of Geath, word of his deed had gone ahead of him. They whistled the *Song of the Sparrowhawk* as he went by, they vied to have him spend the night and tell his dragon-tale. When at last he came to Serd, the ship's master of whom he asked passage out to Roke bowed as he answered, 'A privilege to me, Lord Wizard, and an honour to my ship!'

So Ged turned his back on the Ninety Isles; but even as the ship turned from Serd Inner Port and raised sail, a wind came up hard from the east against her. It was strange, for the wintry sky was clear and the weather had seemed settled mild that morning. It was only thirty miles from Serd to Roke, and they sailed on; and when the wind still rose, they still sailed on. The little ship, like most traders of the Inmost Sea, bore the high fore-and-aft sail that can be turned to catch a headwind, and her master was a handy seaman, proud of his skill. So tacking now north now south they worked eastward. Clouds and rain came up on the wind, which veered and gusted so wildly that there was considerable danger of the ship jibing. 'Lord Sparrowhawk,' said the ship's master to the young man, whom he had beside him in the place of honour in the stern, though small dignity could be kept up under that wind and rain that wet them all to a miserable sleekness in their sodden cloaks – 'Lord Sparrowhawk, might you say a word to this wind, maybe?'

'How near are we to Roke?'

'Better than half-way. But we've made no headway at all this past hour, Sir.'

Ged spoke to the wind, it blew less hard, and for a while they went on fairly enough. Then sudden great gusts came whistling out of the south, and meeting these they were driven back westward again. The clouds broke and boiled in the sky, and the ship's master roared out ragefully. 'This fool's gale blows all ways at once! Only a magewind will get us through this weather, Lord.'

Ged looked glum at that, but the ship and her men were in danger for him, so he raised up the magewind into her sail. At once the ship began to cleave straight to the east, and the ship's master began to look cheerful again. But little by little, though Ged kept up the spell, the magewind slackened, growing feebler, until the ship seemed to hang still on the waves for a minute, her sail drooping, amid all the tumult of the rain and gale. Then with a thunder-crack the boom came swinging round and she jibed and jumped northward like a scared cat.

Ged grabbed hold of a stanchion, for she lay almost over on her side, and shouted out, 'Turn back to Serd, master!'

The master cursed and shouted that he would not: 'A wizard aboard, and I the best seaman of the Trade, and this the handiest ship I ever sailed – turn back?'

Then, the ship turning again almost as if a whirlpool had caught her keel, he too grabbed hold of the sternpost to keep aboard, and Ged said to him, 'Leave me at Serd and sail where you like. It's not against your ship this wind blows, but against me.'

'Against you, a wizard of Roke?'

'Have you never heard of the Roke-wind, master?'

'Aye, that keeps off evil powers from the Isle of the Wise, but what has that to do with you, a Dragontamer?'

93

'That is between me and my shadow,' Ged answered shortly, as a wizard will; and he said no more as they went swiftly, with a steady wind and under clearing skies, back over the sea to Serd.

There was a heaviness and a dread in his heart as he went up from the wharves of Serd. The days were shortening into winter, and dusk came soon. With dusk Ged's uneasiness always grew, and now the turning of each street seemed a threat to him, and he had to steel himself not to keep looking back over his shoulder at what might be coming behind him. He went to the Sea-House of Serd, where travellers and merchants ate together of good fare provided by the township, and might sleep in the long raftered hall; such is the hospitality of the thriving islands of the Inmost Sea.

He saved a bit of meat from his dinner, and by the firepit afterwards he coaxed the otak out of the fold of his hood where it had cowered all that day, and tried to get it to eat, petting it and whispering to it, 'Hoeg, hoeg, little one, silent one ...' But it would not eat, and crept into his pocket to hide. By that, by his own dull uncertainty, by the very look of the darkness in the corners of the great room, he knew that the shadow was not far from him.

No one in this place knew him: they were travellers, from other isles, who had not heard the *Song of the Sparrowhawk*. None spoke to him. He chose a pallet at last and lay down, but all night long he lay with open eyes there in the raftered hall among the sleep of strangers. All night he tried to choose his way, to plan where he should go, what he should do: but each choice, each plan was blocked by a foreboding of doom. Across each way he might go lay the shadow. Only Roke was clear of it: and to Roke he could not go, forbidden by the high, enwoven, ancient spells that kept the perilous island safe. That the Roke-wind had risen against him was proof the thing that hunted him must be very close upon him now.

That thing was bodiless, blind to sunlight, a creature of a lightless, placeless, timeless realm. It must grope after him through the days and across the seas of the sunlit world, and could take visible shape only in dream and darkness. It had as yet no substance or being that the light of the sun would shine on; and so it is sung in the *Deed of Hode*, 'Daybreak makes all earth and sea, from shadow brings forth form, driving dream to the dark kingdom.' But if once the shadow caught up with Ged it could draw his power out of him, and take from him the very weight and warmth and life of his body and the will that moved him.

That was the doom he saw lying ahead on every road. And he knew that he might be tricked towards that doom: for the shadow, growing stronger always as it was nearer him, might even now have strength enough to put evil powers or evil men to its own use – showing him false portents, or speaking with a stranger's voice. For all he knew, in one of these men who slept in this corner or that of the raftered hall of the Sea-House tonight, the dark thing lurked, finding a foothold in a dark soul and there waiting and watching Ged and feeding, even now, on his weakness, on his uncertainty, on his fear.

It was past bearing. He must trust to chance, and run wherever chance took him. At the first cold hint of dawn he got up and went in haste under the dimming stars down to the wharves of Serd, resolved only to take the first ship outward bound that would have him. A galley was loading turbie-oil; she was to sail at sunrise, bound for Havnor Great Port. Ged asked passage of her master. A wizard's staff is passport and payment on most ships. They took him aboard willingly, and within that hour the ship set forth. Ged's spirits lifted with the first lifting of the forty long oars, and the drumbeat that kept the stroke made a brave music to him.

And yet he did not know what he would do in Havnor, or where he would run from there. Northward was as good as any direction. He was a Northerner himself; maybe he would find some ship to take him on to Gont from Havnor, and he might see Ogion again. Or he might find some ship going far out into the Reaches, so far the shadow would lose him and give up the hunt. Beyond such vague ideas as these, there was no plan in his head, and he saw no one course that he must follow. Only he must run ...

Those forty oars carried the ship over a hundred and fifty miles of wintry sea before sunset of the second day out from Serd. They came in to port at Orrimy on the east shore of the great land Hosk, for these trade-galleys of the Inmost Sea keep to the coasts and lie overnight in harbour whenever they can. Ged went ashore, for it was still daylight, and he roamed the steep streets of the port-town, aimless and brooding.

Orrimy is an old town, built heavily of stone and brick, walled against the lawless lords of the interior of Hosk Island; the warehouses on the docks are like forts, and the merchants' houses are towered and fortified. Yet to Ged wandering through the streets those ponderous mansions seemed like veils, behind which lay an empty dark; and people who passed him, intent on their business, seemed not real men but voiceless shadows of men. As the sun set he came down to the wharves again, and even there in the broad red light and wind of the day's end, sea and land alike to him seemed dim and silent.

'Where are you bound, Lord Wizard?'

So one hailed him suddenly from behind. Turning he saw a man dressed in grey, who carried a staff of heavy wood that was not a wizard's staff. The stranger's face was hidden by his hood from the red light, but Ged felt the unseen eyes meet his. Starting back he raised his own yew-staff between him and the stranger.

Mildly the man asked, 'What do you fear?'

'What follows behind me.'

'So? But I'm not your shadow.'

Ged stood silent. He knew that indeed this man, whatever he was, was not what he feared; he was no shadow or ghost or gebbeth-creature. Amidst the dry silence and shadowiness that had come over the world, he even kept a voice and some solidity. He put back his hood now. He had a strange, seamed, bald head, a lined face. Though age had not sounded in his voice, he looked to be an old man.

'I do not know you,' said the man in grey, 'yet I think perhaps we do not meet by chance. I heard a tale once of a young man, a scarred man, who won through darkness to great dominion, even to kingship. I do not know if that is your tale. But I will tell you this: go to the Court of the Terrenon, if you need a sword to fight shadows with. A staff of yew-wood will not serve your need.'

Hope and mistrust struggled in Ged's mind as he listened. A

wizardly man soon learns that few indeed of his meetings are chance ones, be they for good or for ill.

'In what land is the Court of the Terrenon?'

'In Osskil.'

At the sound of that name Ged saw for a moment, by a trick of memory, a black raven on green grass who looked up at him sidelong with an eye like polished stone, and spoke; but the words were forgotten.

'That land has something of a dark name,' Ged said, looking ever at the man in grey, trying to judge what kind of man he was. There was a manner about him that hinted of the sorcerer, even of the wizard; and yet boldly as he spoke to Ged, there was a queer beaten look about him, the look almost of a sick man, or a prisoner, or a slave.

'You are from Roke,' he answered. 'The wizards of Roke give a dark name to wizardries other than their own.'

'What man are you?'

'A traveller; a trader's agent from Osskil; I am here on business,' said the man in grey. When Ged asked him no more he quietly bade the young man good night, and went off up the narrow stepped street above the quays.

Ged turned, irresolute whether to heed this sign or not, and looked to the north. The red light was dying out fast from the hills and from the windy sea. Grey dusk came, and on its heels the night.

Ged went in sudden decision and haste along the quays to a fisherman who was folding his nets down in his dory, and hailed him: 'Do you know any ship in this port bound north – to Semel, or the Enlades?'

'The longship yonder's from Osskil, she might be stopping at the Enlades.'

In the same haste Ged went on to the great ship the fisherman had pointed to, a longship of sixty oars, gaunt as a snake, her high bent prow carven and inlaid with discs of loto-shell, her oarport-covers painted red, with the rune Sifl sketched on each in black. A grim, swift ship she looked, and all in sea-trim, with all her crew aboard. Ged sought out the ship's master and asked passage to Osskil of him.

'Can you pay?'

'I have some skill with winds.'

'I am a weatherworker myself. You have nothing to give? no money?'

In Low Torning the Isle-Men had paid Ged as best they could with the ivory pieces used by traders in the Archipelago; he would take only ten pieces, though they wanted to give him more. He offered these now to the Osskilian, but he shook his head. 'We do not use those counters. If you have nothing to pay, I have no place aboard for you.'

'Do you need arms? I have rowed in a galley.'

'Aye, we're short two men. Find your bench then,' said the ship's master, and paid him no more heed.

So, laying his staff and his bag of books under the rowers' bench, Ged became for ten bitter days of winter an oarsman of that Northern ship. They left Orrimy at daybreak, and that day Ged thought he could never keep up his work. His left arm was somewhat lamed by the old wounds in his shoulder, and all his rowing in the channels about Low Torning had not trained him for the relentless pull and pull and pull at the long galley-oar to the beat of the drum. Each stint at the oars was of two or three hours, and then a second shift of oarsmen took the benches, but the time of rest seemed only long enough for all Ged's muscles to stiffen, and then it was back to the oars. And the second day of it was worse; but after that he hardened to the labour, and got on well enough.

There was no such comradeship among this crew as he had found aboard *Shadow* when he first went to Roke. The crewmen of Andradean and Gontish ships are partners in the trade, working together for a common profit, whereas traders of Osskil use slaves and bondsmen or hire men to row, paying them with small coins of gold. Gold is a great thing in Osskil. But it is not a source of good fellowship there, or amongst the dragons, who also prize it highly. Since half this crew were bondsmen, forced to work, the ship's officers were slavemasters, and harsh ones. They never laid their whips on the back of an oarsman who worked for pay or passage; but there will not be much friendliness in a crew of whom some are whipped and others are not. Ged's fellows said little to one another, and less to him. They were mostly men from Osskil, speaking not the Hardic tongue of the Archipelago but a dialect of their own, and they were dour men, pale-skinned with black drooping moustaches and lank hair. *Kelub*, the red one, was Ged's name among them. Though they knew he was a wizard they showed him no regard, but rather a kind of cautious spitefulness. And he himself was in no mood for making friends. Even on his bench, caught up in the mighty rhythm of the rowing, one oarsman among sixty in a ship racing over void grey seas, he felt himself exposed, defenceless. When they came into strange ports at nightfall and he rolled himself in his cloak to sleep, weary as he was he would dream, wake, dream again; evil dreams, that he could not recall waking, though they seemed to hang about the ship and the men of the ship, so that he mistrusted each one of them.

All the Osskilian freemen wore a long knife at the hip, and one day as his oar-shift shared their noon meal one of these men asked Ged, 'Are you slave or oathbreaker, Kelub?'

'Neither.'

'Why no knife, then? Afraid to fight?' said the man, Skiorh, jeering.

'No.'

'Your little dog fight for you?'

'Otak,' said another who listened. 'No dog, that is otak,' and he said something in Osskilian that made Skiorh scowl and turn away. Just as he turned Ged saw a change in his face, a slurring and shifting of the features, as if for a moment something had changed him, used him, looking out through his eyes sidelong at Ged. Yet the next minute Ged saw him full-face, and he looked as usual, so that Ged told himself that what he had seen was his own fear, his own dread reflected in the other's eyes. But that night as they lay in port in Esen he dreamed, and Skiorh walked in his dream. Afterwards he avoided the man as best he could, and it seemed also that Skiorh kept away from him, and no more words passed between them.

The snow-crowned mountains of Havnor sank away behind them

southward, blurred by the mists of early winter. They rowed on past the mouth of the Sea of Éa where long ago Elfarran was drowned, and past the Enlades. They lay two days in port at Berila, the City of Ivory, white above its bay in the west of myth-haunted Enlad. At all ports they came to, the crewmen were kept aboard the ship, and set no foot on land. Then as a red sun rose they rowed out on the Osskil Sea, into the northeast winds that blow unhindered from the islandless vastness of the North Reach. Through that bitter sea they brought their cargo safe, coming the second day out of Berila into port at Neshum, the trade-city of Eastern Osskil.

Ged saw a low coast lashed by rainy wind, a grey town crouching behind the long stone breakwaters that made its harbour, and behind the town treeless hills under a snow-darkened sky. They had come far from the sunlight of the Inmost Sea.

Longshoremen of the Sea-Guild of Neshum came aboard to unload the cargo – gold, silver, jewellery, fine silks and Southern tapestries, such precious stuff as the lords of Osskil hoard – and the freemen of the crew were dismissed. Ged stopped one of them to ask his way; up until now the distrust he felt of all of them had kept him from saying where he was bound, but now, afoot and alone in a strange land, he must ask for guidance. The man went on impatiently saying he did not know, but Skiorh, overhearing, said, 'The Court of the Terrenon? On the Keksemt Moors. I go that road.'

Skiorh's was no company Ged would have chosen, but knowing neither the language nor the way he had small choice. Nor did it much matter, he thought; he had not chosen to come here. He had been driven, and now was driven on. He pulled his hood up over his head, took up his staff and bag, and followed the Osskilian through the streets of the town and upward into the snowy hills. The little otak would not ride on his shoulder, but hid in the pocket of his sheepskin tunic, under his cloak, as was its wont in cold weather. The hills stretched out into bleak rolling moorlands as far as the eye could see. They walked in silence and the silence of winter lay on all the land.

'How far?' Ged asked after they had gone some miles, seeing no sight of village or farm in any direction, and thinking that they had no food with them. Skiorh turned his head a moment, pulling up his own hood, and said, 'Not far.'

It was an ugly face, pale, coarse, and cruel, but Ged feared no man though he might fear where such a man would guide him. He nodded and they went on. Their road was only a scar through the waste of thin snow and leafless bushes. From time to time other tracks crossed it or branched from it. Now that the chimney-smoke of Neshum was hidden behind the hills in the darkening afternoon there was no sign at all of what way they should go, or had gone. Only the wind blew always from the east. And when they had walked for several hours Ged thought he saw, away off on the hills in the northwest where their way tended, a tiny scratch against the sky, like a tooth, white. But the light of the short day was fading, and on the next rise of the road he could make out the thing, tower or tree or whatever, no more clearly than before.

'Do we go there?' he asked, pointing.

Skiorh made no answer but plodded on, muffled in his coarse cloak with its peaked, furred Osskilian hood. Ged strode on beside him. They had come far, and he was drowsy with the steady pace of their walking and with the long weariness of hard days and nights in the ship. It began to seem to him that he had walked forever and would walk forever beside this silent being through a silent darkening land. Caution and intention were dulled in him. He walked as in a long, long dream, going no place.

The otak stirred in his pocket, and a little vague fear also woke and stirred in his mind. He forced himself to speak. 'Darkness comes, and snow. How far, Skiorh?'

After a pause the other answered, without turning, 'Not far.'

But his voice sounded not like a man's voice, but like a beast, hoarse and lipless, that tries to speak.

Ged stopped. All around stretched empty hills in the late, dusk light. Sparse snow whirled a little falling. 'Skiorh!' he said, and the other halted, and turned. There was no face under the peaked hood.

Before Ged could speak spell or summon power, the gebbeth spoke, saying in its hoarse voice, 'Ged!'

Then the young man could work no transformation, but was

locked in his true being, and must face the gebbeth thus defenceless. Nor could he summon any help in this alien land, where nothing and no one was known to him and would come at his call. He stood alone, with nothing between him and his enemy but the staff of yew-wood in his right hand.

The thing that had devoured Skiorh's mind and possessed his flesh made the body take a step towards Ged, and the arms came groping out towards him. A rage of horror filled Ged and he swung up and brought down his staff whistling on the hood that hid the shadow-face. Hood and cloak collapsed down nearly to the ground under that fierce blow as if there was nothing in them but wind, and then writhing and flapping stood up again. The body of a gebbeth has been drained of true substance and is something like a shell or a vapour in the form of a man, an unreal flesh clothing the shadow which is real. So jerking and billowing as if blown on the wind the shadow spread its arms and came at Ged, trying to get hold of him as it had held him on Roke Knoll: and if it did would cast aside the husk of Skiorh and enter into Ged, devouring him out from within, owning him, which was its whole desire. Ged struck at it again with his heavy, smoking staff, beating it off, but it came again and he struck again, and then dropped the staff that blazed and smouldered, burning his hand. He backed away, then all at once turned and ran.

He ran, and the gebbeth followed a pace behind him, unable to outrun him yet never dropping behind. Ged never looked back. He ran, he ran, through that vast dusk land where there was no hiding place. Once the gebbeth in its hoarse whistling voice called him again by name, but though it had taken his wizard's power thus, it had no power over his body's strength, and could not make him stop. He ran.

Night thickened about the hunter and the hunted, and snow blew fine across the path that Ged could no longer see. The pulse hammered in his eyes, the breath burned in his throat; he was no longer really running but stumbling and staggering ahead: and yet the tireless pursuer seemed unable to catch him, coming always just behind him. It had begun to whisper and mumble at him, calling to him, and he knew that all his life that whispering had been in his ears, just under the threshold of hearing, but now he could hear it, and he must yield, he must give in, he must stop. Yet he laboured on, struggling up a long, dim slope. He thought there was a light somewhere before him, and he thought he heard a voice in front of him, above him somewhere, calling 'Come ! Come !'

He tried to answer but he had no voice. The pale light grew certain, shining through a gateway straight before him : he could not see the walls, but he saw the gate. At the sight of it he halted, and the gebbeth snatched at his cloak, fumbled at his sides trying to catch hold of him from behind. With the last strength in him Ged plunged through that faint-shining door. He tried to turn to shut it behind him against the gebbeth, but his legs would not hold him up. He staggered, reaching for support. Lights swam and flashed in his eyes. He felt himself falling, and he felt himself caught even as he fell; but his mind, utterly spent, slid away into the dark.

7. *The Hawk's Flight*

GED woke, and for a long time he lay aware only that it was pleasant to wake, for he had not expected to wake again, and very pleasant to see light, the large plain light of day all about him. He felt as if he were floating on that light, or drifting in a boat on very quiet waters. At last he made out that he was in bed, but no such bed as he had ever slept in. It was set upon a frame held by four tall carven legs and the mattresses were great silk sacks of down, which was why he thought he was floating, and over it all a crimson canopy hung to keep out drafts. On two sides the curtain was tied back, and Ged looked out at a room with walls of stone and floor of stone. Through three high windows he saw the moorland, bare and brown, snow-patched here and there, in the mild sunlight of winter. The room must be high above the ground, for it looked a great way over the land.

A coverlet of downfilled satin slid aside as Ged sat up, and he saw himself clothed in a tunic of silk and cloth-of-silver like a lord. On a chair beside the bed, boots of glove-leather and a cloak lined with pellawi-fur were laid ready for him. He sat a while, calm and dull as one under an enchantment, and then stood up, reaching for his staff. But he had no staff.

His right hand, though it had been salved and bound, was burned on palm and fingers. Now he felt the pain of it, and the soreness of all his body.

He stood without moving a while again. Then he whispered, not aloud and not hopefully, 'Hoeg ... hoeg ...' For the little fierce loyal creature too was gone, the little silent soul that once had led him back from death's dominion. Had it still been with him last night when he ran? Was that last night, was it many nights ago? He did not know. It was all dim and obscure in his mind, the gebbeth, the burning staff, the running, the whispering, the gate.

None of it came back clearly to him. Nothing even now was clear. He whispered his pet's name once more, but without hope of answer, and tears rose in his eyes.

A little bell rang somewhere far away. A second bell rang in a sweet jangle just outside the room. A door opened behind him, across the room, and a woman came in. 'Welcome, Sparrowhawk,' she said smiling.

She was young and tall, dressed in white and silver, with a net of silver crowning her hair that fell straight down like a fall of black water.

Stiffly, Ged bowed.

'You don't remember me, I think.'

'Remember you, Lady?'

He had never seen a beautiful woman dressed to match her beauty but once in his life: that Lady of O who had come with her Lord to the Sunreturn festival at Roke. She had been like a slight, bright candle-flame, but this woman was like the white new moon.

'I thought you would not,' she said smiling. 'But forgetful as you may be, you're welcome here as an old friend.'

'What place is this?' Ged asked, still stiff and slow-tongued. He found it hard to speak to her and hard to look away from her. The princely clothes he wore were strange to him, the stones he stood on were unfamiliar, the very air he breathed was alien; he was not himself, not the self he had been.

'This keep is called the Court of the Terrenon. My lord, who is called Benderesk, is sovereign of this land from the edge of the Keksemt Moors north to the Mountains of Os, and keeper of the precious stone called Terrenon. As for myself, here in Osskil they call me Serret, Silver in their language. And you, I know, are sometimes called Sparrowhawk, and were made wizard in the Isle of the Wise.'

Ged looked down at his burned hand and said presently, 'I do not know what I am. I had power, once. I have lost it, I think.'

'No! you have not lost it, or only to regain it tenfold. You are safe here from what drove you here, my friend. There are mighty walls about this tower and not all of them are built of stone. Here you can rest, finding your strength again. Here you may also find a different strength, and a staff that will not burn to ashes in your hand. An evil way may lead to a good end, after all. Come with me now, let me show you our domain.'

She spoke so sweetly that Ged hardly heard her words, moved by the promise of her voice alone. He followed her.

His room was high up indeed in the tower that rose like a sharp tooth from its hilltop. Down winding stairs of marble he followed Serret, through rich rooms and halls, past high windows that looked north, west, south, east over the low brown hills that went on houseless and treeless and changeless, clear to the sunwashed winter sky. Only far to the north small white peaks stood sharp against the blue, and southward one could guess the shining of the sea.

Servants opened doors and stood aside for Ged and the lady; pale, dour Osskilians they were all. She was light of skin, but unlike them she spoke Hardic well, even, it seemed to Ged, with the accent of Gont. Later that day she brought him before her husband Benderesk, Lord of the Terrenon. Thrice her age, bone-white, bone-thin, with clouded eyes, Lord Benderesk greeted Ged with grim cold courtesy, bidding him stay as guest however long he would. Then he had little more to say, asking Ged nothing of his voyages or of the enemy that had hunted him here; nor had the Lady Serret asked anything of these matters.

If this was strange, it was only part of the strangeness of this place and of his presence in it. Ged's mind never seemed quite to clear. He could not see things plainly. He had come to this tower-keep by chance, and yet the chance was all design; or he had come by design and yet all the design had merely chanced to come about. He had set out northward: a stranger in Orrimy had told him to seek help here; an Osskilian ship had been waiting for him; Skiorh had guided him. How much of this was the work of the shadow that hunted him? Or was none of it: had he and his hunter both been drawn here by some other power, he following that lure and the shadow following him, and seizing on Skiorh for its weapon when the moment came? That must be it, for certainly the shadow was, as Serret had said, barred from the Court of the Terrenon. He had felt no sign or threat of its lurking presence since he wakened in the tower. But what then had brought him here? For this was no place one came to by chance, even in the dullness of his thoughts he began to see that. No other stranger came to these gates. The tower stood aloof and remote, its back turned on the way to Neshum that was the nearest town. No man came to the keep, none left it. Its windows looked down on desolation.

From those windows Ged looked out, as he kept by himself in his high tower-room, day after day, dull and heartsick and cold. It was always cold in the tower, for all the carpets and the tapestried hangings and the rich furred clothing and the broad marble fireplaces they had. It was a cold that got into the bone, into the marrow, and would not be dislodged. And in Ged's heart a cold shame settled also and would not be dislodged, as he thought always how he had faced his enemy and been defeated and had run. In his mind all the Masters of Roke gathered, Gensher the Archmage frowning in their midst, and Nemmerle was with them, and Ogion, and even the witch who had taught him his first spell: all of them gazed at him and he knew he had failed their trust in him. He would plead, saying, 'If I had not run away the shadow would have possessed me: it had already all Skiorh's strength, and part of mine, and I could not fight it: it knew my name, I had to run away. A wizard-gebbeth would be a terrible power for evil and ruin. I had to run away.' But none of those who listened in his mind would answer him. And he would watch the snow falling, thin and ceaseless, on the empty lands below the window, and feel the dull cold grow within him, till it seemed no feeling was left to him except a kind of weariness.

So he kept to himself for many days out of sheer misery. When he did come down out of his room, he was silent and stiff. The beauty of the Lady of the Keep confused his mind, and in this rich, seemly, orderly, strange Court, he felt himself to be a goatherd born and bred.

They let him alone when he wanted to be alone, and when he could not stand to think his thoughts and watch the falling snow any longer, often Serret met with him in one of the curving halls, tapestried and firelit, lower in the tower, and there they would talk. There was no merriment in the Lady of the Keep, she never laughed though she often smiled; yet she could put Ged at ease almost with one smile. With her he began to forget his stiffness and his shame. Before long they met every day to talk, long, quietly, idly, a little apart from the serving-women who always accompanied Serret, by the fireplace or at the window of the high rooms of the tower.

The old lord kept mostly in his own apartments, coming forth mornings to pace up and down the snowy inner courtyards of the castle-keep like an old sorcerer who has been brewing spells all night. When he joined Ged and Serret for supper he sat silent, looking up at his young wife sometimes with a hard, covetous glance. Then Ged pitied her. She was like a white deer caged, like a white bird wing-clipped, like a silver ring on an old man's finger. She was an item of Benderesk's hoard. When the lord of the keep left them Ged stayed with her, trying to cheer her solitude as she had cheered his.

'What is this jewel that gives your keep its name?' he asked her as they sat talking over their emptied gold plates and gold goblets in the cavernous, candle-lit dining-hall.

'You have not heard of it? It is a famous thing.'

'No. I know only that the lords of Osskil have famous treasuries.'

'Ah, this jewel outshines them all. Come, would you like to see it?'

She smiled, with a look of mockery and daring, as if a little afraid of what she did, and led the young man from the hall, out through the narrow corridors of the base of the tower, and down stairs underground to a locked door he had not seen before. This she unlocked with a silver key, looking up at Ged with that same smile as she did so, as if she dared him to come on with her. Beyond the door was a short passage and a second door, which she unlocked with a gold key, and beyond that again a a third door, which she unlocked with one of the Great Words of unbinding. Within that last door her candle showed them a small room like a dungeon-cell: floor, walls, ceiling all rough stone, unfurnished, blank.

'Do you see it?' Serret asked.

As Ged looked round the room his wizard's eye caught one stone of those that made the floor. It was rough and dank as the rest, a heavy unshapen paving-stone; yet he felt the power of it as if it spoke to him aloud. And his breath caught in his throat, and a sickness came over him for a moment. This was the foundingstone of the tower. This was the central place, and it was cold, bitter cold; nothing could ever warm the little room. This was a very ancient thing: an old and terrible spirit was prisoned in that block of stone. He did not answer Serret yes or no, but stood still, and presently, with a quick curious glance at him, she pointed out the stone. 'That is the Terrenon. Do you wonder that we keep so precious a jewel locked away in our deepest hoardroom?'

Still Ged did not answer, but stood dumb and wary. She might almost have been testing him; but he thought she had no notion of the stone's nature, to speak of it so lightly. She did not know enough of it to fear it. 'Tell me of its powers,' he said at last.

'It was made before Segoy raised the islands of the world from the Open Sea. It was made when the world itself was made, and will endure until the end of the world. Time is nothing to it. If you lay your hand upon it and ask a question of it, it will answer, according to the power that is in you. It has a voice, if you know how to listen. It will speak of things that were, and are, and will be. It told of your coming, long before you came to this land. Will you ask a question of it now?'

'No.'

'It will answer you.'

'There is no question I would ask it.'

'It might tell you,' Serret said in her soft voice, 'how you will defeat your enemy.'

Ged stood mute.

'Do you fear the stone?' she asked as if unbelieving; and he answered, 'Yes.'

In the deadly cold and silence of the room encircled by wall after wall of spellwork and of stone, in the light of the one candle she held, Serret glanced at him again with gleaming eyes. 'Sparrowhawk,' she said, 'you are not afraid.'

'But I will not speak with that spirit,' Ged replied, and looking full at her spoke with a grave boldness: 'My lady, that spirit is sealed in a stone, and the stone is locked by binding-spell and blinding-spell and charm of lock and ward and triple fortress-walls in a barren land, not because it is precious, but because it can work great evil. I do not know what they told you of it when you came here. But you who are young and gentle-hearted should never touch the thing, or even look on it. It will not work you well.'

'I have touched it. I have spoken to it, and heard it speak. It does me no harm.'

She turned away and they went out through the doors and passages till in the torchlight of the broad stairs of the tower she blew out her candle. They parted with few words.

That night Ged slept little. It was not the thought of the shadow that kept him awake; rather that thought was almost driven from his mind by the image, ever returning, of the Stone on which this tower was founded, and by the vision of Serret's face bright and shadowy in the candlelight, turned to him. Again and again he felt her eyes on him, and tried to decide what look had come into those eyes when he refused to touch the Stone, whether it had been disdain or hurt. When he lay down to sleep at last the silken sheets of the bed were cold as ice, and ever he wakened in the dark thinking of the Stone and of Serret's eyes.

Next day he found her in the curving hall of grey marble, lit now by the westering sun, where often she spent the afternoon at games or at the weaving-loom with her maids. He said to her, 'Lady Serret, I affronted you. I am sorry for it.'

'No,' she said musingly, and again, 'No ...' She sent away the serving-women who were with her, and when they were alone she turned to Ged. 'My guest, my friend,' she said, 'you are very clear-sighted, but perhaps you do not see all that is to be seen. In Gont, in Roke they teach high wizardries. But they do not teach all wizardries. This is Osskil, Ravenland: it is not a Hardic land: mages do not rule it, nor do they know much of it. There are happenings here not dealt with by the loremasters of the South, and things here not named in the Namers' lists. What one does not know, one fears. But you have nothing to fear here in the Court of the Terrenon. A weaker man would, indeed. Not you. You are one born with the power to control that which is in the sealed room. This I know. It is why you are here now.'

'I do not understand.'

'That is because my lord Benderesk has not been wholly frank with you. I will be frank. Come, sit by me here.'

He sat down beside her on the deep, cushioned windowledge. The dying sunlight came level through the window, flooding them with a radiance in which there was no warmth; on the moorlands below, already sinking into shadow, last night's snow lay unmelted, a dull white pall over the earth.

She spoke now very softly. 'Benderesk is Lord and Inheritor of the Terrenon, but he cannot use the thing, he cannot make it wholly serve his will. Nor can I, alone or with him. Neither he nor I has the skill and power. You have both.'

'How do you know that?'

'From the Stone itself! I told you that it spoke of your coming. It knows its master. It has waited for you to come. Before ever you were born it waited for you, for the one who could master it. And he who can make the Terrenon answer what he asks and do what he wills, has power over his own destiny: strength to crush any enemy, mortal or of the other world: foresight, knowledge, wealth, dominion, and a wizardry at his command that could humble the Archmage himself! As much of that, as little of that as you choose, is yours for the asking.'

Once more she lifted her strange bright eyes to him, and her gaze pierced him so that he trembled as if with cold. Yet there was fear in her face, as if she sought his help but was too proud to ask it. Ged was bewildered. She had put her hand on his as she spoke; its touch was light, it looked narrow and fair on his dark, strong hand. He said, pleading, 'Serret! I have no such power as you think – what I had once, I threw away. I cannot help you, I am no use to you. But I know this, the Old Powers of earth are not for men to use. They were never given into our hands, and in our hands they work only ruin. Ill means, ill end. I was not drawn here, but driven here, and the force that drove me works to my undoing. I cannot help you.'

'He who throws away his power is filled sometimes with a far greater power,' she said, smiling, as if his fears and scruples were childish ones. 'I may know more than you of what brought you here. Did not a man speak to you in the streets of Orrimy? He was a messenger, a servant of the Terrenon. He was a wizard once himself, but he threw away his staff to serve a power greater than any mage's. And you came to Osskil, and on the moors you tried to fight a shadow with your wooden staff; and almost we could not save you, for that thing that follows you is more cunning than we deemed, and had taken much strength from you already ... Only shadow can fight shadow. Only darkness can defeat the dark. Listen Sparrowhawk! what do you need, then, to defeat that shadow, which waits for you outside these walls?'

'I need what I cannot know. Its name.'

'The Terrenon, that knows all births and deaths and beings before and after death, the unborn and the undying, the bright world and the dark one, will tell you that name.'

'And the price?'

'There is no price. I tell you it will obey you, serve you as your slave.'

Shaken and tormented, he did not answer. She held his hand now in both of hers, looking into his face. The sun had fallen into the mists that dulled the horizon, and the air too had grown dull, but her face grew bright with praise and triumph as she watched him and saw his will shaken within him. Softly she whispered, 'You will be mightier than all men, a king among men. You will rule, and I will rule with you –'

Suddenly Ged stood up, and one step forward took him where he could see, just around the curve of the long room's wall, beside the door, the Lord of the Terrenon who stood listening and smiling a little.

Ged's eyes cleared, and his mind. He looked down at Serret. 'It is light that defeats the dark,' he said stammering, – 'light.'

As he spoke he saw, as plainly as if his words were the light that showed him, how indeed he had been drawn here, lured here, how they had used his fear to lead him on, and how they would, once they had him, have kept him. They had saved him from the shadow, indeed, for they did not want him to be possessed by the shadow until he had become a slave of the Stone. Once his will was captured by the power of the Stone, then they would let the shadow into the walls, for a gebbeth was a better slave than a man. If he had once touched the Stone, or spoken to it, he would have been utterly lost. Yet, even as the shadow had not quite been able to catch up with him and seize him, so the Stone had not been able to use him – not quite. He had almost yielded, but not quite. He had not consented. It is very hard for evil to take hold of the unconsenting soul.

He stood between the two who had yielded, who had consented, looking from one to the other as Benderesk came forward.

'I told you,' the Lord of the Terrenon said dry-voiced to his lady, 'that he would slip from your hands, Serret. They are clever fools, your Gontish sorcerers. And you are a fool too, woman of Gont, thinking to trick both him and me, and rule us both by your beauty, and use the Terrenon to your own ends. But I am the Lord of the Stone, I, and this I do to the disloyal wife : *Ekavroe ai oelwantar –*' It was a spell of Changing, and Benderesk's long hands were raised to shape the cowering woman into some hideous thing, swine or dog or drivelling hag. Ged stepped forward and struck the lord's hand down with his own, saying as he did so only one short word. And though he had no staff, and stood on alien ground and evil ground, the domain of a dark power, yet his will prevailed. Benderesk stood still, his clouded eyes fixed hateful and unseeing upon Serret.

'Come,' she said in a shaking voice, 'Sparrowhawk, come, quick, before he can summon the Servants of the Stone –'

As if in echo a whispering ran through the tower, through the stones of the floor and walls, a dry trembling murmur, as if the earth itself should speak.

Seizing Ged's hand Serret ran with him through the passages and halls, down the long twisted stairs. They came out into the court-yard where a last silvery daylight still hung above the soiled, trodden snow. Three of the castle-servants barred their way, sullen and questioning, as if they had been suspecting some plot of these two against their master. 'It grows dark, Lady,' one said, and another, 'You cannot ride out now.'

'Out of my way, filth!' Serret cried, and spoke in the sibilant Osskilian speech. The men fell back from her and crouched down to the ground, writhing, and one of them screamed aloud.

'We must go out by the gate, there is no other way out. Can you see it? Can you find it, Sparrowhawk?'

She tugged at his hand, yet he hesitated. 'What spell did you set on them?'

'I ran hot lead in the marrow of their bones, they will die of it. Quick, I tell you, he will loose the Servants of the Stone, and I cannot find the gate – there is a great charm on it. Quick!'

Ged did not know what she meant, for to him the enchanted gate was as plain to see as the stone archway of the court through which he saw it. He led Serret through the one, across the untrodden snow of the forecourt, and then, speaking a word of Opening, he led her through the gate of the wall of spells.

She changed as they passed through that doorway out of the silvery twilight of the Court of the Terrenon. She was not less beautiful in the drear light of the moors, but there was a fierce witchlook to her beauty; and Ged knew her at last – the daughter of the Lord of the Re Albi, daughter of a sorceress of Osskil, who had mocked him in the green meadows above Ogion's house, long ago, and had sent him to read that spell which loosed the shadow. But he spent small thought on this, for he was looking about him now with every sense alert, looking for that enemy, the shadow which would be waiting for him somewhere outside the magic walls. It might be gebbeth still, clothed in Skiorh's death, or it might be hidden in the gathering darkness, waiting to seize him and merge its shapelessness with his living flesh. He sensed its nearness, yet did not see it. But as he looked he saw some small dark thing half buried in snow, a few paces from the gate. He stooped, and then softly picked it up in his two hands. It was the otak, its fine short fur all clogged with blood and its small body light and stiff and cold in his hands.

'Change yourself! Change yourself, they are coming!' Serret shrieked, seizing his arm and pointing to the tower that stood behind them like a tall white tooth in the dusk. From slit windows near its base dark creatures were creeping forth, flapping long wings, slowly beating and circling up over the walls towards Ged and Serret where they stood on the hillside, unprotected. The rattling whisper they had heard inside the keep had grown louder, a tremor and moaning in the earth under their feet.

Anger welled up in Ged's heart, a hot rage of hate against all the cruel deathly things that tricked him, trapped him, hunted him down. 'Change yourself!' Serret screamed at him, and she with a quick-gasped spell shrank into a grey gull, and flew. But Ged stooped and plucked a blade of wild grass that poked up dry and frail out of the snow where the otak had lain dead. This blade he held up, and as he spoke aloud to it in the True Speech it lengthened, and thickened, and when he was done he held a great staff, a wizard's staff, in his hand. No banefire burned red along it when the black, flapping creatures from the Court of the Terrenon swooped over him and he struck their wings with it: it blazed only with the white magefire that does not burn but drives away the dark.

The creatures returned to the attack: botched beasts, belonging to ages before bird or dragon or man, long since forgotten by the daylight but recalled by the ancient, malign, unforgetful power of the Stone. They harried Ged, swooping at him. He felt the scythe-sweep of their talons about him and sickened in their dead stench. Fiercely he parried and struck, fighting them off with the fiery staff that was made of his anger and a blade of wild grass. And suddenly they all rose up like ravens frightened from carrion and wheeled away, flapping, silent, in the direction that Serret in her gull-shape had flown. Their vast wings seemed slow, but they flew fast, each downbeat driving them mightily through the air. No gull could long outmatch that heavy speed.

Quick as he had done at Roke, Ged took the shape of a great hawk; not the sparrowhawk they called him but the Pilgrim Falcon that flies like arrow, like thought. On barred, sharp, strong wings he flew, pursuing his pursuers. The air darkened and among the clouds stars shone brightening. Ahead he saw the black ragged flock all driving down in upon one point in mid-air. Beyond that black clot the sea lay, pale with last ashy gleam of day. Swift and straight the hawk-Ged shot towards the creatures of the Stone, and they scattered as he came amongst them as waterdrops scatter from a cast pebble. But they had caught their prey. Blood was on the beak of this one and white feathers stuck to the claws of another, and no gull skimmed beyond them over the pallid sea.

Already they were turning on Ged again, coming quick and ungainly with iron beaks stretched out agape. He, wheeling once above them, screamed the hawk's scream of defiant rage, and then shot on across the low beaches of Osskil, out over the breakers of the sea.

The creatures of the Stone circled a while croaking, and one by one beat back ponderously inland over the moors. The Old Powers will not cross over the sea, being bound each to an isle, a certain place, cave or stone or welling spring. Back went the black emanations to the tower-keep, where maybe the Lord of the Terrenon, Benderesk, wept at their return, and maybe laughed. But Ged went on, falcon-winged, falcon-mad, like an unfalling arrow, like an unforgotten thought, over the Osskil Sea and eastward into the wind of winter and the night.

Ogion the Silent had come home late to Re Albi from his autumn wanderings. More silent, more solitary than ever he had become as the years went on. The new Lord of Gont down in the city below had never got a word out of him, though he had climbed clear up to the Falcon's Nest to seek the help of the mage in a certain piratic venture towards the Andrades. Ogion who spoke to spiders on their webs and had been seen to greet trees courteously never said a word to the Lord of the Isle, who went away discontented. There was perhaps some discontent or unease also in Ogion's mind, for he had spent all summer and autumn alone up on the mountain, and only now near Sunreturn was come back to his hearthside.

The morning after his return he rose late, and wanting a cup of rushwash tea he went out to fetch water from the spring that ran a

little way down the hillside from his house. The margins of the
spring's small lively pool were frozen, and the sere moss among the
rocks was traced with flowers of frost. It was broad daylight, but
the sun would not clear the mighty shoulder of the mountain for
an hour yet: all western Gont, from sea-beaches to the peak, was
sunless, silent, and clear in the winter morning. As the mage stood
by the spring looking out over the falling lands and the harbour
and the grey distances of the sea, wings beat above him. He looked
up, raising one arm a little. A great hawk came down with loud-
beating wings and lighted on his wrist. Like a trained hunting-bird
it clung there, but it wore no broken leash, no band or bell. The
claws dug hard in Ogion's wrist; the barred wings trembled; the
round, gold eye was dull and wild.

'Are you messenger or message?' Ogion said gently to the hawk.
'Come on with me –' As he spoke the hawk looked at him. Ogion
was silent a minute. 'I named you once, I think,' he said, and then
strode to his house and entered, bearing the bird still on his wrist.
He made the hawk stand on the hearth in the fire's heat, and
offered it water. It would not drink. Then Ogion began to lay a
spell, very quietly, weaving the web of magic with his hands more
than with words. When the spell was whole and woven he said
softly, – 'Ged,' – not looking at the falcon on the hearth. He waited
some while, then turned, and got up, and went to the young man
who stood trembling and dull-eyed before the fire.

Ged was richly and outlandishly dressed in fur and silk and
silver, but the clothes were torn and stiff with sea-salt, and he stood
gaunt and stooped, his hair lank about his scarred face.

Ogion took the soiled, princely cloak off his shoulders, led him to
the alcove-room where his prentice once had slept and made him lie
down on the pallet there, and so with a murmured sleep-charm left
him. He had said no word to him, knowing that Ged had no human
speech in him now.

As a boy, Ogion like all boys had thought it would be a very
pleasant game to take by art-magic whatever shape one liked, man
or beast, tree or cloud, and so to play at a thousand beings. But as

a wizard he had learned the price of the game, which is the peril of losing one's self, playing away the truth. The longer a man stays in a form not his own, the greater this peril. Every prentice-sorcerer learns the tale of the wizard Bordger of Way, who delighted in taking bear's shape, and did so more and more often until the bear grew in him and the man died away, and he became a bear, and killed his own little son in the forests, and was hunted down and slain. And no one knows how many of the dolphins that leap in the waters of the Inmost Sea were men once, wise men, who forgot their wisdom and their name in the joy of the restless sea.

Ged had taken hawk-shape in fierce distress and rage, and when he flew from Osskil there had been but one thought in his mind : to outfly both Stone and shadow, to escape the cold treacherous lands, to go home. The falcon's anger and wildness were like his own, and had become his own, and his will to fly had become the falcon's will. Thus he had passed over Enlad, stooping down to drink at a lonely forest pool, but on the wing again at once, driven by fear of the shadow that came behind him. So he had crossed the great sea-lane called the Jaws of Enlad, and gone on and on, east by south, the hills of Oranéa faint to his right and the hills of Andrad fainter to his left, and before him only the sea; until at last, ahead, there rose up out of the waves one unchanging wave, towering always higher, the white peak of Gont. In all the sunlight and the dark of that great flight he had worn the falcon's wings, and looked through the falcon's eyes, and forgetting his own thoughts he had known at last only what the falcon knows; hunger, the wind, the way he flies.

He flew to the right haven. There were few on Roke and only one on Gont who could have made him back into a man.

He was savage and silent when he woke. Ogion never spoke to him, but gave him meat and water and let him sit hunched by the fire, grim as a great, weary, sulking hawk. When night came he slept. On the third morning he came in to the fireside where the mage sat gazing at the flames, and said, 'Master . . .'

'Welcome, lad,' said Ogion.

'I have come back to you as I left : a fool,' the young man said, his voice harsh and thickened. The mage smiled a little and motioned Ged to sit across the hearth from him, and set to brewing them some tea.

Snow was falling, the first of the winter here on the lower slopes of Gont. Ogion's windows were shuttered fast, but they could hear the wet snow as it fell soft on the roof, and the deep stillness of snow all about the house. A long time they sat there by the fire, and Ged told his old master the tale of the years since he had sailed from Gont aboard the ship called *Shadow*. Ogion asked no questions, and when Ged was done he kept silent for a long time, calm, pondering. Then he rose, and set out bread and cheese and wine on the table, and they ate together. When they had done and had set the room straight, Ogion spoke.

'Those are bitter scars you bear, lad,' he said.

'I have no strength against the thing,' Ged answered.

Ogion shook his head but said no more for a time. At length, 'Strange,' he said: 'You had strength enough to outspell a sorcerer in his own domain, there in Osskil. You had strength enough to withstand the lures and fend off the attack of the servants of an Old Power of Earth. And at Pendor you had strength enough to stand up to a dragon.'

'It was luck I had in Osskil, not strength,' Ged replied, and he shivered again as he thought of the dreamlike deathly cold of the Court of the Terrenon. 'As for the dragon, I knew his name. The evil thing, the shadow that hunts me, has no name.'

'All things have a name,' said Ogion, so certainly that Ged dared not repeat what the Archmage Gensher had told him, that such evil forces as he had loosed were nameless. The Dragon of Pendor, indeed, had offered to tell him the shadow's name, but he put little trust in the truth of that offer, nor did he believe Serret's promise that the Stone would tell him what he needed to know.

'If the shadow has a name,' he said at last, 'I do not think it will stop and tell it to me ...'

'No,' said Ogion. 'Nor have you stopped and told it your name. And yet it knew it. On the moors in Osskil it called you by your name, the name I gave you. It is strange, strange ...'

He fell to brooding again. At last Ged said, 'I came here for counsel, not for refuge, Master. I will not bring this shadow upon you, and it will soon be here if I stay. Once you drove it from this very room –'

'No; that was but the foreboding of it, the shadow of a shadow. I could not drive it forth, now. Only you could do that.'

'But I am powerless before it. Is there any place . . .' His voice died away before he had asked the question.

'There is no safe place,' Ogion said gently. 'Do not transform yourself again, Ged. The shadow seeks to destroy your true being. It nearly did so, driving you into hawk's being. No, where you should go, I do not know. Yet I have an idea of what you should do. It is a hard thing to say to you.'

Ged's silence demanded truth, and Ogion said at last, 'You must turn around.'

'Turn around?'

'If you go ahead, if you keep running, wherever you run you will meet danger and evil, for it drives you, it chooses the way you go. You must choose. You must seek what seeks you. You must hunt the hunter.'

Ged said nothing.

'At the spring of the River Ar I named you,' the mage said, 'a stream that falls from the mountain to the sea. A man would know the end he goes to, but he cannot know it if he does not turn, and return to his beginning, and hold that beginning in his being. If he would not be a stick whirled and whelmed in the stream, he must be the stream itself, all of it, from its spring to its sinking in the sea. You returned to Gont, you returned to me, Ged. Now turn clear round, and seek the very source, and that which lies before the source. There lies your hope of strength.'

'There, Master?' Ged said with terror in his voice – 'Where?'

Ogion did not answer.

'If I turn,' Ged said after some time had gone by, 'if as you say I hunt the hunter, I think the hunt will not be long. All its desire is to meet me face to face. And twice it has done so, and twice defeated me.'

'Third time is the charm,' said Ogion.

Ged paced the room up and down, from fireside to door, from door to fireside. 'And if it defeats me wholly,' he said, arguing perhaps with Ogion perhaps with himself, 'it will take my knowledge and my power, and use them. It threatens only me, now. But if it enters into me and possesses me it will work great evil through me.'

'That is true. If it defeats you.'

'Yet if I run again, it will as surely find me again ... And all my strength is spent in the running.' Ged paced on a while, and then suddenly turned, and kneeling down before the mage he said, 'I have walked with great wizards and have lived on the Isle of the Wise, but you are my true master Ogion.' He spoke with love, and with a sombre joy.

'Good,' said Ogion. 'Now you know it. Better now than never, But you will be my master, in the end.' He got up, and built up the fire to a good blaze, and hung the kettle over it to boil, and then pulling on his sheepskin coat said, 'I must go look after my goats. Watch the kettle for me, lad.'

When he came back in, all snow-powdered and stamping snow from his goatskin boots, he carried a long, rough shaft of yew-wood. All the end of the short afternoon, and again after their supper, he sat working by lamplight on the shaft with knife and rubbing-stone and spell-craft. Many times he passed his hands along the wood as if seeking any flaw. Often as he worked he sang softly. Ged, still weary, listened, and as he grew sleepy he thought himself a child in the witch's hut in Ten Alders village, on a snowy night in the firelit dark, the air heavy with herb-scent and smoke, and his mind all adrift on dreams as he listened to the long soft singing of spells and deeds of heroes who fought against dark powers and won, or lost, on distant islands long ago.

'There,' said Ogion, and handed the finished staff to him. 'The Archmage gave you yew-wood, a good choice, and I kept to it. I meant the shaft for a longbow, but it's better this way. Good night, my son.'

As Ged, who found no words to thank him, turned away to his alcove-room, Ogion watched him and said, too soft for Ged to hear, 'O my young falcon, fly well!'

In the cold dawn when Ogion woke, Ged was gone. Only he had left in wizardly fashion a message of silver-scrawled runes on the hearthstone, that faded even as Ogion read them: 'Master, I go hunting.'

8. Hunting

GED had set off down the road from Re Albi in the winter dark before sunrise, and before noon he came to the Port of Gont. Ogion had given him decent Gontish leggings and shirt and vest of leather and linen to replace his Osskilian finery, but Ged had kept for his winter journey the lordly cloak lined with pellawi-fur. So cloaked, empty-handed but for the dark staff that matched his height, he came to the Land Gate, and the soldiers lounging against the carven dragons there did not have to look twice at him to see the wizard. They drew aside their lances and let him enter without question, and watched him as he went on down the street.

On the quays and in the House of the Sea-Guild he asked of ships that might be going out north or west to Enlad, Andrad, Oranéa. All answered him that no ship would be leaving Gont Port now, so near Sunreturn, and at the Sea-Guild they told him that even fishingboats were not going out through the Armed Cliffs in the untrusty weather.

They offered him dinner at the buttery there in the Sea-Guild; a wizard seldom has to ask for his dinner. He sat a while with those longshoremen, shipwrights, and weatherworkers, taking pleasure in their slow, sparse conversation, their grumbling Gontish speech. There was a great wish in him to stay here on Gont, and forgoing all wizardry and venture, forgetting all power and horror, to live in peace like any man on the known, dear ground of his home land. That was his wish; but his will was other. He did not stay long in the Sea-Guild, nor in the city, after he found there would be no ships out of port. He set out walking along the bay shore till he came to the first of the small villages that lie north of the City of Gont, and there he asked among the fishermen till he found one that had a boat to sell.

The fisherman was a dour old man. His boat, twelve foot long and clinker-built, was so warped and sprung as to be scarce sea-worthy, yet he asked a high price for her : the spell of sea-safety for a year laid on his own boat, himself, and his son. For Gontish fishermen fear nothing, not even wizards, only the sea.

That spell of sea-safety which they set much store by in the Northern Archipelago never saved a man from storm-wind or storm-wave, but, cast by one who knows the local seas and the ways of a boat and the skills of the sailor, it weaves some daily safety about the fisherman. Ged made the charm well and honestly, working on it all that night and the next day, omitting nothing, sure and patient, though all the while his mind was strained with fear and his thoughts went on dark paths seeking to imagine how the shadow would appear to him next, and how soon, and where. When the spell was made whole and cast, he was very weary. He slept that night in the fisherman's hut in a whale-gut hammock, and got up at dawn smelling like a dried herring, and went down to the cove under Cutnorth Cliff where his new boat lay.

He pushed it into the quiet water by the landing, and water began to well softly into it at once. Stepping into the boat light as a cat Ged set straight the warped boards and rotten pegs, working both with tools and incantations, as he had used to do with Pech-varry in Low Torning. The people of the village gathered in silence, not too close, to watch his quick hands and listen to his soft voice. This job too he did well and patiently until it was done and the boat was sealed and sound. Then he set up his staff that Ogion had made him for a mast, stayed it with spells, and fixed across it a yard of sound wood. Downward from this yard he wove on the wind's loom a sail of spells, a square sail white as the snows on Gont Peak above. At this the women watching sighed with envy. Then stand-ing by the mast Ged raised up the magewind lightly. The boat moved out upon the water, turning towards the Armed Cliffs across the great bay. When the silent watching fishermen saw that leaky rowboat slip out under sail as quick and neat as a sandpiper taking wing, then they raised a cheer, grinning and stamping in the cold wind on the beach; and Ged looking back a moment saw them cheer-

ing him on, under the dark jagged bulk of Cutnorth Cliff, above
which the snowy fields of the Mountain rose up into cloud.

He sailed across the bay and out between the Armed Cliffs on to
the Gontish Sea, there setting his course northwestwards to pass
north of Oranéa, returning as he had come. He had no plan or
strategy in this but the retracing of his course. Following his falcon-
flight across the days and winds from Osskil, the shadow might
wander or might come straight, there was no telling. But unless it
had withdrawn again wholly into the dream-realm, it should not
miss Ged coming openly, over open sea, to meet it.

On the sea he wished to meet it, if meet it he must. He was not
sure why this was, yet he had a terror of meeting the thing again
on dry land. Out of the sea there rise storms and monsters, but no
evil powers: evil is of earth. And there is no sea, no running of
river or spring, in the dark land where once Ged had gone. Death
is the dry place. Though the sea itself was a danger to him in the
hard weather of the season, that danger and change and instability
seemed to him a defence and chance. And when he met the shadow
in this final end of his folly, he thought, maybe at least he could
grip the thing even as it gripped him, and drag it with the weight of
his body and the weight of his own death down into the darkness of
the deep sea, from which, so held, it might not rise again. So at least
his death would put an end to the evil he had loosed by living.

He sailed a rough chopping sea above which clouds drooped and
drifted in vast mournful veils. He raised no magewind now but used
the world's wind, which blew keen from the northwest; and so
long as he maintained the substance of his spell-woven sail often
with a whispered word, the sail itself set and turned itself to catch
the wind. Had he not used that magic he would have been hard put
to keep the crank little boat on such a course, on that rough sea.
On he went, and kept keen look-out on all sides. The fisherman's
wife had given him two loaves of bread and a jar of water, and after
some hours, when he was first in sight of Kameber Rock, the only
isle between Gont and Oranéa, he ate and drank, and thought gratefully of the silent Gontishwoman who had given him the food. On

past the dim glimpse of land he sailed, tacking more westerly now, in a faint dank drizzle that over land might be a light snow. There was no sound at all but the small creaking of the boat and light slap of waves on her bow. No boat or bird went by. Nothing moved but the ever-moving water and the drifting clouds, the clouds that he remembered dimly as flowing all about him as he, a falcon, flew east on this same course he now followed to the west; and he had looked down on the grey sea then as now he looked up at the grey air.

Nothing was ahead when he looked ahead. He stood up, chilled, weary of this gazing and peering into empty muck. 'Come then,' he muttered, 'come on, what do you wait for, Shadow?' There was no answer, no darker motion among the dark mists and waves. Yet he knew more and more surely now that the thing was not far off, seeking blindly down his cold trail. And all at once he shouted out aloud, 'I am here, I Ged the Sparrowhawk, and I summon my shadow!'

The boat creaked, the waves lisped, the wind hissed a little on the white sail. The moments went by. Still Ged waited, one hand on the yew-wood mast of his boat, staring into the icy drizzle that slowly drove in ragged lines across the sea from the north. The moments went by. Then, far off in the rain over the water, he saw the shadow coming.

It had done with the body of the Osskilian oarsman Skiorh, and not as gebbeth did it follow him through the winds and over sea. Nor did it wear that beast-shape in which he had seen it on Roke Knoll, and in his dreams. Yet it had a shape now, even in the day-light. In its pursuit of Ged and in its struggle with him on the moors it had drawn power from him, sucking him into itself: and it may be that his summoning of it, aloud in the light of day, had given to it or forced upon it some form and semblance. Certainly it had now some likeness to a man, though being shadow it cast no shadow. So it came over the sea, out of the Jaws of Enlad towards Gont, a dim ill-made thing pacing uneasy on the waves, peering down the wind as it came; and the cold rain blew through it.

Because it was half blinded by the day, and because he had

called it, Ged saw it before it saw him. He knew it, as it knew him, among all beings, all shadows.

In the terrible solitude of the winter sea Ged stood and saw the thing he feared. The wind seemed to blow it farther from the boat, and the waves ran under it bewildering his eye, and ever and again it seemed closer to him. He could not tell if it moved or not. It had seen him, now. Though there was nothing in his mind but horror and fear of its touch, the cold black pain that drained his life away, yet he waited, unmoving. Then all at once speaking aloud he called the magewind strong and sudden into his white sail, and his boat leapt across the grey waves straight at the lowering thing that hung upon the wind.

In utter silence the shadow, wavering, turned and fled.

Upwind it went, northward. Upwind Ged's boat followed, shadow-speed against mage-craft, the rainy gale against them both. And the young man yelled to his boat, to the sail and the wind and the waves ahead, as a hunter yells to his hounds when the wolf runs in plain sight before them, and he brought into that spell-woven sail a wind that would have split any sail of cloth and that drove his boat over the sea like a scud of blown foam, closer always to the thing that fled.

Now the shadow turned, making a half-circle, and appearing all at once more loose and dim, less like a man more like mere smoke blowing on the wind, it doubled back and ran downwind with the gale, as if it made for Gont.

With hand and spell Ged turned his boat, and it leaped like a dolphin from the water, rolling, in that quick turn. Faster than before he followed, but the shadow grew ever fainter to his eyes. Rain, mixed with sleet and snow, came stinging across his back and his left cheek, and he could not see more than a hundred yards ahead. Before long, as the storm grew heavier, the shadow was lost to sight. Yet Ged was sure of its track as if he followed a beast's track over snow, instead of a wraith fleeing over water. Though the wind blew his way now he held the singing magewind in the sail, and flake-foam shot from the boat's blunt prow, and she slapped the water as she went.

For a long time hunted and hunter held their weird, fleet course, and the day was darkening fast. Ged knew that at the great pace he had gone these past hours he must be south of Gont, heading past it towards Spevy or Torheven, or even past these islands out into the open Reach. He could not tell. He did not care. He hunted, he followed, and fear ran before him.

All at once he saw the shadow for a moment not far from him. The world's wind had been sinking, and the driving sleet of the storm had given way to a chill, ragged, thickening mist. Through this mist he glimpsed the shadow, fleeing somewhat to the right of his course. He spoke to wind and sail and turned the tiller and pursued, though again it was a blind pursuit: the fog thickened fast, boiling and tattering where it met with the spellwind, closing down all round the boat, a featureless pallor that deadened light and sight. Even as Ged spoke the first word of a clearing-charm, he saw the shadow again, still to the right of his course, but very near, and going slowly. The fog blew through the faceless vagueness of its head, yet it was shaped like a man, only deformed and changing, like a man's shadow. Ged veered the boat once more, thinking he had run his enemy to ground: in that instant it vanished, and it was his boat that ran aground, smashing up on shoal rocks that the blowing mist had hidden from his sight. He was pitched nearly out, but grabbed hold on the mast-staff before the next breaker struck. This was a great wave, which threw the little boat up out of the water and brought her down on a rock, as a man might lift up and crush a snail's shell.

Stout and wizardly was the staff Ogion had shaped. It did not break, and buoyant as a dry log it rode the water. Still grasping it Ged was pulled back as the breakers streamed back from the shoal, so that he was in deep water and saved, till the next wave, from battering on the rocks. Salt-blinded and choked, he tried to keep his head up and to fight the enormous pull of the sea. There was sand beach a little aside of the rocks; he glimpsed this a couple of times as he tried to swim free of the rising of the next breaker. With all his strength and with the staff's power aiding him he struggled to make for that beach. He got no nearer. The surge and recoil of the swells tossed him back and forth like a rag, and the cold of the deep sea drew warmth fast from his body, weakening him till he could not move his arms. He had lost sight of rocks and beach alike, and did not know what way he faced. There was only a tumult of water around him, under him, over him, blinding him, strangling him, drowning him.

A wave swelling in under the ragged fog took him and rolled him over and over and flung him up like a stick of driftwood on the sand.

There he lay. He still clutched the yew-wood staff with both hands. Lesser waves dragged at him, trying to tug him back down the sand in their outgoing rush, and the mist parted and closed above him, and later a sleety rain beat on him.

After a long time he moved. He got up on hands and knees, and began slowly crawling up the beach, away from the water's edge. It was black night now, but he whispered to the staff, and a little werelight clung about it. With this to guide him he struggled forward, little by little, up towards the dunes. He was so beaten and broken and cold that this crawling through the wet sand in the whistling, sea-thundering dark was the hardest thing he had ever had to do. And once or twice it seemed to him that the great noise of the sea and the wind all died away and the wet sand turned to dust under his hands, and he felt the unmoving gaze of strange stars on his back: but he did not lift his head, and he crawled on, and after a while he heard his own gasping breath, and felt the bitter wind beat the rain against his face.

The moving brought a little warmth back into him at last, and after he had crept up into the dunes, where the gusts of rainy wind came less hard, he managed to get up on his feet. He spoke a stronger light out of the staff, for the world was utterly black, and then leaning on the staff he went on, stumbling and halting, half a mile or so inland. Then on the rise of a dune he heard the sea, louder

again, not behind him but in front: the dunes sloped down again
to another shore. This was no island he was on but a mere reef, a bit
of sand in the midst of the ocean.

He was too worn out to despair, but he gave a kind of sob and
stood there, bewildered, leaning on his staff, for a long time. Then
doggedly he turned to the left, so the wind would be at his back at
least, and shuffled down the high dune, seeking some hollow among
the ice-rimed, bowing sea-grass where he could have a little shelter.
As he held up the staff to see what lay before him, he caught a dull
gleam at the farthest edge of the circle of werelight: a wall of rain-
wet wood.

It was a hut or shed, small, and rickety as if a child had built it.
Ged knocked on the low door with his staff. It remained shut. Ged
pushed it open and entered, stooping nearly double to do so. He
could not stand upright inside the hut. Coals lay red in the firepit,
and by their dim glow Ged saw a man with white, long hair, who
crouched in terror against the far wall, and another, man or woman
he could not tell, peering from a heap of rags or hides on the floor.

'I won't hurt you,' Ged whispered.

They said nothing. He looked from one to the other. Their eyes
were blank with terror. When he laid down his staff, the one under
the pile of rags hid whimpering. Ged took off his cloak that was
heavy with water and ice, stripped naked and huddled over the firepit. 'Give me something to wrap myself in,' he said. He was hoarse,
and could hardly speak for the chattering of his teeth and the long
shudders that shook him. If they heard him, neither of the old ones
answered. He reached out and took a rag from the bed-heap – a
goat-hide, it might have been years ago, but it was now all tatters
and black grease. The one under the bed-heap moaned with fear, but
Ged paid no heed. He rubbed himself dry and then whispered, 'Have
you wood? Build up the fire a little, old man. I come to you in need,
I mean you no harm.'

The old man did not move, watching him in a stupor of fear.

'Do you understand me? Do you speak no Hardic?' Ged paused,
and then asked, 'Kargad?'

At that word, the old man nodded all at once, one nod, like a sad old puppet on strings. But as it was the only word Ged knew of the Kargish language, it was the end of their conversation. He found wood piled by one wall, built up the fire himself, and then with gestures asked for water, for swallowing seawater had sickened him and now he was parched with thirst. Cringing, the old man pointed to a great shell that held water, and pushed towards the fire another shell in which were strips of smoke-dried fish. So, cross-legged close by the fire, Ged drank and ate a little, and as some strength and sense began to come back into him, he wondered where he was. Even with the magewind he could not have sailed clear to the Kargad Lands. This islet must be out in the Reach, east of Gont but still west of Karego-At. It seemed strange that people dwelt on so small and forlorn a place, a mere sand-bar; maybe they were cast-aways; but he was too weary to puzzle his head about them then.

He kept turning his cloak to the heat. The silvery pellawi-fur dried fast, and as soon as the wool of the facing was at least warm, if not dry, he wrapped himself in it and stretched out by the firepit. 'Go to sleep, poor folk,' he said to his silent hosts, and laid his head down on the floor of sand, and slept.

Three nights he spent on the nameless isle, for the first morning when he woke he was sore in every muscle and feverish and sick. He lay like a log of driftwood in the hut by the firepit all that day and night. The next morning he woke still stiff and sore, but re-covered. He put back on his salt-crusted clothes, for there was not enough water to wash them, and going out into the grey windy morning looked over this place whereto the shadow had tricked him.

It was a rocky sandbar a mile wide at its widest and a little longer than that, fringed all about with shoals and rocks. No tree or bush grew on it, no plant but the bowing sea-grass. The hut stood in a hollow of the dunes, and the old man and woman lived there alone in the utter desolation of the empty sea. The hut was built, or piled up rather, of driftwood planks and branches. The water came from a little brackish well beside the hut; their food was fish and shellfish, fresh or dried, and rockweed. The tattered hides in the hut, and a little store of bone needles and fishhooks, and the sinew for fishlines and firedrill, came not from goats as Ged had thought at first, but from spotted seal; and indeed this was the kind of place where the seal will go to raise their pups in summer. But no one else comes to such a place. The old ones feared Ged not because they thought him a spirit, and not because he was a wizard, but only because he was a man. They had forgotten that there were other people in the world.

The old man's sullen dread never lessened. When he thought Ged was coming close enough to touch him, he would hobble away, peering back with a scowl around his bush of dirty white hair. At first the old woman had whimpered and hidden under her rag-pile whenever Ged moved, but as he had lain dozing feverishly in the dark hut, he saw her squatting to stare at him with a strange, dull, yearning look; and after a while she had brought him water to drink. When he sat up to take the shell from her she was scared and dropped it, spilling all the water, and then she wept, and wiped her eyes with her long whitish-grey hair.

Now she watched him as he worked down on the beach, shaping driftwood and planks from his boat that had washed ashore into a new boat, using the old man's crude stone adze and a binding-spell. This was neither a repair nor a boat-building, for he had not enough proper wood, and must supply all his wants with pure wizardry. Yet the old woman did not watch his marvellous work so much as she watched him, with that same craving look in her eyes. After a while she went off, and came back presently with a gift: a handful of mussels she had gathered on the rocks. Ged ate them as she gave them to him, sea-wet and raw, and thanked her. Seeming to gain courage, she went to the hut and came back with something again in her hands, a bundle wrapped up in a rag. Timidly, watching his face all the while, she unwrapped the thing and held it up for him to see.

It was a little child's dress of silk brocade stiff with seed-pearls, stained with salt, yellow with years. On the small bodice the pearls were worked in a shape Ged knew: the double arrow of the God-Brothers of the Kargad Empire, surmounted by a king's crown.

The old woman, wrinkled, dirty, clothed in an ill-sewn sack of sealskin, pointed at the little silken dress and at herself, and smiled:

a sweet, unmeaning smile, like a baby's. From some hiding place sewn in the skirt of the dress she took a small object, and this she held out to Ged. It was a bit of dark metal, a piece of broken jewellery perhaps, the half-circle of a broken ring. Ged looked at it, but she gestured that he take it, and was not satisfied until he took it; then she nodded and smiled again; she had made him a present. But the dress she wrapped up carefully in its greasy rag-coverings, and she shuffled back to the hut to hide the lovely thing away.

Ged put the broken ring into his tunic-pocket with almost the same care, for his heart was full of pity. He guessed now that these two might be children of some royal house of the Kargad Empire; a tyrant or usurper who feared to shed kingly blood had sent them to be cast away, to live or die, on an uncharted islet far from Karego-At. One had been a boy of eight or ten, maybe, and the other a stout baby princess in a dress of silk and pearls; and they had lived, and lived on alone, forty years, fifty years, on a rock in the ocean, prince and princess of Desolation.

But the truth of this guess he did not learn until, years later, the quest of the Ring of Erreth-Akbe led him to the Kargad Lands, and to the Tombs of Atuan.

His third night on the isle lightened to a calm, pale sunrise. It was the day of Sunreturn, the shortest day of the year. His little boat of wood and magic, scraps and spells, was ready. He had tried to tell the old ones that he would take them to any land, Gont or Spevy or the Torikles; he would have left them even on some lonely shore of Karego-At, had they asked it of him, though Kargish waters were no safe place for an Archipelagan to venture. But they would not leave their barren isle. The old woman seemed not to understand what he meant with his gestures and quiet words; the old man did understand, and refused. All his memory of other lands and other men was a child's nightmare of blood and giants and screaming: Ged could see that in his face, as he shook his head and shook his head.

So Ged that morning filled up a sealskin pouch with water at the well, and since he could not thank the old ones for their fire and food, and had no present for the old woman as he would have liked, he did what he could, and set a charm on that salty unreliable spring. The water rose up through the sand as sweet and clear as any mountain spring in the heights of Gont, nor did it ever fail. Because of it, that place of dunes and rocks is charted now and bears a name; sailors call it Springwater Isle. But the hut is gone, and the storms of many winters have left no sign of the two who lived out their lives there and died alone.

They kept hidden in the hut, as if they feared to watch, when Ged ran his boat out from the sandy south end of the isle. He let the world's wind, steady from the north, fill his sail of spellcloth, and went speedily forth over the sea.

Now this sea-quest of Ged's was a strange matter, for as he well knew, he was a hunter who knew neither what the thing was that he hunted, nor where in all Earthsea it might be. He must hunt it by guess, by hunch, by luck, even as it had hunted him. Each was blind to the other's being, Ged as baffled by impalpable shadows as the shadow was baffled by daylight and by solid things. One certainty only Ged had: that he was indeed the hunter now and not the hunted. For the shadow, having tricked him on to the rocks, might have had him at its mercy all the while he lay half-dead on the shore and blundered in the stormy dunes; but it had not waited for that chance. It had tricked him and fled away at once, not daring now to face him. In this he saw that Ogion had been right: the shadow could not draw on his power, so long as he was turned against it. So he must keep against it, keep after it, though its track was cold across these wide seas, and he had nothing at all to guide him but the luck of the world's wind blowing southward, and a dim guess or notion in his mind that south or east was the right way to follow.

Before nightfall he saw away off on his left hand the long, faint shoreline of a great land, which must be Karego-At. He was in the very sea-roads of those white barbaric folk. He kept a sharp watch out for any Kargish longship or galley; and he remembered, as he sailed through red evening, that morning of his boyhood in Ten Alders village, the plumed warriors, the fire, the mist. And thinking of that day he saw all at once with a qualm at his heart how the shadow had tricked him with his own trick, bringing that mist about him on the sea as if bringing it out of his own past, blinding him to danger and fooling him to his death.

He kept his course to the southeast, and the land sank out of sight as night came over the eastern edge of the world. The hollows of the waves all were full of darkness while the crests shone yet with a clear ruddy reflection of the west. Ged sang aloud the Winter Carol and such cantos of the *Deed of the Young King* as he remembered, for those songs are sung at the Festival of Sunreturn. His voice was clear but it fell to nothing in the vast silence of the sea. Darkness came quickly and the winter stars.

All that longest night of the year he waked, watching the stars rise upon his left hand and wheel overhead and sink into far black waters on the right, while always the long wind of winter bore him southward over an unseen sea. He could sleep for only a moment now and then, with a sharp awakening. This boat he sailed was in truth no boat but a thing more than half charm and sorcery, and the rest of it mere planks and driftwood which, if he let slack the shaping-spells and the binding-spell upon them, would soon enough lapse and scatter and go drifting off as a little flotsam on the waves. The sail too, woven of magic and the air, would not long stay against the wind if he slept, but would turn to a puff of wind itself. Ged's spells were cogent and potent, but when the matter on which such spells work is small, the power that keeps them working must be renewed from moment to moment: so he slept not that night. He would have gone easier and swifter as a falcon or dolphin, but Ogion had advised him not to change his shape, and he knew the value of Ogion's advice. So he sailed southward under the west-going stars, and the long night passed slowly, until the first day of the new year brightened all the sea.

Soon after the sun rose he saw land ahead, but he was making little way towards it. The world's wind had dropped with daybreak. He raised a light magewind into his sail, to drive him towards that land. At the sight of it, fear had come into him again, the sinking dread that urged him to turn away, to run away. And he followed that fear as a hunter follows the signs, the broad, blunt, clawed tracks of the bear, that may at any moment turn on him from the thickets. For he was close now : he knew it.

It was a queer-looking land that loomed up over the sea as he drew nearer and nearer. What had from afar seemed to be one sheer mountainwall, was split into several long steep ridges, separate isles perhaps, between which the sea ran in narrow sounds or channels. Ged had pored over many charts and maps in the Tower of the Master Namer on Roke, but those had been mostly of the Archipelago and the inner seas. He was out in the East Reach now, and did not know what this island might be. Nor had he much thought for that. It was fear that lay ahead of him, that lurked hiding from him or waiting for him among the slopes and forests of the island, and straight for it he steered.

Now the dark forest-crowned cliffs gloomed and towered high over the boat, and spray from the waves that broke against the rocky headlands blew spattering against his sail, as the magewind bore him between two great capes into a sound, a sea-lane that ran on before him deep into the island, no wider than the length of two galleys. The sea, confined, was restless and fretted at the steep shores. There were no beaches, for the cliffs dropped straight down into the water that lay darkened by the cold reflection of their heights. It was windless, and very silent.

The shadow had tricked him on to the moors in Osskil, and tricked him in the mist on to the rocks, and now would there be a third trick? Had he driven the thing here, or had it drawn him here, into a trap? He did not know. He knew only the torment of dread, and the certainty that he must go ahead and do what he had set out to do : hunt down the evil, follow his terror to its source. Very cautiously he steered, watching before him and behind him and up and down the cliffs on either hand. He had left the sunlight of the new day behind him on the open sea. All was dark here. The opening between the headlands seemed a remote, bright gateway when he glanced back. The cliffs loomed higher and ever higher overhead as he approached the mountain-root from which they sprang, and the lane of water grew narrower. He peered ahead into the dark cleft, and left and right up the great, cavern-pocked, boulder-tumbled slopes where trees crouched with their roots half in air. Nothing moved. Now he was coming to the end of the inlet, a high blank wrinkled mass of rock against which, narrowed to the width of a little creek, the last sea-waves lapped feebly. Fallen boulders and rotten trunks and the roots of gnarled trees left only a tight way to steer. A trap: a dark trap under the roots of the silent mountain, and he was in the trap. Nothing moved before him or above him. All was deathly still. He could go no further.

He turned the boat around, working her carefully round with spell and with makeshift oar lest she knock up against the underwater rocks or be entangled in the outreaching roots and branches, till she faced outward again; and he was about to raise up a wind to take him back as he had come, when suddenly the words of the spell froze on his lips, and his heart went cold within him. He looked back over his shoulder. The shadow stood behind him in the boat.

Had he lost one instant, he had been lost; but he was ready, and lunged to seize and hold the thing which wavered and trembled there within arm's reach. No wizardry would serve him now, but only his own flesh, his life itself, against the unliving. He spoke no word, but attacked, and the boat plunged and pitched from his sudden turn and lunge. And a pain ran up his arms into his breast, taking away his breath, and an icy cold filled him, and he was blinded; yet in his hands that seized the shadow there was nothing – darkness, air.

He stumbled forward, catching the mast to stay his fall, and light came shooting back into his eyes. He saw the shadow shudder away from him and shrink together, then stretch hugely up over him, over the sail, for an instant. Then like black smoke on the wind it recoiled and fled, formless, down the water towards the bright gate between the cliffs.

Ged sank to his knees. The little spell-patched boat pitched again, rocked itself to stillness, drifting on the uneasy waves. He crouched in it, numb, unthinking, struggling to draw breath, until at last cold water welling under his hands warned him that he must see to his boat, for the spells binding it were growing weak. He stood up, holding on to the staff that made the mast and rewove the binding-spell as best he could. He was chilled and weary; his hands and arms ached sorely, and there was no power in him. He wished he might be down there in that dark place where sea and mountain met and sleep, sleep on the restless rocking water.

He could not tell if this weariness were a sorcery laid on him by the shadow as it fled, or came of the bitter coldness of its touch, or was from mere hunger and want of sleep and expense of strength; but he struggled against it, forcing himself to raise up a light mage-wind into the sail and follow down the dark sea-way where the shadow had fled.

All terror was gone. All joy was gone. It was a chase no longer. He was neither hunted nor hunter, now. For the third time they had met and touched: he had of his own will turned to the shadow, seeking to hold it with living hands. He had not held it, but he had forged between them a bond, a link that had no breaking-point. There was no need to hunt the thing down, to track it, nor would its flight avail it. Neither could escape. When they had come to the time and place for their last meeting, they would meet.

But until that time, and elsewhere than that place, there would never be any rest or peace for Ged, day or night, on earth or sea. He knew now, and the knowledge was hard, that his task had never been to undo what he had done, but to finish what he had begun.

He sailed out from between the dark cliffs, and on the sea was broad, bright morning, with a fair wind blowing from the north.

He drank what water he had left in the sealskin pouch, and steered around the westernmost headland until he came into a wide strait between it and a second island lying to the west. Then he knew the place, calling to mind sea-charts of the East Reach. These were the Hands, a pair of lonely isles that reach their mountain-fingers northward towards the Kargad Lands. He sailed on between the two, and as the afternoon darkened with storm-clouds coming up from the north he came to shore, on the southern coast of the west isle. He had seen there was a little village there, above the beach where a stream came tumbling down to the sea, and he cared little what welcome he got if he could have water, fire's warmth, and sleep.

The villagers were rough shy people, awed by a wizard's staff, wary of a strange face, but hospitable to one who came alone, over sea, before a storm. They gave him meat and drink in plenty, and the comfort of firelight and the comfort of human voices speaking his own Hardic tongue, and last and best they gave him hot water to wash the cold and saltness of the sea from him, and a bed where he could sleep.

9. *Iffish*

GED spent three days in that village of the West Hand, recovering himself, and making ready a boat built not of spells and sea-wrack but of sound wood well pegged and caulked, with a stout mast and sail of her own, that he might sail easily and sleep when he needed. Like most boats of the North and the Reaches she was clinker-built, with planks overlapped and clenched one upon the other for strength in the high seas; every part of her was sturdy and well-made. Ged reinforced her wood with deep-inwoven charms, for he thought he might go far in that boat. She was built to carry two or three men, and the old man who owned her said that he and his brothers had been through high seas and foul weather with her and she had ridden all gallantly.

Unlike the shrewd fisherman of Gont, this old man, for fear and wonder of his wizardry, would have given the boat to Ged. But Ged paid him for it in sorcerer's kind, healing his eyes of the cataracts that were in the way of blinding him. Then the old man, rejoicing, said to him, 'We called the boat *Sanderling*, but do you call her *Lookfar*, and paint eyes aside her prow, and my thanks will look out of that blind wood for you and keep you from rock and reef. For I had forgotten how much light there is in the world, till you gave it back to me.'

Other works Ged also did in his days in that village under the steep forests of the Hand, as his power came back into him. These were such people as he had known as a boy in the Northward Vale of Gont, though poorer even than those. With them he was at home, as he would never be in the courts of the wealthy, and he knew their bitter wants without having to ask. So he laid charms of heal and ward on children who were lame or sickly, and spells of increase on the villagers' scrawny flocks of goats and sheep; he set the rune Simn on the spindles and looms, the boat's oars and tools of bronze and stone they brought him, that these might do their work well; and the rune Pirr he wrote on the roof-trees of the huts, which protects the house and its folk from fire, wind, and madness.

When his boat *Lookfar* was ready and well stocked with water and dried fish, he stayed yet one more day in the village, to teach to their young chanter the *Deed of Morred* and the *Havnorian Lay*. Very seldom did any Archipelagan ship touch at the Hands; songs made a hundred years ago were news to those villagers, and they craved to hear of heroes. Had Ged been free of what was laid on him he would gladly have stayed there a week or a month to sing them what he knew, that the great songs might be known on a new isle. But he was not free, and the next morning he set sail, going straight south over the wide seas of the Reach. For southward the shadow had gone. He need cast no finding-charm to know this : he knew it, as certainly as if a fine unreeling cord bound him and it together, no matter what miles and seas and lands might lie between. So he went certain, unhurried, and unhopeful on the way he must go, and the wind of winter bore him to the south.

He sailed a day and a night over the lonesome sea, and on the second day he came to a small isle, which they told him was called Vemish. The people in the little port looked at him askance, and soon their sorcerer came hurrying. He looked hard at Ged, and then he bowed, and said in a voice that was both pompous and wheedling, 'Lord Wizard ! forgive my temerity, and honour us by accepting of us anything you may need for your voyage – food, drink, sailcloth, rope, – my daughter is fetching to your boat at this moment a brace of fresh-roasted hens – I think it prudent, however, that you continue on your way from here as soon as it meets your convenience to do so. The people are in some dismay. For not long ago, the day before yesterday, a person was seen crossing our humble isle afoot from north to south, and no boat was seen to come with him aboard it nor no boat was seen to leave with him aboard it, and it did not seem that he cast any shadow. Those who saw this person tell me that he bore some likeness to yourself.'

At that, Ged bowed his own head, and turned and went back to the docks of Vemish and sailed out, not looking back. There was no profit in frightening the islanders or making an enemy of their sorcerer. He would rather sleep at sea again, and think over this news the sorcerer had told him, for he was sorely puzzled by it.

The day ended, and the night passed with cold rain whispering over the sea all through the dark hours, and a grey dawn. Still the mild north wind carried *Lookfar* on. After noon the rain and mist blew off, and the sun shone from time to time; and late in the day Ged saw right athwart his course the low blue hills of a great island, brightened by that drifting winter sunlight. The smoke of hearthfires lingered blue over the slate roofs of little towns among those hills, a pleasant sight in the vast sameness of the sea.

Ged followed a fishing-fleet in to their port, and going up the streets of the town in the golden winter evening he found an inn called *The Harrekki*, where firelight and ale and roast ribs of mutton warmed him body and soul. At the tables of the inn there were a couple of other voyagers, traders of the East Reach, but most of the men were townsfolk come there for good ale, news, and conversation. They were not rough timid people like the fisher-folk of the Hands, but true townsmen, alert and sedate. Surely they knew Ged for a wizard, but nothing at all was said of it, except that the inn-keeper in talking (and he was a talkative man) mentioned that this town, Ismay, was fortunate in sharing with other towns of the island the inestimable treasure of an accomplished wizard trained at the School on Roke, who had been given his staff by the Archmage himself, and who, though out of town at the moment, dwelt in his ancestral home right in Ismay itself, which, therefore, stood in no need of any other practitioner of the High Arts. 'As they say *two staffs in one town must come to blows,* isn't it so, Sir?' said the inn-keeper, smiling and full of cheer. So Ged was informed that as journeyman-wizard, one seeking a livelihood from sorcery, he was not wanted here. Thus he had got a blunt dismissal from Vemish and a bland one from Ismay, and he wondered at what he had been told about the kindly ways of the East Reach. This isle was Iffish, where his friend Vetch had been born. It did not seem so hospitable a place as Vetch had said.

And yet he saw that they were, indeed, kindly faces enough. It was only that they sensed what he knew to be true : that he was set apart from them, cut off from them, that he bore a doom upon him and followed after a dark thing. He was like a cold wind blowing through the firelit room, like a black bird carried by on a storm from foreign lands. The sooner he went on, taking his evil destiny with him, the better for these folk.

'I am on quest.' he said to the innkeeper. 'I will be here only a night or two.' His tone was bleak. The innkeeper, with a glance at the great yew-staff in the corner, said nothing at all for once, but filled up Ged's cup with brown ale till the foam ran over the top.

Ged knew that he should spend only the one night in Ismay. There was no welcome for him there, or anywhere. He must go where he was bound. But he was sick of the cold empty sea and the silence where no voice spoke to him. He told himself he would spend one day in Ismay, and on the morrow go. So he slept late; when he woke a light snow was falling, and he idled about the lanes and by-ways of the town to watch the people busy at their doings. He watched children bundled in fur capes playing at snow-castle and building snowmen; he heard gossips chatting across the street from open doors, and watched the bronze-smith at work with a little lad red-faced and sweating to pump the long bellows-sleeves at the smelting pit; through windows lit with a dim ruddy gold from within as the short day darkened he saw women at their looms, turning a moment to speak or smile to child or husband there in the warmth within the house. Ged saw all these things from outside and apart, alone, and his heart was very heavy in him, though he would not admit to himself that he was sad. As night fell he still lingered in the streets, reluctant to go back to the inn. He heard a man and a girl talking together merrily as they came down the street past him towards the town square, and all at once he turned, for he knew the man's voice.

He followed and caught up with the pair, coming up beside them in the late twilight lit only by distant lantern-gleams. The girl stepped back, but the man stared at him and then flung up the staff he carried, holding it between them as a barrier to ward off the threat or act of evil. And that was somewhat more than Ged could bear. His voice shook a little as he said, 'I thought you would know me, Vetch.'

Even then Vetch hesitated for a moment.

'I do know you,' he said, and lowered the staff and took Ged's hand and hugged him round the shoulders – 'I do know you! Welcome, my friend, welcome! What a sorry greeting I gave you, as if you were a ghost coming up from behind – and I have waited for you to come, and looked for you –'

'So you are the wizard they boast of in Ismay? I wondered –'

'Oh, yes, I'm their wizard; but listen, let me tell you why I didn't know you, lad. Maybe I've looked too hard for you. Three days ago – were you here three days ago, on Iffish?'

'I came yesterday.'

'Three days ago, in the street in Quor, the village up there in the hills, I saw you. That is, I saw a presentment of you or an imitation of you, or maybe simply a man who looks like you. He was ahead of me, going out of town, and he turned a bend in the road even as I saw him. I called and got no answer, I followed and found no one; nor any tracks; but the ground was frozen. It was a queer thing, and now seeing you come up out of the shadows like that I thought I was tricked again. I am sorry, Ged.' He spoke Ged's true name softly, so that the girl who stood waiting a little way behind him would not hear it.

Ged also spoke low, to use his friend's true name: 'No matter, Estarriol. But this is myself, and I am glad to see you . . .'

Vetch heard, perhaps, something more than simple gladness in his voice. He had not yet let go of Ged's shoulder, and he said now, in the True Speech, 'In trouble and from darkness you come, Ged, yet your coming is joy to me.' Then he went on in his Reach-accented Hardic, 'Come on, come home with us, we're going home, it's time to get in out of the dark! – This is my sister, the youngest of us, prettier than I am as you see, but much less clever: Yarrow she's called. Yarrow, this is the Sparrowhawk, the best of us and my friend.'

'Lord Wizard,' the girl greeted him, and decorously she bobbed her head and hid her eyes with her hands to show respect, as women did in the East Reach; her eyes when not hidden were clear, shy, and curious. She was perhaps fourteen years old, dark like her brother, but very slight and slender. On her sleeve there clung, winged and taloned, a dragon no longer than her hand.

They set off down the dusky street together, and Ged remarked as they went along, 'In Gont they say Gontish women are brave, but I never saw a maiden there wear a dragon for a bracelet.'

This made Yarrow laugh, and she answered him straight, 'This is only a harrekki, have you no harrekki on Gont?' Then she got shy for a moment and hid her eyes.

'No, nor no dragons. Is not the creature a dragon?'

'A little one, that lives in oak trees, and eats wasps and worms and sparrows' eggs – it grows no greater than this. Oh, Sir, my brother has told me often of the pet you had, the wild thing, the otak – do you have it still?'

'No. No longer.'

Vetch turned to him as if with a question, but he held his tongue and asked nothing till much later, when the two of them sat alone over the stone firepit of Vetch's house.

Though he was the chief wizard in the whole island of Iffish, Vetch made his home in Ismay, this small town where he had been born, living with his youngest brother and sister. His father had been a sea-trader of some means, and the house was spacious and strong-beamed, with much homely wealth of pottery and fine weaving and vessels of bronze and brass on carven shelves and chests. A great Taonian harp stood in one corner of the main room, and Yarrow's tapestry-loom in another, its tall frame inlaid with ivory. There Vetch for all his plain quiet ways was both a powerful wizard and a lord in his own house. There were a couple of old servants, prospering along with the house, and the brother, a cheerful lad, and Yarrow, quick and silent as a little fish, who served the two friends their supper and ate with them, listening to their talk, and afterwards slipped off to her own room. All things here were well-founded, peaceful, and assured: and Ged looking about him at the firelit room said, 'This is how a man should live,' and sighed.

'Well, it's one good way,' said Vetch. 'There are others. Now, lad, tell me if you can what things have come to you and gone from you since we last spoke, two years ago. And tell me what journey you are on, since I see well that you won't stay long with us this time.'

Ged told him, and when he was done Vetch sat pondering for a long while. Then he said, 'I'll go with you, Ged.'

'No.'

'I think I will.'

'No, Estarriol. This is no task or bane of yours. I began this evil course alone. I will finish it alone. I do not want any other to suffer from it – you least of all, you who tried to keep my hand from the evil act in the very beginning, Estarriol –'

'Pride was ever your mind's master,' his friend said smiling, as if they talked of a matter of small concern to either. 'Now think: it is your quest, assuredly, but if the quest fail, should there not be another there who might bear warning to the Archipelago? For the shadow would be a fearful power then. And if you defeat the thing, should there not be another there who will tell of it in the Archipelago, that the Deed may be known and sung? I know I can be of no use to you; yet I think I should go with you.'

So entreated Ged could not deny his friend, but he said, 'I should not have stayed this day here. I knew it, but I stayed.'

'Wizards do not meet by chance, lad,' said Vetch. 'And after all, as you said yourself, I was with you at the beginning of your journey. It is right that I should follow you to its end.' He put new wood on the fire, and they sat gazing into the flames a while.

'There is one I have not heard of since that night on Roke Knoll, and I had no heart to ask any at the School of him: Jasper I mean.'

'He never won his staff. He left Roke that same summer, and went to the Island of O to be sorcerer in the Lord's household at O-Tokne. I know no more of him than that.'

Again they were silent, watching the fire and enjoying (since it was a bitter night) the warmth on their legs and faces as they sat on the broad coping of the firepit, their feet almost among the coals.

Ged said at last, speaking low, 'There is a thing that I fear, Estarriol. I fear it more if you are with me when I go. There in the

Hands in the dead end of the inlet I turned upon the shadow, it was within my hands' reach, and I seized it – I tried to seize it. And there was nothing I could hold. I could not defeat it. It fled, I followed. But that may happen again, and yet again, I have no power over the thing. There may be neither death nor triumph to end this quest; nothing to sing of; no end. It may be I must spend my life running from sea to sea and land to land on an endless vain venture, a shadowquest.'

'Avert!' said Vetch, turning his left hand in the gesture that turns aside the ill chance spoken of. For all his sombre thoughts this made Ged grin a little, for it is rather a child's charm than a wizard's; there was always such village innocence in Vetch. Yet also he was keen, shrewd, direct to the centre of a thing. He said now, 'That is a grim thought and I trust a false one. I guess rather that what I saw begin, I may see end. Somehow you will learn its nature, its being, what it is, and so hold and bind and vanquish it. Though that is a hard question: what it is ... There is a thing that worries me, I do not understand it. It seems the shadow now goes in your shape, or a kind of likeness of you at least, as they saw it on Vemish and as I saw it here in Iffish. How may that be, and why, and why did it never do so in the Archipelago?'

'They say, *Rules change in the Reaches.*'

'Aye, a true saying, I can tell you. There are good spells I learned on Roke that have no power here, or go all awry; and also there are spells worked here I never learned on Roke. Every land has its own powers and the farther one goes from the Inner Lands, the less one can guess about those powers and their governance. But I do not think it is only that which works this change in the shadow.'

'Nor do I. I think that, when I ceased to flee from it and turned against it, that turning of my will upon it gave it shape and form, even though the same act prevented it from taking my strength from me. All my acts have their echo in it; it is my creature.'

'In Osskil it named you, and so stopped any wizardry you might have used against it. Why did it not do so again, there in the Hands?'

'I do not know. Perhaps it is only from my weakness that it draws the strength to speak. Almost with my own tongue it speaks : for how did it know my name? How did it know my name? I have racked my brains on that over all the seas since I left Gont, and I cannot see the answer. Maybe it cannot speak at all in its own form or formlessness, but only with borrowed tongue, as a gebbeth. I do not know.'

'Then you must beware meeting it in gebbeth-form a second time.'

'I think,' Ged replied, stretching out his hands to the red coals as if he felt an inward chill, 'I think I will not. It is bound to me now as I am to it. It cannot get so far free of me as to seize any other man and empty him of will and being, as it did Skiorh. It can possess me. If ever I weaken again, and try to escape from it, to break the bond, it will possess me. And yet, when I held it with all the strength I had, it became mere vapour, and escaped from me ... And so it will again, and yet it cannot really escape, for I can always find it. I am bound to the foul cruel thing, and will be forever, unless I can learn the word that masters it : its name.'

Brooding his friend asked, 'Are there names in the dark realms?'

'Gensher the Archmage said there are not. My master Ogion said otherwise.'

'*Infinite are the arguments of mages*,' Vetch quoted, with a smile that was somewhat grim.

'She who served the Old Power on Osskil swore that the Stone would tell me the shadow's name, but that I count for little. However there was also a dragon, who offered to trade that name for his own, to be rid of me; and I have thought that, where mages argue, dragons may be wise.'

'Wise, but unkind. But what dragon is this? You did not tell me you had been talking with dragons since I saw you last.'

They talked together late that night, and though always they came back to the bitter matter of what lay before Ged, yet their pleasure in being together overrode all; for the love between them was strong and steadfast, unshaken by time or chance. In the morning Ged woke beneath his friend's roof, and while he was still drowsy he felt such wellbeing as if he were in some place wholly defended from evil and harm. All day long a little of this dream-peace clung to his thoughts, and he took it, not as a good omen, but as a gift. It seemed likely to him that leaving this house he would leave the last haven he was to know, and so while the short dream lasted he would be happy in it.

Having affairs he must see to before he left Iffish, Vetch went off to the other villages of the island with the lad who served him as prentice-sorcerer. Ged stayed with Yarrow and her brother, called Murre, who was between her and Vetch in age. He seemed not much more than a boy, for there was no gift or scourge of mage-power in him, and he had never been anywhere but Iffish, Tok, and Holp, and his life was easy and untroubled. Ged watched him with wonder and some envy, and exactly so he watched Ged: to each it seemed very queer that the other, so different, yet was his own age, nineteen years. Ged marvelled how one who had lived nineteen years could be so carefree. Admiring Murre's comely, cheerful face he felt himself to be all lank and harsh, never guessing that Murre envied him even the scars that scored his face, and thought them the track of a dragon's claws and the very rune and sign of a hero.

The two young men were thus somewhat shy with each other, but as for Yarrow she soon lost her awe of Ged, being in her own house and mistress of it. He was very gentle with her, and many were the questions she asked of him, for Vetch, she said, would never tell her anything. She kept busy those two days making dry wheatcakes for the voyagers to carry, and wrapping up dried fish and meat and other such provender to stock their boat, until Ged told her to stop, for he did not plan to sail clear to Selidor without a halt.

'Where is Selidor?'

'Very far out in the Western Reach, where dragons are as common as mice.'

'Best stay in the East then, our dragons are as small as mice. There's your meat, then; you're sure that's enough? Listen, I don't understand: you and my brother both are mighty wizards, you wave your hand and mutter and the thing is done. Why do you get hungry, then? When it comes suppertime at sea, why not say, *Meat-pie!* and the meat-pie appears, and you eat it?'

'Well, we could do so. But we don't much wish to eat our words, as they say. *Meat-pie!* is only a word, after all ... We can make it odorous, and savourous, and even filling, but it remains a word. It fools the stomach and gives no strength to the hungry man.'

'Wizards, then, are not cooks,' said Murre, who was sitting across the kitchen hearth from Ged, carving a box-lid of fine wood; he was a woodworker by trade, though not a very zealous one.

'Nor are cooks wizards, alas,' said Yarrow on her knees to see if the last batch of cakes baking on the hearth-bricks was getting brown. 'But I still don't understand, Sparrowhawk. I have seen my brother, and even his prentice, make light in a dark place only by saying one word: and the light shines, it is bright, not a word but a light you can see your way by!'

'Aye,' Ged answered. 'Light is a power. A great power by which we exist, but which exists beyond our needs, in itself. Sunlight and starlight are time, and time is light. In the sunlight, in the days and years, life is. In a dark place life may call upon the light, naming it. – But usually when you see a wizard name or call upon some thing, some object to appear, that is not the same, he calls upon no power greater than himself, and what appears is an illusion only. To summon a thing that is not there at all, to call it by speaking its true name, that is a great mastery, not lightly used. Not for mere hunger's sake. Yarrow, your little dragon has stolen a cake.'

Yarrow had listened so hard, gazing at Ged as he spoke, that she had not seen the harrekki scuttle down from its warm perch on the kettle-hook over the hearth and seize a wheatcake bigger than itself. She took the small scaly creature on her knee and fed it bits and crumbs, while she pondered what Ged had told her.

'So then you would not summon up a real meat-pie lest you disturb what my brother is always talking about – I forget its name –'

'Equilibrium,' Ged replied soberly, for she was very serious.

'Yes. But, when you were shipwrecked, you sailed from the place in a boat woven mostly of spells, and it didn't leak water. Was it illusion?'

'Well, partly it was illusion, because I am uneasy seeing the sea through great holes in my boat, so I patched them for the looks of the thing. But the strength of the boat was not illusion, nor summoning, but made with another kind of art, a binding-spell. The wood was bound as one whole, one entire thing, a boat. What is a boat but a thing that doesn't leak water?'

'I've bailed some that do,' said Murre.

'Well, mine leaked, too, unless I was constantly seeing to the spell.' He bent down from his corner seat and took a cake from the bricks, and juggled it in his hands. 'I too have stolen a cake.'

'You have burned fingers, then. And when you're starving on the waste water between the far isles you'll think of that cake and say, Ah! had I not stolen that cake I might eat it now, alas! – I shall eat my brother's, so he can starve with you –'

'Thus is Equilibrium maintained,' Ged remarked, while she took and munched a hot, half-toasted cake; and this made her giggle and choke. But presently looking serious again she said, 'I wish I could truly understand what you tell me. I am too stupid.'

'Little sister,' Ged said, 'it is I that have no skill explaining. If we had more time –'

'We will have more time,' Yarrow said. 'When my brother comes back home, you will come with him, for a while at least, won't you?'

'If I can,' he answered gently.

There was a little pause; and Yarrow asked, watching the harrekki climb back to its perch, 'Tell me just this, if it is not a secret: what other great powers are there besides the light?'

'It is no secret. All power is one in source and end, I think. Years and distances, stars and candles, water and wind and wizardry, the craft in a man's hand and the wisdom in a tree's root: they all arise together. My name, and yours, and the true name of the sun, or a spring of water, or an unborn child, all are syllables of the great word that is very slowly spoken by the shining of the stars. There is no other power. No other name.'

Staying his knife on the carved wood, Murre asked, 'What of death?'

The girl listened, her shining black head bent down.

'For a word to be spoken,' Ged answered slowly, 'there must be silence. Before, and after.' Then all at once he got up, saying, 'I have no right to speak of these things. The word that was mine to say I said wrong. It is better that I keep still; I will not speak again. Maybe there is no true power but the dark.' And he left the fireside and the warm kitchen, taking up his cloak and going out alone into the drizzling cold rain of winter in the streets.

'He is under a curse,' Murre said, gazing somewhat fearfully after him.

'I think this voyage he is on leads him to his death,' the girl said, 'and he fears that, yet he goes on.' She lifted her head as if she watched, through the red flame of the fire, the course of a boat that came through the seas of winter alone, and went on out into empty seas. Then her eyes filled with tears a moment, but she said nothing.

Vetch came home the next day, and took his leave of the notables of Ismay, who were most unwilling to let him go off to sea in midwinter on a mortal quest not even his own; but though they might reproach him, there was nothing at all they could do to stop him. Growing weary of old men who nagged him, he said, 'I am yours, by parentage and custom and by duty undertaken towards you. I am your wizard. But it is time you recalled that, though I am a servant, I am not your servant. When I am free to come back I will come back : till then farewell.'

At daybreak, as grey light welled up in the east from the sea, the two young men set forth in *Lookfar* from the harbour of Ismay, raising a brown, strong-woven sail to the north wind. On the dock Yarrow stood and watched them go, as sailors' wives and sisters stand on all the shores of all Earthsea watching their men go out on the sea, and they do not wave or call aloud, but stand still in hooded cloak of grey or brown, there on the shore that dwindles smaller and smaller from the boat while the water grows wide between.

10. The Open Sea

THE haven now was sunk from sight and *Lookfar's* painted eyes, wave-drenched, looked ahead on seas ever wider and more desolate. In two days and nights the companions made the crossing from Iffish to Soders Island, a hundred miles of foul weather and contrary winds. They stayed in port there only briefly, long enough to refill a waterskin, and to buy a tar-smeared sailcloth to protect some of their gear in the undecked boat from seawater and rain. They had not provided this earlier, because ordinarily a wizard looks after such small conveniences by way of spells, the very least and commonest kind of spells, and indeed it takes little more magic to freshen seawater and so save the bother of carrying fresh water. But Ged seemed most unwilling to use his craft, or to let Vetch use his. He said only, 'It's better not,' and his friend did not ask or argue. For as the wind first filled their sail, both had felt a heavy foreboding, cold as that winter wind. Haven, harbour, peace, safety, all that was behind. They had turned away. They went now a way in which all events were perilous, and no acts were meaningless. On the course on which they were embarked, the saying of the least spell might change chance and move the balance of power and of doom : for they went now towards the very centre of that balance, towards the place where light and darkness meet. Those who travel thus say no word carelessly.

Sailing out again and coasting round the shores of Soders, where white snowfields faded up into foggy hills, Ged took the boat southward again, and now they entered waters where the great traders of the Archipelago never come, the outmost fringes of the Reach.

Vetch asked no question about their course, knowing that Ged did not choose it but went as he must go. As Soders Island grew small and pale behind them, and the waves hissed and smacked under the prow, and the great grey plain of water circled them all round clear to the edge of the sky, Ged asked, 'What lands lie ahead this course?

'Due south of Soders there are no lands at all. Southeast you go a long way and find little : Pelimer, Kornay, Gosk, and Astowell which is also called Lastland. Beyond it, the Open Sea.'

'What to the southwest?'

'Rolameny, which is one of our East Reach isles, and some small islets round about it; then nothing till you enter the South Reach : Rood, and Toom, and the Isle of the Ear where men do not go.'

'We may,' Ged said wryly.

'I'd rather not,' said Vetch – 'that is a disagreeable part of the world, they say, full of bones and portents. Sailors say that there are stars to be seen from the waters by the Isle of the Ear and Far Sorr that cannot be seen anywhere else, and that have never been named.'

'Aye, there was a sailor on the ship that brought me first to Roke who spoke of that. And he told me tales of the Raft-Folk in the far South Reach, who never come to land but once a year, to cut the great logs for their rafts, and the rest of the year, all the days and months, they drift on the currents of ocean, out of sight of land. I'd like to see those raft-villages.'

'I would not,' said Vetch grinning. 'Give me land, and land-folk; the sea in its bed and I in mine . . .'

'I wish I could have seen all the cities of the Archipelago,' Ged said as he held the sail-rope, watching the wide grey wastes before them. 'Havnor at the world's heart, and Éa where the myths were born, and Shelieth of the Fountains on Way; all the cities and the great lands. And the small lands, the strange lands of the Outer Reaches, them too. To sail right down the Dragons' Run, away in the west. Or to sail north into the ice-floes, clear to Hogen Land. Some say that is a land greater than all the Archipelago, and others say it is mere reefs and rocks with ice between. No one knows. I should like to see the whales in the northern seas . . . But I cannot. I must go where I am bound to go, and turn my back on the bright shores. I was in too much haste, and now have no time left. I traded all the sunlight and the cities and the distant lands for a handful of power, for a shadow, for the dark.' So, as the mageborn will, Ged made his fear and regret into a song, a brief lament, half-sung, that was not for himself alone; and his friend replying spoke the hero's words from the *Deed of Erreth-Akbe*, 'O may I see the earth's bright hearth once more, the white towers of Havnor ...'

So they sailed on their narrow course over the wide forsaken waters. The most they saw that day was a school of silver pannies swimming south, but never a dolphin leapt nor did the flight of gull or murre or tern break the grey air. As the east darkened and the west grew red, Vetch brought out food and divided it between them and said, 'Here's the last of the ale. I drink to the one who thought to put the keg aboard for thirsty men in cold weather : my sister Yarrow.'

At that Ged left off his bleak thoughts and his gazing ahead over the sea, and he saluted Yarrow more earnestly, perhaps, than Vetch. The thought of her brought to his mind the sense of her wise and childish sweetness. She was not like any person he had known. (What young girl had he ever known at all? but he never thought of that.) 'She is like a little fish, a minnow, that swims in a clear creek,' he said, '– defenceless, yet you cannot catch her.'

At this Vetch looked straight at him, smiling. 'You are a mage born,' he said. 'Her true name is Kest.' In the Old Speech, *kest* is minnow, as Ged well knew; and this pleased him to the heart. But after a while he said in a low voice, 'You should not have told me her name, maybe.'

But Vetch, who had not done so lightly, said, 'Her name is safe with you as mine is. And, besides, you knew it without my telling you ...'

Red sank to ashes in the west, and ash-grey sank to black. All the sea and sky were wholly dark. Ged stretched out in the bottom of the boat to sleep, wrapped in his cloak of wool and fur. Vetch, holding the sail-rope, sang softly from the *Deed of Enlad*, where the song tells how the mage Morred the White left Havnor in his oarless longship and coming to the island Soléa saw Elfarran in the orchards in the spring. Ged slept before the song came to the sorry end of their love, Morred's death, the ruin of Enlad, the seawaves, vast and bitter, whelming the orchards of Soléa. Towards midnight he woke, and watched again while Vetch slept. The little boat ran sharp over choppy seas, fleeing the strong wind that leaned on her sail, running blind through the night. But the overcast had broken, and before dawn the thin moon shining between brown-edged clouds shed a weak light on the sea.

'The moon wanes to her dark,' Vetch murmured, awake in the dawn, when for a while the cold wind dropped. Ged looked up at the white half-ring above the paling eastern waters, but said nothing. The dark of the moon that follows first after Sunreturn is called the Fallows, and is the contrary pole of the days of the Moon and the Long Dance in summer. It is an unlucky time for travellers and for the sick; children are not given their true name during the Fallows, and no Deeds are sung, nor swords nor edge-tools sharpened, nor oaths sworn. It is the dark axis of the year, when things done are ill done.

Three days out from Soders they came, following sea-birds and shore-wrack, to Pelimer, a small isle humped high above the high grey seas. Its people spoke Hardic, but in their own fashion, strange even to Vetch's ears. The young men came ashore there for fresh water and a respite from the sea, and at first were well received, with wonder and commotion. There was a sorcerer in the main town of the island, but he was mad. He would talk only of the great serpent that was eating at the foundations of Pelimer so that soon the island must go adrift like a boat cut from her moorings, and slide out over the edge of the world. At first he greeted the young wizards courteously, but as he talked about the serpent he began to look askance at Ged; and then he fell to railing at them there in the street, calling them spies and servants of the Sea-Snake. The Pelimerians looked dourly at them after that, since though mad he was their sorcerer. So Ged and Vetch made no long stay, but set forth again before nightfall, going always south and east.

In these days and nights of sailing Ged never spoke of the shadow, nor directly of his quest; and the nearest Vetch came to asking any question was (as they followed the same course farther and farther out and away from the known lands of Earthsea) – 'Are you sure? –' To this Ged answered only, 'Is the iron sure where the magnet lies?' Vetch nodded and they went on, no more being said by either. But from time to time they talked of the crafts and devices that mages of old days had used to find out the hidden name of baneful powers and beings: how Nereger of Paln had learned the Black Mage's name from overhearing the conversation of dragons, and how Morred had seen his enemy's name written by falling raindrops in the dust of the battlefield of the Plains of Enlad. They spoke of finding-spells, and invocations, and those Answerable Questions which only the Master Patterner of Roke can ask. But often Ged would end by murmuring the words which Ogion had said to him on the shoulder of Gont Mountain in an autumn long ago: 'To hear, one must be silent . . .' And he would fall silent, and ponder, hour after hour, always watching the sea ahead of the boat's way. Sometimes it seemed to Vetch that his friend saw, across the waves and miles and grey days yet to come, the thing they followed and the dark end of their voyage.

They passed between Kornay and Gosk in foul weather, seeing neither isle in the fog and rain, and knowing they had passed them only on the next day when they saw ahead of them an isle of pinnacled cliffs above which sea-gulls wheeled in huge flocks whose mewing clamour could be heard from far over the sea. Vetch said, 'That will be Astowell, from the look of it. Lastland. East and south of it the charts are empty.'

'Yet they who live there may know of farther lands,' Ged answered.

'Why do you say so?' Vetch asked, for Ged had spoken uneasily; and his answer to this again was halting and strange. 'Not there,' he said, gazing at Astowell ahead, and past it, or through it – 'Not there. Not on the sea. Not on the sea but on dry land: what land? Before the springs of the open sea, beyond the sources, behind the gates of daylight –'

Then he fell silent, and when he spoke again it was in an ordinary voice, as if he had been freed from a spell or a vision, and had no clear memory of it.

The port of Astowell, a creek-mouth between rocky heights, was

on the northern shore of the isle, and all the huts of the town faced
north and west; it was as if the island turned its face, though from
so far away, always towards Earthsea, towards mankind.

Excitement and dismay attended the arrival of strangers, in a
season when no boat had ever braved the seas round Astowell. The
women all stayed in the wattle huts, peering out the door, hiding
their children behind their skirts, drawing back fearfully into the
darkness of the huts as the strangers came up from the beach. The
men, lean fellows ill-clothed against the cold, gathered in a solemn
circle about Vetch and Ged, and each one held a stone hand-axe or
a knife of shell. But once their fear was past they made the strangers
very welcome, and there was no end to their questions. Seldom did
any ship come to them even from Soders and Rolameny, they having
nothing to trade for bronze or fine wares; they had not even any
wood. Their boats were coracles woven of reed, and it was a brave
sailor who would go as far as Gosk or Kornay in such a craft. They
dwelt all alone here at the edge of all the maps. They had no witch
or sorcerer, and seemed not to recognize the young wizards' staffs
for what they were, admiring them only for the precious stuff they
were made of, wood. Their chief or Isle-Man was very old, and he
alone of his people had ever before seen a man born in the Archipelago. Ged, therefore, was a marvel to them; the men brought
their little sons to look at the Archipelagan, so they might remember him when they were old. They had never heard of Gont, only of
Havnor and Êa, and took him for a Lord of Havnor. He did his best
to answer their questions about the white city he had never seen.
But he was restless as the evening wore on, and at last he asked the
men of the village, as they sat crowded round the firepit in the
lodgehouse in the reeking warmth of the goat-dung and broom-
faggots that were all their fuel, 'What lies eastward of your
land?'

They were silent, some grinning others grim.

The old Isle-Man answered, 'The sea.'

'There is no land beyond?'

'This is Lastland. There is no land beyond. There is nothing but
water till world's edge.'

'These are wise men, father,' said a younger man, 'seafarers, voyagers. Maybe they know of a land we do not know of.'

'There is no land east of this land,' said the old man, and he looked long at Ged, and spoke no more to him.

The companions slept that night in the smoky warmth of the lodge. Before daylight Ged roused his friend, whispering, 'Estarriol, wake. We cannot stay, we must go.'

'Why so soon?' Vetch asked, full of sleep.

'Not soon – late. I have followed too slow. It has found the way to escape me, and so doom me. It must not escape me, for I must follow it however far it goes. If I lose it I am lost.'

'Where do we follow it?'

'Eastward. Come. I filled the waterskins.'

So they left the lodge before any in the village was awake, except a baby that cried a little in the darkness of some hut, and fell still again. By the vague starlight they found the way down to the creek-mouth, and untied *Lookfar* from the rock cairn where she had been made fast, and pushed her out into the black water. So they set out eastward from Astowell into the Open Sea, on the first day of the Fallows, before sunrise.

That day they had clear skies. The world's wind was cold and gusty from the northeast, but Ged had raised the magewind: the first act of magery he had done since he left the Isle of the Hands. They sailed very fast due eastward. The boat shuddered with the great, smoking, sunlit waves that hit her as she ran, but she went gallantly as her builder had promised, answering the magewind as true as any spell-enwoven ship of Roke.

Ged spoke not at all that morning, except to renew the power of the wind-spell or to keep a charmed strength in the sail, and Vetch finished his sleep, though uneasily, in the stern of the boat. At noon they ate. Ged doled their food out sparingly, and the portent of this was plain, but both of them chewed their bit of salt fish and wheaten cake, and neither said anything.

All afternoon they cleaved eastward never turning nor slackening pace. Once Ged broke his silence, saying, 'Do you hold with those who think the world is all landless sea beyond the Outer Reaches, or with those who imagine other Archipelagoes or vast undiscovered lands on the other face of the world?'

'At this time,' said Vetch, 'I hold with those who think the world has but one face, and he who sails too far will fall off the edge of it.'

Ged did not smile; there was no mirth left in him. 'Who knows what a man might meet, out there? Not we, who keep always to our coasts and shores.'

'Some have sought to know, and have not returned. And no ship has ever come to us from lands we do not know.'

Ged made no reply.

All that day, all that night they went driven by the powerful wind of magery over the great swells of ocean, eastward. Ged kept watch from dusk till dawn, for in darkness the force that drew or drove him grew stronger yet. Always he watched ahead, though his eyes in the moonless night could see no more than the painted eyes aside the boat's blind prow. By daybreak his dark face was grey with weariness, and he was so cramped with cold that he could hardly stretch out to rest. He said whispering, 'Hold the magewind from the west, Estarriol,' and then he slept.

There was no sunrise, and presently rain came beating across the bow from the northeast. It was no storm, only the long, cold winds and rains of winter. Soon all things in the open boat were wet through, despite the sailcloth cover they had bought; and Vetch felt as if he too were soaked clear to the bone; and Ged shivered in his sleep. In pity for his friend, and perhaps for himself, Vetch tried to turn aside for a little that rude ceaseless wind that bore the rain. But though, following Ged's will, he could keep the magewind strong and steady, his weatherworking had small power here so far from land, and the wind of the Open Sea did not listen to his voice.

And at this a certain fear came into Vetch, as he began to wonder how much wizardly power would be left to him and Ged, if they went on and on away from the lands where men were meant to live.

Ged watched again that night, and all night held the boat eastward. When day came the world's wind slackened somewhat, and the sun shone fitfully; but the great swells ran so high that *Lookfar* must tilt and climb up them as if they were hills, and hang at the hillcrest and plunge suddenly, and climb up the next again, and the next, and the next, unending.

In the evening of that day Vetch spoke out of long silence. 'My friend,' he said, 'you spoke once as if sure we would come to land at last. I would not question your vision but for this, that it might be a trick, a deception made by that which you follow, to lure you on farther than a man can go over ocean. For our power may change and weaken on strange seas. And a shadow does not tire, or starve, or drown.'

They sat side by side on the thwart, yet Ged looked at him now as if from a distance, across a wide abyss. His eyes were troubled, and he was slow to answer.

At last he said, 'Estarriol, we are coming near.'

Hearing his words his friend knew them to be true. He was afraid, then. But he put his hand on Ged's shoulder and said only, 'Well, then, good; that is good.'

Again that night Ged watched, for he could not sleep in the dark. Nor would he sleep when the third day came. Still they ran with that ceaseless, light, terrible swiftness over the sea, and Vetch wondered at Ged's power that could hold so strong a magewind hour after hour, here on the Open Sea where Vetch felt his own power all weakened and astray. And they went on, and on, until it seemed to Vetch that what Ged had spoken would come true, and they were going beyond the sources of the sea and eastward behind the gates of daylight. Ged stayed forward in the boat, looking ahead as always. But he was not watching the ocean now, or not the ocean that Vetch saw, a waste of heaving water to the rim of the sky. In Ged's eyes there was a dark vision that overlapped and veiled the grey sea and the grey sky, and the darkness grew, and the veil thickened. None of this was visible to Vetch, except when he looked at his friend's face; then he too saw the darkness for a moment. They went on, and on. And it was as if, though one wind drove them in one boat, Vetch went east over the world's sea, while Ged went alone into a realm where there was no east or west, no rising or setting of the sun, or of the stars.

Ged stood up suddenly in the prow, and spoke aloud. The mage-wind dropped. *Lookfar* lost headway, and rose and fell on the vast surges like a chip of wood. Though the world's wind blew strong as ever straight from the north now, the brown sail hung slack, unstirred. And so the boat hung on the waves, swung by their great slow swinging, but going no direction.

Ged said, 'Take down the sail,' and Vetch did so quickly, while Ged unlashed the oars and set them in the locks and bent his back to rowing.

Vetch, seeing only the waves heaving up and down clear to the end of sight, could not understand why they went now by oars; but he waited, and presently he was aware that the world's wind was growing faint and the swells diminishing. The climb and plunge of the boat grew less and less, till at last she seemed to go forward under Ged's strong oar-strokes over water that lay almost still, as in a land-locked bay. And though Vetch could not see what Ged saw, when between his strokes he looked ever and again over his shoulder at what lay before the boat's way – though Vetch could not see the dark slopes beneath unmoving stars, yet he began to see with his wizard's eye a darkness that welled up in the hollows of the waves all around the boat, and he saw the billows grow low and sluggish as they were choked with sand.

If this were an enchantment of illusion, it was powerful beyond belief; to make the Open Sea seem land. Trying to collect his wits and courage, Vetch spoke the Revelation-Spell, watching between each slow-syllabled word for change or tremor of illusion in this strange drying and shallowing of the abyss of ocean. But there was none. Perhaps the spell, though it should affect only his vision and not the magic at work about them, had no power here. Or perhaps there was no illusion, and they had come to world's end.

Unheeding, Ged rowed always slower, looking over his shoulder, choosing a way among channels or shoals and shallows that he alone could see. The boat shuddered as her keel dragged. Under that keel lay the vast deeps of the sea, yet they were aground. Ged drew the oars up rattling in their locks, and that noise was terrible, for there was no other sound. All sounds of water, wind, wood, sail were gone, lost in a huge profound silence that might have been unbroken for ever. The boat lay motionless. No breath of wind moved. The sea had turned to sand, shadowy, unstirred. Nothing moved in the dark sky or on the dry unreal ground that went on and on into gathering darkness all around the boat as far as eye could see.

Ged stood up, and took his staff, and lightly stepped over the side of the boat. Vetch thought to see him fall and sink down in the sea, the sea that surely was there behind this dry, dim veil that hid away water, sky, and light. But there was no sea any more. Ged walked away from the boat. The dark sand showed his footprints where he went, and whispered a little under his step.

His staff began to shine, not with the werelight but with a clear white glow, that soon grew so bright that it reddened his fingers where they held the radiant wood.

He strode forward, away from the boat, but in no direction. There were no directions here, no north or south or east or west, only towards and away.

To Vetch, watching, the light he bore seemed like a great slow star that moved through the darkness. And the darkness about it thickened, blackened, drew together. This also Ged saw, watching always ahead through the light. And after a while he saw at the faint outermost edge of the light a shadow that came towards him over the sand.

At first it was shapeless, but as it drew nearer it took on the look of a man. An old man it seemed, grey and grim, coming towards Ged; but even as Ged saw his father the smith in that figure, he saw that it was not an old man but a young one. It was Jasper: Jasper's insolent handsome young face, and silver-clasped grey cloak, and stiff stride. Hateful was the look he fixed on Ged across the dark intervening air. Ged did not stop, but slowed his pace, and as he went forward he raised his staff up a little higher. It brightened, and in its light the look of Jasper fell from the figure that approached, and it became Pechvarry. But Pechvarry's face was all bloated and pallid like the face of a drowned man, and he reached out his hand strangely as if beckoning. Still Ged did not stop, but went forward,

163

though there were only a few yards left between them now. Then the thing that faced him changed utterly, spreading out to either side as if it opened enormous thin wings, and it writhed, and swelled, and shrank again. Ged saw in it for an instant Skiorh's white face, and then a pair of clouded, staring eyes, and then suddenly a fearful face he did not know, man or monster, with writhing lips and eyes that were like pits going back into black emptiness.

At that Ged lifted up the staff high, and the radiance of it brightened intolerably, burning with so white and great a light that it compelled and harrowed even that ancient darkness. In that light all form of man sloughed off the thing that came towards Ged. It drew together and shrank and blackened, crawling on four short taloned legs upon the sand. But still it came forward, lifting up to him a blind unformed snout without lips or ears or eyes. As they came right together it became utterly black in the white mage-radiance that burned about it, and it heaved itself upright. In silence, man and shadow met face to face, and stopped.

Aloud and clearly, breaking that old silence, Ged spoke the shadow's name, and in the same moment the shadow spoke without lips or tongue, saying the same word: 'Ged.' And the two voices were one voice.

Ged reached out his hands, dropping his staff, and took hold of his shadow, of the black self that reached out to him. Light and darkness met, and joined, and were one.

But to Vetch, watching in terror through the dark twilight from far off over the sand, it seemed that Ged was overcome, for he saw the clear radiance fail and grow dim. Rage and despair filled him, and he sprang out on the sand to help his friend or die with him, and ran towards that small fading glimmer of light in the empty dusk of the dry land. But as he ran the sand sank under his feet, and he struggled in it as in quicksand, as through a heavy flow of water: until with a roar of noise and a glory of daylight, and the bitter cold of winter, and the bitter taste of salt, the world was restored to him and he floundered in the sudden, true, and living sea.

Nearby the boat rocked on the grey waves, empty. Vetch could see nothing else on the water; the battering wave-tops filled his eyes and blinded him. No strong swimmer, he struggled as best he could to the boat, and pulled himself up into her. Coughing and trying to wipe away the water that streamed from his hair, he looked about desperately, not knowing now which way to look. And at last he made out something dark among the waves, a long way off across what had been sand and now was wild water. Then he leapt to the oars and rowed mightily to his friend, and catching Ged's arms helped and hauled him up over the side.

Ged was dazed and his eyes stared as if they saw nothing, but there was no hurt to be seen on him. His staff, black yew-wood, all radiance quenched, was grasped in his right hand, and he would not let go of it. He said no word. Spent and soaked and shaking he lay huddled up against the mast, never looking at Vetch who raised the sail and turned the boat to catch the north-east wind. He saw nothing of the world until, straight ahead of their course, in the sky that darkened where the sun had set, between long clouds in a bay of clear blue light, the new moon shone : a ring of ivory, a rim of horn, reflected sunlight shining across the ocean of the dark.

Ged lifted his face and gazed at that remote bright crescent in the west.

He gazed for a long time, and then he stood up erect, holding his staff in his two hands as a warrior holds his long sword. He looked about at the sky, the sea, the brown swelling sail above him, his friend's face.

'Estarriol,' he said, 'look, it is done. It is over.' He laughed. 'The wound is healed,' he said, 'I am whole, I am free.' Then he bent over and hid his face in his arms, weeping like a boy.

Until that moment Vetch had watched him with an anxious dread, for he was not sure what had happened there in the dark land. He did not know if this was Ged in the boat with him, and his hand had been for hours ready to the anchor, to stave in the boat's planking and sink her there in midsea, rather than carry back to the harbours of Earthsea the evil thing that he feared might have taken Ged's look and form. Now when he saw his friend and heard him speak, his doubt vanished. And he began to see the truth, that Ged had neither lost nor won but, naming the shadow of his death with his own name, had made himself whole : a man : who, knowing his whole true self, cannot be used or possessed by any power other than himself, and whose life therefore is lived for life's sake and never in the service of ruin, or pain, or hatred, or the dark. In the *Creation of Éa* which is the oldest song, it is said, 'Only in silence the word, only in dark the light, only in dying life: bright the hawk's flight on the empty sky.' That song Vetch sang aloud now as he held the boat westward, going before the cold wind of the winter night that blew at their backs from the vastness of the Open Sea.

Eight days they sailed and eight again, before they came in sight of land. Many times they had to refill their waterskin with spell-sweetened water of the sea; and they fished, but even when they called out fisherman's charms they caught very little, for the fish of the Open Sea do not know their own names and pay no heed to magic. When they had nothing left to eat but a few scraps of smoked meat Ged remembered what Yarrow had said when he stole the cake from the hearth, that he would regret his theft when he came to hunger on the sea; but hungry as he was the remembrance pleased him. For she had also said that he, with her brother, would come home again.

The magewind had borne them for only three days eastward, yet sixteen days they sailed westward to return. No men have ever returned from so far out on the Open Sea as did the young wizards Estarriol and Ged in the Fallows of winter in their open fishing-boat. They met no great storms, and steered steadily enough by the compass and by the star Tolbegren, taking a course somewhat northward of their outbound way. Thus they did not come back to Astowell, but passing by Far Toly and Sneg without sighting them, first raised land off the southernmost cape of Koppish. Over the waves they saw cliffs of stone rise like a great fortress. Seabirds cried wheeling over the breakers, and smoke of the hearthfires of small villages drifted blue on the wind.

From there the voyage to Iffish was not long. They came in to Ismay harbour on a still, dark evening before snow. They tied up

the boat *Lookfar* that had borne them to the coasts of death's kingdom and back, and went up through the narrow streets to the
wizard's house. Their hearts were very light as they entered into the
firelight and warmth under that roof; and Yarrow ran to meet
them, crying with joy.

If Estarriol of Iffish kept his promise and made a song of that first great deed of Ged's, it has been lost. There is a tale told in the East Reach of a boat that ran aground, days out from any shore, over the abyss of ocean. In Iffish they say it was Estarriol who sailed that boat, but in Tok they say it was two fishermen blown by a storm far out on the Open Sea, and in Holp the tale is of a Holpish fisherman, and tells that he could not move his boat from the unseen sands it grounded on, and so wanders there yet. So of the song of the Shadow there remain only a few scraps of legend, carried like driftwood from isle to isle over the long years. But in the *Deed of Ged* nothing is told of that voyage nor of Ged's meeting with the shadow, before ever he sailed the Dragon's Run unscathed, or brought back the Ring of Erreth-Akbe from the Tombs of Atuan to Havnor, or came at last to Roke once more, as Archmage of all the islands of the world.

THE TOMBS OF ATUAN

FOR THE REDHEAD FROM

TELLURIDE

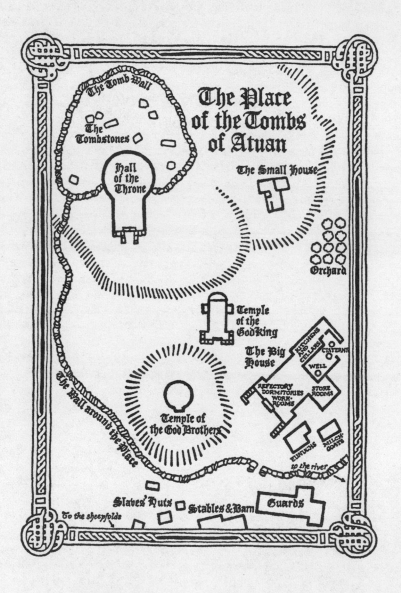

The Place
of the Tombs
of Atuan

The Tomb Wall

The Tombstones

Hall
of the
Throne

The Small House

Orchard

Temple of the
Godking

The Big
House

KITCHENS AND CELLARS

CISTERNS

WELL

REFECTORY
DORMITORIES
WORK-ROOMS

STORE ROOMS

The Wall around the Place

Temple of
the God Brothers

EUNUCHS

MILCH GOATS

to the river

Slaves' Huts

Stables & Barn

Guards

To the sheepfolds

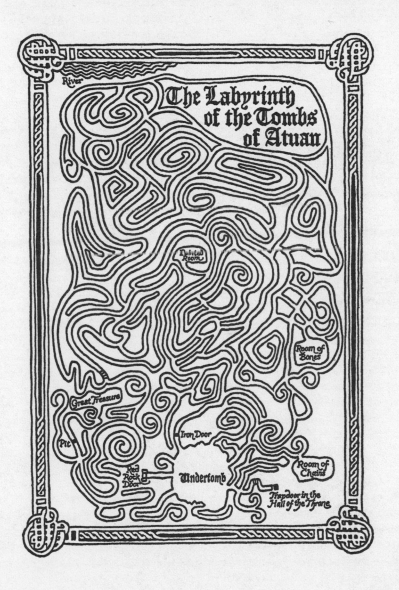

The Labyrinth
of the Tombs
of Atuan

River

Painted
Room

Room of
Bones

Great Treasure

Iron Door

Pit

Red
Rock
Door

Undertomb

Room of
Chains

Trapdoor in the
Hall of the Throne

Prologue

'COME home, Tenar! Come home!'

In the deep valley, in the twilight, the apple trees were on the eve of blossoming; here and there among the shadowed boughs one flower had opened early, rose and white, like a faint star. Down the orchard aisles, in the thick, new, wet grass, the little girl ran for the joy of running; hearing the call she did not come at once, but made a long circle before she turned her face towards home. The mother waiting in the doorway of the hut, with the firelight behind her, watched the tiny figure running and bobbing like a bit of thistle-down blown over the darkening grass beneath the trees.

By the corner of the hut, scraping clean an earth-clotted hoe, the father said, 'Why do you let your heart hang on the child? They're coming to take her away next month. For good. Might as well bury her and be done with it. What's the good of clinging to one you're bound to lose? She's no good to us. If they'd pay for her when they took her, that would be something, but they won't. They'll take her and that's an end of it.'

The mother said nothing, watching the child who had stopped to look up through the trees. Over the high hills, above the orchards, the evening star shone piercing clear.

'She isn't ours, she never was since they came here and said she must be the Priestess at the Tombs. Why can't you see that?' The man's voice was harsh with complaint and bitterness. 'You have four others. They'll stay here, and this one won't. So, don't set your heart on her. Let her go!'

'When the time comes,' the woman said, 'I will let her go.' She bent to meet the child who came running on little, bare, white feet across the muddy ground, and gathered her up in her arms. As she turned to enter the hut she bent her head to kiss the child's hair, which was black; but her own hair, in the flicker of firelight from the hearth, was fair.

The man stood outside, his own feet bare and cold on the ground, the clear sky of spring darkening above him. His face in the dusk was full of grief, a dull, heavy, angry grief that he would never find the words to say. At last he shrugged, and followed his wife into the firelit room that rang with children's voices.

1. The Eaten One

ONE high horn shrilled and ceased. The silence that followed was shaken only by the sound of many footsteps keeping time with a drum struck softly at a slow heart-pace. Through cracks in the roof of the Hall of the Throne, gaps between columns where a whole section of masonry and tile had collapsed, unsteady sunlight shone aslant. It was an hour after sunrise. The air was still and cold. Dead leaves of weeds that had forced up between marble pavement-tiles were outlined with frost, and crackled, catching on the long black robes of the priestesses.

They came, four by four, down the vast hall between double rows of columns. The drum beat dully. No voice spoke, no eye watched. Torches carried by black-clad girls burned reddish in the shafts of sunlight, brighter in the dusk between. Outside, on the steps of the Hall of the Throne, the men stood, guards, trumpeters, drummers; within the great doors only women had come, dark-robed and hooded, walking slowly four by four towards the empty throne.

Two came, tall women looming in their black, one of them thin and rigid, the other heavy, swaying with the planting of her feet. Between these two walked a child of about six. She wore a straight white shift. Her head and arms and legs were bare, and she was barefoot. She looked extremely small. At the foot of the steps leading up to the throne, where the others now waited in dark rows, the two tall women halted. They pushed the child forward a little.

The throne on its high platform seemed to be curtained on each side with great webs of blackness dropping from the gloom of the roof; whether these were curtains, or only denser shadows, the eye could not make certain. The throne itself was black, with a dull glimmer of precious stones or gold on the arms and back, and it was huge. A man sitting in it would have been dwarfed; it was not of human dimensions. It was empty. Nothing sat in it but shadows.

177

Alone, the child climbed up four of the seven steps of red-veined marble. They were so broad and high that she had to get both feet on to one step before attempting the next. On the middle step, directly in front of the throne, stood a large, rough block of wood, hollowed out on top. The child knelt on both knees and fitted her head into the hollow, turning it a little sideways. She knelt there without moving.

A figure in a belted gown of white wool stepped suddenly out of the shadows at the right of the throne and strode down the steps to the child. His face was masked with white. He held a sword of polished steel five feet long. Without word or hesitation he swung the sword, held in both hands, up over the little girl's neck. The drum stopped beating.

As the blade swung to its highest point and poised, a figure in black darted out from the left side of the throne, leapt down the stairs, and stayed the sacrificer's arms with slenderer arms. The sharp edge of the sword glittered in mid-air. So they balanced for a moment, the white figure and the black, both faceless, dancer-like above the motionless child whose white neck was bared by the parting of her black hair.

In silence each leapt aside and up the stairs again, vanishing in the darkness behind the enormous throne. A priestess came forward and poured out a bowl of some liquid on the steps beside the kneeling child. The stain looked black in the dimness of the hall.

The child got up and descended the four stairs laboriously. When she stood at the bottom, the two tall priestesses put on her a black robe and hood and mantle, and turned her around again to face the steps, the dark stain, the throne.

'O let the Nameless Ones behold the girl given to them, who is verily the one born ever nameless. Let them accept her life and the years of her life until her death, which is also theirs. Let them find her acceptable. Let her be eaten!'

Other voices, shrill and harsh as trumpets, replied: 'She is eaten! She is eaten!'

The little girl stood looking from under her black cowl up at the throne. The jewels inset in the huge clawed arms and the back were glazed with dust, and on the carven back were cobwebs and whitish stains of owl droppings. The three highest steps directly before the throne, above the step on which she had knelt, had never been climbed by mortal feet. They were so thick with dust that they looked like one slant of grey soil, the planes of the red-veined marble wholly hidden by the unstirred, untrodden siftings of how many years, how many centuries.

'She is eaten! She is eaten!'

Now the drum, abrupt, began to sound again, beating a quicker pace.

Silent and shuffling, the procession formed and moved away from the throne, eastward towards the bright, distant square of the doorway. On either side, the thick double columns, like the calves of immense pale legs, went up to the dusk under the ceiling. Among the priestesses, and now all in black like them, the child walked, her small bare feet treading solemnly over the frozen weeds, the icy stones. When sunlight slanting through the ruined roof flashed across her way, she did not look up.

Guards held the great doors wide. The black procession came out into the thin, cold light and wind of early morning. The sun dazzled, swimming above the eastern vastness. Westward, the mountains caught its yellow light, as did the façade of the Hall of the Throne. The other buildings, lower on the hill, still lay in purplish shadow, except for the Temple of the God-Brothers across the way on a little knoll: its roof, newly gilt, flashed the day back in glory. The black line of priestesses, four by four, wound down the Hill of the Tombs, and as they went they began softly to chant. The tune was on three notes only, and the word that was repeated over and over was a word so old it had lost its meaning, like a signpost still standing when the road is gone. Over and over they chanted the empty word. All that day of the Remaking of the Priestess was filled with the low chanting of women's voices, a dry unceasing drone.

The little girl was taken from room to room, from temple to temple. In one place salt was placed upon her tongue; in another she knelt facing west while her hair was cut short and washed with oil and scented vinegar; in another she lay face down on a slab of black marble behind an altar while shrill voices sang a lament for the dead. Neither she nor any of the priestesses ate food or drank water all that day. As the evening star set, the little girl was put to bed, naked between sheepskin rugs, in a room she had never slept in before. It was in a house that had been locked for years, unlocked only that day. The room was higher than it was long, and had no windows. There was a dead smell in it, still and stale. The silent women left her there in the dark.

She held still, lying just as they had put her. Her eyes were wide open. She lay so for a long time.

She saw light shake on the high wall. Someone came quietly along the corridor, shielding a rushlight so it showed no more light than a firefly. A husky whisper : 'Ho, are you there, Tenar?'

The child did not reply.

A head poked through the doorway, a strange head, hairless as a peeled potato, and of the same yellowish colour. The eyes were like potato-eyes, brown and tiny. The nose was dwarfed by great, flat slabs of cheek, and the mouth was a lipless slit. The child stared unmoving at this face. Her eyes were large, dark, and fixed.

'Ho, Tenar, my little honeycomb, there you are !' The voice was husky, high as a woman's voice but not a woman's voice. 'I shouldn't be here, I belong outside the door, on the porch, that's where I go. But I had to see how my little Tenar is, after all the long day of it, eh, how's my poor little honeycomb?'

He moved towards her, noiseless and burly, and put out his hand as if to smooth back her hair.

'I am not Tenar any more,' the child said, staring up at him. His hand stopped; he did not touch her.

'No,' he said, after a moment, whispering. 'I know, I know. Now you're the little Eaten One. But I . . .'

She said nothing.

'It was a hard day for a little one,' the man said, shuffling, the tiny light flickering in his big yellow hand.

'You should not be in this House, Manan.'

'No. No. I know. I shouldn't be in this House. Well, good night, little one . . . Good night.'

The child said nothing. Manan slowly turned around and went away. The glimmer died from the high cell walls. The little girl, who had no name any more but *Arha*, the Eaten One, lay on her back looking steadily at the dark.

2. The Wall around the Place

A S she grew older she lost all remembrance of her mother, without knowing she had lost it. She belonged here, at the Place of the Tombs; she had always belonged here. Only sometimes in the long evenings of July as she watched the western mountains, dry and lion-coloured in the afterglow of sunset, she would think of a fire that had burned on a hearth, long ago, with the same clear yellow light. And with this came a memory of being held, which was strange, for here she was seldom even touched; and the memory of a pleasant smell, the fragrance of hair freshly washed and rinsed in sage-scented water, fair long hair, the colour of sunset and firelight. That was all she had left.

She knew more than she remembered, of course, for she had been told the whole story. When she was seven or eight years old, and first beginning to wonder who indeed this person called 'Arha' was, she had gone to her guardian, the Warden Manan, and said, 'Tell me how I was chosen, Manan.'

'Oh, you know all that, little one.'

And indeed she did; the tall, dry-voiced priestess Thar had told her till she knew the words by heart, and she recited them : 'Yes, I know. At the death of the One Priestess of the Tombs of Atuan, the ceremonies of burial and purification are completed within one month by the moon's calendar. After this certain of the Priestesses and Wardens of the Place of the Tombs go forth across the desert, among the towns and villages of Atuan, seeking and asking. They seek the girl-child who was born on the night of the Priestess' death. When they find such a child, they wait and they watch. The child must be sound of body and of mind, and as it grows it must not suffer from rickets nor the smallpox nor any deformity, nor become blind. If it reaches the age of five years unblemished, then it is known that the body of the child is indeed the new body of the Priestess who died. And the child is made known to the Godking in Awabath, and brought here to her Temple and instructed for a year. And at the year's end she is taken to the Hall of the Throne and her name is given back to those who are her Masters, the Nameless Ones : for she is the nameless one, the Priestess Ever Reborn.'

This was all word for word as Thar had told her, and she had never dared ask for a word more. The thin priestess was not cruel, but she was very cold and lived by an iron law, and Arha was in awe of her. But she was not in awe of Manan, far from it, and she would command him, 'Now tell me how I was chosen!' And he would tell her again.

'We left here, going north and west, in the third day of the moon's waxing; for Arha-that-was had died in the third day of the last moon. And first we went to Tenacbah, which is a great city, though those who've seen both say it's no more to Awabath than a flea to a cow. But it's big enough for me, there must be ten hundred houses in Tenacbah ! And we went on to Gar. But nobody in those cities had a baby girl born to them on the third day of the moon a month before; there were some had boys, but boys won't do . . . So we went into the hill country north of Gar, to the towns and villages. That's my own land. I was born in the hills there, where the rivers run, and the land is green. Not in this desert.' Manan's husky voice would get a strange sound when he said that, and his small eyes would be quite hidden in their folds; he would pause a little, and at last go on. 'And so we found and spoke to all those who were parents of babies born in the last months. And some would lie to us. "Oh yes, surely our baby girl was born on the moon's third day !" For poor folk, you know, are often glad to get rid of girl-babies. And there were others who were so poor, living in lonely huts in the valleys of the hills, that they kept no count of days and scarce knew how to tell the turn of time, so they could not say for certain how old their baby was. But we could always come at the truth, by asking long enough. But it was slow work. At last we found a girl-child, in a village of ten houses, in the orchard-vales westward of

Entat. Eight months old she was, so long had we been looking. But she had been born on the night that the Priestess of the Tombs had died, and within the very hour of her death. And she was a fine baby, sitting up on her mother's knee and looking with bright eyes at all of us, crowding into the one room of the house like bats into a cave! The father was a poor man. He tended the apple trees of the rich man's orchard, and had nothing of his own but five children and a goat. Not even the house was his. So there we all crowded in, and you could tell by the way the priestesses looked at the baby and spoke among themselves that they thought they had found the Reborn One at last. And the mother could tell this too. She held the baby and never said a word. Well, so, the next day we came back. And look here! The little bright-eyed baby lying in a cot of rushes weeping and screaming, and all over its body weals and red rashes of fever, and the mother wailing louder than the baby, "Oh! Oh! My babe hath the Witch-Fingers on her!" That's how she said it; the smallpox she meant. In my village, too, they called it the Witch-Fingers. But Kossil, she who is now the High Priestess of the God-king, she went to the cot and picked up the baby. The others had all drawn back, and I with them; I don't value my life very high, but who enters a house where smallpox is? But she had no fear, not that one. She picked up the baby and said, "It has no fever." And she spat on her finger and rubbed at the red marks, and they came off. They were only berry juice. The poor silly mother had thought to fool us and keep her child!' Manan laughed heartily at this; his yellow face hardly changed, but his sides heaved. 'So, her husband beat her, for he was afraid of the wrath of the priestesses. And soon we came back to the desert, but each year one of the people of the Place would return to the village among the apple orchards, and see how the child got on. So five years passed, and then Thar and Kossil made the journey, with the Temple guards, and soldiers of the red helmet sent by the Godking to escort them safely. They brought the child back here, for it was indeed the Priestess of the Tombs reborn, and here it belonged. And who was the child, eh, little one?'

'Me,' said Arha, looking off into the distance as if to see something she could not see, something gone out of sight.

Once she asked, 'What did the ... the mother do, when they came to take the child away?'

But Manan didn't know; he had not gone with the priestesses on that final journey.

And she could not remember. What was the good in remembering? It was gone, all gone. She had come where she must come. In all the world she knew only one place: the Place of the Tombs of Atuan.

In her first year there she had slept in the big dormitory with the other novices, girls between four and fourteen. Even then Manan had been set apart among the Ten Wardens as her particular guardian, and her cot had been in a little alcove, partly separated from the long, low-beamed main room of the dormitory in the Big House where the girls giggled and whispered before they slept, and yawned and plaited one another's hair in the grey light of morning. When her name was taken from her and she became Arha, she slept alone in the Small House, in the bed and in the room that would be her bed and her room for the rest of her life. That house was hers, the House of the One Priestess, and no one might enter it without her permission. When she was quite little still, she enjoyed hearing people knock submissively on her door, and saying, 'You may come in,' and it annoyed her that the two High-Priestesses, Kossil and Thar, took her permission for granted and entered her house without knocking.

The days went by, the years went by, all alike. The girls of the Place of the Tombs spent their time at classes and disciplines. They did not play any games. There was no time for games. They learned the sacred songs and the sacred dances, the histories of the Kargad Lands, and the mysteries of whichever of the gods they were dedicated to: the Godking who ruled in Awabath, or the Twin Brothers, Atwah and Wuluah. Of them all, only Arha learned the rites of the Nameless Ones, and these were taught her by one person, Thar, the High Priestess of the Twin Gods. This took her away from the others for an hour or more daily, but most of her day, like theirs, was spent simply working. They learned how to spin and weave the wool of their flocks, and how to plant and harvest and prepare the food they always ate: lentils, corn ground to a coarse meal for porridge or a fine flour for unleavened bread, onions, cabbages, goat-cheese, apples, and honey.

The best thing that could happen was to be allowed to go fishing in the murky green river that flowed through the desert a half-mile north-east of the Place; to take along an apple or a cold bannock for lunch and sit all day in the dry sunlight among the reeds, watching the slow green water run and the cloud-shadows change slowly on the mountains. But if you squealed with excitement when the line tensed and you swung in a flat, glittering fish to flop on the river bank and drown in air, then Mebbeth would hiss like an adder, 'Be still, you screeching fool!' Mebbeth, who served in the Godking's temple, was a dark woman, still young, but hard and sharp as obsidian. Fishing was her passion. You had to keep on her good side, and never make a sound, or she would not take you out to fish again; and then you'd never get to the river except to fetch water in summer when the wells ran low. That was a dreary business, to trudge through the searing white heat a half-mile down to the river, fill the two buckets on their carrying pole, and then set off as fast as possible uphill to the Place. The first hundred yards were easy, but then the buckets began to grow heavier, and the pole burned your shoulders like a bar of hot iron, and the light glared on the dry road, and every step was harder and slower. At last you got to the cool shade of the back courtyard of the Big House by the vegetable patch, and dumped the buckets into the great cistern with a splash. And then you had to turn around to do it all over again, and again, and again.

Within the precincts of the Place – that was all the name it had or needed, for it was the most ancient and sacred of all places in the Four Lands of the Kargish Empire – a couple of hundred people lived, and there were many buildings: three temples, the Big House and the Small House, the quarters of the eunuch wardens, and close outside the wall the guards' barracks and many slaves' huts, the storehouses and sheep pens and goat pens and farm buildings. It looked like a little town, seen from a distance, from up on the dry hills westward where nothing grew but sage, wire-grass in straggling clumps, small weeds and desert herbs. Even from away off on the eastern plains, looking up one might see the gold roof of the Temple of the Twin Gods wink and glitter beneath the mountains like a speck of mica in a shelf of rock.

That temple itself was a cube of stone, plastered white, windowless, with a low porch and door. Showier, and centuries newer, was the Temple of the Godking a little below it, with a high portico and a row of thick white columns with painted capitals – each one a solid log of cedar, brought on shipboard from Hur-at-Hur where there are forests, and dragged by the straining of twenty slaves across the barren plains to the Place. Only after a traveller aproaching from the east had seen the gold roof and the bright columns would he see, higher up on the Hill of the Place, above them all, tawny and ruinous as the desert itself, the oldest of the temples of his race : the huge, low Hall of the Throne, with patched walls and flattish, crumbling dome.

Behind the Hall and encircling the whole crest of the hill ran a massive wall of rock, laid without mortar, and half fallen down in many places. Inside the loop of the wall several black stones eighteen or twenty feet high stuck up like huge fingers out of the earth. Once the eye saw them it kept returning to them. They stood there full of meaning, and yet there was no saying what they meant. There were nine of them. One stood straight, the others leaned more or less, two had fallen. They were crusted with grey and orange lichen as if splotched with paint, all but one, which was naked and black, with a dull gloss to it. It was smooth to the touch, but on the others, under the crust of lichen, vague carvings could be seen, or felt with the fingers – shapes, signs. These nine stones were the Tombs of Atuan. They had stood there, it was said, since the time of the first men, since Earthsea was created. They had been planted in the darkness when the lands were raised up from the ocean's depths. They were older by far than the Godkings of Kargad, older than the Twin Gods, older than light. They were the tombs of those who ruled before the world of men came to be, the ones not named, and she who served them had no name.

She did not go among them often, and no one else ever set foot on that ground where they stood, on the hilltop within the rock wall behind the Hall of the Throne. Twice a year, at the full moon nearest the equinox of spring and of autumn, there was a sacrifice before the Throne and she came out from the low back door of the Hall carrying a great brass basin full of smoking goat's blood; this she must pour out, half at the foot of the standing black stone, half over one of the fallen stones which lay embedded in the rocky dirt, stained by the blood-offering of centuries.

Sometimes Arha went by herself in the early morning and wandered among the Stones trying to make out the dim humps and scratches of the carvings, brought out more clearly by the low angle of the light; or she would sit there and look up at the mountains westward, and down at the roofs and walls of the Place all laid out below, and watch the first stirrings of activity around the Big House and the guards' barracks, and the flocks of sheep and goats going off to their sparse pastures by the river. There was never anything to do among the Stones. She went only because it was permitted her to go there, because there she was alone. It was a dreary place. Even in the heat of noon in the desert summer there was a coldness about it. Sometimes the wind whistled a little between the two stones that stood closest together, leaning together as if telling secrets. But no secret was told.

From the Tomb Wall another, lower rock wall ran, making a long irregular semicircle about the Hill of the Place and then trailing off northward towards the river. It did not so much protect the Place, as cut it in two: on one side the temples and houses of the priestesses and wardens, on the other the quarters of the guards and of the slaves who farmed and herded and foraged for the Place. None of these ever crossed the wall, except that on certain very holy festivals the guards, and their drummers and players of the horn, would attend the procession of the priestesses; but they did not enter the portals of the temples. No other men set foot upon the inner ground of the Place. There had once been pilgrimages, kings and chieftains coming from the Four Lands to worship there; the first Godking, a century and a half ago, had come to enact the rites of his own temple. Yet even he could not enter among the Tombstones, even he had had to eat and sleep outside the wall around the Place.

One could climb that wall easily enough, fitting toes into crevices. The Eaten One and a girl called Penthe were sitting up on the wall one afternoon in late spring. They were both twelve years old. They were supposed to be in the weaving room of the Big House, a huge stone attic; they were supposed to be at the great looms always warped with dull black wool, weaving black cloth for robes. They had slipped outside for a drink at the well in the courtyard, and then Arha had said, 'Come on!' and had led the other girl down the hill, around out of sight of the Big House, to the wall. Now they sat on top of it, ten feet up, their bare legs dangling down on the outside, looking over the flat plains that went on and on to the east and north.

'I'd like to see the sea,' said Penthe.

'What for?' said Arha, chewing the bitter stem of a weed she had picked from the wall. The barren land was just past its flowering. All the small desert blossoms, yellow and rose and white, low-growing and quick-flowering, were going to seed, scattering tiny plumes and parasols of ash white on the wind, dropping their hooked, ingenious burrs. The ground under the apple trees of the orchard was a drift of bruised white and pink. The branches were green, the only green trees within miles of the Place. Everything else, from horizon to horizon, was a dull, tawny, desert colour, except that the mountains had a silvery bluish tinge from the first buds of the flowering sage.

'Oh, I don't know what for. I'd just like to see something different. It's always the same here. Nothing happens.'

'All that happens everywhere, begins here,' said Arha.

'Oh, I know ... But I'd like to see some of it happening!'

Penthe smiled. She was a soft, comfortable-looking girl. She scratched the soles of her bare feet on the sunwarmed rocks, and after a while went on, 'You know, I used to live by the sea when I was little. Our village was right behind the dunes, and we used to go down and play on the beach sometimes. Once I remember we saw a fleet of ships going by, way out at sea. We ran and told the village and everybody came to see. The ships looked like dragons with red wings. Some of them had real necks, with dragon heads. They came sailing by Atuan, but they weren't Kargish ships. They came from the west, from the Inner Lands, the headman said. Everybody came down to watch them. I think they were afraid they might land. They just went by, nobody knew where they were going. Maybe to make war in Karego-At. But think of it, they really came from the sorcerers' islands, where all the people are the colour of dirt and they can all cast a spell on you easy as winking.'

'Not on me,' Arha said fiercely. 'I wouldn't have looked at them. They're vile accursed sorcerers. How dare they sail so close to the Holy Land?'

'Oh, well, I suppose the Godking will conquer them some day and make them all slaves. But I wish I could see the sea again. There used to be little octopuses in the tide pools, and if you shouted "Boo!" at them they turned all white. There comes that old Manan, looking for you.'

Arha's guard and servant was coming slowly along the inner side of the wall. He would stoop to pull a wild onion, of which he held a large, limp bunch, then straighten up and look about him with his small, dull, brown eyes. He had grown fatter with the years, and his hairless yellow skin glistened in the sun.

'Slide down on the men's side,' Arha hissed, and both girls wriggled lithe as lizards down the far side of the wall until they could cling there just below the top, invisible from the inner side. They heard Manan's slow footsteps coming by.

'Hoo! Hoo! Potato face!' crooned Arha, a whispering jeer faint as the wind among the grasses.

The heavy tread halted. 'Ho there,' said the uncertain voice. 'Little one? Arha?'

Silence.

Manan went forward.

'Hoo-oo! Potato face!'

'Hoo, potato belly!' Penthe whispered in imitation, and then moaned, trying to suppress giggles.

'Somebody there?'

190

Silence.

'Oh well, well, well,' the eunuch sighed, and his slow feet went on. When he was gone over the shoulder of the slope, the girls scrambled back up on to the top of the wall. Penthe was pink with sweat and giggles, but Arha looked savage.

'The stupid old bellwether, following me around everywhere!'

'He has to,' Penthe said reasonably. 'It's his job, looking after you.'

'Those I serve look after me. I please them; I need please nobody else. These old women and half-men, these people should leave me alone. I am the One Priestess!'

Penthe stared at the other girl. 'Oh,' she said feebly, 'oh, I know you are, Arha –'

'Then they should let me be. And not order me about all the time!'

Penthe said nothing for a while, but sighed, and sat swinging her plump legs and gazing at the vast, pale lands below, that rose so slowly to a high, vague, immense horizon.

'You'll be giving the orders pretty soon, you know,' she said at last, quietly. 'In two more years we won't be children any more. We'll be fourteen. I'll go into the Godking's temple, and things will be about the same for me. But you'll really be the High Priestess then. Even Kossil and Thar will have to obey you.'

The Eaten One said nothing. Her face was set, her eyes under black brows caught the light of the sky in a pale glitter.

'We ought to go back,' Penthe said.

'No.'

'But the weaving mistress might tell Thar. And soon it'll be time for the Nine Chants.'

'I'm staying here. You stay, too.'

'They won't punish you, but they will punish me,' Penthe said in her mild way. Arha did not reply. Penthe sighed, and stayed. The sun was sinking into haze high above the plains. Far away on the long gradual slant of the land, sheep bells clanked faintly and lambs bleated. The spring wind blew in dry, faint gusts, sweet-smelling.

The Nine Chants were nearly over when the two girls returned. Mebbeth had seen them sitting on the 'Men's Wall' and had reported this to her superior, Kossil, High Priestess of the Godking.

Kossil was heavy-footed, heavy-faced. Without expression in face or voice she spoke to the two girls, telling them to follow her. She led them through the stone hallways of the Big House, out of the front door, up the knoll to the Temple of Atwah and Wuluah. There she spoke with the High Priestess of that temple, Thar, tall and dry and thin as the legbone of a deer.

Kossil said to Penthe, 'Take off your gown.'

She whipped the girl with a bundle of reed canes, which cut the skin a little. Penthe bore this patiently with silent tears. She was sent back to the weaving room without supper, and the next day also she would go without food. 'If you are found climbing over the Men's Wall again,' Kossil said, 'there will be very much worse things than this that will happen to you. Do you understand, Penthe?' Kossil's voice was soft, but not kindly. Penthe said, 'Yes,' and slipped away, cowering and flinching as her heavy clothing rubbed the cuts on her back.

Arha had stood beside Thar to watch the whipping. Now she watched Kossil clean the canes of the whip.

Thar said to her, 'It is not fitting that you are seen climbing and running with other girls. You are Arha.'

She stood sullen and did not reply.

'It is better that you do only what is needful for you to do. You are Arha.'

For a moment the girl raised her eyes to Thar's face, then to Kossil's, and there was a depth of hate or rage in her look that was terrible to see. But the thin priestess showed no concern; rather she confirmed, leaning forward a little, almost whispering, 'You are Arha. There is nothing left. It was all eaten.'

'It was all eaten,' the girl repeated, as she had repeated daily, all the days of her life since she was six.

Thar bowed her head slightly; so did Kossil, as she put away the whip. The girl did not bow, but turned submissively and left.

After the supper of potatoes and spring onions, eaten in silence in

the narrow, dark refectory, after the chanting of the evening
hymns, and the placing of the sacred words upon the doors, and the
brief Ritual of the Unspoken, the work of the day was done. Now
the girls might go up to the dormitory and play games with dice and
sticks, so long as the single rushlight burned, and whisper in the
dark from bed to bed. Arha set off across the courts and slopes of
the Place as she did every night, to the Small House where she slept
alone.

The night wind was sweet. The stars of spring shone thick, like
drifts of daisies in spring meadows, like the glittering of light on
the April sea. But the girl had no memory of meadows or the sea.
She did not look up.

'Ho there, little one !'

'Manan,' she said indifferently.

The big shadow shuffled up beside her, starlight glinting on his
hairless pate.

'Were you punished?'

'I can't be punished.'

'No . . . That's so . . .'

'They can't punish me. They don't dare.'

He stood with his big hands hanging, dim and bulky. She smelled
wild onion, and the sweaty, sagey smell of his old black robes,
which were torn at the hem, and too short for him.

'They can't touch me. I am Arha,' she said in a shrill, fierce voice,
and burst into tears.

The big, waiting hands came up and drew her to him, held her
gently, smoothed her braided hair. 'There, there. Little honeycomb,
little girl . . .' She heard the husky murmur in the deep hollow of
his chest, and clung to him. Her tears stopped soon, but she held on
to Manan as if she could not stand up.

'Poor little one,' he whispered, and picking the child up carried
her to the doorway of the house where she slept alone. He set her
down.

'All right now, little one?'

She nodded, turned from him, and entered the dark house.

3. The Prisoners

KOSSIL'S steps sounded along the hallway of the Small House, even and deliberate. The tall, heavy figure filled the doorway of the room, shrank as the priestess bowed down touching one knee to the floor, swelled as she straightened to her full height.

'Mistress.'

'What is it, Kossil?'

'I have been permitted to look after certain matters pertaining to the Domain of the Nameless Ones, until now. If you so desire, it is now time for you to learn, and see, and take charge of these matters, which you have not yet remembered in this life.'

The girl had been sitting in her windowless room, supposedly meditating, actually doing nothing and thinking almost nothing. It took some time for the fixed, dull, haughty expression of her face to change. Yet it did change, though she tried to conceal it. She said, with a certain slyness, 'The Labyrinth?'

'We will not enter the Labyrinth. But it will be necessary to cross the Undertomb.'

There was a tone in Kossil's voice that might have been fear, or might have been a pretence of fear, intended to frighten Arha. The girl stood up without haste and said indifferently, 'Very well.' But in her heart, as she followed the heavy figure of the Godking's priestess, she exulted: At last! At last! I shall see my own domain at last!

She was fifteen. It was over a year since she had made her crossing into womanhood and at the same time had come into her full powers as the One Priestess of the Tombs of Atuan, highest of all high priestesses of the Kargad Lands, one whom not even the Godking himself might command. They all bowed the knee to her now, even grim Thar and Kossil. All spoke to her with elaborate deference. But nothing had changed. Nothing happened. Once the ceremonies of her consecration were over, the days went on as they had always gone. There was wool to be spun, black cloth to be woven, meal to be ground, rites to be performed; the Nine Chants must be sung nightly, the doorways blessed, the Stones fed with goat's blood twice a year, the dances of the dark of the moon danced before the Empty Throne. And so the whole year had passed, just as the years before it had passed, and were all the years of her life to pass so?

Her boredom rose so strong in her sometimes that it felt like terror: it took her by the throat. Not long ago she had been driven to speak of it. She had to talk, she thought, or she would go mad. It was Manan she talked to. Pride kept her from confiding in the other girls, and caution kept her from confessing to the older women, but Manan was nothing, a faithful old bellwether; it didn't matter what she said to him. To her surprise he had had an answer for her.

'Long ago,' he said, 'you know, little one, before our four lands joined together into an empire, before there was a Godking over us all, there were a lot of lesser kings, princes, chiefs. They were always quarrelling with each other. And they'd come here to settle their quarrels. That was how it was, they'd come from our land Atuan, and from Karego-At, and Atnini, and even from Hur-at-Hur, all the chiefs and princes with their servants and their armies. And they'd ask you what to do. And you'd go before the Empty Throne, and give them the counsel of the Nameless Ones. Well, that was long ago. After a while the Priest-Kings came to rule all of Karego-At, and soon they were ruling Atuan; and now for four or five lifetimes of men the Godkings have ruled all the four lands together, and made them an empire. And so things are changed. The Godking can put down the unruly chiefs, and settle all the quarrels himself. And being a god, you see, he doesn't have to consult the Nameless Ones very often.'

Arha stopped to think this over. Time did not mean very much, here in the desert land, under the unchanging Stones, leading a life that had been led in the same way since the beginning of the world. She was not accustomed to thinking about things changing, old ways dying and new ones arising. She did not find it comfortable to look at things in that light. 'The powers of the Godking are much less than the powers of the Ones I serve,' she said, frowning.

'Surely ... Surely ... But one doesn't go about saying that to a god, little honeycomb. Nor to his priestess.'

And catching his small, brown, twinkling eye, she thought of Kossil, High Priestess of the Godking, whom she had feared ever since she first came to the Place; and she took his meaning.

'But the Godking, and his people, are neglecting the worship of the Tombs. No one comes.'

'Well, he sends prisoners here to sacrifice. He doesn't neglect that. Nor the gifts due to the Nameless Ones.'

'Gifts! His temple is painted fresh every year, there's a hundred-weight of gold on the altar, the lamps burn attar of roses! And look at the Hall of the Throne – holes in the roof, and the dome cracking, and the walls full of mice, and owls, and bats ... But all the same it will outlast the Godking and all his temples, and all the kings that come after him. It was there before them, and when they're all gone it will still be there. It is the centre of things.'

'It is the centre of things.'

'There are riches there; Thar tells me about them sometimes. Enough to fill the Godking's temple ten times over. Gold and tro-phies given ages ago, a hundred generations, who knows how long. They're all locked away in the pits and vaults, underground. They won't take me there yet, they keep me waiting and waiting. But I know what it's like. There are rooms underneath the Hall, under-neath the whole Place, under where we stand now. There's a great maze of tunnels, a Labyrinth. It's like a great dark city, under the hill. Full of gold, and the swords of old heroes, and old crowns, and bones, and years, and silence.'

She spoke as if in trance, in rapture. Manan watched her. His slabby face never expressed much but stolid, careful sadness; it was sadder than usual now. 'Well, and you're mistress of all that,' he said. 'The silence, and the dark.'

'I am. But they won't show me anything, only the rooms above ground, behind the Throne. They haven't even shown me the en-trances to the places underground; they just mumble about them sometimes. They're keeping my own domain from me! Why do they make me wait and wait?'

'You are young. And perhaps,' Manan said in his husky alto, 'perhaps they're afraid, little one. It's not their domain, after all. It's yours. They are in danger when they enter there. There's no mortal that doesn't fear the Nameless Ones.'

Arha said nothing, but her eyes flashed. Again Manan had shown her a new way of seeing things. So formidable, so cold, so strong had Thar and Kossil always seemed to her, that she had never even imagined their being afraid. Yet Manan was right. They feared those places, those powers of which Arha was part, to which she belonged. They were afraid to go into the dark places, lest they be eaten.

Now, as she went with Kossil down the steps of the Small House and up the steep winding path towards the Hall of the Throne, she recalled that conversation with Manan, and exulted again. No matter where they took her, what they showed her, she would not be afraid. She would know her way.

A little behind her on the path, Kossil spoke. 'One of my mistress's duties, as she knows, is the sacrifice of certain prisoners, criminals of noble birth, who by sacrilege or treason have sinned against our lord the Godking.'

'Or against the Nameless Ones,' said Arha.

'Truly. Now it is not fitting that the Eaten One while yet a child should undertake this duty. But my mistress is no longer a child. There are prisoners in the Room of Chains, sent a month ago by the grace of our lord the Godking from his city Awabath.'

'I did not know prisoners had come. Why did I not know?'

'Prisoners are brought at night, and secretly, in the way prescribed of old in the rituals of the Tombs. It is the secret way my mistress will follow, if she takes the path that leads along the wall.'

Arha turned off the path to follow the great wall of stones that bounded the Tombs behind the domed hall. The rocks it was built of were massive; the least of them would outweigh a man, and the largest were big as wagons. Though unshapen they were carefully fitted and interlocked. Yet in places the height of the wall had slipped down and the rocks lay in a shapeless heap. Only a vast span of time could do that, the desert centuries of fiery days and frozen nights, the millennial, imperceptible movements of the hills themselves.

'It is very easy to climb the Tomb Wall,' Arha said as they went along beneath it.

'We have not men enough to rebuild it,' Kossil replied.

'We have men enough to guard it.'

'Only slaves. They cannot be trusted.'

'They can be trusted if they're frightened. Let the penalty be the same for them as for the stranger they allow to set foot on the holy ground within the wall.'

'What is that penalty?' Kossil did not ask to learn the answer. She had taught the answer to Arha, long ago.

'To be decapitated before the Throne.'

'Is it my mistress's will that a guard be set upon the Tomb Wall?'

'It is,' the girl answered. Inside her long black sleeves her fingers clenched with elation. She knew Kossil did not want to spare a slave to this duty of watching the wall, and indeed it was a useless duty, for what strangers ever came here? It was not likely that any man would wander, by mischance or intent, anywhere within a mile of the Place without being seen; he certainly would get nowhere near the Tombs. But a guard was an honour due to them, and Kossil could not well argue against it. She must obey Arha.

'Here,' said her cold voice.

Arha stopped. She had often walked this path around the Tomb Wall, and knew it as she knew every foot of the Place, every rock and thorn and thistle. The great rock wall reared up thrice her height to the left; to the right the hill shelved away into a shallow, arid valley, which soon rose again towards the foothills of the western range. She looked over all the ground nearby, and saw nothing that she had not seen before.

'Under the red rocks, mistress.'

A few yards down the slope an outcropping of red lava made a stair or little cliff in the hill. When she went down to it and stood on the level before it, facing the rocks, Arha realized that they looked like a rough doorway, four feet high.

'What must be done?'

She had learned long ago that in the holy places it is no use trying to open a door until you know how the door is opened.

'My mistress has all the keys to the dark places.'

Since the rites of her coming of age, Arha had worn on her belt an iron ring on which hung a little dagger and thirteen keys, some long and heavy, some small as fishhooks. She lifted the ring and spread the keys. 'That one,' Kossil said, pointing; and then placed her thick forefinger on a crevice between two red, pitted rock-surfaces.

The key, a long shaft of iron with two ornate wards, entered the crevice. Arha turned it to the left, using both hands, for it was stiff to move; yet it turned smoothly.

'Now?'

'Together –'

Together they pushed at the rough rock face to the left of the keyhole. Heavily, but without catch and with very little noise, an uneven section of the red rock moved inward until a narrow slit was opened. Inside it was blackness.

Arha stooped and entered.

Kossil, a heavy woman heavily clothed, had to squeeze through the narrow opening. As soon as she was inside she backed against the door and, straining, pushed it shut.

It was absolutely black. There was no light. The dark seemed to press like wet felt upon the open eyes.

They crouched, almost doubled over, for the place they stood in was not four feet high, and so narrow that Arha's groping hands touched damp rock at once to right and left.

'Did you bring a light?'

She whispered, as one does in the dark.

'I brought no light,' Kossil replied, behind her. Kossil's voice too was lowered, but it had an odd sound to it, as if she were smiling. Kossil never smiled. Arha's heart jumped; the blood pounded in her throat. She said to herself, fiercely : This is my place, I belong here, I will not be afraid !

Aloud she said nothing. She started forward; there was only one way to go. It went into the hill, and downwards.

Kossil followed, breathing heavily, her garments brushing and scraping against rock and earth.

All at once the roof lifted: Arha could stand straight, and stretching out her hands she felt no walls. The air, which had been close and earthy, touched her face with a cooler dampness, and faint movements in it gave the sense of a great expanse. Arha took a few cautious steps forward into the utter blackness. A pebble, slipping under her sandalled foot, struck another pebble, and the tiny sound wakened echoes, many echoes, minute, remote, yet more remote. The cavern must be immense, high and broad, yet not empty: something in its darkness, surfaces of invisible objects or partitions, broke the echo into a thousand fragments.

'Here we must be beneath the Stones,' the girl said whispering, and her whisper ran out into the hollow blackness and frayed into threads of sound as fine as spiderweb, that clung to the hearing for a long time.

'Yes. This is the Undertomb. Go on. I cannot stay here. Follow the wall to the left. Pass three openings.'

Kossil's whisper hissed (and the tiny echoes hissed after it). She was afraid, she was indeed afraid. She did not like to be here among the Nameless Ones, in their tombs, in their caves, in the dark. It was not her place, she did not belong here.

'I shall come here with a torch,' Arha said, guiding herself along the wall of the cavern by the touch of her fingers, wondering at the strange shapes of the rock, hollows and swellings and fine curves and edges, rough as lace here, smooth as brass there: surely this was carven work. Perhaps the whole cavern was the work of sculptors of the ancient days.

'Light is forbidden here.' Kossil's whisper was sharp. Even as she said it, Arha knew it must be so. This was the very home of darkness, the inmost centre of the night.

Three times her fingers swept across a gap in the complex, rocky blackness. The fourth time she felt for the height and width of the opening, and entered it. Kossil came behind.

In this tunnel, which went upwards again at a slight slant, they passed an opening on the left, and then at a branching way took the right: all by feel, by groping, in the blindness of the under-earth and the silence inside the ground. In such a passageway as this, one must reach out almost constantly to touch both sides of the tunnel lest one of the openings that must be counted be missed, or the forking of the way go unnoticed. Touch was one's whole guidance; one could not see the way, but held it in one's hands.

'Is this the Labyrinth?'

'No. This is the lesser maze, which is beneath the Throne.'

'Where is the entrance to the Labyrinth?'

Arha liked this game in the dark, she wanted a greater puzzle to be set her.

'The second opening we passed in the Undertomb. Feel for a door to the right now, a wooden door, perhaps we've passed it already –'

Arha heard Kossil's hands fumbling uneasily along the wall, scraping on the rough rock. She kept her fingertips light against the rock, and in a moment felt the smooth grain of wood beneath them. She pushed on it, and the door creaked open easily. She stood for a moment blind with light.

They entered a large low room, walled with hewn stone and lighted by one fuming torch hung from a chain. The place was foul with the torch-smoke that had no outlet. Arha's eyes stung and watered.

'Where are the prisoners?'

'There.'

At last she realized that the three heaps of something on the far side of the room were men.

'The door isn't locked. Is there no guard?'

'None is needed.'

She went a little further into the room, hesitant, peering through the smoky haze. The prisoners were manacled by both ankles and one wrist to great rings driven into the rock of the wall. If one of them wanted to lie down, his chained arm must remain raised, hanging from the manacle. Their hair and beards had made a matted tangle which, together with the shadows, hid their faces. One of them half lay, the other two sat or squatted. They were naked. The smell from them was stronger even than the reek of smoke.

One of them seemed to be watching Arha; she thought she saw the glitter of eyes, then was not sure. The others had not moved or lifted their heads.

She turned away. 'They are not men any more,' she said.

'They were never men. They were demons, beast-spirits, who plotted against the sacred life of the Godking!' Kossil's eyes shone with the reddish torchlight.

Arha looked again at the prisoners, awed and curious. 'How could a man attack a god? How was it? You: how could you dare attack a living god?'

The one man stared at her through the black brush of his hair, but said nothing.

'Their tongues were cut out before they were sent from Awabath,' Kossil said. 'Do not speak to them, mistress. They are defilement. They are yours, but not to speak to, nor to look at, nor to think upon. They are yours to give to the Nameless Ones.'

'How are they to be sacrificed?'

Arha no longer looked at the prisoners. She faced Kossil instead, drawing strength from the massive body, the cold voice. She felt dizzy, and the reek of smoke and filth made her sick, yet she seemed to think and speak with perfect calm. Had she not done this many times before?

'The Priestess of the Tombs knows best what manner of death will please her Masters, and it is hers to choose. There are many ways.'

'Let Gobar the captain of the guards hew off their heads. And the blood will be poured out before the Throne.'

'As if it were a sacrifice of goats?' Kossil seemed to be sneering at her lack of imagination. She stood dumb. Kossil went on, 'Besides, Gobar is a man. No man can enter the Dark Places of the Tombs, surely my mistress remembers that? If he enters, he does not leave ...'

'Who brought them here? Who feeds them?'

'The wardens who serve my temple, Duby and Uahto: they are eunuchs and may enter here on the services of the Nameless Ones, as I may. The Godking's soldiers left the prisoners bound outside the wall, and I and the wardens brought them in through the Prisoners' Door, the door in the red rocks. So it is always done. The food and water is lowered from a trapdoor in one of the rooms behind the Throne.'

Arha looked up and saw, beside the chain from which the torch hung, a wooden square set into the stone ceiling. It was far too small for a man to crawl through, but a rope lowered from it would come down just within reach of the middle prisoner of the three. She looked away again quickly.

'Let them not bring any more food or water, then. Let the torch go out.'

Kossil bowed. 'And the bodies, when they die?'

'Let Duby and Uahto bury them in the great cavern that we passed through, the Undertomb,' the girl said, her voice becoming quick and high. 'They must do it in the dark. My Masters will eat the bodies.'

'It shall be done.'

'Is this well, Kossil?'

'It is well, mistress.'

'Then let us go,' Arha said, very shrill. She turned and hurried back to the wooden door, and out of the Room of Chains into the blackness of the tunnel. It seemed sweet and peaceful as a starless night, silent, without sight, or light, or life. She plunged into the clean darkness, hurried forward through it like a swimmer through water. Kossil hastened along, behind her and getting farther behind, panting, lumbering. Without hesitation Arha repeated the missed and taken turnings as they had come, skirted the vast echoing Undertomb, and crept, bent over, up the last long tunnel to the shut door of rock. There she crouched down and felt for the long key on the ring at her waist. She found it, but could not find the keyhole. There was no pinprick of light in the invisible wall before her. Her fingers groped over it seeking lock or bolt or handle and finding nothing. Where must the key go? How could she get out?

'Mistress!'

Kossil's voice, magnified by echoes, hissed and boomed far behind her.

'Mistress, the door will not open from inside. There is no way out. There is no return.'

Arha crouched against the rock. She said nothing.

'Arha!'

'I am here.'

'Come!'

She came, crawling on hands and knees along the passage, like a dog, to Kossil's skirts.

'To the right. Hurry! I must not linger here. It is not my place. Follow me.'

Arha got to her feet, and held on to Kossil's robes. They went forward, following the strangely carven wall of the cavern to the right for a long way, then entering a black gap in the blackness. They went upward now, in tunnels, by stairs. The girl still clung to the woman's robe. Her eyes were shut.

There was light, red through her eyelids. She thought it was the torchlit room full of smoke again, and did not open her eyes. But the air smelt sweetish, dry and mouldy, a familiar smell; and her feet were on a staircase steep almost as a ladder. She let go Kossil's robe, and looked. A trapdoor was open over her head. She scrambled through it after Kossil. It let her into a room she knew, a little stone cell containing a couple of chests and iron boxes, in the warren of rooms behind the Throne Room of the Hall. Daylight glimmered grey and faint in the hallway outside its door.

'The other, the Prisoners' Door, leads only into the tunnels. It does not lead out. This is the only way out. If there is any other way I do not know of it, nor does Thar. You must remember it for yourself, if there is one. But I do not think there is.' Kossil still spoke in an undertone, and with a kind of spitefulness. Her heavy face within the black cowl was pale, and damp with sweat.

'I don't remember the turnings to this way out.'

'I'll tell them to you. Once. You must remember them. Next time I will not come with you. This is not my place. You must come alone.'

The girl nodded. She looked up into the older woman's face, and thought how strange it looked, pale with scarcely mastered fear and yet triumphant, as if Kossil gloated over her weakness.

'I will come alone after this,' Arha said, and then trying to turn away from Kossil she felt her legs give way, and saw the room turn over. She fainted in a little black heap at the priestess's feet.

'You'll learn,' Kossil said, still breathing heavily, standing motionless. 'You'll learn.'

4. Dreams and Tales

ARHA was not well for several days. They treated her for fever. She kept to her bed, or sat in the mild autumn sunlight on the porch of the Small House, and looked up at the western hills. She felt weak and stupid. The same ideas occurred to her again and again. She was ashamed of having fainted. No guard had been set upon the Tomb Wall, but now she would never dare ask Kossil about that. She did not want to see Kossil at all: never. It was because she was ashamed of having fainted.

Often, in the sunlight, she would plan how she was going to behave next time she went into the dark places under the hill. She thought many times about what kind of death she should command for the next set of prisoners, more elaborate, better suited to the rituals of the Empty Throne.

Each night, in the dark, she woke up screaming, 'They aren't dead yet! They are still dying!'

She dreamed a great deal. She dreamed that she had to cook food, great cauldrons full of savoury porridge, and pour it all out into a hole in the ground. She dreamed that she had to carry a full bowl of water, a deep brass bowl, through the dark, to someone who was thirsty. She could never get to this person. She woke, and she herself was thirsty, but she did not go and get a drink. She lay awake, eyes open, in the room without windows.

One morning Penthe came to see her. From the porch Arha saw her approach the Small House with a careless, purposeless air, as if she just happened to be wandering that way. If Arha had not spoken she would not have come up the steps. But Arha was lonely, and spoke.

Penthe made the deep bow required of all who approached the Priestess of the Tombs, and then plopped down on the steps below Arha and made a noise like 'Phewph!' She had got quite tall and plump; anything she did turned her cherry pink, and she was pink now from walking.

'I heard you were ill. I saved you some apples.' She suddenly produced a rush net containing six or eight perfect yellow apples, from somewhere under her voluminous black robe. She was now consecrated to the service of the Godking, and served in his temple under Kossil; but she wasn't yet a priestess, and still did lessons and chores with the novices. 'Poppe and I sorted the apples this year, and I saved the very best ones. They always dry all the really good ones. Of course they keep best, but it seems such a waste. Aren't they pretty?'

Arha felt the pale gold satin skins of the apples, looked at the twigs to which brown leaves still delicately clung. 'They are pretty.'

'Have one,' said Penthe.

'Not now. You do.'

Penthe selected the smallest, out of politeness, and ate it in about ten juicy, skilful, interested bites.

'I could eat all day,' she said. 'I never get enough. I wish I could be a cook instead of a priestess. I'd cook better than that old skin-flint Nathabba, and besides, I'd get to lick the pots ... Oh, did you hear about Munith? She was supposed to be polishing those brass pots they keep the rose oil in, you know, those long thin sort of jars with stoppers. And she thought she was supposed to clean the insides too, so she stuck her hand in, with a rag around it, you know, and then she couldn't get it out. She tried so hard it got all puffed up and swollen at the wrist, you know, so that she really was stuck. And she went galloping all over the dormitories yelling, 'I can't get it off! I can't get it off!' And Punti's so deaf now he thought it was a fire, and started screeching at the other wardens to come and rescue the novices. And Uahto was milking and came running out of the pen to see what was the matter, and left the gate open, and all the milch-goats got out and came charging into the courtyard and ran into Punti and the wardens and the little girls, and Munith waving this brass pot around on the end of her arm and having hysterics, and they were all sort of rushing around down there when Kossil came down from the temple. And she said, "What's this? What's this?"'

Penthe's fair, round face took on a repulsive sneer, not at all like Kossil's cold expression, and yet somehow so like Kossil that Arha gave a snort of almost terrified laughter.

' "What's this? What's all this?" Kossil said. And then – and then the brown goat *butted* her –' Penthe dissolved in laughter, tears welled in her eyes. 'And M-Munith hit the, the goat with the p-p-pot –'

Both girls rocked back and forth in spasms of giggling, holding their knees, choking.

'And Kossil turned around and said, "What's this? What's this?" to the – to the – to the goat . . .' The end of the tale was lost in laughter. Penthe finally wiped her eyes and nose and absent-mindedly started on another apple.

To laugh so hard made Arha feel a little shaky. She calmed herself down, and after a while asked, 'How did you come here, Penthe?'

'Oh, I was the sixth girl my mother and father had, and they just couldn't bring up so many and marry them all off. So when I was seven they brought me to the Godking's temple and dedicated me. That was in Ossawa. They had too many novices there, I suppose, because pretty soon they sent me on here. Or may be they thought I'd make a specially good priestess or something. But they were wrong about that!' Penthe bit her apple with a cheerful, rueful face.

'Would you rather not have been a priestess?'

'Would I rather! Of course! I'd rather marry a pig-herd and live in a ditch. I'd rather anything than stay buried alive here all my born days with a mess of women in a perishing old desert where nobody ever comes! But there's no good *wishing* about it, because I've been consecrated now and I'm stuck with it. But I do hope that in my next life I'm a dancing-girl in Awabath! Because I will have earned it.'

Arha looked down at her with a dark steady gaze. She did not understand. She felt that she had never seen Penthe before, never looked at her and seen her, round and full of life and juice as one of her golden apples, beautiful to see.

'Doesn't the Temple mean anything to you?' she asked, rather harshly.

Penthe, always submissive and easily bullied, did not take alarm this time. 'Oh, I know your Masters are very important to you,' she said with an indifference that shocked Arha. 'That makes some sense, anyhow, because you're their one special servant. You weren't just consecrated, you were specially born. But look at me. Am I supposed to feel so much awe and so on about the Godking? After all he's just a man, even if he does live in Awabath in a palace ten miles round with gold roofs. He's about fifty years old, and he's bald. You can see in all the statues. And I'll bet you he has to cut his toenails, just like any other man. I know perfectly well that he's a god, too. But what I think is, he'll be much godlier after he's dead.'

Arha agreed with Penthe, for secretly she had come to consider the self-styled Divine Emperors of Kargad as upstarts, false gods trying to filch the worship due to the true and everlasting Powers. But there was something underneath Penthe's words with which she didn't agree, something wholly new to her, frightening to her. She had not realized how very different people were, how differently they saw life. She felt as if she had looked up and suddenly seen a whole new planet hanging huge and populous right outside the window, an entirely strange world, one in which the gods did not matter. She was scared by the solidity of Penthe's unfaith. Scared, she struck out.

'That's true. My Masters have been dead a long long time; and they were never men ... Do you know, Penthe, I could call you into the service of the Tombs.' She spoke pleasantly, as if offering her friend a better choice.

The pink went right out of Penthe's cheeks.

'Yes,' she said, 'you could. But I'm not ... I'm not the sort that would be good at that.'

'Why?'

'I am afraid of the dark,' Penthe said in a low voice.

Arha made a little sound of scorn, but she was pleased. She had made her point. Penthe might disbelieve in the gods, but she feared the unnameable powers of the dark – as did every mortal soul.

'I wouldn't do that unless you wanted to, you know,' Arha said. A long silence fell between them.

'You're getting to be more and more like Thar,' Penthe said in her soft dreamy way. 'Thank goodness you're not getting like Kossil! But you're so strong. I wish I were strong. I just like eating . . .'

'Go ahead,' Arha said, superior and amused, and Penthe slowly consumed a third apple down to the seeds.

The demands of the endless ritual of the Place brought Arha out of her privacy a couple of days later. Twin kids had been born out of season to a she-goat, and were to be sacrificed to the Twin God-Brothers as the custom was: an important rite, at which the First Priestess must be present. Then it was dark of the moon, and the ceremonies of the darkness must be performed before the Empty Throne. Arha breathed in the drugging fumes of herbs burning in broad trays of bronze before the Throne, and danced, solitary in black. She danced for the unseen spirits of the dead and the unborn and as she danced the spirits crowded the air around her, following the turn and spin of her feet and the slow, sure gestures of her arms. She sang the songs whose words no man understood, which she had learned syllable by syllable, long ago, from Thar. A choir of priestesses hidden in the dusk behind the great double row of columns echoed the strange words after her, and the air in the vast ruinous room hummed with voices, as if the crowding spirits repeated the chants again and again.

The Godking in Awabath sent no more prisoners to the Place, and gradually Arha ceased to dream of the three now long since dead and buried in shallow graves in the great cavern under the Tombstones.

She summoned up her courage to return to that cavern. She must go back there: the Priestess of the Tombs must be able to enter her own domain without terror, to know its ways.

The first time she entered the trapdoor was hard; yet not so hard as she had feared. She had schooled herself up to it so well, had so determined that she would go alone and keep her nerve, that when she came there she was almost dismayed to find that there was nothing to be afraid of. Graves might be there, but she could not see them; she could not see anything. It was black; it was silent. And that was all.

Day after day she went there, always entering by the trapdoor in the room behind the Throne, until she knew well the whole circuit of the cavern, with its strange sculptured walls – as well as one can know what one cannot see. She never left the walls, for in striking out across the great hollow she might soon lose her sense of direction in the darkness, and so, blundering back at last to the wall, not know where she was. For as she had learned the first time, the important thing down in the dark places was to know which turnings and openings one had passed, and which were to come. It must be done by counting, for they were all alike to the groping hands. Arha's memory had been well trained, and she found no difficulty to this odd trick of finding one's way by touch and number, instead of by sight and common sense. She soon knew by heart all the corridors that opened off the Undertomb, the lesser maze that lay under the Hall of the Throne and the hilltop. But there was one corridor she never entered: the second left from the red rock entrance, that one which, if she entered mistaking it for one she knew, she might never find her way out of again. Her longing to enter it, to learn the Labyrinth, grew steadily, but she restrained it until she had learned all she could about it, above ground.

Thar knew little about it but the names of certain of its rooms, and the list of directions, of turns made and missed, for getting to these rooms. She would tell these to Arha, but she would never draw them in the dust or even with the gesture of a hand in the air; and she herself had never followed them, had never entered the Labyrinth. But when Arha asked her, 'What is the way from the iron door that stands open to the Painted Room?' or 'How does the way run from the Room of Bones to the tunnel by the river?' – then Thar would be silent a little, and then recite the strange directions she had learned long before from Arha-that-was: so many crossings passed, so many left-hand turns taken, and so on, and so on. And all these Arha got by heart, as Thar had, often on the first listening. When she lay in bed nights she would repeat them to herself, trying to imagine the places, the rooms, the turnings.

Thar showed Arha the many spy holes that opened into the maze, in every building and temple of the Place, and even under rocks out of doors. The spiderweb of stone-walled tunnels underlay all the Place and even beyond its walls; there were miles of tunnels, down there in the dark. No person there but she, the two High Priestesses, and their special servants, the eunuchs Manan, Uahto, and Duby, knew of the existence of this maze that lay beneath every step they took. There were vague rumours of it among the others; they all knew that there were caves or rooms of some sort under the Tombstones. But none of them was very curious about anything to do with the Nameless Ones and the places sacred to them. Perhaps they felt that the less they knew, the better. Arha of course had been intensely curious, and knowing that there were spy holes into the Labyrinth, had sought for them; yet they were so well concealed, in the pavements of the floors or in the desert ground, that she had never found one, not even the one in her own Small House, until Thar showed it to her.

One night in early spring she took a candle lantern and went down with it, unlit, through the Undertomb to the second passage to the left of the passage from the red rock door.

In the dark, she went some thirty paces down the passage, and then passed through a doorway, feeling the iron frame set in the rock: the limit, until now, of her explorations. Past the Iron Door she went a long way along the tunnel, and when at last it began to curve to the right, she lit her candle and looked about her. For light was permitted, here. She was no longer in the Undertomb. She was in a place less sacred, though perhaps more dreadful. She was in the Labyrinth.

The raw, blank walls and vault and floor of rock surrounded her in the small sphere of candlelight. The air was dead. Before her and behind her the tunnel stretched off into darkness.

All the tunnels were the same, crossing and recrossing. She kept careful count of her turnings and passings, and recited Thar's directions to herself, though she knew them perfectly. For it would not do to get lost in the Labyrinth. In the Undertomb and the short passages around it, Kossil or Thar might find her, or Manan come seeking for her, for she had taken him there several times. Here, none of them had ever been : only she herself. Little good it would do her if they came to the Undertomb and called aloud, and she was lost in some spiralling tangle of tunnels half a mile away. She imagined how she might hear the echo of voices calling her, echoing down every corridor, and she would try to come to them, but, lost, would only become farther lost. So vividly did she imagine this that she stopped, thinking she heard a distant voice calling. But there was nothing. And she would not get lost. She was very careful; and this was her place, her own domain. The powers of the dark, the Nameless Ones, would guide her steps here, just as they would lead astray any other mortal who dared enter the Labyrinth of the Tombs.

She did not go far into it that first time, but far enough that the strange, bitter, yet pleasurable certainty of her utter solitude and independence there grew strong in her, and led her back, and back again, and each time farther. She came to the Painted Room, and the Six Ways, and followed the long Outmost Tunnel, and penetrated the strange tangle that led to the Room of Bones.

'When was the Labyrinth made?' she asked Thar, and the stern, thin priestess answered, 'Mistress, I do not know. No one knows.'

'Why was it made?'

'For the hiding away of the treasures of the Tombs, and for the punishment of those who tried to steal those treasures.'

'All the treasures I've seen are in the rooms behind the Throne, and the basements under it. What lies in the Labyrinth?'

'A far greater and more ancient treasure. Would you look on it?'

'Yes.'

'None but you may enter the Treasury of the Tombs. You may take your servants into the Labyrinth, but not into the Treasury. If even Manan entered there, the anger of the dark would waken; he

would not leave the Labyrinth alive. There you must go alone, forever. I know where the Great Treasure is. You told me the way, fifteen years ago, before you died, so that I would remember and tell
you when you returned. I can tell you the way to follow in the
Labyrinth, beyond the Painted Room; and the key to the Treasury
is that silver one on your ring, with a figure of a dragon on the haft.
But you must go alone.'

'Tell me the way.'

Thar told her, and she remembered, as she remembered all that
was told her. But she did not go to see the Great Treasure of the
Tombs. Some feeling that her will or her knowledge was not yet
complete held her back. Or perhaps she wanted to keep something
in reserve, something to look forward to, that cast a glamour over
those endless tunnels through the dark that ended always in blank
walls or bare dusty cells. She would wait awhile before she saw her
treasures.

After all, had she not seen them before?

It still made her feel strange when Thar and Kossil spoke to her
of things she had seen or said before she died. She knew that indeed
she had died, and had been reborn in a new body at the hour of her
old body's death : not only once, fifteen years ago, but fifty years
ago, and before that, and before that, back down the years and hundreds of years, generation before generation, to the very beginning
of years when the Labyrinth was dug, and the Stones were raised,
and the First Priestess of the Nameless Ones lived in this Place and
danced before the Empty Throne. They were all one, all those lives
and hers. She was the First Priestess. All human beings were forever reborn, but only she, Arha, was reborn forever as herself. A
hundred times she had learned the ways and turnings of the Labyrinth and had come to the hidden room at last.

Sometimes she thought she remembered. The dark places under
the hill were so familiar to her, as if they were not only her domain,
but her home. When she breathed in the drug-fumes to dance at
dark of the moon, her head grew light and her body was no longer
hers; then she danced across the centuries, barefoot in black robes,
and knew that the dance had never ceased.

Yet it was always strange when Thar said, 'You told me before you died . . .'

Once she asked, 'Who were those men that came to rob the Tombs? Did any ever do so?' The idea of robbers had struck her as exciting, but improbable. How could they come secretly to the Place? Pilgrims were very few, fewer even than prisoners. Now and then new novices or slaves were sent from lesser temples of the Four Lands, or a small group came to bring some offering of gold or rare incense to one of the temples. And that was all. Nobody came by chance, or to buy and sell, or to sightsee, or to steal; nobody came but under orders. Arha did not even know how far it was to the nearest town, twenty miles or more; and the nearest town was a small one. The Place was guarded and defended by emptiness, by solitude. Anybody crossing the desert that surrounded it, she thought, would have as much chance of going unseen as a black sheep in a snowfield.

She was with Thar and Kossil, with whom much of her time was spent now when she was not in the Small House or alone under the hill. It was a stormy, cold night in April. They sat by a tiny fire of sage on the hearth in the room behind the Godking's temple, Kossil's room. Outside the doorway, in the hall, Manan and Duby played a game with sticks and counters, tossing a bundle of sticks and catching as many as possible on the back of the hand. Manan and Arha still sometimes played that game, in secret, in the inner courtyard of the Small House. The rattle of dropping sticks, the husky mumbles of triumph and defeat, the small crackle of the fire, were the only sounds when the three priestesses fell silent. All round beyond the walls reached the profound silence of the desert night. From time to time came the patter of a sparse, hard shower of rain.

'Many came to rob the Tomb, long ago; but none ever did so,' said Thar. Taciturn as she was, she liked now and then to tell a story, and often did so as part of Arha's instruction. She looked tonight as if a story might be drawn out of her.

'How would any man dare?'

'*They* would dare,' Kossil said. 'They were sorcerers, wizard-folk from the Inner Lands. That was before the Godkings ruled the Kargad Lands; we were not so strong then. The wizards used to sail from the west to Karego-At and Atuan to plunder the towns on the coast, loot the farms, even come into the Sacred City Awabath. They came to kill dragons, they said, but they stayed to rob towns and temples.'

'And their great heroes would come among us to test their swords,' Thar said, 'and work their ungodly spells. One of them, a mighty sorcerer and dragonlord, the greatest of them all, came to grief here. It was long ago, very long ago, but the tale is still remembered, and not only in this place. The sorcerer was named Erreth-Akbe, and he was both king and wizard in the West. He came to our lands, and in Awabath he joined with certain Kargish rebel lords, and fought for the rule of the city with the High Priest of the Inmost Temple of the Twin Gods. Long they fought, the man's sorcery against the lightning of the gods, and the temple was destroyed around them. At last the High Priest broke the sorcerer's witching-staff, broke in half his amulet of power, and defeated him. He escaped from the city and from the Kargish lands, and fled clear across Earthsea to the farthest west; and there a dragon slew him, because his power was gone. And since that day the power and might of the Inner Lands has ever waned. Now the High Priest was named Intathin, and he was the first of the house of Tarb, that lineage from which, after the fulfilment of the prophecies and the centuries, the Priest-Kings of Karego-At were descended, and from them, the Godkings of all Kargad. So it was that since the day of Intathin the power and might of the Kargish lands has ever grown. Those who came to rob the Tombs, they were sorcerers, trying and trying to get back the broken amulet of Erreth-Akbe. But it is still here, where the High Priest put it for safekeeping. And so are their bones . . .' Thar pointed at the ground under her feet.

'And the other half lost forever.'

'How lost?' asked Arha.

'The one half, in Intathin's hand, was given by him to the Treasury of the Tombs, where it should lie safe forever. The other remained in the sorcerer's hand, but he gave it before he fled to a petty king, one of the rebels, named Thoreg of Hupun. I do not know why he did so.'

'To cause strife, to make Thoreg proud,' Kossil said. 'And so it did. The descendants of Thoreg rebelled again when the house of Tarb ruled; and yet again they took arms against the first Godking, refusing to acknowledge him as either king or god. They were an accursed, ensorcelled race. They are all dead now.'

Thar nodded. 'The father of our present Godking, the Lord Who Has Arisen, put down that family of Hupun, and destroyed their palaces. When that was done, the half-amulet, which they had kept ever since the days of Erreth-Akbe and Intathin, was lost. No one knows what became of it. And that was a lifetime ago.'

'It was thrown out as rubbish, no doubt,' Kossil said. 'They say it doesn't look like anything of value, the Ring of Erreth-Akbe. A curse upon it and upon all the things of the wizard-folk!' Kossil spat into the fire.

'Have you seen the half that is here?' Arha asked of Thar.

The thin woman shook her head. 'It is in that treasury to which none may come but the One Priestess. It may be the greatest of all the treasures there; I do not know. I think perhaps it is. For hundreds of years the Inner Lands sent thieves and wizards here to try to steal it back, and they would pass by open coffers of gold, seeking that one thing. It is very long since Erreth-Akbe and Intathin lived, and yet still the story is known and told, both here and in the West. Most things grow old and perish, as the centuries go on and on. Very few are the precious things that remain precious, or the tales that are still told.'

Arha brooded awhile and said, 'They must have been very brave men, or very stupid, to enter the Tombs. Don't they know the powers of the Nameless Ones?'

'No,' Kossil said in her cold voice. 'They have no gods. They work magic, and think they are gods themselves. But they are not. And when they die, they are not reborn. They become dust and bone, and their ghosts whine on the wind a little while till the wind blows them away. They do not have immortal souls.'

'But what is this magic they work?' Arha asked, enthralled. She did not remember having said once that she would have turned away and refused to look at the ships from the Inner Lands. 'How do they do it? What does it do?'

'Tricks, deceptions, jugglery,' Kossil said.

'Somewhat more,' said Thar, 'if the tales be true even in part. The wizards of the West can raise and still the winds, and make them blow whither they will. On that, all agree, and tell the same tale. That is why they are great sailors; they can put the wind of magic in their sails, and go where they will, and hush the storms at sea. And it is said that they can make light at will, and darkness; and change rocks to diamonds, and lead to gold; that they can build a great palace or a whole city in one instant, at least in seeming; that they can turn themselves into bears, or fish, or dragons, just as they please.'

'I do not believe all that,' said Kossil. 'That they are dangerous, subtle with trickery, slippery as eels, yes. But they say that if you take his wooden staff away from a sorcerer, he has no power left. Probably there are evil runes written on the staff.'

Thar shook her head again. 'They carry a staff, indeed, but it is only a tool for the power they bear within them.'

'But how do they get the power?' Arha asked. 'Where does it come from?'

'Lies,' Kossil said.

'Words,' said Thar. 'So I was told by one who once had watched a great sorcerer of the Inner Lands, a Mage as they are called. They had taken him prisoner, raiding to the West. He showed them a stick of dry wood, and spoke a word to it. And lo! it blossomed. And he spoke another word, and lo! it bore red apples. And he spoke one more word, and stick, blossoms, apples, and all vanished, and with them the sorcerer. With one word he had gone as a rainbow goes, like a wink, without a trace; and they never found him on that isle. Was that mere jugglery?'

'It's easy to fool fools,' Kossil said.

Thar said no more, avoiding argument; but Arha was loath to have the subject dropped. 'What do the wizard-folk look like,' she asked, 'are they truly black all over, with white eyes?'

'They are black and vile. I have never seen one,' Kossil said with satisfaction, shifting her heavy bulk on the low stool and spreading her hands to the fire.

'May the Twin Gods keep them afar,' Thar muttered.

'They will never come here again,' said Kossil. And the fire sputtered, and the rain spattered on the roof, and outside the gloomy doorway Manan cried shrilly, 'Ahah! A half for me, a half!'

5. *Light under the Hill*

As the year was rounding again towards winter, Thar died. In the summer a wasting disease had come upon her; she who had been thin grew skeletal, she who had been grim now did not speak at all. Only to Arha would she talk, sometimes, when they were alone together; then even that ceased, and she went silently into the dark. When she was gone, Arha missed her sorely. If Thar had been stern, she had never been cruel. It was pride she had taught to Arha, not fear.

Now there was only Kossil.

A new High Priestess for the Temple of the Twin Gods would come in spring from Awabath; until then, Arha and Kossil between them were the rulers of the Place. The woman called the girl 'Mistress', and should obey her if commanded. But Arha had learned not to command Kossil. She had the right to do so, but not the strength; it would take very great strength to stand up against Kossil's jealousy of a higher status than her own, her hatred of anything she herself did not control.

Since Arha had learned (from gentle Penthe) of the existence of unfaith, and had accepted it as a reality even though it frightened her, she had been able to look at Kossil much more steadily, and to understand her. Kossil had no true worship in her heart of the Nameless Ones or of the gods. She held nothing sacred but power. The Emperor of the Kargad Lands now held the power, and therefore he was indeed a godking in her eyes, and she would serve him well. But to her the temples were mere show, the Tombstones were rocks, the Tombs of Atuan were dark holes in the ground, terrible but empty. She would do away with the worship of the Empty Throne, if she could. She would do away with the first Priestess, if she dared.

Arha had come to face even this last fact quite steadily. Perhaps

Thar had helped her to see it, though she had never said anything directly. In the first stages of her illness, before the silence came upon her, she had asked Arha to come to her every few days, and had talked to her, telling her much about the doings of the Godking and his predecessor, and the ways of Awabath – matters which she should as an important priestess know, but which were not often flattering to the Godking and his court. And she had spoken of her own life, and described what the Arha of the previous life had looked like and done; and sometimes, not often, she had mentioned what might be the difficulties and dangers of Arha's present life. Not once did she mention Kossil by name. But Arha had been Thar's pupil for eleven years, and needed no more than a hint or a tone to understand, and to remember.

After the gloomy commotion of the Rites of Mourning was over, Arha took to avoiding Kossil. When the long works and rituals of the day were done, she went to her solitary dwelling; and whenever there was time, she went to the room behind the Throne, and opened the trapdoor, and went down into the dark. In daytime and nighttime, for it made no difference there, she pursued a systematic exploration of her domain. The Undertomb, with its great weight of sacredness, was utterly forbidden to any but priestesses and their most trusted eunuchs. Any other, man or woman, who ventured there would certainly be struck dead by the wrath of the Nameless Ones. But among all the rules she had learned, there was no rule forbidding entry to the Labyrinth. There was no need. It could be entered only from the Undertomb; and anyway, do flies need rules to tell them not to enter a spider's web?

So she took Manan often into the nearer regions of the Labyrinth, that he might learn the ways. He was not at all eager to go there, but as always he obeyed her. She made sure that Duby and Uahto, Kossil's eunuchs, knew the way to the Room of Chains and the way out of the Undertomb, but no more; she never took them into the Labyrinth. She wanted no one but Manan, utterly faithful to her, to know those secret ways. For they were hers, hers alone, forever. She had begun her full exploration with the Labyrinth. All the autumn she spent many days walking those endless corridors, and still there were regions of them she had never come to. There was a weariness in that tracing of the vast, meaningless web of ways; the legs got tired and the mind got bored, forever reckoning up the turnings and the passages behind and to come. It was wonderful, laid out in the solid rock underground like the streets of a great city; but it had been made to weary and confuse the mortal walking in it, and even its priestess must feel it to be nothing, in the end, but a great trap.

So, more and more as winter deepened, she turned her thorough exploration to the Hall itself, the altars, the alcoves behind and beneath the altars, the rooms of chests and boxes, the contents of the chests and boxes, the passages and attics, the dusty hollow under the dome where hundreds of bats nested, the basements and underbasements that were the anterooms of the corridors of darkness.

Her hands and sleeves perfumed with the dry sweetness of a musk that had fallen to powder lying for eight centuries in an iron chest, her brow smeared with the clinging black of cobweb, she would kneel for an hour to study the carvings on a beautiful, time-ruined coffer of cedar wood, the gift of some king ages since to the Nameless Powers of the Tombs. There was the king, a tiny stiff figure with a big nose, and there was the Hall of the Throne with its flat dome and porch columns, carved in delicate relief on the wood by some artist who had been dust for how many hundred years. There was the One Priestess, breathing in the drug-fumes from the trays of bronze and prophesying or advising the king, whose nose was broken off in this frame; the face of the Priestess was too small to have clear features, yet Arha would imagine that the face was her own face. She wondered what she had told the king with the big nose, and whether he had been grateful.

She had favourite places in the Hall of the Throne, as one might have favourite spots to sit in a sunny house. She often went to a little half-loft over one of the robing rooms in the hinder part of the Hall. There ancient gowns and costumes were kept, left from the days when great kings and lords came to worship at the Place of the

Tombs of Atuan, acknowledging a domain greater than their own or any man's. Sometimes their daughters, the princesses, had put on these soft white silks, embroidered with topaz and dark amethyst, and had danced with the Priestess of the Tombs. There were little painted ivory tables in one of the treasuries, showing such a dance, and the lords and kings waiting outside the Hall, for then as now no man ever set foot on the ground of the Tombs. But the maidens might come in, and dance with the Priestess, in white silk. The Priestess herself wore rough cloth, homespun black, always, then and now; but she liked to come and finger the sweet, soft stuff, rotten with age, the unperishing jewels tearing from the cloth by their own slight weight. There was a scent in these chests different from all the musks and incenses of the temples of the Place: a fresher scent, fainter, younger.

In the treasure rooms she would spend a night learning the contents of a single chest, jewel by jewel, the rusted armour, the broken plumes of helms, the buckles and pins and brooches, bronze, silver-gilt, and solid gold.

Owls, undisturbed by her presence, sat on the rafters and opened and shut their yellow eyes. A bit of starlight shone in between tiles of the roof; or the snow came sifting down, fine and cold as those ancient silks that fell to nothing at hand's touch.

One night late in the winter, it was too cold in the Hall. She went to the trapdoor, raised it, swung down on to the steps, and closed it above her. She set off silently on the way she now knew so well, the passage to the Undertomb. There, of course, she never bore a light; if she carried a lantern, from going in the Labyrinth or in the dark of night above ground, she extinguished it before she came near the Undertomb. She had never seen that place, never in all the generations of her priestesshood. In the passage now, she blew out the candle in the lamp she carried, and without slowing her pace at all went forward in the pitch dark, easy as a little fish in dark water. Here, winter or summer, there was no cold, no heat: always the same even chill, a little damp, changeless. Up above, the great frozen winds of winter whipped the snow over the desert.

Here there was no wind, no season; it was close, it was still, it was safe.

She was going to the Painted Room. She liked sometimes to go there and study the strange wall drawings that leapt out of the dark at the gleam of her candle: men with long wings and great eyes, serene and morose. No one could tell her what they were, there were no such paintings elsewhere in the Place, but she thought she knew; they were the spirits of the damned, who are not reborn. The Painted Room was in the Labyrinth, so she must pass through the cavern beneath the Tombstones first. As she approached it down the slanting passage, a faint grey bloomed, a bare hint and glimmer, the echo of an echo of a distant light.

She thought her eyes were tricking her, as they often did in that utter blackness. She closed them, and the glimmering vanished. She opened them, and it reappeared.

She had stopped and was standing still. Grey, not black. A dull edge of pallor, just visible, where nothing could be visible, where all must be black.

She took a few steps forward and put out her hand to that angle of the tunnel wall; and, infinitely faint, saw the movement of her hand.

She went on. This was strange beyond thought, beyond fear, this faint blooming of light where no light had ever been, in the inmost grave of darkness. She went noiseless on bare feet, black-clothed. At the last turn of the corridor she halted; then very slowly took the last step, and looked, and saw.

– Saw what she had never seen, not though she had lived a hundred lives: the great vaulted cavern beneath the Tombstones, not hollowed by man's hand but by the powers of the Earth. It was jewelled with crystals and ornamented with pinnacles and filigrees of white limestone where the waters under earth had worked, eons since: immense, with glittering roof and walls, sparkling, delicate, intricate, a palace of diamonds, a house of amethyst and crystal, from which the ancient darkness had been driven out by glory.

Not bright, but dazzling to the dark-accustomed eye, was the light that worked this wonder. It was a soft gleam, like marshlight,

that moved slowly across the cavern, striking a thousand scintilla-
tions from the jewelled roof and shifting a thousand fantastic shadows along the carven walls.

The light burned at the end of a staff of wood, smokeless, un-
consuming. The staff was held by a human hand. Arha saw the
face beside the light; the dark face: the face of a man.

She did not move.

For a long time he crossed and recrossed the vast cave. He moved
as if he sought something, looking behind the lacy cataracts of
stone, studying the several corridors that led out of the Undertomb,
yet not entering them. And still the Priestess of the Tombs stood
motionless, in the black angle of the passage, waiting.

What was hardest for her to think, perhaps, was that she was
looking at a stranger. She had very seldom seen a stranger. It
seemed to her that this must be one of the wardens – no, one of the
men from over the wall, a goatherd or guard, a slave of the Place;
and he had come to see the secrets of the Nameless Ones, maybe to
steal something from the Tombs . . .

To steal something. To rob the Dark Powers. Sacrilege: the word
came slowly into Arha's mind. This was a man, and no man's foot
must ever touch the soil of the Tombs, the Holy Place. Yet he had
come here into the hollow place that was the heart of the Tombs.
He had entered in. He had made light where light was forbidden,
where it had never been since world's beginning. Why did the
Nameless Ones not strike him down?

He was standing now looking down at the rocky floor, which
was cut and troubled. One could see that it had been opened and
reclosed. The sour sterile clods dug up for the graves had not all
been stamped down again.

Her Masters had eaten those three. Why did they not eat this
one? What were they waiting for?

For their hands to act, for their tongue to speak . . .

'Go! Go! Begone!' she screamed all at once at the top of her
voice. Great echoes shrilled and boomed across the cavern, seeming
to blur the dark, startled face that turned towards her, and, for one
moment across the shaken splendour of the cavern, saw her. Then

the light was gone. All splendour gone. Blind dark, and silence.

Now she could think again. She was released from the spell of light.

He must have come in by the red rock door, the Prisoners' Door, so he would try to escape by it. Light and silent as the soft-winged owls she ran the half-circuit of the cavern to the low tunnel that led to the door which opened only inwards. She stopped there at the entrance of the tunnel. There was no draft of wind from outside; he had not left the door fixed open behind him. It was shut, and if he was in the tunnel, he was trapped there.

But he was not in the tunnel. She was sure of it. So close, in that cramped place, she would have heard his breath, felt the warmth and pulse of his life itself. There was no one in the tunnel. She stood erect, and listened. Where had he gone?

The darkness pressed like a bandage on her eyes. To have seen the Undertomb confused her; she was bewildered. She had known it only as a region defined by hearing, by hand's touch, by drifts of cool air in the dark; a vastness; a mystery, never to be seen. She had seen it, and the mystery had given place, not to horror, but to beauty, a mystery deeper even than that of the dark.

She went slowly forward now, unsure. She felt her way to the left, to the second passageway, the one that led into the Labyrinth. There she paused and listened.

Her ears told her no more than her eyes. But, as she stood with one hand on either side of the rock archway, she felt a faint, obscure vibration in the rock, and on the chill, stale air was the trace of a scent that did not belong there: the smell of the wild sage that grew on the desert hills, overhead, under the open sky.

Slow and quiet she moved down the corridor, following her nose.

After perhaps a hundred paces she heard him. He was almost as silent as she, but he was not so surefooted in the dark. She heard a slight scuffle, as if he had stumbled on the uneven floor and recovered himself at once. Nothing else. She waited awhile and then went slowly on, touching her right-hand finger-tips very lightly to the wall. At last a rounded bar of metal came under them. There she stopped, and felt up the strip of iron until, almost as high as she could reach, she touched a projecting handle of rough iron. This, suddenly, with all her strength, she dragged downward.

There was a fearful grinding and a clash. Blue sparks leapt out in a falling shower. Echoes died away, quarrelling, down the corridor behind her. She put out her hands and felt, only a few inches before her face, the pocked surface of an iron door.

She drew a long breath.

Returning slowly up the tunnel to the Undertomb, and keeping its wall to her right, she went on to the trapdoor in the Hall of the Throne. She did not hasten, and went silently, though there was no need for silence any more. She had caught her thief. The door that he had gone through was the only way into or out of the Labyrinth; and it could be opened only from the outer side.

He was down there now, in the darkness underground, and he would never come out again.

Walking slowly and erect, she went past the Throne into the long columned hall. There, where one bronze bowl on the high tripod brimmed with the red glow of charcoal, she turned and approached the seven steps that led up to the Throne.

On the lowest step she knelt, and bowed her forehead down to the cold, dusty stone, littered with mouse bones dropped by the hunting owls.

'Forgive me that I have seen Your darkness broken,' she said, not speaking the words aloud. 'Forgive me that I have seen Your tombs violated. You will be avenged. O my Masters, death will deliver him to you, and he will never be reborn!'

Yet even as she prayed, in her mind's eye she saw the quivering radiance of the lighted cavern, life in the place of death; and instead of terror at the sacrilege and rage against the thief, she thought only how strange it was, how strange . . .

'What must I tell Kossil?' she asked herself as she came out into the blast of the winter wind and drew her cloak about her. 'Nothing. Not yet. I am mistress of the Labyrinth. This is no business of the Godking's. I'll tell her after the thief is dead, perhaps. How must I kill him? I should make Kossil come and watch him die.

She's fond of death. What is it he was seeking? He must be mad. How did he get in? Kossil and I have the only keys to the red rock door and the trapdoor. He must have come by the red rock door. Only a sorcerer could open it. A sorcerer –'

She halted, though the wind almost buffeted her off her feet.

'He is a sorcerer, a wizard of the Inner Lands, seeking the amulet of Erreth-Akbe.'

And there was such an outrageous glamour in this, that she grew warm all over, even in that icy wind, and laughed out loud. All around her the Place, and the desert around it, was black and silent; the wind keened; there were no lights down in the Big House. Thin, invisible snow flicked past on the wind.

'If he opened the red rock door with sorcery, he can open others. He can escape.'

This thought chilled her for a moment, but it did not convince her. The Nameless Ones had let him enter. Why not? He could not do any harm. What harm is a thief who can't leave the scene of his theft? Spells and black powers he must have, and strong ones no doubt, since he had got that far; but he would not get farther. No spell cast by mortal man could be stronger than the will of the Nameless Ones, the presences in the Tombs, the Kings whose Throne was empty.

To reassure herself of this, she hastened on down to the Small House. Manan was asleep on the porch, rolled up in his cloak and the ratty fur blanket that was his winter bed. She entered quietly, so as not to awaken him, and without lighting any lamp. She opened a little locked room, a mere closet at the end of the hall. She struck a flint spark long enough to find a certain place on the floor, and kneeling, pried up one tile. A bit of heavy, dirty cloth, only a few inches square, was revealed to her touch. This she slipped aside noiselessly. She started back, for a ray of light shot upward, straight into her face.

After a moment, very cautiously, she looked into the opening. She had forgotten that he carried that queer light on his staff. She had been expecting at most to hear him, down there in the dark. She had forgotten the light, but he was where she had expected him to be : right beneath the spy hole, at the iron door that blocked his escape from the Labyrinth.

He was standing there, one hand on his hip, the other holding out at an angle the wooden staff, as tall as he was, to the tip of which clung the soft will-o'-the-wisp. His head, which she looked down upon from six feet above, was cocked a bit to the side. His clothes were those of any winter traveller or pilgrim, a short heavy cloak, a leather tunic, leggings of wool, laced sandals; there was a light pack on his back, a water bottle slung from it, a knife sheathed at his hip. He stood there still as a statue, easy and thoughtful.

Slowly he raised his staff from the ground, and held the bright tip of it out towards the door, which Arha could not see from her spy hole. The light changed, growing smaller and brighter, an intense brilliance. He spoke aloud. The language he spoke was strange to Arha, but stranger to her than the words was the voice, deep and resonant.

The light on the staff brightened, flickered, dimmed. For a moment it died quite away, and she could not see him.

The pale violet marshlight reappeared, steady, and she saw him turn away from the door. His spell of opening had failed. The powers that held the lock fast on that door were stronger than any magic he possessed.

He looked about him, as if thinking, now what?

The tunnel or corridor in which he stood was about five feet wide. Its roof was from twelve to fifteen feet above the rough rock floor. The walls here were of dressed stone, laid without mortar but very carefully and closely, so that one could scarcely slip a knife-tip into the joints. They leaned inward increasingly as they rose, forming a vault.

There was nothing else.

He started forward. One stride took him out of Arha's range of vision. The light died away. She was about to replace the cloth and the tile, when again the soft shaft of light rose up out of the floor before her. He had come back to the door. Perhaps he had realized that if he once left it and entered the maze, he was not very likely to find it again.

He spoke, one word only, in a low voice. 'Emenn,' he said, and then again, louder, 'Emenn!' And the iron door rattled in its jambs, and low echoes rolled down the vaulted tunnel like thunder, and it seemed to Arha that the floor beneath her shook.

But the door stayed fast.

He laughed then, a short laugh, that of a man who thinks, 'What a fool I've made of myself!' He looked around the walls once more, and as he glanced upwards Arha saw the smile lingering on his dark face. Then he sat down, unslung his pack, got out a piece of dry bread, and munched on it. He unstopped his leather bottle of water and shook it; it looked light in his hand, as if nearly empty. He replaced the stopper without drinking. He put the pack behind him for a pillow, pulled his cloak around him, and lay down. His staff was in his right hand. As he lay back, the little wisp or ball of light floated upward from the staff and hung dimly behind his head, a few feet off the ground. His left hand was on his breast, holding something that hung from a heavy chain around his neck. He lay there quite comfortable, legs crossed at the ankle; his gaze wandered across the spy hole and away; he sighed and closed his eyes. The light grew slowly dimmer. He slept.

The clenched hand on his breast relaxed and slipped aside, and the watcher above saw then what talisman he wore on the chain: a bit of rough metal, crescent-shaped, it seemed.

The faint glimmer of his sorcery died away. He lay in silence and the dark.

Arha replaced the cloth and reset the tile in its place, rose cautiously and slipped away to her room. There she lay long awake in the wind-loud darkness, seeing always before her the crystal radiance that had shimmered in the house of death, the soft unburning fire, the stones of the tunnel wall, the quiet face of the man asleep.

6. The Man Trap

NEXT day, when she had finished with her duties at the various temples, and with her teaching of the sacred dances to the novices, she slipped away to the Small House and, darkening the room, opened the spy hole and peered down it. There was no light. He was gone. She had not thought he would stay so long at the unavailing door, but it was the only place she knew to look. How was she to find him now that he had lost himself?

The tunnels of the Labyrinth, by Thar's account and her own experience, extended in all their windings, branchings, spirals, and dead ends, for more than twenty miles. The blind alley that lay farthest from the Tombs was not much more than a mile away in a straight line, probably. But down underground, nothing ran straight. All the tunnels curved, split, rejoined, branched, interlaced, looped, traced elaborate routes that ended where they began, for there was no beginning, and no end. One could go, and go, and go, and still get nowhere, for there was nowhere to get to. There was no centre, no heart of the maze. And once the door was locked, there was no end to it. No direction was right.

Though the ways and turnings to the various rooms and regions were firm in Arha's memory, even she had taken with her on her longer explorations a ball of fine yarn, and let it unravel behind her, and rewound it as she followed it returning. For if one of the turns and passages that must be counted were missed, even she might be lost. A light was no help, for there were no landmarks. All the corridors, all the doorways and openings, were alike.

He might have gone miles by now, and yet not be forty feet from the door where he had entered.

She went to the Hall of the Throne, and the Twin Gods' temple, and to the cellar under the kitchens, and, choosing a moment when she was alone, looked through each of those spy holes down into the cold, thick dark. When night came, freezing and blazing with stars, she went to certain places on the Hill and raised up certain stones, cleared away the earth, peered down again, and saw the starless darkness underground.

He was there. He must be there. Yet he had escaped her. He would die of thirst before she found him. She would have to send Manan into the maze to find him, once she was sure he was dead. That was unbearable to think of. As she knelt in the starlight on the bitter ground of the Hill, tears of rage rose in her eyes.

She went to the path that led back down the slope to the Temple of the Godking. The columns with their carved capitals shone white with hoar-frost in the starlight, like pillars of bone. She knocked at the rear door, and Kossil let her in.

'What brings my mistress?' said the stout woman, cold and watchful.

'Priestess, there is a man within the Labyrinth.'

Kossil was taken off guard; for once something had occurred that she did not expect. She stood and stared. Her eyes seemed to swell a little. It flitted across Arha's mind that Kossil looked very like Penthe imitating Kossil, and a wild laugh rose up in her, was repressed, and died away.

'A man? In the Labyrinth?'

'A man, a stranger.' Then as Kossil continued to look at her with disbelief, she added, 'I know a man by sight, though I have seen few.'

Kossil disdained her irony. 'How came a man there?'

'By witchcraft, I think. His skin is dark, perhaps he is from the Inner Lands. He came to rob the Tombs. I found him first in the Undertomb, beneath the very Stones. He ran to the entrance of the Labyrinth when he became aware of me, as if he knew where he went. I locked the iron door behind him. He made spells, but that did not open the door. In the morning he went on into the maze. I cannot find him now.'

'Has he a light?'

'Yes.'

'Water?'

'A little flask, not full.'

'His candle will be burned down already.' Kossil pondered. 'Four or five days. Maybe six. Then you can send my wardens down to drag the body out. The blood should be fed to the Throne and the –'

'No,' Arha said with sudden, shrill fierceness. 'I wish to find him alive.'

The priestess looked down at the girl from her heavy height. 'Why?'

'To make – to make his dying longer. He has committed sacrilege against the Nameless Ones. He has defiled the Undertomb with light. He came to rob the Tombs of their treasures. He must be punished with worse than lying down in a tunnel alone and dying.'

'Yes,' Kossil said, as if deliberating. 'But how will you catch him, mistress? That is chancy. There is no chance about the other. Is there not a room full of bones, somewhere in the Labyrinth, bones of men who entered it and did not leave it? ... Let the Dark Ones punish him in their own way, in their own ways, the black ways of the Labyrinth. It is a cruel death, thirst.'

'I know,' the girl said. She turned and went out into the night, pulling her hood up over her head against the hissing, icy wind. Did she not know?

It had been childish of her, and stupid, to come to Kossil. She would get no help there. Kossil herself knew nothing, all she knew was cold waiting and death at the end of it. She did not understand. She did not see that the man must be found. It must not be the same as with those others. She could not bear that again. Since there must be death let it be swift, in daylight. Surely it would be more fitting that this thief, the first man in centuries brave enough to try to rob the Tombs, should die by sword's edge. He did not even have an immortal soul to be reborn. His ghost would go whining through the corridors. He could not be let die of thirst there alone in the dark.

Arha slept very little that night. The next day was filled with rites and duties. She spent the night going, silent and without lantern, from one spy hole to another in all the dark buildings of the Place, and on the windswept hill. She went to the Small House to bed at last, two or three hours before dawn, but still she could not rest. On the third day, late in the afternoon, she walked out alone to the desert, towards the river that now lay low in the winter drought, with ice among the reeds. A memory had come to her that once, in the autumn, she had gone very far in the Labyrinth, past the Six-Cross, and all along one long curving corridor she had heard behind the stones the sound of running water. Might not a man athirst, if he came that way, stay there? There were spy holes even out here; she had to search for them, but Thar had shown her each one, last year, and she refound them without much trouble. Her recall of place and shape was like that of a blind person : she seemed to feel her way to each hidden spot, rather than to look for it. At the second, the farthest of all from the Tombs, when she pulled up her hood to cut out light, and put her eye to the hole cut in a flat pan of rock, she saw below her the dim glimmer of the wizardly light.

He was there, half out of sight. The spy hole looked down at the very end of the blind alley. She could see only his back, and bent neck, and right arm. He sat near the corner of the walls, and was picking at the stones with his knife, a short dagger of steel with a jewelled grip. The blade of it was broken short. The broken point lay directly under the spy hole. He had snapped it trying to pry apart the stones, to get at the water he could hear running, clear and murmurous in that dead stillness under earth, on the other side of the impenetrable wall.

His movements were listless. He was very different, after these three nights and days, from the figure that had stood lithe and calm before the iron door and laughed at his own defeat. He was still obstinate, but the power was gone out of him. He had no spell to stir those stones aside, but must use his useless knife. Even his sorcerer's light was wan and dim. As Arha watched, the light flickered; the man's head jerked and he dropped the dagger. Then doggedly he picked it up and tried to force the broken blade between the stones.

Lying among ice-bound reeds on the riverbank, unconscious of where she was or what she was doing, Arha put her mouth to the cold mouth of rock, and cupped her hands around to hold the sound in. 'Wizard!' she said, and her voice slipping down the stone throat whispered coldly in the tunnel underground.

The man started and scrambled to his feet, so going out of the circle of her vision when she looked for him. She put her mouth to the spy hole again and said, 'Go back along the river wall to the second turn. The first turn left. Pass two to the right, take the third. Pass one to the right, take the second. Then left; then right. Stay there in the Painted Room.'

As she moved to look again, she must have let a shaft of daylight shoot through the spy hole into the tunnel for a moment, for when she looked he was back in the circle of her vision and staring upwards at the opening. His face, which she now saw to be scarred in some way, was strained and eager. The lips were parched and black, the eyes bright. He raised his staff, bringing the light closer and closer to her eyes. Frightened, she drew back, stopped the spy hole with its rock lid and litter of covering stones, rose, and went back swiftly to the Place. She found her hands were shaky, and sometimes a giddiness swept over her as she walked. She did not know what to do.

If he followed the directions she had given him, he would come back in the direction of the iron door, to the room of pictures. There was nothing there, no reason for him to go there. There was a spy hole in the ceiling of the Painted Room, a good one, in the treasury of the Twin Gods' temple; perhaps that was why she had thought of it. She did not know. Why had she spoken to him?

She could let a little water for him down one of the spy holes, and then call him to that place. That would keep him alive longer. As long as she pleased, indeed. If she put down water and a little food now and then, he would go on and on, days, months, wandering in the Labyrinth; and she could watch him through the spy holes, and tell him where water was to be found, and sometimes tell him falsely so he would go in vain, but he would always have to go. That would teach him to mock the Nameless Ones, to swagger his foolish manhood in the burial places of the Immortal Dead!

But so long as he was there, she would never be able to enter the

Labyrinth herself. Why not? she asked herself, and replied – Because he might escape by the iron door, which I must leave open behind me ... But he could escape no farther than the Undertomb. The truth was that she was afraid to face him. She was afraid of his power, the arts he had used to enter the Undertomb, the sorcery that kept that light burning. And yet, was that so much to be feared? The powers that ruled in the dark places were on her side, not his. Plainly he could not do much, there in the realm of the Nameless Ones. He had not opened the iron door; he had not summoned magic food, nor brought water through the wall, nor conjured up some demon monster to break down the walls, all of which she had feared he might be able to do. He had not even found his way in three days' wandering to the door of the Great Treasury, which surely he had sought. Arha herself had never yet pursued Thar's directions to that room, putting off and putting off the journey out of a certain awe, a reluctance, a sense that the time had not yet come.

Now she thought, why should he not go that journey for her? He could look all he liked at the treasures of the Tombs. Much good they would do him ! She could jeer at him, and tell him to eat the gold, and drink the diamonds.

With the nervous, feverish hastiness that had possessed her all these three days, she ran to the Twin Gods' temple, unlocked its little vaulted treasury, and uncovered the well-hidden spy hole in the floor.

The Painted Room was below, but pitch dark. The way the man must follow in the maze was much more roundabout, miles longer perhaps; she had forgotten that. And no doubt he was weakened and not going fast. Perhaps he would forget her directions and take the wrong turning. Few people could remember directions from one hearing of them, as she could. Perhaps he did not even understand the tongue she spoke. If so, let him wander till he fell down and died in the dark, the fool, the foreigner, the unbeliever. Let his ghost whine down the stone roads of the Tombs of Atuan until the darkness ate even it ...

Next morning very early, after a night of little sleep and evil dreams, she returned to the spy hole in the little temple. She looked down and saw nothing: blackness. She lowered a candle burning in a little tin lantern on a chain. He was there, in the Painted Room. She saw, past the candle's glare, his legs and one limp hand. She spoke into the spy hole, which was a large one, the size of a whole floor tile: 'Wizard!'

No movement. Was he dead? Was that all the strength he had in him? She sneered; her heart pounded. 'Wizard!' she cried, her voice ringing in the hollow room beneath. He stirred, and slowly sat up, and looked around bewildered. After a while he looked up, blinking at the tiny lantern that swung from his ceiling. His face was terrible to see, swollen, dark as a mummy's face.

He put his hand out to his staff that lay on the floor beside him, but no light flowered on the wood. There was no power left in him.

'Do you want to see the treasure of the Tombs of Atuan, wizard?'

He looked up wearily, squinting at the light of her lantern, which was all he could see. After a while, with a wince that might have begun as a smile, he nodded once.

'Go out of this room to the left. Take the first corridor to the left ...' She rattled off the long series of directions without pause, and at the end said, 'There you will find the treasure which you came for. And there, maybe, you'll find water. Which would you rather have now, wizard?'

He got to his feet, leaning on his staff. Looking up with eyes that could not see her, he tried to say something, but there was no voice in his dry throat. He shrugged a little, and left the Painted Room.

She would not give him any water. He would never find the way to the treasure room, anyway. The instructions were too long for him to remember; and there was the Pit, if he got that far. He was in the dark now. He would lose his way, and would fall down at last and die somewhere in the narrow, hollow, dry halls. And Manan would find him and drag him out. And that was the end. Arha clutched the lid of the spy hole with her hands, and rocked her crouching body back and forth, back and forth, biting her lip as if to bear some dreadful pain. She would not give him any water. She would not give him any water. She would give him death, death, death, death, death.

In that grey hour of her life, Kossil came to her, entering the treasury room with heavy step, bulky in black winter robes.

'Is the man dead yet?'

Arha raised her head. There were no tears in her eyes, nothing to hide.

'I think so,' she said, getting up and dusting her skirts. 'His light has gone out.'

'He may be tricking. The soulless ones are very cunning.'

'I shall wait a day to be sure.'

'Yes, or two days. Then Duby can go down and bring it out. He is stronger than old Manan.'

'But Manan is in the service of the Nameless Ones, and Duby is not. There are places within the Labyrinth where Duby should not go, and the thief is in one of these.'

'Why, then it is defiled already –'

'It will be made clean by his death there,' Arha said. She could see by Kossil's expression that there must be something strange about her own face. 'This is my domain, priestess. I must care for it as my Masters bid me. I do not need more lessons in death.'

Kossil's face seemed to withdraw into the black hood, like a desert tortoise's into its shell, sour and slow and cold. 'Very well, mistress.'

They parted before the altar of the God-Brothers. Arha went, without haste now, to the Small House, and called Manan to accompany her. Since she had spoken to Kossil she knew what must be done.

She and Manan went together up the hill, into the Hall, down into the Undertomb. Straining together at the long handle, they opened the iron door of the Labyrinth. They lit their lanterns there, and entered. Arha led the way to the Painted Room, and from it started on the way to the Great Treasury.

The thief had not got very far. She and Manan had not walked five hundred paces on their tortuous course when they came upon him, crumpled up in the narrow corridor like a heap of rags thrown down. He had dropped his staff before he fell; it lay some distance from him. His mouth was bloody, his eyes half shut.

'He's alive,' said Manan, kneeling, his great yellow hand on the dark throat, feeling the pulse. 'Shall I strangle him, mistress?'

'No. I want him alive. Pick him up and bring him after me.'

'Alive?' said Manan, disturbed. 'What for, little mistress?'

'To be a slave of the Tombs! Be still with your talk and do as I say.'

His face more melancholy than ever, Manan obeyed, hoisting the young man effortlessly up on to his shoulders like a long sack. He staggered along after Arha thus laden. He could not go far at a time under that load. They stopped a dozen times on the return journey for Manan to catch his breath. At each halt the corridor was the same: the greyish-yellow, close-set stones rising to a vault, the uneven rocky floor, the dead air; Manan groaning and panting, the stranger lying still, the two lanterns burning dull in a dome of light that narrowed away into darkness down the corridor in both directions. At each halt Arha dripped some of the water she had brought in a flask into the dry mouth of the man, a little at a time, lest life returning kill him.

'To the Room of Chains?' Manan asked, as they were in the passage that led to the iron door; and at that, Arha thought for the first time where she must take this prisoner. She did not know.

'Not there, no,' she said, sickened as ever by the memory of the smoke and reek and the matted, speechless, unseeing faces. And Kossil might come to the Room of Chains. 'He . . . he must stay in the Labyrinth, so that he cannot regain his sorcery. Where is there a room . . .'

'The Painted Room has a door, and a lock, and a spy hole, mistress. If you trust him with doors.'

'He has no powers, down here. Take him there, Manan.'

So Manan lugged him back, half again as far as they had come, too labouring and breathless to protest. When they entered the Painted Room at last, Arha took off her long, heavy winter cloak of wool, and laid it on the dusty floor. 'Put him on that,' she said.

Manan stared in melancholy consternation, wheezing. 'Little mistress –'

'I want the man to live, Manan. He'll die of the cold, look how he shakes now.'

'Your garment will be defiled. The Priestess's garment. He is an unbeliever, a man,' Manan blurted, his small eyes wrinkling up as if in pain.

'Then I shall burn the cloak and have another woven! Come on, Manan!'

At that he stooped, obedient, and let the prisoner flop off his back on to the black cloak. The man lay still as death, but the pulse beat heavy in his throat, and now and then a spasm made his body shiver as it lay.

'He should be chained,' said Manan.

'Does he look dangerous?' Arha scoffed; but when Manan pointed out an iron hasp set into the stones, to which the prisoner could be fastened, she let him go fetch a chain and band from the Room of Chains. He grumbled off down the corridors, muttering the directions to himself; he had been to and from the Painted Room before this, but never by himself.

In the light of her single lantern the paintings on the four walls seemed to move, to twitch, the uncouth human forms with great drooping wings, squatting and standing in a timeless dreariness.

She knelt and let water drop, a little at a time, into the prisoner's mouth. At last he coughed, and his hands reached up feebly to the flask. She let him drink. He lay back with his face all wet, besmeared with dust and blood, and muttered something, a word or two in a language she did not know.

Manan returned at last, dragging a length of iron links, a great padlock with its key, and an iron band which fitted around the man's waist and locked there. 'It's not tight enough, he can slip out,' he grumbled as he locked the end link on to the ring set in the wall.

'No, look.' Feeling less fearful of her prisoner now, Arha showed that she could not force her hand between the iron band and the man's ribs. 'Not unless he starves longer than four days.'

'Little mistress,' Manan said plaintively, 'I do not question, but

... what good is he as a slave to the Nameless Ones? He is a man, little one.'

'And you are an old fool, Manan. Come along now, finish your fussing.'

The prisoner watched them with bright, weary eyes.

'Where's his staff, Manan? There. I'll take that; it has magic in it. Oh, and this; this I'll take too,' and with a quick movement she seized the silver chain that showed at the neck of the man's tunic, and tore it off over his head, though he tried to catch her arms and stop her. Manan kicked him in the back. She swung the chain over him, out of his reach. 'Is this your talisman, wizard? Is it precious to you? It doesn't look like much, couldn't you afford a better one? I shall keep it safe for you.' And she slipped the chain over her own head, hiding the pendant under the heavy collar of her woollen robe.

'You don't know what to do with it,' he said, very hoarse, and mispronouncing the words of the Kargish tongue, but clearly enough.

Manan kicked him again, and at that he made a little grunt of pain and shut his eyes.

'Leave off, Manan. Come.'

She left the room. Grumbling, Manan followed.

That night, when all the lights of the Place were out, she climbed the hill again, alone. She filled her flask from the well in the room behind the Throne, and took the water and a big, flat, unleavened cake of buckwheat bread down to the Painted Room in the Labyrinth. She set them just within the prisoner's reach, inside the door. He was asleep, and never stirred. She returned to the Small House, and that night she too slept long and sound.

In early afternoon she returned alone to the Labyrinth. The bread was gone, the flask was dry, the stranger was sitting up, his back against the wall. His face still looked hideous with dirt and scabs, but the expression of it was alert.

She stood across the room from him where he could not possibly reach her, chained as he was, and looked at him. Then she looked away. But there was nowhere particular to look. Something prevented her speaking. Her heart beat as if she were afraid. There was no reason to fear him. He was at her mercy.

'It's pleasant to have light,' he said in the soft but deep voice, which perturbed her.

'What's your name?' she asked, peremptory. Her own voice, she thought, sounded uncommonly high and thin.

'Well, mostly I'm called Sparrowhawk.'

'Sparrowhawk? Is that your name?'

'No.'

'What is your name, then?'

'I cannot tell you that. Are you the One Priestess of the Tombs?'

'Yes.'

'What are you called?'

'I am called Arha.'

'The one who has been devoured – is that what it means?' His dark eyes watched her intently. He smiled a little. 'What is your name?'

'I have no name. Do not ask me questions. Where do you come from?'

'From the Inner Lands, the West.'

'From Havnor?'

It was the only name of a city or island of the Inner Lands that she knew.

'Yes, from Havnor.'

'Why did you come here?'

'The Tombs of Atuan are famous among my people.'

'But you're an infidel, an unbeliever.'

He shook his head. 'Oh no, Priestess. I believe in the powers of darkness! I have met the Unnamed Ones, in other places.'

'What other places?'

'In the Archipelago – the Inner Lands – there are places which belong to the Old Powers of the Earth, like this one. But none so great as this one. Nowhere else have they a temple, and a priestess, and such worship as they receive here.'

'You came to worship them,' she said, jeering.

'I came to rob them,' he said.

She stared at his grave face. 'Braggart!'

'I knew it would not be easy.'

'Easy! It cannot be done. If you weren't an unbeliever you'd know that. The Nameless Ones look after what is theirs.'

'What I seek is not theirs.'

'It's yours, no doubt?'

'Mine to claim.'

'What are you then – a god? A king?' She looked him up and down, as he sat chained, dirty, exhausted. 'You are nothing but a thief!'

He said nothing, but his gaze met hers.

'You are not to look at me!' she said shrilly.

'My lady,' he said, 'I do not mean offence. I am a stranger, and a trespasser. I do not know your ways, nor the courtesies due the Priestess of the Tombs. I am at your mercy, and I ask your pardon if I offend you.'

She stood silent, and in a moment she felt the blood rising to her cheeks, hot and foolish. But he was not looking at her and did not see her blush. He had obeyed, and turned away his dark gaze.

Neither spoke for some while. The painted figures all around watched them with sad, blind eyes.

She had brought a stone jug of water. His eyes kept straying to that, and after a time she said, 'Drink, if you like.'

He hitched himself over to the jug at once, and hefting it as lightly as if it were a wine cup, drank a long, long draught. Then he wet a corner of his sleeve, and cleaned the grime and blood-clot and cobweb off his face and hands as best he could. He spent some while at this, and the girl watched. When he was done he looked better, but his catbath had revealed the scars on one side of his face: old scars long healed, whitish on his dark skin, four parallel ridges from eye to jawbone, as if from the scraping talons of a huge claw.

'What is that?' she said. 'That scar.'

He did not answer at once.

'A dragon?' she said, trying to scoff. Had she not come down here to make mock of her victim, to torment him with his helplessness?

'No, not a dragon.'

'You're not a dragonlord, at least, then.'

'No,' he said rather reluctantly, 'I *am* a dragonlord. But the scars were before that. I told you that I had met with the Dark Powers before, in other places of the earth. This on my face is the mark of one of the kinship of the Nameless Ones. But no longer nameless, for I learned his name, in the end.'

'What do you mean? What name?'

'I cannot tell you that,' he said, and smiled, though his face was grave.

'That's nonsense, fool's babble, sacrilege. They are the Nameless Ones! You don't know what you're talking about –'

'I know even better than you, Priestess,' he said, his voice deepening. 'Look again!' He turned his head so she must see the four terrible marks across his cheek.

'I don't believe you,' she said, and her voice shook.

'Priestess,' he said gently, 'you are not very old; you can't have served the Dark Ones very long.'

'But I have. Very long! I am the First Priestess, the Reborn. I have served my masters for a thousand years and a thousand years before that. I am their servant and their voice and their hands. And I am their vengeance on those who defile the Tombs and look upon what is not to be seen! Stop your lying and your boasting, can't you see that if I say one word my guard will come and cut your head off your shoulders? Or if I go away and lock this door, then nobody will come, ever, and you'll die here in the dark, and those I serve will eat your flesh and eat your soul and leave your bones here in the dust?'

Quietly, he nodded.

She stammered, and finding no more to say, swept out of the room and bolted the door behind her with a clang. Let him think she wasn't coming back! Let him sweat, there in the dark, let him curse and shiver and try to work his foul, useless spells!

But in her mind's eye she saw him stretching out to sleep, as she had seen him do by the iron door, serene as a sheep in a sunny meadow.

She spat at the bolted door, and made the sign to avert defilement, and went almost at a run towards the Undertomb.

While she skirted its wall on the way to the trapdoor in the Hall, her fingers brushed along the fine planes and traceries of rock, like frozen lace. A longing swept over her to light her lantern, to see once more, just for a moment, the time-carven stone, the lovely glitter of the walls. She shut her eyes tight and hurried on.

7. The Great Treasure

NEVER had the rites and duties of the day seemed so many, or so petty, or so long. The little girls with their pale faces and furtive ways, the restless novices, the priestesses whose looks were stern and cool but whose lives were all a secret brangle of jealousies and miseries and small ambitions and wasted passions – all these women, among whom she had always lived and who made up the human world to her, now appeared to her as both pitiable and boring.

But she who served great powers, she the priestess of grim Night, was free of that pettiness. She did not have to care about the grinding meanness of their common life, the days whose one delight was likely to be getting a bigger slop of lamb fat over your lentils than your neighbour got ... She was free of the days altogether. Underground, there were no days. There was always and only night.

And in that unending night, the prisoner : the dark man, practiser of dark arts, bound in iron and locked in stone, waiting for her to come or not to come, to bring him water and bread and life, or a knife and a butcher's bowl and death, just as the whim took her.

She had told no one but Kossil about the man, and Kossil had not told anyone else. He had been in the Painted Room three nights and days now, and still she had not asked Arha about him. Perhaps she assumed that he was dead, and that Arha had had Manan carry the body to the Room of Bones. It was not like Kossil to take anything for granted; but Arha told herself that there was nothing strange about Kossil's silence. Kossil wanted everything kept secret, and hated to have to ask questions. And besides, Arha had told her not to meddle in her business. Kossil was simply obeying.

However, if the man was supposed to be dead, Arha could not ask for food for him. So, apart from stealing some apples and dried onions from the cellars of the Big House, she did without food. She had her morning and evening meals sent to the Small House, pretending she wished to eat alone, and each night took the food down to the Painted Room in the Labyrinth, all but the soups. She was used to fasting for a day or up to four days at a time, and thought nothing about it. The fellow in the Labyrinth ate up her meagre portions of bread and cheese and bean as a toad eats a fly : snap ! it's gone. Clearly he could have done so five or six times over; but he thanked her soberly, as if he were her guest and she his hostess at a table such as she had heard of in tales of feasts at the palace of the Godking, all set with roast meats and buttered loaves and wine in crystal. He was very strange.

'What is it like in the Inner Lands?'

She had brought down a little cross-leg folding stool of ivory, so that she would not have to stand while she questioned him, yet would not have to sit down on the floor, on his level.

'Well, there are many islands. Four times forty, they say, in the Archipelago alone, and then there are the Reaches; no man has ever sailed all the Reaches, nor counted all the lands. And each is different from the others. But the fairest of them all, maybe, is Havnor, the great land at the centre of the world. In the heart of Havnor on a broad bay full of ships is the City Havnor. The towers of the city are built of white marble. The house of every prince and merchant has a tower, so they rise up one above the other. The roofs of the houses are red tile, and all the bridges over the canals are covered in mosaic work, red and blue and green. And the flags of the princes are all colours, flying from the white towers. On the highest of all the towers the Sword of Erreth-Akbe is set, like a pinnacle, skyward. When the sun rises on Havnor it flashes first on that blade and makes it bright, and when it sets the Sword is golden still above the evening, for a while.'

'Who was Erreth-Akbe?' she said, sly.

He looked up at her. He said nothing, but he grinned a little. Then as if on second thoughts he said, 'It's true you would know little of him here. Nothing beyond his coming to the Kargish lands, perhaps. And how much of that tale do you know?'

'That he lost his sorcerer's staff and his amulet and his power —

like you,' she answered. 'He escaped from the High Priest and fled into the west, and dragons killed him. But if he'd come here to the Tombs, there had been no need of dragons.'

'True enough,' said her prisoner.

She wanted no more talk of Erreth-Akbe, sensing a danger in the subject. 'He was a dragonlord, they say. And you say you're one. Tell me, what is a dragonlord?'

Her tone was always jeering, his answers direct and plain, as if he took her questions in good faith.

'One whom the dragons will speak with,' he said, 'that is a dragonlord, or at least that is the centre of the matter. It's not a trick of mastering the dragons, as most people think. Dragons have no masters. The question is always the same, with a dragon : will he talk with you or will he eat you? If you can count upon his doing the former, and not doing the latter, why then you're a dragonlord.'

'Dragons can speak?'

'Surely ! In the Eldest Tongue, the language we men learn so hard and use so brokenly, to make our spells of magic and of patterning. No man knows all that language, or a tenth of it. He has not time to learn it. But dragons live a thousand years ... They are worth talking to, as you might guess.'

'Are there dragons here in Atuan?'

'Not for many centuries, I think, nor in Karego-At. But in your northernmost island, Hur-at-Hur, they say there are still large dragons in the mountains. In the Inner Lands they all keep now to the farthest west, the remote West Reach, islands where no men live and few men come. If they grow hungry, they raid the lands to their east; but that is seldom. I have seen the island where they come to dance together. They fly on their great wings in spirals, in and out, higher and higher over the western sea, like a storming of yellow leaves in autumn.' Full of the vision, his eyes gazed through the black paintings on the walls, through the walls and the earth and the darkness, seeing the open sea stretch unbroken to the sunset, the golden dragons on the golden wind.

'You are lying,' the girl said fiercely, 'you are making it up.'

He looked at her, startled. 'Why should I lie, Arha?'

'To make me feel like a fool, and stupid, and afraid. To make yourself seem wise, and brave, and powerful, and a dragonlord and all this and all that. You've seen dragons dancing, and the towers in Havnor, and you know all about everything. And I know nothing at all and haven't been anywhere. But all you know is lies! You are nothing but a thief and a prisoner, and you have no soul, and you'll never leave this place again. It doesn't matter if there's oceans and dragons and white towers and all that, because you'll never see them again, you'll never even see the light of the sun. All I know is the dark, the night underground. And that's all there really is. That's all there is to know, in the end. The silence, and the dark. You know everything, wizard. But I know one thing – the one true thing!'

He bowed his head. His long hands, copper-brown, were quiet on his knees. She saw the fourfold scar on his cheek. He had gone farther than she into the dark; he knew death better than she did, even death ... A rush of hatred for him rose up in her, choking her throat for an instant. Why did he sit there so defenceless and so strong? Why could she not defeat him?

'This is why I have let you live,' she said suddenly, without the least forethought. 'I want you to show me how the tricks of sorcerers are performed. So long as you have some art to show me, you'll stay alive. If you have none, if it's all foolery and lies, why then I'll have done with you. Do you understand?'

'Yes.'

'Very well. Go on.'

He put his head in his hands a minute, and shifted his position. The iron belt kept him from ever getting quite comfortable, unless he lay down flat.

He raised his face at last and spoke very seriously. 'Listen, Arha. I am a Mage, what you call a sorcerer. I have certain arts and powers. That's true. It's also true that here in the Place of the Old Powers, my strength is very little and my crafts don't avail me. Now I could work illusion for you, and show you all kinds of wonders. That's the least part of wizardry. I could work illusions when I was a child; I can do them even here. But if you believe them, they'll frighten you, and you may wish to kill me if fear makes you angry. And if you disbelieve them, you'll see them as only lies and foolery, as you say; and so I forfeit my life again. And my purpose and desire, at the moment, is to stay alive.'

That made her laugh, and she said, 'Oh, you'll stay alive awhile, can't you see that? You are stupid! All right, show me these illusions. I know them to be false and won't be afraid of them. I wouldn't be afraid if they were real, as a matter of fact. But go ahead. Your precious skin is safe, for tonight, anyhow.'

At that he laughed, as she had a moment ago. They tossed his life back and forth between them like a ball, playing.

'What do you wish me to show you?'

'What can you show me?'

'Anything.'

'How you brag and brag!'

'No,' he said, evidently a little stung. 'I do not. I didn't mean to, anyway.'

'Show me something you think worth seeing. Anything!'

He bent his head and looked at his hands awhile. Nothing happened. The tallow candle in her lantern burned dim and steady. The black pictures on the walls, the bird-winged, flightless figures with eyes painted dull red and white, loomed over him and over her. There was no sound. She sighed, disappointed and somehow grieved. He was weak; he talked great things, but did nothing. He was nothing but a good liar, and not even a good thief. 'Well,' she said at last, and gathered her skirts together to rise. The wool rustled strangely as she moved. She looked down at herself, and stood up in startlement.

The heavy black she had worn for years was gone; her dress was of turquoise-coloured silk, bright and soft as the evening sky. It belled out full from her hips, and all the skirt was embroidered with thin silver threads and seed pearls and tiny crumbs of crystal, so that it glittered softly, like rain in April.

She looked at the magician, speechless.

'Do you like it?'

'Where —'

'It's like a gown I saw a princess wear once, at the Feast of Sun-return in the New Palace in Havnor,' he said, looking at it with satisfaction. 'You told me to show you something worth seeing. I show you yourself.'

'Make it — make it go away.'

'You gave me your cloak,' he said as if in reproach. 'Can I give you nothing? Well, don't worry. It's only illusion; see.'

He seemed not to raise a finger, certainly he said no word; but the blue splendour of silk was gone, and she stood in her own harsh black.

She stood still awhile.

'How do I know,' she said at last, 'that you are what you seem to be?'

'You don't,' said he. 'I don't know what I seem, to you.'

She brooded again. 'You could trick me into seeing you as —' She broke off, for he had raised his hand and pointed upward, the briefest sketch of a gesture. She thought he was casting a spell, and drew back quickly towards the door; but following his gesture, her eyes found high in the dark arching roof the small square that was the spy hole from the treasury of the Twin Gods' temple.

There was no light from the spy hole; she could see nothing, hear no one overhead there; but he had pointed, and his questioning gaze was on her.

Both held perfectly still for some time.

'Your magic is mere folly for the eyes of children,' she said clearly. 'It is trickery and lies. I have seen enough. You will be fed to the Nameless Ones. I shall not come again.'

She took her lantern and went out, and sent the iron bolts home firm and loud. The she stopped there outside the door and stood dismayed. What must she do?

How much had Kossil seen or heard? What had they been saying? She could not remember. She never seemed to say what she had intended to say to the prisoner. He always confused her with his talk about dragons, and towers, and giving names to the Nameless, and wanting to stay alive, and being grateful for her cloak to lie on. He never said what he was supposed to say. She had not even asked him about the talisman, which she still wore, hidden against her breast.

That was just as well, since Kossil had been listening.

Well, what did it matter, what harm could Kossil do? Even as she asked herself the question she knew the answer. Nothing is easier to kill than a caged hawk. The man was helpless, chained there in the cage of stone. The Priestess of the Godking had only to send her servant Duby to throttle him tonight; or if she and Duby did not know the Labyrinth this far, all she need do was blow poison-dust down the spy hole into the Painted Room. She had boxes and phials of evil substances, some to poison food or water, some that drugged the air, and killed, if one breathed that air too long. And he would be dead in the morning, and it would all be over. There would never be a light beneath the Tombs again.

Arha hastened through the narrow ways of stone to the entrance from the Undertomb, where Manan waited for her, squatting patient as an old toad in the dark. He was uneasy about her visits to the prisoner. She would not let him come with her all the way, so they had settled on this compromise. Now she was glad that he was there at hand. Him, at least, she could trust.

'Manan, listen. You are to go to the Painted Room, right now. Say to the man that you're taking him to be buried alive beneath the Tombs.' Manan's little eyes lit up. 'Say that aloud. Unlock the chain, and take him to –' She halted, for she had not yet decided where she could best hide the prisoner.

'To the Undertomb,' said Manan, eagerly.

'No, fool. I said to say that, not to do it. Wait –'

What place was safe from Kossil and Kossil's spies? None but the deepest places underground, the holiest and most hidden places of the domain of the Nameless, where she dared not come. Yet would Kossil not dare almost anything? Afraid of the dark places she might be, but she was one who would subdue her fear to gain her ends. There was no telling how much of the plan of the Laby-rinth she might actually have learned, from Thar, or from the

Arha of the previous life, or even from secret explorations of her own in past years; Arha suspected her of knowing more than she pretended to know. But there was one way she surely could not have learned, the best-kept secret.

'You must bring the man where I lead you, and you must do it in the dark. Then when I bring you back here, you will dig a grave in the Undertomb, and make a coffin for it, and put it in the grave empty, and fill in the earth again, yet so that it can be felt and found if someone sought for it. A deep grave. Do you understand?'

'No,' said Manan, dour and fretful. 'Little one, this trickery is not wise. It is not good. There should not be a man here! There will come a punishment –'

'An old fool will have his tongue cut out, yes! Do you dare tell me what is wise? I follow the orders of the Dark Powers. Follow me!'

'I'm sorry, little mistress, I'm sorry . . .'

They returned to the Painted Room. There she waited outside in the tunnel, while Manan entered and unlocked the chain from the hasp in the wall. She heard the deep voice ask, 'Where now, Manan?' and the husky alto answer, sullenly, 'You are to be buried alive, my mistress says. Under the Tombstones. Get up!' She heard the heavy chain crack like a whip.

The prisoner came out, his arms bound with Manan's leather belt. Manan came behind, holding him like a dog on a short leash, but the collar was around his waist and the leash was iron. His eyes turned to her, but she blew out her candle and without a word set off into the dark. She fell at once into the slow but fairly steady pace that she usually kept when she was not using a light in the Labyrinth, brushing her fingertips very lightly but almost constantly along the walls on either side. Manan and the prisoner followed behind, much more awkward because of the leash, shuffling and stumbling along. But in the dark they must go; for she did not want either of them to learn this way.

A left turn from the Painted Room, and pass one opening; take the next right, and pass the opening to the right; then a long curving way, and a flight of steps down, long, slippery, and much too narrow for normal human feet. Farther than these steps she had never gone.

The air was fouler here, very still, with a sharp odour to it. The directions were clear in her mind, even the tones of Thar's voice speaking them. Down the steps (behind her, the prisoner stumbled in the pitch blackness, and she heard him gasp as Manan kept him afoot with a mighty jerk on the chain), and at the foot of the steps turn at once to the left. Hold the left then for three openings, then the first right, then hold to the right. The tunnels curved and angled, none ran straight. 'Then you must skirt the Pit,' said Thar's voice in the darkness of her mind, 'and the way is very narrow.'

She slowed her step, stooped over, and felt before her with one hand along the floor. The corridor now ran straight for a long way, giving false reassurance to the wanderer. All at once her groping hand, which never ceased to touch and sweep the rock before her, felt nothing. There was a stone lip, an edge : beyond the edge, void. To the right the wall of the corridor plunged down sheer into the pit. To the left there was a ledge or kerb, not much more than a hand's-breadth wide.

'There is a pit. Face the wall to the left, press against it, and go sideways. Slide your feet. Keep hold of the chain, Manan ... Are you on the ledge? It grows narrower. Don't put your weight on your heels. So, I'm past the pit. Reach me your hand. There ...'

The tunnel ran in short zigzags with many side openings. From some of these as they passed the sound of their footsteps echoed in a strange way, hollowly; and stranger than that, a very faint draft could be felt, sucking inward. Those corridors must end in pits like the one they had passed. Perhaps there lay, under this low part of the Labyrinth, a hollow place, a cavern so deep and so vast that the cavern of the Undertomb would be little in comparison, a huge black inward emptiness.

But above that chasm, where they went in the dark tunnels, the corridors grew slowly narrower and lower, until even Arha must stoop. Was there no end to this way?

The end came suddenly: a shut door. Going bent over, and a little faster than usual. Arha ran up against it, jarring her head and hands. She felt for the keyhole, then for the small key on her belt-ring, never used, the silver key with the haft shaped like a dragon. It fitted, it turned. She opened the door of the Great Treasure of the Tombs of Atuan. A dry, sour, stale air sighed outward through the dark.

'Manan, you may not enter here. Wait outside the door.'

'He, but not I?'

'If you enter this room, Manan, you will not leave it. That is the law for all but me. No mortal being but I has ever left this room alive. Will you go in?'

'I will wait outside,' said the melancholy voice in the blackness. 'Mistress, mistress, don't shut the door –'

His alarm so unnerved her that she left the door ajar. Indeed the place filled her with a dull dread, and she felt some mistrust of the prisoner, pinioned though he was. Once inside, she struck her light. Her hands trembled. The lantern candle caught reluctantly; the air was close and dead. In the yellowish flicker that seemed bright after the long passages of night, the treasure room loomed about them, full of moving shadows.

There were six great chests, all of stone, all thick with a fine grey dust like the mould on bread; nothing else. The walls were rough, the roof low. The place was cold, with a deep and airless cold that seemed to stop the blood in the heart. There were no cobwebs, only the dust. Nothing lived here, nothing at all, not even the rare, small, white spiders of the Labyrinth. The dust was thick, and every grain of it might be a day that had passed here where there was no time or light: days, months, years, ages all gone to dust.

'This is the place you sought,' Arha said, and her voice was steady. 'This is the Great Treasure of the Tombs. You have come to it. You cannot ever leave it.'

He said nothing, and his face was quiet, but there was in his eyes something that moved her: a desolation, the look of one betrayed.

'You said you wanted to stay alive. This is the only place I know where you can stay alive. Kossil will kill you or make me kill you, Sparrowhawk. But here she cannot reach.'

Still he said nothing.

'You could never have left the Tombs in any case, don't you see? This is no different. And at least you've come to . . . to the end of your journey. What you sought is here.'

He sat down on one of the great chests, looking spent. The trailing chain clanked harshly on the stone. He looked around at the grey walls and the shadows, then at her.

She looked away from him, at the stone chests. She had no wish at all to open them. She did not care what marvels rotted in them.

'You don't have to wear that chain, in here.' She came to him and unlocked the iron belt, and unbuckled Manan's leather belt from his arms. 'I must lock the door, but when I come I will trust you. You know that you *cannot* leave – that you must not try? I am their vengeance, I do their will; but if I fail them – if you fail my trust – then they will avenge themselves. You must not try to leave the room, by hurting me or tricking me when I come. You must believe me.'

'I will do as you say,' he said gently.

'I'll bring food and water when I can. There won't be much. Water enough, but not much food for a while; I'm getting hungry, do you see? But enough to stay alive on. I may not be able to come back for a day or two days, perhaps even longer. I must get Kossil off the track. But I will come. I promise. Here's the flask. Hoard it, I can't come back soon. But I will come back.'

He raised his face to her. His expression was strange. 'Take care, Tenar,' he said.

8. Names

SHE brought Manan back through the winding ways in the dark, and left him in the dark of the Undertomb, to dig the grave that must be there as proof to Kossil that the thief had indeed been punished. It was late, and she went straight to the Small House to bed. In the night she woke suddenly; she remembered that she had left her cloak in the Painted Room. He would have nothing for warmth in that dank vault but his own short cloak, no bed but the dusty stone. A cold grave, a cold grave, she thought miserably, but she was too weary to wake up fully, and soon slipped back into sleep. She began to dream. She dreamt of the souls of the dead on the walls of the Painted Room, the figures like great bedraggled birds with human hands and feet and faces, squatting in the dust of the dark places. They could not fly. Clay was their food and dust their drink. They were the souls of those not reborn, the ancient peoples and the unbelievers, those whom the Nameless Ones devoured. They squatted all around her in the shadows, and a faint creaking or cheeping sound came from them now and then. One of them came up quite close to her. She was afraid at first and tried to draw away, but could not move. This one had the face of a bird, not a human face; but its hair was golden, and it said in a woman's voice, 'Tenar', tenderly, softly, 'Tenar'.

She woke. Her mouth was stopped with clay. She lay in a stone tomb, underground. Her arms and legs were bound with grave clothes and she could not move or speak.

Her despair grew so great that it burst her breast open and like a bird of fire shattered the stone and broke out into the light of day – the light of day, faint in her windowless room.

Really awake this time, she sat up, worn out by that night's dreaming, her mind befogged. She got into her clothes, and went out to the cistern in the walled courtyard of the Small House. She plunged her arms and face, her whole head, into the icy water until her body jumped with cold and her blood raced. Then flinging back her dripping hair she stood erect and looked up into the morning sky.

It was not long past sunrise, a fair winter's day. The sky was yellowish, very clear. High up, so high he caught the sunlight and burned like a fleck of gold, a bird was circling, a hawk or desert eagle.

'I am Tenar,' she said, not aloud, and she shook with cold, and terror, and exultation, there under the open, sun-washed sky. 'I have my name back. I am Tenar!'

The golden fleck veered westward towards the mountains, out of sight. Sunrise gilded the eaves of the Small House. Sheep bells clanked, down in the folds. The smell of wood-smoke and buckwheat porridge from the kitchen chimneys drifted on the fine, fresh wind.

'I am so hungry . . . How did he know? How did he know my name? . . . Oh, I've got to go eat, I'm so hungry . . .'

She pulled up her hood and ran off to breakfast.

Food, after three days of semi-fasting, made her feel solid, gave her ballast; she didn't feel so wild and light-hearted and frightened. She felt quite capable of handling Kossil, after breakfast.

She came up beside the tall, stout figure on the way out of the dining hall of the Big House, and said in a low voice, 'I have done away with the robber . . . What a fine day it is!'

The cold grey eyes looked sidelong at her from the black hood.

'I thought that the Priestess must abstain from eating for three days after a human sacrifice?'

This was true. Arha had forgotten it, and her face showed that she had forgotten.

'He is not dead yet,' she said at last, trying to feign the indifferent tone that had come so easily a moment ago. 'He is buried alive. Under the Tombs. In a coffin. There will be some air, the coffin isn't sealed, it's a wooden one. It will go quite slowly, the dying. When I know he is dead then I'll begin the fast.'

'How will you know?'

Flustered, she hesitated again. 'I will know. The ... My Masters will tell me.'

'I see. Where is the grave?'

'In the Undertomb. I told Manan to dig it beneath the Smooth Stone.' She must not answer so quickly, in that foolish, appeasing tone; she must be on her dignity with Kossil.

'Alive, in a wooden coffin. That's a risky thing with a sorcerer, mistress. Did you make sure his mouth was stopped so he cannot say charms? Are his hands bound? They can weave spells with the motion of a finger, even when their tongues are cut out.'

'There is nothing to his sorcery, it is mere tricking,' the girl said, raising her voice. 'He is buried, and my Masters are waiting for his soul. And the rest does not concern you, priestess!'

This time she had gone too far. Others could hear; Penthe and a couple of other girls, Duby, and the priestess Mebbeth, all were in hearing distance. The girls were all ears, and Kossil was aware of it.

'All that happens here is my concern, mistress. All that happens in his realm is the concern of the Godking, the Man Immortal, whose servant I am. Even into the places underground and into the hearts of men does he search and look, and none shall forbid him entrance!'

'I shall. Into the Tombs no one comes if the Nameless Ones forbid it. They were before your Godking and they will be after him. Speak softly of them, priestess. Do not call their vengeance on you. They will come into your dreams, they will enter the dark places in your mind, and you will go mad.'

The girl's eyes were blazing. Kossil's face was hidden, drawn back into the black cowl. Penthe and the others watched, terrified and enthralled.

'They are old,' Kossil's voice said, not loud, a whistling thread of sound out of the depths of the cowl. 'They are old. Their worship is forgotten, save in this one place. Their power is gone. They are only shadows. They have no power any more. Do not try to frighten me, Eaten One. You are the First Priestess; does that not mean also that you are the last? ... You cannot trick me. I see into your heart. The darkness hides nothing from me. Take care, Arha!'

She turned and went on, with her massive, deliberate steps, crushing the frost-starred weeds under her heavy, sandalled feet, going to the white-pillared house of the Godking.

The girl stood, slight and dark, as if frozen to earth, in the front courtyard of the Big House. Nobody moved, nothing moved, only Kossil, in all the vast landscape of court and temple, hill and desert plain and mountain.

'May the Dark Ones eat your soul, Kossil!' she shouted in a voice like a hawk's scream, and lifting her arm with the hand stretched out stiff, she brought the curse down on the priestess' heavy back, even as she set foot on the steps of her temple. Kossil staggered, but did not stop or turn. She went on, and entered the Godking's door.

Arha spent that day sitting on the lowest step of the Empty Throne. She dared not go into the Labyrinth; she would not go among the other priestesses. A heaviness filled her, and held her there hour after hour in the cold dusk of the great hall. She stared at the pairs of thick pale columns going off into the gloom at the distant end of the hall, and at the shafts of daylight that slanted in from holes in the roof, and at the thick-curling smoke from the bronze tripod of charcoal near the Throne. She made patterns with the little bones of mice on the marble stair, her head bowed, her mind active and yet as if stupefied. Who am I? she asked herself, and got no answer.

Manan came shuffling down the hall between the double rows of columns, when the light had long since ceased to shaft the hall's darkness, and the cold had grown intense. Manan's doughy face was very sad. He stood at a distance from her, his big hands hanging; the torn hem of his rusty cloak dangled by his heel.

'Little mistress.'

'What is it, Manan?' She looked at him with dull affection.

'Little one, let me do what you said ... what you said was done. He must die, little one. He has bewitched you. She will have revenge. She is old and cruel, and you are too young. You have not strength enough.'

'She can't hurt me.'

'If she killed you, even in the sight of all, in the open, there is none in all the Empire who would dare punish her. She is the High Priestess of the Godking, and the Godking rules. But she won't kill you in the open. She will do it by stealth, by poison, in the night.'

'Then I will be born again.'

Manan twisted his big hands together. 'Perhaps she will not kill you,' he whispered.

'What do you mean?'

'She could lock you into a room in the ... down there ... As you have done with him. And you would be alive for years and years, maybe. For years ... And no new Priestess would be born, for you wouldn't be dead. Yet there would be no Priestess of the Tombs, and the dances of the dark of the moon would not be danced, and the sacrifices would not be made, and the blood not poured out, and the worship of the Dark Ones could be forgotten, forever. She and her Lord would like it to be so.'

'*They* would set me free, Manan.'

'Not while they are wrathful at you, little mistress,' Manan whispered.

'Wrathful?'

'Because of him ... The sacrilege not paid for. Oh little one, little one! They do not forgive!'

She sat in the dust of the lowest step, her head bowed. She looked at a tiny thing that she held on her palm, the minute skull of a mouse. The owls in the rafters over the Throne stirred a little; it was darkening towards night.

'Do not go down into the Labyrinth tonight,' Manan said very low. 'Go to your house, and sleep. In the morning go to Kossil, and tell her that you lift the curse from her. And that will be all. You need not worry. I will show her proof.'

'Proof?'

'That the sorcerer is dead.'

She sat still. Slowly she closed her hand, and the fragile skull cracked and collapsed. When she opened her hand it held nothing but splinters of bone and dust.

'No,' she said. She brushed the dust from her palm.

'He must die. He has put a spell on you. You are lost, Arha!'

'He has not put any spell on me. You're old and cowardly, Manan; you're frightened by old women. How do you think you'd come to him and kill him and get your "proof"? Do you know the way clear to the Great Treasure, that you followed in the dark last night? Can you count the turnings and come to the steps, and then the pit, and then the door? Can you unlock that door? . . . Oh, poor old Manan, your wits are all thick. She has frightened you. You go down to the Small House now, and sleep, and forget all these things. Don't worry me forever with talk of death . . . I'll come later. Go on, go on, old fool, old lump.' She had risen, and gently pushed Manan's broad chest, patting him and pushing him to go. 'Good night, good night!'

He turned, heavy with reluctance, and foreboding, but obedient, and trudged down the long hall under the columns and the ruined roof. She watched him go.

When he had gone some while she turned and went around the dais of the Throne, and vanished into the dark behind it.

9. The Ring of Erreth-Akbe

IN the Great Treasury of the Tombs of Atuan, time did not pass. No light; no life; no least stir of spider in the dust or worm in the cold earth. Rock, and dark, and time not passing.

On the stone lid of a great chest the thief from the Inner Lands lay stretched on his back like the carven figure on a tomb. The dust disturbed by his movements had settled on his clothes. He did not move.

The lock of the door rattled. The door opened. Light broke the dead black and a fresher draught stirred the dead air. The man lay inert.

Arha closed the door and locked it from within, set her lantern on a chest, and slowly approached the motionless figure. She moved timorously, and her eyes were wide, the pupils still fully dilated from her long journey through the dark.

'Sparrowhawk!'

She touched his shoulder, and spoke his name again, and yet again.

He stirred then, and moaned. At last he sat up, face drawn and eyes blank. He looked at her unrecognizing.

'It's I, Arha – Tenar. I brought you water. Here, drink.'

He fumbled for the flask as if his hands were numb, and drank, but not deeply.

'How long has it been?' he asked, speaking with difficulty.

'Two days have passed since you came to this room. This is the third night. I couldn't come earlier. I had to steal the food – here it is –' She got out one of the flat grey loaves from the bag she had brought, but he shook his head.

'I'm not hungry. This . . . this is a deathly place.' He put his head in his hands and sat unmoving.

'Are you cold? I brought the cloak from the Painted Room.'

263

He did not answer.

She put the cloak down and stood gazing at him. She was trembling a little, and her eyes were still black and wide.

All at once she sank down on her knees, bowed over, and began to cry, with deep sobs that wrenched her body, but brought no tears.

He got down stiffly from the chest, and bent over her. 'Tenar –'

'I am not Tenar. I am not Arha. The gods are dead, the gods are dead.'

He laid his hands on her head, pushing back the hood. He began to speak. His voice was soft, and the words were in no tongue she had ever heard. The sound of them came into her heart like rain falling. She grew still to listen.

When she was quiet he lifted her, and set her like a child on the great chest where he had lain. He put his hand on hers.

'Why did you weep, Tenar?'

'I'll tell you. It doesn't matter what I tell you. You can't do anything. You can't help. You're dying too, aren't you? So it doesn't matter. Nothing matters. Kossil, the Priestess of the Godking, she was always cruel, she kept trying to make me kill you. The way I killed those others. And I would not. What right has she? And she defied the Nameless Ones and mocked them, and I set a curse upon her. And since then I've been afraid of her, because it's true what Manan said, she doesn't believe in the gods. She wants them to be forgotten, and she'd kill me while I slept. So I didn't sleep. I didn't go back to the Small House. I stayed in the Hall all last night, in one of the lofts, where the dancing dresses are. Before it was light I went down to the Big House and stole some food from the kitchen, and then I came back to the Hall and stayed there all day. I was trying to find out what I should do. And tonight . . . tonight I was so tired, I thought I could go to a holy place and go to sleep, she might be afraid to come there. So I came down to the Undertomb. That great cave where I first saw you. And . . . and she was there. She must have come in by the red rock door. She was there with a lantern. Scratching in the grave that Manan dug, to see if there was a corpse in it. Like a rat in a graveyard, a great fat black rat, digging. And the light burning in the Holy Place, the dark place. And the Nameless Ones did nothing. They didn't kill her or drive her mad. They are old, as she said. They are dead. They are all gone. I am not a priestess any more.'

The man stood listening, his hand still on hers, his head a little bent. Some vigour had come back into his face and stance, though the scars on his cheek showed livid grey, and there was dust yet on his clothes and hair.

'I went past her, through the Undertomb. Her candle made more shadows than light, and she didn't hear me. I wanted to go into the Labyrinth to get away from her. But when I was in it I kept thinking that I heard her following me. All through the corridors I kept hearing somebody behind me. And I didn't know where to go. I thought I would be safe here, I thought my Masters would protect me and defend me. But they don't, they are gone, they are dead . . .'

'It was for them you wept – for their death? But they are here, Tenar, here!'

'How should you know?' she said listlessly.

'Because every instant since I set foot in the cavern under the Tombstones, I have striven to keep them still, to keep them unaware. All my skills have gone to that, I have spent my strength on it. I have filled these tunnels with an endless net of spells, spells of sleep, of stillness, of concealment, and yet still they are aware of me, half aware, half sleeping, half awake. And even so I am all but worn out, striving against them. This is a most terrible place. One man alone has no hope, here. I was dying of thirst when you gave me water, yet it was not the water alone that saved me. It was the strength of the hands that gave it.' As he said that, he turned her hand palm upward in his own for a moment, gazing at it; then he turned away, walked a few steps about the room, and stopped again before her. She said nothing.

'Did you truly think them dead? You know better in your heart. They do not die. They are dark and undying, and they hate the light: the brief, bright light of our mortality. They are immortal, but they are not gods. They never were. They are not worth the worship of any human soul.'

She listened, her eyes heavy, her gaze fixed on the flickering lantern.

'What have they ever given you, Tenar?'

'Nothing,' she whispered.

'They have nothing to give. They have no power of making. All their power is to darken and destroy. They cannot leave this place; they *are* this place; and it should be left to them. They should not be denied nor forgotten, but neither should they be worshipped. The Earth is beautiful, and bright, and kindly, but that is not all. The Earth is also terrible, and dark, and cruel. The rabbit shrieks dying in the green meadows. The mountains clench their great hands full of hidden fire. There are sharks in the sea, and there is cruelty in men's eyes. And where men worship these things and abase themselves before them, there evil breeds; there places are made in the world where darkness gathers, places given over wholly to the Ones whom we call Nameless, the ancient and holy Powers of the Earth before the Light, the powers of the dark, of ruin, of madness ... I think they drove your priestess Kossil mad a long time ago; I think she has prowled these caverns as she prowls the labyrinth of her own self, and now she cannot see the daylight any more. She tells you that the Nameless Ones are dead; only a lost soul, lost to truth, could believe that. They exist. But they are not your Masters. They never were. You are free, Tenar. You were taught to be a slave, but you have broken free.'

She listened, though her expression did not change. He said no more. They were silent; but it was not the silence that had been in that room before she entered. There was the breathing of two of them now, and the movement of life in their veins, and the burning of the candle in its lantern of tin, a tiny, lively sound.

'How is it that you know my name?'

He walked up and down the room, stirring up the fine dust, stretching his arms and shoulders in an effort to shake off the numbing chill.

'Knowing names is my job. My art. To weave the magic of a thing, you see, one must find its true name out. In my lands we keep our true names hidden all our lives long, from all but those whom we trust utterly; for there is great power, and great peril, in a name. Once, at the beginning of time, when Segoy raised the isles of Earthsea from the ocean deeps, all things bore their own true names. And all doing of magic, all wizardry, hangs still upon the knowledge – the relearning, the remembering – of that true and ancient language of the Making. There are spells to learn, of course, ways to use the words; and one must know the consequences, too. But what a wizard spends his life at is finding out the names of things, and finding out how to find out the names of things.'

'How did you find out mine?'

He looked at her a moment, a deep clear glance across the shadows between them; he hesitated a moment. 'I cannot tell you that. You are like a lantern swathed and covered, hidden away in a dark place. Yet the light shines; they could not put out the light. They could not hide you. As I know the light, as I know you, I know your name, Tenar. That is my gift, my power. I cannot tell you more. But tell me this : what will you do now?'

'I don't know.'

'Kossil has found an empty grave, by now. What will she do?'

'I don't know. If I go back up, she can have me killed. It is death for a High Priestess to lie. She could have me sacrificed on the steps of the Throne if she wanted. And Manan would have to really cut off my head this time, instead of just lifting the sword and waiting for the Dark Figure to stop it. But this time it wouldn't stop. It would come down and cut off my head.'

Her voice was dull and slow. He frowned. 'If we stay here long,' he said, 'you are going to go mad, Tenar. The anger of the Nameless Ones is heavy on your mind. And on mine. It's better now that you're here, much better. But it was a long time before you came, and I've used up most of my strength. No one can withstand the Dark Ones long alone. They are very strong.' He stopped; his voice had sunk low, and he seemed to have lost the thread of his speech. He rubbed his hands over his forehead, and presently went to drink from the flask again. He broke off a hunch of bread and sat down on the chest opposite to eat it.

What he said was true; she felt a weight, a pressure on her mind, that seemed to darken and confuse all thought and feeling. Yet she was not terrified, as she had been coming through the corridors alone. Only the utter silence outside the room seemed terrible. Why was that? She had never feared the silence of the underearth before. But never before had she disobeyed the Nameless Ones, never had she set herself against them.

She gave a little whimpering laugh at last. 'Here we sit on the greatest treasure of the Empire,' she said. 'The Godking would give all his wives to have one chest of it. And we haven't even opened a lid to look.'

'I did,' said the Sparrowhawk, chewing.

'In the dark?'

'I made a little light. The werelight. It was hard to do, here. Even with my staff it would have been hard, and without it, it was like trying to light a fire with wet wood in the rain. But it came at last. And I found what I was after.'

She raised her face slowly to look at him. 'The ring?'

'The half-ring. You have the other half.'

'I have it? The other half was lost –'

'And found. I wore it on a chain around my neck. You took it off, and asked me if I couldn't afford a better talisman. The only talisman better than half the Ring of Erreth-Akbe would be the whole. But then, as they say, half a loaf's better than none. So you now have my half, and I have yours.' He smiled at her across the shadows of the tomb.

'You said when I took it, that I didn't know what to do with it.'

'That was true.'

'And you do know?'

He nodded.

'Tell me. Tell me what it is, the ring, and how you came upon the lost half, and how you came here, and why. All this I must know, then maybe I will see what to do.'

'Maybe you will. Very well. What is it, the Ring of Erreth-Akbe? Well, you can see that it's not precious looking, and it's not even a ring. It's too big. An arm-ring, perhaps, yet it seems too small for that. No man knows who it was made for. Elfarran the Fair wore it once, before the Isle of Soléa was lost beneath the sea; and it was old when she wore it. And at last it came into the hands of Erreth-Akbe ... The metal is hard silver, pierced with nine holes. There's a design like waves scratched on the outside, and nine Runes of Power on the inside. The half you have bears four runes and a bit of another; and mine likewise. The break came right across that one symbol, and destroyed it. It is what's been called, since then, the Lost Rune. The other eight are known to Mages: Pirr that protects from madness and from wind and fire, Ges that gives endurance, and so on. But the broken rune was the one that bound the lands. It was the Bond-Rune, the sign of dominion, the sign of peace. No king could rule well if he did not rule beneath that sign. No one knows how it was written. Since it was lost there have been no great kings in Havnor. There have been princes and tyrants, and wars and quarrelling among all the lands of Earthsea.

'So the wise lords and Mages of the Archipelago wanted the Ring of Erreth-Akbe, that they might restore the lost rune. But at last they gave up sending men out to seek it, since none could take the one half from the Tombs of Atuan, and the other half, which Erreth-Akbe gave to a Kargish king, was lost long since. They said there was no use in the search. That was many hundred years ago.

'Now I come into it thus. When I was a little older than you are now, I was on a ... chase, a kind of hunt across the sea. That which I hunted tricked me, so that I was cast up on a desert isle, not far off the coasts of Karego-At and Atuan, south and west of here. It was a little islet, not much more than a sandbar, with long grassy dunes down the middle, and a spring of salty water, and nothing else.

'Yet two people lived there. An old man and woman; brother and sister, I think. They were terrified of me. They had not seen any other human face for – how long? Years, tens of years. But I was in need, and they were kind to me. They had a hut of driftwood, and a fire. The old woman gave me food, mussels she pulled from the rocks at low tide, dried meat of seabirds they killed by throwing stones. She was afraid of me, but she gave me food. Then when I did nothing to frighten her, she came to trust me, and she showed me her treasure. She had a treasure, too ... It was a little dress. All of silk stuff, with pearls. A little child's dress, a princess' dress. She was wearing uncured sealskin.

'We couldn't talk. I didn't know the Kargish tongue then, and they knew no language of the Archipelago, and little enough of their own. They must have been brought there as young children, and left to die. I don't know why, and doubt that they knew. They knew nothing but the island, the wind, and the sea. But when I left she gave me a present. She gave me the lost half of the Ring of Erreth-Akbe.'

He paused for a while.

'I didn't know it for what it was, no more than she did. The greatest gift of this age of the world, and it was given by a poor old foolish woman in sealskins to a silly lout who stuffed it into his pocket and said "Thanks!" and sailed off . . . Well, so I went on, and did what I had to do. And then other things came up, and I went to the Dragons' Run, westward, and so on. But all the time I kept the thing with me, because I felt a gratitude towards that old woman who had given me the only present she had to give. I put a chain through one of the holes pierced in it, and wore it, and never thought about it. And then one day on Selidor, the Farthest Isle, the land where Erreth-Akbe died in his battle with the dragon Orm – on Selidor I spoke with a dragon, one of that lineage of Orm. He told me what I wore upon my breast.

'He thought it very funny that I hadn't known. Dragons think we are amusing. But they remember Erreth-Akbe; him they speak of as if he were a dragon, not a man.

'When I came back to the Inmost Isles, I went at last to Havnor. I was born on Gont, which lies not far west of your Kargish lands, and I had wandered a good deal since, but I had never been to Havnor. It was time to go there. I saw the white towers, and spoke with the great men, the merchants and the princes and the lords of the ancient domains. I told them what I had. I told them that if they liked, I would go seek the rest of the ring in the Tombs of Atuan, in order to find the Lost Rune, the key to peace. For we need peace sorely in the world. They were full of praise; and one of them even gave me money to provision my boat. So I learned your tongue, and came to Atuan.'

He fell silent, gazing before him into the shadows.

'Didn't the people in our towns know you for a Westerner, by your skin, by your speech?'

'Oh, it's easy to fool people,' he said rather absently, 'if you know the tricks. You make some illusion-changes, and nobody but another Mage will see through them. And you have no wizards or Mages here in the Kargish lands. That's a queer thing. You banished all your wizards long ago, and forbade the practice of the Art Magic; and now you scarcely believe in it.'

'I was taught to disbelieve in it. It is contrary to the teachings of the Priest Kings. But I know that only sorcery could have got you to the Tombs, and in at the door of red rock.'

'Not only sorcery, but good advice also. We use writing more than you, I think. Do you know how to read?'

'No. It is one of the black arts.'

He nodded. 'But a useful one,' he said. 'An ancient unsuccessful thief left certain descriptions of the Tombs of Atuan, and instructions for entering, if one were able to use one of the Great Spells of Opening. All this was written down in a book in the treasury of a prince of Havnor. He let me read it. So I got as far as the great cavern –'

'The Undertomb.'

'The thief who wrote the way to enter thought that the treasure was there, in the Undertomb. So I looked there, but I had the feeling that it must be better hidden farther on in the maze. I knew the entrance to the Labyrinth, and when I saw you, I went to it, thinking to hide in the maze and search it. That was a mistake, of course. The Nameless Ones had hold of me already, bewildering my mind. And since then I have grown only weaker and stupider. One must not submit to them, one must resist, keep one's spirits always strong and certain. I learned that a long time ago. But it's hard to do, here, where they are so strong. They are not gods, Tenar. But they are stronger than any man.'

They were both silent for a long time.

'What else did you find in the treasure chests?' she asked dully.

'Rubbish. Gold, jewels, crowns, swords. Nothing to which any man alive has any claim ... Tell me this, Tenar. How were you chosen to be the Priestess of the Tombs?'

'When the First Priestess dies they go looking all through Atuan for a girl-baby born on the night the Priestess died. And they always find one. Because it is the Priestess reborn. When the child is five they bring it here to the Place. And when it is six it is given to the Dark Ones and its soul is eaten by them. And so it belongs to them, and has belonged to them since the beginning days. And it has no name.'

'Do you believe that?'

'I have always believed it.'

'Do you believe it now?'

She said nothing.

Again the shadowy silence fell between them. After a long time she said, 'Tell me ... tell me about the dragons in the West.'

'Tenar, what will you do? We can't sit here telling each other tales until the candle burns out, and the darkness comes again.'

'I don't know what to do. I am afraid.' She sat erect on the stone chest, her hands clenched one in the other, and spoke loudly like one in pain. She said, 'I am afraid of the dark.'

He answered softly. 'You must make a choice. Either you must leave me, lock the door, go up to your altars and give me to your Masters; then go to the Priestess Kossil and make your peace with her – and that is the end of the story – or, you must unlock the door, and go out of it, with me. Leave the Tombs, leave Atuan, and come with me oversea. And that is the beginning of the story. You must be Arha, or you must be Tenar. You cannot be both.'

The deep voice was gentle and certain. She looked through the shadows into his face, which was hard and scarred, but had in it no cruelty, no deceit.

'If I leave the service of the Dark Ones, they will kill me. If I leave this place I will die.'

'You will not die. Arha will die.'

'I cannot...'

'To be reborn one must die, Tenar. It is not so hard as it looks from the other side.'

'They would not let us get out. Ever.'

'Perhaps not. Yet it's worth trying. You have knowledge, and I have skill, and between us we have...' He paused.

'We have the Ring of Erreth-Akbe.'

'Yes, that. But I thought also of another thing between us. Call it trust ... That is one of its names. It is a very great thing. Though each of us alone is weak, having that we are strong, stronger than the Powers of the Dark.' His eyes were clear and bright in his scarred face. 'Listen, Tenar!' he said. 'I came here a thief, an enemy, armed against you; and you showed me mercy, and trusted me. And I have trusted you from the first time I saw your face, for one moment in the cave beneath the Tombs, beautiful in darkness. You have proved your trust in me. I have made no return. I will give you what I have to give. My true name is Ged. And this is yours to keep.' He had risen, and he held out to her a semi-circle of pierced and carven silver. 'Let the ring be rejoined,' he said.

She took it from his hand. She slipped from her neck the silver chain on which the other half was strung, and took it off the chain. She laid the two pieces in her palm so that the broken edges met, and it looked whole.

She did not raise her face.

'I will come with you,' she said.

10. The Anger of the Dark

WHEN she said that, the man named Ged put his hand over hers that held the broken talisman. She looked up startled, and saw him flushed with life and triumph, smiling. She was dismayed and frightened of him. 'You have set us both free,' he said. 'Alone, no one wins freedom. Come, let's waste no time while we still have time! Hold it out again, for a little.' She had closed her fingers over the pieces of silver, but at his request she held them out again on her hand, the broken edges touching.

He did not take them, but put his fingers on them. He said a couple of words, and sweat suddenly sprang out on his face. She felt a queer little tremor on the palm of her hand, as if a small animal sleeping there had moved. Ged sighed; his tense stance relaxed, and he wiped his forehead.

'There,' he said, and picking up the Ring of Erreth-Akbe he slid it over the fingers of her right hand, narrowly over the breadth of the hand, and up on to the wrist. 'There!' and he regarded it with satisfaction. 'It fits. It must be a woman's arm-ring, or a child's.'

'Will it hold?' she murmured, nervously, feeling the strip of silver slip cold and delicate on her thin arm.

'It will. I couldn't put a mere mending charm on the Ring of Erreth-Akbe, like a village witch mending a kettle. I had to use a Patterning, and make it whole. It is whole now as if it had never been broken. Tenar, we must be gone. I'll bring the bag and flask. Wear your cloak, is there anything more?'

As she fumbled at the door, unlocking it, he said, 'I wish I had my staff,' and she replied, still whispering, 'It's just outside the door. I brought it.'

'Why did you bring it?' he asked curiously.

'I thought of . . . taking you to the door. Letting you go.'

'That was a choice you didn't have. You could keep me a slave,

274

and be a slave; or set me free, and come free with me. Come, little one, take courage, turn the key.'

She turned the dragon-hafted key and opened the door on the low, black corridor. She went out of the Treasury of the Tombs with the ring of Erreth-Akbe on her arm, and the man followed her.

There was a low vibration, not quite a noise, in the rock of the walls and floor and vaulting. It was like distant thunder, like something huge falling a great way off.

The hair on her head rose up, and without stopping to reason she blew out the candle in the tin lantern. She heard the man move behind her; his quiet voice said, so close that his breath stirred her hair. 'Leave the lantern. I can make light if need be. What time is it outside?'

'Long past midnight when I came here.'

'We must go forward then.'

But he did not move. She realized that she must lead him. Only she knew the way out of the Labyrinth, and he waited to follow her. She set out, stooping because the tunnel here was so low, but keeping a pretty good pace. From unseen cross-passages came a cold breath and a sharp, dank odour, the lifeless smell of the huge hollowness beneath them. When the passage grew a little higher and she could stand upright, she went slower, counting her steps as they approached the pit. Lightfooted, aware of all her movements, he followed a short way behind her. The instant she stopped, he stopped.

'Here's the pit,' she whispered. 'I can't find the ledge. No, here. Be careful, I think the stones are coming loose . . . No, no, wait – it's loose –' She sidled back to safety as the stones teetered under her feet. The man caught her arm and held her. Her heart pounded. 'The ledge isn't safe, the stones are coming loose.'

'I'll make a little light, and look at them. Maybe I can mend them with the right word. It's all right, little one.'

She thought how strange it was that he called her what Manan had always called her. And as he kindled a faint glow on the end of his staff, like the glow on rotting wood or a star behind fog, and stepped out on to the narrow way beside the black abyss, she saw the bulk looming in the farther dark beyond him, and knew it for Manan. But her voice was caught in her throat as in a noose, and she could not cry out.

As Manan reached out to push him off his shaky perch into the pit beside him, Ged looked up, saw him, and with a shout of surprise or rage struck out at him with the staff. At the shout the light blazed up white and intolerable, straight in the eunuch's face. Manan flung up one of his big hands to shield his eyes, lunged desperately to catch hold of Ged, and missed, and fell.

He made no cry as he fell. No sound came up out of the black pit, no sound of his body hitting the bottom, no sound of his death, none at all. Clinging perilously to the ledge, kneeling frozen at the lip, Ged and Tenar did not move; listened; heard nothing.

The light was a grey wisp, barely visible.

'Come!' Ged said, holding out his hand; she took it, and in three bold steps he brought her across. He quenched the light. She went ahead of him again to lead the way. She was quite numb and did not think of anything. Only after some time she thought, *Is it right or left?*

She stopped.

Halted a few steps behind her, he said softly, 'What is it?'

'I am lost. Make the light.'

'Lost?'

'I have . . . I have lost count of the turnings.'

'I kept count,' he said, coming a little closer. 'A left turn after the pit; then a right, and a right again.'

'Then the next will be right again,' she said automatically, but she did not move. 'Make the light.'

'The light won't show us the way, Tenar.'

'Nothing will. It is lost. We are lost.'

The dead silence closed in upon her whisper, ate it.

She felt the movement and warmth of the other, close to her in the cold dark. He sought her hand and took it. 'Go on, Tenar. The next turn to the right.'

'Make a light,' she pleaded. 'The tunnels twist so . . .'

'I cannot. I have no strength to spare. Tenar, they are – They know that we left the Treasury. They know that we're past the pit. They are seeking us, seeking our will, our spirit. To quench it, to devour it. I must keep that alight. All my strength is going into that. I must withstand them; with you. With your help. We must go on.'

'There is no way out,' she said, but she took one step forward. Then she took another, hesitant as if beneath each step the black hollow void gaped open, the emptiness under the earth. The warm, hard grip of his hand was on her hand. They went forward.

After what seemed a long time they came to the flight of steps. It had not seemed so steep before, the steps hardly more than slimy notches in the rock. But they climbed it, and then went on a little more rapidly, for she knew that the curving passage went a long way without side turnings after the steps. Her fingers, trailing the left-hand wall for guidance, crossed a gap, an opening to the left. 'Here,' she murmured; but he seemed to hold back, as if something in her movements made him doubtful.

'No,' she muttered in confusion, 'not this, it's the next turn to the left. I don't know. I can't do it. There's no way out.'

'We are going to the Painted Room,' the quiet voice said in the darkness. 'How should we go there?'

'The left turn after this.'

She led on. They made the long circuit, past one false lead, to the passage that branched rightwards towards the Painted Room.

'Straight on,' she whispered, and now the long unravelling of the darkness went better, for she knew these passages towards the iron door and had counted their turns a hundred times; the strange weight that lay upon her mind could not confuse her about them, if she did not try to think. But all the time they were getting nearer and nearer to that which weighed upon her and pressed against her; and her legs were so tired and heavy that she whimpered once or twice with the labour of making them move. And beside her the man would breathe deep, and hold the breath, again and again, like one making a mighty effort with all the strength of his body.

Sometimes his voice broke out, hushed and sharp, in a word or fragment of a word. So they came at last to the iron door; and in sudden terror she put out her hand.

The door was open.

'Quick!' she said, and pulled her companion through. Then, on the further side, she halted.

'Why was it open?' she said.

'Because your Masters need your hands to shut it for them.'

'We are coming to . . .' Her voice failed her.

'To the centre of the darkness. I know. Yet we're out of the Labyrinth. What ways out of the Undertomb are there?'

'Only one. The door you entered doesn't open from within. The way goes through the cavern and up passages to a trapdoor in a room behind the Throne. In the Hall of the Throne.'

'Then we must go that way.'

'But she is there,' the girl whispered. 'There in the Undertomb. In the cavern. Digging in the empty grave. I cannot pass her, oh, I cannot pass her again!'

'She will have gone by now.'

'I cannot go there.'

'Tenar, I hold the roof up over our heads, this moment. I keep the walls from closing in upon us. I keep the ground from opening beneath our feet. I have done this since we passed the pit where their servant waited. If I can hold off the earthquake, do you fear to meet one human soul with me? Trust me, as I have trusted you! Come with me now.'

They went forward.

The endless tunnel opened out. The sense of a greater air met them, an enlarging of the dark. They had entered the great cave beneath the Tombstones.

They started to circle it, keeping to the right-hand wall. Tenar had gone only a few steps when she paused. 'What is it?' she murmured, her voice barely passing her lips. There was a noise in the dead, vast, black bubble of air: a tremor or shaking, a sound heard by the blood and felt in the bones. The time-carven walls beneath her fingers thrummed, thrummed.

'Go forward,' the man's voice said, dry and strained. 'Hurry, Tenar.'

As she stumbled forward she cried out in her mind, which was as dark, as shaken as the subterranean vault, 'Forgive me. O my Masters, O unnamed ones, most ancient ones, forgive me, forgive me !'

There was no answer. There had never been an answer.

They came to the passage beneath the Hall, climbed the stairs, came to the last steps up and the trapdoor at their head. It was shut, as she always left it. She pressed the spring that opened it. It did not open.

'It is broken,' she said. 'It is locked.'

He came up past her and put his back against the trap. It did not move.

'It's not locked, but held down by something heavy.'

'Can you open it?'

'Perhaps. I think she'll be waiting there. Has she men with her?'

'Duby and Uahto, maybe other wardens – men cannot come there –'

'I can't make a spell of opening, and hold off the people waiting up there, and withstand the will of the darkness, all at one time,' said his steady voice, considering. 'We must try the other door then, the door in the rocks, by which I came in. She knows that it can't be opened from within?'

'She knows. She let me try it once.'

'Then she may discount it. Come. Come, Tenar !'

She had sunk down on the stone steps, which hummed and shivered as if a great bowstring were being plucked in the depths beneath them.

'What is it – the shaking?'

'Come,' he said, so steady and certain that she obeyed, and crept back down the passages and stairs, back to the dreadful cavern.

At the entrance so great a weight of blind and dire hatred came pressing down upon her, like the weight of the earth itself, that she cowered and without knowing it cried out aloud, 'They are here ! They are here !'

'Then let them know that we are here,' the man said, and from his staff and hands leapt forth a white radiance that broke as a sea-wave breaks in sunlight, against the thousand diamonds of the roof and walls: a glory of light, through which the two fled, straight across the great cavern, their shadows racing from them into the white traceries and the glittering crevices and the empty, open grave. To the low doorway they ran, down the tunnel, stooping over, she first, he following. There in the tunnel the rocks boomed, and moved under their feet. Yet the light was with them still, dazzling. As she saw the dead rock-face before her, she heard over the thundering of the earth his voice speaking one word, and as she fell to her knees his staff struck down, over her head, against the red rock of the shut door. The rocks burned white as if afire, and burst asunder.

Outside them was the sky, paling to dawn. A few white stars lay high and cool within it.

Tenar saw the stars and felt the sweet wind on her face; but she did not get up. She crouched on hands and knees there between the earth and sky.

The man, a strange dark figure in that half-light before the dawn, turned and pulled at her arm to make her get up. His face was black and twisted like a demon's. She cowered away from him, shrieking in a thick voice not her own, as if a dead tongue moved in her mouth, 'No! No! Don't touch me – leave me – Go!' And she writhed back away from him, into the crumbling, lipless mouth of the Tombs.

His hard grip loosened. He said in a quiet voice, 'By the bond you wear I bid you come, Tenar.'

She saw the starlight on the silver of the ring on her arm. Her eyes on that, she rose, staggering. She put her hand in his, and came with him. She could not run. They walked down the hill. From the black mouth among the rocks behind them issued forth a long, long, groaning howl of hatred and lament. Stones fell about them. The ground quivered. They went on, she with her eyes still fixed on the glimmer of starlight on her wrist.

They were in the dim valley westward of the Place. Now they began to climb; and all at once he bade her turn. 'See –'

She turned, and saw. They were across the valley, on a level now with the Tombstones, the nine great monoliths that stood or lay above the cavern of diamonds and graves. The stones that stood were moving. They jerked, and leaned slowly like the masts of ships. One of them seemed to twitch and rise taller; then a shudder went through it, and it fell. Another fell, smashing crossways on the first. Behind them the low dome of the Hall of the Throne, black against the yellow light in the east, quivered. The walls bulged. The whole great ruinous mass of stone and masonry changed shape like clay in running water, sank in upon itself, and with a roar and sudden storm of splinters and dust slid sideways and collapsed. The earth of the valley rippled and bucked; a kind of wave ran up the hillside, and a huge crack opened among the Tombstones, gaping on the blackness underneath, oozing dust like grey smoke. The stones that still stood upright toppled into it and were swallowed. Then with a crash that seemed to echo off the sky itself, the raw black lips of the crack closed together; and the hills shook once, and grew still.

She looked from the horror of earthquake to the man beside her, whose face she had never seen by daylight. 'You held it back,' she said, and her voice piped like the wind in a reed, after that mighty bellowing and crying of the earth. 'You held back the earthquake, the anger of the dark.'

'We must go on,' he said, turning away from the sunrise and the ruined Tombs. 'I am tired, I am cold . . .' He stumbled as they went, and she took his arm. Neither could go faster than a dragging walk. Slowly, like two tiny spiders on a great wall, they toiled up the immense slope of the hill, until at the top they stood on dry ground yellowed by the rising sun and streaked with the long, sparse shadows of the sage. Before them the western mountains stood, their feet purple, their upper slopes gold. The two paused a moment, then passed over the crest of the hill, out of sight of the Place of the Tombs, and were gone.

11. The Western Mountains

TENAR woke, struggling up from bad dreams, out of places where she had walked so long that all the flesh had fallen from her and she could see the double white bones of her arms glimmer faintly in the dark. She opened her eyes to a golden light, and smelled the pungency of sage. A sweetness came into her as she woke, a pleasure that filled her slowly and wholly till it overflowed, and she sat up, stretching her arms out from the black sleeves of her robe, and looked about her in unquestioning delight.

It was evening. The sun was down behind the mountains that loomed close and high to westward, but its afterglow filled all earth and sky: a vast, clear, wintry sky, a vast, barren, golden land of mountains and wide valleys. The wind was down. It was cold, and absolutely silent. Nothing moved. The leaves of the sagebushes nearby were dry and grey, the stalks of tiny dried-up desert herbs prickled her hand. The huge silent glory of light burned on every twig and withered leaf and stem, on the hills, in the air.

She looked to her left and saw the man lying on the desert ground, his cloak pulled round him, one arm under his head, fast asleep. His face in sleep was stern, almost frowning; but his left hand lay relaxed on the dirt, beside a small thistle that still bore its ragged clock of grey fluff and its tiny defence of spikes and spines. The man and the small desert thistle; the thistle and the sleeping man . . .

He was one whose power was akin to, and as strong as, the Old Powers of the earth: one who talked with dragons, and held off earthquakes with his word. And there he lay asleep on the dirt, with a little thistle growing by his hand. It was very strange. Living, being in the world, was a much greater and stranger thing than she had ever dreamed. The glory of the sky touched his dusty hair, and turned the thistle gold for a little while.

The light was slowly fading. As it did so, the cold seemed to grow intenser minute by minute. Tenar got up and began to gather dry sagebrush, picking up fallen twigs, breaking off the tough branches that grew as gnarled and massive, in their scale, as the limbs of oaks. They had stopped here about noon, when it was warm, and they could go no farther for weariness. A couple of stunted junipers, and the westward slope of the ridge they had just descended, had offered shelter enough; they had drunk a little water from the flask, and lain down, and gone to sleep.

There was a litter of larger branches under the little trees, which she gathered. Scooping out a pit in an angle of earth-embedded rocks, she built up a fire, and lit it with her flint and steel. The tinder of sage leaves and twigs caught at once. Dry branches bloomed into rosy flame, scented with resin. Now it seemed quite dark, all around the fire; and the stars were coming out again in the tremendous sky.

The snap and crack of the flames roused the sleeper. He sat up, rubbing his hands over his grimy face, and at last got up stiffly and came close to the fire.

'I wonder –' he said sleepily.

'I know, but we can't last the night here without a fire. It gets too cold.' After a minute she added, 'Unless you have some magic that would keep us warm, or that would hide the fire . . .'

He sat down by the fire, his feet almost in it, his arms round his knees. 'Brr,' he said. 'A fire is much better than magic. I've put a little illusion about us here; if someone comes by, we might look like sticks and stones to him. What do you think? Will they be following us?'

'I fear it, yet I don't think they will. No one but Kossil knew of your being there. Kossil, and Manan. And they are dead. Surely she was in the Hall when it fell. She was waiting at the trapdoor. And the others, the rest, they must think that I was in the Hall or the Tombs, and was crushed in the earthquake.' She too put her arms round her knees, and shuddered. 'I hope the other buildings didn't fall. It was hard to see from the hill, there was so much dust. Surely all the temples and houses didn't fall, the Big House where all the girls sleep.'

'I think not. It was the Tombs that devoured themselves. I saw a gold roof of some temple as we turned away; it still stood. And there were figures down the hill, people running.'

'What will they say, what will they think ... Poor Penthe! She might have to become the High Priestess of the Godking now. And it was always she who wanted to run away. Not I. Maybe now she'll run away.' Tenar smiled. There was a joy in her that no thought nor dread could darken, that same sure joy that had risen in her, waking in the golden light. She opened her bag and took out two small, flat loaves; she handed one across the fire to Ged, and bit into the other. The bread was tough, and sour, and very good to eat.

They munched together in silence awhile.

'How far are we from the sea?'

'It took me two nights and two days coming. It'll take us longer going.'

'I'm strong,' she said.

'You are. And valiant. But your companion's tired,' he said with a smile. 'And we haven't any too much bread.'

'Will we find water?'

'Tomorrow, in the mountains.'

'Can you find food for us?' she asked, rather vaguely and timidly.

'Hunting takes time, and weapons.'

'I meant, with, you know, spells.'

'I can call a rabbit,' he said, poking the fire with a twisted stick of juniper. 'The rabbits are coming out of their holes all around us, now. Evening's their time. I could call one by name, and he'd come. But would you catch and skin and cook a rabbit that you'd called to you thus? Perhaps if you were starving. But it would be a breaking of trust, I think.'

'Yes. I thought, perhaps you could just ...'

'Summon up a supper,' he said. 'Oh, I could. On golden plates, if you like. But that's illusion, and when you eat illusions you end up hungrier than before. It's about as nourishing as eating your own words.' She saw his white teeth flash a moment in the firelight.

'Your magic is peculiar,' she said, with a little dignity of equals, Priestess addressing Mage. 'It appears to be useful only for large matters.'

He laid more wood on the fire, and it flared up in a juniper-scented fireworks of sparks and crackles.

'Can you really call a rabbit?' Tenar inquired suddenly.

'Do you want me to?'

She nodded.

He turned away from the fire and said softly into the immense and starlit dark, 'Kebbo . . . O kebbo . . .'

Silence. No sound. No motion. Only presently, at the very edge of the flickering firelight, a round eye like a pebble of jet, very near the ground. A curve of furry back; an ear, long, alert, upraised.

Ged spoke again. The ear flicked, gained a sudden partner-ear out of the shadow; then as the little beast turned Tenar saw it entire for an instant, the small, soft, lithe hop of it returning unconcerned to its business in the night.

'Ah!' she said, letting out her breath. 'That's lovely.' Presently she asked, 'Could I do that?'

'Well –'

'It is a secret,' she said at once, dignified again.

'The rabbit's *name* is a secret. At least, one should not use it lightly for no reason. But what is not a secret, but rather a gift, or a mystery, do you see, is the power of calling.'

'Oh,' she said, 'that you have. I know!' There was a passion in her voice, not hidden by pretended mockery. He looked at her and did not answer.

He was indeed still worn out by his struggle against the Nameless Ones; he had spent his strength in the quaking tunnels. Though he had won, he had little spirit left for exultation. He soon curled up again, as near the fire as he could get, and slept.

Tenar sat feeding the fire and watching the blaze of the winter constellations from horizon to horizon until her head grew giddy with splendour and silence, and she dozed off.

They both woke. The fire was dead. The stars she had watched were now far over the mountains and new ones had risen in the east. It was the cold that woke them, the dry cold of the desert night, the wind like a knife of ice. A veil of cloud was coming over the sky from the southwest.

The gathered firewood was almost gone. 'Let's walk,' Ged said, 'it's not long till dawn.' His teeth chattered so that she could hardly understand him. They set out, climbing the long slow slope westward. The bushes and rocks showed black in starlight, and it was as easy to walk as in the day. After a cold first while, the walking warmed them; they stopped crouching and shivering, and began to go easier. So by sunrise, they were on the first rise of the western mountains, which had walled in Tenar's life till then.

They stopped in a grove of trees whose golden, quivering leaves still clung to the boughs. He told her they were aspens; she knew no trees but juniper, and the sickly poplars by the river-springs, and the forty apple trees of the orchard of the Place. A small bird among the aspens said 'dee, dee', in a small voice. Under the trees ran a stream, narrow but powerful, shouting, muscular over its rocks and falls, too hasty to freeze. Tenar was almost afraid of it. She was used to the desert where things are silent and move slowly: sluggish rivers, shadows of clouds, vultures circling.

They divided a piece of bread and a last crumbling bit of cheese for breakfast, rested a little, and went on.

By evening they were up high. It was overcast and windy, freezing weather. They camped in the valley of another stream, where there was plenty of wood, and this time built up a sturdy fire of logs by which they could keep fairly warm.

Tenar was happy. She had found a squirrel's cache of nuts, exposed by the falling of a hollow tree: a couple of pounds of fine walnuts and a smooth-shelled kind that Ged, not knowing the Kargish name, called *ubir*. She cracked them one by one between a flat stone and a hammerstone, and handed every second nutmeat to the man.

'I wish we could stay here,' she said, looking down at the windy, twilit valley between the hills. 'I like this place.'

'This is a good place,' he agreed.

'People would never come here.'

'Not often ... I was born in the mountains,' he said, 'on the Mountain of Gont. We shall pass it, sailing to Havnor, if we take the northern way. It's beautiful to see it in winter, rising all white out of the sea, like a greater wave. My village was by just such a stream as this one. Where were you born, Tenar?'

'In the north of Atuan, in Entat, I think. I can't remember it.'

'They took you so young?'

'I was five. I remember a fire on a hearth, and ... nothing else.'

He rubbed his jaw, which though it had acquired a sparse beard, was at least clean; despite the cold, both of them had washed in the mountain streams. He rubbed his jaw and looked thoughtful and severe. She watched him, and never could she have said what was in her heart as she watched him, in the firelight, in the mountain dusk.

'What are you going to do in Havnor?' he said, asking the question of the fire, not of her. 'You are – more than I had realized – truly reborn.'

She nodded, smiling a little. She felt newborn.

'You should learn the language, at least.'

'Your language?'

'Yes.'

'I'd like to.'

'Well, then. This is *kabat*,' and he tossed a little stone into the lap of her black robe.

'Kabat. Is that in the dragon-tongue?'

'No, no. You don't want to work spells, you want to talk with other men and women!'

'But what is a pebble in the dragon's tongue?'

'*Tolk*,' he said. 'But I am not making you my apprentice sorcerer. I'm teaching you the language people speak in the Archipelago, the Inner Lands. I had to learn your language before I came here.'

'You speak it oddly.'

'No doubt. Now, *arkemmi kabat*,' and he held out his hands for her to give him the pebble.

'Must I go to Havnor?' she said.

'Where else would you go, Tenar?'

She hesitated.

'Havnor is a beautiful city,' he said. 'And you bring it the ring, the sign of peace, the lost treasure. They'll welcome you in Havnor as a princess. They'll do you honour for the great gift you bring them, and bid you welcome, and make you welcome. They are a noble and generous people in that city. They'll call you the White Lady because of your fair skin, and they'll love you the more because you are so young. And because you are beautiful. You'll have a hundred dresses like that one I showed you by illusion, but real ones. You'll meet with praise and gratitude, and love. You who have known nothing but solitude and envy and the dark.'

'There was Manan,' she said, defensive, her mouth trembling just a little. 'He loved me and was kind to me, always. He protected me as well as he knew how, and I killed him for it; he fell into the black pit. I don't want to go to Havnor. I don't want to go there. I want to stay here.'

'Here – in Atuan?'

'In the mountains. Where we are now.'

'Tenar,' he said in his grave, quiet voice, 'we'll stay then. I haven't my knife, and if it snows it will be hard. But so long as we can find food –'

'No. I know we can't stay. I'm merely being foolish,' Tenar said, and got up, scattering walnut shells, to lay new wood on the fire. She stood thin and very straight in her torn, dirt-stained gown and cloak of black. 'All I know is of no use now,' she said, 'and I haven't learned anything else. I will try to learn.'

Ged looked away, wincing as if in pain.

Next day they crossed the summit of the tawny range. In the pass a hard wind blew, with snow in it, stinging and blinding. It was not until they had come down a long way on the other side, out from under the snow clouds of the peaks, that Tenar saw the land beyond the mountain wall. It was all green – green of pines, of grasslands, of sown fields and fallows. Even in the dead of winter, when the thickets were bare and the forest full of grey boughs, it was a green land, humble and mild. They looked down on it from a high, rocky slant of the mountainside. Wordless, Ged pointed to the west, where the sun was getting low behind a thick cream and roil of clouds. The sun itself was hidden, but there was a glitter on the horizon, almost like the dazzle of the crystal walls of the Undertomb, a kind of joyous shimmering off on the edge of the world.

'What is that?' the girl said and he: 'The sea.'

Shortly afterwards, she saw a less wonderful thing than that, but wonderful enough. They came on a road, and followed it; and it brought them by dusk into a village: ten or a dozen houses strung along the road. She looked at her companion in alarm when she realized they were coming among men. She looked, and did not see him. Beside her, in Ged's clothing, and with his gait, and in his shoes, strode another man. He had a white skin, and no beard. He glanced at her; his eyes were blue. He winked.

'Will I fool 'em?' he said. 'How are your clothes?'

She looked down at herself. She had on a countrywoman's brown skirt and jacket, and a large red woollen shawl.

'Oh,' she said, stopping short. 'Oh, you are – you *are* Ged!' As she said his name she saw him perfectly clearly, the dark, scarred face she knew, the dark eyes; yet there stood the milk-faced stranger.

'Don't say my true name before others. Nor will I say yours. We are brother and sister, come from Tenacbah. And I think I'll ask for a bite of supper if I see a kindly face.' He took her hand and they entered the village.

They left it next morning with full stomachs, after a pleasant sleep in a hayloft.

'Do Mages often beg?' asked Tenar, on the road between green fields, where goats and little spotted cattle grazed.

'Why do you ask?'

'You seemed used to begging. In fact you were good at it.'

'Well, yes. I've begged all my life, if you look at it that way. Wizards don't own much, you know. In fact nothing but their staff and clothing, if they wander. They are received and given food and shelter, by most people, gladly. They do make some return.'

'What return?'

'Well, that woman in the village. I cured her goats.'

'What was wrong with them?'

'They both had infected udders. I used to herd goats when I was a boy.'

'Did you tell her you'd cured them?'

'No. How could I? Why should I?'

After a pause she said, 'I see your magic is not good only for large things.'

'Hospitality,' he said, 'kindness to a stranger, that's a very large, thing. Thanks are enough, of course. But I was sorry for the goats.'

In the afternoon they came by a large town. It was built of clay brick, and walled round in the Kargish fashion, with overhanging battlements, watchtowers at the four corners, and a single gate, under which drovers were herding a big flock of sheep. The red tile roofs of a hundred or more houses poked up over the walls of yellowish brick. At the gate stood two guards in the red-plumed helmets of the Godking's service. Tenar had seen men in such helmets come, once a year or so, to the Place, escorting offerings of slaves or money to the Godking's temple. When she told Ged that, as they passed by outside the walls, he said, 'I saw them too, as a boy. They came raiding to Gont. They came into my village, to plunder it. But they were driven off. And there was a battle down by Armouth, on the shore; many men were killed, hundreds, they say. Well, perhaps now that the ring is rejoined and the Lost Rune remade, there will be no more such raiding and killing between the Kargish Empire and the Inner Lands.'

'It would be foolish if such things went on,' said Tenar. 'What would the Godking ever do with so many slaves?'

Her companion appeared to ponder this awhile. 'If the Kargish lands defeated the Archipelago, you mean?'

She nodded.

'I don't think that would be likely to happen.'

'But look how strong the Empire is – that great city, with its walls, and all its men. How could your lands stand against them, if they attacked?'

'That is not a very big city,' he said cautiously and gently. 'I too would have thought it tremendous, when I was new from my mountain. But there are many, many cities in Earthsea, among which this is only a town. There are many, many lands. You will see them, Tenar.'

She said nothing. She trudged along the road, her face set.

'It is marvellous to see them: the new lands rising from the sea as your boat comes towards them. The farmlands and forests, the cities with their harbours and palaces, the market-places where they sell everything in the world.'

She nodded. She knew he was trying to hearten her, but she had left joy up in the mountains, in the twilit valley of the stream. There was a dread in her now that grew and grew. All that lay ahead of her was unknown. She knew nothing but the desert and the Tombs. What good was that? She knew the turning of a ruined maze, she knew the dances danced before a fallen altar. She knew nothing of forests, or cities, or the hearts of men.

She said suddenly, 'Will you stay with me there?'

She did not look at him. He was in his illusory disguise, a white-skinned Kargish countryman, and she did not like to see him so. But his voice was unchanged, the same voice that had spoken in the darkness of the Labyrinth.

He was slow to answer. 'Tenar, I go where I am sent. I follow my calling. It has not yet let me stay in any land for long. Do you see that? I do what I must do. Where I go, I must go alone. So long as you need me, I'll be with you in Havnor. And if you ever need me again, call me. I will come. I would come from my grave if you called me, Tenar! But I cannot stay with you.'

She said nothing. After a while he said, 'You will not need me long, there. You will be happy.'

She nodded, accepting, silent.

They went on side by side towards the sea.

12. *Voyage*

HE had hidden his boat in a cave on the side of a great rocky headland, Cloud Cape it was called by the villagers nearby, one of whom gave them a bowl of fish stew for their supper. They made their way down the cliffs to the beach in the last light of the grey day. The cave was a narrow crack that went back into the rock for about thirty feet; its sandy floor was damp, for it lay just above the high-tide mark. Its opening was visible from sea, and Ged said they should not light a fire lest the night-fishermen out in their small craft along shore should see it and be curious. So they lay miserably on the sand, which seemed so soft between the fingers and was rock-hard to the tired body. And Tenar listened to the sea, a few yards below the cave mouth, crashing and sucking and booming on the rocks, and the thunder of it down the beach eastward for miles. Over and over and over it made the same sounds, yet never quite the same. It never rested. On all the shores of all the lands in all the world, it heaved itself in these unresting waves, and never ceased, and never was still. The desert, the mountains: they stood still. They did not cry out forever in a great, dull voice. The sea spoke forever, but its language was foreign to her. She did not understand.

In the first grey light, when the tide was low, she roused from uneasy sleep and saw the wizard go out of the cave. She watched him walk, barefoot and with belted cloak, on the black-haired rocks below, seeking something. He came back, darkening the cave as he entered. 'Here,' he said, holding out a handful of wet, hideous things like purple rocks with orange lips.

'What are they?'

'Mussels, off the rocks. And those two are oysters, even better. Look – like this.' With the little dagger from her keyring, which she had lent him up in the mountains, he opened a shell and ate the orange mussel with seawater as its sauce.

'You don't even cook it? You eat it alive!'

She would not look at him while he, shamefaced but undeterred, went on opening and eating the shellfish one by one.

When he was done, he went back into the cave to the boat, which lay prow forward, kept from the sand by several long driftwood logs. Tenar had looked at the boat the night before, mistrustfully and without comprehension. It was much larger than she had thought boats were, three times her own length. It was full of objects she did not know the use of, and it looked dangerous. On either side of its nose (which is what she called the prow) an eye was painted; and in her half-sleep she had constantly felt the boat staring at her.

Ged rummaged about inside it a moment and came back with something: a packet of hard bread, well wrapped to keep dry. He offered her a large piece.

'I'm not hungry.'

He looked into her sullen face.

He put the bread away, wrapping it as before, and then sat down in the mouth of the cave. 'About two hours till the tide's back in,' he said. 'Then we can go. You had a restless night, why don't you sleep now.'

'I'm not sleepy.'

He made no answer. He sat there, in profile to her, cross-legged in the dark arch of rocks; the shining heave and movement of the sea was beyond him as she watched him from deeper in the cave. He did not move. He was still as the rocks themselves. Stillness spread out from him, like rings from a stone dropped in the water. His silence became not absence of speech, but a thing in itself, like the silence of the desert.

After a long time Tenar got up and came to the mouth of the cave. He did not move. She looked down at his face. It was as if cast in copper – rigid, the dark eyes not shut, but looking down, the mouth serene.

He was as far beyond her as the sea.

Where was he now, on what way of the spirit did he walk? She could never follow him.

He had made her follow him. He had called her by her name, and she had come crouching to his hand, as the little wild desert rabbit had come to him out of the dark. And now that he had the ring, now that the Tombs were in ruin and their priestess forsworn forever, now he didn't need her, and went away where she could not follow. He would not stay with her. He had fooled her, and would leave her desolate.

She reached down and with one swift gesture plucked from his belt the little steel dagger she had given him. He moved no more than a robbed statue.

The dagger blade was only four inches long, sharp on one side; it was the miniature of a sacrificial knife. It was part of the garments of the Priestess of the Tombs, who must wear it along with the ring of keys, and a belt of horsehair, and other items some of which had no known purpose. She had never used the dagger for anything, except that in one of the dances performed at dark of the moon she would throw and catch it before the Throne. She had liked that dance; it was a wild one, with no music but the drumming of her own feet. She had used to cut her fingers, practising it, till she got the trick of catching the knife handle every time. The little blade was sharp enough to cut a finger to the bone, or to cut the arteries of a throat. She would serve her Masters still, though they had betrayed her and forsaken her. They would guide and drive her hand in the last act of darkness. They would accept the sacrifice.

She turned upon the man, the knife held back in her right hand behind her hip. As she did so he raised his face slowly and looked at her. He had the look of one come from a long way off, one who has seen terrible things. His face was calm but full of pain. As he gazed up at her and seemed to see her more and more clearly, his expression cleared. At last he said, 'Tenar', as if in greeting, and reached up his hand to touch the band of pierced and carven silver on her wrist. He did this as if reassuring himself, trustingly. He did not pay attention to the dagger in her hand. He looked away, at the waves, which heaved deep over the rocks below, and said with effort, 'It's time . . . Time we were going.'

At the sound of his voice the fury left her. She was afraid.

'You'll leave them behind, Tenar. You're going free now,' he said, getting up with sudden vigour. He stretched, and belted his cloak tight again. 'Give me a hand with the boat. She's up on logs, for rollers. That's it, push ... again. There, there, enough. Now be ready to hop in when I say "hop". This is a tricky place to launch from – once more. There! In you go!' – and leaping in after her, he caught her as she overbalanced, sat her down in the bottom of the boat, braced his legs wide, and standing to the oars sent the boat shooting out on an ebb wave over the rocks, out past the roaring foam-drenched head of the cape, and so to sea.

He shipped the oars when they were well away from shoal water, and stepped the mast. The boat looked very small, now that she was inside it and the sea was outside it.

He put up the sail. All the gear had a look of long, hard use, though the dull red sail was patched with great care and the boat was as clean and trim as could be. They were like their master: they had gone far, and had not been treated gently.

'Now,' he said, 'now we're away, now we're clear, we're clean gone, Tenar. Do you feel it?'

She did feel it. A dark hand had let go its lifelong hold upon her heart. But she did not feel joy, as she had in the mountains. She put her head down in her arms and cried, and her cheeks were salt and wet. She cried for the waste of her years in bondage to a useless evil. She wept in pain, because she was free.

What she had begun to learn was the weight of liberty. Freedom is a heavy load, a great and strange burden for the spirit to under-take. It is not easy. It is not a gift given, but a choice made, and the choice may be a hard one. The road goes upward towards the light; but the laden traveller may never reach the end of it.

Ged let her cry, and said no word of comfort; nor when she was done with tears and sat looking back towards the low blue land of Atuan, did he speak. His face was stern and alert, as if he were alone; he saw to the sail and the steering, quick and silent, looking always ahead.

In the afternoon he pointed rightward of the sun, towards which they now sailed. 'That is Karego-At,' he said, and Tenar following his gesture saw the distant loom of hills like clouds, the great island of the Godking. Atuan was out of sight behind them. Her heart was very heavy. The sun beat in her eyes like a hammer of gold.

Supper was dry bread, and dried smoked fish, which tasted vile to Tenar, and water from the boat's cask, which Ged had filled at a stream on Cloud Cape beach the evening before. The winter night came down soon and cold upon the sea. Far off to northward they saw for a while the tiny glitter of lights, yellow firelight in distant villages on the shore of Karego-At. These vanished in a haze that rose up from the ocean, and they were alone in the starless night over deep water.

She had curled up in the stern; Ged lay down in the prow, with the water cask for a pillow. The boat moved on steadily, the low swells slapping her sides a little, though the wind was only a faint breath from the south. Out here, away from the rocky shores, the sea too was silent; only as it touched the boat did it whisper a little.

'If the wind is from the south,' Tenar said, whispering because the sea did, 'doesn't the boat sail north?'

'Yes, unless we tack. But I've put the mage-wind in her sail, to the west. By tomorrow morning we should be out of Kargish waters. Then I'll let her go by the world's wind.'

'Does it steer itself?'

'Yes,' Ged replied with gravity, 'given the proper instructions. She doesn't need many. She's been in the open sea, beyond the farthest isle of the East Reach; she's been to Selidor where Erreth-Akbe died, in the farthest West. She's a wise crafty boat, my *Lookfar*. You can trust her.'

In the boat moved by magic over the great deep, the girl lay looking up into the dark. All her life she had looked into the dark; but this was a vaster darkness, this night on the ocean. There was no end to it. There was no roof. It went on out beyond the stars. No earthly Powers moved it. It had been before light, and would be after. It had been before life, and would be after. It went on beyond evil.

In the dark, she spoke : 'The little island, where the talisman was given you, is that in this sea?'

'Yes,' his voice answered out of the dark. 'Somewhere. To the south, perhaps. I could not find it again.'

'I know who she was, the old woman who gave you the ring.'

'You know?'

'I was told the tale. It is part of the knowledge of the First Priestess. Thar told it to me, first when Kossil was there, then more fully when we were alone; it was the last time she talked to me before she died. There was a noble house in Hupun who fought against the rise of the High Priests in Awabath. The founder of the house was King Thoreg, and among the treasures he left his descendants was the half-ring, which Erreth-Akbe had given him.'

'That indeed is told in the *Deed of Erreth-Akbe*. It says ... in your tongue it says, "When the ring was broken, half remained in the hands of the High Priest Intathin, and half in the hero's hand. And the High Priest sent the broken half to the Nameless, to the Ancient of the Earth in Atuan, and it went into the dark, into the lost places. But Erreth-Akbe gave the broken half into the hands of the maiden Tiarath, daughter of the wise king, saying : 'Let it remain in the light in the maiden's dowry, let it remain in this land until it be rejoined.' So spoke the hero before he sailed to the west." '

'So it must have gone from daughter to daughter of that house, over all the years. It was not lost as your people thought. But as the High Priests made themselves into the Priest-Kings, and then when the Priest-Kings made the Empire and began to call themselves God-kings, all this time the house of Thoreg grew poorer and weaker. And at last, so Thar told me, there were only two of the lineage of Thoreg left, little children, a boy and a girl. The Godking in Awabath then was the father of him who rules now. He had the children stolen from their palace in Hupun. There was a prophecy that one of the descendants of Thoreg of Hupun would bring about the fall of the Empire in the end, and that frightened him. He had the children stolen away, and taken to a lonely isle somewhere out in the middle of the sea, and left there with nothing but the clothes they wore and a little food. He feared to kill them by knife or strangling or poison; they were of kingly blood, and murder of kings brings a curse even on the gods. They were named Ensar and Anthil. It was Anthil who gave you the broken ring.'

He was silent a long while. 'So the story comes whole,' he said at last, 'even as the ring is made whole. But it is a cruel story, Tenar. The little children, that isle, the old man and woman I saw ... They scarcely knew human speech.'

'I would ask you something.'

'Ask.'

'I do not wish to go to the Inner Lands, to Havnor. I do not belong there, in the great cities among foreign men. I do not belong to any land. I betrayed my own people. I have no people. And I have done a very evil thing. Put me alone on an island, as the king's children were left, on a lone isle where there are no people, where there is no one. Leave me, and take the ring to Havnor. It is yours, not mine. It has nothing to do with me. Nor have your people. Let me be by myself!'

Slowly, gradually, yet startling her, a light dawned like a small moonrise in the blackness before her : the wizardly light that came at his command. It clung to the end of his staff, which he held upright as he sat facing her in the prow. It lit the bottom of the sail, and the gunwales, and the planking, and his face, with a silvery glow. He was looking straight at her.

'What evil have you done, Tenar?'

'I ordered that three men be shut in a room beneath the Throne, and starved to death. They died of hunger and thirst. They died, and are buried there in the Undertomb. The Tombstones fell on their graves.' She stopped.

'Is there more?'

'Manan.'

'That death is on my soul.'

'No. He died because he loved me, and was faithful. He thought he was protecting me. He held the sword above my neck. When I was little he was kind to me – when I cried –' She stopped again, for the tears rose hard in her, yet she would cry no more. Her hands were clenched on the black folds of her dress. 'I was never kind to him,' she said. 'I will not go to Havnor. I will not go with you. Find some isle where no one comes, and put me there, and leave me. The evil must be paid for. I am *not* free.'

The soft light, greyed by sea mist, glimmered between them.

'Listen, Tenar. Heed me. You were the vessel of evil. The evil is poured out. It is done. It is buried in its own tomb. You were never made for cruelty and darkness; you were made to hold light, as a lamp burning holds and gives its light. I found the lamp unlit; I won't leave it on some desert island like a thing found and cast away. I'll take you to Havnor and say to the princes of Earthsea, "Look! In the place of darkness I found the light, her spirit. By her an old evil was brought to nothing. By her I was brought out of the grave. By her the broken was made whole, and where there was hatred there will be peace." '

'I will not,' Tenar said in agony. 'I cannot. It's not true !'

'And after that,' he went on quietly, 'I'll take you away from the princes and the rich lords; for it's true that you have no place there. You are too young, and too wise. I'll take you to my own land, to Gont where I was born, to my old master Ogion. He's an old man now, a very great Mage, a man of quiet heart. They call him "the Silent". He lives in a small house on the great cliffs of Re Albi, high over the sea. He keeps some goats, and a garden patch. In autumn he goes wandering over the island, alone, in the forests, on the mountainsides, through the valleys of the rivers. I lived there once with him, when I was younger than you are now. I didn't stay long, I hadn't the sense to stay. I went off seeking evil and sure enough I found it ... But you come escaping evil; seeking freedom; seeking silence for a while, until you find your own way. There you will find kindness and silence, Tenar. There the lamp will burn out of the wind awhile. Will you do that?'

The sea mist drifted grey between their faces. The boat lifted lightly on the long waves. Around them was the night and under them the sea.

'I will,' she said with a long sigh. And after a long time, 'Oh, I wish it were sooner ... that we could go there now ...'

'It won't be long, little one.'

'Will you come there, ever?'

'When I can I will come.'

The light had died away; it was all dark around them.

They came, after the sunrises and sunsets, the still days and the icy winds of their winter voyage, to the Inmost Sea. They sailed the crowded lanes among great ships, up the Ebavnor Straits and into the bay that lies locked in the heart of Havnor, and across the bay to Havnor Great Port. They saw the white towers, and all the city white and radiant in snow. The roofs of the bridges and the red roofs of the houses were snow-covered, and the rigging of the hundred ships in the harbour glittered with ice in the winter sun. News of their coming had run ahead of them, for *Lookfar's* patched red sail was known in those seas; a great crowd had gathered on the snowy quays, and coloured pennants cracked above the people in the bright, cold wind.

Tenar sat in the stern, erect, in her ragged cloak of black. She looked at the ring around her wrist, then at the crowded, many-coloured shore and the palaces and the high towers. She lifted up her right hand, and sunlight flashed on the silver of the ring. A cheer went up, faint and joyous on the wind, over the restless water. Ged brought the boat in. A hundred hands reached to catch the rope he flung up to the mooring. He leapt up on to the pier and turned, holding out his hand to her, 'Come!' he said smiling, and she rose, and came. Gravely she walked beside him up the white streets of Havnor, holding his hand, like a child coming home.

THE FARTHEST SHORE

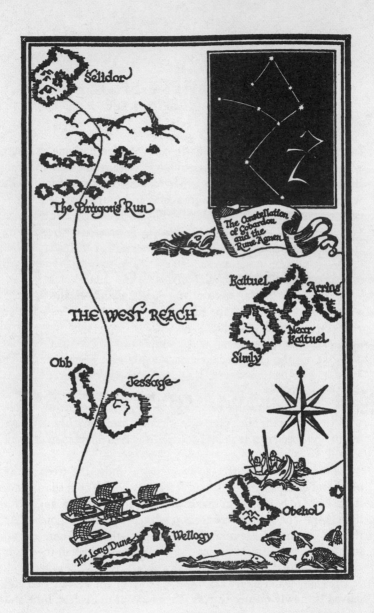

1. The Rowan Tree

IN the Court of the Fountain the sun of March shone through young leaves of ash and elm, and water leapt and fell through shadow and clear light. About that roofless court stood four high walls of stone. Behind those were rooms and courts, passages, corridors, towers, and at last the heavy outmost walls of the Great House of Roke, which would stand any assault of war, or earthquake, or the sea itself, being built not only of stone, but of incontestable magic. For Roke is the Isle of the Wise, where the art magic is taught; and the Great House is the school and central place of wizardry; and the central place of the House is that small court far within the walls, where the fountain plays and the trees stand in rain or sun or starlight.

The tree nearest the fountain, a well-grown rowan, had humped and cracked the marble pavement with its roots. Veins of bright green moss filled the cracks, spreading up from the grassy plot around the basin. A boy sat there on the low hump of marble and moss, his gaze following the fall of the fountain's central jet. He was nearly a man, but still a boy; slender, dressed richly. His face might have been cast in golden bronze, it was so finely moulded and so still.

Behind him, fifteen feet away perhaps, under the trees at the other end of the small central lawn, a man stood, or seemed to stand; it was hard to be certain in that flickering shift of shadow and warm light. Surely he was there, a man in white, standing motionless. As the boy watched the fountain, so he watched the boy. There was no sound or movement but the play of leaves and the play of the water and its continual song.

The man walked forward. A wind stirred the rowan tree and moved its newly opened leaves. The boy leapt to his feet, lithe and startled. He faced the man and bowed to him. 'My Lord Archmage,' he said.

The man stopped before him, a short, straight, vigorous figure in a hooded cloak of white wool. Above the folds of the laid-down hood his face was reddish-dark, hawk-nosed, seamed on one cheek with old scars. The eyes were bright and fierce. Yet he spoke gently. 'It's a pleasant place to sit, the Court of the Fountain,' he said, and, forestalling the boy's apology, 'You have travelled far, and have not rested. Sit down again.'

He knelt on the white rim of the basin and held out his hand to the ring of glittering drops that fell from the higher bowl of the fountain, letting the water run through his fingers. The boy sat down again on the humped tiles, and for a minute neither spoke.

'You are the son of the Prince of Enlad and the Enlades,' the Archmage said, 'heir of the Principality of Morred. There is no older heritage in all Earthsea, and none fairer. I have seen the orchards of Enlad in the Spring, and the golden roofs of Berila ... How are you called?'

'I am called Arren.'

'That would be a word in the dialect of your land. What is it in our common speech?'

The boy said, 'Sword.'

The Archmage nodded. There was silence again, and then the boy said, not boldly, but without timidity, 'I had thought the Archmage knew all languages.'

The man shook his head, watching the fountain.

'And all names ...'

'All names? Only Segoy who spoke the First Word, raising up the isles from the deep sea, knew all names. To be sure,' and the bright, fierce gaze was on Arren's face, 'if I needed to know your true name, I would know it. But there's no need. Arren I will call you; and I am Sparrowhawk. Tell me, how was your voyage here?'

'Too long.'

'The winds blew ill?'

'The winds blew fair, but the news I bear is ill, Lord Sparrowhawk.'

'Tell it then,' the Archmage said, gravely, but like one yielding to a child's impatience; and while Arren spoke, he looked again at the crystal curtain of water-drops falling from the upper basin into the lower, not as if he did not listen, but as if he listened to more than the boy's words.

'You know, my lord, that the prince my father is a wizardly man, being of the lineage of Morred, and having spent a year here on Roke in his youth. Some power he has, and knowledge, though he seldom uses his arts, being concerned with the ruling and ordering of his realm, and the governance of cities, and matters of trade. The fleets of our island go westward, even into the West Reach, trading for sapphires and ox-hides and tin, and early this winter a sea-captain returned to our city Berila with a tale that came to my father's ears, so that he had the man sent for and heard him tell it.' The boy spoke quickly, with assurance. He had been trained by civil, courtly people, and did not have the self-consciousness of the young. 'The sea-captain said that on the isle of Narveduen, which is some five hundred miles west of us by the ship-lanes, there was no more magic. Spells had no power there, he said, and the words of wizardry were forgotten. My father asked him if it was that all the sorcerers and witches had left that isle, and he answered, No : there were some there who had been sorcerers, but they cast no more spells, not even so much as a charm for kettlemending or the finding of a lost needle. And my father asked, Were not the folk of Narveduen dismayed? And the sea-captain said again, No, they seemed uncaring. And indeed, he said, there was sickness among them, and their autumn harvest had been poor, and still they seemed careless. He said – I was there, when he spoke to the prince – he said, "They were like sick men, like a man who has been told he must die within the year, and tells himself it is not true, and he will live forever. They go about," he said, "without looking at the world." When other traders returned they repeated the tale that Narveduen had become a poor land and had lost the arts of wizardry. But all this was mere tales of the Reach, which are always strange, and only my father gave it much thought. Then in the New Year, in the Festival of the Lambs that we hold in Enlad, when the shepherds' wives come into the city bringing the firstlings of the flocks, my father named the wizard Root to say the spells of increase over the lambs. But Root came back to our hall distressed, and laid his staff down, and said, "My Lord, I cannot say the spells." My father questioned him, but he could say only, "I have forgotten the words and the patterning." So my father went to the market-place and said the spells himself, and the festival was completed. But I saw him come home to the palace that evening, and he looked grim and weary, and he said to me, "I said the words, but I do not know if they had meaning," And indeed there's trouble among the flocks this spring, the ewes dying in birth, and many lambs born dead, and some are ... deformed.' The boy's easy, eager voice dropped; he winced as he said the word, and swallowed. 'I saw some of them,' he said. There was a pause.

'My father believes that this matter, and the tale of Narveduen, show some evil at work in our part of the world. He desires the counsel of the Wise.'

'That he sent you proves that his desire is urgent,' said the Arch-mage. 'You are his only son, and the voyage from Enlad to Roke is not short. Is there more to tell?'

'Only some old wives' tales from the hills.'

'What do the old wives say?'

'That all the fortunes witches read in smoke and waterpools tell of ill, and that their love-potions go amiss. But these are people without true wizardry.'

'Fortune-telling and love-potions are not of much account, but old women are worth listening to. Well, your message will indeed be discussed by the Masters of Roke. But I do not know, Arren, what counsel they may give your father. For Enlad is not the first land from which such tidings have come.'

Arren's trip from the north, down past the great isle Havnor and through the Inmost Sea to Roke, was his first voyage. Only in these last few weeks had he seen lands that were not his own homeland, and become aware of distance and diversity and recognized that there was a great world beyond the pleasant hills of Enlad, and many people in it. He was not yet used to thinking widely, and so it was a while before he understood.

'Where else?' he asked then, a little dismayed. For he had hoped to bring a prompt cure home to Enlad.

'In the South Reach, first. Latterly even in the south of the Archipelago, in Wathort. There is no more magic done in Wathort, men say. It is hard to be sure. That land has long been rebellious and piratical, and to hear a Southern trader is to hear a liar, as they say. Yet the story is always the same : The springs of wizardry have run dry.'

'But here on Roke –'

'Here on Roke we have felt nothing of this. We are defended here from storm, and change, and all ill chance. Too well defended, perhaps. Prince, what will you do now?'

'I shall go back to Enlad when I can bring my father some clear word of the nature of this evil, and of its remedy.'

Once more the Archmage looked at him, and this time, for all his training, Arren looked away. He did not know why, for there was nothing unkind in the gaze of those dark eyes. They were impartial, calm, compassionate.

All in Enlad looked up to his father, and he was his father's son. No man ever looked at him thus, not as Arren Prince of Enlad, son of the Ruling Prince, but as Arren alone. He did not like to think that he feared the Archmage's gaze, but he could not meet it. It seemed to enlarge the world yet again around him, and now not only Enlad sank into insignificance, but he himself, so that in the eyes of the Archmage he was only a small figure, very small, in a vast scene of sea-girt lands over which hung darkness.

He sat picking at the vivid moss that grew in the cracks of the marble flagstones, and presently he said, hearing his voice, which had deepened only in the last couple of years, sound thin and husky : 'And I shall do as you bid me.'

'Your duty is to your father, not to me,' the Archmage said.

His eyes were still on Arren, and now the boy looked up. As he had made his act of submission he had forgotten himself, and now he saw the Archmage : the greatest wizard of all Earthsea, the man who had capped the Black Well of Fundaur, and won the Ring of Erreth-Akbe from the Tombs of Atuan, and built the deep-founded seawall of Nepp; the sailor who knew the seas from Astowell to Selidor; the only living Dragonlord. There he knelt beside a fountain, a short man and not young, a quiet-voiced man, with eyes as deep as evening.

Arren scrambled up from sitting and knelt down formally on both knees, all in haste. 'My lord,' he said stammering, 'let me serve you!'

His self-assurance was gone, his face was flushed, his voice shook.

At his hip he wore a sword in a sheath of new leather figured with inlay of red and gold; but the sword itself was plain, with a worn cross-hilt of silvered bronze. This he drew forth, all in haste, and offered the hilt to the Archmage, as a liegeman to his prince.

The Archmage did not put out his hand to touch the swordhilt. He looked at it, and at Arren. 'That is yours, not mine,' he said. 'And you are no man's servant.'

'But my father said that I might stay on Roke until I learned what this evil is, and maybe some mastery – I have no skill, I don't think I have any power, but there were mages among my forefathers – if I might in some way learn to be of use to you –'

'Before your ancestors were mages,' the Archmage said, 'they were kings.'

He stood up and came with silent, vigorous step to Arren, and taking the boy's hand made him rise. 'I thank you for your offer of service, and though I do not accept it now, yet I may, when we have taken counsel on these matters. The offer of a generous spirit is not one to refuse lightly. Nor is the sword of the son of Morred to be lightly turned aside! ... Now go. The lad who brought you here will see that you eat and bathe, and rest. Go on,' and he pushed Arren gently between the shoulder blades, a familiarity no one had ever taken before, and which the young prince would have resented from anyone else; but the Archmage's touch was like an accolade.

Arren was an active boy, delighting in games, taking pride and pleasure in the skills of body and mind, apt at his duties of ceremony and governing, which were neither light nor simple. Yet he had never given himself entirely to anything. All had come easy to him, and he had done all easily; it had all been a game, and he had played at loving. But now the depths of him were wakened, not by a game or dream, but by honour, danger, wisdom, by a scarred face and a quiet voice and a dark hand holding, careless of its power, the staff of yew that bore near the grip, in silver set in black wood, the Lost Rune of the Kings.

So the first step out of childhood is made all at once, without looking before or behind, without caution, and nothing held in reserve.

Forgetting courtly farewells he hurried to the doorway, awkward, radiant, obedient. And Ged the Archmage watched him go.

Ged stood a while by the fountain under the ash tree, then raised his face to the sunwashed sky. 'A gentle messenger for bad news,' he said half aloud, as if talking to the fountain. It did not listen, but went on talking in its own silver tongue, and he listened to it a while. Then going to another doorway, which Arren had not seen, and which indeed very few eyes would have seen no matter how close they looked, he said, 'Master Doorkeeper.'

A little man of no age appeared. Young he was not, so that one had to call him old but the word did not suit him. His face was dry, and coloured like ivory, and he had a pleasant smile that made long curves in his cheeks. 'What's the matter, Ged?' said he.

For they were alone, and he was one of the seven persons in the world who knew the Archmage's name. The others were the Master Namer of Roke; and Ogion the Silent, the wizard of Re Albi, who long ago on the mountain of Gont had given Ged that name; and the White Lady of Gont, Tenar of the Ring; and a village wizard in Iffish called Vetch; and in Iffish again, a house-carpenter's wife, mother of three girls, ignorant of all sorcery but wise in other things, who was called Yarrow; and finally, on the other side of Earthsea, in the farthest west, two dragons: Orm Embar and Kalessin.

'We should meet tonight,' the Archmage said. 'I'll go to the Patterner. And I'll send to Kurremkarmerruk, so that he'll put his lists away and let his students rest one evening, and come to us, if not in flesh. Will you see to the others?'

'Aye,' said the Doorkeeper, smiling, and was gone; and the

Archmage also was gone; and the fountain talked to itself all serene and never ceasing in the sunlight of early spring.

Somewhere to the west of the Great House of Roke, and often somewhere south of it, the Immanent Grove is usually to be seen. There is no place for it on maps, and there is no way to it except for those who know the way to it. But even novices and townsfolk and farmers can see it, always at a certain distance, a wood of high trees whose leaves have a hint of gold in their greenness even in the spring. And they consider – the novices, the townsfolk, the farmers – that the Grove moves about in a mystifying manner. But in this they are mistaken for the Grove does not move. Its roots are the roots of being. It is all the rest that moves.

Ged walked over the fields from the Great House. He took off his white cloak, for the sun was at noon. A farmer ploughing a brown hillside raised his hand in salute, and Ged replied the same way. Small birds went up into the air and sang. The sparkweed was just coming into flower in the fallows and beside the roads. Far up, a hawk cut a wide arc on the sky. Ged glanced up, and raised his hand again. Down shot the bird in a rush of windy feathers and stooped straight to the offered wrist, gripping with yellow claws. It was no sparrowhawk but a big Enderfalcon of Roke, a white-and-brown-barred fishing hawk. It looked sidelong at the Archmage with one round, bright-gold eye, then clashed its hooked beak and stared at him straight on with both round, bright-gold eyes. 'Fearless.' the man said to it in the tongue of the Making, 'fearless.'

The big hawk beat its wings and gripped with its talons, gazing at him.

'Go then, brother, fearless one.'

The farmer, away off on the hillside under the bright sky, had stopped to watch. Once last autumn he had watched the Archmage take a wild bird on his wrist, and then in the next moment had seen no man, but two hawks mounting on the wind.

This time they parted as the farmer watched : the bird to the high air, the man walking on across the muddy fields.

He came to the path that led to the Immanent Grove, a path that led always straight and direct no matter how time and the world bent awry about it, and following it came soon into the shadow of the trees.

The trunks of some of these were vast. Seeing them one could believe at last that the Grove never moved : they were like immemorial towers grey with years, their roots were like the roots of mountains. Yet these, the most ancient, were some of them thin of leaf, with branches that had died. They were not immortal. Among the giants grew sapling trees, tall and vigorous with bright crowns of foliage, and seedlings, slight leafy wands no taller than a girl.

The ground beneath the trees was soft, rich with the rotten leaves of all the years. Ferns and small woodland plants grew in it, but there was no kind of tree but the one, which had no name in the Hardic tongue of Earthsea. Under the branches the air smelled earthy and fresh, and had a taste in the mouth like live springwater.

In a glade which had been made years before by the falling of an enormous tree Ged met the Master Patterner, who lived within the Grove and seldom or never came forth from it. His hair was yellow as butter; he was no Archipelagan. Since the restoral of the Ring of Erreth-Akbe, the barbarians of Kargad had ceased their forays and had struck some bargains of trade and peace with the Inner Lands. They were not friendly folk, and held aloof. But now and then a young warrior or merchant's son came westward by himself, drawn by love of adventure or craving to learn wizardry. Such had been the Master Patterner ten years ago, a sword-begirt, red-plumed young savage from Karego-At, arriving at Roke on a rainy morning and telling the Doorkeeper in imperious and scanty Hardic, 'I come to learn !' And now he stood in the green-gold light under the trees, a tall man and fair, with long fair hair, and strange green eyes, the Master Patterner of Earthsea.

It may be that he too knew Ged's name, but if so he never spoke it. They greeted each other in silence.

'What are you watching there?' the Archmage asked, and the other answered, 'A spider.'

Between two tall grassblades in the clearing a spider had spun a web, a circle delicately suspended. The silver threads caught the sunlight. In the centre the spinner waited, a grey-black thing no larger than the pupil of an eye.

'She too is a patterner,' Ged said, studying the artful web.

'What is evil?' asked the younger man.

The round web, with its black centre, seemed to watch them both.

'A web we men weave,' Ged answered.

In this wood no birds sang. It was silent in the noon light, and hot. About them stood the trees and shadows.

'There is word from Narveduen and Enlad : the same.'

'South and south-west. North and north-west,' said the Patterner, never looking from the round web.

'We shall come here this evening. This is the best place for counsel.'

'I have no counsel.' The Patterner looked now at Ged, and his greenish eyes were cold. 'I am afraid,' he said. 'There is fear. There is fear at the roots.'

'Aye,' said Ged. 'We must look to the deep springs, I think. We have enjoyed the sunlight too long, basking in that peace which the healing of the Ring brought, accomplishing small things, fishing the shallows. Tonight we must question the depths.' And so he left the Patterner alone, gazing still at the spider in the sunny grass.

At the edge of the Grove, where the leaves of the great trees reached out over ordinary ground, he sat with his back against a mighty root, his staff across his knees. He shut his eyes as if resting, and sent a sending of his spirit over the hills and fields of Roke, northward, to the sea-assaulted cape where the Isolate Tower stands.

'Kurremkarmerruk,' he said in spirit, and the Master Namer looked up from the thick book of names of roots and herbs and leaves and seeds and petals which he was reading to his pupils, and said, 'I am here, my lord.'

Then he listened, a big, thin, old man, white-haired under his dark hood; and the students at their writing-tables in the tower room looked up at him and glanced at one another.

'I will come,' Kurremkarmerruk said, and bent his head to his book again, saying, 'Now the petal of the flower of moly hath a

312

name, which is *iebera*, and so also the sepal, which is *partonath*; and stem and leaf and root hath each his name . . .'

But under his tree the Archmage Ged, who knew all the names of moly, withdrew his sending, and stretched out his legs more comfortably, and kept his eyes shut, and presently fell asleep in the leaf-spotted sunlight.

2. The Masters of Roke

THE School on Roke is where boys who show promise in sorcery are sent from all the Inner Lands of Earthsea to learn the highest arts of magic. There they become proficient in the various kinds of sorcery, learning names, and runes, and skills, and spells, and what should and what should not be done, and why. And there, after long practice, and if hand and mind and spirit all keep pace together, they may be named wizard, and receive the staff of power. True wizards are made only on Roke; and since there are sorcerers and witches on all the isles, and the uses of magic are as needful to their people as bread and as delightful as music, so the School of Wizardry is a place held in reverence. The nine mages who are the Masters of the School are considered the equals of the great princes of the Archipelago. Their master, the warden of Roke, the Archmage, is held to be accountable to no man at all, except the King of All the Isles: and that only by an act of fealty, by heart's gift, for not even a king could constrain so great a mage to serve the common law, if his will were otherwise. Yet even in the kingless centuries the Archmages of Roke kept fealty and served that common law. All was done on Roke as it had been done for many hundred years; a place safe from all trouble it seemed, and the laughter of boys rang in the echoing courts and down the broad, cold corridors of the Great House.

Arren's guide about the School was a stocky lad whose cloak was clasped at the neck with silver, in token that he had passed his novicehood and was a proven sorcerer, studying to gain his staff. He was called Gamble. 'Because,' said he, 'my parents had six girls, and the seventh child, my father said, was a gamble against Fate.' He was an agreeable companion, quick of mind and tongue. At another time Arren would have enjoyed his humour, but today his mind was too full. He did not pay very much attention, in fact. And

Gamble, with a natural wish to be given credit for existence, began to take advantage of the guest's absentmindedness. He told him strange facts about the School, and then told him strange lies about the School, and to all of them Arren said 'Oh yes' or 'I see', until Gamble thought him a royal idiot.

'Of course they don't cook in here,' he said, showing Arren past the huge stone kitchen all alive with the glitter of copper cauldrons and the clatter of chopping-knives and the eye-prickling smell of onions. 'It's just for show. We come to the refectory, and everybody charms up whatever he wants to eat. Saves dishwashing, too.'

'Yes, I see,' said Arren politely.

'Of course novices who haven't learned the spells yet often lose a good deal of weight, their first months here; but they learn. There's one boy from Havnor who always tries for roast chicken, but all he ever gets is millet mush. He can't seem to get his spells past millet mush. He did get a dried haddock along with it, yesterday.' Gamble was getting hoarse with the effort to push his guest into incredulity. He gave up, and stopped talking.

'Where . . . what land does the Archmage come from?' said that guest, not even looking at the mighty gallery through which they were walking, all carven on wall and arched ceiling with the Thousand-leaved Tree.

'Gont,' said Gamble. 'He was a village goatherd there.'

Now, at this plain and well-worn fact, the boy from Enlad turned and looked with disapproving unbelief at Gamble. 'A goatherd?'

'That's what most Gontishmen are, unless they're pirates or sorcerers. I didn't say he was a goatherd now, you know!'

'But how would a goatherd become Archmage?'

'The same way a prince would! By coming to Roke and outdoing all the Masters, by stealing the Ring in Atuan, by sailing the Dragon's Run, by being the greatest wizard since Erreth-Akbe – how else?'

They came out of the gallery by the north door. Late afternoon lay warm and bright on the furrowed hills and the roofs of Thwil Town and the bay beyond. There they stood to talk. Gamble said, 'Of course that's all long ago, now. He hasn't done much since he was named Archmage. They never do. They just sit on Roke and watch the Equilibrium, I suppose. And he's quite old now.'

'Old? How old?'

'Oh, forty or fifty.'

'Have you seen him?'

'Of course I've seen him,' Gamble said sharply. The royal idiot seemed also to be a royal snob.

'Often?'

'No. He keeps to himself. But when I first came to Roke I saw him, in the Fountain Court.'

'I spoke with him there today,' Arren said. His tone made Gamble look at him, and then answer him fully: 'It was three years ago. And I was so frightened I never really looked at him. I was pretty young, of course. But it's hard to see things clearly in there. I remember his voice, mostly, and the fountain running.' After a moment he added, 'He does have a Gontish accent.'

'If I could speak to dragons in their own language,' Arren said, 'I wouldn't care about my accent.'

At that Gamble looked at him with a degree of approval, and asked, 'Did you come here to join the school, prince?'

'No. I carried a message from my father to the Archmage.'

'Enlad is one of the Principalities of the Kingship, isn't it?'

'Enlad, Ilien, and Way. Havnor and Éa, once, but the line of descent from the kings has died out in those lands. Ilien traces the descent from Gemal Sea-born through Maharion. Way, from Akambar and the House of Shelieth. Enlad, the oldest, from Morred through his son Serriadh and the House of Enlad.'

Arren recited these genealogies with a dreamy air, like a well-trained scholar whose mind is on another subject.

'Do you think we'll see a king in Havnor again in our lifetime?'

'I never thought about it much.'

'In Ark, where I come from, people think about it. We're part of the Principality of Ilien now, you know, since peace was made. How long has it been, seventeen years, or eighteen, since the Ring of the King's Rune was returned to the Tower of the Kings in Havnor? Things were better for a while then, but now they're worse than ever. It's time there was a king again on the throne of Earthsea, to wield the Sign of Peace. People are tired of wars and raids and merchants who overprice and princes who overtax and all the confusion of unruly powers. Roke guides, but it can't rule. The Balance lies here, but the Power should lie in the king's hands.'

Gamble spoke with real interest, all foolery set aside, and Arren's attention was finally caught. 'Enlad is a rich and peaceful land,' he said slowly. 'It has never entered into these rivalries. We hear of the troubles in other lands. But there's been no king on the throne in Havnor since Maharion died: eight hundred years. Would the lands indeed accept a king?'

'If he came in peace and in strength; if Roke and Havnor recognized his claim.'

'And there is a prophecy that must be fulfilled, isn't there? Maharion said that the next king must be a mage.'

'The Master Chanter's a Havnorian and interested in the matter, and he's been dinning the words into us for three years now. Maharion said, *He shall inherit my throne who has crossed the dark land living and come to the far shores of the day.*'

'Therefore a mage.'

'Yes, since only a wizard or mage can go among the dead in the dark land and return. Though they do not *cross* it. At least, they always speak of it as if it had only one boundary, and beyond that, no end. What are *the far shores of the day*, then? But so runs the prophecy of the Last King, and therefore some day one will be born to fulfil it. And Roke will recognize him, and the fleets and armies and nations will come together to him. Then there will be majesty again in the centre of the world, in the Tower of the Kings of Havnor. I would come to such a one, I would serve a true king with all my heart and all my art,' said Gamble, and then laughed and shrugged, lest Arren think he spoke with overmuch emotion. But Arren looked at him with friendliness, thinking, 'He would feel towards the king as I do towards the Archmage.' Aloud he said, 'A king would need such men as you about him.'

They stood, each thinking his own thoughts, yet companionable, until a gong rang sonorous in the Great House behind them.

'There!' said Gamble. 'Lentil and onion soup tonight. Come on.'

'I thought you said they didn't cook,' said Arren, still dreamy, following.

'Oh, sometimes – by mistake –'

No magic was involved in the dinner, though plenty of substance was. After it they walked out over the fields in the soft blue of the dusk. 'This is Roke Knoll,' Gamble said as they began to climb a rounded hill. The dewy grass brushed their legs, and down by the marshy Thwilburn there was a chorus of little toads to welcome the first warmth and the shortening, starry nights.

There was a mystery in that ground. Gamble said softly, 'This hill was the first that stood above the sea, when the First Word was spoken.'

'And it will be the last to sink, when all things are unmade,' said Arren.

'Therefore a safe place to stand on,' Gamble said, shaking off awe; but then he cried, awestruck. 'Look! The Grove!'

South of the Knoll a great light was revealed on the earth, like moonrise, but the thin moon was already settling westward over the hill's top; and there was a flickering in this radiance, like the movement of leaves in the wind.

'What is it?'

'It comes from the Grove – the Masters must be there. They say it burned so, with a light like moonlight, when they met to choose the Archmage five years ago. But why are they meeting now? Is it the news you brought?'

'It may be,' said Arren.

Gamble, excited and uneasy, wanted to return to the Great House to hear any rumour of what the Council of the Masters portended. Arren went with him, but looked back often at that strange radiance till the slope hid it, and there was only the new moon setting, and the stars of spring.

Alone in the dark in the stone cell that was his sleeping-room, Arren lay with eyes open. He had slept on a bed all his life, under soft furs; even in the twenty-oared galley in which he had come from Enlad they had provided their young prince with more comfort than this – a straw pallet on the stone floor, and a ragged blanket of felt. But he noticed none of it. 'I am at the centre of the world,' he thought. 'The Masters are talking in the holy place. What will they do? Will they weave a great magic to save magic? Can it be true that wizardry is dying out of the world? Is there a danger that threatens even Roke? I will stay here. I will not go home. I would rather sweep his room than be a prince in Enlad. Would he let me stay as a novice? But perhaps there will be no more teaching of the art of magic, no more learning of the true names of things. My father has the gift of wizardry, but I do not; perhaps it is indeed dying out of the world. Yet I would stay near *him*, even if he lost his power and his art. Even if I never saw him. Even if he never said another word to me.' But his ardent imagination swept him on past that, so that in a moment he saw himself face to face with the Archmage once more in the court beneath the rowan tree, and the sky was dark, and the tree leafless, and the fountain silent: and he said, 'My lord, the storm is on us, yet I will stay by thee, and serve thee,' and the Archmage smiled at him ... But there imagination failed, for he had not seen that dark face smile.

In the morning he rose, feeling that yesterday he had been a boy, today he was a man. He was ready for anything. But when it came, he stood gaping. 'The Archmage wishes to speak to you, Prince Arren,' said a little novice-lad at his doorway, waited a moment, and ran off before Arren could collect his wits to answer.

He made his way down the tower staircase and through stone corridors towards the Fountain Court, not knowing where he should go. An old man met him in the corridor, smiling so that deep furrows ran down his cheeks from nose to chin: the same who had met him yesterday at the door of the Great House when he first came up from the harbour, and had required him to say his true name before he entered. 'Come this way,' said the Master Door-keeper.

The halls and passages in this part of the building were silent, empty of the rush and racket of the boys that enlivened the rest. Here one felt the great age of the walls. The enchantment with which the ancient stones were laid and protected was here palpable.

Runes were graven on the walls at intervals, cut deep, some inlaid with silver. Arren had learned the Runes of Hardic from his father, but none of these did he know, though certain of them seemed to hold a meaning that he almost knew, or had known and could not quite remember.

'Here you are, lad,' said the Doorkeeper, who made no account of titles such as Lord or Prince. Arren followed him into a long, low-beamed room, where on one side a fire burned in a stone hearth, its flames reflecting in the oaken floor, and on the other side pointed windows let in the heavy light of a foggy morning. Before the hearth stood a group of men. All looked at him as he entered, but among them he saw only one, the Archmage. He stopped, and bowed, and stood dumb.

'These are the Masters of Roke, Arren,' said the Archmage, 'seven of the nine. The Patterner will not leave his Grove, and the Namer is in his tower, thirty miles to the north. All of them know your errand here. My lords, this is the son of Morred.'

No pride roused in Arren at that phrase, but only a kind of dread. He was proud of his lineage, but thought of himself only as an heir of princes, one of the House of Enlad. Morred, from whom that house descended, had been dead two thousand years. His deeds were matter of legends, not of this present world. It was as if the Archmage had named him son of myth, inheritor of dreams.

He did not dare look up at the faces of the eight men. He stared at the iron-shod foot of the Archmage's staff, and felt the blood ringing in his ears.

'Come, let us breakfast together,' said the Archmage, and led them to a table set beneath the windows. There was milk and sour beer, bread, new butter, and cheese. Arren sat with them and ate.

He had been among noblemen, landholders, rich merchants, all his life. His father's hall in Berila was full of them: men who owned much, who bought and sold much, rich in the things of the world. They ate and drank wine, and talked loud; many disputed, many flattered, most sought something for themselves. Young as he was, Arren had learned a good deal about the manners and disguises of humanity. But he had never been among such men as these. They ate bread, and talked little, and their faces were quiet. If they sought something, it was not for themselves. Yet they were men of great power : that, too, Arren recognized.

Sparrowhawk the Archmage sat at the head of the table and seemed to listen to what was said, and yet there was a silence about him, and no one spoke to him. Arren was let alone also, so that he had time to recover himself. On his left was the Doorkeeper, and on his right a grey-haired man with a kindly look who said to him at last, 'We are countrymen, Prince Arren. I was born in eastern Enlad, by the Forest of Aol.'

'I have hunted in that forest,' Arren replied, and they spoke together a little of the woods and towns of the Isle of the Myths, so that Arren was comforted by the memory of his home.

When the meal was done they drew together once more before the hearth, some sitting and some standing, and there was a little silence.

'Last night,' the Archmage said, 'we met in council. Long we talked, yet resolved nothing. I would hear you say now, in the morning light, whether you uphold or gainsay your judgement of the night.'

'That we resolved nothing,' said the Master Herbal, a stocky, dark-skinned man with calm eyes, 'is itself a judgement. In the Grove are patterns found; but we found nothing there but argument.'

'Only because we could not see the pattern plain,' said the grey-haired mage of Enlad, the Master Changer. 'We do not know enough. Rumours from Wathort; news from Enlad. Strange news, and should be looked to. But to raise a great fear on so little a foundation is unneedful. Our power is not threatened only because a few sorcerers have forgotten their spells.'

'So say I,' said a lean, keen-eyed man, the Master Windkey. 'Have we not all our powers? Do not the trees of the Grove grow and put forth leaves? Do not the storms of heaven obey our word? Who can fear for the art of wizardry, which is the oldest of the arts of man?'

'No man,' said the Master Summoner, deep-voiced and tall,

young, with a dark and noble face, 'no man, no power, can bind the action of wizardry, or still the words of power. For they are the very words of the Making, and one who could silence them could unmake the world.'

'Aye, and one who could do that would not be on Wathort or Narveduen,' said the Changer. 'He would be here at the gates of Roke, and the end of the world would be at hand ! We've not come to that pass yet.'

'Yet there is something wrong,' said another, and they looked at him : deep-chested, solid as an oaken cask, he sat by the fire, and the voice came from him soft and true as the note of a great bell. He was the Master Chanter. 'Where is the king that should be in Havnor? Roke is not the heart of the world. That tower is, on which the sword of Erreth-Akbe is set, and in which stands the throne of Serriadh, of Akambar, of Maharion. Eight hundred years has the heart of the world been empty ! We have the crown, but no king to wear it. We have the Lost Rune, the King's Rune, the Rune of Peace, restored to us, but have we peace? Let there be a king upon the throne, and we will have peace, and even in the farthest Reaches the sorcerers will practise their arts with untroubled mind, and there will be order, and a due season to all things.'

'Aye,' said the Master Hand, a slight, quick man, modest of bearing but with clear and seeing eyes. 'I am with you, Chanter. What wonder that wizardry goes astray, when all else goes astray? If the whole flock wander, will our black sheep stay by the fold?'

At that the Doorkeeper laughed, but he said nothing.

'Then to you all,' said the Archmage, 'it seems that there is nothing very wrong; or if there is, it lies in this, that our lands are ungoverned or ill-governed, so that all the arts and high skills of men suffer from neglect. With that much I agree. Indeed it is because the South is all but lost to peaceful commerce, that we must depend on rumour; and who has any safe word from the West Reach, save this from Narveduen? If ships went forth and came back safely as of old, if our lands of Earthsea were well-knit, we might know how things stand in the remote places, and so could act. And I think we should act! For, my lords, when the Prince of Enlad tells us that he spoke the words of the Making in a spell, and yet did not know their meaning as he spoke them; when the Master Patterner says that there is fear at the roots, and will say no more: is this so little a foundation for anxiety? When a storm begins, it is only a little cloud on the horizon.'

'You have a sense for the black things, Sparrowhawk,' said the Doorkeeper. 'You ever did. Say what you think is wrong.'

'I do not know. There is a weakening of power. There is a want of resolution. There is a dimming of the sun. I feel, my lords – I feel as if we who sit here talking, were all wounded mortally, and while we talk and talk our blood runs softly from our veins . . .'

'And you would be up and doing.'

'I would,' said the Archmage.

'Well,' said the Doorkeeper, 'can the owls keep the hawk from flying?'

'But where would you go?' the Changer asked and the Chanter answered him : 'To seek our king and bring him to his throne!'

The Archmage looked keenly at the Chanter, but answered only, 'I would go where the trouble is.'

'South, or west,' said the Master Windkey.

'And north and east if need be,' said the Doorkeeper.

'But you are needed here, my lord,' said the Changer. 'Rather than to go seeking blindly among unfriendly peoples, on strange seas, would it not be wiser to stay here, where all magic is strong, and find out by your arts what this evil or disorder is?'

'My arts do not avail me,' the Archmage said. There was that in his voice which made them all look at him, sober and with uneasy eyes. 'I am the Warder of Roke. I do not leave Roke lightly. I wish that your counsel and my own were the same; but that is not to be hoped for, now. The judgement must be mine; and I must go.'

'To that judgement we yield,' said the Summoner.

'And I go alone. You are the Council of Roke, and it must not be broken. Yet one I will take with me, if he will come.' He looked at Arren. 'You offered me your service, yesterday. Last night the

Master Patterner said, "Not by chance does any man come to the shores of Roke. Not by chance is a son of Morred the bearer of this news." And no other word had he for us all the night. Therefore I ask you, Arren, will you come with me?'

'Yes, my lord,' said Arren, with a dry throat.

'The prince your father surely would not let you go into this peril,' said the Changer somewhat sharply, and to the Archmage, 'The lad is young, and not trained in wizardry.'

'I have years and spells enough for both of us,' Sparrowhawk said in a dry voice. 'Arren, what of your father?'

'He would let me go.'

'How can you know?' asked the Summoner.

Arren did not know where he was being required to go, nor when, nor why. He was bewildered, and abashed by these grave, honest, terrible men. If he had had time to think he could not have said anything at all. But he had no time to think; and the Archmage asked him, 'Will you come with me?'

'When my father sent me here he said to me, "I fear a dark time is coming on the world, a time of danger. So I send you rather than any other messenger, for you can judge whether we should ask the help of the Isle of the Wise in this matter, or offer the help of Enlad to them." So if I am needed, therefore I am here.'

At that he saw the Archmage smile. There was great sweetness in his smile, though it was brief. 'Do you see?' he said to the seven mages. 'Could age, or wizardry add anything to this?'

Arren felt that they looked on him approvingly then, but with a kind of pondering or wondering look, still. The Summoner spoke, his arched brows straightened to a frown : 'I do not understand it, my lord. That you are bent on going, yes. You have been caged here five years. But always before you were alone; you have always gone alone. Why, now, companioned?'

'I never needed help before,' said Sparrowhawk, with an edge of threat or irony in his voice. 'And I have found a fit companion.' There was a dangerousness about him, and the tall Summoner asked him no more questions, though he still frowned.

But the Master Herbal, calm-eyed and dark like a wise and patient ox, rose from his seat and stood monumental. 'Go, my lord,' he said, 'and take the lad. And all our trust goes with you.'

One by one the others gave assent quietly, and by ones and twos withdrew, until only the Summoner was left of the seven. 'Sparrowhawk,' he said, 'I do not seek to question your judgement. Only I say : if you are right, if there is imbalance and the peril of great evil, then a voyage to Wathort, or into the West Reach, or to the world's end, will not be far enough. Where you may have to go, can you take this companion, and is it fair to him?'

They stood apart from Arren, and the Summoner's voice was lowered, but the Archmage spoke openly : 'It is fair.'

'You are not telling me all you know,' the Summoner said.

'If I knew, I would speak. I know nothing. I guess much.'

'Let me come with you.'

'One must guard the gates.'

'The Doorkeeper does that –'

'Not only the gates of Roke. Stay here, and watch the sunrise to see if it be bright, and watch at the wall of stones to see who crosses it and where their faces are turned. There is a breach, Thorion, there is a break, a wound, and it is this I go to seek. If I am lost then maybe you will find it. But wait. I bid you wait for me.' He was speaking now in the Old Speech, the language of the Making, in which all true spells are cast and on which all the great acts of magic depend; but very seldom is it spoken in conversation, except among the dragons. The Summoner made no further argument or protest, but bowed his tall head quietly both to the Archmage and to Arren, and departed.

The fire crackled in the hearth. There was no other sound. Outside the windows the fog pressed formless and dim.

The Archmage stared into the flames, seeming to have forgotten Arren's presence. The boy stood at some distance from the hearth, not knowing if he should take his leave or wait to be dismissed, irresolute and somewhat desolate, feeling again like a small figure in a dark, illimitable, confusing space.

'We'll go first to Hort Town,' said Sparrowhawk, turning his back to the fire. 'News gathers there from all the South Reach, and we may find a lead. Your ship still waits in the bay. Speak to the master, let him carry word to your father. I think we should leave as soon as maybe. At daybreak tomorrow. Come to the steps by the boathouse.'

'My lord, what –' His voice stuck a moment. 'What is it you seek?'

'I don't know, Arren.'

'Then –'

'Then how shall I seek it? Neither do I know that. Maybe it will seek me.' He grinned a little at Arren, but his face was like iron in the grey light of the windows.

'My lord,' Arren said, and his voice was steady now, 'it is true I come of the lineage of Morred, if any tracing of lineage so old be true. And if I can serve you I will count it the greatest chance and honour of my life, and there is nothing I would rather do. But I fear that you mistake me for something more than I am.'

'Maybe,' said the Archmage.

'I have no great gifts or skills. I can fence with the short sword and the noble sword. I can sail a boat. I know the court-dances and the country-dances. I can mend a quarrel between courtiers. I can wrestle, I am a poor archer, and skilful at the game of net-ball. I can sing, and play the harp and lute. And that is all. There is no more. What use will I be to you? The Master Summoner is right –'

'Ah, you saw that, did you? He's jealous. He claims the privilege of older loyalty.'

'And greater skill, my lord.'

'Then you'd rather he went with me, and you stayed behind?'

'No! But I fear –'

'Fear what?'

Tears sprang to the boy's eyes. 'To fail you,' he said.

The Archmage turned around again to the fire. 'Sit down, Arren,' he said, and the boy came to the stone corner-seat of the hearth. 'I did not mistake you for a wizard, or a warrior, or any finished thing. What you are I do not know, though I'm glad to know that you can sail a boat ... What you will be, no one knows. But this much I do know : you are the son of Morred and of Serriadh.'

326

Arren was silent. 'That is true, my lord,' he said at last. 'But ...' The Archmage said nothing, and he had to finish his sentence: 'But I am not Morred. I am only myself.'

'You take no pride in your lineage?'

'Yes, I take pride in it – because it makes me a prince, it is a responsibility, a thing that must be lived up to –'

The Archmage nodded sharply. 'That is what I meant. To deny the past is to deny the future. A man does not make his destiny: he accepts it, or denies it. If the rowan's roots are shallow it bears no crown.' At this Arren looked up startled, for his true name, Lebannen, meant the rowan tree. But the Archmage had not said his name. 'Your roots are deep,' he went on. 'You have strength, and you must have room, room to grow. Thus I offer you, instead of a safe trip home to Enlad, an unsafe voyage to an unknown end. You need not come. The choice is yours. But I offer you the choice. For I am tired of safe places, and roofs, and walls around me.' He ended abruptly, looking about him with piercing, unseeing eyes. Arren saw the deep restlessness of the man, and it frightened him. Yet fear sharpens exhilaration, and it was with a leap of the heart that he answered, 'My lord, I choose to go with you.'

Arren left the Great House with his heart and mind full of wonder. He told himself that he was happy, but the word did not seem to suit. He told himself that the Archmage had called him strong, a man of destiny, and that he was proud of such praise; but he was not proud. Why not? The most powerful wizard in the world had told him, 'Tomorrow we sail to the edge of doom,' and he nodded his head and came: should he not feel pride? But he did not. He felt only wonder.

He went down through the steep wandering streets of Thwil Town, found his ship's master on the quays, and said to him, 'I sail tomorrow with the Archmage, to Wathort and the South Reach. Tell the Prince my father that when I am released from this service I will come home to Berila.'

The ship's captain looked dour. He knew how the bringer of such news might be received by the Prince of Enlad. 'I must have writing about it from your hand, prince,' he said. Seeing the justice in that,

Arren hurried off – he felt that all must be done instantly – and found a strange little shop where he purchased inkstone and a brush and a piece of soft pape , thick as felt; then he hurried back to the quays and sat down on the wharfside to write to his parents. When he thought of his mother holding this same piece of paper, reading the letter, a distress came into him. She was a blithe patient woman, but Arren knew that he was the foundation of her contentment, that she longed for his quick return. There was no way to comfort her for his long absence. His letter was dry and brief. He signed with the sword-rune, sealed the letter with a bit of pitch from a caulking-pot near by and gave it to the ship's master. Then, 'Wait!' he said, as if the ship were ready to sail that instant, and ran back up the cobbled streets to the strange little shop. He had trouble finding it, for there was something shifty about the streets of Thwil; it almost seemed that the turnings were different every time. He came on the right street at last, and darted into the shop under the strings of red clay beads that ornamented its doorway. When he was buying ink and paper he had noticed, on a tray of clasps and brooches, a silver brooch in the shape of a wild rose; and his mother was called Rose. 'I'll buy that,' he said in his hasty, princely way.

'Ancient silverwork of the Isle of O. I can see you are a judge of the old crafts,' said the shopkeeper, looking at the hilt – not the handsome sheath – of Arren's sword. 'That will be four in ivory.'

Arren paid the rather high price unquestioning; he had in his purse plenty of the ivory counters that serve as money in the Inner Lands. The idea of a gift for his mother pleased him; the act of buying pleased him; as he left the shop he set his hand on the pommel of his sword, with a touch of swagger.

His father had given him that sword on the eve of his departure from Enlad. He had received it solemnly, and had worn it, as if it were a duty to wear it, even aboard ship. He was proud of the weight of it at his hip, the weight of its great age on his spirit. For it was the sword of Serriadh who was the son of Morred and Elfarran; there was none older in the world except the sword of Erreth-Akbe, which was set atop the Tower of the Kings in Havnor. This had never been laid away or hoarded up, but worn: yet was unworn by the centuries, unweakened, because it had been forged with a great power of enchantment. Its history said that it never had been drawn, nor ever could be drawn, except in the service of life. For no purpose of bloodlust or revenge or greed, in no war for gain, would it let itself be wielded. From it, the greatest treasure of his family, Arren had received his use-name: Arrendek he had been called as a child, 'the little Sword'.

He had not used the sword, nor had his father, nor his grandfather. There had been peace in Enlad for a long time.

And now, in the street of the strange town of the Wizards' Isle, the sword's handle felt strange to him when he touched it. It was awkward to his hand, and cold. Heavy, the sword hindered his walk, dragged at him. And the wonder he had felt was still in him but had gone cold. He went back down to the quay, and gave the brooch to the ship's master for his mother and bade him farewell and a safe voyage home. Turning away he pulled his cloak over the sheath that held the old, unyielding weapon, the deadly thing he had inherited. He did not feel like swaggering any more. 'What am I doing?' he said to himself as he climbed the narrow ways, not hurrying now, to the fortress-bulk of the Great House above the town. 'How is it that I'm not going home? Why am I seeking something I don't understand, with a man I don't know?'

And he had no answer to his questions.

3. Hort Town

In the darkness before dawn Arren dressed in clothing that had been given him, seaman's garb, well worn but clean, and hurried down through the silent halls of the Great House to the eastern door, carven of horn and dragon's tooth. There the Doorkeeper let him out, and pointed the way that he should take, smiling a little. He followed the topmost street of the town and then a path that led down to the boathouses of the School, south along the bayshore from the docks of Thwil. He could just make out his way. Trees, roofs, hills bulked as dim masses within dimness; the dark air was utterly still and very cold; everything held still, held itself withdrawn and obscure. Only over the dark sea eastward was there one faint clear line: the horizon, tipping momently towards the unseen sun.

He came to the boathouse steps. No one was there, nothing moved. In his bulky sailor's coat and wool cap he was warm enough, but he shivered, standing on the stone steps in the darkness, waiting.

The boathouses loomed black above black water, and suddenly from them there came a dull, hollow sound, a booming knock, repeated three times. Arren's hair stirred on his scalp. A long shadow glided out onto the water, silently. It was a boat and it slid softly towards the pier. Arren ran down the steps and onto the pier, and leapt down into the boat.

'Take the tiller,' said the Archmage, a lithe shadowy figure in the prow, 'and hold her steady while I get the sail up.'

They were out on the water already, the sail opening like a white wing from the mast, catching the growing light. 'A west wind to save us rowing out of the bay, that's a parting gift from the Master Windkey, I don't doubt. Watch her, lad, she steers very light! So then. A west wind and a clear dawn for the Balance-Day of spring.'

'Is this boat *Lookfar*?' Arren had heard of the Archmage's boat in songs and tales.

'Aye,' said the other, busy with ropes. The boat bucked and veered as the wind freshened; Arren set his teeth and tried to keep her steady.

'She steers very light, but somewhat wilful, lord.'

The Archmage laughed. 'Let her have her will; she is wise also. Listen, Arren,' and he paused, kneeling on the thwart to face Arren, 'I am no lord now, nor you a prince. I am a trader called Hawk, and you're my nephew, learning the seas with me, called Arren; for we hail from Enlad. From what town? A large one, lest we meet a townsman.'

'Temere, on the south coast? They trade to all the Reaches.'

The Archmage nodded.

'But,' said Arren cautiously, 'you don't have quite the accent of Enlad.'

'I know. I have a Gontish accent,' his companion said, and laughed, looking up at the brightening east. 'But I think I can borrow what I need from you. So we come from Temere in our boat *Dolphin*, and I am neither lord, nor mage, nor Sparrowhawk, but — how am I called?'

'Hawk, my lord.'

Then Arren bit his tongue.

'Practice, nephew,' said the Archmage. 'It takes practice. You've never been anything but a prince. While I have been many things, and last of all, and maybe least, an Archmage ... We go south looking for emmel-stone, that blue stuff they carve charms of. I know they value it in Enlad. They make it into charms against rheums, sprains, stiff necks, and slips of the tongue.'

After a moment Arren laughed, and as he lifted his head the boat lifted on a long wave, and he saw the rim of the sun against the edge of the ocean, a flare of sudden gold, before them.

Sparrowhawk stood with one hand on the mast, for the little boat leaped on the choppy waves, and facing the sunrise of the equinox of spring he chanted. Arren did not know the Old Speech, the tongue of wizards and dragons, but he heard praise and rejoicing in

331

the words, and there was a great striding rhythm in them like the rise and fall of tides or the balance of the day and night each succeeding each forever. Gulls cried on the wind, and the shores of Thwil Bay slid past to right and left, and they entered on the long waves, full of light, of the Inmost Sea.

From Roke to Hort Town is no great voyage, but they spent three nights at sea. The Archmage had been urgent to be gone, but once gone, he was more than patient. The winds turned contrary as soon as they were away from the charmed weather of Roke, but he did not call a mage-wind into their sails, as any weatherworker could have done; instead, he spent hours teaching Arren how to manage the boat in a stiff head-wind, in the rock-fanged sea east of Issel. The second night out it rained, the rough cold rain of March, but he said no spell to keep it off them. On the next night as they lay outside the entrance to Hort Harbour in a calm, cold, foggy darkness, Arren thought about this, and reflected that in this short time he had known him, the Archmage had done no magic at all.

He was a peerless sailor, though. Arren had learned more in three days' sailing with him, than in ten years of boating and racing on Berila Bay. And mage and sailor are not so far apart; both work with the powers of sky and sea, and bend great winds to the use of their hands, bringing near what was remote. Archmage or Hawk the sea-trader, it came to much the same thing.

He was a rather silent man, though perfectly good-humoured. No clumsiness of Arren's fretted him; he was companionable; there could be no better shipmate, Arren thought. But he would go into his own thoughts and be silent for hours on end, and then when he must speak there was a harshness in his voice, and he would look right through Arren. This did not weaken the love the boy felt for him, but maybe it lessened liking somewhat; it was a little awesome. Perhaps Sparrowhawk felt this, for in that foggy night off the shores of Wathort he began to talk to Arren, rather haltingly, about himself. 'I do not want to go among men again, tomorrow,' he said. 'I've been pretending that I am free ... That nothing's wrong in the world. That I'm not Archmage, not even sorcerer. That I'm Hawk of Temere, without responsibilities or privileges, owing nothing to anyone . . .' He stopped and after a while went on, 'Try to choose carefully, Arren, when the great choices must be made. When I was young I had to choose between the life of being and the life of doing. And I leapt at the latter like a trout to a fly. But each deed you do, each act, binds you to itself and to its consequences, and makes you act again and yet again. Then very seldom do you come upon a space, a time like this, between act and act, when you may stop and simply be. Or wonder who, after all, you are.'

How could such a man, thought Arren, be in doubt as to who and what he was? He had believed such doubts were reserved for the young, who had not done anything yet.

They rocked in the great, cool darkness.

'That's why I like the sea,' said Sparrowhawk's voice in that darkness.

Arren understood him; but his own thoughts ran ahead, as they had been doing all these three days and nights, to their quest, the aim of their sailing. And since his companion was in a mood to talk, at last, he asked, 'Do you think we will find what we seek in Hort Town?'

Sparrowhawk shook his head, perhaps meaning no, perhaps meaning that he did not know.

'Can it be a kind of pestilence, a plague, that drifts from land to land, blighting the crops and the flocks and men's spirits?'

'A pestilence is a motion of the great balance, of the Equilibrium itself; this is different. There is the stink of evil in it. We may suffer for it when the balance of things rights itself, but we do not lose hope, and forego art, and forget the words of the Making. Nature is not unnatural. This is not a righting of the balance, but an upsetting of it. There is only one creature who can do that.'

'A man?' Arren said, tentative.

'We men.'

'How?'

'By an unmeasured desire for life.'

'For life? But it isn't wrong to want to live?'

'No. But when we crave power over life – endless wealth, unassailable safety, immortality – then desire becomes greed. And if knowledge allies itself to that greed, then comes evil. Then the balance of the world is swayed, and ruin weighs heavy in the scale.'

Arren brooded over this a while, and said at last, 'Then you think it is a man we seek?'

'A man, and a mage. Aye, I think so.'

'But I had thought, from what my father and teachers taught, that the great arts of wizardry were dependent on the Balance, the Equilibrium of things, and so could not be used for evil.'

'That,' said Sparrowhawk somewhat wryly, 'is a debatable point. *Infinite are the arguments of mages* ... Every land of Earthsea knows of witches who cast unclean spells, sorcerers who use their art to win riches. But there is more. The Firelord, who sought to undo the darkness and stop the sun at noon, was a great mage; even Erreth-Akbe could scarcely defeat him. The Enemy of Morred was another such. When he came, whole cities knelt to him; armies fought for him. The spell he wove against Morred was so mighty that even when he was slain it could not be halted, and the island of Soléa was overwhelmed by the sea, and all on it perished. Those were men in whom great strength and knowledge served the will to evil, and fed upon it. Whether the wizardry that serves a better end may always prove the stronger, we do not know. We hope.'

There is a certain bleakness in finding hope where one expected certainty. Arren found himself unwilling to stay on these cold summits. He said after a little while, 'I see why you say that only men do evil, I think. Even sharks are innocent, they kill because they must.'

'That is why nothing can resist us. Only one thing in the world can resist an evil-hearted man. And that is another man. In our shame is our glory. Only our spirit, which is capable of evil, is capable of overcoming it.'

'But the dragons,' said Arren. 'Do they not do great evil? Are they innocent?'

'The dragons! The dragons are avaricious, insatiable, treacherous; without pity, without remorse. But are they evil? Who am I to judge the acts of dragons? ... They are wiser than men are. It is with them as with dreams, Arren. We men dream dreams, we work magic, we do good, we do evil. The dragons do not dream. They are dreams. They do not work magic: it is their substance, their being. They do not do: they are.'

'In Serilune,' said Arren, 'is the skin of Bar Oth, killed by Keor Prince of Enlad three hundred years ago. No dragons have ever come to Enlad since that day. I saw the skin of Bar Oth. It is heavy as iron, and so large that if it were spread out it would cover all the marketplace of Serilune, they said. The teeth are as long as my fore-arm. Yet they said Bar Oth was a young dragon, not full grown.'

'There is a desire in you,' said Sparrowhawk, 'to see dragons.'

'Yes.'

'Their blood is cold, and venomous. You must not look into their eyes. They are older than mankind ...' He was silent a while, and then went on, 'And though I came to forget or regret all I have ever done, yet I would remember that once I saw the dragons aloft on the wind at sunset above the western isles; and I would be content.'

Both were silent then, and there was no sound but the whispering of the water with the boat, and no light. So at last, there on the deep waters, they slept.

In the bright haze of morning they came into Hort Harbour, where a hundred craft were moored or setting forth; fishermen's boats, crabbers, trawlers, trading-ships, two galleys of twenty oars, one great sixty-oared galley in bad repair, and some lean, long sailing-ships with high triangular sails designed to catch the upper airs in the hot calms of the South Reach. 'Is that a ship of war?' Arren asked as they passed one of the twenty-oared galleys, and his companion answered, 'A slaver, I judge from the chain-bolts in her hold. They sell men in the South Reach.'

Arren pondered this a minute, then went to the gear-box and took from it his sword, which he had wrapped well and stowed away on the morning of their departure. He uncovered it; he stood indecisive, the sheathed sword on his two hands, the belt dangling from it.

'It's no sea-trader's sword,' he said. 'The scabbard is too fine.'

Sparrowhawk, busy at the tiller, shot him a look. 'Wear it if you like.'

'I thought it might be wise.'

'As swords go, that one is wise,' said his companion, his eyes alert on their passage through the crowded bay. 'Is it not a sword reluctant to be used?'

Arren nodded. 'So they say. Yet it has killed. It has killed men.' He looked down at the slender, handworn hilt. 'It has, but I have not. It makes me feel a fool. It is too much older than I ... I shall take my knife,' he ended, and rewrapping the sword shoved it down deep in the gear-box. His face was perplexed and angry. Sparrowhawk said nothing, till he said, 'Will you take the oars now, lad. We're heading for the pier there by the stairs.'

Hort Town, one of the Seven Great Ports of the Archipelago, rose from its noisy waterfront up the slopes of three steep hills in a jumble of colour. The houses were of clay plastered in red, orange, yellow, white; the roofs were of purplish-red tile; pendick-trees in flower made masses of dark red along the upper streets. Gaudy striped awnings stretched from roof to roof, shading narrow market-places. The quays were bright with sunlight; the streets running back from the waterfront were like dark slots full of shadows and people and noise.

When they had tied up the boat, Sparrowhawk stooped over as if to check the knot, beside Arren, and he said, 'Arren, there are people in Wathort who know me pretty well; so watch me, that you may know me.' When he straightened up there was no scar on his face. His hair was quite grey; his nose was thick and somewhat snub; and instead of a yew staff his own height, he carried a wand of ivory, which he tucked away inside his shirt. 'Dost know me?' he said to Arren with a broad smile, and he spoke with the accent of Enlad. 'Hast never seen thy nuncle before this?'

Arren had seen wizards at the court of Berila change their faces when they mimed the *Deed of Morred*, and knew it was only an illusion; he kept his wits about him, and was able to say, 'Oh aye, nuncle Hawk!'

But, while the mage bickered with the harbour guardsman over the fee for docking and guarding the boat, Arren kept looking at him to make sure that he did know him. And as he looked, the transformation troubled him more, not less. It was too complete; this was not the Archmage at all, this was no wise guide and leader ... The guardsman's fee was high, and Sparrowhawk grumbled as he paid, and strode away with Arren, still grumbling. 'A test of my patience,' he said. 'Pay that swagbellied thief to guard my boat! when half a spell would do twice the job! Well, this is the price of disguise ... And I've forgot my proper speech, have I not, nevvy?'

They were walking up a crowded, smelly, gaudy street lined with shops, little more than booths, whose owners stood in the doorways among heaps and festoons of wares, loudly proclaiming the beauty and cheapness of their pots, hosiery, hats, spades, pins, purses, kettles, baskets, knives, ropes, bolts, bedlinens, and every other kind of hardware and drygoods. 'Is it a fair?'

'Eh?' said the snub-nosed man, bending his grizzled head.

'Is it a fair, nuncle?'

'Fair? No, no. They keep it up all year round, here. Keep your fishcakes, mistress, I have breakfasted!' And Arren tried to shake off a man with a tray of little brass vases, who followed at his heels whining, 'But, try, handsome young master, they won't fail you, breath as sweet as the roses of Numima, charming the women to you, try them, young sealord, young prince ...'

All at once Sparrowhawk was between Arren and the pedlar, saying, 'What charms are these?'

'Not charms!' the man winced, shrinking away from him. 'I sell no charms, seamaster! Only syrups to sweeten the breath after drink or hazia-root – only syrups, great prince!' He cowered right down onto the pavement stones, his tray of vases clinking and clattering, some of them tipping so that a drop of the sticky stuff inside oozed out, pink or purple, over the lip.

Sparrowhawk turned away without speaking, and went on with Arren. Soon the crowds thinned and the shops grew wretchedly poor, little kennels displaying as all their wares a handful of bent nails, a broken pestle and an old carding-comb. This poverty disgusted Arren less than the rest; in the rich end of the street he had felt choked, suffocated, by the pressure of things to be sold and voices screaming to him to buy, buy. And the pedlar's abjectness had shocked him. He thought of the cool, bright streets of his Northern town. No man in Berila, he thought, would have grovelled to a stranger like that. 'These are a foul folk!' he said.

'This way, nevvy,' was all his companion's answer. They turned aside into a passage between high, red, windowless housewalls, which ran along the hillside and through an archway garlanded with decaying banners, out again into the sunlight in a steep square, another market-place, crowded with booths and stalls and swarming with people and flies.

Around the edges of the square a number of men and women were sitting or lying on their backs, motionless. Their mouths had a curious blackish look, as if they had been bruised, and around their lips flies swarmed and gathered in clusters like bunches of dried currants.

'So many,' said Sparrowhawk's voice, low and hasty as if he too had got a shock; but when Arren looked at him there was the blunt bland face of the hearty trader Hawk, showing no concern.

'What's wrong with those people?'

'Hazia. It soothes and numbs, letting the body be free of the mind. And the mind roams free. But when it returns to the body it needs more hazia ... And the craving grows; and the life is short, for the stuff is poison. First there is a trembling, and later paralysis, and then death.'

Arren looked at a woman sitting with her back to a sun-warmed wall; she had raised her hand as if to brush away the flies from her face, but the hand made a jerky, circular motion in the air, as if she had quite forgotten about it and it was moved only by the repeated surging of a palsy or shaking in the muscles. The gesture was like an incantation emptied of all intention, a spell without meaning.

Hawk was looking at her too, expressionless. 'Come on!' he said.

He led on across the market-place to an awning-shaded booth. Stripes of sunlight coloured green, orange, lemon, crimson, azure, fell across the cloths and shawls and woven belts displayed, and danced multitudinous in the tiny mirrors that bedecked the high, feathered headdress of the woman who sold the stuff. She was big, and she chanted in a big voice, 'Silks, satins, canvases, furs, felts, woollens, fleecefells of Gont, gauzes of Sowl, silks of Lorbanery! Hey, you Northern men, take off your duffle-coats, don't you see the sun's out? How's this to take home to a girl in far Havnor? Look at it, silk of the South, fine as the mayfly's wing!' She had flipped open with deft hands a bolt of gauzy silk, pink shot with threads of silver.

'Nay, mistress, we're not wed to queens,' said Hawk, and the woman's voice rose to a blare: 'So what do you dress your women-folk in, burlap? sailcloth? Misers that won't buy a bit of silk for a poor woman freezing in the everlasting Northern snow! How's this then, a Gontish fleecefell, to help you keep her warm on winter nights!' She flung out over the counterboard a great cream and brown square, woven of the silky hair of the goats of the north-eastern isles. The pretended trader put out his hand and felt it; and he smiled.

'Aye, you're a Gontishman?' said the blaring voice, and the headdress nodding sent a thousand coloured dots spinning over the canopy and the cloth.

'This is Andradean work; see? There's but four warp-strings to the finger's width. Gont uses six or more. But tell me why you've turned from working magic to selling fripperies. When I was here years since I saw you pulling flames out of men's ears, and then you made the flames turn into birds and golden bells, and that was a finer trade than this one.'

'It was no trade at all,' the big woman said, and for a moment Arren was aware of her eyes, hard and steady as agates, looking at him and Hawk from out of the glitter and restlessness of her nodding feathers and flashing mirrors.

'It was pretty, that pulling fire out of ears,' said Hawk in a dour but simple-minded tone. 'I thought to show it to my nevvy.'

'Well now look you,' said the woman less harshly, leaning her broad brown arms and heavy bosom on the counter. 'We don't do those tricks any more. People don't want 'em. They've seen through 'em. These mirrors now, I see you remember my mirrors,' and she tossed her head so that the reflected dots of coloured light whirled dizzily about them, 'well, you can puzzle a man's mind with the flashing of the mirrors, and with words, and with other tricks I won't tell you, till he thinks he sees what he don't see, what isn't there. Like the flames and golden bells, or the suits of clothes I used to deck sailormen in, cloth of gold with diamonds like apricots, and off they'd swagger like the King of All the Isles . . . But it was tricks, fooleries. You can fool men. They're like chickens charmed by a snake, by a finger held before 'em. Men are like chickens. But then in the end they know they've been fooled and fuddled, and they get angry, and lose their pleasure in such things. So I turned to this trade, and maybe all the silks aren't silks nor all the fleeces Gontish, but all the same they'll wear – they'll wear! They're real, and not mere lies and air, like the suits of cloth of gold.'

'Well, well,' said Hawk, 'then there's none left in all Hort Town to pull fire out of ears or do any magic like they did?'

At his last words the woman frowned; she straightened up and began to fold the fleecefell carefully. 'Those who want lies and visions chew hazia,' she said. 'Talk to them if you like!' She nodded to the unmoving figures around the square.

'But there were sorcerers, they that charmed the winds for seamen and put spells of fortune on their cargoes. Are they all turned to other trades?'

But she in sudden fury came blaring in over his words, 'There's a sorcerer if you want one, a great one, a wizard with a staff and all – see him there? He sailed with Egre himself, making winds and finding fat galleys, so he said, but it was all lies, and Captain Egre gave him his just reward at last, he cut his right hand off. And there he sits now, see him, with his mouth full of hazia and his belly full of air. Air and lies! Air and lies! That's all there is to your magic, Seacaptain Goat!'

'Well, well, mistress,' said Hawk with obdurate mildness, 'I was only asking.' She turned her broad back with a great dazzle of whirling mirror-dots, and he ambled off, Arren beside him.

His amble was purposeful. It brought them near the man she had pointed out. He sat propped against a wall, staring at nothing; the dark, bearded face had been very handsome once. The wrinkled wrist-stump lay on the pavement stones in the hot, bright sunlight, shameful.

There was some commotion among the booths behind them, but Arren found it hard to look away from the man; a loathing fascination held him. 'Was he really a wizard?' he asked very low.

'He may be the one called Hare, who was weatherworker for the pirate Egre. They were famous thieves – Here, stand clear, Arren !' A man running full tilt out from among the booths nearly slammed into them both. Another came trotting by, struggling under the weight of a great folding tray loaded with cords and braids and laces. A booth collapsed with a crash; awnings were being pushed over or taken down hurriedly; knots of people shoved and wrestled through the market-place, voices rose in shouts and screams. Above them all rang the blaring yell of the woman with the headdress of mirrors; Arren glimpsed her wielding some kind of pole or stick against a bunch of men, fending them off with great sweeps like a swordsman at bay. Whether it was a quarrel that had spread and become a riot, or an attack by a gang of thieves, or a fight between two rival lots of pedlars, there was no telling; people rushed by with armfuls of goods that could be loot or their own property saved from looting, there were knife-fights, fist-fights, and brawls all over the square. 'That way,' said Arren, pointing to a side street that led out of the square near them, and started for it, for it was clear that they had better get out at once; but his companion caught his arm. Arren looked back, and saw that the man Hare was struggling to his feet. When he got himself erect he stood swaying a moment, and then without a look around him set off around the edge of the square, trailing his single hand along the house-walls as if to guide or support himself. 'Keep him in sight,' Sparrowhawk said, and they set off following. No one molested them or the man they followed, and in a minute they were out of the market-square, going down-hill in the silence of a narrow, twisting street.

Overhead the attics of the houses almost met across the street, cutting out light; underfoot the stones were slippery with water and refuse. Hare went along at a good pace, though he kept trailing his hand along the walls like a blind man. They had to keep pretty close behind him lest they lose him at a cross-street. The excitement of the chase came into Arren suddenly; his senses were all alert, as they were during a stag-hunt in the forests of Enlad; he saw vividly each face they passed, and breathed in the sweet stink of the city, a smell of garbage, incense, carrion and flowers. As they threaded their way across a broad, crowded street he heard a drum beat, and caught a glimpse of a line of naked men and women, chained each to the next by wrist and waist, matted hair hanging over their faces; one glimpse and they were gone, as he dodged after Hare down a flight of steps and out into a narrow square, empty but for a few women gossiping at the fountain.

There Sparrowhawk caught up with Hare and set a hand on his shoulder, at which Hare cringed as if scalded, wincing away, and backed into the shelter of a massive doorway. There he stood shivering, and stared at them with the unseeing eyes of the hunted.

'Are you called Hare?' asked Sparrowhawk, and he spoke in his own voice, which was harsh in quality, but gentle in intonation. The man said nothing, seeming not to heed or not to hear. 'I want something of you,' Sparrowhawk said. Again no response. 'I'll pay for it.'

A slow reaction : 'Ivory or gold?'

'Gold.'

'How much?'

'The wizard knows the spell's worth.'

Hare's face flinched and changed, coming alive for an instant, so quickly that it seemed to flicker, then clouding again into blankness. 'That's all gone,' he said, 'all gone.' A coughing fit bent him over; he spat black. When he straightened up he stood passive, shivering, seeming to have forgotten what they were talking about.

Again Arren watched him in fascination. The angle in which he stood was formed by two giant figures flanking a doorway, statues whose necks were bowed under the weight of a pediment and whose knot-muscled bodies emerged only partially from the wall, as if they had tried to struggle out of stone into life and had failed partway. The door they guarded was rotten on its hinges; the house, once a palace, was derelict. The gloomy, bulging faces of the giants were chipped and lichen-grown. Between these ponderous figures the man called Hare stood slack and fragile, his eyes as dark as the windows of the empty house. He lifted up his maimed arm between himself and Sparrowhawk and whined, 'Spare a little for a poor cripple, master ...'

The mage scowled as if in pain, or shame; Arren felt he had seen his true face for a moment under the disguise. He put his hand again on Hare's shoulder and said a few words, softly, in the wizardly tongue that Arren did not understand.

But Hare understood. He clutched at Sparrowhawk with his one hand, and stammered, 'You can still speak – speak – Come with me, come –'

The mage glanced at Arren, then nodded.

They went down by steep streets into one of the valleys between Hort Town's three hills. The ways became narrower, darker, quieter as they descended. The sky was a pale strip between the overhanging eaves, and the house-walls to either hand were dank. At the bottom of the gorge a stream ran, stinking like an open sewer; between arched bridges houses crowded along its banks, and into the dark doorway of one of these houses Hare turned aside, vanishing like a candle blown out. They followed him.

The unlit stairs creaked and swayed beneath their feet. At the head of the stairs Hare pushed open a door, and they could see where they were : an empty room with a straw-stuffed mattress in one corner and one unglazed, shuttered window that let in a little dusty light.

Hare turned to face Sparrowhawk and caught at his arm again. His lips worked. He said at last, stammering, 'Dragon ... Dragon ...'

Sparrowhawk returned his look steadily, saying nothing.

'I cannot speak,' Hare said, and he let go his hold on Sparrowhawk's arm and crouched down on the empty floor, weeping.

The mage knelt by him and spoke to him softly in the Old Speech. Arren stood by the shut door, his hand on his knifehilt. The

343

grey light and the dusty room, the two kneeling figures, the soft strange sound of the mage's voice speaking the language of the dragons, all came together as does a dream, having no relation to what happens outside it or to time passing.

Slowly Hare stood up. He dusted his knees with his single hand, and hid the maimed arm behind his back. He looked around him, looked at Arren; he was seeing what he looked at, now. He turned away presently and sat down on his mattress. Arren remained standing, on guard; but, with the simplicity of one whose childhood was totally unfurnished, Sparrowhawk sat down cross-legged on the bare floor. 'Tell me how you lost your craft, and the language of your craft,' he said.

Hare did not answer for a while. He began to beat his mutilated arm against his thigh in a restless, jerky way, and at last he said, forcing the words out in bursts, 'They cut off my hand. I can't weave the spells. They cut off my hand. The blood ran out, ran dry.'

'But that was after you'd lost your power, Hare, or else they could not have done it.'

'Power ...'

'Power over the winds, and the waves, and men. You called them by their names and they obeyed you.'

'Yes. I remember being alive,' the man said in a soft hoarse voice. 'And I knew the words, and the names ...'

'Are you dead now?'

'No. Alive. Alive. Only once I was a dragon ... I'm not dead. I sleep sometimes. Sleep comes very close to death, everyone knows that. The dead walk in dreams, everyone knows that. They come to you alive, and they say things. They walk out of death into the dreams. There's a way. And if you go on far enough there's a way back all the way. All the way. You can find it if you know where to look. And if you're willing to pay the price.'

'What price is that?' Sparrowhawk's voice floated on the dim air like the shadow of a falling leaf.

'Life - what else? What can you buy life with, but life?' Hare rocked back and forth on his pallet, a cunning, uncanny brightness

in his eyes. 'You see,' he said, 'they can cut off my hand. They can
cut off my head. It doesn't matter. I can find the way back. I know
where to look. Only men of power can go there.'

'Wizards, you mean?'

'Yes.' Hare hesitated, seeming to attempt the word several times;
he could not say it. 'Men of power,' he repeated. 'And they must –
and they must give it up. Pay.'

Then he fell sullen, as if the word 'pay' had at last roused associ-
ations, and he had realized that he was giving information away
instead of selling it. Nothing more could be got from him, not even
the hints and stammers about 'a way back' which Sparrowhawk
seemed to find meaningful, and soon enough the mage stood up.
'Well, half answers beat no answer,' he said, 'and the same with
payment,' and, deft as a conjuror, he flipped a gold piece onto the
pallet in front of Hare.

Hare picked it up. He looked at it, and Sparrowhawk, and Arren,
with jerky movements of his head. 'Wait,' he stammered. As soon as
the situation changed he lost his grip of it, and now groped miserably after what he wanted to say. 'Tonight,' he said at last. 'Wait.
Tonight. I have hazia.'

'I don't need it.'

'To show you – To show you the way. Tonight. I'll take you. I'll
show you. You can get there, because you ... you're ...' He groped
for the word until Sparrowhawk said, 'I am a wizard.'

'Yes! So we can – we can get there. To the way. When I dream.
In the dream. See? I'll take you. You'll go with me, to the ... to
the way.'

Sparrowhawk stood, solid and pondering, in the middle of the
dim room. 'Maybe,' he said at last. 'If we come, we'll be here by
dark.' Then he turned to Arren, who opened the door at once, eager
to be gone.

The dank overshadowed street seemed bright as a garden after
Hare's room. They struck out for the upper city by the shortest way,
a steep stairway of stone between ivy-grown house-walls. Arren
breathed in and out like a sea-lion – 'Ugh! – Are you going back
there?'

'Well, I will, if I can't get the same information from a less risky source. He's likely to set an ambush for us.'

'But aren't you defended against thieves and so on?'

'Defended?' said Sparrowhawk. 'What do you mean? D'you think I go about wrapped up in spells like an old woman afraid of rheumatism? I haven't the time for it. I hide my face to hide our quest; that's all. We can look out for each other. But the fact is we're not going to be able to keep out of danger on this journey.'

'Of course not,' Arren said stiffly, angry, angered in his pride. 'I did not seek to do so.'

'That's just as well,' the mage said, inflexible, and yet with a kind of good humour that appeased Arren's temper. Indeed, he was startled by his own anger; he had never thought to speak thus to the Archmage. But then, this was and was not the Archmage, this Hawk with the snub nose and square, ill-shaven cheeks, whose voice was sometimes one man's voice and sometimes another's : a stranger, unreliable.

'Does it make sense, what he told you?' Arren asked, for he did not look forward to going back to that dim room above the stinking river. 'All that fibblefabble about being alive and dead and coming back with his head cut off?'

'I don't know if it makes sense. I wanted to talk with a wizard who has lost his power. He says that he hasn't lost it but given it – traded it. For what? Life for life, he said. Power for power. No, I don't understand him, but he is worth listening to.'

Sparrowhawk's steady reasonableness shamed Arren further. He felt himself petulant and nervous, like a child. Hare had fascinated him, but now that fascination was broken he felt a sick disgust, as if he had eaten something vile. He resolved not to speak again until he had controlled his temper. Next moment he missed his step on the worn, slick stairs, slipped, recovering himself scraping his hands on the stones. 'Oh curse this filthy town !' he broke out in rage. And the mage replied dryly, 'No need to, I think.'

There was indeed something very wrong about Hort Town, wrong in the very air, so that one might think seriously that it lay under a curse; and yet this was not a presence of any quality but rather an absence, a weakening of all qualities, like a sickness that soon infected the spirit of any visitor. Even the warmth of the afternoon sun was sickly, too heavy a heat for March. The squares and streets bustled with activity and business, but there was neither order nor prosperity. Goods were poor, prices high, and the markets were unsafe for vendors and buyers alike, being full of thieves and roaming gangs. Not many women were on the streets, and then mostly in groups. It was a city without law or governance. Talking with people, Arren and Sparrowhawk soon learned that there was in fact no council or mayor or lord left in Hort Town. Some of those who had used to rule the city had died, and some had resigned, and some had been assassinated; various chiefs lorded it over various quarters of the city, the harbour guardsmen ran the port and lined their pockets, and so on. There was no centre left to the city. The people, for all their restless activity, seemed purposeless. Craftsmen seemed to lack the will to work well; even the robbers robbed because it was all they knew how to do. All the brawl and brightness of a great port-city was there, on the surface, but all about the edges of it sat the hazia-eaters, motionless. And under the surface things did not seem entirely real, not even the faces, the sounds, the smells. They would fade, from time to time during that long, warm afternoon while Sparrowhawk and Arren walked the streets and talked with this person and that. They would fade quite away, the striped awnings, the dirty cobbles, the coloured walls, and all vividness of being would be gone, leaving the city a dream city, empty and dreary in the hazy sunlight.

Only at the top of the town where they went to rest a while in late afternoon did this sickly mood of daydream break for a while. 'This is not a town for luck,' Sparrowhawk had said some hours ago, and now after hours of aimless wandering and fruitless conversations with strangers, he looked tired and grim. His disguise was wearing a little thin; a certain hardness and darkness could be seen through the bluff sea-trader's face. Arren had never been able to shake off the morning's irritability. They sat down on the coarse turf of the hilltop under the eaves of a grove of pendick trees, dark-leaved and budded thickly with red buds, some open. From there they saw nothing of the city but its tile roofs multitudinously scaling downward to the sea. The bay opened its arms wide, slate blue beneath the spring haze, reaching on to the edge of air. No lines were drawn, no boundaries. They sat gazing at that immense blue space. Arren's mind cleared, opening out to meet and celebrate the world.

When they went to drink from a little stream nearby, running clear over brown rocks from its spring in some princely garden on the hill behind them, he drank deep, and doused his head right under the cold water. Then he got up and declaimed the lines from the *Deed of Morred,*

> *Praised are the Fountains of Shelieth, the silver harp*
> *of the waters,*
> *But blest in my name forever this stream that*
> *stanched my thirst!*

Sparrowhawk laughed at him, and he also laughed. He shook his head like a dog, and the bright spray flew out fine in the last gold sunlight.

They had to leave the grove and go down into the streets again, and when they had made their supper at a stall that sold greasy fishcakes, night was getting heavy in the air. Darkness came fast in the narrow streets. 'We'd better go, lad,' said Sparrowhawk, and Arren said, 'To the boat?' but knew it was not to be the boat but to the house above the river and the empty, dusty, terrible room.

Hare was waiting for them in the doorway.

He lighted an oil lamp to show them up the black stairs. Its tiny flame trembled continually as he held it, throwing vast, quick shadows up the walls.

He had got another sack of straw for his visitors to sit on, but Arren took his place on the bare floor by the door. The door opened outward, and to guard it he should have sat himself down outside it: but that pitchblack hall was more than he could stand, and he wanted to keep an eye on Hare. Sparrowhawk's attention, and perhaps his powers, were going to be turned on what Hare had to tell him, or show him; it was up to Arren to keep alert for trickery.

Hare held himself straighter, and trembled less; he had cleaned his mouth and teeth; he spoke sanely enough, at first, though with excitement. His eyes in the lamplight were so dark that they seemed, like the eyes of animals, to show no whites. He disputed earnestly with Sparrowhawk, urging him to eat hazia. 'I want to take you, take you with me. We've got to go the same way. Before long I'll be going whether you're ready or not. You must have the hazia to follow me.'

'I think I can follow you.'

'Not where I'm going. This isn't ... spell-casting.' He seemed unable to say the words 'wizard' or wizardry'. 'I know you can get to the – place, you know, the wall. But it isn't there. It's a different way.'

'If you go, I can follow.'

Hare shook his head. His handsome, ruined face was flushed; he glanced over at Arren often, including him, though he spoke only to Sparrowhawk. 'Look: there are two kinds of man, aren't there? Our kind, and the rest. The ... dragons, and the others. People without power are only half alive. They don't count. They don't know what they dream, they're afraid of the dark. But the others, the lords of men, aren't afraid to go into the dark. We have strength.'

'So long as we know the names of things.'

'But names don't matter there – that's the point, that's the point! It isn't what you do, what you know, that you need. Spells are no good. You have to forget all that, to let it go. That's where eating hazia helps, you forget the names, you let the forms of things go, you go straight to the reality. I'm going to be going pretty soon now; if you want to find out where you ought to do as I say. I say as he does. You must be a lord of men to be a lord of life. You have to find the secret. I could tell you its name but what's a name? A name isn't real, the real, the real forever. Dragons can't go there. Dragons die. They all die. I took so much tonight you'll never catch me. Not a patch on me. Where I get lost you can lead me. Remember what the secret is? Remember? No death. No death – no! No sweaty bed and rotting coffin, no more, never. The blood dries up like the dry river and it's gone. No fear. No death. The names are

349

gone and the words and the fear gone. Show me where I can get lost, show me, lord ...'

So he went on, in a choked rapture of words that was like the chanting of a spell and yet made no spell, no whole, no sense. Arren listened, listened, striving to understand. If only he could understand! Sparrowhawk should do as he said and take the drug, this once, so that he could find out what Hare was talking about, the mystery that he would not or could not speak. Why else were they here? But then (Arren looked from Hare's ecstatic face to the other profile) perhaps the mage understood already ... Hard as rock, that profile. Where was the snub nose, the bland look? Hawk the sea-trader was gone, forgotten. It was the mage, the Archmage, who sat there.

Hare's voice now was a crooning mumble, and he rocked his body as he sat cross-legged. His face had grown haggard and his mouth slack. Facing him, in the tiny, steady light of the oil lamp set on the floor between them, the other never spoke, but he had reached out and taken Hare's hand, holding him. Arren had not seen him reach out. There were gaps in the order of events, gaps of non-existence – drowsiness, it must be. Surely some hours had passed, it might be near midnight. If he slept, would he too be able to follow Hare into his dream, and come to the place, the secret way? Perhaps he could. It seemed quite possible now. But he was to guard the door. He and Sparrowhawk had scarcely spoken of it, but both were aware that in having them come back at night Hare might have planned some ambush; he had been a pirate, he knew robbers. They had said nothing, but Arren knew that he was to stand guard, for while the mage made this strange journey of the spirit he would be defenceless. But like a fool he had left his sword on board the boat, and how much good would his knife be if that door swung suddenly open behind him? But that would not happen: he could listen, and hear. Hare was not speaking any more, both men were utterly silent, the whole house was silent. Nobody could come up those swaying stairs without some noise. He could speak, if he heard a noise: shout aloud, and the trance would break, and Sparrowhawk would turn and defend himself and Arren with all the vengeful lightning of a wizard's rage ... When Arren had sat down at the door Sparrowhawk had looked at him, only a glance, approval: approval and trust. He was the guard. There was no danger if he kept on guard. But it was hard, hard to keep watching those two faces, the little pearl of lamp-flame between them on the floor, both silent now, both still, their eyes open but not seeing the light or the dusty room, not seeing the world, but some other world of dream or death ... to watch them, and not try to follow them ...

There, in the vast, dry darkness, there one stood beckoning. *Come*, he said, the tall lord of shadows. In his hand he held a tiny flame no larger than a pearl, held it out to Arren, offering life. Slowly Arren took one step towards him, following.

4. Magelight

DRY, his mouth was dry. There was the taste of dust in his mouth. His lips were covered with dust.

Without lifting his head from the floor he watched the shadow-play. There were the big shadows that moved and stooped, swelled and shrank, and fainter ones that ran around the walls and ceiling swiftly mocking them. There was a shadow in the corner, and a shadow on the floor, and neither of these moved.

The back of his head began to hurt. At the same time, what he saw came clear to his mind, in one flash, frozen in an instant: Hare slumped in a corner with his head on his knees, Sparrowhawk sprawled on his back, a man kneeling over Sparrowhawk, another tossing gold pieces into a bag, a third standing watching. The third man held a lantern in one hand and a dagger in the other, Arren's dagger.

If they talked he did not hear them. He heard only his own thoughts, which told him immediately and unhesitatingly what to do. He obeyed them at once. He crawled forward very slowly a couple of feet, darted out his left hand and grabbed the bag of loot, leapt to his feet, and made for the stairs with a hoarse yell. He plunged downstairs in the blind dark without missing a step, without even feeling them under his feet, as if he were flying. He broke out into the street and ran fullspeed into the dark.

The houses were black hulks against stars. Starlight gleamed faintly on the river to his right, and though he could not see where the streets led, he could make out street-crossings, and so turn and double on his track. They had followed him, he could hear them behind him, not very far behind. They were unshod, and their panting breathing was louder than their footfalls. He would have laughed if he had had time; he knew at last what it was like to be the hunted instead of the hunter, the leader of the chase, the quarry. It was to be alone, and to be free. He swerved to the right and dodged stooping across a high-parapeted bridge, slipped into a sidestreet, around a corner, back to the riverside and along it for a way, across another bridge. His shoes were loud on the cobblestones, the only sound in all the city; he paused at the bridge abutment to unlace them, but the strings were knotted, and the hunt had not lost him. The lantern glittered a second across the river, the soft, heavy, running feet came on. He could not get away from them, he could only outrun them, keep going, keep ahead, and get them away from the dusty room, far away ... They had stripped his coat off him, along with his dagger and he was in shirt-sleeves, light and hot, his head swimming and the pain in the back of his skull pointing and pointing with each stride, and he ran, and he ran ... The bag hindered him. He flung it down suddenly, a loose gold piece flying out and striking the stones with a clear ring. 'Here's your money!' he yelled, his voice hoarse and gasping. He ran on. And all at once the street ended. No cross streets, no stars before him, a dead end. Without pausing he turned back and ran at his pursuers. The lantern swung wild in his eyes, and he yelled defiance as he came at them.

There was a lantern swinging back and forth before him, a faint spot of light in a great moving greyness. He watched it for a long time. It grew fainter, and at last a shadow passed before it, and when the shadow went on the light was gone. He grieved for it a little; or perhaps he was grieving for himself because he knew he must wake up now.

The lantern, dead, still swung against the mast to which it was fixed. All around, the sea brightened with the coming sun. A drum beat. Oars creaked heavily, regularly; the wood of the ship cried and creaked in a hundred little voices; a man up in the prow called something to the sailors behind him. The men chained with Arren in the after hold were all silent. Each wore an iron band around his waist, and manacles on his wrists, and both these bonds were linked by a short heavy chain to the bonds of the next man; the belt of iron was also chained to a bolt in the deck, so that the man could sit, or crouch, but could not stand. They were too close together to lie down, jammed together in the small cargo-hold. Arren was in the forward port corner. If he lifted his head high his eyes were on a level with the decking between hold and rail, a couple of feet wide.

He did not remember much of last night past the chase and the dead-end street. He had fought, and been knocked down and trussed up, and carried somewhere. A man with a strange whispering voice had spoken; there had been a place like a smithy, a forge-fire leaping red . . . he could not recall it. He knew, though, that this was a slave-ship, and that he had been taken to be sold.

It did not mean much to him. He was too thirsty. His body ached and his head hurt. When the sun rose the light sent lances of pain into his eyes.

Along in mid-morning they were given a quarter of bread each and a long drink from a leather flask, held to their lips by a man with a sharp, hard face. His neck was clasped by a broad, gold-studded leather band like a dog's collar, and when Arren heard him speak he recognized the weak, strange, whistling voice.

Drink and food eased his bodily wretchedness for a while, and cleared his head. He looked for the first time at the faces of his fellow slaves, three in his row and four close behind. Some sat with their heads on their raised knees; one was slumped over, sick or drugged. The one next to Arren was a fellow of twenty or so with a broad, flat face. 'Where are they taking us?' Arren said to him.

The fellow looked at him – their faces were not a foot apart – and grinned, shrugging, and Arren thought he meant he did not know; but then he jerked his manacled arms as if to gesture, and opened his still grinning mouth to show, where the tongue should be, only a black root.

'It'll be Showl,' said one behind Arren, and another, 'Or the Market at Amrun,' and then the man with the collar, who seemed to be everywhere on the ship, was bending above the hold hissing, 'Be still if you don't want to be sharkbait,' and all of them were still.

Arren tried to imagine these places, Showl, the Market of Amrun. They sold slaves there. They stood them out in front of the buyers, no doubt, like oxen or rams for sale in Berila Market-place.

He would stand there, wearing chains. Somebody would buy him and lead him home, and they would give him an order; and he would refuse to obey. Or obey, and try to escape. And he would be killed, one way or the other. It was not that his soul rebelled at the thought of slavery, he was much too sick and bewildered for that; it was simply that he knew he could not do it, that within a week or two he would die or be killed. Though he saw and accepted this as a fact it frightened him, so that he stopped trying to think ahead. He stared down at the foul black planking of the hold between his feet, and felt the heat of the sun on his naked shoulders, and felt the thirst drying out his mouth and narrowing his throat again.

The sun sank, night came on clear and cold. The sharp stars came out. The drum beat like a slow heart, keeping the oar-stroke, for there was no breath of wind. Now the cold became the greatest misery. Arren's back gained a little warmth from the cramped legs of the man behind him, and his left side from the mute beside him, who sat hunched up, humming a grunting rhythm all on one note. The rowers changed shift, the drum beat again. Arren had longed for the darkness, but he could not sleep; his bones ached, and he could not change position. He sat aching, shivering, parched, staring up at the stars, which jerked across the sky with every stroke the oarsmen took, slid to their places and were still, jerked again, slid, paused...

The man with the collar and another stood between the after hold and the mast; the little swinging lantern on the mast sent gleams between them and silhouetted their heads and shoulders. 'Fog, you pig's bladder,' said the weak hateful voice of the man with the collar, 'what's a fog doing in the Southing Straits this time of year? Curse the luck!'

The drum beat. The stars jerked, slid, paused. Beside Arren the tongueless man shuddered all at once and raising his head let out a nightmare scream, a terrible, formless noise. 'Quiet there!' roared the second man by the mast. The mute shuddered again and was silent, munching with his jaws.

Stealthily the stars slid forward into nothingness.

The mast wavered and vanished. A cold grey blanket seemed to drop over Arren's back. The drum faltered, then resumed its beat, but slower.

'Thick as curdled milk,' said the hoarse voice somewhere above Arren. 'Keep up the stroke there! there's no shoals for twenty miles!' A horny, scarred foot appeared out of the fog, paused an instant close to Arren's face, then with one step vanished.

In the fog there was no sense of forward motion, only of swaying, and the tug of the oars. The throb of the stroke-drum was muffled. It was clammy cold. The mist condensing in Arren's hair ran down into his eyes; he tried to catch the drops with his tongue, and breathed the damp air with open mouth, trying to assuage his thirst. But his teeth chattered. The cold metal of a chain swung against his thigh, and burned like fire where it touched. The drum beat, and beat, and ceased.

It was silent.

'Keep the beat! What's amiss?' roared the hoarse, whistling voice from the prow. No answer came.

The ship rolled a little on the quiet sea. Beyond the dim rails was nothing: blank. Something grated against the ship's side. The noise was loud in that dead, weird silence and darkness. 'We're aground,' one of the prisoners whispered, but the silence closed in on his voice.

The fog grew bright, as if a light were blooming in it. Arren saw the heads of men chained by him clearly, the tiny moisture-drops shining in their hair. Again the ship swayed, and he strained as far up as his chains would let him, stretching his neck, to see forward in the ship. The fog glowed over the deck like the moon behind thin cloud, cold and radiant. The oarsmen sat like carved statues. Crewmen stood in the waist of the ship, their eyes shining a little. Alone on the port side stood a man, and it was from him that the light came, from the face, and hands, and staff that burned like molten silver.

At the feet of the radiant man a dark shape was crouched.

Arren tried to speak, and could not. Clothed in that majesty of light, the Archmage came to him ,and knelt down on the deck. Arren felt the touch of his hand, and heard his voice. He felt the bonds on his wrists and body give way; all through the hold there was a rattling of chains. But no man moved; only Arren tried to stand, but he could not, being cramped with long immobility. The Archmage's strong grip was on his arm, and with that help he crawled up out of the cargo-hold, and huddled on the deck.

The Archmage strode away from him, and the misty splendour glowed on the unmoving faces of the oarsmen. He halted by the man who had crouched down by the port rail.

'I do not punish,' said the hard, clear voice, cold as the cold magelight in the fog. 'But in the cause of justice, Egre, I take this much upon myself: I bid your voice be dumb until the day you find a word worth speaking.'

He came back to Arren and helped him to get to his feet. 'Come on now, lad,' he said, and with his help Arren managed to hobble forward, and half-scramble, half-fall down into the boat that rocked there below the ship's side: *Lookfar*, her sail like a moth's wing in the fog.

In the same silence and dead calm the light died away, and the boat turned and slipped from the ship's side. Almost at once the galley, the dim mast-lantern, the immobile oarsmen, the hulking black side, were gone. Arren thought he heard voices break out in cries but the sound was thin and soon lost. A little longer, and the fog began to thin and tatter, blowing by in the dark. They came out under the stars, and silent as a moth *Lookfar* fled through the clear night over the sea.

Sparrowhawk had covered Arren with blankets, and given him water; he sat with his hand on the boy's shoulder when he fell suddenly to weeping. He said nothing, but there was a gentleness, a steadiness, in the touch of his hand. Comfort came slowly into Arren: warmth, the soft motion of the boat, heart's ease.

He looked up at his companion. No unearthly radiance clung to the dark face. He could barely see him, against the stars.

The boat fled on, charm-guided. Waves whispered as if in surprise along her sides.

'Who is the man with the collar?'

'Lie still. A sea-robber, Egre. He wears that collar to hide a scar

357

where his throat was slit once. It seems his trade has sunk from piracy to slaving. But he took the bear's cub this time.' There was a slight ring of satisfaction in the dry, quiet voice.

'How did you find me?'

'Wizardry, bribery . . . I wasted time. I did not like to let it be known that the Archmage and Warden of Roke was ferreting about the slums of Hort Town. I wish still I could have kept up my disguise. But I had to track down this man and that man, and when at last I found that the slaver had sailed before daybreak, I lost my temper. I took *Lookfar* and spoke the wind into her sail, in the dead calm of the day, and glued the oars of every ship in that bay fast into the oarlocks – for a while – How they'll explain that, if wizardry's all lies and air, is their problem. But in my haste and anger I missed and overpassed Egre's ship, which had gone east of south to miss the shoals. Ill done was all I did this day. There is no luck in Hort Town . . . Well I made a spell of finding at last, and so came on the ship in the darkness. Should you not sleep now?'

'I'm all right, I feel much better.' A light fever had replaced Arren's chill, and he did indeed feel well, his body languid but his mind racing lightly from one thing to another. 'How soon did you wake up? What happened to Hare?'

'I woke with daylight; and lucky I have a hard head; there's a lump and a cut like a split cucumber behind my ear. I left Hare in the drug-sleep.'

'I failed my guard –'

'But not by falling asleep.'

'No.' Arren hesitated. 'It was – I was –'

'You were ahead of me; I saw you,' Sparrowhawk said strangely. 'And so they crept in and tapped us on the head like lambs at the shambles, took gold, good clothes, and the saleable slave, and left. It was you they were after, lad. You'd fetch the price of a farm in Amrun Market.'

'They didn't tap me hard enough. I woke up. I did give them a run. I spilt their loot all over the street, too, before they cornered me.' Arren's eyes glittered.

'You woke while they were there – and ran? Why?'

'To get them away from you.' The surprise in Sparrowhawk's voice suddenly struck Arren's pride, and he added fiercely, 'I thought it was you they were after. I thought they might kill you. I grabbed their bag so they'd follow me, and shouted out, and ran. And they followed me.'

'Aye – they would!' That was all Sparrowhawk said, no word of praise, though he sat and thought a while. Then he said, 'Did it not occur to you I might be dead already?'

'No.'

'Murder first and rob after, is the safer course.'

'I didn't think of that. I only thought of getting them away from you.'

'Why?'

'Because you might be able to defend us, to get us both out of it, if you had time to wake up. Or get yourself out of it, anyway. I was on guard and I failed my guard. I tried to make up for it. You are the one I was guarding. You are the one that matters. I'm along to guard, or whatever you need – it's you who'll lead us, who can get to wherever it is we must go, and put right what's gone wrong.'

'Is it?' said the mage. 'I thought so myself, until last night. I thought I had a follower, but I followed you, my lad.' His voice was cool and perhaps a little ironic. Arren did not know what to say. He was indeed completely confused. He had thought that his fault of falling into sleep or trance on guard could scarcely be atoned by his feat of drawing off the robbers from Sparrowhawk: it now appeared that the latter had been a silly act, whereas going into trance at the wrong moment had been wonderfully clever.

'I am sorry, my lord,' he said at last, his lips rather stiff and the need to cry not easily controlled again, 'that I failed you. And you have saved my life –'

'And you mine, maybe,' said the mage harshly. 'Who knows? They might have slit my throat when they were done. No more of that, Arren. I am glad you are with me.'

He went to their stores-box, then, and lit their little charcoal

stove, and busied himself with something. Arren lay and watched
the stars, and his emotions cooled and his mind ceased racing. And
he saw then that what he had done, and what he had not done, was
not going to receive judgement from Sparrowhawk. He had done it;
Sparrowhawk accepted it as done. 'I do not punish,' he had said,
cold-voiced, to Egre. Neither did he reward. But he had come for
Arren in all haste across the sea, unleashing the power of his wizardry for his sake; and he would do so again. He was to be depended
on.

He was worth all the love Arren had for him, and all the trust.
For the fact was that he trusted Arren. What Arren did, was right.

He came back now, handing Arren a cup of steaming hot wine.
'Maybe that'll put you to sleep. Take care, it'll scald your tongue.'

'Where did the wine come from? I never saw a wineskin
aboard –'

'There's more in *Lookfar* than meets the eye,' Sparrowhawk said,
sitting down beside him, and Arren heard him laugh, briefly and
almost silently, in the dark.

Arren sat up to drink the wine. It was very good, refreshing body
and spirit. He said, 'Where are we going now?'

'Westward.'

'Where did you go with Hare?'

'Into the darkness. I never lost him, but he was lost. He wandered
on the outer borders, in the endless barrens of delirium and nightmare. His soul piped like a bird in those dreary places, like a seagull
crying far from the sea. He is no guide. He has always been lost. For
all his craft in sorcery he has never seen the way before him, seeing
only himself.'

Arren did not understand all of this; nor did he want to understand it now. He had been drawn a little way into that 'darkness' of
which wizards spoke, and he did not want to remember it; it was
nothing to do with him. Indeed he did not want to sleep, lest he see
it again in dream, and see that dark figure, a shadow holding out a
pearl, whispering, 'Come.'

'My lord,' he said, his mind veering away rapidly to another subject, 'why –'

'Sleep!' said Sparrowhawk with mild exasperation.

'I can't sleep my lord. I wondered why you didn't free the other slaves.'

'I did. I left none bound on that ship.'

'But Egre's men had weapons. If you had bound *them* –'

'Aye, if I had bound them? There were but six. The oarsmen were chained slaves, like you. Egre and his men may be dead by now, or chained by the others to be sold as slaves; but I left them free to fight, or bargain. I am no slave-taker.'

'But you know them to be evil men –'

'Was I to join them therefore? To let their acts rule my own? I will not make their choices for them, nor will I let them make mine for me!'

Arren was silent, pondering this. Presently the mage said, speaking softly, 'Do you see, Arren, how an act is not, as young men think, like a rock that one picks up and throws, and it hits or misses, and that's the end of it. When that rock is lifted the earth is lighter, the hand that bears it heavier. When it is thrown the circuits of the stars respond, and where it strikes or falls the universe is changed. On every act the balance of the whole depends. The winds and seas, the powers of water and earth and light, all that these do, and all that the beasts and green things do, is well done, and rightly done. All these act within the Equilibrium. From the hurricane and the great whale's sounding to the fall of a dry leaf and the gnat's flight, all they do is done within the balance of the whole. But we, in so far as we have power over the world and over one another, we must *learn* to do what the leaf and the whale and the wind do of their own nature. We must learn to keep the balance. Having intelligence, we must not act in ignorance. Having choice, we must not act without responsibility. Who am I – though I have the power to do it – to punish and reward, playing with men's destinies?'

'But then,' the boy said, frowning at the stars, 'is the balance to be kept by doing nothing? Surely a man must act, even not knowing all the consequences of his act, if anything is to be done at all?'

'Never fear. It is much easier for men to act than to refrain from acting. We will continue to do good, and to do evil ... But if there were a king over us all again, and he sought counsel of a mage, as in the days of old, and I were that mage, I would say to him : My lord, do nothing because it is righteous, or praiseworthy, or noble, to do so; do nothing because it seems good to do so; do only that which you must do, and which you cannot do in any other way.'

There was that in his voice which made Arren turn to watch him as he spoke. He thought that the radiance of light was shining again from his face, seeing the hawk nose and the scarred cheek, the dark, fierce eyes. And Arren looked at him with love but also with fear, thinking, 'He is too far above me.' Yet as he gazed he became aware at last that it was no magelight, no cold glory of wizardry, that lay shadowless on every line and plane of the man's face, but light itself : morning, the common light of day. There was a power greater than his own. And the years had been no kinder to Sparrowhawk than to any man. Those were lines of age; and he looked tired, as the light grew ever stronger. He yawned . . .

So gazing, and wondering, and pondering, Arren fell asleep at last. But Sparrowhawk sat by him watching the dawn come and the sun rise, even as one might study a treasure for something gone amiss in it, a jewel flawed, a child sick.

5. Sea Dreams

LATE in the morning Sparrowhawk took the magewind from the sail and let his boat go by the world's wind, which blew softly to the south and west. Far off to the right the hills of southern Wathort slipped away and fell behind, growing blue and small, like misty waves above the waves.

Arren woke. The sea basked in the hot, gold noon, endless water under endless light. In the stern of the boat Sparrowhawk sat naked except for a loincloth and a kind of turban made from sailcloth. He was singing softly, striking his palms on the thwart as if it were a drum, in a light monotonous rhythm. The song he sang was no spell of wizardry, no chant of Deed of heroes or kings, but a lilting drone of nonsense words, such as a boy might sing as he herded goats through the long, long afternoons of summer, in the high hills of Gont, alone.

From the sea's surface a fish leaped up and glided through the air for many yards on stiff, shimmering vanes like the wings of dragon-flies.

'We're in the South Reach,' Sparrowhawk said, when his song was done. 'A strange part of the world, where the fish fly, and the dolphins sing, they say. But the water's mild for swimming, and I have an understanding with the sharks. Wash the touch of the slave-taker from you.'

Arren was sore in every muscle, and loath to move at first. Also he was an unpractised swimmer, for the seas of Enlad are bitter, so that one must fight with them rather than swim in them, and is soon exhausted. This bluer sea was cold at first plunge, then delightful. Aches dropped away from him. He thrashed by *Lookfar's* side like a young sea-serpent. Spray flew up in fountains. Sparrowhawk joined him, swimming with a firmer stroke. Docile and protective, *Lookfar* waited for them, white-winged on the shining water. A fish leaped from sea to air; Arren pursued it; it dived, leapt up again, swimming in air, flying in the sea, pursuing him.

Golden and supple, the boy played and basked in the water and the light until the sun touched the sea. And dark and spare, with the economy of gesture and the terse strength of age, the man swam, and kept the boat on course, and rigged up an awning of sailcloth, and watched the swimming boy and the flying fish with an impartial tenderness.

'Where are we heading?' Arren asked in the late dusk, after eating largely salt meat and hardbread, and already sleepy again.

'Lorbanery,' Sparrowhawk replied, and the soft meaningless syllables were the last word Arren heard that night, so that his dreams of the early night wove themselves about it. He dreamed he was walking in drifts of soft, pale-coloured stuff, shreds and threads of pink and gold and azure, and felt a foolish pleasure; someone told him, 'These are the silkfields of Lorbanery, where it never gets dark.' But later, in the fag-end of night, when the stars of autumn shone in the sky of spring, he dreamed that he was in a ruined house. It was dry there. Everything was dusty, and festooned with ragged, dusty webs. Arren's legs were tangled in the webs, and they drifted across his mouth and nostrils, stopping his breath. And the worst horror of it was that he knew the high, ruined room was that hall where he had breakfasted with the Masters, in the Great House on Roke.

He woke all in dismay, his heart pounding, his legs cramped against a thwart. He sat up, trying to get away from the evil dream. In the east there was not yet light, but a dilution of darkness. The mast creaked; the sail, still taut to the north-east breeze, glimmered high and faint above him. In the stern his companion slept sound and silent. Arren lay down again, and dozed till clear day woke him.

This day the sea was bluer and quieter than he had ever imagined it could be, the water so mild and clear that swimming in it was half like gliding or floating upon air; strange it was, and dreamlike.

In the noontime he asked, 'Do wizards make much account of dreams?'

Sparrowhawk was fishing. He watched his line attentively. After a long time he said, 'Why?'

'I wondered if there's ever truth in them.'

'Surely.'

'Do they foretell truly?'

But the mage had a bite, and ten minutes later when he had landed their lunch, a splendid silver-blue sea bass, the question was clean forgotten.

In the afternoon as they lazed under the awning rigged to give shelter from the imperious sun, Arren asked, 'What do we seek in Lorbanery?'

'That which we seek,' said Sparrowhawk.

'In Enlad,' said Arren after a while, 'we have a story about the boy whose schoolmaster was a stone.'

'Aye? ... What did he learn?'

'Not to ask questions.'

Sparrowhawk snorted, as if suppressing a laugh, and sat up. 'Very well!' he said. 'Though I prefer to save talking till I know what I'm talking about. Why is there no more magic done in Hort Town, and in Narveduen, and maybe throughout all the Reaches? That's what we seek to learn, is it not?'

'Yes.'

'Do you know the old saying, *Rules change in the Reaches?* Seamen use it, but it is a wizard's saying, and it means that wizardry itself depends on place. A true spell on Roke may be mere words on Iffish. The language of the Making is not everywhere remembered; here one word, there another. And the weaving of spells is itself interwoven with the earth and the water, the winds, the fall of light, of the place where it is cast. I once sailed into the East, so far that neither wind nor water heeded my command, being ignorant of their true names; or more likely it was I that was ignorant. For the world is very large, the Open Sea going on past all knowledge; and there are worlds beyond the world. Over these abysses of space and in the long extent of time, I doubt whether any word that can be spoken would bear, everywhere and forever, its weight of meaning and its power; unless it were that First Word which Segoy spoke, making all, or the Final Word which has not been nor will be spoken until all things are unmade ... So, even within this world of our Earthsea, the little islands that we know, there are differences, and mysteries, and changes. And the place least known and fullest of mysteries is the South Reach. Few wizards of the Inner Lands have come among these people. They do not welcome wizards, having – so it is believed – their own kinds of magic. But the rumours of these are vague, and it may be that the art magic was never well known here, not fully understood. If so, it would be easily undone by one who set himself to the undoing of it, and sooner weakened than our wizardry of the Inner Lands. And then we might hear tales of the failure of magic in the South. For discipline is the channel in which our acts run strong and deep; where there is no direction, the deeds of men run shallow, and wander, and are wasted. So that fat woman of the mirrors has lost her art, and thinks she never had it. And so Hare takes his hazia and thinks he has gone farther than the greatest mages go, when he has barely entered the fields of dream and is already lost ... But where is it that he *thinks* he goes? What is it he looks for? What is it that has swallowed up his wizardry? We have had enough of Hort Town, I think, so we go farther south, to Lorbanery, to see what the wizards do there, to find out what it is that we must find out ... Does that answer you?'

'Yes, but –'

'Then let the stone be still a while!' said the mage. And he sat by the mast in the yellowish glowing shade of the awning, and looked out to sea, to the west, as the boat sailed softly southward through the afternoon. He sat erect, and still. The hours passed. Arren swam a couple of times, slipping quietly into the water from the stern of the boat, for he did not like to cross the line of that dark gaze which, looking west over the sea, seemed to see far beyond the bright horizon-line, beyond the blue of air, beyond the boundaries of light.

Sparrowhawk came back from his silence at last, and spoke, though not more than a word at a time. Arren's upbringing had made him quick to sense mood disguised by courtesy or by reserve; he knew his companion's heart was heavy. He asked no more questions, and in the evening he said, 'If I sing will it disturb your thoughts?' Sparrowhawk replied with an effort at joking, 'That depends upon the singing.'

Arren sat with his back against the mast, and sang. His voice was no longer high and sweet as when the music master of the Hall of Berila had trained it years ago, striking the harmonies on his tall harp; nowadays the higher tones of it were husky, and the deep tones had the resonance of a viol, dark and clear. He sang the Lament for the White Enchanter, that song which Elfarran made when she knew of Morred's death and waited for her own. Not often is that song sung, nor lightly. Sparrowhawk listened to the young voice, strong, sure, and sad between the red sky and the sea, and the tears came into his eyes, blinding.

Arren was silent for a while after that song; then he began to sing lesser, lighter tunes, softly, beguiling the great monotony of windless air and heaving sea and failing light, as night came on.

When he ceased to sing everything was still, the wind down, the waves small, wood and rope barely creaking. The sea lay hushed, and over it the stars came out one by one. Piercing bright to the south a yellow light appeared and sent a shower and splintering of gold across the water.

'Look! a beacon!' Then after a minute, 'Can it be a star?'

Sparrowhawk gazed at it a while, and finally said, 'I think it must be the star Gobardon. It can be seen only in the South Reach. Gobardon means Crown. Kurremkarmerruk taught us that, sailing still farther south, one would bring one by one eight more stars clear of the horizon under Gobardon, making a great constellation, some say of a running man, others say of the rune Agnen. The rune of Ending.'

They watched it clear the restless sea-horizon and shine forth steadily.

'You sang Elfarran's song,' Sparrowhawk said, 'as if you knew her grief, and made me know it too ... Of all the histories of Earthsea that one has always held me most. The great courage of Morred against despair; and Serriadh who was born beyond despair, the gentle king. And her, Elfarran. When I did the greatest evil I have ever done, yet it was to her beauty that I thought I turned; and I saw her – for a moment I saw Elfarran.'

A cold thrill went up Arren's back. He swallowed and sat silent, looking at the splendid, baleful, topaz-yellow star.

'Which of the heroes is yours?' the mage asked, and he answered, 'Erreth-Akbe.'

'He was indeed the greatest.'

'But it is his death I think of: alone, fighting the dragon Orm on the shore of Selidor. He might have ruled all Earthsea. Yet he chose that instead.'

The mage did not answer. Each followed his own thoughts a while. Then Arren asked, still watching yellow Gobardon, 'Then it is true that the dead can be brought back to life by magery?'

'They can be brought back into life,' the mage said.

'But is it ever done? How is it done?'

His companion seemed to answer with very great reluctance. 'By the spells of Summoning,' he said, and scowled, or winced, as he spoke. Arren thought he would say no more, but presently he went on. 'Such spells are in the Lore of Paln. The Master Summoner will not teach or use that Lore. It has been used seldom; and never wisely, I think. The great spells of it were made by the Grey Mage of Paln, a thousand years ago. He summoned up the spirits of the heroes and mages, even Erreth-Akbe, to give counsel to the Lords of Paln in their wars and government.'

'And what happened?'

'The counsel of the dead is not profitable to the living. Paln came on evil times. The Grey Mage was driven forth. He died nameless.'

The mage spoke reluctantly, but he did speak, as if he felt Arren had a right to be answered; and Arren pressed on – 'Then no one uses those spells now?'

'I have known only one man who used them freely.'

'Who was he?'

'He lived in Havnor. They accounted him a mere sorcerer, but in native power he was a great mage. He made money from his art, showing any who paid him whatever spirit they asked to see, dead wife or husband or child, filling his house with unquiet shadows of old centuries, the fair women of the days of the Kings. I saw him summon from the Dry Land my own old master who was Archmage in my youth, Nemmerle, for a trick to entertain the idle. And the great soul came at his call, like a dog to heel. I was angry, and challenged him. I was not Archmage then. I said, "You compel the dead to come into your house. Will you come with me to theirs?" And I made him come, though he fought me with all his will, and changed his shape, and wept aloud in the darkness.'

'So you killed him?' Arren whispered, enthralled.

'No! I made him follow me, and come back with me. He was afraid. He who summoned up the dead so easily was more afraid of death – his own death – than any man I ever knew. At the wall of stones ... But I tell you more than a novice ought to know. And you're not even a novice.' Through the dusk the keen eyes returned Arren's gaze, abashing him. 'No matter,' said the Archmage. 'There is a wall of stones, then, at a certain place on the bourne. Across it the spirit goes at death, and a living man may cross it and return again, if he knows the way ... By the wall of stones this man crouched down, on the side of the living. He clung to the stones with his hands, and wept and moaned. I made him go on. His fear made me sick and angry. I should have known by that that I did wrong. I was possessed by anger and by vanity. He was strong, and I was eager to prove that I was stronger.'

'What did he do afterwards – when you came back?'

'Grovelled, and swore never to use the Pelnish Lore again, and kissed my hand, and would have killed me if he dared.'

'What became of him?'

'He went west from Havnor, to Paln perhaps; I heard no more of him. He was white-haired when I knew him, though still a quick, long-armed man, like a wrestler. He would be dead by now. I cannot even bring to mind his name.'

'His true name?'

'No! that I can remember –' Then he paused, and for the space of three heartbeats was utterly still.

'They call him Cob, in Havnor,' he said in a changed, careful voice. It had grown too dark for expression to be seen. Arren saw him turn and look at the yellow star, now higher above the waves and casting across them a broken trail of gold as slender as a spider's thread. After a time he said, 'It's not only in dreams, Arren, that we find ourselves facing what is yet to be in what was long forgotten, and speaking what seems nonsense because we will not see its meaning.'

6. Lorbanery

SEEN across ten miles of sunlit water, Lorbanery was green, green as the bright moss by a fountain's rim. Close to, it broke into leaves, and tree-trunks, and shadows, and roads, and houses, and the faces and clothing of people and dust, and all that goes to make up an island inhabited by men. Yet still, over all, it was green : for every acre of it that was not built or walked upon was given up to the low, round-topped hurbah trees, on the leaves of which feed the little worms that spin the silk that is made into thread and woven by the men, and women, and children of Lorbanery. At dusk the air there is full of small grey bats who feed on the little worms. They eat many, but are suffered to do so, and not killed by the silk-weavers; who indeed account it a deed of very evil omen to kill the grey-winged bats. For if human beings live off the worms, they say, surely small bats have the right to do so.

The houses were curious, with little windows set randomly, and thatches of hurbah-twigs, all green with moss and lichens. It had been a wealthy isle, as isles of the Reach go, and this was still to be seen in the well-painted and well-furnished houses, in the great spinning wheels and looms in the cottages and worksheds, and in the stone piers of the little harbour of Sosara, where several trading galleys might have docked. But there were no galleys in the harbour. The paint on the houses was faded, and there was no new furniture, and most of the wheels and looms were still, with dust on them, and spiderwebs between pedal and pedal, between warp and frame.

'Sorcerers?' said the mayor of Sosara village, a short man with a face as hard and brown as the soles of his bare feet. 'There's no sorcerers in Lorbanery. Nor ever was.'

'Who'd have thought it?' said Sparrowhawk admiringly. He was sitting with eight or nine of the villagers, drinking hurbahberry wine, a thin and bitter vintage. He had of necessity told them that he was in the South Reach hunting emmel-stone, but he had in no way disguised himself or his companion, except that Arren had left his sword hidden in the boat, as usual, and if Sparrowhawk had his staff about him it was not to be seen. The villagers had been sullen and hostile at first, and were disposed to turn sullen and hostile again at any moment; only Sparrowhawk's adroitness and authority had forced a grudging acceptance from them. 'Wonderful men with trees you must have here,' he said now. 'What do they do about a late frost on the orchards?'

'Nothing,' said a skinny man at the end of the row of villagers. They all sat in line with their backs against the inn wall, under the eaves of the thatch. Just past their bare feet the large, soft rain of April pattered on the earth.

'Rain's the peril, not frost,' the mayor said. 'Rots the wormcases. No man's going to stop rain falling. Nor ever did.' He was belligerent against sorcerers and sorcery : some of the others seemed more wistful on the subject. 'Never did used to rain this time of year,' one of them said, 'when the old fellow was alive.'

'Who? Old Mildi? Well, he's not alive. He's dead,' said the mayor.

'Used to call him the Orcharder,' the skinny man said. 'Aye. Called him the Orcharder,' said another one. Silence descended, like the rain.

Inside the window of the one-roomed inn Arren sat. He had found an old lute hung on the wall, a long-necked, three-stringed lute such as they play in the Isle of Silk, and he was playing with it now, learning to draw its music from it, not much louder than the patter of rain on the thatch.

'In the markets of Hort Town,' said Sparrowhawk, 'I saw stuff sold as silk of Lorbanery. Some of it was silk. But none of it was silk of Lorbanery.'

'The seasons have been poor,' said the skinny man. 'Four years, five years now.'

'Five years it is since Fallows Eve,' said an old man in a munching

372

self-satisfied voice, 'since old Mildi died, aye, die he did, and not near the age I am. Died on Fallows Eve he did.'

'Scarcity puts up the prices,' said the mayor. 'For one bolt of semi-fine blue-dyed we get now what we used to get for three bolts.'

'If we get it. Where's the ships? And the blue's false,' said the skinny man, thus bringing on a half-hour argument concerning the quality of the dyes they used in the great worksheds.

'Who makes the dyes?' Sparrowhawk asked, and a new hassle broke out. The upshot of it was that the whole process of dyeing had been overseen by a family who, in fact, called themselves wizards; but if they ever had been wizards they had lost their art, and nobody else had found it, as the skinny man remarked sourly. For they all agreed, except the mayor, that the famous blue dyes of Lorbanery and the unmatchable crimson, the 'dragon's fire' worn by Queens in Havnor long ago, were not what they had been. Something had gone out of them. The unseasonable rains were at fault, or the dye-earths, or the refiners. 'Or the eyes,' said the skinny man, 'of men who couldn't tell the true azure from blue mud,' and he glared at the mayor. The mayor did not take up the challenge; they fell silent again.

The thin wine seemed only to acidify their tempers, and their faces looked glum. There was no sound now but the rustle of rain on the uncountable leaves of the orchards of the valley, and the whisper of the sea down at the end of the street, and the murmur of the lute in the darkness within doors.

'Can he sing, that girlish lad of yours?' asked the mayor.

'Aye, he can sing. Arren; sing a measure for us, lad.'

'I cannot get this lute to play out of the minor,' said Arren at the window, smiling. 'It wants to weep. What would you hear, my hosts?'

'Something new,' growled the mayor.

The lute thrilled a little; he had the touch of it already. 'This might be new here,' he said. Then he sang.

> 'By the white Straits of Soléa
> and the bowed red branches

> *that bent their blossoms over*
> *her bowed head, heavy*
> *with sorrow for her lost lover*
> *by the red branch and the white branch*
> *and the sorrow unceasing*
> *do I swear, Serriadh,*
> *son of my mother and of Morred,*
> *to remember the wrong done*
>   *forever, forever.'*

They were still: the bitter faces and the shrewd, the hardworked hands and bodies. They sat still in the warm rainy Southern dusk, and heard that song like the cry of the grey swan of the cold seas of Éa, yearning, bereft. For a while after the song was over they kept still.

'That's queer music,' said one, uncertainly.

Another, reassured as to the absolute centrality of the isle of Lorbanery in all time and space, said, 'Foreign music's always queer and gloomy.'

'Give us some of yours,' said Sparrowhawk. 'I'd like to hear a cheery stave myself. The lad will always sing of old dead heroes.'

'I'll do that,' said the last speaker, and hemmed a bit, and started out to sing about a lusty, trusty barrel of wine, and a hey, ho, and about we go! But nobody joined him in the chorus, and he went flat on the hey, ho.

'There's no more proper singing,' he said angrily. 'It's the young people's fault, always chopping and changing the way things are done, and not learning the old songs.'

'It's not that,' said the skinny man, 'there's no more proper anything. Nothing goes right any more.'

'Aye, aye, aye,' wheezed the oldest one, 'the luck's run out. That's what. The luck's run out.'

After that there was not much to say. The villagers departed by twos and threes, until Sparrowhawk was left alone outside the window, and Arren inside it. And then Sparrowhawk laughed, at last. But it was not a merry laugh.

The innkeeper's shy wife came and spread out beds for them on the floor, and went away, and they lay down to sleep. But the high rafters of the room were an abode of bats. In and out the unglazed windows the bats flew all night long, chittering very high. Only at dawn did they return and settle, each composing itself in a little, neat, grey package hanging from a rafter upside down.

Perhaps it was the restlessness of the bats that made Arren's sleep uneasy. It was many nights now since he had slept ashore; his body was not used to the immobility of earth, and insisted to him as he fell asleep that he was rocking, rocking ... and then the world would fall out from underneath him and he would wake with a great start. When at last he got to sleep he dreamed he was chained in the hold of the slaver's ship; there were others with him, but they were all dead. He woke from this dream more than once, struggling to get free of it, but falling to sleep at once re-entered into it. At last it seemed to him that he was all alone on the ship, but still chained so that he could not move. Then a curious, slow voice spoke in his ear. 'Loose your bonds,' it said. 'Loose your bonds.' He tried to move then, and moved: he stood up. He was on some vast, dim moor, under a heavy sky. There was horror in the earth, in the thick air, an enormity of horror. This place was fear, was fear itself, and he in it, and no paths. He must find the way, but there were no paths, and he was tiny, like a child, like an ant and the place was huge, endless. He tried to walk, stumbled, woke.

The fear was inside him, now that he was awake, and he was not inside it : yet it was no less huge and endless. He felt choked by the black darkness of the room, and looked for stars in the dim square that was the window, but though the rain had ceased there were no stars. He lay awake, and was afraid, and the bats flew in and out on noiseless leather wings. Sometimes he heard their thin voices at the very limit of his hearing.

The morning came bright, and they were early up. Sparrowhawk inquired earnestly for emmel-stone. Though none of the townsfolk knew what emmel-stone was, they all had theories about it, and quarrelled over them; and he listened, though he listened for news of something other than emmel-stones. At last he and Arren took a way that the mayor suggested to them, towards the quarries where the blue dye-earth was dug. But on the way Sparrowhawk turned aside.

'This will be the house,' he said. 'They said that that family of dyers and discredited magicians lives on this road.'

'Is it any use to talk to them?' said Arren, remembering Hare all too well.

'There is a centre to this bad luck,' said the mage, harshly. 'There is a place where the luck runs out. I need a guide to that place!' And he went on, and Arren must follow.

The house stood apart among its own orchards, a fine building of stone, but it and all its acreage had gone long uncared for. Cocoons of ungathered silkworms hung discoloured among the ragged branches, and the ground beneath was thick with papery litter of dead grubs and moths. All about the house under the close-set trees there hung an odour of decay, and as they came to it Arren suddenly remembered the horror that had been on him in the night.

Before they reached the door it was flung open. Out charged a grey-haired woman, glaring with reddened eyes and shouting, 'Out, curse you, thieves slanderers lackwits liars and misbegotten fools! Get out, out, go! The ill chance be on you forever!'

Sparrowhawk stopped looking somewhat amazed, and quickly raised his hand in a curious gesture. He said one word, 'Avert!'

At that the woman stopped yelling. She stared at him.

'Why did you do that?'

'To turn your curse aside.'

She stared a while longer and said at last, hoarsely, 'Foreigners?'

'From the North.'

She came forward. At first Arren had been inclined to laugh at her, an old woman screeching on her doorstep, but close to her he felt only shame. She was foul and ill-clothed, and her breath stank, and her eyes had a terrible stare of pain.

'I have no power to curse,' she said. 'No power.' She imitated Sparrowhawk's gesture. 'They still do that, where you come from?'

He nodded. He watched her steadily, and she returned his gaze.

Presently her face began to work and change, and she said, 'Where's thy stick?'

'I do not show it here, sister.'

'No, you should not. It will keep you from life. Like my power, it kept me from life. So I lost it. I lost all the things I knew, all the words and names. They came by little strings like spiderwebs out of my eyes and mouth. There is a hole in the world, and the light is running out of it. And the words go with the light. Did you know that? My son sits staring all day at the dark, looking for the hole in the world. He says he would see better if he were blind. He has lost his hand as a dyer. We were the Dyers of Lorbanery. Look!' She shook before them her muscular, thin arms, stained to the shoulder with a faint, streaky mixture of ineradicable dyes. 'It never comes off the skin,' she said, 'but the mind washes clean. It won't hold the colours. Who are you?'

Sparrowhawk said nothing. Again his eyes held the woman's; and Arren, standing aside, watched uneasily.

All at once she trembled and said in a whisper, 'I know thee —'

'Aye. Like knows like, sister.'

It was strange to see how she pulled away from the mage in terror, wanting to flee him, and yearned towards him as if to kneel at his feet.

He took her hand and held her. 'Would you have your power back, the skills, the names? I can give you that.'

'You are the Great Man,' she whispered. 'You are the King of the Shadows, the Lord of the Dark Place —'

'I am not. I am no king. I am a man, a mortal, your brother and your like.'

'But you will not die?'

'I will.'

'But you will come back, and live for ever.'

'Not I. Nor any man.'

'Then you are not — not the Great One in the darkness,' she said, frowning, and looking at him a little askance, with less fear. 'But you are a Great One. Are there two? What is your name?'

377

Sparrowhawk's stern face softened a moment. 'I cannot tell you that,' he said gently.

'I'll tell you a secret,' she said. She stood straighter now, facing him, and there was the echo of an old dignity in her voice and bearing. 'I do not want to live, and live, and live forever. I would rather have back the names of things. But they are all gone. Names don't matter now. There are no more secrets. Do you want to know my name?' Her eyes filled with light, her fists clenched, she leaned forward and whispered: 'My name is Akaren.' Then she screamed aloud, 'Akaren! Akaren! My name is Akaren! Now they all know my secret name, my true name, and there are no secrets, and there is no truth, and there is no death – death – death – death!' She screamed the word sobbing, and spittle flew from her lips.

'Be still, Akaren!'

She was still. Tears ran down her face, which was dirty, and streaked with locks of her uncombed grey hair.

Sparrowhawk took that wrinkled, tear-blubbered face between his hands, and very lightly, very tenderly, kissed her on the eyes. She stood motionless, her eyes closed. Then with his lips close to her ear he spoke a little in the Old Speech, and once more kissed her, and let her go.

She opened her eyes, and looked at him a while with a brooding, wondering gaze. So a newborn child looks at its mother; so a mother looks at her child. She turned slowly and went to her door, and entered it, and closed it behind her: all in silence, with the still look of wonder on her face.

In silence the mage turned and started back towards the road. Arren followed him. He dared ask no question. Presently the mage stopped, there in the ruined orchard, and said, 'I took her name from her, and gave her a new one. And thus in some sense a re-birth. There was no other help or hope for her.'

His voice was strained and stifled.

'She was a woman of power,' he went on. 'No mere witch or potion-maker, but a woman of art and skill, using her craft for the making of the beautiful, a proud woman, and honourable. That was her life. And it is all wasted.' He turned abruptly away, walked off into the orchard aisles, and there stood beside a tree-trunk, his back turned.

Arren waited for him in the hot, leaf-speckled sunlight. He knew that Sparrowhawk was ashamed to burden Arren with his emotion; and indeed there was nothing the boy could do or say. But his heart went out utterly to his companion, not now with that first romantic ardour and adoration, but painfully as if a link were drawn forth from the very inmost of it and forged into an unbreaking bond. For in this love he now felt there was compassion : without which love is untempered, and is not whole, and does not last.

Presently Sparrowhawk returned to him through the green shade of the orchard. Neither said anything, and they went on side by side. It was hot already; last night's rain had dried and dust rose under their feet on the road. Earlier the day had seemed dreary and insipid to Arren, as if infected by his dreams; now he took pleasure in the bite of the sunlight and the relief of shade, and enjoyed walking without brooding about their destination.

This was just as well, for they accomplished nothing. The afternoon was spent in talking with the men who mined the dye-ores, and bargaining for some bits of what was said to be emmel-stone. As they trudged back to Sosara with the late sun pounding on their heads and necks, Sparrowhawk remarked, 'It's blue malachite; but I doubt they'll know the difference in Sosara either.'

'They're strange here,' Arren said. 'It's that way with everything, they don't know the difference. Like what one of them said to the headman last night. 'You wouldn't know the true azure from blue mud ...' They complain about bad times, but they don't know when the bad times began : they say the work's shoddy, but they don't improve it; they don't even know the difference between an artisan and a spell-worker, between handcraft and the art magic. It's as if they had no lines and distinctions and colours clear in their heads. Everything's the same to them, everything's grey.'

'Aye,' said the mage, thoughtfully. He stalked along for a while, his head hunched between his shoulders, hawklike; though a short man he walked with a long stride. 'What is it they're missing?'

Arren said without hesitation, 'Joy in life.'

379

'Aye,' said Sparrowhawk again, accepting Arren's statement and pondering it for some time. 'I'm glad,' he said at last, 'that you can think for me, lad ... I feel tired and stupid. I've been sick at heart since this morning, since we talked to her who was Akaren. I do not like waste and destruction. I do not want an enemy. If I must have an enemy I do not want to seek him, and find him, and meet him ... If one must hunt, the prize should be a treasure, not a detestable thing.'

'An enemy, my lord,' said Arren.

Sparrowhawk nodded.

'When she talked about the Great Man, the King of Shadows –?'

Sparrowhawk nodded again. 'I think so,' he said. 'I think we must come not only to a place, but to a person. This is evil, evil, what passes on this island, this loss of craft and pride, this joylessness, this waste. This is the work of an evil will. But a will not even bent here, not even noticing Akaren, or Lorbanery. The track we hunt is the track of wreckage, as if we followed a runaway cart down a mountainside, and watched it set off an avalanche.'

'Could she – Akaren – tell you more about this enemy – who he is and where he is, or what he is?'

'Not now, lad,' the mage said in a soft but rather bleak voice. 'No doubt she could have. In her madness there was still wizardry. Indeed her madness was her wizardry. But I could not hold her to answer me. She was in too much pain.'

And he walked on with his head somewhat hunched between his shoulders, as if he himself were enduring, and longing to avoid, some pain.

Arren turned, hearing a scuffling of feet behind them on the road. A man was running after them, a good way off but catching up fast. The dust of the road and his long wiry hair made aureoles of red about him in the westering light, and his long shadow hopped fantastically along the trunks and aisles of the orchards by the road. 'Listen !' he shouted. 'Stop ! I found it ! I found it !'

He caught up with them in a rush. Arren's hand went first to the air where his swordhilt might have been, then to the air where his lost knife had been, and then made itself into a fist, all in half a second. He scowled and moved forward. The man was a full head taller than Sparrowhawk, and broad-shouldered, and a panting, raving, wild-eyed madman. 'I found it !' he kept saying while Arren, trying to dominate him by a stern threatening voice and attitude, said, 'What do you want?' The man tried to get around him, to Sparrowhawk; Arren stepped in front of him again.

'You are the Dyer of Lorbanery,' Sparrowhawk said.

Then Arren felt he had been a fool, trying to protect his companion; and he stepped aside, out of the way. For at six words from the mage, the madman stopped his panting and the clutching gesture of his big, stained hands· his eyes grew quieter; he nodded his head.

'I was the dyer,' he said, 'but now I can't dye.' Then he looked askance at Sparrowhawk, and grinned; he shook his head with its reddish, dusty bush of hair. 'You took away my mother's name,' he said. 'Now I don't know her, and she doesn't know me. She loves me well enough still, but she's left me. She's dead.'

Arren's heart contracted, but he saw that Sparrowhawk merely shook his head a little. 'No, no,' he said, 'she's not dead.'

'But she will be. She'll die.'

'Aye. That's a consequence of being alive,' the mage said. The Dyer seemed to puzzle over this for a minute, and then came right up to Sparrowhawk, seized his shoulders, and bent over him. He moved so fast that Arren could not prevent him, but he did come up very close, and so heard his whisper, I found the hole in the darkness. The King was standing there. He watches it, he rules it. He had a little flame, a little candle in his hand. He blew on it, and it went out. Then he blew on it again and it burned ! It burned !'

Sparrowhawk made no protest at being held and whispered at. He simply asked, 'Where were you when you saw that?'

'In bed.'

'Dreaming?'

'No.'

'Across the wall?'

'No,' the Dyer said, in a suddenly sober tone, and as if uncomfortable. He let the mage go, and took a step back from him. 'No, I – I don't know where it is. I found it. But I don't know where.'

'That's what I'd like to know,' said Sparrowhawk.

'I can help you.'

'How?'

'You have a boat. You came here on it, you're going on. Are you going on west? That's the way. The way to the place where he comes out. There has to be a place, a place *here*, because he's alive – not just the spirits, the ghosts, that come over the wall, not like that, – you can't bring anything but souls over the wall but this is the body, this is the flesh immortal. I saw the flames rise in the darkness at his breath, the flame that was out. I saw that.' The man's face was transfigured, a wild beauty in it in the long red-gold light. 'I know that he hath overcome death. I know it. I gave my wizardry to know it. I was a wizard once ! And you know it, and you are going there. Take me with you.'

The same light shone on Sparrowhawk's face, but left it unmoved and harsh. 'I am trying to go there,' he said.

'Let me go with you !'

Sparrowhawk nodded briefly. 'If you're there when we sail,' he said, as coldly as before.

The Dyer backed away from him another step, and stood watching him, the exaltation in his face clouding slowly over until it was replaced by a strange, heavy look; it was as if reasoning thought were labouring to break through the storm of words and feelings and visions that confused him. Finally he turned around without a word and began to run back down the road, into the haze of dust that had not yet settled on his tracks. Arren drew a long breath of relief.

Sparrowhawk also sighed, though not as if his heart were any easier. 'Well,' he said. 'Strange roads have strange guides. Let's go on.'

Arren fell into step beside him. 'You won't take him with us?' he asked.

'That's up to him.'

With a flash of anger Arren thought: It's up to me, also. But he did not say anything, and they went on together in silence.

They were not well received on their return to Sosara. Everything on a little island like Lorbanery is known as soon as it is done, and no doubt they had been seen turning aside to the Dyer's House, and talking to the madman on the road. The innkeeper served them uncivilly, and his wife acted scared to death of them. In the evening when the men of the village came to sit under the eaves of the inn, they made much display of not speaking to the foreigners, and being very witty and merry among themselves. But they had not much wit to pass around, and soon ran short of jollity. They all sat in silence for a long time, and at last the mayor said to Sparrow-hawk, 'Did you find your blue rocks?'

'I found some blue rocks,' Sparrowhawk replied politely.

'Sopli showed you where to find 'em, no doubt.'

Ha, ha, ha, went the other men, at this masterstroke of irony.

'Sopli would be the red-haired man?'

'The madman. You called on his mother in the morning.'

'I was looking for a wizard,' said the wizard.

The skinny man, who sat nearest him, spat into the darkness. 'What for?'

'I thought I might find out about what I'm looking for.'

'People come to Lorbanery for silk,' the mayor said. 'They don't come for stones. They don't come for charms. Or armwavings and jibber-jabber and sorcerers' tricks. Honest folk live here and do honest work.'

'That's right. He's right,' said others.

'And we don't want any other sort here, people from foreign parts snooping about and prying into our business.'

'That's right. He's right,' came the chorus.

'If there was any sorcerer around that wasn't crazy we'd give him an honest job in the sheds, but they don't know how to do honest work.'

'They might, if there were any to do,' said Sparrowhawk. 'Your sheds are empty, the orchards are untended, the silk in your warehouses was all woven years ago. What do you do, here in Lorbanery?'

'We look after our own business,' the mayor snapped, but the skinny man broke in excitedly, 'Why don't the ships come, tell us that! What are they doing in Hort Town? Is it because our work's been shoddy? —' He was interrupted by angry denials. They shouted at one another, jumped to their feet, the mayor shook his fist in Sparrowhawk's face, another drew a knife. Their mood had gone wild. Arren was on his feet at once, and looked at Sparrowhawk expecting to see him stand up in the sudden radiance of the magelight and strike them dumb with his revealed power. But he did not. He sat there, and looked from one to another, and listened to their menaces. And gradually they fell quiet, as if they could not keep up anger any more than they could keep up merriment. The knife was sheathed, the threats turned to sneers. They began to go off like dogs leaving a dog-fight, some strutting and some sneaking.

When the two were left alone Sparrowhawk got up, and came inside the inn, and took a long draught of water from the jug beside the door. 'Come, lad,' he said. 'I've had enough of this.'

'To the boat?'

'Aye.' He put down two trade-counters of silver on the window sill to pay for their lodging, and hoisted up their light pack of clothing. Arren was tired and sleepy, but he looked around the room of the inn, stuffy and bleak, and all aflitter up in the rafters with the restless bats; he thought of last night in that room, and followed Sparrowhawk willingly. He thought, too, as they went down Sosara's one dark street, that going now they would give the madman Sopli the slip. But when they came to the harbour he was waiting for them on the pier.

'There you are,' said the mage. 'Get aboard, if you want to come.'

Without a word Sopli got down into the boat and crouched beside the mast. like a big unkempt dog. At this Arren rebelled. 'My lord!' he said. Sparrowhawk turned; they stood face to face on the pier above the boat.

'They are all mad on this island, but I thought you were not. Why do you take him?'

384

'As a guide.'

'A guide – to more madness? To death by drowning or a knife in the back?'

'To death, but by what road I do not know.'

Arren spoke with heat, and though Sparrowhawk answered quietly there was something of a fierce note in his voice. He was not used to being questioned. But ever since Arren tried to protect him from the madman on the road that afternoon, and had seen how vain and unneeded his protection was, he had felt a bitterness and all that uprush of devotion he had felt in the morning was spoilt and wasted. He was unable to protect Sparrowhawk; he was not permitted to make any decisions; he was unable, or was not permitted, even to understand the nature of their quest. He was merely dragged along on it, useless as a child. But he was not a child.

'I would not quarrel with you, my lord,' he said as coldly as he could. 'But this – this is beyond reason !'

'It is beyond all reason. We go where reason will not take us. Will you come, or will you not?'

Tears of anger sprang into Arren's eyes. 'I said I would come with you and serve you. I do not break my word.'

'That is well,' the mage said grimly, and made as if to turn away. Then he faced Arren again. 'I need you, Arren; and you need me. For I will tell you now that I believe this way we go is yours to follow, not out of obedience or loyalty to me, but because it was yours to follow before you ever saw me; before you ever set foot on Roke; before you sailed from Enlad. You cannot turn back from it.'

His voice had not softened. Arren answered him as grimly, 'How should I turn back, with no boat, here on the edge of the world?'

'This is the edge of the world? No, that is farther on. We may yet come to it.'

Arren nodded once, and swung down into the boat. Sparrowhawk loosed the line and spoke a light wind into the sail. Once away from the looming, empty docks of Lorbanery the air blew cool and clean out of the dark north, and the moon broke silver from the sleek sea before them, and rode upon their left as they turned southward to coast the isle.

7. *The Madman*

THE madman, the Dyer of Lorbanery, sat huddled up against the
mast, his arms wrapped around his knees and his head hunched
down. His mass of wiry hair looked black in the moonlight. Sparrowhawk had rolled himself up in a blanket and gone to sleep in the
stern of the boat. Neither of them stirred. Arren sat up in the prow;
he had sworn to himself to watch all night. If the mage chose to
assume that their lunatic passenger would not assault him, or
Arren, in the night, that was all very well for him; Arren, however,
would make his own assumptions, and undertake his own responsibilities.

But the night was very long, and very calm. The moonlight
poured down, changeless. Huddled by the mast, Sopli snored, long,
soft snores. Softly the boat moved onward; softly Arren slid into
sleep. He started awake at once, and saw the moon scarcely higher;
he abandoned his self-righteous guardianship, made himself comfortable and went to sleep.

He dreamed again, as he seemed always to do on this voyage, and
at first the dreams were fragmentary but strangely sweet and reassuring. In place of *Lookfar's* mast a tree grew, with great arching
arms of foliage; swans guided the boat, swooping on strong wings
before it; far ahead, over the beryl-green sea, shone a city of white
towers. Then he was in one of those towers, climbing the steps
which spiralled upward, running up them lightly and eagerly.
These scenes changed and recurred and led into others, which passed
without trace; but suddenly he was in the dreaded dull twilight on
the moors, and the horror grew in him until he could not breathe.
But he went forward, because he must go forward. After a long time
he realized that to go forward here was to go in a circle and come
round on one's own tracks again. Yet he must get out, get away; it
grew more and more urgent. He began to run. As he ran the circles

narrowed in and the ground began to slant. He was running in the darkening gloom, faster and faster, around the sinking inner lip of a pit, an enormous whirlpool sucking down to darkness; and as he knew this, his foot slipped, and he fell.

'What's the matter, Arren?'

Sparrowhawk spoke to him from the stern. Grey dawn held the sky and sea still.

'Nothing.'

'The nightmare?'

'Nothing.'

Arren was cold, and his right arm ached from having been cramped under him. He shut his eyes against the growing light and thought, 'He hints of this and hints of that, but he will never tell me clearly where we're going, or why, or why I should go there. And now he drags this madman with us. Which is maddest, the lunatic or I, for coming with him? The two of them may understand each other, it's the wizards who are mad now, he said. I could have been at home by now, at home in the Hall in Berila, in my room with the carven walls, and the red rugs on the floor, and a fire in the hearth, waking up to go out a-hawking with my father. Why did I come with him? Why did he bring me? Because it's my way to go, he says, but that's wizard's talk, making things seem great by great words. But the meaning of the words is always somewhere else. If I have any way to go, it's to my home, not wandering senselessly across the Reaches. I have duties at home, and am shirking them. If he really thinks there is some enemy of wizardry at work, why did he come alone, with me? He might have brought another mage to help him – a hundred of them. He could have brought an army of warriors, a fleet of ships. Is this how a great peril is met, by sending out an old man and a boy in a boat? This is mere folly. He is mad himself; it is as he said, he seeks death. He seeks death, and wants to take me with him. But I am not mad and not old, I will not die, I will not go with him.'

He sat up on his elbow, looking forward. The moon that had risen before them as they left Sosara Bay was again before them, sinking. Behind, in the east, day came wan and dull. There were no clouds, but a faint sickly overcast. Later in the day the sun grew hot, but it shone veiled, without splendour.

All day long they coasted Lorbanery, low and green to their right hand. A light wind blew off the land and filled their sail. Towards evening they passed a long last cape; the breeze died down. Sparrowhawk spoke the magewind into the sail, and like a falcon loosed from the wrist *Lookfar* started and fled forward eagerly, putting the Isle of Silk behind.

Sopli the Dyer had cowered in the same place all day, evidently afraid of the boat and afraid of the sea, seasick and wretched. He spoke now, hoarsely. 'Are we going west?'

The sunset was right in his face; but Sparrowhawk, patient with his stupidest questions, nodded.

'To Obehol?'

'Obehol lies west of Lorbanery.'

'A long way west. Maybe the place is there.'

'What is it like, the place?'

'How do I know? How could I see? It's not on Lorbanery! I hunted it for years, four years, five years, in the dark, at night, shutting my eyes, always with him calling *Come, come,* but I couldn't come. I'm no lord of wizards who can tell the ways in the dark. But there's a place to come to in the light, under the sun, too. That's what Mildi and my mother wouldr.'t understand. They kept looking in the dark. Then old Mildi died, and my mother lost her mind. She forgot the spells we use in the dyeing, and it affected her mind. She wanted to die, but I told her to wait. Wait till I find the place. There must be a place. If the dead can come back to life in the world there must be a place in the world where it happens.'

'Are the dead coming back to life?'

'I thought you knew such things,' Sopli said after a pause, looking askance at Sparrowhawk.

'I seek to know them.'

Sopli said nothing. The mage suddenly looked at him, a direct compelling gaze, though his tone was gentle : 'Are you looking for a way to live forever, Sopli?'

Sopli returned his gaze for a moment; then he hid his shaggy, brownish-red head in his arms, locking his hands across his ankles, and rocked himself a little back and forth. It seemed that when he was frightened he took this position, and when he was in it he would not speak or take any notice of what was said. Arren turned away from him in despair and disgust. How could they go on, with Sopli, for days or weeks, in an eighteen-foot boat? It was like sharing a body with a diseased soul . . .

Sparrowhawk came up beside him in the prow, and knelt with one knee on the thwart, looking into the sallow evening. He said, 'The man has a gentle spirit.'

Arren did not answer this. He asked coldly, 'What is Obehol? I never heard the name.'

'I know its name and place on the charts; no more . . . Look there : the companions of Gobardon !'

The great topaz-coloured star was higher in the south now, and beneath it, just clearing the dim sea, shone a white star to the left and a bluish-white one to the right, forming a triangle.

'Have they names?'

'The Master Namer did not know. Maybe the men of Obehol and Wellogy have names for them. I do not know. We go now into strange seas, Arren, under the Sign of Ending.'

The boy did not answer, looking with a kind of loathing at the bright, nameless stars above the endless water.

As they sailed westward day after day the warmth of the southern spring lay on the waters, and the sky was clear. Yet it seemed to Arren that there was a dullness in the light, as if it fell aslant through glass. The sea was lukewarm when he swam, bringing little refreshment. Their salt food had no savour. There was no freshness or brightness in anything, unless it were at night, when the stars burned with a greater radiance than he had ever seen in them. He would lie and watch them till he slept. Sleeping, he would dream : always the dream of the moors, or the pit, or a valley hemmed round by cliffs, or a long road going downwards under a low sky; always the dim light, and the horror in him, and the hopeless effort to escape.

He never spoke of this to Sparrowhawk. He did not speak of anything important to him, nothing but the small daily incidents of their sailing; and Sparrowhawk, who had always had to be drawn out, was now habitually silent.

Arren saw now what a fool he had been to entrust himself body and soul to this restless and secretive man, who let impulse move him and made no effort to control his life, nor even to save it. For now the fey mood was on him; and that, Arren thought, was because he dared not face his own failure – the failure of wizardry as a great power among men.

It was clear now that to those who knew the secrets, there were not many secrets to that art magic from which Sparrowhawk, and all the generations of sorcerers and wizards, had made much fame and power. There was not much more to it than the use of wind and weather, the knowledge of healing herbs, and a skilful show of such illusions as mists and lights and shape-changes, which could awe the ignorant, but which were mere tricks. Reality was not changed. There was nothing in magery that gave a man true power over men; nor was it any use against death. The mages lived no longer than ordinary men. All their secret words could not put off for one hour the coming of their death.

Even in small matters magery was not worth counting on. Sparrowhawk was always miserly about employing his arts; they went by the world's wind whenever they might, they fished for food, and spared their water, like any sailors. After four days of interminable tacking into a fitful headwind, Arren asked him if he would not speak a little following wind into the sail, and when he shook his head, said, 'Why not?'

'I would not ask a sick man to run a race,' said Sparrowhawk, 'nor lay a stone on an overburdened back.' It was not clear whether he spoke of himself, or of the world at large. Always his answers were grudging, hard to understand. There, thought Arren, lay the very heart of wizardry: to hint at mighty meanings while saying nothing at all, and to make doing nothing at all seem the very crown of wisdom.

Arren had tried to ignore Sopli, but it was impossible; and in any case he soon found himself in a kind of alliance with the madman. Sopli was not so mad, or not so simply mad, as his wild hair and fragmented talk made him appear. Indeed the maddest thing about him was perhaps his terror of the water. To come into a boat had taken desperate courage, and he never really got the edge worn off his fear; he kept his head down so much so that he would not have to see the water heaving and lapping about him, and the frail little shell of the boat. To stand up in the boat made him giddy; he clung to the mast. The first time Arren decided on a swim and dived off the prow, Sopli shouted out in horror; when Arren came climbing back into the boat, the poor man was green with shock. 'I thought you were drowning yourself,' he said, and Arren had to laugh.

In the afternoon, when Sparrowhawk sat meditating, unheeding and unhearing, Sopli came hitching cautiously over the thwarts to Arren. He said in a low voice, 'You don't want to die, do you?'

'Of course not.'

'He does,' Sopli said, with a little shift of his lower jaw towards Sparrowhawk.

'Why do you say that?'

Arren took a lordly tone, which indeed came naturally to him, and Sopli accepted it as natural, though he was ten or fifteen years older than Arren. He replied with ready civility, though in his usual fragmentary way, 'He wants to get to the secret place. But I don't know why. He doesn't want ... He doesn't believe in ... the promise.'

'What promise?'

Sopli glanced up at him sharply, something of his ruined manhood in his eyes; but Arren's will was stronger. He answered very low, 'You know. Life. Eternal life.'

A great chill went through Arren's body. He remembered his dreams, the moor, the pit, the cliffs, the dim light. That was death, that was the horror of death. It was from death he must escape, must find the way. And on the doorsill stood the figure crowned with shadow, holding out a little light no larger than a pearl, the glimmer of immortal life. Arren met Sopli's eyes for the first time : light brown eyes, very clear; in them he saw that he had understood at last, and that Sopli shared his knowledge.

'He,' the Dyer said, with his twitch of the jaw towards Sparrow-hawk, 'he won't give up his name. Nobody can take his name through. The way is too narrow.'

'Have you seen it?'

'In the dark, in my mind. That's not enough. I want to get there, I want to see it. In the world, with my eyes. What if I – what if I died and couldn't find the way, the place? Most people can't find it, they don't even know it's there, there's only some of us have the power. But it's hard, because you have to give the power up to get there . . . No more words. No more names. It is too hard to do in the mind. And when you – die, your mind – dies.' He stuck each time on the word. 'I want to *know* I can come back. I want to be there. On the side of life. I want to live, to be safe. I hate – I hate this water . . .'

The Dyer drew his limbs together as a spider does when falling, and hunched his wiry-red head down between his shoulders, to shut out the sight of the sea.

But Arren did not shun his conversation after that, knowing that Sopli shared not only his vision, but his fear; and that, if worst came to worst, Sopli might aid him against Sparrowhawk.

Always they sailed, slowly in the calms and fitful breezes, to the west, where Sparrowhawk pretended that Sopli guided them. But Sopli did not guide them, he who knew nothing of the sea, had never seen a chart, never been in a boat, dreaded the water with a sick dread. It was the mage who guided them, and led them deliber-ately astray. Arren saw this now, and saw the reason for it. The Archmage knew that they, and others like them, were seeking eter-nal life, and had been promised it or drawn towards it, and might find it. In his pride, his overweening pride as Archmage, he feared lest they might gain it; he envied them, and feared them, and would have no man greater than himself. He meant to sail out onto the Open Sea beyond all lands until they were utterly astray and could never come back to the world, and where they would die of thirst. For he would die himself, to prevent them from eternal life.

Every now and then there would come a moment, when Sparrowhawk spoke to Arren of some small matter of managing the boat or swam with him in the warm sea or bade him good night under the great stars, when all these ideas seemed utter nonsense to the boy. He would look at his companion and see him, that hard, harsh, patient face, and he would think, 'This is my lord and friend.' And it seemed unbelievable to him that he had doubted. But a little while later he would be doubting again, and he and Sopli would exchange glances warning each other of their mutual enemy.

Every day the sun shone hot, yet dull. Its light lay like a gloss on the slow-heaving sea. The water was blue, the sky blue without change or shading. The breezes blew and died, and they turned the sail to catch them, and slowly crept on towards no end.

One afternoon they had at last a light following wind; and Sparrowhawk pointed upward, near sunset, saying, 'Look.' High above the mast a line of sea-geese wavered like a black rune drawn across the sky. The geese flew westward: and following, on the next day *Lookfar* came in sight of a great island.

'That's it,' Sopli said. 'That island. We must go there.'

'The place you seek is there?'

'Yes. We must land there. This is as far as we can go.'

'This land will be Obehol. Beyond it in the South Reach is another island, Wellogy. And in the West Reach are islands lying farther west than Wellogy. Are you certain, Sopli?'

The Dyer of Lorbanery grew angry, so that the wincing look came back into his eyes; but he did not talk madly, Arren thought, as he had when they first spoke with him many days ago on Lorbanery. 'Yes. We must land here. We have gone far enough. The place we seek is here. Do you want me to swear that I know it? Shall I swear by my name?'

'You cannot,' Sparrowhawk said, his voice hard, looking up at Sopli who was taller than he; Sopli had stood up, holding on tight to the mast, to look at the land ahead. 'Don't try, Sopli.'

The Dyer scowled as if in rage or pain. He looked at the

mountains lying blue with distance before the boat, over the heaving, trembling plain of water, and said, 'You took me as guide. This is the place. We must land here.'

'We'll land in any case, we must have water,' said Sparrowhawk, and went to the tiller. Sopli sat down in his place by the mast, muttering. Arren heard him say, 'I swear by my name. By my name,' many times, and each time he said it, he scowled again as if in pain.

They beat closer to the island on a northwind, and coasted it seeking a bay or landing, but the breakers beat thunderous in the hot sunlight on all the northern shore. Inland green mountains stood baking in that light, tree-clothed to the peaks.

Rounding a cape they came at last in sight of a deep crescent bay with white sand beaches. Here the waves came in quietly, their force held off by the cape, and a boat might land. No sign of human life was visible on the beach or in the forests above it; they had not seen a boat, a roof, a wisp of smoke. The light breeze dropped as soon as *Lookfar* entered the bay. It was still, silent, hot. Arren took the oars, Sparrowhawk steered. The creak of the oars in the locks was the only sound. The green peaks loomed above the bay, closing in around. The sun laid sheets of white-hot light on the water. Arren heard the blood drumming in his ears. Sopli had left the safety of the mast and crouched in the prow, holding onto the gunwales, staring and straining forward to the land. Sparrowhawk's dark, scarred face shone with sweat as if it had been oiled; his glance shifted continually from the low breakers to the foliage-screened bluffs above.

'Now,' he said to Arren and the boat. Arren struck three great strokes with the oars, and lightly *Lookfar* came up on the sand. Sparrowhawk leapt out to push the boat clear up on the last impetus of the waves. As he put his hands out to push he stumbled and half fell, catching himself against the stern. With a mighty strain he dragged the boat back into the water on the outward wash of the wave, and floundered in over the gunwale as she hung between sea and shore. 'Row!' he gasped out, and crouched on all fours, streaming with water and trying to get his breath. He was holding a spear – a bronze-headed throwing spear two feet long.

Where had he got it? Another spear appeared as Arren hung bewildered on the oars; it struck a thwart edgewise, splintering the wood, and rebounded end over end. On the low bluffs over the beach, under the trees, figures moved, darting and crouching. There were little whistling, whirring noises in the air. Arren suddenly bent his head between his shoulders, bent his back, and rowed with powerful strokes : two to clear the shallows, three to turn the boat, and away.

Sopli, in the prow of the boat, behind Arren's back, began to shout. Arren's arms were seized suddenly so that the oars shot up out of the water, and the butt end of one struck him in the pit of the stomach, so that for a moment he was blind and breathless. 'Turn back ! Turn back !' Sopli was shouting. The boat leapt in the water all at once, and rocked. Arren turned as soon as he had got his grip on the oars again, furious. Sopli was not in the boat.

All around them the deep water of the bay heaved and dazzled in the sunlight.

Stupidly, Arren looked behind him again, then at Sparrowhawk crouching in the stern. 'There,' Sparrowhawk said, pointing alongside, but there was nothing, only the sea and the dazzle of the sun. A spear from a throwing-stick fell short of the boat by a few yards, entered the water noiselessly, vanished. Arren rowed ten or twelve hard strokes, then backed water, and looked once more at Sparrowhawk.

Sparrowhawk's hands and left arm were bloody; he held a wad of sailcloth to his shoulder. The bronze-headed spear lay in the bottom of the boat. He had not been holding it when Arren first saw it; it had been standing out from the hollow of his shoulder where the point had gone in. He was scanning the water between them and the white beach, where some tiny figures hopped and wavered in the heat-glare. At last he said, 'Go on.'

'Sopli —'

'He never came up.'

'Is he drowned?' Arren asked unbelieving.

Sparrowhawk nodded.

Arren rowed on until the beach was only a white line beneath the forests and the great green peaks. Sparrowhawk sat by the tiller, holding the wad of cloth to his shoulder but paying no heed to it.

'Did a spear hit him?'

'He jumped.'

'But he – he couldn't swim. He was afraid of the water!'

'Aye. Mortally afraid. He wanted ... He wanted to come to land.'

'Why did they attack us? Who are they?'

'They must have thought us enemies. Will you ... give me a hand with this a moment?' Arren saw then that the cloth he held pressed against his shoulder was soaked and vivid.

The spear had struck between the shoulder-joint and collar-bone, tearing one of the great veins, so that it bled heavily. Under his direction Arren tore strips from a linen shirt and made shift to bandage the wound. Sparrowhawk asked him for the spear, and when Arren laid it on his knees he put his right hand over the blade, long and narrow like a willow leaf, of crudely hammered bronze; he made as if to speak, but after a minute he shook his head. 'I have no strength for spells,' he said. 'Later. It will be all right. Can you get us out of this bay, Arren?'

Silently the boy returned to the oars. He bent his back to the work, and soon, for there was strength in his smooth, lithe frame, he brought *Lookfar* out of the crescent bay into open water. The long noon calm of the Reach lay on the sea. The sail hung back. The sun glared through a veil of haze, and the green peaks seemed to shake and throb in the great heat. Sparrowhawk had stretched out in the bottom of the boat, his head propped against the thwart by the tiller; he lay still, lips and eyelids half-parted. Arren did not like to look at his face, but stared over the boat's stern. Heat-haze wavered above the water, as if veils of cobweb were spun out over the sky. His arms trembled with fatigue, but he rowed on.

'Where are you taking us?' Sparrowhawk asked hoarsely, sitting up a little. Turning, Arren saw the crescent bay curving its green arms about the boat once more, and the white line of the beach ahead, and the mountains gathered in the air above. He had turned the boat around without knowing it.

'I can't row any more,' he said, and stowed the oars, and went and crouched in the prow. He kept thinking Sopli was behind him in the boat, by the mast. They had been many days together and his death had been too sudden, too reasonless to be understood. Nothing was to be understood.

The boat hung swaying on the water, the sail slack on the spar. The tide, beginning to enter the bay, turned her slowly broadside to the current and pushed her by little nudges in and in, towards the distant white line of the beach.

'*Lookfar*,' the mage said caressingly, and a word or two in the Old Speech; and softly the boat rocked and nosed outward and slipped over the blazing sea away from the arms of the bay.

But as slowly and softly, in less than an hour, she ceased to make way, and again the sail hung back. Arren looked back in the boat and saw his companion lying as before, but his head had dropped back a little and his eyes were closed.

All this while Arren had felt a heavy, sickly horror, which grew on him and held him from action as if winding his body in fine threads, and dimming his mind. No courage rose up in him to fight against the fear, only a kind of dull resentment against his lot.

He should not let the boat drift here near the rocky shores of a land whose people attacked strangers; this was clear to his mind, but it did not mean much. What was he to do instead? Row the boat back to Roke? He was lost, utterly lost beyond hope, in the vastness of the Reach. He could never bring the boat back through those weeks of voyage to any friendly land. Only with the mage's guidance could he do it, and Sparrowhawk was hurt and helpless, as suddenly and meaninglessly as Sopli was dead. His face was changed, lax-featured and yellowish; he might be dying. Arren thought he should go and move him under the awning to keep the sunlight off him, and give him water; men who had lost blood needed to drink. But they had been short of water for days; the barrel was almost empty. What did it matter? There was no good in anything, no use. The luck had run out.

Hours went by, the sun beat down, the greyish heat wrapped Arren round. He sat unmoving.

A breath of cool passed across his forehead. He looked up. It was evening: the sun was down, the west dull red. *Lookfar* moved slowly under a mild breeze from the east, skirting the steep, wooded shores of Obehol.

Arren went back in the boat and looked after his companion, arranging him a pallet under the awning, and giving him water to drink. He did these things hurriedly, and kept his eyes from the bandage, which was in need of changing, for the wound had not wholly ceased to bleed. Sparrowhawk, in the languor of weakness, did not speak; even as he drank eagerly, his eyes closed and he slipped into sleep again, that being the greater thirst. He lay silent; and when in the darkness the breeze died, no magewind replaced it, and again the boat rocked idly on the smooth, heaving water. But now the mountains that loomed to the right were black against a sky gorgeous with stars, and for a long time Arren gazed at them. Their outlines seemed familiar to him, as if he had seen them before, as if he had known them all his life.

When he lay down to sleep he faced southward, and there, well up in the sky above the blank sea, burned the star Gobardon. Beneath it were the two forming a triangle with it, and beneath these three had risen in a straight line, forming a greater triangle. Then, slipping free of the liquid plains of black and silver, two more followed as the night wore on; they were yellow like Gobardon, though fainter, slanting from right to left from the right base of the triangle. So there were eight of the nine stars which were supposed to make the figure of a man, or the Hardic rune Agnen. To Arren's eyes there was no man in the pattern, unless, as starfigures are, he was strangely distorted; but the rune was plain, with hooked arm and cross-stroke, all but the foot, the last stroke to complete it, the star that had not yet risen.

Watching for it, Arren slept.

When he woke in the dawn, *Lookfar* had drifted farther from Obehol. A mist hid the shores and all but the peaks of the mountains, and thinned out into a haze above the violet waters of the south, dimming the last stars.

He looked at his companion. Sparrowhawk breathed unevenly,

as when pain moves under the surface of sleep not quite breaking it. His face was lined and old in the cold shadowless light. Arren looking at him saw a man with no power left in him, no wizardry, no strength, not even youth, nothing. He had not saved Sopli, nor turned away the spear from himself. He had brought them into peril, and had not saved them. Now Sopli was dead, and he dying, and Arren would die. Through this man's fault; and in vain, for nothing.

So Arren looked at him with the clear eyes of despair, and saw nothing.

No memory stirred in him of the fountain under the rowan tree, or of the white magelight on the slave-ship in the fog, or of the weary orchards of the House of the Dyers. Nor did any pride or stubbornness of will wake in him. He watched dawn come over the quiet sea, where low, great swells ran coloured like pale amethyst, and it was all like a dream, pallid, with no grip or vigour of reality. And at the depths of the dream and of the sea, there was nothing – a gap, a void. There were no depths.

The boat moved forward irregularly and slowly, following the fitful humour of the wind. Behind, peaks of Obehol shrank black against the rising sun, from which the wind came, bearing the boat away from land, away from the world, out onto the open sea.

8. *The Children of the Open Sea*

TOWARDS the middle of that day Sparrowhawk stirred, and asked for water. When he had drunk he asked, 'Where are we heading?' For the sail was taut above him, and the boat dipped like a swallow on the long swells.

'West, or north by west.'

'I'm cold,' Sparrowhawk said. The sun blazed down, filling the boat with heat.

Arren said nothing.

'Try to hold west. Wellogy, west of Obehol. Land there. We need water.'

The boy looked forward, over the empty sea.

'What's the matter, Arren?'

He said nothing.

Sparrowhawk tried to sit up, and failing that, to reach his staff that lay by the gear-box; but it was out of his reach, and when he tried to speak again the words halted on his dry lips. The blood broke out anew under the soaked and crusted bandage, making a little spider's thread of crimson on the dark skin of his chest. He drew breath sharply and closed his eyes.

Arren looked at him, but without feeling, and not for long. He went forward and resumed his crouching position in the prow, gazing forward. His mouth was very dry. The east wind that now blew steadily over the open sea was as dry as a desert wind. There were only two or three pints of water left in their cask; these were, in Arren's mind, for Sparrowhawk, not for himself; it never occurred to him to drink from that water. He had set out fishing lines, having learned since they left Lorbanery that raw fish fulfils both thirst and hunger; but there was never anything on the lines. It did not matter. The boat moved on over the desert of water. Over the boat, slowly, yet winning the race in the end by the width of heaven, the sun moved also from east to west.

Once Arren thought he saw a blue height in the south that might have been land, or cloud; the boat had been running somewhat north of west for hours. He did not try to tack and turn, but let her go on. The land might or might not be real; it did not matter. To him all the vast fiery glory of wind and light and ocean was dim and false.

Darkness came, and light again, and dark, and light, like drumbeats on the tight-stretched canvas of the sky.

He trailed his hand in the water over the side of the boat. For an instant he saw that, vivid : his hand pale greenish beneath the living water. He bent and sucked the wet off his fingers. It was bitter, burning his lips painfully, but he did it again. Then he was sick, and crouched down vomiting, but only a little bile burned his throat. There was no more water to give Sparrowhawk, and he was afraid to go near him. He lay down, shivering despite the heat. It was all silent, dry, and bright : terribly bright. He hid his eyes from the light.

They stood in the boat, three of them, stalk-thin and angular, great-eyed, like strange, dark herons or cranes. Their voices were thin, like birds' voices. He did not understand them. One knelt above him with a dark bladder on his arm, and tipped from it into Arren's mouth : it was water. Arren drank avidly, choked, drank again till he had drained the container. Then he looked about, and struggled to his feet, saying, 'Where is, where is he?' For in *Lookfar* with him were only the three strange, slender men.

They looked at him uncomprehending.

'The other man,' he croaked, his raw throat and stiff-caked lips unfit to form the words, 'my friend –'

One of them understood his distress if not his words, and putting a slight hand on his arm, pointed with the other. 'There,' he said, reassuring.

Arren looked. And he saw, ahead of the boat and northward of her, some gathered in close and others strung far out across the sea, rafts: so many rafts that they lay like autumn leaves on a pool. Low to the water, each bore one or two cabins or huts near the centre, and several had masts stepped. Like leaves they floated, rising and falling very softly as the vast swells of the western ocean passed under them. The lanes of water shone like silver between them, and over them towered great violet and golden rainclouds, darkening the west.

'There,' the man said, pointing to a great raft near Lookfar.

'Alive?'

They all looked at him, and at last one understood. 'Alive. He is alive.' At this Arren began to weep, a dry sobbing, and one of the men took his wrist in a strong and narrow hand and drew him out of Lookfar and onto a raft to which the boat had been made fast. The raft was so great and buoyant that it did not dip even slightly to their weight. The man led Arren across it while one of the others reached out with a heavy gaff tipped with a curving whaleshark's tooth and hauled a near-by raft closer, till they could step the gap. There he led Arren to the shelter or cabin, which was open on one side and closed with woven screens on the fourth. 'Lie down,' he said, and beyond that Arren knew nothing at all.

He was lying on his back, stretched out flat, gazing up at a rough green roof dappled with tiny dots of light. He thought he was in the apple orchards of Semermine, where the princes of Enlad pass their summers, in the hills behind Berila; he thought he was lying in the thick grass at Semermine, looking up at the sunlight between apple boughs.

After a while he heard the slap and jostle of water in the hollow places underneath the raft, and the thin voices of the raft-people speaking a tongue that was the common Hardic of the Archipelago, but much changed in sounds and rhythms, so that it was hard to understand; and so he knew where he was – out beyond the Archipelago, beyond the Reach, beyond all isles, lost on the open sea. But still he was untroubled, lying as comfortably as if he lay in the grass in the orchards of his home.

He thought after a while that he ought to get up, and did so, finding his body very thin and burnt-looking, and his legs shaky but serviceable. He pushed aside the woven hanging that made the walls of the shelter and stepped out into the afternoon. It had rained while he slept. The wood of the raft, great, smooth-shapen, squared logs, fit close and caulked, was dark with wet, and the hair of the thin, half-naked people was black and lank from the rain. But half the sky was clear where the sun stood in the west, and the clouds now rode to the far north-east in heaps of silver.

One of the men came up to Arren, warily, stopping some feet from him. He was slight and short, no taller than a boy of twelve; his eyes were long, large, and dark. He carried a spear with a barbed ivory head.

Arren said to him, 'I owe my life to you and your people.'

The man nodded.

'Will you take me to my companion?'

Turning away, the raft-man raised his voice in a high, piercing cry like the call of a seabird. Then he squatted down on his heels as if to wait, and Arren did the same.

The rafts had masts, though the mast of the one they were on was not stepped. On these, sails could be run up, small compared to the breadth of the raft, of a brown material, not canvas or linen but a fibrous stuff that looked not woven but beaten together, as felt is made. A raft some quarter mile away let the brown sail down from the crosstree by ropes and slowly worked its way, gaffing and poling off the other rafts between, till it came alongside the one Arren was on. When there was only three feet of water between, the man beside Arren got up and nonchalantly hopped across. Arren did the same and landed awkwardly on all fours; there was no spring left in his knees. He picked himself up, and found the little man looking at him, not with amusement, but with approval: Arren's composure had evidently won his respect.

This raft was larger and higher out of the water than any other, made of logs forty feet in length and four or five feet wide, blackened and smooth with use and weather. Strangely carven statues of wood stood about the several shelters or enclosures on it, and tall poles bearing tufts of seabirds' feathers stood at the four corners.

His guide took him to the smallest of the shelters, and there he saw Sparrowhawk lying asleep.

Arren sat down inside the shelter. His guide went back to the other raft, and nobody bothered him. After an hour or so a woman from the other raft brought him food: a kind of cold fish-stew with bits of transparent green stuff in it, salty but good; and a small cup of water, stale, tasting pitchy from the caulking of the barrel. He saw by the way she gave him the water that it was a treasure that she gave him, a thing to be honoured. He drank it respectfully and asked for no more, though he could have drunk ten times the cupful.

Sparrowhawk's shoulder had been skilfully bandaged; he slept deep and easily. When he woke up his eyes were clear. He looked at Arren, and smiled the sweet, joyous smile that was always startling on his hard face. Arren felt suddenly like weeping again. He put his hand on Sparrowhawk's hand and said nothing.

One of the raft-folk approached, and squatted down in the shade of the large shelter near by: a kind of temple, it appeared to be, with a square design of great complexity above the doorway, and the doorjambs made of logs carved in the shape of grey whales sounding. This man was short and thin like the others, boy-like in frame, but his face was strong-featured and weathered by the years. He wore nothing but a loincloth, but dignity clothed him amply. 'He must sleep,' he said, and Arren left Sparrowhawk and came to him.

'You are the chief of this folk,' Arren said, knowing a prince when he saw one.

'I am,' the man said, with a short nod. Arren stood before him, erect and unmoving. Presently the man's dark eyes met his briefly: 'You are a chief also,' he observed.

'I am,' Arren answered. He would have liked very much to know how the raft-man knew it, but remained impassive. 'But I serve my lord, there.'

The chief of the raft-folk said something Arren did not understand at all: certain words changed out of recognition, or names he did not know; then he said, 'Why came you into Balatran?'

'Seeking —'

But Arren did not know how much to say, nor indeed what to say. All that had happened, and the matter of their quest, seemed very long ago, and was confused in his mind. At last he said, 'We came to Obehol. They attacked us when we came to land. My lord was hurt.'

'And you?'

'I was not hurt,' Arren said, and the cold self-possession he had learnt in his courtly childhood served him well. 'But there was — there was something like a madness. One who was with us drowned himself. There was a fear —' He stopped, and stood silent.

The chief watched him with black, opaque eyes. At last he said, 'You come by chance here, then.'

'Yes. Are we still in the South Reach?'

'Reach? No. The islands —' The chief moved his slender black hand in an arc, no more than a quarter of the compass, north to east. 'The islands are there,' he said. 'All the islands.' Then showing all the evening sea before them, from north through west to south, he said, 'The sea.'

'What land are you from, lord?'

'No land. We are the Children of the Open Sea.'

Arren looked at his keen face. He looked about him at the great raft with its temple and its tall idols, each carved from a single tree, great god-figures mixed of dolphin, fish, man, and seabird; at the people busy at their work, weaving, carving, fishing, cooking on raised platforms, tending babies; at the other rafts, seventy at least, scattered out over the water in a great circle perhaps a mile across. It was a town: smoke rising in thin wisps from distant houses, the voices of children high on the wind. It was a town, and under its floors was the abyss.

'Do you never come to land?' the boy asked in a low voice.

'Once a year. We go to the Long Dune. We cut wood there and refit the rafts. That is in autumn, and after that we follow the grey whales north. In winter we go apart, each raft alone. In the spring we come to Balatran, and meet. There is going from raft to raft then, there are marriages, the Long Dance is held. These are the

Roads of Balatran; from here the great current bears south. In summer we drift south upon the great current, until we see the Great Ones, the grey whales, turning northward. Then we follow them, returning at last to the beaches of Emah on the Long Dune, for a little while.'

'This is most wonderful, my lord,' said Arren. 'Never did I hear of such a people as yours. My home is very far from here. Yet there too, in the island of Enlad, we dance the Long Dance on midsummer eve.'

'You stamp the earth down, and make it safe,' the chief said dryly. 'We dance on the deep sea.'

After a time he asked, 'How is he called, your lord?'

'Sparrowhawk,' Arren said. The chief repeated the syllables, but they clearly had no meaning for him. And that more than any other thing made Arren understand that his tale was true, that these people lived on the sea year in, year out, on the open sea past any land or scent of land, beyond the flight of the land birds, outside the knowledge of men.

'There was death in him,' the chief said. 'He must sleep. You go back to Star's raft; I will send for you.' He stood up. Though perfectly sure of himself, he was apparently not quite sure what Arren was, whether he should treat him as an equal or as a boy. Arren preferred the latter, in this situation, and accepted his dismissal; but then faced a problem of his own. The rafts had drifted apart again, and a hundred yards of satiny water rippled between the two.

The chief of the Children of the Open Sea spoke to him once more, briefly. 'Swim,' he said.

Arren let himself gingerly into the water. Its cool was pleasant on his sun-baked skin. He swam across and hauled himself out on the other raft, to find a group of five or six children and young people watching him with undisguised interest. A very small girl said, 'You swim like a fish on a hook.'

'How should I swim?' asked Arren, a little mortified, but polite; indeed he could not have been rude to a human being so very small. She looked like a polished mahogany statuette, fragile, exquisite.

'Like this !' she cried, and dived like a seal into the dazzle and liquid roil of the waters. Only after a long time, and at an improbable distance, did he hear her shrill cry and see her black, sleek head above the surface.

'Come on,' said a boy who was probably Arren's age, though he looked not more than twelve in height and build : a grave-faced fellow, with a blue crab tattooed all across his back. He dived, and all dived, even the three-year-old; so Arren had to, and did so, trying not to splash.

'Like an eel,' said the boy, coming up by his shoulder.

'Like a dolphin,' said a pretty girl with a pretty smile, and vanished in the depths.

'Like me !' squeaked the three-year-old, bobbing like a bottle.

So that evening until dark, and all the next long golden day, and the days that followed, Arren swam and talked and worked with the young people of Star's raft. And of all the events of his voyage since that morning of the equinox when he and Sparrowhawk left Roke, this seemed to him in some way the strangest; for it had nothing to do with all that had gone before, in the voyage or in all his life; and even less to do with what was yet to come. At night, lying down to sleep among the others under the stars, he thought, 'It is as if I were dead, and this is an after-life, here in the sunlight, beyond the edge of the world, among the sons and daughters of the sea . . .' Before he slept he would look in the far south for the yellow star and the figure of the Rune of Ending, and always he saw Gobardon, and the lesser or the greater triangle; but it rose later now, and he could not keep his eyes open till the whole figure stood free of the horizon. By night and by day the rafts drifted southward, but there was never any change in the sea, for the ever-changing does not change; the rainstorms of May passed over, and at night the stars shone, and all day the sun.

He knew that their life could not be lived always in this dream-like ease. He asked of winter, and they told him of the long rains and the mighty swells, the single rafts, each separated from all the rest, drifting and plunging along through the grey and darkness, week after week after week. Last winter in a month-long storm they had seen waves so great they were 'like thunderclouds', they said, for they had not seen hills : from the back of one the next could be seen, immense, miles away, rushing hugely towards them. Could the rafts ride such seas? he asked, and they said yes, but not always. In the spring when they gathered at the Roads of Balatran there would be two rafts missing, or three, or six . . .

They married very young. Bluecrab, the boy tattooed with his namesake, and the pretty girl Albatross were man and wife, though he was just seventeen and she two years younger; there were many such marriages between the rafts. Many babies crept and toddled about the rafts, tied by long leashes to the four posts of the central shelter, all crawling into it in the heat of the day and sleeping in wriggling heaps. The older children tended the younger, and men and women shared in all the work. All took their turn at gathering the great brown-leaved sea-weeds, the nilgu of the Roads, fringed like fern and eighty or a hundred feet long. All worked together at pounding the nilgu into cloth and braiding the coarse fibres for ropes and nets; at fishing, and drying the fish, and shaping whale-ivory into tools, and all the other tasks of the rafts. But there was always time for swimming and for talking, and never a time by which a task must be finished. There were no hours : only whole days, whole nights. After a few such days and nights it seemed to Arren that he had lived on the raft for time uncountable, and Obehol was a dream, and behind that were fainter dreams, and in some other world he had lived on land and been a prince in Enlad.

When he was summoned at last to the chief's raft, Sparrowhawk looked at him a while and said, 'You look like that Arren whom I saw in the Court of the Fountain : sleek as a golden seal. It suits you here, lad.'

'Aye, my lord.'

'But where is here? We have left places behind us. We have sailed off the maps . . . Long ago I heard tell of the Raft-Folk, but thought it only one more tale of the South Reach, a fancy without substance. Yet we were rescued by that fancy, and our lives saved by a myth.'

He spoke smilingly, as though he had shared in that timeless ease of life in the summer light; but his face was gaunt, and in his eyes lay an unlighted darkness. Arren saw that, and faced it.

'I betrayed –' he said, and stopped. 'I betrayed your trust in me.'

'How so, Arren?'

'There – at Obehol. When for once you needed me. You were hurt, and needed my help. I did nothing. The boat drifted, and I let her drift. You were in pain and I did nothing for you. I saw land – I saw land, and did not even try to turn the boat –'

'Be still, lad,' the mage said with such firmness that Arren obeyed. And presently, 'Tell me what you thought at that time.'

'Nothing, my lord – nothing! I thought there was no use in doing anything. I thought your wizardry was gone – no, that it had never been. That you had tricked me.' The sweat broke out on Arren's face and he had to force his voice, but he went on. 'I was afraid of you. I was afraid of death. I was so afraid of it I would not look at you, because you might be dying. I could think of nothing, except that there was – there was a way of not dying, for me, if I could find it. But all the time life was running out, as if there was a great wound and the blood running from it – such as you had. But this was in everything. And I did nothing, nothing, but try to hide from the horror of dying.'

He stopped, for saying the truth aloud was unendurable. It was not shame that stopped him, but fear, the same fear. He knew now why this tranquil life in sea and sunlight on the rafts seemed to him like an after-life or a dream, unreal. It was because he knew in his heart that reality was empty: without life, or warmth, or colour, or sound: without meaning. There were no heights or depths. All this lovely play of form and light and colour on the sea and in the eyes of men, was no more than that: a playing of illusions on the shallow void.

They passed, and there remained the shapelessness and the cold. Nothing else.

Sparrowhawk was looking at him, and he had looked down to avoid that gaze. But there spoke in him unexpectedly a little voice of courage, or perhaps of mockery. It was arrogant, and pitiless, and it said, Coward! Coward! Will you throw even this away?

So he looked up, with a great effort of will, and met his companion's eyes.

Sparrowhawk reached out and took his hand in a hard grasp, so that both by eye and by flesh they touched.

'Lebannen,' he said. He had never spoken Arren's true name, nor had Arren told it to him. 'Lebannen, this is. And thou art. There is no safety. There is no end. The word must be heard in silence. There must be darkness to see the stars. The dance is always danced above the hollow place, above the terrible abyss.'

Arren would have drawn away from him, but the mage did not release him. 'I failed you,' he said. 'I will fail you again. I have not strength enough!'

'You have strength enough.' Sparrowhawk's voice seemed tender, but in it was that same hardness that had risen in the depths of Arren's own shame, mocking. 'What you love, you will love. What you undertake, you will do. You are to be relied on. Small wonder if you have not learned that yet; you have had only seventeen years to learn it. But consider, Lebannen. To refuse death is to refuse life.'

'But I sought death!' Arren lifted his head and stared at Sparrowhawk. 'Like Sopli —'

'Sopli was not seeking death. He sought an end to the fear of death.'

'But there is a way. The way he looked for. Sopli. And Hare, and the others. The way back to life, life without death. You – you above all – you must know of that way –'

'I do not know it.'

'But the others, the wizards –'

'I know what they think they seek. But I know that they will die, as Sopli did. That I will die. That you will die.'

The hard grip still held Arren.

'And I prize that knowledge. It is a great gift. It is the gift of selfhood. For only that is ours which we are willing to lose. That selfhood, our torment and glory, our humanity, does not endure. It changes and it goes, a wave on the sea. Would you have the sea grow still and the tides cease to save one wave, to save yourself? Would you give up the craft of your hands, and the passion of your heart, and the hunger of your mind, to buy safety?'

'Safety,' Arren repeated.

'Aye,' the mage said. 'Safety.'

He released Arren then; let his hand go, and looked away from him, leaving him alone, though they still sat face to face.

'I do not know,' Arren said at last. 'I do not know what I seek, or where I go, or who I am.'

'I know who you are,' Sparrowhawk said in that same low, hard voice. 'You are my guide. In your innocence and courage, in your unwisdom and your loyalty, you are my guide – the child I sent before me into the dark. It is your fear I follow. You have thought me harsh to you. You never knew how harsh. I use your love as a man burns a candle, burns it away, to light his steps. And we must go on. We must go on. We must go all the way. We must come to the place where the springs run dry, the place to which your mortal terror draws you.'

'Where is it, my lord?'

'I do not know.'

'I cannot lead you there. But I will come with you.'

The mage's gaze on him was sombre, unfathomable.

'But if I should fail again, and betray you –'

'I will trust you, son of Morred.'

Then both were silent.

Above them the tall carven idols rocked very slightly against the blue Southern sky, dolphin bodies, gulls' wings folded, human faces with staring eyes of shell.

Sparrowhawk got up stiffly, for he was still far from being fully healed of his wound. 'I am tired of sitting about,' he said, 'I shall grow fat in idleness.' He began to pace the length of the raft, and Arren joined him. They talked a little as they walked; Arren told Sparrowhawk how he spent his days, who his friends among the raft-folk were. Sparrowhawk's restlessness was greater than his strength, which soon gave out. He stopped by a girl who was weaving nilgu on her loom behind the House of the Great Ones, asking her to seek out the chief for him, and then returned to his shelter. There the chief of the raft-folk came and greeted him with courtesy, which the mage returned; and all three of them sat down together on the spotted sealskin rugs of the shelter.

'I have thought,' the chief began, slowly and with a civil solemnity, 'of the things you have told me. Of how men think to come back from death into their own bodies, and seeking to do this forget the worship of the gods and neglect their bodies and go mad. This is an evil matter and a great folly. Also I have thought, what has it to do with us? We have nothing to do with other men, their islands and their ways, their makings and unmakings. We live on the sea and our lives are the sea's. We do not hope to save them, we do not seek to lose them. Madness does not come here. We do not come to land, nor do the land-folk come to us. When I was young, we spoke sometimes with men who came on boats to the Long Dune, when we were there to cut the raft-logs and build the winter shelters. Often we saw sails from Ohol and Welwai (so he called Obehol and Wellogy) following the grey whales in the autumn. Often they followed our rafts from afar, for we know the roads and meeting-places of the Great Ones in the sea. But that is all I ever saw of the land-folk, and now they come no longer. Maybe they have all gone mad and fought with one another. Two years ago on the Long Dune looking north to Welwai we saw for three days the smoke of a great burning. And if that were so, what is it to us? We are the Children of the Open Sea. We go the sea's way.'

'Yet seeing a landsman's boat adrift you came to it,' said the mage.

'Some among us said it was not wise to do so, and would have let the boat drift on to sea's end,' the chief answered in his high, impassive voice.

'You were not one of them.'

'No. I said, though they be land-folk, yet we will help them, and so it was done. But with your undertakings we have nothing to do. If there is a madness among the land-folk, the land-folk must deal with it. We follow the road of the Great Ones. We cannot help you in your search. So long as you wish to stay with us you are welcome. It is not many days till the Long Dance; after it we return northward, following the eastern current that by summer's end will bring us round again to the seas by the Long Dune. If you will stay with us and be healed of your hurt, this will be well. Or if you will take your boat and go your way, this too will be well.'

The mage thanked him, and the chief got up, slight and stiff as a heron, and left them alone together.

'In innocence there is no strength against evil,' said Sparrowhawk, a little wryly. 'But there is strength in it for good ... We shall stay with them a while, I think, till I am cured of this weakness.'

'That is wise,' said Arren. Sparrowhawk's physical frailty had shocked and moved him; he had determined to protect the man from his own energy and urgency, to insist that they wait at least until he was free of pain before they went on.

The mage looked at him, somewhat startled by the compliment.

'They are kind, here,' Arren pursued, not noticing. 'They seem to be free of that sickness of soul they had in Hort Town, and the other islands. Maybe there is no island where we would have been helped and welcomed, as these lost people have done.'

'You may well be right.'

'And they lead a pleasant life, in summer ...'

'They do. Though to eat cold fish one's whole life long, and never to see a pear-tree in blossom, or taste of a running spring, would be wearisome at last!'

So Arren returned to Star's raft, and worked and swam and basked with the other young people, and talked with Sparrowhawk in the cool of the evening, and slept under the stars. And the days wore on towards the Long Dance of midsummer's eve, and the great rafts drifted slowly southward on the currents of the open sea.

9. Orm Embar

ALL night long, the shortest night of the year, torches burned on the rafts which lay gathered in a great circle under the thick-starred sky, so that a ring of fires flickered on the sea. The raft-folk danced, using no drum or flute or any music but the rhythm of bare feet on the great rocking rafts, and the thin voices of their chanters ringing plaintive in the vastness of their dwelling-place the sea. There was no moon that night, and the bodies of the dancers were dim in the starlight and torchlight. Now and again one flashed like a fish leaping, a youth vaulting from one raft to the next: long leaps, and high, and they vied with one another, trying to circle all the ring of rafts and dance on each, and so come round before the break of day.

Arren danced with them, for the Long Dance is held on every isle of the Archipelago, though the steps and songs may vary. But as the night drew on, and many dancers dropped out and settled down to watch or doze, and the voices of the chanters grew husky, he came with a group of high-leaping lads to the chief's raft, and there stopped, while they went on.

Sparrowhawk sat with the chief and the chief's three wives, near the temple. Between the carven whales that made its doorway sat a chanter whose high voice had not flagged all night long. Tireless he sang, tapping his hands on the wooden deck to keep time.

'What does he sing of?' Arren asked the mage, for he could not follow the words, which were all held long, with trills and strange catches on the note.

'Of the grey whales, and the albatross, and the storm ... They do not know the songs of the heroes and the kings. They do not know the name of Erreth-Akbe. Earlier he sang of Segoy, how he established the lands amid the sea; that much they remember of the lore of men. But the rest is all of the sea.'

Arren listened; he heard the singer imitate the whistling cry of the dolphin, weaving his song about it. He watched Sparrowhawk's profile against the torchlight, black and firm as rock, and saw the liquid gleam of the chief's wives' eyes as they chatted softly, and felt the long slow dip of the raft on the quiet sea, and slipped gradually towards sleep.

He roused all at once : the chanter had fallen silent. Not only the one near whom they sat, but all the others, on the rafts near and far. The thin voices had died away like a far-off piping of seabirds, and it was still.

Arren looked over his shoulder to the east, expecting dawn. But only the old moon rode low, just rising, golden among the summer stars.

Then looking southward he saw, high up, yellow Gobardon, and below it the eight companions, even to the last : the rune of Ending clear and fiery above the sea. And turning to Sparrowhawk, he saw the dark face turned to those same stars.

'Why do you cease?' the chief was asking the singer. 'It is not daybreak, not even dawn.'

The man stammered and said, 'I do not know.'

'Sing on ! The Long Dance is not ended.'

'I do not know the words,' the chanter said, and his voice rose high as if in terror. 'I cannot sing. I have forgotten the song.'

'Sing another, then !'

'There are no more songs. It is ended,' the chanter cried, and bent forward till he crouched on the decking; and the chief stared at him in amazement.

The rafts rocked beneath their sputtering torches, all silent. The silence of the ocean enclosed the small stir of life and light upon it, and swallowed it. No dancer moved.

It seemed to Arren then that the splendour of the stars dimmed, and yet no daylight was in the east. A horror came on him, and he thought, 'There will be no sunrise. There will be no day.'

The mage stood up. As he did so a faint light, white and quick, ran along his staff, burning clearest in the rune that was set in silver in the wood. 'The dance is not ended,' he said, 'nor the night. Arren, sing.'

Arren would have said, 'I cannot, lord!' – but instead he looked at the nine stars in the south, and drew a deep breath and sang. His voice was soft and husky at first, but it grew stronger as he sang, and the song was that oldest song, of the Creation of Éa, and the balancing of the dark and the light, and the making of green lands by him who spoke the first word, the Eldest Lord, Segoy.

Before the song was ended the sky had paled to greyish-blue, and in it only the moon and Gobardon still burned faintly, and the torches hissed in the wind of dawn. Then, the song done, Arren was silent; and the dancers who had gathered to listen returned quietly from raft to raft, as the light brightened in the east.

'That is a good song,' the chief said. His voice was uncertain, though he strove to speak impassively. 'It would not be well to end the Long Dance before it is completed. I will have the lazy chanters beaten with nilgu thongs.'

'Comfort them rather,' Sparrowhawk said. He was still afoot, and his tone was stern. 'No singer chooses silence. Come with me, Arren.'

He turned to go to the shelter, and Arren followed him. But the strangeness of that daybreak was not yet done, for even then, as the eastern rim of the sea grew white, there came from the north flying a great bird: so high up that its wings caught the sunlight that had not shone upon the world yet, and beat in strokes of gold upon the air. Arren cried out, pointing. The mage looked up, startled. Then his face became fierce and exulting, and he shouted out aloud, '*Nam hietha arw Ged arkvaissa!*' – which in the Speech of the Making is, If thou seekest Ged here find him.

And like a golden plummet dropped, with wings held high outstretched, vast and thundering on the air, with talons which might seize an ox as if it were a mouse, with a curl of steamy flame streaming from long nostrils, the dragon, stooped like a falcon on the rocking raft.

The raft-folk cried out; some cowered down, some leapt into the sea, and some stood still, watching, in a wonder that surpassed fear.

The dragon hovered above them. Ninety feet, maybe, was he from tip to tip of his vast membranous wings, that shone in the new sunlight like gold-shot smoke, and the length of his body was no less, but lean, arched like a greyhound, clawed like a lizard, and snake-scaled. Along the narrow spine went a row of jagged darts, like rose-thorns in shape, but at the hump of the back three feet in height, and so diminishing that the last at the tail-tip was no longer than the blade of a little knife. These thorns were grey, and the scales of the dragon were iron-grey, but there was a glitter of gold in them. His eyes were green and slitted.

Moved by fear for his people to forget fear for himself, the chief of the raft-folk came from his shelter with a harpoon such as they used in the hunt of whales : it was longer than himself, and pointed with a great barbed point of ivory. Poising it on his small sinewy arm he ran forward to gain the impetus to hurl it up and strike the dragon's narrow, light-mailed belly that hung above the raft. Arren waking from stupor saw him, and plunging forward caught his arm and came down in a heap with him and the harpoon. 'Would you anger him with your silly pins?' he gasped. 'Let the Dragonlord speak first!'

The chief, half the wind knocked out of him, stared stupidly at Arren, and at the mage, and at the dragon. But he did not say anything. And then the dragon spoke.

None there but Ged to whom it spoke could understand it, for dragons speak only in the Old Speech, which is their tongue. The voice was soft and hissing, almost like a cat's when he cries out softly in rage, but huge, and there was a terrible music in it. Whoever heard that voice stopped still, and listened.

The mage answered briefly, and again the dragon spoke, poising above him on slight-shifting wings : even, thought Arren, like a dragonfly poised on the air.

Then the mage answered one word, '*Memeas*,' I will come; and he lifted up his staff of yew-wood. The dragon's jaws opened, and a coil of smoke escaped them in a long arabesque. The gold wings clapped like thunder, making a great wind that smelled of burning : and he wheeled and flew hugely to the north.

It was quiet on the rafts, with a little thin piping and wailing of children, and women comforting them; and men climbed aboard out of the sea somewhat shamefaced; and the forgotten torches burned in the first rays of the sun.

The mage turned to Arren. His face had a light in it that might have been joy or stark anger, but he spoke quietly. 'Now we must go, lad. Say your farewells, and come.' He turned to thank the chief of the raft-folk and bid him farewell, and then went from the great raft across three others, as they still lay close ingathered for the dancing, till he came to the one to which *Lookfar* was tied. So the boat had followed the raft-town in its long slow drift into the south, rocking along empty behind; but the Children of the Open Sea had filled its empty cask with hoarded rainwater, and made up its stock of provisions, wishing thus to honour their guests; for many of them believed Sparrowhawk to be one of the Great Ones, who had taken on the form of a man instead of the form of a whale. When Arren joined him he had the sail up. Arren loosed the rope and leapt into the boat, and in that instant she veered from the raft and her sail stiffened as in a high wind, though only the breeze of sunrise blew. She heeled turning and sped off northward on the dragon's track, light as a blown leaf on the wind.

When Arren looked back he saw the raft-town as a tiny scattering, like sticks and chips of wood afloat: the shelters and the torchpoles. Soon these were lost in the dazzle of early sunlight on the water. *Lookfar* fled forward. When her bow bit the waves, fine crystal spray flew and made him squint.

Under no wind of earth could that small boat have sailed so fast, unless in storm, and then might have foundered in the stormwaves. This was no wind of earth, but the mage's word and power, that sent her forth so fleet.

He stood a long time by the mast, with watchful eyes. At last he sat down in his old place by the tiller, and laid one hand upon it, and looked at Arren.

'That was Orm Embar,' he said, 'the Dragon of Selidor, kin to the great Orm who slew Erreth-Akbe and was slain by him.'

'Was he hunting, lord?' said Arren; for he was not certain whether the mage had spoken to the dragon in welcome or in threat.

'Hunting me. What dragons hunt, they find. He came to ask my help.' He laughed shortly. 'And that's a thing I would not believe if any told me : that a dragon turned to a man for help. And of them all, that one ! He is not the oldest, though he is very old, but he is the mightiest of his kind. He does not hide his name, as dragons and men must do. He has no fear that any can gain power over him. Nor does he deceive, in the way of his kind. Long ago, on Selidor, he let me live, and he told me a great truth; he told me how the Rune of Kings might be refound. To him I owe the Ring of Erreth-Akbe. But never did I think to repay such a debt, to such a creditor !'

'What does he ask?'

'To show me the way I seek,' said the mage, more grimly. And after a pause, 'He said, "In the west there is another Dragonlord; he works destruction on us, and his power is greater than ours." I said, "Even than thine, Orm Embar?" and he said, "Even than mine. I need thee : follow in haste." And so bid, I obeyed.'

'You know no more than that?'

'I will know more.'

Arren coiled up the mooring line, and stowed it, and saw to other small matters about the boat, but all the while the tension of excitement sang in him like a tightened bowstring, and it sang in his voice when he spoke at last. 'This is a better guide,' he said, 'than the others !'

Sparrowhawk looked at him, and laughed. 'Aye,' he said. 'This time we will not go astray, I think.'

So those two began their great race across the ocean. A thousand miles and more it was from the uncharted seas of the raft-folk to the island Selidor, which lies of all the lands of Earthsea the farthest west. Day after day rose shining from the clear horizon, and sank into the red west, and under the gold arch of the sun and the silver wheeling of the stars the boat ran northward, all alone on the sea.

Sometimes the thunderclouds of high summer massed far off, casting purple shadows down on the horizon; then Arren would watch the mage as he stood up and with voice and hand called those clouds to drift towards them, and to loosen their rain down on the boat. The lightning would leap among the clouds, and the thunder would bellow, and still the mage stood with upraised hand, until the rain came pouring down on him, and on Arren, and into the vessels they had set out, and into the boat, and onto the sea, flattening the waves with its violence. He and Arren would grin with pleasure, for of food they had enough if none to spare, but water they needed. And the furious splendour of the storm that obeyed the mage's word delighted them.

Arren wondered at this power which his companion now used so lightly, and once he said, 'When we began our voyage, you used to work no charms.'

'The first lesson on Roke, and the last, is Do what is needful. And no more!'

'The lessons in between, then, must consist in learning what is needful.'

'They do. One must consider the Balance. But when the Balance itself is broken – then one considers others things. Above all, haste.'

'But how is it that all the wizards of the South – and elsewhere by now – even the chanters of the rafts – all have lost their art, but you keep yours?'

'Because I desire nothing beyond my art,' Sparrowhawk said.

And after some time he added, more cheerfully, 'And if I am soon to lose it, I shall make the best of it while it lasts.'

There was indeed a kind of lightheartedness in him now, a pure pleasure in his skill, which Arren, seeing him always so careful, had not guessed. The mind of the magician takes delight in tricks; a mage is a trickster. Sparrowhawk's disguise in Hort Town, which had so troubled Arren, had been a game to him; a very slight game, too, for one who could transform not just his face and voice at will, but his body and very being, becoming as he chose a fish, a dolphin, a hawk. And once he said, 'Look, Arren: I'll show you Gont,' and had him look at the surface of their water-cask, which he had opened, and which was full to the brim. Many simple sorcerers can cause an image to appear on the water-mirror, and so he had done : a great peak, cloud-wreathed, rising from a grey sea. Then the image changed, and Arren saw plainly a cliff of that mountain isle. It was as if he was a bird, gull or falcon, hanging on the wind off shore and

looking across the wind at that cliff that towered from the breakers
for two thousand feet. On the high shelf of it was a little house.
'That is Re Albi,' said Sparrowhawk, 'and there lives my master,
Ogion, he who stilled the earthquake long ago. He tends his goats,
and gathers herbs, and keeps his silence. I wonder if he still walks
on the mountain; he is very old now. But I would know, surely I
would know, even now, if Ogion died . . .' There was no certainty
in his voice; for a moment the image wavered, as if the cliff itself
were falling. It cleared, his voice cleared : 'He used to go up into the
forests alone, in late summer and in autumn. So he came first to me,
when I was a brat in a mountain village, and gave me my name.
And my life with it.' The image of the water-mirror now showed as
if the watcher were a bird among the forest branches, looking out
to steep sunlit meadows beneath the rock and snow of the peak,
looking inward along a steep road going down in a green, gold-shot
darkness. 'There is no silence like the silence of those forests,'
Sparrowhawk said, yearning.

The image faded, and there was nothing but the blinding disc of
the noon sun reflected in the water in the cask.

'There,' Sparrowhawk said looking at Arren with a strange, mocking look, 'there, if I could ever go back there, not even you could
follow me.'

Land lay ahead, low and blue in the afternoon like a bank of
mist. 'Is it Selidor?' Arren asked, and his heart beat fast, but the
mage answered, 'Obb, I think, or Jessage. We're not halfway yet,
lad.'

That night they sailed the straits between those two islands. They
saw no lights, but there was a reek of smoke in the air, so heavy that
their lungs grew raw with breathing it. When day came and they
looked back, the eastern isle, Jessage, looked burnt and black as far
as they could see inland from the shore, and a haze hung blue and
dull above it.

'They have burnt the fields,' Arren said.

'Aye. And the villages. I have smelled that smoke before.'

'Are they savages, here in the West?'

Sparrowhawk shook his head. 'Farmers; townsmen.'

Arren stared at the black ruin of the land, the withered trees of orchards against the sky; and his face was hard. 'What harm have the trees done them?' he said. 'Must they punish the grass for their own faults? Men are savages, who would set a land afire because they have a quarrel with other men.'

'They have no guidance,' Sparrowhawk said. 'No king; and the kingly men, and the wizardly men, all drawn aside and drawn into their own minds, hunting the door through death. So it was in the South, and so I guess it to be here.'

'And this is one man's doing – the one the dragon spoke of? It seems not possible.'

'Why not? If there were a King of the Isles, he would be one man. And he would rule. One man may as easily destroy, as govern; be King, or Anti-King.'

There was again that note in his voice of mockery, or challenge, which roused Arren's temper.

'A king has servants, soldiers, messengers, lieutenants. He governs through his servants. Where are the servants of this – Anti-King?'

'In our minds, lad. In our minds. The traitor, the self, the self that cries *I want to live, let the world rot so long as I can live!* The little traitor soul in us, in the dark, like the spider in a box. He talks to all of us. But only some understand him. The wizards, the singers, the makers. And the heroes, the ones who seek to be themselves. To be oneself is a rare thing, and a great one. To be oneself forever, is that not greater still?'

Arren looked straight at Sparrowhawk. 'You mean that it is not greater. But tell me why. I was a child when I began this voyage. I did not believe in death. I have learned something, not much maybe but something, I have learned to believe in death. But I have not learned to rejoice over it, to welcome my death, or yours. If I love life shall I not hate the end of it?'

Arren's fencing-master in Berila had been a man of about sixty, short, bald, and cold. Arren had disliked him for years, though he knew him for a great swordsman. But one day in practice he had caught his master off guard and disarmed him: and he never forgot the incredulous, incongruous happiness that had suddenly gleamed in the master's cold face, the hope, the joy – an equal, at last an equal! From that day on the fencing-master had trained him mercilessly, and whenever they fenced the same relentless smile would be on the old man's face, brightening as Arren fought him harder. It was on Sparrowhawk's face now.

'Life without end,' the mage said. 'Life without death. Immortality. Every soul desires it, and its health is the strength of its desire. But be careful, Arren. You are one who might achieve your desire.'

'And then?'

'And then – this. This blight upon the lands. The arts of man forgotten. The singer tongueless. The eye blind. And then? A false king ruling. Ruling forever. And over the same subjects forever. No births; no new lives. No children. Only what is mortal bears life, Arren. Only in death is there rebirth. The Balance is not a stillness. It is a movement – an eternal becoming.'

'But how can the Balance of the Whole be endangered by one man's acts, one man's life? Surely it is not possible, it would not be allowed –' He halted.

'Who allows? Who forbids?'

'I do not know.'

'Nor I.'

Almost sullenly, doggedly, Arren asked, 'Then how is it you are so sure?'

'I know how much evil one man can do,' Sparrowhawk said, and his scarred face frowned, but rather as if in pain than in anger. 'I know it because I have done it. I have done the same evil, moved by the same pride. I opened the door between the worlds. Only a crack, a little crack, only to prove that I was stronger than death itself. I was young, and had not met death – like you ... It took the strength of the Archmage Nemmerle, it took his mastery and his life, to shut that door. You can see the mark that night left on me, on my face. But him it killed. Oh, the door between the light and the darkness can be opened, Arren; it takes strength, but it can be done. But to shut it again, there's a different story.'

'But what you did surely was not the same –'

'Why? Because I am a good man?' That coldness like the fencer's sword was in Sparrowhawk's eye again. 'What is a good man, Arren? Is a good man one who would not do evil, who would not open a door to the darkness, who has no darkness in him? Look again, lad. Look a little farther. You'll need what you learn, to go where you must go. Look into yourself! Did you not hear a voice say *Come*? Did you not follow?'

'I did. But I – I thought that voice was his.'

'It was his. And it was yours. How could he speak to you, and to all those who know how to listen, but in your own voice?'

'Why do you not hear it, then?'

'Because I will not!' Sparrowhawk said fiercely. 'I was born to power, even as you were. But you are young. You stand on the borders of possibility, in the shadowland, in the realm of dream, and you hear the voice saying *Come*. As I did once. But I am old. I have made my choices, I have done what I must do. I stand in daylight facing my own death. And I know that there is only one power worth having. And that is the power, not to take, but to accept. Not to have, but to give.'

Jessage was far behind them now, a blue stain on the sea.

'Then I am his servant,' Arren said.

'You are. And I am yours.'

'But who is he, then? What is he?'

'A man, I think.'

'That man you spoke of once – the sorcerer of Havnor, who summoned up the dead? Is it he?'

'It may well be.'

'But he was old, you said, when you knew him years ago ... Would he not have died by now?'

'Maybe,' Sparrowhawk said.

And they said no more.

That night the sea was full of fire. The sharp waves thrown back by *Lookfar*'s prow, and the movement of every fish through the surface water, were all outlined and alive with light. Arren sat with his arm on the gunwale and his head on his arm, watching those curves and whorls of silver radiance. He put his hand in the water and raised it again, and light ran softly from his fingers. 'Look,' he said, 'I too am a wizard.'

'That gift you have not,' said his companion.

'Much good I shall be to you without it,' said Arren, gazing at the restless shimmer of the waves, 'when we meet our enemy.'

For he had hoped – from the very beginning he had hoped – that the reason why the Archmage had chosen him and him alone for this voyage was that he had some inborn power, descended from his ancestor Morred, which would in the ultimate need and the blackest hour be revealed : and so he would save himself, and his lord, and all the world, from the enemy. But lately he had looked once more at that hope, and it was as if he saw it from a great distance; it was like remembering that, when he was a very little boy, he had had a burning desire to try on his father's crown, and had wept when he was forbidden to. This hope was as ill-timed, as childish. There was no magery in him. There never would be.

The time might come, indeed, when he could, when he must, put on his father's crown, and rule as Prince of Enlad. But that seemed a small thing now, and his home a small place, and remote. There was no disloyalty in this. Only his loyalty had grown greater, being fixed upon a greater model and a broader hope. He had learned his own weakness, also, and by it had learned to measure his strength; and he knew that he was strong. But what use was strength, if he had no gift, nothing to offer, still, to his lord, but his service and his steady love? Where they were going, would those be enough?

Sparrowhawk said only, 'To see a candle's light one must take it into a dark place.' With that Arren tried to comfort himself; but he did not find it very comforting.

Next morning when they woke the air was grey and the water was grey. Over the mast the sky brightened to the blue of an opal, for the fog lay low. To Northern men such as Arren of Enlad and Sparrowhawk of Gont, the fog was welcome, like an old friend. Softly it enclosed the boat so that they could not see far, and it was to them like being in a familiar room after many weeks of bright and barren space and the wind blowing. They were coming back into their own climate, and were now perhaps at the latitude of Roke.

And some seven hundred miles east of those fog-clad waters where *Lookfar* sailed, clear sunlight shone on the leaves of the trees of the Immanent Grove, on the green crown of Roke Knoll, and on the high slate roofs of the Great House.

In a room in the south tower, a magicians' workroom cluttered with retorts and alembics and great-bellied, crook-necked bottles, thick-walled furnaces and tiny heating-lamps, tongs, bellows, stands, pliers, files, pipes, a thousand boxes and vials and stoppered jugs marked with Hardic or more secret runes, and all such paraphernalia of alchemy, glass-blowing, metal-refining, and the arts of healing, in that room among the much-encumbered tables and benches stood the Master Changer and the Master Summoner of Roke.

In his hands the grey-haired Changer held a great stone like a diamond uncarved. It was a rock-crystal, coloured faintly deep within with amethyst and rose, but clear as water. Yet as the eye looked into that clarity it found unclarity, and neither reflection nor image of what was real round about, but only planes and depths ever deeper, until it was led quite into dream and found no way out. This was the Stone of Shelieth. It had long been kept by the princes of Way, sometimes as a mere bauble of their treasury, sometimes as a charm for sleep, sometimes for a more baneful purpose: for those who looked too long and without understanding into that endless depth of crystal, might go mad. But the Archmage Gensher of Way, coming to Roke, had brought with him the Stone of Shelieth, for in the hands of a mage it held great truth.

Yet the truth varies with the man.

Therefore the Changer, holding it and looking through its bossed, uneven surface into the infinite, pale-coloured, shimmering depths, spoke aloud to tell what he saw. 'I see the earth, even as though I stood on Mount Onn in the centre of the world and beheld all beneath my feet, even to the farthest isle of the farthest Reaches, and beyond. And all is clear. I see ships in the lanes of Ilien, and the hearthfires of Torheven, and the roofs of this tower where we stand now. But past Roke, nothing. In the south, no lands. In the west, no lands. I cannot see Wathort where it should be, nor any isle of the West Reach, even so close as Pendor. And Osskil and Ebosskil, where are they? There is a mist on Enlad, a greyness, like a spider's web. Each time I look more islands are gone, and the sea where they were is empty and unbroken, even as it was before the Making –' and his voice stumbled on the last word as if it came with difficulty to his lips.

He set the stone down on its ivory stand, and stood away from it. His kindly face looked drawn. He said, 'Tell me what you see.'

The Master Summoner took up the crystal in his hands and turned it slowly as if seeking on its rough, glassy surface an entrance of vision. A long time he handled it, his face intent. At last he set it down and said, 'Changer, I see little. Fragments, glimpses, making no whole.'

The grey-haired Master clenched his hands. 'Is that not strange in itself?'

'How so?'

'Are your eyes often blind?' the Changer cried, as if enraged. 'Do you not see that there is,' and he stammered several times before he could speak, 'that there is a hand upon your eyes, even as there is a hand over my mouth?'

The Summoner said, 'You are overwrought, my lord.'

'Summon the Presence of the Stone,' said the Changer, controlling himself, but speaking somewhat stifled.

'Why?'

'Why, because I ask you.'

'Come, Changer, do you dare me – like boys before a bear's den? Are we children?'

'Yes! Before what I see in the Stone of Shelieth, I am a child – a frightened child. Summon the Presence of the Stone. Must I beg you, my lord?'

'No,' said the tall Master, but he frowned, and turned from the older man. Then stretching wide his arms in the great gesture that begins the spells of his art, he raised his head and spoke the syllables of invocation. As he spoke, a light grew within the Stone of

427

Shelieth. The room darkened about it: shadows gathered. When the shadows were deep and the stone was very bright, he brought his hands together, and lifted the crystal before his face, and looked into its radiance.

He was silent some while, and then spoke, 'I see the Fountains of Shelieth,' he said softly. 'The pools and basins and the waterfalls, the silver-curtained dripping caves where ferns grow in banks of moss, the rippled sands, the leaping up of the waters and the running of them, the outwelling of deep springs from earth, the mystery and sweetness of the source, the spring ...' He fell silent again, and stood so for a time, his face pale as silver in the light of the stone. Then he cried aloud wordlessly, and dropping the crystal with a crash fell to his knees, his face hidden in his hands.

There were no shadows. Summer sunlight filtered the jumbled room. The great stone lay beneath a table in the dust and litter, unharmed.

The Summoner reached out blindly, catching at the other man's hand like a child. He drew a deep breath. At last he got up, leaning a little on the Changer, and said with unsteady lips and some attempt to smile, 'I will not take your dares again, my lord.'

'What saw you, Thorion?'

'I saw the fountains. I saw them sink down, and the streams run dry, and the lips of the springs of water draw back. And underneath all was black, and dry. You saw the sea before the Making, but I saw the ... what comes after ... I saw the Unmaking.' He wet his lips. 'I wish that the Archmage were here,' he said.

'I wish that we were there with him.'

'Where? There is none that can find him now.' The Summoner looked up at the windows that showed the blue, untroubled sky. 'No sending can come to him, no summoning reach him. He is there where you saw an empty sea. He is coming to the place where the springs run dry. He is where our arts do not avail ... Yet maybe even now there are spells that might reach to him, some of those in the Lore of Paln.'

'But those are spells whereby the dead are brought among the living.'

'Some bring the living among the dead.'

'You do not think him dead?'

'I think he goes towards death, and is drawn towards it. And so are we all. Our power is going from us, and our strength, and our hope and luck. The springs are running dry.'

The Changer gazed at him a while with a troubled face. 'Do not seek to send to him, Thorion,' he said at last. 'He knew what he sought long before we knew it. To him the world is even as this Stone of Shelieth : he looks and sees what is and what must be ... We cannot help him. The great spells have grown very perilous, and of all there is most danger in the Lore of which you spoke. We must stand fast as he bade us, and look to the walls of Roke, and the remembering of the Names.'

'Aye,' said the Summoner. 'But I must go and think on this.' And he left the tower room, walking somewhat stiffly and holding his noble, dark head high.

In the morning the Changer sought him. Entering his room after vain knocking, he found him stretched asprawl on the stone floor, as if he had been hurled backward by a heavy blow. His arms were flung wide as if in the gesture of invocation, but his hands were cold, and his open eyes saw nothing. Though the Changer knelt by him and called him with a mage's authority, saying his name, Thorion, thrice over, yet he lay still. He was not dead, but there was in him only so much life as kept his heart beating very slowly, and a little breath in his lungs. The Changer took his hands, and holding them whispered, 'O Thorion, I forced you to look into the Stone. This is my doing !' Then going hastily from the room he said aloud to those he met, Masters and students, 'The enemy has reached among us, into Roke the well-defended, and has stricken our strength at its heart !' Though he was a gentle man, he looked so fey and cold that those who saw him feared him. 'Look to the Master Summoner,' he said. 'Though who will summon back his spirit since he the master of his art is gone?'

He went towards his own chamber, and they all drew back to let him pass.

The Master Healer was sent for. He had them lay Thorion the

Summoner abed, and cover him warmly; but he brewed no herb of healing, nor did he sing any of the chants that aid the sick body or the troubled mind. One of his pupils was with him, a young boy not yet made sorcerer, but promising in the arts of healing, and he asked, 'Master, is there nothing to be done for him?'

'Not on this side of the wall,' said the Master Healer. Then, recalling to whom he spoke, he said, 'He is not ill, lad; but even if this were a fever of illness of the body, I do not know if our craft would much avail. It seems there is no savour in my herbs of late; and though I say the words of our spells, there is no virtue in them.'

'That is like what the Master Chanter said yesterday. He stopped in the middle of a song he was teaching us, and said, "I do not know what the song means." And he walked out of the room. Some of the boys laughed, but I felt as if the floor had sunk out from under me.'

The Healer looked at the boy's blunt, clever face, and then down at the Summoner's face, cold and rigid. 'He will come back to us,' he said. 'The songs will not be forgotten.'

But that night the Changer went from Roke. No one saw the manner of his going. He slept in a room with a window looking out into a garden; the window was open in the morning, and he was gone. They thought he had transformed himself, with his own skill of form-change, into a bird or beast, or a mist or wind even, for no shape or substance was beyond his art, and so had fled from Roke, perhaps to seek for the Archmage. Some, knowing how the shape-changer may be caught in his own spells if there is any failure of skill or will, feared for him, but they said nothing of their fears.

So there were three of the Masters lost to the Council of the Wise. As the days passed and no news ever came of the Archmage, and the Summoner lay like one dead, and the Changer did not return, a chill and gloom grew in the Great House. The boys whispered among themselves, and some of them spoke of leaving Roke, for they were not being taught what they had come to learn. 'Maybe,' said one, 'they were all lies from the beginning, these secret arts and powers. Of the Masters, only the Master Hand still does his tricks, and these, we all know, are frank illusion. And now the others hide, or refuse to do anything, because their tricks have been revealed.' Another, listening, said, 'Well, what is wizardry? What is this art magic, beyond a show of seeming? Has it ever saved a man from death, or given long life, even? Surely if the mages have the power they claim to have, they'd all live forever!' And he and the other boys fell to telling over the deaths of the great mages, how Morred had been killed in battle, and Nereger by the Grey Mage, and Erreth-Akbe by a dragon, and Gensher, the last Archmage, by mere sickness, in his bed, like any man. Some of the boys listened gladly, having envious hearts; others listened and were wretched.

All this time the Master Patterner stayed alone in the Grove, and let none enter it.

But the Doorkeeper, though seldom seen, was not changed. He bore no shadow in his eyes. He smiled, and kept the doors of the Great House against its lord's return.

10. The Dragons' Run

ON the seas of the outermost West Reach that Lord of the Island of the Wise, waking cramped and stiff in a small boat in a cold, bright morning, sat up and yawned. And after a moment, pointing north, he said to his yawning companion, 'There! Two islands, do you see them? The southmost of the isles of the Dragons' Run.'

'You have a hawk's eyes, lord,' said Arren, peering through sleep over the sea, and seeing nothing.

'Therefore I am the Sparrowhawk,' the mage said; he was still cheerful, seeming to shrug off forethought and foreboding. 'Can't you see them?'

'I see gulls,' said Arren, after rubbing his eyes and searching all the blue-grey horizon before the boat.

The mage laughed. 'Could even a hawk see gulls at twenty miles' distance?'

As the sun brightened above the eastern mists, the tiny wheeling flecks in the air that Arren watched seemed to sparkle, like gold-dust shaken in water, or dust-motes in a sunbeam. And then Arren realized that they were dragons.

As Lookfar approached the islands Arren saw the dragons soaring and circling on the morning wind, and his heart leapt up with them with a joy, a joy of fulfilment, that was like pain. All the glory of mortality was in that flight. Their beauty was made up of terrible strength, and utter wildness, and the grace of reason. For these were thinking creatures, with speech, and ancient wisdom: in the patterns of their flight there was a fierce, willed concord.

Arren did not speak, but he thought: I do not care what comes after; I have seen the dragons on the wind of morning.

At times the patterns jarred, and the circles broke, and often in flight one dragon or another would jet from its nostrils a long streak of fire that curved and hung on the air a moment repeating the curve and brightness of the dragon's long, arching body. Seeing that, the mage said, 'They are angry. They dance their anger on the wind.'

And presently he said, 'Now we're in the hornet's nest.' For the dragons had seen the little sail on the waves, and first one, then another, broke from the whirlwind of their dancing and came stretched long and level on the air, rowing with great wings, straight towards the boat.

The mage looked at Arren, who sat at the tiller, since the waves ran rough and counter. The boy held it steady with a steady hand, though his eyes were on the beating of those wings. As if satisfied, Sparrowhawk turned again, and standing by the mast, let the mage-wind drop from the sail. He lifted up his staff and spoke aloud.

At the sound of his voice and the words of the Old Speech, some of the dragons wheeled in mid-flight, scattering, and returned to the isles. Others halted and hovered, the sword-like claws of their fore-arms outstretched but checked. One, dropping low over the water, flew slowly on towards them : in two wing-strokes it was over the boat. The mailed belly scarcely cleared the mast. Arren saw the wrinkled, un-armoured flesh between the inner shoulder-joint and breast, which, with the eye, is the dragon's only vulnerable part, unless the spear that strikes be mightily enchanted. The smoke that rolled from the long, toothed mouth choked him, and with it came a carrion stench that made him wince and retch.

The shadow passed. It returned, as low as before, and this time Arren felt the furnace-blast of breath before the smoke. He heard Sparrowhawk's voice, clear and fierce. The dragon passed over. Then all were gone, streaming back to the isles like fiery cinders on a gust of wind.

Arren caught his breath, and wiped his forehead, which was covered with cold sweat. Looking at his companion he saw his hair had gone white : the dragon's breath had burnt and crisped the ends of the hairs. And the heavy cloth of the sail was scorched brown along one side.

'Your head is somewhat singed, lad.'

'So is yours, lord.'

Sparrowhawk passed his hand over his hair, surprised. 'So it is ! – That was an insolence; but I seek no quarrel with these creatures. They seem mad, or bewildered. They did not speak. Never have I met a dragon who did not speak before it struck, if only to torment its prey ... Now we must go forward. Do not look them in the eye, Arren. Turn aside your face if you must. We'll go with the world's wind, it blows fair from the south, and I may need my art for other things. Hold her as she goes.'

Lookfar moved forward and soon had on her left a distant island, and on her right the twin isles they had seen first. These rose up into low cliffs, and all the stark rock was whitened with the droppings of the dragons and of the black-headed terns that nested fearlessly amongst them.

The dragons had flown up high, and circled in the upper air as vultures circle. Not one stooped down again to the boat. Sometimes they cried out to one another, high and harsh across the gulfs of air, but if there were words in their crying Arren could not make them out.

The boat rounded a short promontory, and he saw on the shore what he took for a moment to be a ruined fortress. It was a dragon. One black wing was bent under it and the other stretched out vast across the sand and into the water, so that the come and go of waves moved it a little to and fro in a mockery of flight. The long snake-body lay full length on the rock and sand. One foreleg was missing, and the armour and flesh were torn from the great arch of the ribs, and the belly was torn open, so that the sand for yards about was blackened with the poisoned dragon-blood. Yet the creature still lived. So great a life is in dragons that only an equal power of wizardry can kill them swiftly. The green-gold eyes were open, and as the boat sailed by, the lean, huge head moved a little, and with a rattling hiss steam mixed with blood spray shot from his nostrils.

The beach between the dying dragon and the sea's edge was tracked and scored by the feet and heavy bodies of its kind, and its entrails were trodden into the sand.

Neither Arren nor Sparrowhawk spoke until they were well clear of that island and heading across the choppy, restless channel of the Dragons' Run, full of reefs and pinnacles and shapes of rock, towards the northern islands of the double chain. Then Sparrowhawk said, 'That was an evil sight,' and his voice was bleak and cold.

'Do they ... eat their own kind?'

'No. No more than we do. They have been driven mad. Their speech has been taken from them. They who spoke before men spoke, they who are older than any living thing, the Children of Segoy, – they have been driven to the dumb terror of the beasts. Ah! Kalessin! where have your wings borne you? Have you lived to see your race learn shame?' His voice rang like struck iron, and he looked upward, searching the sky. But the dragons were behind, circling lower now above the rocky isles and the bloodstained beach, and overhead was nothing but the blue sky and the sun of noon.

There was then no man living who had sailed the Dragons' Run, or seen it, except the Archmage. Twenty years ago and more, he had sailed the length of it from east to west and back again. It was a nightmare and a marvel, to a sailor. The water was a maze of blue channels and green shoals, and among these, by hand and word and most vigilant care, he and Arren now picked their boat's way, between the rocks and reefs. Some of these lay low, under or half-under the wash of the waves, covered with anemone and barnacle and ribbony seafern; like water-monsters, shelled or sinuous. Others stood up in cliff and pinnacle sheer from the sea, and there were arches and half-arches, carven towers, fantastic shapes of animals, boars' backs and serpents' heads, all huge, deformed, diffuse, as if life writhed half-conscious in the rock. The sea-waves beat on them with a sound like breathing, and they were wet with the bright, bitter spray. In one such rock from the south there was plainly visible the hunched shoulders and heavy, noble head of a man, stooped in pondering thought above the sea; but when the boat had passed it, looking back from the north, all man was gone from it and the massive rocks revealed a cave in which the sea rose and fell making a hollow, clapping thunder; and there seemed to be a word, a syllable, in that sound. As they sailed on, the garbling echoes lessened and this syllable came more clearly; so that Arren said, 'Is there a voice in the cave?'

'The sea's voice.'

'But it speaks a word.'

Sparrowhawk listened; he glanced at Arren, and back at the cave. 'How do you hear it?'

'As saying the sound *ahm*.'

'In the Old Speech that signifies the beginning, or long ago. But I hear it as *ohb*, which is a way of saying the end. – Look ahead there!' he ended abruptly, even as Arren warned him, 'Shoal water!' And, though *Lookfar* picked her way like a cat among the dangers, they were busy with the steering for some time, and slowly the cave forever thundering out its enigmatic word fell behind them.

Now the water deepened and they came out from among the phantasmagoria of the rocks; and ahead of them loomed an island like a tower. Its cliffs were black, and made up of many cylinders or great pillars pressed together, with straight edges and plane surfaces, rising three hundred feet sheer from the water.

'That is the Keep of Kalessin,' said the mage. 'So the dragons named it to me, when I was here long ago.'

'Who is Kalessin?'

'The eldest . . .'

'Did he build this place?'

'I do not know. I don't know if it was built. Nor how old he is. I say "he", but I do not even know that . . . To Kalessin, Orm Embar is like a yearling kid. And you and I are like mayflies.' He scanned the terrific palisades, and Arren looked up at them uneasily, thinking how a dragon might drop from that far, black rim and be upon them almost with its shadow. But no dragon came. They passed slowly through the still waters in the lee of the rock, hearing nothing but the whisper and clap of shadowed waves on the columns of basalt. The water here was deep, without reef or rock; Arren handled the boat, and Sparrowhawk stood up in the prow, searching the cliffs and the bright sky ahead.

The boat passed out at last from the shadow of the Keep of Kalessin into the sunlight of late afternoon. They were across the Dragons' Run. The mage lifted his head, like one who sees what he had looked to see, and across that great space of gold before them came on golden wings the dragon Orm Embar.

Arren heard Sparrowhawk's cry to him: *Aro Kalessin?* He guessed the meaning of that, but could make no sense of what the dragon answered. Yet hearing the Old Speech he felt always that he was on the point of understanding, almost understanding: as if it were a language he had forgotten, not one he had never known. In speaking it the mage's voice was much clearer than when he spoke Hardic, and seemed to make a kind of silence about it, as does the softest touch on a great bell. But the dragon's voice was like a gong, both deep and shrill, or the hissing thrum of cymbals.

Arren watched his companion stand there in the narrow prow, speaking with the monstrous creature that hovered above him filling half the sky; and a kind of rejoicing pride came into the boy's heart, to see how small a thing a man is, how frail, and how terrible. For the dragon could have torn the man's head from his shoulders with one stroke of his taloned foot, he could have crushed and sunk the boat as a stone sinks a floating leaf, if it were only size that mattered. But Sparrowhawk was as dangerous as Orm Embar: and the dragon knew it.

The mage turned his head. 'Lebannen,' he said, and the boy got up and came forward, though he wanted to go not one boat's length, not one step, closer to those fifteen-foot jaws and the long, slit-pupilled, yellow-green eyes that burned upon him from the air.

Sparrowhawk said nothing to him, but put a hand on his shoulder, and spoke again to the dragon, briefly.

'Lebannen,' said the vast voice with no passion in it. '*Agni Lebannen!*'

He looked up; the pressure of the mage's hand reminded him, and he avoided the gaze of the green-gold eyes.

He could not speak the Old Speech; but he was not dumb. 'I greet thee, Orm Embar, Lord Dragon,' he said clearly, as one prince greets another.

Then there was a silence, and Arren's heart beat hard and laboured. But Sparrowhawk, standing by him, smiled.

After that the dragon spoke again, and Sparrowhawk replied; and this seemed long to Arren. At last it was over, and suddenly. The dragon sprang aloft with a wingbeat that all but heeled the boat over, and was off. Arren looked at the sun, and found it seemed no nearer setting than before; the time had not really been long. But the mage's face was the colour of wet ashes, and his eyes glittered as he turned to Arren. He sat down on the thwart.

'Well done, lad,' he said hoarsely. 'It is not easy – talking to dragons.'

Arren got them food, for they had not eaten all day; and the mage said no more until they had eaten and drunk. By then the sun was low to the horizon, though in these northern latitudes, and not long past midsummer, night came late and slowly.

'Well,' he said at last, 'Orm Embar has, after his fashion, told me much. He says that the one we seek is, and is not, on Selidor ... It is hard for a dragon to speak plainly. They do not have plain minds. And even when one of them would speak the truth to a man, which is seldom, he does not know how truth looks to a man. So I asked him, "Even as thy father Orm is on Selidor?" For as you know, there Orm and Erreth-Akbe died in their battle. And he answered, "No and yes. You will find him on Selidor, but not on Selidor."' Sparrowhawk paused and pondered, chewing on a crust of hardbread. 'Maybe he meant that though the man is not on Selidor, yet I must go there to get to him. Maybe ... I asked him then of the other dragons. He said that this man has been among them, having no fear of them, for though killed he re-arises from death, in his body, alive. Therefore they fear him as a creature outside nature; and their fear gives his wizardry hold over them, and he takes the Speech of the Making from them, leaving them prey to their own wild nature. So they devour one another, or take their own lives, plunging into the sea – a loathly death for the fire-serpent, the beast of wind and fire. Then I said, "Where is their lord Kalessin?" and all he would answer was, "In the West," which might mean that Kalessin had flown away to the other lands which dragons say lie

farther than ever ship has sailed; or it may not mean that. So then I
ceased my questions, and he asked his, saying, "I flew over Kaltuel
returning north, and over the Toringates. On Kaltuel I saw villagers
killing a baby on an altar stone, and on Ingat I saw a sorcerer killed
by his townsfolk throwing stones at him. Will they eat the baby,
think you, Ged? Will the sorcerer come back from death and throw
stones at his townsfolk?" I thought he mocked me, and was about
to speak in anger, but he was not mocking. He said, "The sense has
gone out of things. There is a hole in the world and the sea is running out of it. The light is running out. We will be left in the dry
land. There will be no more speaking, and no more dying." So at
last I saw what he would say to me.'

Arren did not see it; and moreover was sorely troubled. For
Sparrowhawk, in repeating the dragon's words, had named himself
by his own true name, unmistakably. This brought unwelcome into
Arren's mind the memory of that tormented woman of Lorbanery
crying out, 'My name is Akaren!' If the powers of wizardry, and
of music, and speech, and trust, were weakening and withering
among men, if an insanity of fear was coming on them so that,
like the dragons bereft of reason, they turned on each other to
destroy: if all this were so, would his lord escape it? Was he so
strong?

He did not look strong, sitting hunched over his supper of bread
and smoked fish, with hair greyed and fire-singed, and slight hands,
and a tired face.

Yet the dragon feared him.

'What irks you, lad?'

Only the truth would do, with him.

'My lord, you spoke your name.'

'Oh, aye. I forgot I had not done so earlier. You will need my true
name, if we go where we must go.' He looked up, chewing, at Arren.
'Did you think I grew senile, and went about babbling my name,
like old bleared men past sense and shame? Not yet, lad!'

'No,' said Arren, so confused that he could say nothing else. He
was very weary: the day had been long, and full of dragons. And
the way ahead grew dark.

'Arren,' said the mage – 'No: Lebannen: where we go, there is no hiding. There all bear their own true names.'

'The dead cannot be hurt,' said Arren sombrely.

'But it is not only there, not in death only, that men take their names. Those who can be most hurt, the most vulnerable: those who have given love, and do not take it back: they speak each other's names. The faithful-hearted, the givers of life ... You are worn out, lad. Lie down and sleep. There's nothing to do now but keep the course all night. And by morning we shall see the last island of the world.'

In his voice was an insuperable gentleness. Arren curled up in the prow, and sleep began to come into him at once. He heard the mage begin a soft, almost whispering chant, not in the Hardic tongue but in the words of the Making; and as he began to understand at last, and to remember what the words meant, just before he understood them, he fell fast asleep.

Silently the mage stowed away their bread and meat, looked to the lines, made all trim in the boat, and then, taking the guideline of the sail in hand and sitting down on the after thwart, he set the magewind strong in the sail. Tireless, *Lookfar* sped north, an arrow over the sea.

He looked down at Arren. The boy's sleeping face was lit redgold by the long sunset, the rough hair was wind-stirred. The soft, easy, princely look of the boy who had sat by the fountain of the Great House a few months since was gone; this was a thinner face, and harder, and much stronger. But it was not less beautiful.

'I have found none to follow in my way,' Ged the Archmage said aloud to the sleeping boy or to the empty wind. 'None but thee. And thou must go thy way, not mine. Yet will thy kingship be, in part, my own. For I knew thee first. I knew thee first! They will praise me more for that in afterdays than for anything I did of magery ... If there will be afterdays. For first we two must stand upon the balance-point, the very fulcrum of the world. And if I fall, you fall, and all the rest ... For a while, for a while. No darkness lasts forever. And even there, there are stars ... Oh, but I should like to see thee crowned in Havnor, and the sunlight on the

Tower of the Sword, and on the Ring we brought for thee from Atuan, from the dark tombs, Tenar and I, before ever thou wast born!'

He laughed then, and turning to face the north, he said to himself, in the common tongue, 'A goatherd to set the heir of Morred on his throne! Will I never learn?'

Presently, as he sat with the guide-rope in his hand and watched the full sail strain reddened in the last light of the west, he spoke again softly. 'Not in Havnor would I be, and not in Roke. It is time to be done with power. To drop the old toys, and go on. It is time that I went home. I would see Tenar. I would see Ogion, and speak with him before he dies, in the house on the cliffs of Re Albi. I crave to walk on the mountain, the mountain of Gont, in the forests, in the autumn when the leaves are bright. There is no kingdom like the forests. It is time I went there, went in silence, went alone. And maybe there I would learn at last what no act, or power can teach me, what I have never learned.'

The whole west blazed up in a fury and glory of red, so that the sea was crimson and the sail above it bright as blood; and then the night came quietly on. All that night long the boy slept and the man waked, gazing forward steadily into the dark. There were no stars.

11. Selidor

WAKING in the morning Arren saw before the boat, dim and low along the blue west, the shores of Selidor.

In the Hall in Berila were old maps that had been made in the days of the Kings, when traders and explorers had sailed from the Inner Lands and the Reaches had been better known. A great map of the North and West was laid in mosaic on two walls of the Prince's throne-room, with the isle of Enlad in gold and grey above the throne; and Arren saw it in his mind's eye as he had seen it a thousand times in boyhood. North of Enlad was Osskil, and west of it Ebosskil, and south of that Semel and Paln; and there the Inner Lands ended, and there was nothing but the pale blue-green mosaic of the empty sea, set here and there with a tiny dolphin or a whale. Then at last, after the corner where the north wall met the west wall, there was Narveduen, and beyond it three lesser islands. And then the empty sea again, on and on; until the very edge of the wall, and the end of the map, and there was Selidor, and beyond it, nothing.

He could recall it vividly, the curving shape of it, with a great bay in the heart of it, opening narrowly to the east. They had not come so far north as that, but were steering now for a deep cove in the southernmost cape of the island, and there, while the sun was still low in the haze of morning, they came to land.

So ended their great run from the Roads of Balatran to the Western Isle. The stillness of the earth was strange to them, when they had beached *Lookfar*, and walked after so long on solid ground.

Ged climbed a low dune, grass-crowned, the crest of it leaning out over the steep slope, bound into cornices by the tough roots of the grass. When he reached the summit he stood still, looking west and north. Arren stopped at the boat to put on his shoes, which he had not worn for many days, and he took his sword out of the gear-box and buckled it on, this time with no questions in his mind as to whether or not he should do so. Then he climbed up beside Ged to look at the land.

The dunes ran inland, low and grassy, for half a mile or so, and then there were lagoons, thick with sedge and saltreeds, and beyond those, low hills lay yellow-brown and empty out of sight. Beautiful and desolate was Selidor. Nowhere on it was there any mark of man, his work or habitation. There were no beasts to be seen, and the reed-filled lakes bore no flocks of gulls or wild geese or any bird.

They descended the inland side of the dune, and the slope of sand cut off the noise of the breakers and the sound of the wind, so that it became still.

Between the outmost dune and the next was a dell of clean sand, sheltered, the morning sun shining warm on its western slope. 'Lebannen,' the mage said, for he used Arren's true name now, 'I could not sleep last night, and now I must. Stay with me and keep watch.' He lay down in the sunlight, for the shade was cold; put his arm over his eyes: sighed, and slept. Arren sat down beside him. He could see nothing but the white slopes of the dell, and the dune-grass bowing at the top against the misty blue of the sky, and the yellow sun. There was no sound except the muted murmur of the surf, and sometimes the wind gusting moved the particles of sand with a faint whispering.

Arren saw what might have been an eagle flying very high, but it was not an eagle. It circled and stooped, and down it came with that thunder and shrill whistle of outspread golden wings. It alighted on huge talons on the summit of the dune. Against the sun the great head was black, with fiery glints.

The dragon crawled a little way down the slope, and spoke. 'Agni Lebannen,' it said.

Standing between it and Ged, Arren answered: 'Orm Embar.' And he held his bare sword in his hand.

It did not feel heavy, now. The smooth, worn hilt was comfortable in his hand; it fitted. The blade had come lightly, eagerly, from the sheath. The power of it, the age of it, were on his side, for he knew now what use to make of it. It was his sword.

443

The dragon spoke again, but Arren could not understand. He glanced back at his sleeping companion, whom all the rush and thunder had not awakened, and said to the dragon, 'My lord is weary; he sleeps.'

At that Orm Embar crawled and coiled on down to the bottom of the dell. He was heavy on the ground, not lithe and free as when he flew, but there was a sinister grace in the slow placing of his great taloned feet and the curving of his thorny tail. Once there he drew his legs beneath him, lifted up his huge head, and was still : like a dragon carved on a warrior's helm. Arren was aware of his yellow eye, not ten feet away, and of the faint reek of burning that hung about him. This was no carrion stink; dry and metallic, it accorded with the faint odours of the sea and the salt sand, a cleanly, wild smell.

The sun rising higher struck the flanks of Orm Embar, and he burned like a dragon made of iron and gold.

Still Ged slept, relaxed, taking no more notice of the dragon than a sleeping farmer of his hound.

So an hour passed, and Arren, starting, found the mage had sat up beside him.

'Have you got so used to dragons that you fall asleep between their paws?' said Ged, and laughed, and yawned. Then rising he spoke to Orm Embar in the dragon's speech.

Before Orm Embar answered, he too yawned – perhaps in sleepiness, perhaps in rivalry – and that was a sight that few have lived to remember : the rows of yellow-white teeth as long and sharp as swords, the forked, red, fiery tongue twice the length of a man's body, the fuming cavern of the throat.

Orm Embar spoke, and Ged was about to answer, when both turned to look at Arren. They had heard, clear in the silence, the hollow whisper of steel on sheath. Arren was looking up at the lip of the dune behind the mage's head, and his sword was ready in his hand.

There stood, bright lit by sunlight, the faint wind stirring his garments slightly, a man. He stood still as a carven figure except for that flutter of the hem and hood of his light cloak. His hair was long and black, falling in a mass of glossy curls; he was broad-shouldered and tall, a strong, comely man. His eyes seemed to look out over them, at the sea. He smiled.

'Orm Embar I know,' he said. 'And you also I know, though you have grown old since I last saw you, Sparrowhawk. You are Archmage now, they tell me. You have grown great, as well as old. And you have a young servant with you : a prentice mage, no doubt, one of those who learn wisdom on the Isle of the Wise. What do you two here, so far from Roke and the invulnerable walls that protect the Masters from all harm?'

'There is a breach in greater walls than those,' said Ged, clasping both hands on his staff and looking up at the man. 'But will you not come to us in the flesh, so that we may greet one whom we have long sought?'

'In the flesh?' said the man, and smiled again. 'Is mere flesh, body, butcher's meat, of such account between two mages? No, let us meet mind to mind, Archmage.'

'That, I think, we cannot do. – Lad, put up your sword. It is but a sending, an appearance, no true man. As well draw blade against the wind. – In Havnor, when your hair was white, you were called Cob. But that was only a use-name. How shall we call you when we meet you?'

'You will call me Lord,' said the tall figure on the dune's edge.

'Aye, and what else?'

'King and Master.'

At that Orm Embar hissed, a loud and hideous sound, and his great eyes gleamed; yet he turned his head away from the man, and sank crouching in his tracks, as if he could not move.

'And where shall we come to you, and when?'

'In my domain, and at my pleasure.'

'Very well,' said Ged, and lifting up his staff moved it a little towards the tall man – and the man was gone, like a candle-flame blown out.

Arren stared, and the dragon rose up mightily on his four crooked legs, his mail clanking and the lips writhing back from his teeth. But the mage leaned on his staff again.

'It was only a sending. A presentment or image of the man. It can speak and hear, but there's no power in it, save what our fear may lend it. Nor is it even true in seeming, unless the sender so wishes. We have not seen what he now looks like, I guess.'

'Is he near, do you think?'

'Sendings do not cross water. He is on Selidor. But Selidor is a great island: broader than Roke or Gont, and near as long as Enlad. We may seek him long.'

Then the dragon spoke. Ged listened, and turned to Arren. 'Thus says the Lord of Selidor: "I have come back to my own land, nor will I leave it. I will find the Unmaker and bring you to him, that together we may abolish him." And have I not said that what a dragon hunts, he finds?'

Thereupon Ged went down on one knee before the great creature, as a liegeman kneels before a king, and thanked him in his own tongue. The breath of the dragon, so close, was hot on his bowed head.

Orm Embar dragged his scaly weight up the dune once more, and beat his wings, and took the air.

Ged brushed the sand from his clothes, and said to Arren, 'Now you have seen me kneel. And maybe you'll see me kneel once more, before the end.'

Arren did not ask what he meant; in their long companionship he had learned that there was reason in the mage's reserve. Yet it seemed to him that there was evil omen in the words.

They crossed over the dune to the beach once more to make sure the boat lay high above the reach of tide or storm, and to take from her cloaks for the night and what food they had left. Ged paused a minute by the slender prow which had borne him over strange seas so long, so far; he laid his hand on it, but he set no spell and said no word. Then they struck inland, northward, once again, towards the hills.

They walked all day, and at evening camped by a stream that wound down towards the reed-choked lakes and marshes. Though it was full summer the wind blew chill, coming from the west, from the endless landless reaches of the open sea. A mist veiled the sky, and no stars shone above the hills on which no hearth-fire or window-light had ever gleamed.

In the darkness Arren woke. Their small fire was dead, but a westering moon lit the land with a grey misty light. In the stream-valley and on the hillside about it stood a great multitude of people, all still, all silent, their faces turned towards Ged and Arren. Their eyes caught no light of the moon.

Arren dared not speak, but he put his hand on Ged's arm. The mage stirred, and sat up saying, 'What's the matter?' He followed Arren's gaze, and saw the silent people.

They were all clothed darkly, men and women alike. Their faces could not be clearly seen in the faint light, but it seemed to Arren that among those who stood nearest them in the valley, across the little stream, there were some whom he knew, though he could not say their names.

Ged stood up, the cloak falling from him. His face and hair and shirt shone silvery pale, as if the moonlight gathered itself to him. He held out his arm in a wide gesture and said aloud, 'O you who have lived, go free! I break the bond that holds you: *Anvassa mane harw pennodathe!*'

For a moment they stood still, the multitude of silent people. They turned away slowly, and seemed to walk into the grey darkness, and were gone.

Ged sat down. He drew a deep breath. He looked at Arren, and put his hand on the boy's shoulder, and his touch was warm and firm. 'There's nothing to fear, Lebannen,' he said, gently, mockingly. 'They were only the dead.'

Arren nodded, though his teeth were chattering and he felt cold to his very bones. 'How did,' he began, but his jaw and lips would not obey him yet.

Ged understood him. 'They came at his summoning. This is what he promises: eternal life. At his word they may return. At his bidding they must walk upon the hills of life, though they cannot stir a blade of grass.'

'Is he – is he then dead, too?'

Ged shook his head, brooding. 'The dead cannot summon the

447

dead back into the world. No, he has the powers of a living man; and more ... But if any thought to follow him, he tricked them. He keeps his power for himself. He plays King of the Dead; and not only of the dead ... But they were only shadows.'

'I don't know why I fear them,' Arren said with shame.

'You fear them because you fear death, and rightly : for death is terrible, and must be feared,' the mage said. He laid new wood on the fire, and blew on the small coals under the ashes. A little flare of brightness bloomed on the twigs of brushwood, a grateful light to Arren. 'And life also is a terrible thing,' Ged said, 'and must be feared, and praised.'

They both sat back, wrapping their cloaks close about them. They were silent a while. Then Ged spoke very gravely. 'Lebannen, how long he may tease us here with sendings and with shadows, I do not know. But you know where he will go at last.'

'Into the dark land.'

'Aye. Among them.'

'I have seen them now. I will go with you.'

'Is it faith in me that moves you? You may trust my love, but do not trust my strength. For I think I have met my match.'

'I will go with you.'

'But if I am defeated, if my power or my life is spent, I cannot guide you back; you cannot return alone.'

'I will return with you.'

At that Ged said, 'You enter your manhood at the gate of death.' And then he said that word or name by which the dragon had twice called Arren, speaking it very low : 'Agni – Agni Lebannen.'

After that they spoke no more, and presently sleep came back into them, and they lay down by their small and briefly-burning fire.

The next morning they walked on, going north and west; this was Arren's decision, not Ged's, who said, 'Choose us our way, lad; the ways are all alike to me.' They made no haste, for they had no goal, waiting for some sign from Orm Embar. They followed the lowest, outermost range of hills, mostly within sight of the ocean. The grass was dry and short, blowing and blowing for ever in the wind. The hills rose up golden and forlorn upon their right, and on their left lay the salt marshes and the western sea. Once they saw swans flying, far away in the south. No other breathing creature did they see all that day. A kind of weariness of dread, of waiting for the worst, grew in Arren all day long. Impatience and a dull anger rose in him. He said after hours of silence, 'This land is as dead as the land of death itself!'

'Do not say that,' the mage said sharply. He strode on a while and then went on, in a changed voice, 'Look at this land; look about you. This is your kingdom, the kingdom of life. This is your immortality. Look at the hills, the mortal hills. They do not endure forever. The hills with the living grass on them, and the streams of water running ... In all the world, in all the worlds, in all the immensity of time, there is no other like each of those streams, rising cold out of the earth where no eye sees it, running through the sunlight and the darkness to the sea. Deep are the springs of being, deeper than life, than death ...'

He stopped, but in his eyes as he looked at Arren and at the sunlit hills there was a great, wordless, grieving love. And Arren saw that, and seeing it saw him, saw him for the first time whole, as he was.

'I cannot say what I mean,' Ged said unhappily.

But Arren thought of that first hour in the Fountain Court, of the man who had knelt by the running water of the fountain; and joy, as clear as that remembered water, welled up in him. He looked at his companion and said, 'I have given my love to what is worthy of love. Is that not the kingdom, and the unperishing spring?'

'Aye, lad,' said Ged, gently, and with pain.

They went on together in silence. But Arren saw the world now with his companion's eyes, and saw the living splendour that was revealed about them in the silent, desolate land, as if by a power of enchantment surpassing any other, in every blade of the windbowed grass, every shadow, every stone. So when one stands in a cherished place for the last time before a voyage without return, he sees it all whole, and real, and dear, as he has never seen it before and never will see it again.

As evening came on serried lines of clouds rose from the west, borne on great winds from the sea, and burned fiery before the sun, reddening it as it sank. As he gathered brushwood for their fire in a creek-valley, in that red light, Arren glanced up and saw a man standing not ten feet from him. The man's face looked vague and strange, but Arren knew him, the Dyer of Lorbanery, Sopli, who was dead.

Behind him stood others, all with sad, staring faces. They seemed to speak, but Arren could not hear their words, only a kind of whispering blown away by the west wind. Some of them came towards him slowly.

He stood and looked at them, and again at Sopli; and then he turned his back on them, and stooped, and picked up one more stick of brushwood, though his hands shook. He added it to his load, and picked up another, and one more. Then he straightened, and looked back. There was no one in the valley, only the red light burning on the grass. He returned to Ged, and set down his load of firewood, but he said nothing of what he had seen.

All that night, in the misty darkness of that land empty of living souls, when he woke from fitful sleep he heard about him the whispering of the souls of the dead. He steadied his will, and did not listen, and slept again.

Both he and Ged woke late, when the sun, already a hand's breadth above the hills, broke free at last from fog and brightened the cold land. As they ate their small morning meal the dragon came, wheeling above them in the air. Fire shot from his jaws, and smoke and sparks from his red nostrils; his teeth gleamed like blades of ivory in that lurid glare. But he said nothing, though Ged hailed him, crying in his language, 'Hast found him, Orm Embar?'

The dragon threw back his head and arched his body strangely, raking the wind with his razor talons. Then he set off flying fast to the west, looking back at them as he went.

Ged gripped his staff, and struck it on the ground. 'He cannot speak,' he said. 'He cannot speak! The words of the Making are taken from him, and he is left like an adder, like a tongueless worm, his wisdom dumb. Yet he can lead, and we can follow!' Swinging up their light packs on their backs they strode westward across the hills as Orm Embar had flown.

Eight miles or more they went, not slackening that first swift steady pace. Now the sea lay on either hand, and they walked on a long, falling ridge-back that ran down at last through dry reeds and winding creek-beds to an outcurving beach of sand, coloured like ivory. This was the westernmost cape of all the lands, the end of earth.

Orm Embar crouched on that ivory sand, his head low like an angry cat's and his breath coming in gasps of fire. Some way before him, between him and the long, low breakers of the sea, stood a thing like a hut or shelter, white, as if built of long-bleached drift-wood. But there was no driftwood on this shore which faced no other land. As they came closer Arren saw that the ramshackle walls were built up of great bones: whales' bones, he thought at first, and then saw the white triangles edged like knives, and knew they were the bones of a dragon.

They came to the place. Sunlight on the sea glittered through crevices between the bones. The lintel of the doorway was a thigh-bone longer than a man. On it stood a human skull, staring with hollow eyes at the hills of Selidor.

They stopped there, and as they looked up at the skull a man came out of the doorway under it. He wore an armour of gilt bronze, in an ancient fashion; it was rent as if by hatchet blows, and the jewelled scabbard of his sword was empty. His face was stern, with arched black brows and narrow nose; his eyes were dark, keen, and sorrowful. There were wounds on his arms, and in his throat and side; they bled no longer, but they were mortal wounds. He stood erect and still, and looked at them.

Ged took one step towards him. They were somewhat alike, thus face to face.

'Thou art Erreth-Akbe,' Ged said. The other gazed at him steadily, and nodded once, but did not speak.

'Even thou, even thou must do his bidding.' Rage was in Ged's voice. 'O my lord, and best and bravest of us all, rest in thy honour and in death!' And raising his hands Ged brought them down in a

great gesture, saying again those words he had spoken to the multi-
tudes of the dead. His hands left behind on the air a moment a
broad bright track. When it was gone the armoured man was gone,
and only the sun dazzled on the sand where he had stood.

Ged struck at the house of bones with his staff, and it fell and
vanished away. Nothing of it was left but one great rib-bone that
stuck up out of the sand.

He turned to Orm Embar. 'Is it here, Orm Embar? Is this the
place?'

The dragon opened his mouth and made a huge gasping hiss.

'Here on the last shore of the world. That is well!' Then holding
his black yew staff in his left hand, Ged opened his arms in a
gesture of invocation, and spoke. Though he spoke in the language
of the Making, yet Arren understood, at last, as all who hear that
invocation must understand, for it has power over all: 'Now do I
summon you and here, my enemy, before my eyes and in the flesh,
and bind you by the word that will not be spoken till time's end, to
come!'

But where the name of him summoned should have been spoken,
Ged said only: *My enemy*.

A silence followed, as if the sound of the sea had faded. It seemed
to Arren that the sun failed and dimmed, though it stood high in a
clear sky. A darkness came over the beach, as though one looked
through smoked glass; directly before Ged it grew very dark, and
it was hard to see what was there. It was as if nothing was there,
nothing the light could fall on, a formlessness.

Out of it came a man, suddenly. It was the same man they had
seen upon the dune, black-haired and long-armed, lithe and tall. He
held now a long rod or blade of steel, graven all down its length
with runes, and he tilted this towards Ged as he faced him. But
there was something strange in the look of his eyes, as if they were
sun-dazzled and could not see.

'I come,' he said, 'at my own choosing, in my own way. You
cannot summon me, Archmage. I am no shadow. I am alive. I only
am alive! You think you are, but you are dying, dying. Do you
know what this is I hold? It is the staff of the Grey Mage; he who

silenced Nereger; the Master of my art. But I am the Master now. And I have had enough of playing games with you.' With that he suddenly reached out the steel blade to touch Ged, who stood as if he could not move, and could not speak. Arren stood a pace behind him, and all his will was to move, but he could not stir, he could not even put his hand on his sword-hilt, and his voice was stopped in his throat.

But over Ged and Arren, over their heads, vast and fiery, the great body of the dragon came in one writhing leap, and plunged down full force upon the other, so that the charmed steel blade entered into the dragon's mailed breast to its full length : but the man was borne down under his weight and crushed and burned.

Rising up again from the sand, arching his back and beating his vaned wings, Orm Embar vomited out gouts of fire, and screamed. He tried to fly, but he could not fly. Malign and cold, the metal lay in his heart. He crouched, and the blood ran black and poisonous, steaming, from his mouth, and the fire died in his nostrils till they became like pits of ash. He laid down his great head on the sand.

So died Orm Embar where his forefather Orm died, on the bones of Orm buried in the sand.

But where he had struck his enemy to earth, there lay something ugly and shrivelled, like the body of a big spider dried up in its web. It had been burned by the dragon's breath, and crushed by his taloned feet. Yet, as Arren watched, it moved. It crawled away a little from the dragon.

The face lifted up towards them. There was no comeliness left in it, only ruin, old age that had outlived old age. The mouth was withered. The sockets of the eyes were empty, and had long been empty. So Ged and Arren saw at last the living face of their enemy.

It turned away. The burnt, blackened arms reached out, and a darkness gathered into them, that same shapeless darkness that swelled and dimmed the sunlight. Between the arms of the Unmaker it was like an archway or a gate, though dim and without outline; and through it was neither pale sand nor ocean, but a long slope of darkness going down into the dark.

There the crushed, crawling figure went, and when it came into the darkness it seemed suddenly to rise up, and move swiftly, and it was gone.

'Come, Lebannen,' said Ged, laying his right hand on the boy's arm, and they went forward into the dry land.

12. The Dry Land

THE yew-wood staff in the mage's hand shone in the dull, lowering darkness with a silver gleam. Another slight glimmering movement caught Arren's eye: a flicker of light along the blade of the sword he held naked in his hand. As the dragon's act and death broke the binding spell, he had drawn his sword, there on the beach of Selidor. And here, though he was no more than a shadow, he was a living shadow, and bore the shadow of his sword.

There was no other brightness anywhere. It was like a late twilight under clouds at the end of November, a dour, chill, dull air in which one could see, but not clearly and not far. Arren knew the place, the moors and barrens of his hopeless dreams; but it seemed to him that he was farther, immensely farther, than he had ever been in dream. He could make out nothing distinctly, except that he and his companion stood on the slope of a hill, and before them was a low wall of stones, no higher than a man's knee.

Ged still kept his right hand on Arren's arm. He moved forward now, and Arren went with him; they stepped over the wall of stones.

Formless, the long slope fell away before them, descending into the dark.

But overhead, where Arren had thought to see a heavy overcast of cloud, the sky was black, and there were stars. He looked at them, and it seemed as if his heart shrank small and cold within him. They were no stars that he had ever seen. Unmoving they shone, unwinking. They were those stars that do not rise, nor set, nor are they ever hidden by any cloud, nor does any sunrise dim them. Still and small they shine on the dry land.

Ged set off walking down the far side of the hill of being, and pace by pace Arren went with him. There was terror in him, and yet so resolved was his heart and so intent his will that the fear did not

455

rule him, nor was he even very clearly aware of it; only it was as if something deep within him grieved, like an animal shut up in a room and chained.

It seemed that they walked down that hill-slope for a long way, but perhaps it was a short way; for there was no passing of time there, where no wind blew and the stars did not move. They came then into the streets of one of the cities that are there, and Arren saw the houses with windows that are never lit, and in certain doorways standing, with quiet faces and empty hands, the dead.

The market places were all empty. There was no buying and selling there, no gaining and spending. Nothing was used; nothing was made. Ged and Arren went through the narrow streets alone, though a few times they saw a figure at the turning of another way, distant and hardly to be seen in the gloom. At sight of the first of these Arren started and raised his sword to point, but Ged shook his head and went on. Arren saw then that the figure was a woman, who moved slowly, not fleeing from them.

All those whom they saw – not many, for the dead are many, but that land is large – stood still, or moved slowly and with no purpose. None of them bore wounds, as had the semblance of Erreth-Akbe summoned into daylight at the place of his death. No marks of illness were on them. They were whole, and healed. They were healed of pain, and of life. They were not loathsome as Arren had feared they would be, not frightening in the way he had thought they would be. Quiet were their faces, freed from anger and desire, and there was in their shadowed eyes no hope.

Instead of fear, then, great pity rose up in Arren, and if fear underlay it, it was not for himself, but for us all. For he saw the mother and child who had died together, and they were in the dark land together; but the child did not run, nor did it cry, and the mother did not hold it, nor even look at it. And those who had died for love passed each other in the streets.

The potter's wheel was still, the loom empty, the stove cold. No voice ever sang.

The dark streets between dark houses led on and on, and they passed through them. The sound of their feet was the only sound.

It was cold. Arren had not noticed that cold at first, but it crept into his spirit, which was, here, also his flesh. He felt very weary. They must have come a long way. Why go on? he thought, and his steps lagged a little.

Ged stopped suddenly, turning to face a man who stood at the crossing of two streets. He was slender and tall, with a face that Arren thought he had seen, but could not remember where. Ged spoke to him, and no other voice had broken the silence since they stepped across the wall of stones: 'O Thorion, my friend, how come you here!'

And he put out his hands to the Summoner of Roke.

Thorion made no answering gesture. He stood still, and his face was still; but the silvery light on Ged's staff struck deep in his enshadowed eyes, making a little light there, or meeting it. Ged took the hand he did not offer, and said again, 'What do you here, Thorion? You are not of this kingdom yet. Go back!'

'I followed the undying one. I lost my way.' The Summoner's voice was soft and dull, like that of a man who speaks in sleep.

'Upward: towards the wall,' said Ged, pointing the way he and Arren had come, the long, dark, descending street. At that there was a tremor in Thorion's face, as if some hope had entered into him like a sword, intolerable.

'I cannot find the way,' he said. 'My lord, I cannot find the way.'

'Maybe thou shalt,' Ged said, and embraced him, and then went forward. Thorion stood still at the crossroads, behind him.

As they went on it seemed to Arren that in this timeless dusk there was, in truth, neither forward nor back, no east nor west, no way to go. Was there a way out? He thought how they had come down the hill, always descending, no matter how they turned; and still in the dark city the streets went downward, so that to return to the wall of stones they need only climb, and at the hill's top they would find it. But they did not turn. Side by side, they went on. Did he follow Ged? Or did he lead him?

They came out of the city. The country of the innumerable dead was empty. No tree or thorn or blade of grass grew in the stony earth under the unsetting stars.

There was no horizon, for the eye could not see so far into the gloom; but ahead of them the small, still stars were absent from the sky over a long space above the ground, and this starless space was jagged and sloped like a chain of mountains. As they went on the shapes were more distinct: high peaks, weathered by no wind or rain. There was no snow on them to gleam in starlight. They were black. The sight of them struck desolation into Arren's heart. He looked away from them. But he knew them; he recognized them; his eyes were drawn back to them. Each time he looked at those peaks he felt a cold weight in his breast, and his nerve came near to failing. Still he walked on, always downward, for the land fell away, descending towards the mountains' feet. At last he said, 'My lord, what are ...' He pointed at the mountains, for he could not go on speaking; his throat was dry.

'They border on the world of light,' Ged answered, 'even as does the wall of stones. They have no name but Pain. There is a road across them. It is forbidden to the dead. It is not long. But it is a bitter road.'

'I am thirsty,' Arren said, and his companion answered, 'Here they drink dust.'

They went on.

It seemed to Arren that his companion's gait had slowed somewhat, and sometimes he hesitated. He himself felt no more hesitation, though the weariness had not ceased to grow in him. They must go down, they must go on. They went on.

Sometimes they passed through other towns of the dead, where the dark roofs made angles against the stars, which stood forever in the same place above them. After the towns was the empty land again, where nothing grew. As soon as they had come out of a town, it was lost in the darkness. Nothing could be seen, before or behind, except the mountains that grew ever nearer, towering before them. To their right the formless slope fell away as it had done, how long ago? when they crossed the wall of stones. 'What lies that way?' Arren murmured to Ged, for he craved the sound of speech, but the mage shook his head: 'I do not know. It may be a way without an end.'

458

In the direction they went the slope seemed to be growing less, and always less. The ground under their feet gritted harshly, like lava-dust. Still they went on, and now Arren never thought of returning, or of how they might return. Nor did he think of stopping, though he was very weary. Once he tried to lighten the numb darkness and weariness and horror within him by thinking of his home; but he could not remember what sunlight looked like, nor his mother's face. There was nothing to do but go on. And he went on.

He felt the ground level under his feet; and beside him Ged hesitated. Then he too stopped. The long descent was over : this was the end; there was no way further, no need to go on.

They were in the valley directly under the Mountains of Pain. There were rocks underfoot, and boulders about them, rough to the touch like scoria, as if this narrow valley might be the dry bed of a river of water that had once run here, or the course of a river of fire long since cold, from the volcanoes that reared their black, unmerciful peaks above.

He stood still, there in the narrow valley in the dark, and Ged stood still beside him. They stood like the aimless dead, gazing at nothing, silent. Arren thought, with a little dread but not much, 'We have come too far.'

It did not seem to matter much.

Speaking his thoughts, Ged said, 'We have come too far to turn back.' His voice was soft, but the ring of it was not wholly muted by the great gloomy hollowness around them, and at the sound of it Arren roused a little. Had they not come here to meet the one they sought?

A voice in the darkness said, 'You have come too far.'

Arren answered it, saying, 'Only too far is far enough.'

'You have come to the Dry River,' said the voice. 'You cannot go back to the wall of stones. You cannot go back to life.'

'Not that way,' said Ged, speaking into the darkness. Arren could hardly see him, though they stood side by side, for the mountains under which they stood cut out half the starlight, and it seemed as if the current of the Dry River was darkness itself. 'But we would learn your way.'

There was no answer.

'We meet as equals here. If you are blind, Cob, yet we are in the dark.'

There was no answer.

'We cannot hurt you here; we cannot kill you. What is there to fear?'

'I have no fear,' said the voice in the darkness. Then slowly, glimmering a little as with that light that sometimes clung to Ged's staff, the man appeared standing some way upstream from Ged and Arren, among the great dim masses of the boulders. He was tall, broad-shouldered and long-armed, like that figure which had appeared to them on the dune and on the beach of Selidor, but older; the hair was white, and thickly matted over the high forehead. So he appeared in the spirit, in the kingdom of death, not burnt by the dragon's fire, not maimed; but not whole. The sockets of his eyes were empty.

'I have no fear,' he said. 'What should a dead man fear?' He laughed. The sound of laughter rang so false and uncanny, there in that narrow stony valley under the mountains, that Arren's breath failed him for a moment. But he gripped his sword, and listened.

'I do not know what a dead man should fear,' Ged answered. 'Surely not death? Yet it seems you fear it. For you have found a way to escape from it.'

'I have. I live: my body lives.'

'Not well,' the mage said dryly. 'Illusion might hide age; but Orm Embar was not gentle with that body.'

'I can mend it. I know secrets of healing and of youth, no mere illusions. What do you take me for? Because you are called Archmage, do you take me for a village sorcerer? I who alone among all mages found the Way of Immortality, which no other ever found!'

'Maybe we did not seek it,' said Ged.

'You sought it. All of you. You sought it and could not find it, and so made wise words about acceptance and balance and the equilibrium of life and death. But they were words – lies to cover your failure – to cover your fear of death! What man would not live forever, if he could? And I can. I am immortal. I did what you could not do, and therefore I am your master: and you know it. Would you know how I did it, Archmage?'

'I would.'

Cob came a step closer. Arren noticed that, though the man had no eyes, his manner was not quite that of the stone-blind; he seemed to know exactly where Ged and Arren stood, and to be aware of both of them, though he never turned his head to Arren. Some wizardly second-sight he might have, such as that hearing and seeing which sendings and presentments had: something which gave him an awareness, though it might not be true sight.

'I was in Paln,' he said to Ged, 'after you, in your pride, thought you had humbled me and taught me a lesson. Oh, a lesson you taught me, indeed, but not the one you meant to teach! There I said to myself: I have seen death now, and I will not accept it. Let all stupid nature go its stupid course, but I am a man, better than nature, above nature. I will not go that way, I will not cease to be myself! And so determined, I took the Pelnish Lore again, but found only hints and smatterings of what I needed. So I rewove it and remade it, and made a spell – the greatest spell that has ever been made. The greatest and the last!'

'In working that spell, you died.'

'Yes! I died. I had the courage to die, to find out what you cowards could never find – the way back from death. I opened the door that had been shut since the beginning of time. And now I come freely to this place, and freely return to the world of the living. Alone of all men in all time I am Lord of the Two Lands. And the door I opened is open not only here, but in the minds of the living, in the depths and unknown places of their being, where we are all one in the darkness. They know it, and they come to me. And the dead too must come to me, all of them, for I have not lost the magery of the living: they must climb over the wall of stones when I bid them, all the souls, the lords, the mages, the proud women; back and forth from life to death, at my command. All must come to me, the living and the dead, I who died and live!'

'Where do they come to you, Cob? Where is that you are?'

'Between the worlds.'

'But that is neither life nor death. What is life, Cob?'

'Power.'

'What is love?'

'Power,' the blind man repeated heavily, hunching up his shoulders.

'What is light?'

'Darkness!'

'What is your name?'

'I have none.'

'All in this land bear their true name.'

'Tell me yours, then!'

'I am named Ged. And you?'

The blind man hesitated, and said, 'Cob.'

'That was your use-name, not your name. Where is your name? Where is the truth of you? Did you leave it in Paln where you died? You have forgotten much, O Lord of the Two Lands. You have forgotten light, and love, and your own name.'

'I have your name now, and power over you, Ged the Archmage – Ged who was Archmage when he was alive!'

'My name is no use to you,' Ged said. 'You have no power over me at all. I am a living man; my body lies on the beach of Selidor, under the sun, on the turning earth. And when that body dies, I will be here: but only in name, in name alone, in shadow. Do you not understand? Did you never understand, you who called up so many shadows from the dead, who summoned all the hosts of the perished, even my lord Erreth-Akbe, wisest of us all? Did you not understand that he, even he, is but a shadow and a name? His death did not diminish life. Nor did it diminish him. He is there – *there*, not here! Here is nothing, dust and shadows. There, he is the earth and sunlight, the leaves of trees, the eagle's flight. He is alive. And all who ever died, live; they are reborn, and have no end, nor will there be an end. All, save you. For you would not have death. You lost death, you lost life, in order to save yourself. Yourself! Your immortal self! What is it? Who are you?'

'I am myself. My body will not decay and die –'

'A living body suffers pain, Cob; a living body grows old; it dies. Death is the price we pay for our life, and for all life.'

'I do not pay it! I can die and in that moment live again! I cannot be killed, I am immortal, I alone am myself for ever!'

'Who are you, then?'

'The Immortal One.'

'Say your name.'

'The King.'

'Say my name. I told it to you but a minute since. Say my name!'

'You are not real. You have no name. Only I exist.'

'You exist, without name, without form. You cannot see the light of day; you cannot see the dark. You sold the green earth and the sun and stars to save yourself. But you have no self. All that which you sold, that is yourself. You have given everything for nothing. And so now you seek to draw the world to you, all that light and life you lost, to fill up your nothingness. But it cannot be filled. Not all the songs of earth, not all the stars of heaven, could fill your emptiness.'

Ged's voice rang like iron, there in the cold valley under the mountains, and the blind man cringed away from him. He lifted up his face, and the dim starlight shone on it; he looked as if he wept, but he had no tears, having no eyes. His mouth opened and shut, full of darkness, but no words came out of it, only a groaning. At last he said one word, barely shaping it with his contorted lips, and the word was 'Life'.

'I would give you life if I could, Cob. But I cannot. You are dead. But I can give you death.'

'No!' the blind man screamed aloud, and then he said, 'No, no,' and crouched down sobbing, though his cheeks were as dry as the stony river-course where only night, and no water, ran. 'You cannot. No one can ever set me free. I opened the door between the worlds and I cannot shut it. No one can shut it. It will never be shut again. It draws, it draws me. I must come back to it. I must go through it, and come back here, into the dust and cold and silence. It sucks at me and sucks at me. I cannot leave it. I cannot close it.

It will suck all the light out of the world in the end. All the rivers will be like the Dry River. There is no power anywhere that can close the door I opened!'

Very strange was the mixture of despair and vindictiveness, terror and vanity, in his words and voice.

Ged said only, 'Where is it?'

'That way. Not far. You can go there. But you cannot do anything there. You cannot shut it. If you spent all your power in that one act, it would not be enough. Nothing is enough.'

'Maybe,' Ged answered. 'Though you chose despair, remember we have not yet done so. Take us there.'

The blind man raised his face, in which fear and hatred struggled visibly. Hatred triumphed. 'I will not,' he said.

At that Arren stepped forward, and he said, 'You will.'

The blind man held still. The cold silence and the darkness of the realm of the dead surrounded them, surrounded their words.

'Who are you?'

'My name is Lebannen.'

Ged spoke: 'You who call yourself King, do you not know who this is?'

Again Cob held utterly still. Then he said, gasping a little as he spoke, 'But he is dead – You are dead. You cannot go back. There is no way out. You are caught here!' As he spoke the glimmer of light died away from him, and they heard him turn in the darkness and go away from them into it, hastily. 'Give me light, my lord!' Arren cried, and Ged held up his staff above his head, letting the white light break open that old darkness, full of rocks and shadows, among which the tall, stooped figure of the blind man hurried and dodged, going upstream from them with a strange, unseeing, unhesitating gait. After him Arren came, sword in hand; and after him, Ged.

Soon Arren had outdistanced his companion, and the light was very faint, much interrupted by the boulders and the turnings of the riverbed; but the sound of Cob's going, the sense of his presence ahead, was guide enough. He drew closer, slowly, as the way became steeper. They were climbing in a steep gorge choked with stones;

the Dry River, narrowing to its head, wound between sheer banks. Rocks clattered under their feet, and under their hands, for they must clamber. Arren sensed the final narrowing in of the banks, and with a lunge forward came up to Cob and caught his arm, halting him there: a kind of basin of rocks five or six feet wide, what might have been a pool if ever water ran there; and above it a tumbled cliff of rock and slag. In that cliff there was a black hole, the source of the Dry River.

Cob did not try to pull away from him. He stood quite still, while the light of Ged's approach brightened on his eyeless face. He had turned that face to Arren. 'This is the place,' he said at last, a kind of smile forming on his lips. 'This is the place you seek. See it? There you can be reborn. All you need to do is follow me. You will live immortally. We shall be kings together.'

Arren looked at that dry, dark springhead, the mouth of dust, the place where a dead soul, crawling into earth and darkness, was born again dead: abominable it was to him, and he said in a harsh voice, struggling with deadly sickness, 'Let it be shut!'

'It will be shut,' Ged said, coming beside them: and the light blazed up now from his hands and face as if he were a star fallen on earth in that endless night. Before him the dry spring, the door yawned open. It was wide, and hollow, but whether deep or shallow there was no telling. There was nothing in it for the light to fall on, for the eye to see. It was void. Through it was neither light nor dark, neither life nor death. It was nothing. It was a way that led nowhere.

Ged raised up his hands and spoke.

Arren still held Cob's arm; the blind man had laid his free hand against the rocks of the cliff-wall. Both stood still, caught in the power of the spell.

With all the skill of his life's training, and with all the strength of his fierce heart, Ged strove to shut that door, to make the world whole once more. And under his voice and the command of his shaping hands the rocks drew together, painfully, trying to be whole, to meet; they drew together. But at the same time the light weakened and weakened, dying out from his hands and from his face, dying out from his yew staff, until only a glimmer of it clung there. By that faint light Arren saw that the door was nearly closed.

Under his hand the blind man felt the rocks move, felt them come together: and felt also the art and power giving itself up, spending itself, spent – And all at once he shouted, 'No!' and broke from Arren's grasp, lunged forward and caught Ged in his blind powerful grasp. Bearing Ged down under his weight he closed his hands on his throat to strangle him.

Arren raised up the sword of Serriadh, and brought the blade down straight and hard on the bowed neck beneath the matted hair.

The living spirit has weight in the world of the dead, and the shadow of his sword has an edge. The blade made a great wound, severing Cob's spine. Black blood leapt out lit by the sword's own light.

But there is no good in killing a dead man; and Cob was dead, years dead. The wound closed, swallowing its blood. The blind man stood up very tall, groping out with his long arms at Arren, his face writhing with rage and hatred: as if he had just now perceived who his true enemy and rival was.

So horrible to see was this recovery from a deathblow, this inability to die, more horrible than any dying, that a rage of loathing swelled up in Arren, a berserk fury, and swinging up the sword he struck again with it, a full terrible downward blow. Cob fell with skull split open and face masked with blood, yet Arren was upon him at once, to strike again, before the wound could close, to strike until he killed . . .

Beside him Ged, struggling to his knees, spoke one word.

At the sound of his voice Arren was stopped, as if a hand had grasped his sword-arm. The blind man, who had begun to rise, also held utterly still. Ged got to his feet; he swayed a little. When he could hold himself erect he faced the cliff.

'Be thou made whole!' he said in a clear voice, and with his staff he drew in lines of fire across the gate of rocks a figure: the rune Agnen, the rune of Ending, which closes roads and is drawn on coffin lids. And there was then no gap or void place among the boulders. The door was shut.

The earth of the Dry Land trembled under their feet, and across the unchanging, barren sky a long roll of thunder ran, and died away.

'By the word that will not be spoken until time's end I summoned thee. By the word that was spoken at the making of things I now release thee. Go free !' And bending over the blind man, who was crouched on his knees, Ged whispered in his ear, under the white tangled hair.

Cob stood up. He looked about him slowly, with seeing eyes. He looked at Arren, and then at Ged. He spoke no word, but gazed at them with dark eyes. There was no anger in his face, no hate, no grief. Slowly he turned, and went off down the course of the Dry River, and soon was gone from sight.

There was no more light on Ged's yew-staff, nor in his face. He stood there in the darkness. When Arren came to him he caught at the young man's arm to hold himself upright. For a moment a spasm of dry sobbing shook him. 'It is done,' he said, 'it is all gone.'

'It is done, dear lord. We must go.'

'Aye. We must go home.'

Ged was like one bewildered or exhausted. He followed Arren back down the rivercourse, stumbling along with difficulty and slowly among the rocks and boulders. Arren stayed with him. When the banks of the Dry River were low and the ground was less steep, he turned towards the way they had come, the long, formless slope that led up into the dark. Then he turned away.

Ged said nothing. As soon as they halted he had sunk down sitting on a lava-boulder, forspent, his head hanging.

Arren knew that the way they had come was closed to them. They could only go on. They must go all the way. Even too far is not far enough, he thought. He looked up at the black peaks, cold and silent against the unmoving stars, terrible; and once more that ironic, mocking voice of his will spoke to him, unrelenting: 'Will you stop halfway, Lebannen?'

467

He went to Ged and said very gently, 'We must go on, my lord.'

Ged said nothing, but he stood up.

'We must go by the mountains, I think.'

'Thy way, lad,' Ged said in a hoarse whisper. 'Help me.'

So they set out up the slopes of dust and scoria into the mountains, Arren helping his companion along as well as he could. It was black dark in the combes and gorges, so that he had to feel the way ahead, and it was hard for him to give Ged support at the same time. Walking was hard, a stumbling matter; but when they had to climb and clamber as the slopes grew steeper, that was harder still. The rocks were rough, burning the hands like molten iron. Yet it was cold, and got colder as they went higher. There was a torment in the touch of this earth. It seared like live coals: a fire burned within the mountains. But the air was always cold, and always dark. There was no sound. No wind blew. The sharp rocks broke under their hands, gave way under their feet. Black and sheer the spurs and chasms went up in front of them and fell away beside them into blackness. Behind, below, the kingdom of the dead was lost. Ahead, above, the peaks and rocks stood out against the stars. And nothing moved in all the length and breadth of those black mountains, except the two mortal souls.

Ged often stumbled or missed his footing, in weariness. His breath came harder and harder, and when his hands came hard against the rocks he gasped in pain. To hear him cry out thus wrung Arren's heart. He tried to keep him from falling. But often the way was too narrow for them to go abreast, or Arren had to go in front and seek out a footing. And at last, on a high slope that ran up to the stars, Ged slipped and fell forward, and did not get up.

'My lord,' Arren said, kneeling by him, and then spoke his name: 'Ged.'

He did not move or answer.

Arren lifted him in his arms and carried him up that high slope. At the end of it there was level ground for some way ahead. Arren laid his burden down, and dropped down beside him, exhausted and in pain, past hope. This was the summit of the pass between the two black peaks, for which he had been struggling. This was the pass, and the end. There was no way further. The end of the level ground was the edge of a cliff : beyond it the darkness went on forever, and the small stars hung unmoving in the black gulf of the sky.

Endurance may outlast hope. He crawled forward, when he was able to do so, doggedly. He looked over the edge of darkness. And below him, only a little way below, he saw the beach of ivory sand; the white and amber waves were curling and breaking in foam on it, and across the sea the sun setting in a haze of gold.

Arren turned back to the dark. He went back. He lifted Ged up as best he could, and struggled forward with him until he could not go any farther. Here all things ceased to be : thirst, and pain, and the dark, and the sun's light, and the sound of the breaking sea.

13. The Stone of Pain

WHEN Arren woke a grey fog hid the sea and the dunes and hills of Selidor. The breakers came murmuring in a low thunder out of the fog and withdrew murmuring into it again. The tide was in, and the beach much narrower than when they had first come here; the last small foam-lines of the waves came and licked at Ged's outflung left hand as he lay face down on the sand. His clothes and hair were wet, and Arren's clothes clung icy to his body; as if once at least the sea had broken over them. Of Cob's dead body there was no trace. Maybe the waves had drawn it out to sea. But behind Arren, when he turned his head, huge and dim in the mist the grey body of Orm Embar bulked like a ruined tower.

Arren got up, shuddering with chill; he could barely stand, for cold, and stiffness, and a dizzy weakness like that which comes of lying a long time unmoving. He staggered like a drunken man. As soon as he could control his limbs he went to Ged and managed to pull him a little way up the sand above the waves' reach, but that was all he could do. Very cold, very heavy, Ged seemed to him; he had borne him over the boundary from death into life, but maybe in vain. He put his ear to Ged's breast, but could not still the shaking in his own limbs and the chattering of his teeth to listen for the heartbeat. He stood up again, and tried to stamp to bring some warmth back into his legs, and finally, trembling and dragging his legs like an old man, set off to find their packs. They had dropped them beside a little stream running down from the ridge of the hills, a long time ago, when they came down to the house of bones. It was that stream he sought, for he could not think of anything but water, fresh water.

Before he expected it he came to the stream, as it descended onto the beach and wandered mazy and branching like a tree of silver to the sea's edge. There he dropped down and drank, with his face in the water, and his hands in the water, sucking up the water into his mouth and into his spirit.

At last he sat up, and as he did so he saw on the far side of the stream, immense, a dragon.

Its head, the colour of iron, stained as with red rust at nostril and eye socket and jowl, hung facing him, almost over him. The talons sank deep into the soft wet sand on the edge of the stream. The folded wings were partly visible, like sails, but the length of the dark body was lost in the fog.

It did not move. It might have been crouching there for hours, or for years, or for centuries. It was carven of iron, shaped from rock – but the eyes, the eyes he dared not look into, the eyes like oil coiling on water, like yellow smoke behind glass, the opaque, profound, and yellow eyes watched Arren.

There was nothing he could do; so he stood up. If the dragon would kill him, it would; and if it did not, he would try to help Ged, if there was any help for him. He stood up, and started to walk up the rivulet to find their packs.

The dragon did nothing. It crouched unmoving, and watched. Arren found the packs, and filled both the skin bottles at the stream, and went back across the sand to Ged. After he had taken only a few steps away from the stream, the dragon was lost in the thick fog.

He gave Ged water, but could not rouse him. He lay lax and cold, his heavy head on Arren's arm. His dark face was greyish, the nose and cheek-bones and the old scar standing out harshly. Even his body looked thin and burned, as if half consumed.

Arren sat there on the damp sand, his companion's head on his knees. The fog made a vague soft sphere about them, lighter overhead. Somewhere in the fog was the dead dragon Orm Embar, and the live dragon was waiting by the stream. And somewhere across Selidor the boat *Lookfar*, with no provisions in her, lay on another beach. And then the sea, eastward. Three hundred miles to any other land of the West Reach, maybe; a thousand to the Inmost

471

Sea. A long way. 'As far as Selidor,' they used to say on Enlad. The old stories told to children, the myths, began, 'As long ago as forever and as far away as Selidor, there lived a prince . . .'

He was the prince. But in the old stories, that was the beginning; and this seemed to be the end.

He was not downcast. Though very tired, and grieving for his companion, he felt not the least bitterness or regret. Only there was no longer anything he could do. It had all been done.

When his strength came back into him, he thought, he would try surf-fishing with the line from his pack; for once his thirst was quenched he had begun to feel the gnawing hunger, and their food was gone, all but one packet of hardbread. He would save that, for if he soaked and softened it in water he might be able to feed some of it to Ged.

And that was all there was left to do. Beyond that he could not see; the mist was all about him.

He felt about in his pockets as he sat there, huddled with Ged in the fog, to see if he had anything useful. In his tunic pocket was a hard, sharp-edged thing. He drew it forth and looked at it, puzzled. It was a small stone, black, porous, hard. He almost tossed it away. Then he felt the edges of it in his hand, rough and searing, and felt the weight of it, and knew it for what it was, a bit of rock from the Mountains of Pain. It had caught in his pocket as he climbed or when he crawled to the edge of the pass with Ged. He held it in his hand, the unchanging thing, the stone of pain. He closed his hand on it, and held it. And he smiled then, a smile both sombre and joyous, knowing, for the first time in his life, and alone, and unpraised, and at the end of the world, victory.

The mists thinned and moved. Far out through them he saw sunlight on the open sea. The dunes and hills came and went, colourless and enlarged by the veils of fog. Sunlight struck bright on the body of Orm Embar, magnificent in death.

The iron-black dragon crouched, never moving, on the far side of the stream.

Past noon the sun grew clear and warm, burning the last blur of

mist out of the air. Arren threw off his wet clothes and let them
dry, and went naked save for his sword-belt and sword. He let the
sun dry Ged's clothing likewise, but though the great healing comfortable flood of heat and light poured down on Ged, yet he lay
still.

There was a noise as of metal rubbing against metal, the grating
whisper of crossed swords. The iron-coloured dragon had risen on
its crooked legs. It moved, and crossed the rivulet, with a soft
hissing sound as it dragged its long body through the sand. Arren
saw the wrinkles at the shoulder joints, and the mail of the flanks
scored and scarred like the armour of Erreth-Akbe, and the long
teeth yellowed and blunt. In all this, and in its sure, ponderous
movements, and in a deep frightening calmness that it had, he saw
the sign of age : of great age, of years beyond remembering. So when
the dragon stopped some few feet from where Ged lay, and Arren
stood up between the two, he said, in Hardic for he did not know
the Old Speech, 'Art thou Kalessin?'

The dragon said no word, but it seemed to smile. Then, lowering
its huge head and sticking out its neck, it looked down at Ged, and
spoke his name.

Its voice was huge, and soft, and smelt like a blacksmith's
forge.

Again it spoke, and once more; and at the third time, Ged opened
his eyes. After a while he tried to sit up, but could not. Arren knelt
by him and supported him. Then Ged spoke. 'Kalessin,' he said,
'senvanissai'n ar Roke!' He had no more strength after speaking; he
leaned his head on Arren's shoulder and shut his eyes.

The dragon made no reply. It crouched as before, not moving.
The fog was coming in again, dimming the sun as it went down to
the sea.

Arren dressed, and wrapped Ged in his cloak. The tide which had
drawn far out was coming in again, and he thought to carry his
companion up to dryer ground on the dunes, for he felt his strength
coming back.

But as he bent to lift Ged up, the dragon put out a great mailed
foot, almost touching him. The talons of that foot were four, with a

spur behind such as a cock's foot has, but these were spurs of steel, and as long as scythe-blades.

'Sobriost,' said the dragon, like a January wind through frozen reeds.

'Let my lord be. He has saved us all, and doing so has spent his strength, and maybe his life with it. Let him be!'

So Arren spoke, fiercely and with command. He had been over-awed and frightened too much, he had been filled up with fear, and had got sick of it and would not have it any more. He was angry with the dragon for its brute strength and size, its unjust advantage. He had seen death, he had tasted death, and no threat had power over him.

The old dragon Kalessin looked at him from one long, awful, golden eye. There were ages beyond ages in the depths of that eye; the morning of the world was deep in it. Though Arren did not look into it, he knew that it looked upon him with profound and mild hilarity.

'Arw sobriost,' said the dragon, and its rusty nostrils widened so that the banked and stifled fire deep within them glittered.

Arren had his arm under Ged's shoulders, having been in the act of lifting him when Kalessin's movement stopped him, and now he felt Ged's head turn a little, and heard his voice: 'It means, mount here.'

For a while Arren did not move. This was all folly. But there was the great taloned foot, set like a step in front of him; and above it, the crook of the elbow joint; and above that, the jutting shoulder, and the musculature of the wing where it sprang from the shoulder-blade; four steps; a stairway. And there in front of the wings and the first great iron thorn of the spine-armour, in the hollow of the neck there was place for a man to sit astride, or two men. If they were mad, and past hope, and given up to folly.

'Mount!' said Kalessin in the speech of the Making.

So Arren stood up and helped his companion to stand. Ged held his head erect, and with Arren's arms to guide him climbed up those strange steps. Both sat down astride in the rough-mailed hollow of the dragon's neck, Arren behind, ready to support Ged if he needed it. Both felt the warmth come into them, a welcome heat like the sun's heat, where they touched the dragon's hide: life burned in fire beneath that iron armour.

Arren saw that they had left the mage's staff of yew lying half-buried in the sand; the sea was creeping in to take it. He made to get down for it, but Ged stopped him. 'Leave it. I spent all wizardry at that dry spring, Lebannen. I am no mage now.'

Kalessin turned and looked at them sidelong; the ancient laughter was in its eye. Whether Kalessin was male or female, there was no telling; what Kalessin thought, there was no knowing. Slowly the wings lifted and unfurled. They were not gold like Orm Embar's wings but red, dark red, dark as rust or blood, or the crimson silk of Lorbanery. The dragon raised its wings, carefully, lest it unseat its puny riders. Carefully it gathered in the spring of its great haunches, and leapt like a cat up into the air, and the wings beat down and bore them above the fog that drifted over Selidor.

Rowing with those crimson wings in the evening air Kalessin wheeled out over the open sea, and turned to the east and flew.

In the days of high summer on the island of Ully a great dragon was seen flying low, and later in Usidero, and in the north of Ontuego. Though dragons are dreaded in the West Reach, where people know them all too well, yet after this one had passed over and the villagers had come out of their hiding places, those who had seen it said, 'The dragons are not all dead, as we thought. Maybe the wizards are not all dead, either. Surely there was a great splendour in that flight; maybe it was the Eldest.'

Where Kalessin touched to land none saw. In those far islands there are forests and wild hills to which few men ever come, and where even the descent of a dragon might go unseen.

But in the Ninety Isles there was screaming and disarray. Men rowed westward among the little islands crying, 'Hide! Hide! The Dragon of Pendor has broken his word! The Archmage has perished, and the Dragon is come devouring!'

Without landing, without looking down, the great iron-coloured worm flew over the little islands and the little towns and farms, and deigned not even a belch of fire for such small fry. So it passed over Geath, and over Serd, and crossed the straits of the Inmost Sea, and came within sight of Roke.

Never in the memory of man, scarcely in the memory of legend, had any dragon braved the walls visible and invisible of the well-defended isle. Yet this one did not hesitate, but flew on ponderous wings and heavily over the western shore of Roke, and above the villages and fields, to the green hill that rises over Thwil town. There at last it stooped softly to the earth, and raised its red wings and folded them, and crouched on the summit of Roke Knoll.

The boys came running out of the Great House. Nothing could have stopped them. But for all their youth they were slower than their Masters, and came second to the Knoll. When they came the Patterner was there, come from his Grove, his fair hair bright in the sun. With him was the Changer, who had returned two nights before in the shape of a great sea-osprey, lame-winged and weary; long he had been caught by his own spells in that form, and could not come into his own shape again until he came into the Grove, on that night when the balance was restored and the broken was made whole. The Summoner, gaunt and frail, only one day risen from his bed, had come; and beside him stood the Doorkeeper. And the other Masters of the Isle of the Wise were there.

They saw the riders dismount, one aiding the other. They saw them look about with a look of strange contentment, grimness, and wonder. The dragon crouched like stone while they clambered down from its back and stood beside it. It turned its head a little while the Archmage spoke to it, and briefly answered him. Those who watched saw the sidelong look of the yellow eye, cold and full of laughter. Those who understood heard the dragon say, 'I have brought the young king to his kingdom, and the old man to his home.'

'A little farther yet, Kalessin,' Ged replied. 'I have not gone where I must go.' He looked down at the roofs and towers of the Great House in the sunlight, and he seemed to smile a little. Then he turned to Arren, who stood tall and slight, in worn clothes, and not wholly steady on his legs from the weariness of the long ride and the bewilderment of all that had passed. In the sight of them all there Ged knelt to him, down on both knees, and bowed his grey head.

Then he stood up and kissed the young man on the cheek, saying, 'When you come to your throne in Havnor, my lord and dear companion, rule long, and well.'

He looked again at the Masters and the young wizards and the boys and the townsfolk gathered on the slopes and at the foot of the Knoll. His face was quiet, and in his eyes there was something like that laughter in the eyes of Kalessin. Turning from them all he mounted up again by the dragon's foot and shoulder, and took his seat reinless between the great peaks of the wings, on the neck of the dragon. The red wings lifted with a drumming rattle, and Kalessin the Eldest sprang into the air. Fire came from the dragon's jaws, and smoke, and the sound of thunder and the storm-wind was in the beating of its wings. It circled the hill once and flew off, north and eastward, towards that quarter of Earthsea where stands the mountain isle of Gont.

The Doorkeeper, smiling, said, 'He has done with doing. He goes home.'

And they watched the dragon fly between the sunlight and the sea till it was out of sight.

The Deed of Ged tells that he who had been Archmage came to the crowning of the King of All the Isles in the Tower of the Sword in Havnor at the world's heart. The song tells that when the ceremony of crowning was over and the festival began, he left the company and went down alone to the port of Havnor. There lay out on the water a boat, worn and beaten by storm and the weather of years; she had no sail up, and was empty. Ged called the boat by name, Lookfar, and she came to him. Entering the boat from the pier Ged turned his back on land, and without wind or sail or oar the boat moved; it took him from harbour and from haven, westward among the isles, westward over sea; and no more is known of him.

But in the island of Gont they tell the story otherwise, saying that it was the young King, Lebannen, who came seeking Ged to bring him to the coronation. But he did not find him at Gont Port or at Re Albi. No one could say where he was, only that he had gone afoot up into the forests of the mountain. Often he went so, they said, and did not return for many months, and no man knew the roads of his solitude. Some offered to seek for him, but the King forbade them, saying, 'He rules a greater kingdom than do I.' And so he left the mountain, and took ship, and returned to Havnor, to be crowned.

TEHANU

Kemay
Tutok Bay
Kedun
Oskres
Selt
Korry   Up Selt
Desi Port
Ketoleka
Var
Solwes
Allege
Essary
Kebas
Re Albi
Gont Port
Tettego
Etreke   Valmouth

Norvale
Up Norvale
Ten Alders   Medu   Lotin
Chodur
At
Toss
East Port
Wiss   Tant
Overk
Beach Springs
Lissu
Down Wiss
Kahedanan
Kaheda   Oak Village

Kameber

THE ISLAND OF GONT

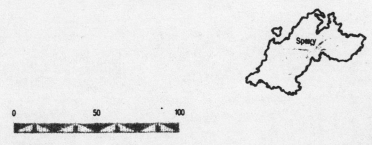

Spevy

0   50   100

1. A Bad Thing

After Farmer Flint of the Middle Valley died, his widow stayed on at the farmhouse. Her son had gone to sea and her daughter had married a merchant of Valmouth, so she lived alone at Oak Farm. People said she had been some kind of great person in the foreign land she came from, and indeed the mage Ogion used to stop by Oak Farm to see her; but that didn't count for much, since Ogion visited all sorts of nobodies.

She had a foreign name, but Flint had called her Goha, which is what they call a little white web-spinning spider on Gont. That name fit well enough, she being white-skinned and small and a good spinner of goat's-wool and sheep fleece. So now she was Flint's widow, Goha, mistress of a flock of sheep and the land to pasture them, four fields, an orchard of pears, two tenants' cottages, the old stone farmhouse under the oaks, and the family graveyard over the hill where Flint lay, earth in his earth.

'I've generally lived near tombstones,' she said to her daughter.

'Oh, mother, come live in town with us!' said Apple, but the widow would not leave her solitude.

'Maybe later, when there are babies and you'll need a hand,' she said, looking with pleasure at her grey-eyed daughter. 'But not now. You don't need me. And I like it here.'

When Apple had gone back to her young husband, the widow closed the door and stood on the stone-flagged floor of the kitchen of the farmhouse. It was dusk, but she did not light the lamp, thinking of her own husband lighting the lamp: the hands, the spark, the intent, dark face in the catching glow. The house was silent.

'I used to live in a silent house, alone,' she thought. 'I will do so again.' She lighted the lamp.

In a late afternoon of the first hot weather, the widow's old friend Lark came out from the village, hurrying along the dusty lane. 'Goha,' she said, seeing her weeding in the bean patch, 'Goha, it's a bad thing. It's a very bad thing. Can you come?'

'Yes,' the widow said. 'What would the bad thing be?'

Lark caught her breath. She was a heavy, plain, middle-aged woman, whose name did not fit her body any more. But once she had been a slight and pretty girl, and she had befriended Goha, paying no attention to the villagers who gossiped about that white-faced Kargish witch Flint had brought home; and friends they had been ever since.

'A burned child,' she said.

'Whose?'

'Tramps'.'

Goha went to shut the farmhouse door, and they set off along the lane, Lark talking as they went. She was short of breath and sweating. Tiny seeds of the heavy grasses that lined the lane stuck to her cheeks and forehead, and she brushed at them as she talked. 'They've been camped in the river meadows all the month. A man, passed himself off as a tinker, but he's a thief, and a woman with him. And another man, younger, hanging around with them most of the time. Not working, any of 'em. Filching and begging and living off the woman. Boys from downriver were bringing them farmstuff to get at her. You know how it is now, that kind of thing. And gangs on the roads and coming by farms. If I were you, I'd lock my door, these days. So this one, this younger fellow, comes into the village, and I was out in front of our house, and he says, "The child's not well." I'd barely seen a child with them, a little ferret of a thing, slipped out of sight so quick I wasn't sure it was there at all. So I said, "Not well? A fever?" And the fellow says, "She hurt herself, lighting the fire," and then before I'd got myself ready to go with him he'd made off. Gone. And when I went out there by the river, the other pair was gone too. Cleared out. Nobody. All their traps and trash gone too. There was just their camp-fire, still smouldering, and just by it – partly in it – on the ground –'

Lark stopped talking for several steps. She looked straight ahead, not at Goha.

'They hadn't even put a blanket over her,' she said.

She strode on.

'She'd been pushed into the fire while it was burning,' she said. She swallowed, and brushed at the sticking seeds on her hot face. 'I'd say maybe she fell, but if she'd been awake she'd have tried to save herself. They beat her and thought they'd killed her, I guess, and wanted to hide what they'd done to her, so they –'

She stopped again, went on again.

'Maybe it wasn't him. Maybe he pulled her out. He came to get help for her, after all. It must have been the father. I don't know. It doesn't matter. Who's to know? Who's to care? Who's to care for the child? Why do we do what we do?'

Goha asked in a low voice, 'Will she live?'

'She might,' Lark said. 'She might well live.'

After a while, as they neared the village, she said, 'I don't know why I had to come to you. Ivy's there. There's nothing to be done.'

'I could go to Valmouth, for Beech.'

'Nothing he could do. It's beyond . . . beyond help. I got her warm. Ivy's given her a potion and a sleeping charm. I carried her home. She must be six or seven but she didn't weigh what a two-year-old would. She never really waked. But she makes a sort of gasping . . . I know there isn't anything you can do. But I wanted you.'

'I want to come,' Goha said. But before they entered Lark's house, she shut her eyes and held her breath a moment in dread.

Lark's children had been sent outdoors, and the house was silent. The child lay unconscious on Lark's bed. The village witch, Ivy, had smeared an ointment of witch hazel and heal-all on the lesser burns, but had not touched the right side of the face and head and the right hand, which had been charred to the bone. She had drawn the rune Pirr above the bed, and left it at that.

'Can you do anything?' Lark asked in a whisper.

Goha stood looking down at the burned child. Her hands were still. She shook her head.

'You learned healing, up on the mountain, didn't you?' Pain and shame and rage spoke through Lark, begging for relief.

'Even Ogion couldn't heal this,' the widow said.

Lark turned away, biting her lip, and wept. Goha held her, stroking her grey hair. They held each other.

The witch Ivy came in from the kitchen, scowling at the sight of Goha. Though the widow cast no charms and worked no spells, it was said that when she first came to Gont she had lived at Re Albi as a ward of the mage, and that she knew the Archmage of Roke, and no doubt had foreign and uncanny powers. Jealous of her prerogative, the witch went to the bed and busied herself beside it, making a mound of something in a dish and setting it afire so that it smoked and reeked while she muttered a curing charm over and over. The rank herbal smoke made the burned child cough and half rouse, flinching and shuddering. She began to make a gasping noise, quick, short, scraping breaths. Her one eye seemed to look up at Goha.

Goha stepped forward and took the child's left hand in hers. She spoke in her own language. 'I served them and I left them,' she said. 'I will not let them have you.'

The child stared at her or at nothing, trying to breathe, and trying again to breathe, and trying again to breathe.

2. Going to the Falcon's Nest

It was more than a year later, in the hot and spacious days after the Long Dance, that a messenger came down the road from the north to Middle Valley asking for the widow Goha. People in the village put him on the path, and he came to Oak Farm late in the afternoon. He was a sharp-faced, quick-eyed man. He looked at Goha and at the sheep in the fold beyond her and said, 'Fine lambs. The Mage of Re Albi sends for you.'

'He sent you?' Goha inquired, disbelieving and amused. Ogion, when he wanted her, had quicker and finer messengers: an eagle calling, or only his own voice saying her name quietly – *Will you come?*

The man nodded. 'He's sick,' he said. 'Will you be selling off any of the ewe lambs?'

'I might. You can talk to the shepherd if you like. Over by the fence there. Do you want supper? You can stay the night here if you want, but I'll be on my way.'

'Tonight?'

This time there was no amusement in her look of mild scorn. 'I won't be waiting about,' she said. She spoke for a minute with the old shepherd, Clearbrook, and then turned away, going up to the house built into the hillside by the oak grove. The messenger followed her.

In the stone-floored kitchen, a child whom he looked at once and quickly looked away from served him milk, bread, cheese, and green onions, and then went off, never saying a word. She reappeared beside the woman, both shod for travel and carrying light leather packs. The messenger followed them out, and the widow locked the farm-house door. They all set off together, he on his business, for the message from Ogion had been a mere favour added to the serious matter of buying a breeding ram for the Lord of Re Albi; and the woman and the burned child bade him farewell where the lane turned off to the village. They went on up the road he had come down, northward and then west into the foothills of Gont Mountain.

They walked until the long summer twilight began to darken. They left the narrow road then and made camp in a dell down by a stream that ran quick and quiet, reflecting the pale evening sky between thickets of scrub willow. Goha made a bed of dry grass and willow leaves, hidden among the thickets like a hare's form, and rolled the child up in a blanket on it. 'Now,' she said, 'you're a cocoon. In the morning you'll be a butterfly and hatch out.' She lighted no fire, but lay in her cloak beside the child and watched the stars shine one by one and listened to what the stream said quietly, until she slept.

When they woke in the cold before the dawn, she made a small fire and heated a pan of water to make oatmeal gruel for the child and herself. The little ruined butterfly came shivering from her cocoon, and Goha cooled the pan in the dewy grass so that the child could hold it and drink from it. The east was brightening above the high, dark shoulder of the mountain when they set off again.

They walked all day at the pace of a child who tired easily. The woman's heart yearned to make haste, but she walked slowly. She was not able to carry the child any long distance, and so to make the way easier for her she told her stories.

'We're going to see a man, an old man, called Ogion,' she told her as they trudged along the narrow road that wound upward through the forests. 'He's a wise man, and a wizard. Do you know what a wizard is, Therru?'

If the child had had a name, she did not know it or would not say it. Goha called her Therru.

She shook her head.

'Well, neither do I,' said the woman. 'But I know what they can do. When I was young – older than you, but young – Ogion was my father, the way I'm your mother now. He looked after me and tried to teach me what I needed to know. He stayed with me when he'd rather have been wandering by himself. He liked to walk, all along these roads like we're doing now, and in the forests, in the wild places. He went everywhere on the mountain, looking at things, listening. He always listened, so they called him the Silent. But he used to talk to me. He told me stories. Not only the great stories everybody learns, the heroes and the kings and the things that happened long ago and far away, but stories only he knew.' She walked on a way before she went on. 'I'll tell you one of those stories now.

'One of the things wizards can do is turn into something else – take another form. Shape-changing, they call it. An ordinary sorcerer can make himself look like somebody else, or like an animal, just so you don't know for a minute what you're seeing – as if he'd put on a mask. But the wizards and mages can do more than that. They can be the mask, they can truly change into another being. So a wizard, if he wanted to cross the sea and had no boat, might turn himself into a gull and fly across. But he has to be careful. If he stays a bird, he begins to think what a bird thinks and forget what a man thinks, and he might fly off and be a gull and never a man again. So they say there was a great wizard once who liked to turn himself into a bear, and did it too often, and became a bear, and killed his own little son; and they had to hunt him down and kill him. But Ogion used to joke about it, too. Once when the mice got into his pantry and ruined the cheese, he caught one with a tiny mousetrap spell, and he held the mouse up like this and looked it in the eye and said, "I told you not to play mouse!" And for a minute I thought he meant it . . .

'Well, this story is about something like shape-changing but Ogion said it was beyond all shape-changing he knew, because it was about being two things, two beings, at once, and in the same form, and he said that this is beyond the power of wizards. But he met with it in a little village around on the northwest coast of Gont, a place called Kemay. There was a woman there, an old fisherwoman, not a witch, not learned; but she made songs. That's how Ogion came to hear of her. He was wandering there, the way he did, going along the coast, listening; and he heard somebody singing, mending a net or caulking a boat and singing as they worked:

> Farther west than west
> beyond the land
> my people are dancing
> on the other wind.

'It was the tune and the words both that Ogion heard, and he had never heard them before, so he asked where the song came from. And from one answer to another, he went along to where somebody said, "Oh, that's one of the songs of the Woman of Kemay." So he went along to Kemay, the little fishing port where the woman lived, and he found her house down by the harbour. And he knocked on the door with his mage's staff. And she came and opened the door.

'Now you know, you remember when we talked about names, how children have child-names, and everybody has a use-name, and maybe a nickname too. Different people may call you differently. You're my Therru, but maybe you'll have a Hardic use-name when you get older. But also, when you come into your womanhood, you will, if all be rightly done, be given your true name. It will be given you by one of true power, a wizard or a mage, because that is their power, their art – naming. And that's the name you'll maybe never tell another person, because your own self is in your true name. It is your strength, your power; but to another it is risk and burden, only to be given in utmost need and trust. But a great mage, knowing all names, may know it without your telling him.

'So Ogion, who is a great mage, stood at the door of the little house there by the seawall, and the old woman opened the door. Then Ogion stepped back, and he held up his oak staff, and put up his hand, too, like this, as if trying to protect himself from the heat of a fire, and in his amazement and fear he said her true name aloud — "Dragon!"

'In that first moment, he told me, it was no woman he saw at all in the doorway, but a blaze and glory of fire, and a glitter of gold scales and talons, and the great eyes of a dragon. They say you must not look into a dragon's eyes.

'Then that was gone, and he saw no dragon, but an old woman standing there in the doorway, a bit stooped, a tall old fisherwoman with big hands. She looked at him as he did at her. And she said, "Come in, Lord Ogion."

'So he went in. She served him fish soup, and they ate, and then they talked by her fire. He thought that she must be a shape-changer, but he didn't know, you see, whether she was a woman who could change herself into a dragon, or a dragon who could change itself into a woman. So he asked her at last, "Are you woman or dragon?" And she didn't say, but she said, "I'll sing you a story I know."'

Therru had a little stone in her shoe. They stopped to get that out, and went on, very slowly, for the road was climbing steeply between cut banks of stone overhung by thickets where the cicadas sang in the summer heat.

'So this is the story she sang to him, to Ogion.

'When Segoy raised the islands of the world from the sea in the beginning of time, the dragons were the first born of the land and the wind blowing over the land. So the Song of the Creation tells. But her song told also that then, in the beginning, dragon and human were all one. They were all one people, one race, winged, and speaking the True Language.

'They were beautiful, and strong, and wise, and free.

'But in time nothing can be without becoming. So among the dragon-people some became more and more in love with flight and wildness, and would have less and less to do with the works of making, or with study and learning, or with houses and cities. They wanted only to fly farther and farther, hunting and eating their kill, ignorant and uncaring, seeking more freedom and more.

'Others of the dragon-people came to care little for flight, but gathered up treasure, wealth, things made, things learned. They built houses, strongholds to keep their treasures in, so they could pass all they gained to their children, ever seeking more increase and more. And they came to fear the wild ones, who might come flying and destroy all their dear hoard, burn it up in a blast of flame out of mere carelessness and ferocity.

'The wild ones feared nothing. They learned nothing. Because they were ignorant and fearless, they could not save themselves when the flightless ones trapped them as animals and killed them. But other wild ones would come flying and set the beautiful houses afire, and destroy, and kill. Those that were strongest, wild or wise, were those who killed each other first.

'Those who were most afraid, they hid from the fighting, and when there was no more hiding they ran from it. They used their skills of making and made boats and sailed east, away from the western isles where the great winged ones made war among the ruined towers.

'So those who had been both dragon and human changed, becoming two peoples – the dragons, always fewer and wilder, scattered by their endless, mindless greed and anger, in the far islands of the Western Reach; and the human folk, always more numerous in their rich towns and cities, filling up the Inner Isles and all the south and east. But among them there were some who saved the learning of the dragons – the True Language of the Making – and these are now the wizards.

'But also, the song said, there are those among us who know they once were dragons, and among the dragons there are some who know their kinship with us. And these say that when the one people were becoming two, some of them, still both human and dragon, still winged, went not east but west, on over the Open Sea, till they came to the other side of the world. There they live in peace, great winged beings both wild and wise, with human mind and dragon heart. And so she sang,

> Farther west than west
> beyond the land
> my people are dancing
> on the other wind.

'So that was the story told in the song of the Woman of Kemay, and it ended with those words.

'Then Ogion said to her, "When I first saw you I saw your true being. This woman who sits across the hearth from me is no more than the dress she wears."

'But she shook her head and laughed, and all she would say was, "If only it were that simple!"

'So then after a while Ogion came back to Re Albi. And when he told me the story, he said to me, "Ever since that day, I have wondered if anyone, man or dragon, has been farther west than west; and who we are, and where our wholeness lies." ... Are you getting hungry, Therru? There's a good sitting place, it looks like, up there where the road turns. Maybe from there we'll be able to see Gont

Port, away down at the foot of the mountain. It's a big city, even bigger than Valmouth. We'll sit down when we get to the turn, and rest a bit.'

From the high corner of the road they could indeed look down the vast slopes of forest and rocky meadow to the town on its bay, and see the crags that guarded the entrance to the bay, and the boats on the dark water like wood-chips or water beetles. Far ahead on their road and still somewhat above it, a cliff jutted out from the mountainside: the Overfell, on which was the village of Re Albi, the Falcon's Nest.

Therru made no complaints, but when presently Goha said, 'Well, shall we go on?' the child, sitting there between the road and the gulfs of sky and sea, shook her head. The sun was warm, and they had walked a long way since their breakfast in the dell.

Goha brought out their water bottle, and they drank again; then she brought out a bag of raisins and walnuts and gave it to the child.

'We're in sight of where we're going,' she said, 'and I'd like to be there before dark, if we can. I'm anxious to see Ogion. You'll be very tired, but we won't walk fast. And we'll be there safe and warm tonight. Keep the bag, tuck it in your belt. Raisins make your legs strong. Would you like a staff – like a wizard – to help you walk?'

Therru munched and nodded. Goha took out her knife and cut a strong shoot of hazel for the child, and then seeing an alder fallen above the road, broke off a branch of it and trimmed it to make herself a stout, light stick.

They set off again, and the child trudged along, beguiled by raisins. Goha sang to amuse them both, love songs and shepherd's songs and ballads she had learned in the Middle Valley; but all at once her voice hushed in the middle of a tune. She stopped, putting out her hand in a warning gesture.

The four men ahead of them on the road had seen her.

494

There was no use trying to hide in the woods till they went on or went by.

'Travellers,' she said quietly to Therru, and walked on. She took a good grip on her alder stick.

What Lark had said about gangs and thieves was not just the complaint each generation makes that things aren't what they used to be and the world's going to the dogs. In the last several years there had been a loss of peace and trust in the towns and countrysides of Gont. Young men behaved like strangers among their own people, abusing hospitality, stealing, selling what they stole. Beggary was common where it had been rare, and the unsatisfied beggar threatened violence. Women did not like to go alone in the streets and roads, nor did they like that loss of freedom. Some of the young women ran off to join the gangs of thieves and poachers. Often they came home within the year, sullen, bruised, and pregnant. And among village sorcerers and witches there was rumour of matters of their profession going amiss: charms that had always cured did not cure; spells of finding found nothing, or the wrong thing; love potions drove men into frenzies not of desire but of murderous jealousy. And worse than this, they said, people who knew nothing of the art of magic, the laws and limits of it and the dangers of breaking them, were calling themselves people of power, promising wonders of wealth and health to their followers, promising even immortality.

Ivy, the witch of Goha's village, had spoken darkly of this weakening of magic, and so had Beech, the sorcerer of Valmouth. He was a shrewd and modest man, who had come to help Ivy do what little could be done to lessen the pain and scarring of Therru's burns. He had said to Goha, 'I think a time in which such things as this occur must be a time of ruining, the end of an age. How many hundred years since there was a king in Havnor? It can't go on so. We must turn to the centre again or be lost, island against island, man against man, father against child . . . ' He had glanced at her, somewhat timidly, yet with his clear, shrewd look. 'The Ring of Erreth-Akbe is restored to the Tower in Havnor,' he said. 'I know who brought it there . . . That was the sign, surely, that was the sign of the new age to come! But we haven't acted on it. We have no king. We have no centre. We must find our heart, our strength. Maybe the Archmage will act at last.' And he added, with confidence, 'After all, he is from Gont.'

But no word of any deed of the Archmage, or any heir to the Throne in Havnor, had come; and things went badly on.

So it was with fear and a grim anger that Goha saw the four men on the road before her step two to each side, so that she and the child would have to pass between them.

As they went walking steadily forward, Therru kept very close beside her, holding her head bent down, but she did not take her hand.

One of the men, a big-chested fellow with coarse black hairs on his upper lip drooping over his mouth, began to speak, grinning a little. 'Hey, there,' he said, but Goha spoke at the same time and louder. 'Out of my way!' she said, raising her alder stick as if it were a wizard's staff – 'I have business with Ogion!' She strode between the men and straight on, Therru trotting beside her. The men, mistaking effrontery for witchery, stood still. Ogion's name perhaps still held power. Or perhaps there was a power in Goha, or in the child. For when the two had gone by, one of the men said, 'Did you see that?' and spat and made the sign to avert evil.

'Witch and her monster brat,' another said. 'Let 'em go!'

Another, a man in a leather cap and jerkin, stood staring for a moment while the others slouched on their way. His face looked sick and stricken, yet he seemed to be turning to follow the woman and child, when the hairy-lipped man called to him, 'Come on, Handy!' and he obeyed.

Out of sight around the turn of the road, Goha had picked up Therru and hurried on with her until she had to set her down and stand gasping. The child asked no questions and made no delays. As soon as Goha could go on again, the child walked as fast as she could beside her, holding her hand.

'You're red,' she said. 'Like fire.'

She spoke seldom, and not clearly, her voice being very hoarse; but Goha could understand her.

'I'm angry,' Goha said with a kind of laugh. 'When I'm angry I turn red. Like you people, you red people, you barbarians of the western lands . . . Look, there's a town there ahead, that'll be Oak Springs. It's the only village on this road. We'll stop there and rest a little. Maybe we can get some milk. And then, if we can go on, if you think you can walk on up to the Falcon's Nest, we'll be there by nightfall, I hope.'

The child nodded. She opened her bag of raisins and walnuts and ate a few. They trudged on.

The sun had long set when they came through the village and to Ogion's house on the cliff-top. The first stars glimmered above a dark mass of clouds in the west over the high horizon of the sea. The sea wind blew, bowing short grasses. A goat bleated in the pastures behind the low, small house. The one window shone dim yellow.

Goha stood her stick and Therru's against the wall by the door, and held the child's hand, and knocked once.

There was no answer.

She pushed the door open. The fire on the hearth was out, cinders and grey ashes, but an oil lamp on the table made a tiny seed of light, and from his mattress on the floor in the far corner of the room Ogion said, 'Come in, Tenar.'

3. Ogion

She bedded down the child on the cot in the western alcove. She built up the fire. She went and sat down beside Ogion's pallet, cross-legged on the floor.

'No one looking after you!'

'I sent 'em off,' he whispered.

His face was as dark and hard as ever, but his hair was thin and white, and the dim lamp made no spark of light in his eyes.

'You could have died alone,' she said, fierce.

'Help me do that,' the old man said.

'Not yet,' she pleaded, stooping, laying her forehead on his hand.

'Not tonight,' he agreed. 'Tomorrow.'

He lifted his hand to stroke her hair once, having that much strength.

She sat up again. The fire had caught. Its light played on the walls and low ceiling and sent shadows to thicken in the corners of the long room.

'If Ged would come,' the old man murmured.

'Have you sent to him?'

'Lost,' Ogion said. 'He's lost. A cloud. A mist over the lands. He went into the west. Carrying the branch of the rowan tree. Into the dark mist. I've lost my hawk.'

'No, no, no,' she whispered. 'He'll come back.'

They were silent. The fire's warmth began to penetrate them both, letting Ogion relax and drift in and out of sleep, letting Tenar find rest pleasant after the long day afoot. She rubbed her feet and her aching shoulders. She had carried Therru part of the last long climb, for the child had begun to gasp with weariness as she tried to keep up.

Tenar got up, heated water, and washed the dust of the road from her. She heated milk, and ate bread she found in Ogion's larder, and came back to sit by him. While he slept, she sat thinking, watching his face and the firelight and the shadows.

She thought how a girl had sat silent, thinking, in the night, a long time ago and far away, a girl in a windowless room, brought up to know herself only as the one who had been eaten, priestess and servant of the powers of the darkness of the earth. And there had been a woman who would sit up in the peaceful silence of a farmhouse when husband and children slept, to think, to be alone an hour. And there was the widow who had carried a burned child here, who sat by the side of the dying, who waited for a man to return. Like all women, any woman, doing what women do. But it was not by the names of the servant or the wife or the widow that Ogion had called her. Nor had Ged, in the darkness of the Tombs. Nor – longer ago, farther away than all – had her mother, the mother she remembered only as the warmth and lion-colour of firelight, the mother who had given her her name.

'I am Tenar,' she whispered. The fire, catching a dry branch of pine, leapt up in a bright yellow tongue of flame.

Ogion's breathing became troubled and he struggled for air. She helped him as she could till he found some ease. They both slept for a while, she drowsing by his dazed and drifting silence, broken by strange words. Once in the deep night he said aloud, as if meeting a friend in the road, 'Are you here, then? Have you seen him?' And again, when Tenar roused herself to build up the fire, he began to speak, but this time it seemed he spoke to someone in his memory of years long gone, for he said clearly as a child might, 'I tried to help her, but the roof of the house fell down. It fell on them. It was the earthquake.' Tenar listened. She too had seen earthquake. 'I tried to help!' said the boy in the old man's voice, in pain. Then the gasping struggle to breathe began again.

At first light Tenar was wakened by a sound she thought at first was the sea. It was a great rushing of wings. A flock of birds was flying over, low, so many that their wings stormed and the window was darkened by their quick shadows. It seemed they circled the house once and then were gone. They made no call or cry, and she did not know what birds they were.

People came that morning from the village of Re Albi, which Ogion's house stood apart from to the north. A goatgirl came, and a woman for the milk of Ogion's goats, and others to ask what they might do for him. Moss, the village witch, fingered the alder stick and the hazel switch by the door and peered in hopefully, but not even she ventured to come in, and Ogion growled from his pallet, 'Send 'em away! Send 'em all away!'

He seemed stronger and more comfortable. When little Therru woke, he spoke to her in the dry, kind, quiet way Tenar remembered. The child went out to play in the sun, and he said to Tenar, 'What is the name you call her?'

He knew the True Language of the Making, but he had never learned any Kargish at all.

'*Therru* means burning, the flaming of fire,' she said.

'Ah, ah,' he said, and his eyes gleamed, and he frowned. He seemed to grope for words for a moment. 'That one,' he said. 'That one – they will fear her.'

'They fear her now,' Tenar said bitterly.

The mage shook his head.

'Teach her, Tenar,' he whispered. 'Teach her all! – Not Roke. They are afraid – Why did I let you go? Why did you go? To bring her here – too late?'

'Be still, be still,' she told him tenderly, for he struggled with words and breath and could find neither. He shook his head, and gasped, 'Teach her!' and lay still.

He would not eat, and only drank a little water. In the

middle of the day he slept. Waking in the late afternoon, he said, 'Now, daughter,' and sat up.

Tenar took his hand, smiling at him.

'Help me get up.'

'No, no.'

'Yes,' he said. 'Outside. I can't die indoors.'

'Where would you go?'

'Anywhere. But if I could, the forest path,' he said. 'The beech above the meadow.'

When she saw he was able to get up and determined to get outdoors, she helped him. Together they got to the door, where he stopped and looked around the one room of his house. In the dark corner to the right of the doorway his tall staff leaned against the wall, shining a little. Tenar reached out to give it to him, but he shook his head. 'No,' he said, 'not that.' He looked around again as if for something missing, forgotten. 'Come on,' he said at last.

When the bright wind from the west blew on his face and he looked out at the high horizon, he said, 'That's good.'

'Let me get some people from the village to make a litter and carry you,' she said. 'They're all waiting to do something for you.'

'I want to walk,' the old man said.

Therru came around the house and watched solemnly as Ogion and Tenar went, step by step, and stopping every five or six steps for Ogion to gasp, across the tangled meadow towards the woods that climbed steep up the mountainside from the inner side of the cliff-top. The sun was hot and the wind cold. It took them a very long time to cross that meadow. Ogion's face was grey and his legs shook like the grass in the wind when they got at last to the foot of a big young beech tree just inside the forest, a few yards up the beginning of the mountain path. There he sank down between the roots of the tree, his back against its trunk. For a long time he could not move or speak, and his heart, pounding and faltering, shook his body. He nodded finally and whispered, 'All right.'

Therru had followed them at a distance. Tenar went to her and held her and talked to her a little. She came back to Ogion. 'She's bringing a rug,' she said.

'Not cold.'

'*I'm* cold.'

There was the flicker of a smile on her face.

The child came lugging a goat's-wool blanket. She whispered to Tenar and ran off again.

'Heather will let her help milk the goats, and look after her,' Tenar said to Ogion. 'So I can stay here with you.'

'Never one thing, for you,' he said in the hoarse whistling whisper that was all the voice he had left.

'No. Always at least two things, and usually more,' she said. 'But I am here.'

He nodded.

For a long time he did not speak, but sat back against the tree trunk, his eyes closed. Watching his face, Tenar saw it change as slowly as the light changed in the west.

He opened his eyes and gazed through a gap in the thickets at the western sky. He seemed to watch something, some act or deed, in that far, clear, golden space of light. He whispered once, hesitant, as if unsure, 'The dragon –'

The sun was down, the wind fallen.

Ogion looked at Tenar.

'Over,' he whispered with exultation. 'All changed! – Changed, Tenar! Wait – wait here, for –' A shaking took his body, tossing him like the branch of a tree in a great wind. He gasped. His eyes closed and opened, gazing beyond her. He laid his hand on hers; she bent down to him; he spoke his name to her, so that after his death he might be truly known.

He gripped her hand and shut his eyes and began once more the struggle to breathe, until there was no more breath. He lay then like one of the roots of the tree, while the stars came out and shone through the leaves and branches of the forest.

Tenar sat with the dead man in the dusk and dark. A lantern gleamed like a firefly across the meadow. She had laid the woollen blanket across them both, but her hand that held his hand had grown cold, as if it held a stone. She touched her forehead to his hand once more. She stood up, stiff and dizzy, her body feeling strange to her, and went to meet and guide whoever was coming with the light.

That night his neighbours sat with Ogion, and he did not send them away.

The mansion house of the Lord of Re Albi stood on an outcrop of rocks on the mountainside above the Overfell. Early in the morning, long before the sun had cleared the mountain, the wizard in the service of that lord came down through the village; and very soon after, another wizard came toiling up the steep road from Gont Port, having set out in darkness. Word had come to them that Ogion was dying, or their power was such that they knew of the passing of a great mage.

The village of Re Albi had no sorcerer, only its mage, and a witchwoman to perform the lowly jobs of finding and mending and bonesetting, which people would not bother the mage with. Aunty Moss was a dour creature, unmarried, like most witches, and unwashed, with greying hair tied in curious charm-knots, and eyes red-rimmed from herb smoke. It was she who had come across the meadow with the lantern, and with Tenar and the others she had watched the night by Ogion's body. She had set a wax candle in a glass shade, there in the forest, and had burned sweet oils in a dish of clay; she had said the words that should be said, and done what should be done. When it came to touching the body to prepare it for burial, she had looked once at Tenar as if for permission, and then had gone on with her offices. Village witches usually saw to the homing, as they called it, of the dead, and often to the burial.

When the wizard came down from the mansion house, a tall young man with a silvery staff of pinewood, and the other one came up from Gont Port, a stout middle-aged man with a short yew staff, Aunty Moss did not look at them with her bloodshot eyes, but ducked and bowed and drew back, gathering up her poor charms and witcheries.

When she had laid out the corpse as it should lie to be buried, on the left side with the knees bent, she had put in the upturned left hand a tiny charm-bundle, something wrapped in soft goatskin and tied with coloured cord. The wizard of Re Albi flicked it away with the tip of his staff.

'Is the grave dug?' asked the wizard of Gont Port.

'Yes,' said the wizard of Re Albi. 'It is dug in the graveyard of my lord's house,' and he pointed towards the mansion house up on the mountain.

'I see,' said Gont Port. 'I had thought our mage would be buried in all honour in the city he saved from earthquake.'

'My lord desires the honour,' said Re Albi.

'But it would seem –' Gont Port began, and stopped, not liking to argue, but not ready to give in to the young man's easy claim. He looked down at the dead man. 'He must be buried nameless,' he said with regret and bitterness. 'I walked all night, but came too late. A great loss made greater!'

The young wizard said nothing.

'His name was Aihal,' Tenar said. 'His wish was to lie here, where he lies now.'

Both men looked at her. The young man, seeing a middle-aged village woman, simply turned away. The man from Gont Port stared a moment and said, 'Who are you?'

'I'm called Flint's widow, Goha,' she said. 'Who I am is your business to know, I think. But not mine to say.'

At this, the wizard of Re Albi found her worthy of a brief stare. 'Take care, woman, how you speak to men of power!'

'Wait, wait,' said Gont Port, with a patting gesture, trying to calm Re Albi's indignation, and still gazing at Tenar. 'You were – You were his ward, once?'

'And friend,' Tenar said. Then she turned away her head and stood silent. She had heard the anger in her voice as she said that word, 'friend'. She looked down at her friend, a corpse ready for the ground, lost and still. They stood over him, alive and full of power, offering no friendship, only contempt, rivalry, anger.

'I'm sorry,' she said. 'It was a long night. I was with him when he died.'

'It is not –' the young wizard began, but unexpectedly old Aunty Moss interrupted him, saying loudly, 'She was. Yes, she was. Nobody else but her. He sent for her. He sent young Townsend the sheep-dealer to tell her come, clear down round the mountain, and he waited his dying till she did come and was with him, and then he died, and he died where he would be buried, here.'

'And,' said the older man, '– and he told you –?'

'His name.' Tenar looked at them, and do what she would, the incredulity on the older man's face, the contempt on the other's, brought out an answering disrespect in her. 'I said that name,' she said. 'Must I repeat it to you?'

To her consternation she saw from their expressions that in fact they had not heard the name, Ogion's true name; they had not paid attention to her.

'Oh!' she said. 'This is a bad time – a time when even such a name can go unheard, can fall like a stone! Is listening not power? Listen, then: his name was Aihal. His name in death is Aihal. In the songs he will be known as Aihal of Gont. If there are songs to be made any more. He was a silent man. Now he's very silent. Maybe there will be no songs, only silence. I don't know. I'm very tired. I've lost my father and dear friend.' Her voice failed; her throat closed on a sob. She turned to go. She saw on the forest path the little charm-bundle Aunty Moss had made. She picked it up, knelt down by the corpse, kissed the open palm of the left hand, and laid the bundle on it. There on her knees she looked up once more at the two men. She spoke quietly.

'Will you see to it,' she said, 'that his grave is dug here, where he desired it?'

First the older man, then the younger, nodded.

She got up, smoothing down her skirt, and started back across the meadow in the morning light.

4. Kalessin

'Wait,' Ogion, who was Aihal now, had said to her, just before the wind of death had shaken him and torn him loose from living. 'Over – all changed,' he had whispered, and then, 'Tenar, wait –' But he had not said what she should wait for. The change he had seen or known, perhaps; but what change? Was it his own death he meant, his own life that was over? He had spoken with joy, exulting. He had charged her to wait.

'What else have I to do?' she said to herself, sweeping the floor of his house. 'What else have I ever done?' And, speaking to her memory of him, 'Shall I wait here, in your house?'

'Yes,' said Aihal the Silent, silently, smiling.

So she swept out the house and cleaned the hearth and aired the mattresses. She threw out some chipped crockery and a leaky pan, but she handled them gently. She even put her cheek against a cracked plate as she took it out to the midden, for it was evidence of the old mage's illness this past year. Austere he had been, living as plain as a poor farmer, but when his eyes were clear and his strength in him, he would never have used a broken plate or let a pan go unmended. These signs of his weakness grieved her, making her wish she had been with him to look after him. 'I would have liked that,' she said to her memory of him, but he said nothing. He never would have anybody to look after him but himself. Would he have said to her, 'You have better things to do?' She did not know. He was silent. But that she did right to stay here in his house, now, she was certain.

Shandy and her old husband, Clearbrook, who had been

at the farm in Middle Valley longer than she herself had, would look after the flocks and the orchard; the other couple on the farm, Tiff and Sis, would get the field crops in. The rest would have to take care of itself for a while. Her raspberry canes would be picked by the neighbourhood children. That was too bad; she loved raspberries. Up here on the Overfell, with the sea wind always blowing, it was too cold to grow raspberries. But Ogion's little old peach tree in the sheltered nook of the house wall facing south bore eighteen peaches, and Therru watched them like a mousing cat till the day she came in and said in her hoarse, unclear voice, 'Two of the peaches are all red and yellow.'

'Ah,' said Tenar. They went together to the peach tree and picked the two first ripe peaches and ate them there, unpeeled. The juice ran down their chins. They licked their fingers.

'Can I plant it?' said Therru, looking at the wrinkled stone of her peach.

'Yes. This is a good place, near the old tree. But not too close. So they both have room for their roots and branches.'

The child chose a place and dug the tiny grave. She laid the stone in it and covered it over. Tenar watched her. In the few days they had been living here, Therru had changed, she thought. She was still unresponsive, without anger, without joy; but since they had been here her awful vigilance, her immobility, had almost imperceptibly relaxed. She had desired the peaches. She had thought of planting the stone, of increasing the number of peaches in the world. At Oak Farm she was unafraid of two people only, Tenar and Lark; but here she had taken quite easily to Heather, the goatherd of Re Albi, a bawling-voiced, gentle lackwit of twenty, who treated the child very much as another goat, a lame kid. That was all right. And Aunty Moss was all right too, no matter what she smelled like.

When Tenar had first lived in Re Albi, twenty-five years

ago, Moss had not been an old witch but a young one. She had ducked and bowed and grinned at 'the young lady', 'the White Lady', Ogion's ward and student, never speaking to her but with the utmost respect. Tenar had felt that respect to be false, a mask for an envy and dislike and distrust that were all too familiar to her from women over whom she had been placed in a position of superiority, women who saw themselves as common and her as uncommon, as privileged. Priestess of the Tombs of Atuan or foreign ward of the Mage of Gont, she was set apart, set above. Men had given her power, men had shared their power with her. Women looked at her from outside, sometimes rivalrous, often with a trace of ridicule.

She had felt herself the one left outside, shut out. She had fled from the Powers of the desert tombs, and then she had left the powers of learning and skill offered her by her guardian, Ogion. She had turned her back on all that, gone to the other side, the other room, where the women lived, to be one of them. A wife, a farmer's wife, a mother, a householder, undertaking the power that a woman was born to, the authority allotted her by the arrangements of mankind.

And there in the Middle Valley, Flint's wife, Goha, had been welcome, all in all, among the women; a foreigner to be sure, white-skinned and talking a bit strange, but a notable housekeeper, an excellent spinner, with well-behaved, well-grown children and a prospering farm: respectable. And among men she was Flint's woman, doing what a woman should do: bed, breed, bake, cook, clean, spin, sew, serve. A good woman. They approved of her. Flint did well for himself after all, they said. I wonder what a white woman's like, white all over? their eyes said, looking at her, until she got older and they no longer saw her.

Here, now, it was all changed, there was none of all that. Since she and Moss had kept the vigil for Ogion together, the witch had made it plain that she would be

her friend, follower, servant, whatever Tenar wanted
her to be. Tenar was not at all sure what she wanted Aunty
Moss to be, finding her unpredictable, unreliable, incomprehensible, passionate, ignorant, sly, and dirty. But Moss got
on with the burned child. Perhaps it was Moss who was
working this change, this slight easing, in Therru. With
her, Therru behaved as with everyone – blank, unanswer-
ing, docile in the way an inanimate thing, a stone, is
docile. But the old woman had kept at her, offering her
little sweets and treasures, bribing, coaxing, wheedling.
'Come with Aunty Moss now, dearie! Come along and
Aunty Moss'll show you the prettiest sight you ever
saw . . .'

Moss's nose leaned out over her toothless jaws and thin
lips; there was a wart on her cheek the size of a cherry pit;
her hair was a grey-black tangle of charm-knots and wisps;
and she had a smell as strong and broad and deep and
complicated as the smell of a fox's den. 'Come into the
forest with me, dearie!' said the old witches in the tales
told to the children of Gont. 'Come with me and I'll show
you such a pretty sight!' And then the witch shut the child
in her oven and baked it brown and ate it, or dropped it
into her well, where it hopped and croaked dismally for
ever, or put it to sleep for a hundred years inside a great
stone, till the King's Son should come, the Mage Prince, to
shatter the stone with a word, wake the maiden with a
kiss, and slay the wicked witch . . .

'Come with me, dearie!' And she took the child into the
fields and showed her a lark's nest in the green hay, or
into the marshes to gather white hallows, wild mint, and
blueberries. She did not have to shut the child in an oven,
or change her into a monster, or seal her in stone. That
had all been done already.

She was kind to Therru, but it was a wheedling kindness,
and when they were together it seemed that she talked to
the child a great deal. Tenar did not know what Moss was

telling or teaching her, whether she should let the witch fill the child's head with stuff. *Weak as woman's magic, wicked as woman's magic,* she had heard said a hundred times. And indeed she had seen that the witchery of such women as Moss or Ivy was often weak in sense and sometimes wicked in intent or through ignorance. Village witches, though they might know many spells and charms and some of the great songs, were never trained in the High Arts or the principles of magery. No woman was so trained. Wizardry was a man's work, a man's skill; magic was made by men. There had never been a woman mage. Though some few had called themselves wizard or sorceress, their power had been untrained, strength without art or knowledge, half frivolous, half dangerous.

The ordinary village witch, like Moss, lived on a few words of the True Speech handed down as great treasures from older witches or bought at high cost from sorcerers, and a supply of common spells of finding and mending, much meaningless ritual and mystery-making and gibberish, a solid experiential training in midwifery, bonesetting, and curing animal and human ailments, a good knowledge of herbs mixed with a mess of superstitions – all this built up on whatever native gift she might have of healing, chanting, changing, or spellcasting. Such a mixture might be a good one or a bad one. Some witches were fierce, bitter women, ready to do harm and knowing no reason not to do harm. Most were midwives and healers with a few love potions, fertility charms, and potency spells on the side, and a good deal of quiet cynicism about them. A few, having wisdom though no learning, used their gift purely for good, though they could not tell, as any prentice wizard could, the reason for what they did, and prate of the Balance and the Way of Power to justify their action or abstention. 'I follow my heart,' one of these women had said to Tenar when she was Ogion's ward and pupil. 'Lord Ogion is a great mage. He does you great honour, teaching you. But look and see, child, if all he's taught you isn't finally to follow your heart.'

Tenar had thought even then that the wise woman was right, and yet not altogether right; there was something left out of that. And she still thought so.

Watching Moss with Therru now, she thought Moss was following her heart, but it was a dark, wild, queer heart, like a crow, going its own ways on its own errands. And she thought that Moss might be drawn to Therru not only by kindness but by Therru's hurt, by the harm that had been done her: by violence, by fire.

Nothing Therru did or said, however, showed that she was learning anything from Aunty Moss except where the lark nested and the blueberries grew and how to make cat's cradles one-handed. Therru's right hand had been so eaten by fire that it had healed into a kind of club, the thumb usable only as a pincer, like a crab's claw. But Aunty Moss had an amazing set of cat's cradles for four fingers and a thumb, and rhymes to go with the figures –

> *Churn churn cherry all!*
> *Burn burn bury all!*
> *Come, dragon, come!*

– and the string would form four triangles that flicked into a square ... Therru never sang aloud, but Tenar heard her whispering the chant under her breath as she made the figures, alone, sitting on the doorstep of the mage's house.

And, Tenar thought, what bond linked her, herself, to the child, beyond pity, beyond mere duty to the helpless? Lark would have kept her if Tenar had not taken her. But Tenar had taken her without ever asking herself why. Had she been following her heart? Ogion had asked nothing about the child, but he had said, 'They will fear her.' And Tenar had replied, 'They do,' and truly. Maybe she herself feared the child, as she feared cruelty, and rape, and fire. Was fear the bond that held her?

'Goha,' Therru said, sitting on her heels under the peach tree, looking at the place in the hard summer dirt where she had planted the peach stone, 'what are dragons?'

'Great creatures,' Tenar said, 'like lizards, but longer than a ship – bigger than a house. With wings, like birds. They breathe out fire.'

'Do they come here?'

'No,' Tenar said.

Therru asked no more.

'Has Aunty Moss been telling you about dragons?' Therru shook her head. 'You did,' she said.

'Ah,' said Tenar. And presently, 'The peach you planted will need water to grow. Once a day, till the rains come.'

Therru got up and trotted off around the corner of the house to the well. Her legs and feet were perfect, unhurt. Tenar liked to see her walk or run, the dark, dusty, pretty little feet on the earth. She came back with Ogion's watering-jug, struggling along with it, and tipped out a small flood over the new planting.

'So you remember the story about when people and dragons were all the same ... It told how the humans came here, eastward, but the dragons all stayed in the far western isles. A long, long way away.'

Therru nodded. She did not seem to be paying attention, but when Tenar, saying 'the western isles', pointed out to the sea, Therru turned her face to the high, bright horizon glimpsed between staked bean-plants and the milking shed.

A goat appeared on the roof of the milking shed and arranged itself in profile to them, its head nobly poised; apparently it considered itself to be a mountain goat.

'Sippy's got loose again,' said Tenar.

'Hesssss! Hesssss!' went Therru, imitating Heather's goat call; and Heather herself appeared by the bean-patch fence, saying 'Hesssss!' up at the goat, which ignored her, gazing thoughtfully down at the beans.

Tenar left the three of them to play the catching-Sippy game. She wandered on past the bean patch towards the edge of the cliff and along it. Ogion's house stood apart from the village and closer than any other house to the edge of the Overfell, here a steep, grassy slope broken by ledges and outcrops of rock, where goats could be pastured. As you went on north the drop grew ever steeper, till it began to fall sheer; and on the path the rock of the great ledge showed through the soil, till a mile or so north of the village the Overfell had narrowed to a shelf of reddish sandstone hanging above the sea that undercut its base two thousand feet below.

Nothing grew at that far end of the Overfell but lichens and rockworts and here and there a blue daisy, wind-stunted, like a button dropped on the rough, crumbling stone. Inland of the cliff's edge to the north and east, above a narrow strip of marshland the dark, tremendous side of Gont Mountain rose up, forested almost to the peak. The cliff stood so high above the bay that one must look down to see its outer shores and the vague lowlands of Essary. Beyond them, in all the south and west, there was nothing but the sky above the sea.

Tenar had liked to go there in the years she had lived in Re Albi. Ogion had loved the forests, but she, who had lived in a desert where the only trees for a hundred miles were a gnarled orchard of peach and apple, hand watered in the endless summers, where nothing grew green and moist and easy, where there was nothing but a mountain and a great plain and the sky – she liked the cliff's edge better than the enclosing woods. She liked having nothing at all over her head.

The lichens, the grey rockwort, the stemless daisies, she liked them too; they were familiar. She sat down on the shelving rock a few feet from the edge and looked out to sea as she had used to do. The sun was hot but the ceaseless wind cooled the sweat on her face and arms. She leaned back on her hands and thought of nothing, sun and wind and sky and sea filling her, making her transparent to sun, wind, sky, sea. But her left hand reminded her of its existence, and she looked round to see what was scratching the heel of her hand. It was a tiny thistle, crouched in a crack in the sandstone, barely lifting its colourless spikes into the light and wind. It nodded stiffly as the wind blew, resisting the wind, rooted in rock. She gazed at it for a long time.

When she looked out to sea again she saw, blue in the blue haze where sea met sky, the line of an island: Oranéa, easternmost of the Inner Isles.

She gazed at that faint dream-shape, dreaming, until a bird flying from the west over the sea drew her gaze. It was not a gull, for it flew steadily, and too high to be a pelican. Was it a wild goose, or an albatross, the great, rare voyager of the open sea, come among the islands? She watched the slow beat of the wings, far out and high in the dazzling air. Then she got to her feet, retreating a little from the cliff's edge, and stood motionless, her heart going hard and her breath caught in her throat, watching the sinuous, iron-dark body borne by long, webbed wings as red as fire, the outreaching claws, the coils of smoke fading behind it in the air.

Straight to Gont it flew, straight to the Overfell, straight to her. She saw the glitter of rust-black scales and the gleam of the long eye. She saw the red tongue that was a tongue of flame. The stink of burning filled the wind, as with a hissing roar the dragon, turning to land on the shelf of rock, breathed out a sigh of fire.

Its feet clashed on the rock. The thorny tail, writhing, rattled, and the wings, scarlet where the sun shone through them, stormed and rustled as they folded down to the mailed flanks. The head turned slowly. The dragon looked at the woman who stood there within reach of its scythe-blade talons. The woman looked at the dragon. She felt the heat of its body.

She had been told that men must not look into a dragon's eyes, but that was nothing to her. It gazed straight at her from yellow eyes under armoured carapaces wide-set above the narrow nose and flaring, fuming nostrils. And her small, soft face and dark eyes gazed straight at it.

Neither of them spoke.

The dragon turned its head aside a little so that she was not destroyed when it did speak, or perhaps it laughed – a great 'Hah!' of orange flame.

Then it lowered its body into a crouch and spoke, but not to her.

'*Ahivaraihe, Ged*,' it said, mildly enough, smokily, with a flicker of the burning tongue; and it lowered its head.

Tenar saw for the first time, then, the man astride its back. In the notch between two of the high sword-thorns that rose in a row down its spine he sat, just behind the neck and above the shoulders where the wings had root. His hands were clenched on the rust-dark mail of the dragon's neck and his head leaned against the base of the sword-thorn, as if he were asleep.

'*Ahi eheraihe, Ged!*' said the dragon, a little louder, its long mouth seeming always to smile, showing the teeth as long as Tenar's forearm, yellowish, with white, sharp tips.

The man did not stir.

The dragon turned its long head and looked again at Tenar.

'*Sobriost*,' it said, in a whisper of steel sliding over steel.

That word of the Language of the Making she knew. Ogion had taught her all she would learn of that tongue. Go up, the dragon said: mount! And she saw the steps to mount. The taloned foot, the crooked elbow, the shoulder-joint, the first musculature of the wing: four steps.

She too said, 'Hah!' but not in a laugh, only trying to

get her breath, which kept sticking in her throat; and she lowered her head a moment to stop her dizzy faintness. Then she went forward, past the talons and the long lipless mouth and the long yellow eye, and mounted the shoulder of the dragon. She took the man's arm. He did not move, but surely he was not dead, for the dragon had brought him here and spoken to him. 'Come on,' she said, and then seeing his face as she loosened the clenched grip of his left hand, 'Come on, Ged. Come on . . .'

He raised his head a little. His eyes were open, but unseeing. She had to climb around him, scratching her legs on the hot, mailed hide of the dragon, and unclench his right hand from a horny knob at the base of the sword-thorn. She got him to take hold of her arms, and so could carry-drag him down those four strange stairs to earth.

He roused enough to try to hold on to her, but there was no strength in him. He sprawled off the dragon on to the rock like a sack unloaded, and lay there.

The dragon turned its immense head and in a completely animal gesture nosed and sniffed at the man's body.

It lifted its head, and its wings too half lifted with a vast, metallic sound. It shifted its feet away from Ged, closer to the edge of the cliff. Turning back the head on the thorned neck, it stared once more directly at Tenar, and its voice like the dry roar of a kiln-fire spoke: '*Thesse Kalessin.*'

The sea wind whistled in the dragon's half-open wings.

'*Thesse Tenar*,' the woman said in a clear, shaking voice.

The dragon looked away, westward, over the sea. It twitched its long body with a clink and clash of iron scales, then abruptly opened its wings, crouched, and leapt straight out from the cliff on to the wind. The dragging tail scored the sandstone as it passed. The red wings beat down, lifted, and beat down, and already Kalessin was far from land, flying straight, flying west.

517

Tenar watched it till it was no larger than a wild goose or a gull. The air was cold. When the dragon had been there it had been hot, furnace-hot, with the dragon's inward fire. Tenar shivered. She sat down on the rock beside Ged and began to cry. She hid her face in her arms and wept aloud. 'What can I do?' she cried. 'What can I do now?'

Presently she wiped her eyes and nose on her sleeve, put back her hair with both hands, and turned to the man who lay beside her. He lay so still, so easy on the bare rock, as if he might lie there for ever.

Tenar sighed. There was nothing she could do, but there was always the next thing to be done.

She could not carry him. She would have to get help. That meant leaving him alone. It seemed to her that he was too near the cliff's edge. If he tried to get up he might fall, weak and dizzy as he would be. How could she move him? He did not rouse at all when she spoke and touched him. She took him under the shoulders and tried to pull him, and to her surprise succeeded; dead weight as he was, the weight was not much. Resolute, she dragged him ten or fifteen feet inland, off the bare rock shelf on to a bit of dirt, where dry bunchgrass gave some illusion of shelter. There she had to leave him. She could not run, for her legs shook and her breath still came in sobs. She walked as fast as she could to Ogion's house, calling out as she approached it to Heather, Moss, and Therru.

The child appeared around the milking shed and stood, as her way was, obedient to Tenar's call but not coming forward to greet or be greeted.

'Therru, run into town and ask anyone to come – anybody strong – There's a man hurt on the cliff.'

Therru stood there. She had never gone alone into the village. She was frozen between obedience and fear. Tenar saw that and said, 'Is Aunty Moss here? Is Heather? The three of us can carry him. Only, quick, quick, Therru!' She felt that if she let Ged lie unprotected there he would surely die. He would be gone when she came back – dead, fallen, taken by dragons. Anything could happen. She must hurry before it happened. Flint had died of a stroke in his fields and she had not been with him. He had died alone. The shepherd had found him lying by the gate. Ogion had died and she could not keep him from dying, she could not give him breath. Ged had come home to die and it was the end of everything, there was nothing left, nothing to be done, but she must do it. 'Quick, Therru! Bring anyone!'

She started shakily towards the village herself, but saw old Moss hurrying across the pasture, stumping along with her thick hawthorn stick. 'Did you call me, dearie?'

Moss's presence was an immediate relief. She began to get her breath and be able to think. Moss wasted no time in questions, but hearing there was a man hurt who must be moved, got the heavy canvas mattress-cover that Tenar had been airing, and lugged it out to the end of the Overfell. She and Tenar rolled Ged on to it and were dragging this conveyance laboriously homeward when Heather came trotting along, followed by Therru and Sippy. Heather was young and strong, and with her help they could lift the canvas like a litter and carry the man to the house.

Tenar and Therru slept in the alcove in the west wall of the long single room. There was only Ogion's bed at the far end, covered now with a heavy linen sheet. There they laid the man. Tenar put Ogion's blanket over him, while Moss muttered charms around the bed, and Heather and Therru stood and stared.

'Let him be now,' said Tenar, leading them all to the front part of the house.

'Who is he?' Heather asked.

'What was he doing on the Overfell?' Moss asked.

'You know him, Moss. He was Ogion's – Aihal's prentice, once.'

The witch shook her head. 'That was the lad from Ten Alders, dearie,' she said. 'The one that's Archmage in Roke, now.'

Tenar nodded.

'No, dearie,' said Moss. 'This looks like him. But isn't him. This man's no mage. Not even a sorcerer.'

Heather looked from one to the other, entertained. She did not understand most things people said, but she liked to hear them say them.

'But I know him, Moss. It's Sparrowhawk.' Saying the name, Ged's use-name, released a tenderness in her, so that for the first time she thought and felt that this was he indeed, and that all the years since she had first seen him were their bond. She saw a light like a star in darkness, underground, long ago, and his face in the light. 'I know him, Moss.' She smiled, and then smiled more broadly. 'He's the first man I ever saw,' she said.

Moss mumbled and shifted. She did not like to contradict 'Mistress Goha', but she was perfectly unconvinced. 'There's tricks, disguises, transformations, changes,' she said. 'Better be careful, dearie. How did he get where you found him, away out there? Did any see him come through the village?'

'None of you – saw –?'

They stared at her. She tried to say 'the dragon' and could not. Her lips and tongue would not form the word. But a word formed itself with them, making itself with her mouth and breath. 'Kalessin,' she said.

Therru was staring at her. A wave of warmth, heat, seemed to flow from the child, as if she were in fever. She said nothing, but moved her lips as if repeating the name, and that fever heat burned around her.

'Tricks!' Moss said. 'Now that our mage is gone there'll be all kinds of tricksters coming round.'

'I came from Atuan to Havnor, from Havnor to Gont, with Sparrowhawk, in an open boat,' Tenar said drily.

'You saw him when he brought me here, Moss. He wasn't archmage then. But he was the same, the same man. Are there other scars like those?'

Confronted, the older woman became still, collecting herself. She glanced at Therru. 'No,' she said. 'But –'

'Do you think I wouldn't know him?'

Moss twisted her mouth, frowned, rubbed one thumb with the other, looking at her hands. 'There's evil things in the world, mistress,' she said. 'A thing that takes a man's form and body, but his soul's gone – eaten –'

'The gebbeth?'

Moss cringed at the word spoken openly. She nodded. 'They do say, once the mage Sparrowhawk came here, long ago, before you came with him. And a thing of darkness came with him – following him. Maybe it still does. Maybe –'

'The dragon who brought him here,' Tenar said, 'called him by his true name. And I know that name.' Wrath at the witch's obstinate suspicion rang in her voice.

Moss stood mute. Her silence was better argument than her words.

'Maybe the shadow on him is his death,' Tenar said. 'Maybe he's dying. I don't know. If Ogion –'

At the thought of Ogion she was in tears again, thinking how Ged had come too late. She swallowed the tears and went to the woodbox for kindling for the fire. She gave Therru the kettle to fill, touching her face as she spoke to her. The seamed and slabby scars were hot to touch, but the child was not feverish. Tenar knelt to make the fire. Somebody in this fine household – a witch, a widow, a cripple, and a half-wit – had to do what must be done, and not frighten the child with weeping. But the dragon was gone, and was there nothing to come any more but death?

5. Bettering

He lay like the dead but was not dead. Where had he been? What had he come through? That night, in firelight, Tenar took the stained, worn, sweat-stiffened clothes off him. She washed him and let him lie naked between the linen sheet and the blanket of soft, heavy goat's-wool. Though a short, slight-built man, he had been compact, vigorous; now he was thin as if worn down to the bone, worn away, fragile. Even the scars that ridged his shoulder and the left side of his face from temple to jaw seemed lessened, silvery. And his hair was grey.

I'm sick of mourning, Tenar thought. Sick of mourning, sick of grief. I will not grieve for him! Didn't he come to me riding the dragon?

Once I meant to kill him, she thought. Now I'll make him live, if I can. She looked at him then with a challenge in her eye, and no pity.

'Which of us saved the other from the Labyrinth, Ged?'

Unhearing, unmoving, he slept. She was very tired. She bathed in the water she had heated to wash him with, and crept into bed beside the little, warm, silky silence that was Therru asleep. She slept, and her sleep opened out into a vast windy space hazy with rose and gold. She flew. Her voice called, 'Kalessin!' A voice answered, calling from the gulfs of light.

When she woke, the birds were chirping in the fields and on the roof. Sitting up she saw the light of morning through the gnarled glass of the low window looking west. There was something in her, some seed or glimmer, too small to look at or think about, new. Therru was still asleep. Tenar sat by her looking out the small window at cloud and sunlight, thinking of her daughter Apple, trying to remember Apple as a baby. Only the faintest glimpse, vanishing as she turned to it – the small, fat body shaking with a laugh, the wispy, flying hair ... And the second baby, Spark he got called as a joke, because he'd been struck off Flint. She did not know his true name. He had been as sickly a child as Apple had been a sound one. Born early and very small, he had nearly died of the croup at two months, and for two years after that it had been like rearing a fledgling sparrow, you never knew if he would be alive in the morning. But he held on, the little spark wouldn't go out. And growing, he became a wiry boy, endlessly active, driven; no use on the farm; no patience with animals, plants, people; using words for his needs only, never for pleasure and the give and take of love and knowledge.

Ogion had come by on his wanderings when Apple was thirteen and Spark eleven. Ogion had named Apple then, in the springs of the Kaheda at the valley's head; beautiful she had walked in the green water, the woman-child, and he had given her her true name, Hayohe. He had stayed on at Oak Farm a day or two, and had asked the boy if he wanted to go wandering a little with him in the forests. Spark merely shook his head. 'What would you do if you could?' the mage had asked him, and the boy said what he had never been able to say to father or mother: 'Go to sea.' So after Beech gave him his true name, three years later, he shipped as a sailor aboard a merchantman trading from Valmouth to Oranéa and North Havnor. From time to time he would come to the farm, but not often and never for long, though at his father's death it would be his property. He was white-skinned like Tenar, but grew tall like Flint, with a narrow face. He had not told his parents his true name. There might never be anyone he told it to. Tenar had not seen him for three years now. He might or might not know of his father's death. He might be dead himself, drowned, but she thought not. He would carry that spark his life over the waters, through the storms.

That was what it was like in her now, a spark; like the bodily certainty of a conception; a change, a new thing. What it was she would not ask. You did not ask. You did not ask a true name. It was given you, or not.

She got up and dressed. Early as it was, it was warm, and she built no fire. She sat in the doorway to drink a cup of milk and watch the shadow of Gont Mountain draw inward from the sea. There was as little wind as there could be on this air-swept shelf of rock, and the breeze had a midsummer feel, soft and rich, smelling of the meadows. There was a sweetness in the air, a change.

'All changed!' the old man had whispered, dying, joyful. Laying his hand on hers, giving her the gift, his name, giving it away.

'Aihal!' she whispered. For answer a couple of goats bleated, out behind the milking shed, waiting for Heather to come. 'Be-eh,' one said, and the other, deeper, metallic, 'Bla-ah! Bla-ah!' Trust a goat, Flint used to say, to spoil anything. Flint, a shepherd, had disliked goats. But Sparrowhawk had been a goatherd, here across the mountain, as a boy.

She went inside. She found Therru standing gazing at the sleeping man. She put her arm around the child, and though Therru usually shrank from or was passive to touch or caress, this time she accepted it and perhaps even leaned a little to Tenar.

Ged lay in the same exhausted, overwhelmed sleep. His face was turned to expose the four white scars that marked it.

'Was he burned?' Therru whispered.

Tenar did not answer at once. She did not know what those scars were. She had asked him long ago, in the Painted Room of the Labyrinth of Atuan, jeering: 'A

524

dragon?' And he had answered seriously, 'Not a dragon. One of the kinship of the Nameless Ones; but I learned his name . . .' And that was all she knew. But she knew what 'burned' meant to the child.

'Yes,' she said.

Therru continued to gaze at him. She had cocked her head to bring her one seeing eye to bear, which made her look like a little bird, a sparrow or a finch.

'Come along, finchling, birdlet, sleep's what he needs, you need a peach. Is there a peach ripe this morning?'

Therru trotted out to see, and Tenar followed her.

Eating her peach, the child studied the place where she had planted the peach pit yesterday. She was evidently disappointed that no tree had grown there, but she said nothing.

'Water it,' said Tenar.

Aunty Moss arrived in the midmorning. One of her skills as a witch-handywoman was basket making, using the rushes of Overfell Marsh, and Tenar had asked her to teach her the art. As a child in Atuan, Tenar had learned how to learn. As a stranger in Gont, she had found that people liked to teach. She had learned to be taught and so to be accepted, her foreignness forgiven.

Ogion had taught her his knowledge, and then Flint had taught her his. It was her habit of life, to learn. There seemed always to be a great deal to be learned, more than she would have believed when she was a prentice-priestess or the pupil of a mage.

The rushes had been soaking, and this morning they were to split them, an exacting but not a complicated business, leaving plenty of attention to spare.

'Aunty,' said Tenar as they sat on the doorstep with the bowl of soaking rushes between them and a mat before them to lay the split ones on, 'how do you tell if a man's a wizard or not?'

Moss's reply was circuitous, beginning with the usual gnomics and obscurities. 'Deep knows deep,' she said, deeply, and 'What's born will speak,' and she told a story about the ant that picked up a tiny end of hair from the floor of a palace and ran off to the ants' nest with it, and in the night the nest glowed underground like a star, for the hair was from the head of the great mage Brost. But only the wise could see the glowing anthill. To common eyes it was all dark.

'One needs training, then,' said Tenar.

Maybe, maybe not, was the gist of Moss's dark reply. 'Some are born with that gift,' she said. 'Even when they don't know it, it will be there. Like the hair of the mage in the hole in the ground, it will shine.'

'Yes,' said Tenar. 'I've seen that.' She split and resplit a reed cleanly and laid the splints on the mat. 'How do you know, then, when a man is *not* a wizard?'

'It's not there,' Moss said, 'it's not there, dearie. The power. See now. If I've got eyes in my head I can see that you have eyes, can't I? And if you're blind I'll see that. And if you've only got one eye, like the little one, or if you've got three, I'll see 'em, won't I? But if I don't have an eye to see with, I won't know if you do till you tell me. But I do. I see, I know. The third eye!' She touched her forehead and gave a loud, dry chuckle, like a hen triumphant over an egg. She was pleased with having found the words to say what she wanted to say. A good deal of her obscurity and cant, Tenar had begun to realize, was mere ineptness with words and ideas. Nobody had ever taught her to think consecutively. Nobody had ever listened to what she said. All that was expected, all that was wanted of her was muddle, mystery, mumbling. She was a witchwoman. She had nothing to do with clear meaning.

'I understand,' Tenar said. 'Then – maybe this is a question you don't want to answer – then when you look at a person with your third eye, with your power, you see their power – or don't see it?'

'It's more a knowing,' Moss said. 'Seeing is just a way of saying it. 'Tisn't like I see you, I see this rush, I see the mountain there. It's a knowing. I know what's in you and not in that poor hollow-headed Heather. I know what's in the dear child and not in him in yonder. I know –' She could not get any farther with it. She mumbled and spat. 'Any witch worth a hairpin knows another witch!' she said finally, plainly, impatiently.

'You recognize each other.'

Moss nodded. 'Aye, that's it. That's the word. Recognize.'

'And a wizard would recognize your power, would know you for a sorceress –'

But Moss was grinning at her, a black cave of a grin in a cobweb of wrinkles.

'Dearie,' she said, 'a man, you mean, a wizardly man? What's a man of power to do with us?'

'But Ogion –'

'Lord Ogion was kind,' Moss said, without irony.

They split rushes for a while in silence.

'Don't cut your thumb on 'em, dearie,' Moss said.

'Ogion taught me. As if I weren't a girl. As if I'd been his prentice, like Sparrowhawk. He taught me the Language of the Making, Moss. What I asked him, he told me.'

'There wasn't no other like him.'

'It was I who wouldn't be taught. I left him. What did I want with his books? What good were they to me? I wanted to live, I wanted a man, I wanted my children, I wanted my life.'

She split reeds neatly, quickly, with her nail.

'And I got it,' she said.

'Take with the right hand, throw away with the left,' the witch said. 'Well, dearie mistress, who's to say? Who's to say? Wanting a man got me into awful troubles more than once. But wanting to get married, never! No, no. None of that for me.'

'Why not?' Tenar demanded.

Taken aback, Moss said simply, 'Why, what man'd marry a witch?' And then, with a sidelong chewing motion of her jaw, like a sheep shifting its cud, 'And what witch'd marry a man?'

They split rushes.

'What's wrong with men?' Tenar inquired cautiously.

As cautiously, lowering her voice, Moss replied, 'I don't know, my dearie. I've thought on it. Often I've thought on it. The best I can say it is like this. A man's in his skin, see, like a nut in its shell.' She held up her long, bent, wet fingers as if holding a walnut. 'It's hard and strong, that shell, and it's all full of him. Full of grand man-meat, man-self. And that's all. That's all there is. It's all him and nothing else, inside.'

Tenar pondered awhile and finally asked, 'But if he's a wizard —'

'Then it's all his power, inside. His power's himself, see. That's how it is with him. And that's all. When his power goes, he's gone. Empty.' She cracked the unseen walnut and tossed the shells away. 'Nothing.'

'And a woman, then?'

'Oh, well, dearie, a woman's a different thing entirely. Who knows where a woman begins and ends? Listen, mistress, I have roots, I have roots deeper than this island. Deeper than the sea, older than the raising of the lands. I go back into the dark.' Moss's eyes shone with a weird brightness in their red rims and her voice sang like an instrument. 'I go back into the dark! Before the moon I was. No one knows, no one knows, no one can say what I am, what a woman is, a woman of power, a woman's power, deeper than the roots of trees, deeper than the roots of islands, older than the Making, older than the moon. Who dares ask questions of the dark? Who'll ask the dark its name?'

The old woman was rocking, chanting, lost in her

incantation; but Tenar sat upright, and split a reed down the centre with her thumbnail.

'I will,' she said.

She split another reed.

'I lived long enough in the dark,' she said.

She looked in from time to time to see that Sparrowhawk was still sleeping. She did so now. When she sat down again with Moss, wanting not to return to what they had been saying, for the older woman looked dour and sullen, she said, 'This morning when I woke up I felt, oh, as if a new wind were blowing. A change. Maybe just the weather. Did you feel that?'

But Moss would not say yes or no. 'Many a wind blows here on the Overfell, some good, some ill. Some bears clouds and some fair weather, and some brings news to those who can hear it, but those who won't listen can't hear. Who am I to know, an old woman without mage-learning, without book-learning? All my learning's in the earth, in the dark earth. Under their feet, the proud ones. Under their feet, the proud lords and mages. Why should they look down, the learned ones? What does an old witchwoman know?'

She would be a formidable enemy, Tenar thought, and was a difficult friend.

'Aunty,' she said, taking up a reed, 'I grew up among women. Only women. In the Kargish lands, far east, in Atuan. I was taken from my family as a little child to be brought up a priestess in a place in the desert. I don't know what name it has, all we called it in our language was just that, the place. The only place I knew. There were a few soldiers guarding it, but they couldn't come inside the walls. And we couldn't go outside the walls. Only in a group, all women and girls, with eunuchs guarding us, keeping the men out of sight.'

'What's those you said?'

'Eunuchs?' Tenar had used the Kargish word without thinking. 'Gelded men,' she said.

The witch stared, and said, '*Tsekh!*' and made the sign to avert evil. She sucked her lips. She had been startled out of her resentment.

'One of them was the nearest to a mother I had there . . . But do you see, Aunty, I never saw a man till I was a woman grown. Only girls and women. And yet I didn't know what women are, because women were all I did know. Like men who live among men, sailors, and soldiers, and mages on Roke – do they know what men are? How can they, if they never speak to a woman?'

'Do they take 'em and do 'em like rams and he-goats,' said Moss, 'like that, with a gelding knife?'

Horror, the macabre, and a gleam of vengeance had won out over both anger and reason. Moss didn't want to pursue any topic but that of eunuchs.

Tenar could not tell her much. She realized that she had never thought about the matter. When she was a girl in Atuan, there had been gelded men; and one of them had loved her tenderly, and she him; and she had killed him to escape from him. Then she had come to the Archipelago, where there were no eunuchs, and had forgotten them, sunk them in darkness with Manan's body.

'I suppose,' she said, trying to satisfy Moss's craving for details, 'that they took young boys, and –' But she stopped. Her hands stopped working.

'Like Therru,' she said after a long pause. 'What's a child for? What's it there for? To be used. To be raped, to be gelded – Listen, Moss. When I lived in the dark places, that was what they did there. And when I came here, I thought I'd come out into the light. I learned the true words. And I had my man, I bore my children, I lived well. In the broad daylight. And in the broad daylight, they did that – to the child. In the meadows by the river. The river that rises from the spring where Ogion named my daughter.

In the sunlight. I am trying to find out where I can live, Moss. Do you know what I mean? What I'm trying to say?'

'Well, well,' the older woman said; and after a while, 'Dearie, there's misery enough without going looking for it.' And seeing Tenar's hands shake as she tried to split a stubborn reed, she said, again, 'Don't cut your thumb on 'em, dearie.'

It was not till the next day that Ged roused at all. Moss, who was very skilful though appallingly unclean as a nurse, had succeeded in spooning some meat-broth into him. 'Starving,' she said, 'and dried up with thirst. Wherever he was, they didn't do much eating and drinking.' And after appraising him again, 'He'll be too far gone already, I think. They get weak, see, and can't even drink, though it's all they need. I've known a great strong man to die like that. All in a few days, shrivelled to a shadow, like.'

But through relentless patience she got a few spoonfuls of her brew of meat and herbs into him. 'Now we'll see,' she said. 'Too late, I guess. He's slipping away.' She spoke without regret, perhaps with relish. The man was nothing to her; a death was an event. Maybe she could bury this mage. They had not let her bury the old one.

Tenar was salving his hands, the next day, when he woke. He must have ridden long on Kalessin's back, for his fierce grip on the iron scales had scoured the skin off his palms, and the inner side of the fingers was cut and recut. Sleeping, he kept his hands clenched as if they would not let go the absent dragon. She had to force his fingers open gently to wash and salve the sores. As she did that, he cried out and started, reaching out, as if he felt himself falling. His eyes opened. She spoke quietly. He looked at her.

'Tenar,' he said without smiling, in pure recognition

beyond emotion. And it gave her pure pleasure, like a sweet flavour or a flower, that there was still one man living who knew her name, and that it was this man.

She leaned forward and kissed his cheek. 'Lie still,' she said. 'Let me finish this.' He obeyed, drifting back into sleep soon, this time with his hands open and relaxed.

Later, falling asleep beside Therru in the night, she thought, But I never kissed him before. And the thought shook her. At first she disbelieved it. Surely, in all the years – Not in the Tombs, but after, travelling together in the mountains – In *Lookfar*, when they sailed together to Havnor – When he brought her here to Gont –?

No. Nor had Ogion ever kissed her, or she him. He had called her daughter, and had loved her, but had not touched her; and she, brought up as a solitary, untouched priestess, a holy thing, had not sought touch, or had not known she sought it. She would lean her forehead or her cheek for a moment on Ogion's open hand, and he might stroke her hair, once, very lightly.

And Ged never even that.

Did I never *think* of it? she asked herself in a kind of incredulous awe.

She did not know. As she tried to think of it, a horror, a sense of transgression, came on her very strongly, and then died away, meaningless. Her lips knew the slightly rough, dry, cool skin of his cheek near the mouth on the right side, and only that knowledge had importance, was of weight.

She slept. She dreamed that a voice called her, 'Tenar! Tenar!' and that she replied, crying like a seabird, flying in the light above the sea; but she did not know what name she called.

Sparrowhawk disappointed Aunty Moss. He stayed alive. After a day or two she gave him up for saved. She came and fed him her broth of goat's-meat and roots and herbs, propping him against her, surrounding him with the powerful smell of her body, spooning life into him, and grumbling. Although he had recognized her and called her by her use-name, and she could not deny that he seemed to be the man called Sparrowhawk, she wanted to deny it. She did not like him. He was all wrong, she said. Tenar respected the witch's sagacity enough that this troubled her, but she could not find any such suspicion in herself, only the pleasure of his being there and of his slow return to life. 'When he's himself again, you'll see,' she said to Moss.

'Himself!' Moss said, and she made that gesture with her fingers of breaking and dropping a nutshell.

He asked, pretty soon, about Ogion. Tenar had dreaded that question. She had told herself and nearly convinced herself that he would not ask, that he would know as mages knew, as even the wizards of Gont Port and Re Albi had known when Ogion died. But on the fourth morning he was lying awake when she came to him, and looking up at her, he said, 'This is Ogion's house.'

'Aihal's house,' she said, as easily as she could; it still was not easy for her to speak the mage's true name. She did not know if Ged had known that name. Surely he had. Ogion would have told him, or had not needed to tell him.

For a while he did not react, and when he spoke it was without expression. 'Then he is dead.'

'Ten days ago.'

He lay looking before him as if pondering, trying to think something out.

'When did I come here?'

She had to lean close to understand him.

'Four days ago, in the evening of the day.'

'There was no one else in the mountains,' he said. Then his body winced and shuddered as if in pain or the intolerable memory of pain. He shut his eyes, frowning, and took a deep breath.

As his strength returned little by little, that frown, the held breath and clenched hands, became familiar to Tenar. Strength returned to him but not ease, not health.

He sat on the doorstep of the house in the sunlight of the summer afternoon. It was the longest journey he had yet taken from the bed. He sat on the threshold, looking out into the day, and Tenar, coming around the house from the bean patch, looked at him. He still had an ashy, shadowy look to him. It was not the grey hair only, but some quality of skin and bone, and there was nothing much to him but that. There was no light in his eyes. Yet this shadow, this ashen man, was the same whose face she had seen first in the radiance of his own power, the strong face with hawk nose and fine mouth, a handsome man. He had always been a proud, handsome man.

She came on towards him.

'The sunlight's what you need,' she said to him, and he nodded, but his hands were clenched as he sat in the flood of summer warmth.

He was so silent with her that she thought maybe it was her presence that troubled him. Maybe he could not be at ease with her as he had used to be. He was Archmage now, after all – she kept forgetting that. And it was twenty-five years since they had walked in the mountains of Atuan and sailed together in *Lookfar* across the eastern sea.

'Where is *Lookfar*?' she asked, suddenly, surprised by the thought of it, and then thought, But how stupid of me! All those years ago, and he's Archmage, he wouldn't have that little boat now.

'In Selidor,' he answered, his face set in its steady and incomprehensible misery.

As long ago as for ever, as far away as Selidor . . .

'The farthest island,' she said; it was half a question.

'The farthest west,' he said.

*

They were sitting at table, having finished the evening meal. Therru had gone outside to play.

'It was from Selidor that you came, then, on Kalessin?'

When she spoke the dragon's name again it spoke itself, shaping her mouth to its shape and sound, making her breath soft fire.

At the name, he looked up at her, one intense glance, which made her realize that he did not usually meet her eyes at all. He nodded. Then, with a laborious honesty, he corrected his assent: 'From Selidor to Roke. And then from Roke to Gont.'

A thousand miles? Ten thousand miles? She had no idea. She had seen the great maps in the treasuries of Havnor, but no one had taught her numbers, distances. *As far away as Selidor* . . . And could the flight of a dragon be counted in miles?

'Ged,' she said, using his true name since they were alone, 'I know you've been in great pain and peril. And if you don't want, maybe you can't, maybe you shouldn't tell me – but if I knew, if I knew something of it, I'd be more help to you, maybe. I'd like to be. And they'll be coming soon from Roke for you, sending a ship for the Archmage, what do I know, sending a dragon for you! And you'll be gone again. And we'll never have talked.' As she spoke she clenched her own hands at the falseness of her tone and words. To joke about the dragon – to whine like an accusing wife!

He was looking down at the table, sullen, enduring, like a farmer after a hard day in the fields faced with some domestic squall.

'Nobody will come from Roke, I think,' he said, and it cost him effort enough that it was a while before he went on. 'Give me time.'

She thought it was all he was going to say, and replied, 'Yes, of course. I'm sorry,' and was rising to clear the table when he said, still looking down, not clearly, 'I have that, now.'

Then he too got up, and brought his dish to the sink,
and finished clearing the table. He washed the dishes while
Tenar put the food away. And that interested her. She had
been comparing him to Flint; but Flint had never washed a
dish in his life. Women's work. But Ged and Ogion had
lived here, bachelors, without women; everywhere Ged
had lived, it was without women; so he did the 'women's
work' and thought nothing about it. It would be a pity,
she thought, if he did think about it, if he started fearing
that his dignity hung by a dishcloth.

Nobody came for him from Roke. When they spoke of
it, there had scarcely been time for any ship but one with
the magewind in her sails all the way; but the days went
on, and still there was no message or sign to him. It
seemed strange to her that they would let their archmage
go untroubled so long. He must have forbidden them to
send to him; or perhaps he had hidden himself here with
his wizardry, so that they did not know where he was, and
so that he could not be recognized. For the villagers paid
curiously little attention to him still.

That no one had come down from the mansion of the
Lord of Re Albi was less surprising. The lords of that
house had never been on good terms with Ogion. Women
of the house had been, so the village tales went, adepts of
dark arts. One had married a northern lord, they said,
who buried her alive under a stone; another had meddled
with the unborn child in her womb, trying to make it a
creature of power, and indeed it had spoken words as it
was born, but it had no bones. 'Like a little bag of skin,'
the midwife whispered in the village, 'a little bag with eyes
and a voice, and it never sucked, but it spoke in some
strange tongue, and died . . .' Whatever the truth of such
tales, the Lords of Re Albi had always held aloof. Companion of the mage Sparrowhawk, ward of the mage Ogion,
bringer of the Ring of Erreth-Akbe to Havnor, Tenar
might have been asked to stay, it would seem, at the

mansion house when she first came to Re Albi; but she had not. She had lived instead, to her own delight, alone in a tiny cottage that belonged to the village weaver, Fan, and she saw the people of the great house seldom and at a distance. There was now no lady of the house at all, Moss told her, only the old lord, very old, and his grandson, and the young wizard, called Aspen, whom they had hired from the School on Roke.

Since Ogion was buried, with Aunty Moss's talisman in his hand, under the beech tree by the mountain path, Tenar had not seen Aspen. Strange as it seemed, he did not know the Archmage of Earthsea was in his own village, or, if he knew it, for some reason kept away. And the wizard of Gont Port, who had also come to bury Ogion, had never come back either. Even if he did not know that Ged was here, surely he knew who she was, the White Lady, who had worn the Ring of Erreth-Akbe on her wrist, who had made whole the Rune of Peace – And how many years ago was that, old woman! she said to herself. Is your nose out of joint?

All the same, it was she who had told them Ogion's true name. It seemed some courtesy was owing.

But wizards, as such, had nothing to do with courtesy. They were men of power. It was only power that they dealt with. And what power had she now? What had she ever had? As a girl, a priestess, she had been a vessel: the power of the dark places had run through her, used her, left her empty, untouched. As a young woman she had been taught a powerful knowledge by a powerful man and had laid it aside, turned away from it, not touched it. As a woman she had chosen and had the powers of a woman, in their time, and the time was past; her wiving and mothering was done. There was nothing in her, no power, for anybody to recognize.

But a dragon had spoken to her. 'I am Kalessin,' it had said, and she had answered, 'I am Tenar.'

'What is a dragonlord?' she had asked Ged, in the dark place, the Labyrinth, trying to deny his power, trying to make him admit hers; and he had answered with the plain honesty that forever disarmed her, 'A man dragons will talk to.'

So she was a woman dragons would talk to. Was that the new thing, the folded knowledge, the light seed, that she felt in herself, waking beneath the small window that looked west?

A few days after that brief conversation at table, she was weeding Ogion's garden patch, rescuing the onions he had set out in spring from the weeds of summer. Ged let himself in the gate in the high fence that kept the goats out, and set to weeding at the other end of the row. He worked awhile and then sat back, looking down at his hands.

'Let them have time to heal,' Tenar said mildly.

He nodded.

The tall staked bean-plants in the next row were flowering. Their scent was very sweet. He sat with his thin arms on his knees, staring into the sunlit tangle of vines and flowers and hanging beanpods. She spoke as she worked: 'When Aihal died, he said, "All changed . . ." And since his death, I've mourned him, I've grieved, but something lifts up my grief. Something is coming to be born – has been set free. I know in my sleep and my first waking, something is changed.'

'Yes,' he said. 'An evil ended. And . . .'

After a long silence he began again. He did not look at her, but his voice sounded for the first time like the voice she remembered, easy, quiet, with the dry Gontish accent.

'Do you remember, Tenar, when we came first to Havnor?'

Would I forget? her heart said, but she was silent for fear of driving him back into silence.

'We brought *Lookfar* in and came up on to the quay –

the steps are marble. And the people, all the people – and you held up your arm to show them the Ring . . .'

– And held your hand; I was terrified beyond terror: the faces, the voices, the colours, the towers and the flags and banners, the gold and silver and music, and all I knew was you – in the whole world all I knew was you, there by me as we walked . . .

'The stewards of the King's House brought us to the foot of the Tower of Erreth-Akbe, through the streets full of people. And we went up the high steps, the two of us alone. Do you remember?'

She nodded. She laid her hands on the earth she had been weeding, feeling its grainy coolness.

'I opened the door. It was heavy, it stuck at first. And we went in. Do you remember?'

It was as if he asked for reassurance – Did it happen? Do I remember?

'It was a great, high hall,' she said. 'It made me think of my Hall, where I was eaten, but only because it was so high. The light came down from windows away up in the tower. Shafts of sunlight crossing like swords.'

'And the throne,' he said.

'The throne, yes, all gold and crimson. But empty. Like the throne in the Hall in Atuan.'

'Not now,' he said. He looked across the green shoots of onion at her. His face was strained, wistful, as if he named a joy he could not grasp. 'There is a king in Havnor,' he said, 'at the centre of the world. What was foretold has been fulfilled. The Rune is healed, and the world is whole. The days of peace have come. He –'

He stopped and looked down, clenching his hands.

'He carried me from death to life. Arren of Enlad. Lebannen of the songs to be sung. He has taken his true name, Lebannen, King of Earthsea.'

'Is that it, then,' she asked, kneeling, watching him – 'the joy, the coming into light?'

He did not answer.

A king in Havnor, she thought, and said aloud, 'A king in Havnor!'

The vision of the beautiful city was in her, the wide streets, the towers of marble, the tiled and bronze roofs, the white-sailed ships in harbour, the marvellous throne room where sunlight fell like swords, the wealth and dignity and harmony, the order that was kept there. From that bright centre, she saw order going outward like the perfect rings on water, like the straightness of a paved street or a ship sailing before the wind: a going the way it should go, a bringing to peace.

'You did well, dear friend,' she said.

He made a little gesture as if to stop her words, and then turned away, pressing his hand to his mouth. She could not bear to see his tears. She bent to her work. She pulled a weed, and another, and the tough root broke. She dug with her hands, trying to find the root of the weed in the harsh soil, in the dark of the earth.

'Goha,' said Therru's weak, cracked voice at the gate, and Tenar looked round. The child's half-face looked straight at her from the seeing eye and the blinded eye. Tenar thought, Shall I tell her that there is a king in Havnor?

She got up and went to the gate to spare Therru from trying to make herself heard. When she lay in the fire unconscious, Beech said, the child had breathed in fire. 'Her voice is burned away,' he explained.

'I was watching Sippy,' Therru whispered, 'but she got out of the broom-pasture. I can't find her.'

It was as long a speech as she had ever made. She was trembling from running and from trying not to cry. We can't all be weeping at once, Tenar said to herself – this is stupid, we can't have this! – 'Sparrowhawk!' she said, turning, 'there's a goat got out.'

He stood up at once and came to the gate.

'Try the springhouse,' he said.

He looked at Therru as if he did not see her hideous scars, as if he scarcely saw her at all: a child who had lost a goat, who needed to find a goat. It was the goat he saw. 'Or she's off to join the village flock,' he said.

Therru was already running to the springhouse.

'Is she your daughter?' he asked Tenar. He had never before said a word about the child, and all Tenar could think for a moment was how very strange men were.

'No, nor my granddaughter. But my child,' she said. What was it that made her jeer at him, jibe at him, again?

He let himself out the gate, just as Sippy dashed towards them, a brown-and-white flash, followed far behind by Therru.

'I Ii!' Ged shouted suddenly, and with a leap he blocked the goat's way, heading her directly to the open gate and Tenar's arms. She managed to grab Sippy's loose leather collar. The goat at once stood still, mild as any lamb, looking at Tenar with one yellow eye and at the onion-rows with the other.

'Out,' said Tenar, leading her out of goat heaven and over to the stonier pasture where she was supposed to be.

Ged had sat down on the ground, as out of breath as Therru, or more so, for he gasped, and was evidently dizzy; but at least he was not in tears. Trust a goat to spoil anything.

'Heather shouldn't have told you to watch Sippy,' Tenar said to Therru. 'Nobody can watch Sippy. If she gets out again, tell Heather, and don't worry. All right?'

Therru nodded. She was looking at Ged. She seldom looked at people, and very seldom at men, for longer than a glance; but she was gazing at him steadily, her head cocked like a sparrow. Was a hero being born?

6. Worsening

It was well over a month since the solstice, but the evenings were still long up on the west-facing Overfell. Therru had come in late from an all-day herbal expedition with Aunty Moss, too tired to eat. Tenar put her to bed and sat with her, singing to her. When the child was overtired she could not sleep, but would crouch in the bed like a paralysed animal, staring at hallucinations till she was in a nightmare state, neither sleeping nor waking, and unreachable. Tenar had found she could prevent this by holding her and singing her to sleep. When she ran out of the songs she had learned as a farmer's wife in Middle Valley, she sang interminable Kargish chants she had learned as a child priestess at the Tombs of Atuan, lulling Therru with the drone and sweet whine of offerings to the Nameless Powers and the Empty Throne that was now filled with the dust and ruin of earthquake. She felt no power in those songs but that of song itself; and she liked to sing in her own language, though she did not know the songs a mother would sing to a child in Atuan, the songs her mother had sung to her.

Therru was fast asleep at last. Tenar slipped her from her lap to the bed and waited a moment to be sure she slept on. Then, after a glance round to be sure she was alone, with an almost guilty quickness, yet with the ceremony of enjoyment, of great pleasure, she laid her narrow, light-skinned hand along the side of the child's face where eye and cheek had been eaten away by fire, leaving slabbed, bald scar. Under her touch all that was gone. The flesh was whole, a child's round, soft, sleeping face. It was as if her touch restored the truth.

Lightly, reluctantly, she lifted her palm, and saw the irremediable loss, the healing that would never be whole.

She bent down and kissed the scar, got up quietly, and went out of the house.

The sun was setting in a vast, pearly haze. No one was about. Sparrowhawk was probably off in the forest. He had begun to visit Ogion's grave, spending hours in that quiet place under the beech tree, and as he got more strength he took to wandering on up the forest paths that Ogion had loved. Food evidently had no savour to him; Tenar had to ask him to eat. Companionship he shunned, seeking only to be alone. Therru would have followed him anywhere, and being as silent as he was she did not trouble him, but he was restless, and presently would send the child home and go on by himself, farther, to what ends Tenar did not know. He would come in late, cast himself down to sleep, and often be gone again before she and the child woke. She would leave him bread and meat to take with him.

She saw him now coming along the meadow path that had been so long and hard when she had helped Ogion walk it for the last time. He came through the luminous air, the wind-bowed grasses, walking steadily, locked in his obstinate misery, hard as stone.

'Will you be about the house?' she asked him, across some distance. 'Therru's asleep. I want to walk a little.'

'Yes. Go on,' he said, and she went on, pondering the indifference of a man towards the exigencies that ruled a woman: that someone must be not far from a sleeping child, that one's freedom meant another's unfreedom, unless some ever-changing, moving balance were reached, like the balance of a body moving forward, as she did now, on two legs, first one then the other, in the practice of that remarkable art, walking ... Then the deepening colours of the sky and the soft insistence of the wind replaced her thoughts. She went on walking, without metaphors, until she came to the sandstone cliffs. There she stopped and watched the sun be lost in the serene, rosy haze.

She knelt and found with her eyes and then with her fingertips a long, shallow, blurred groove in the rock, scored right out to the edge of the cliff: the track of Kalessin's tail. She followed it again and again with her fingers, gazing out into the gulfs of twilight, dreaming. She spoke once. The name was not fire in her mouth this time, but hissed and dragged softly out of her lips, 'Kalessin . . .'

She looked up to the east. The summits of Gont Mountain above the forest were red, catching the light that was gone here below. The colour dimmed as she watched. She looked away and when she looked back the summit was grey, obscure, the forested slopes dark.

She waited for the evening star. When it shone above the haze, she walked slowly home.

Home, not home. Why was she here in Ogion's house not in her own farmhouse, looking after Ogion's goats and onions not her own orchards and flocks? 'Wait,' he had said, and she had waited; and the dragon had come; and Ged was well now – was well enough. She had done her part. She had kept the house. She was no longer needed. It was time she left.

Yet she could not think of leaving this high ledge, this hawk's nest, and going down into the lowlands again, the easy farmlands, the windless inlands, she could not think of that without her heart sinking and darkening. What of the dream she had here, under the small window looking west? What of the dragon who had come to her here?

The door of the house stood open as usual for light and air. Sparrowhawk was sitting without lamp or firelight on a low seat by the swept hearth. He often sat there. She thought it had been his place when he was a boy here, in his brief apprenticeship with Ogion. It had been her place, winter days, when she had been Ogion's pupil.

He looked at her entering, but his eyes had not been on the doorway but beside it to the right, the dark corner behind the door. Ogion's staff stood there, an oaken stick, heavy, worn smooth at the grip, the height of the man himself. Beside it Therru had set the hazel switch and the alder stick Tenar had cut for them when they were walking to Re Albi.

Tenar thought – His staff, his wizard's staff, yew-wood, Ogion gave it to him – Where is it? And at the same time, Why have I not thought of that till now?

It was dark in the house, and seemed stuffy. She was oppressed. She had wished he would stay to talk with her, but now that he sat there she had nothing to say to him, nor he to her.

'I've been thinking,' she said at last, setting straight the four dishes on the oaken sideboard, 'that it's time I was getting back to my farm.'

He said nothing. Possibly he nodded, but her back was turned.

She was tired all at once, wanting to go to bed; but he sat there in the front part of the house, and it was not yet entirely dark; she could not undress in front of him. Shame made her angry. She was about to ask him to go out for a while when he spoke, clearing his throat, hesitant.

'The books. Ogion's books. The Runes and the two Lorebooks. Would you be taking them with you?'

'With me?'

'You were his last student.'

She came over to the hearth and sat down across from him on Ogion's three-legged chair.

'I learned to write the runes of Hardic, but I've forgotten most of that, no doubt. He taught me some of the language the dragons speak. Some of that I remember. But nothing else. I didn't become an adept, a wizard. I got married, you know. Would Ogion have left his books of wisdom to a farmer's wife?'

545

After a pause he said without expression, 'Did he not leave them to someone, then?'

'To you, surely.'

Sparrowhawk said nothing.

'You were his last prentice, and his pride, and friend. He never said it, but of course they go to you.'

'What am I to do with them?'

She stared at him through the dusk. The western window gleamed faint across the room. The dour, relentless, unexplaining rage in his voice roused her own anger.

'You the Archmage ask me? Why do you make a worse fool of me than I am, Ged?'

He got up then. His voice shook. 'But don't you – can't you see – all that is over – is gone!'

She sat staring, trying to see his face.

'I have no power, nothing. I gave it – spent it – all I had. To close – So that – So it's done, done with.'

She tried to deny what he said, but could not.

'Like pouring out a little water,' he said, 'a cup of water on to the sand. In the dry land. I had to do that. But now I have nothing to drink. And what difference, what difference did it make, does it make, one cup of water in all the desert? Is the desert gone? – Ah! Listen! – It used to whisper that to me from behind the door there: Listen, listen! And I went into the dry land when I was young. And I met it there, I became it, I married my death. It gave me life. Water, the water of life. I was a fountain, a spring, flowing, giving. But the springs don't run, there. All I had in the end was one cup of water, and I had to pour it out on the sand, in the bed of the dry river, on the rocks in the dark. So its gone. It's over. Done.'

She knew enough, from Ogion and from Ged himself, to know what land he spoke of, and that though he spoke in images they were not masks of the truth but the truth itself as he had known it. She knew also that she must deny what he said, no matter if it was true. 'You don't give yourself time, Ged,' she said. 'Coming back from death

546

must be a long journey – even on the dragon's back. It will take time. Time and quiet, silence, stillness. You have been hurt. You will be healed.'

For a long while he was silent, standing there. She thought she had said the right thing, and given him some comfort. But he spoke at last.

'Like the child?'

It was like a knife so sharp she did not feel it come into her body.

'I don't know,' he said in the same soft, dry voice, 'why you took her, knowing that she cannot be healed. Knowing what her life must be. I suppose it's a part of this time we have lived – a dark time, an age of ruin, an ending time. You took her, I suppose, as I went to meet my enemy, because it was all you could do. And so we must live on into the new age with the spoils of our victory over evil. You with your burned child, and I with nothing at all.'

Despair speaks evenly, in a quiet voice.

Tenar turned to look at the mage's staff in the dark place to the right of the door, but there was no light in it. It was all dark, inside and out. Through the open doorway a couple of stars were visible, high and faint. She looked at them. She wanted to know what stars they were. She got up and went groping past the table to the door. The haze had risen and not many stars were visible. One of those she had seen from indoors was the white summer star that they called, in Atuan, in her own language, Tehanu. She did not know the other one. She did not know what they called Tehanu here, in Hardic, or what its true name was, what the dragons called it. She knew only what her mother would have called it, Tehanu, Tehanu. Tenar, Tenar . . .

'Ged,' she said from the doorway, not turning, 'who brought you up, when you were a child?'

He came to stand near her, also looking out at the misty horizon of the sea, the stars, the dark bulk of the mountain above them.

'Nobody much,' he said. 'My mother died when I was a baby. There were some older brothers. I don't remember them. There was my father the smith. And my mother's sister. She was the witch of Ten Alders.'

'Aunty Moss,' Tenar said.

'Younger. She had some power.'

'What was her name?'

He was silent.

'I cannot remember,' he said slowly.

After a while he said, 'She taught me the names. Falcon, pilgrim falcon, eagle, osprey, goshawk, sparrowhawk . . .'

'What do you call that star? The white one, up high.'

'The Heart of the Swan,' he said, looking up at it. 'In Ten Alders they called it the Arrow.'

But he did not say its name in the Language of the Making, nor the true names the witch had taught him of hawk, falcon, sparrowhawk.

'What I said – in there – was wrong,' he said softly. 'I shouldn't speak at all. Forgive me.'

'If you won't speak, what can I do but leave you?' She turned to him. 'Why do you think only of yourself? always of yourself? Go outside awhile,' she told him, wrathful. 'I want to go to bed.'

Bewildered, muttering some apology, he went out; and she, going to the alcove, slipped out of her clothes and into the bed, and hid her face in the sweet warmth of Therru's silky nape.

'Knowing what her life must be . . .'

Her anger with him, her stupid denial of the truth of what he told her, rose from disappointment. Though Lark had said ten times over that nothing could be done, yet she had hoped that Tenar could heal the burns; and for all her saying that even Ogion could not have done it, Tenar had hoped that Ged could heal Therru – could lay his hand on the scar and it would be whole and well, the blind eye bright, the clawed hand soft, the ruined life intact.

'Knowing what her life must be . . .'

The averted faces, the signs against evil, the horror and curiosity, the sickly pity and the prying threat, for harm draws harm to it . . . And never a man's arms. Never anyone to hold her. Never anyone but Tenar. Oh, he was right, the child should have died, should be dead. They should have let her go into that dry land, she and Lark and Ivy, meddling old women, softhearted and cruel. He was right, he was always right. But then, the men who had used her for their needs and games, the woman who had suffered her to be used – they had been quite right to beat her unconscious and push her into the fire to burn to death. Only they had not been thorough. They had lost their nerve, they had left some life in her. That had been wrong. And everything she, Tenar, had done was wrong. She had been given to the dark powers as a child: she had been eaten by them, she had been suffered to be eaten. Did she think that by crossing the sea, by learning other languages, by being a man's wife, a mother of children, that by merely living her life, she could ever be anything but what she was – their servant, their food, theirs to use for their needs and games? Destroyed, she had drawn the destroyed to her, part of her own ruin, the body of her own evil.

The child's hair was fine, warm, sweet-smelling. She lay curled up in the warmth of Tenar's arms, dreaming. What wrong could she be? Wronged, wronged beyond all repair, but not wrong. Not lost, not lost, not lost. Tenar held her and lay still and set her mind on the light of her dreaming, the gulfs of bright air, the name of the dragon, the name of the star, Heart of the Swan, the Arrow, Tehanu.

She was combing the black goat for the fine underwool that she would spin and take to a weaver to make into cloth, the silky 'fleecefell' of Gont Island. The old black goat had been combed a thousand times, and liked it, leaning into the dig and pull of the wire comb-teeth. The grey-black combings grew into a soft, dirty cloud, which Tenar at last stuffed into a net bag; she worked some burrs out of the fringes of the goat's ears by way of thanks, and slapped her barrel flank companionably. 'Bah!' the goat said, and trotted off. Tenar let herself out of the fenced pasture and came around in front of the house, glancing over the meadow to make sure Therru was still playing there.

Moss had shown the child how to weave grass baskets, and clumsy as her crippled hand was, she had begun to get the trick of it. She sat there in the meadow grass with her work on her lap, but she was not working. She was watching Sparrowhawk.

He stood a good way off, nearer the cliff's edge. His back was turned, and he did not know anyone was watching him, for he was watching a bird, a young kestrel; and she in turn was watching some small prey she had glimpsed in the grass. She hung beating her wings, wanting to flush the vole or mouse, to panic it into a rush to its nest. The man stood, as intent, as hungry, gazing at the bird. Slowly he lifted his right hand, holding the forearm level, and he seemed to speak, though the wind bore his words away. The kestrel veered, crying her high, harsh, keening cry, and shot up and off towards the forests.

The man lowered his arm and stood still, watching the bird. The child and the woman were still. Only the bird flew, went free.

'He came to me once as a falcon, a pilgrim falcon,' Ogion had said, by the fire, on a winter day. He had been telling her of the spells of Changing, of transformations, of the mage Bordger who had become a bear. 'He flew to me, to my wrist, out of the north and west. I brought him in by the fire here. He could not speak. Because I knew him, I was able to help him; he could put off the falcon, and be a man again. But there was always some hawk in him. They called him Sparrowhawk in his village because the wild hawks would come to him, at his word. Who are we? What is it to be a man? Before he had his name, before he had knowledge, before he had power, the hawk was in him, and the man, and the mage, and more – he was what we cannot name. And so are we all.'

The girl sitting at the hearth, gazing at the fire, listening, saw the hawk; saw the man; saw the birds come to him, come at his word, at his naming them, come beating their wings to hold his arm with their fierce talons; saw herself the hawk, the wild bird.

7. Mice

Townsend, the sheep-buyer who had brought Ogion's message to the farm in Middle Valley, came out one afternoon to the mage's house.

'Will you be selling the goats, now Lord Ogion's gone?'

'I might,' Tenar said neutrally. She had in fact been wondering how, if she stayed in Re Albi, she would get on. Like any wizard, Ogion had been supported by the people his skills and powers served – in his case, anyone on Gont. He had only to ask and what he needed would be given gratefully, a good bargain for the goodwill of a mage; but he never had to ask. Rather he had to give away the excess of food and raiment and tools and livestock and all necessities and ornaments that were offered or simply left on his doorstep. 'What shall I do with them?' he would demand, perplexed, standing with his arms full of indignant, squawking chickens, or yards of tapestry, or pots of pickled beets.

But Tenar had left her living in the Middle Valley. She had not thought when she left so suddenly of how long she might stay. She had not brought with her the seven pieces of ivory, Flint's hoard; nor would that money have been of use in the village except to buy land or livestock, or deal with some trader up from Gont Port peddling pellawi furs or silks of Lorbanery to the rich farmers and little lords of Gont. Flint's farm gave her all she and Therru needed to eat and wear; but Ogion's six goats and his beans and onions had been for his pleasure rather than his need. She had been living off his larder, the gifts of villagers who gave to her for his sake, and the generosity of Aunty Moss. Just yesterday the witch had said, 'Dearie, my ringneck hen's brood's hatched out, and I'll bring you two-three chickies when they begin to scratch. The mage wouldn't keep 'em, too noisy and silly, he said, but what's a house without chickies at the door?'

Indeed her hens wandered in and out of Moss's door freely, and slept on her bed, and enriched the smells of the dark, smoky, reeking room beyond belief.

'There's a brown-and-white yearling nanny will make a fine milch goat,' Tenar said to the sharp-faced man.

'I was thinking of the whole lot,' he said. 'Maybe. Only five or six of 'em, right?'

'Six. They're in the pasture up there if you want to have a look.'

'I'll do that.' But he didn't move. No eagerness, of course, was to be evinced on either side.

'Seen the great ship come in?' he asked.

Ogion's house looked west and north, and from it one could see only the rocky headlands at the mouth of the bay, the Armed Cliffs; but from the village itself at several places one could look down the steep back-and-forth road to Gont Port and see the docks and the whole harbour. Shipwatching was a regular pursuit in Re Albi. There were generally a couple of old men on the bench behind the smithy, which gave the best view, and though they might never in their lives have gone down the fifteen zigzag miles of that road to Gont Port, they watched the comings and goings of ships as a spectacle, strange yet familiar, provided for their entertainment.

'From Havnor, smith's boy said. He was down in Port bargaining for ingots. Come up yesterevening late. The great ship's from Havnor Great Port, he said.'

He was probably talking to keep her mind off the price of goats, and the slyness of his look was probably simply the way his eyes were made. But Havnor Great Port traded little with Gont, a poor and remote island notable only for wizards, pirates, and goats; and something in the words, 'the great ship', troubled or alarmed her, she did not know why.

'He said they say there's a king in Havnor now,' the sheep-buyer went on, with a sidelong glance.

'That might be a good thing,' said Tenar.

Townsend nodded. 'Might keep the foreign riffraff out.'

Tenar nodded her foreign head pleasantly.

'But there's those down in Port won't be pleased, maybe.' He meant the pirate sea-captains of Gont, whose control of the northeastern seas had been increasing of late years to the point where many of the old trade-schedules with the central islands of the Archipelago had been disrupted or abandoned; this impoverished everyone on Gont except the pirates, but that did not prevent the pirates from being heroes in the eyes of most Gontishmen. For all she knew, Tenar's son was a sailor on a pirate ship. And safer, maybe, as such than on a steady merchantman. *Better shark than herring*, as they said.

'There's some who're never pleased no matter what,' Tenar said, automatically following the rules of conversation, but impatient enough with them that she added, rising, 'I'll show you the goats. You can have a look. I don't know if we'll sell all or any.' And she took the man to the broom-pasture gate and left him. She did not like him. It wasn't his fault that he had brought her bad news once and maybe twice, but his eyes slid, and she did not like his company. She wouldn't sell him Ogion's goats. Not even Sippy.

After he had left, bargainless, she found herself uneasy. She had said to him, 'I don't know if we'll sell,' and that had been foolish, to say *we* instead of *I*, when he hadn't asked to speak to Sparrowhawk, hadn't even alluded to him, as a man bargaining with a woman was more than likely to do, especially when she was refusing his offer.

She did not know what they made of Sparrowhawk, of his presence and nonpresence, in the village. Ogion, aloof and silent and in some ways feared, had been their own mage and their fellow-villager. Sparrowhawk they might be proud of as a name, the archmage who had lived awhile in Re Albi and done wonderful things, fooling a dragon in the Ninety Isles, bringing the Ring of Erreth-Akbe back from somewhere or other; but they did not know him. Nor did he know them. He had not gone into the village since he came, only to the forest, the wilderness. She had not thought about it before, but he avoided the village as surely as Therru did.

They must have talked about him. It was a village, and people talked. But gossip about the doings of wizards and mages would not go far. The matter was too uncanny, the lives of men of power were too strange, too different from their own. 'Let be,' she had heard villagers in the Middle Valley say when somebody got to speculating too freely about a visiting weatherworker or their own wizard, Beech – 'Let be. He goes his way, not ours.'

As for herself, that she should have stayed on to nurse and serve such a man of power would not seem a questionable matter to them; again it was a case of, 'Let be.' She had not been very much in the village herself; they were neither friendly nor unfriendly to her. She had lived there once in Weaver Fan's cottage, she was the old mage's ward, he had sent Townsend down round the mountain for her; all that was very well. But then she had come with the child, terrible to look at, who'd walk about in daylight with it by choice? And what kind of woman would be a wizard's pupil, a wizard's nurse? Witchery there, sure enough, and foreign too. But all the same, she was wife to a rich farmer way down there in the Middle Valley; though he was dead and she a widow. Well, who could understand the ways of the witchfolk? Let be, better let be . . .

She met the Archmage of Earthsea as he came past the garden fence. She said, 'They say there's a ship in from the City of Havnor.'

He stopped. He made a movement, quickly controlled, but it had been the beginning of a turn to run, to break and run like a mouse from a hawk.

'Ged!' she said. 'What is it?'

'I can't,' he said. 'I can't face them.'

'Who?'

'Men from him. From the king.'

His face had gone greyish, as when he was first here, and he looked around for a place to hide.

His terror was so urgent and undefended that she thought only how to spare him. 'You needn't see them. If anybody comes I'll send them away. Come back to the house now. You haven't eaten all day.'

'There was a man there,' he said.

'Townsend, pricing goats. I sent *him* away. Come on!'

He came with her, and when they were in the house she shut the door.

'They couldn't harm you, surely, Ged. Why would they want to?'

He sat down at the table and shook his head dully. 'No, no.'

'Do they know you're here?'

'I don't know.'

'What is it you're afraid of?' she asked, not impatiently, but with some rational authority.

He put his hands across his face, rubbing his temples and forehead, looking down. 'I was –' he said. 'I'm not –'

It was all he could say.

She stopped him, saying, 'All right, it's all right.' She dared not touch him lest she worsen his humiliation by any semblance of pity. She was angry at him, and for him. 'It's none of their business,' she said, 'where you are, or who you are, or what you choose to do or not to do! If they come prying they can leave curious.' That was Lark's saying. She had a pang of longing for the company of an ordinary, sensible woman. 'Anyhow, the ship may have

556

nothing at all to do with you. They may be chasing pirates home. It'll be a good thing, too, when the king gets around to doing that ... I found some wine in the back of the cupboard, a couple of bottles, I wonder how long Ogion had it squirrelled away there. I think we'd both do well with a glass of wine. And some bread and cheese. The little one's had her dinner and gone off with Heather to catch frogs. There may be frogs' legs for supper. But bread and cheese for now. And wine. I wonder where it's from, who brought it to Ogion, how old it is?' So she talked along, woman's babble, saving him from having to make any answer or misread any silence, until he had got over the crisis of shame, and eaten a little, and drunk a glass of the old, soft, red wine.

'It's best I go, Tenar,' he said. 'Till I learn to be what I am now.'

'Go where?'

'Up on the mountain.'

'Wandering – like Ogion?' She looked at him. She remembered walking with him on the roads of Atuan, deriding him: 'Do wizards often beg?' And he had answered, 'Yes, but they try to give something in exchange.'

She asked cautiously, 'Could you get on for a while as a weatherworker, or a finder?' She filled his glass full.

He shook his head. He drank wine, and looked away. 'No,' he said. 'None of that. Nothing of that.'

She did not believe him. She wanted to rebel, to deny, to say to him, How can it be, how can you say that – as if you'd forgotten all you know, all you learned from Ogion, and at Roke, and in your travelling! You can't have forgotten the words, the names, the acts of your art. You learned, you earned your power! – She kept herself from saying that, but she murmured, 'I don't understand. How can it all . . .'

'A cup of water,' he said, tipping his glass a little as if to pour it out. And after a while, 'What I don't understand is why he brought me back. The kindness of the young is cruelty . . . So I'm here, I have to get on with it, till I can go back.'

She did not know clearly what he meant, but she heard a note of blame or complaint that, in him, shocked and angered her. She spoke stiffly: 'It was Kalessin that brought you here.'

It was dark in the house with the door closed and only the small western window letting in the late-afternoon light. She could not make out his expression; but presently he raised his glass to her with a shadowy smile, and drank.

'This wine,' he said. 'Some great merchant or pirate must have brought it to Ogion. I never drank its equal. Even in Havnor.' He turned the squat glass in his hands, looking down at it. 'I'll call myself something,' he said, 'and go across the mountain, to Armouth and the East Forest country, where I came from. They'll be making hay. There's always work at haying and harvest.'

She did not know how to answer. Fragile and ill-looking, he would be given such work only out of charity or brutality; and if he got it he would not be able to do it.

'The roads aren't like they used to be,' she said. 'These last years, there's thieves and gangs everywhere. Foreign riffraff, as my friend Townsend says. But it's not safe any more to go alone.'

Looking at him in the dusky light to see how he took this, she wondered sharply for a moment what it must be like never to have feared a human being – what it would be like to have to learn to be afraid.

'Ogion still went –' he began, and then set his mouth; he had recalled that Ogion had been a mage.

'Down in the south part of the island,' Tenar said, 'there's a lot of herding. Sheep, goats, cattle. They drive them up into the hills before the Long Dance, and pasture them there until the rains. They're always needing herders.' She drank a mouthful of the wine. It was like the dragon's name in her mouth. 'But why can't you just stay here?'

'Not in Ogion's house. The first place they'll come.'

'Well, what if they do come? What will they want of you?'

'To be what I was.'

The desolation of his voice chilled her.

She was silent, trying to remember what it was like to have been powerful, to be the Eaten One, the One Priestess of the Tombs of Atuan, and then to lose that, throw it away, become only Tenar, only herself. She thought about how it was to have been a woman in the prime of life, with children and a man, and then to lose all that, becoming old and a widow, powerless. But even so she did not feel she understood his shame, his agony of humiliation. Perhaps only a man could feel so. A woman got used to shame.

Or maybe Aunty Moss was right, and when the meat was out the shell was empty.

Witch-thoughts, she thought. And to turn his mind and her own, and because the soft, fiery wine made her wits and tongue quick, she said, 'Do you know, I've thought – about Ogion teaching me, and I wouldn't go on, but went and found myself my farmer and married him – I thought, when I did that, I thought on my wedding day, Ged will be angry when he hears of this!' She laughed as she spoke.

'I was,' he said.

She waited.

He said, 'I was disappointed.'

'Angry,' she said.

'Angry,' he said.

He poured her glass full.

'I had the power to know power, then,' he said. 'And you – you shone, in that terrible place, the Labyrinth, that darkness . . .'

'Well, then, tell me: what should I have done with my power, and the knowledge Ogion tried to teach me?'

'Use it.'

'How?'

'As the Art Magic is used.'

'By whom?'

'Wizards,' he said, a little painfully.

'Magic means the skills, the arts of wizards, of mages?'

'What else would it mean?'

'Is that all it could ever mean?'

He pondered, glancing up at her once or twice.

'When Ogion taught me,' she said, 'here – at the hearth there – the words of the Old Speech, they were as easy and as hard in my mouth as in his. That was like learning the language I spoke before I was born. But the rest – the lore, the runes of power, the spells, the rules, the raising of the forces – that was all dead to me. Somebody else's language. I used to think, I could be dressed up as a warrior, with a lance and a sword and a plume and all, but it wouldn't fit, would it? What would I do with the sword? Would it make me a hero? I'd be myself in clothes that didn't fit, is all, hardly able to walk.'

She sipped her wine.

'So I took it all off,' she said, 'and put on my own clothes.'

'What did Ogion say when you left him?'

'What did Ogion usually say?'

That roused the shadowy smile again. He said nothing.

She nodded.

After a while, she went on more softly, 'He took me because you brought me to him. He wanted no prentice after you, and he never would have taken a girl but from you, at your asking. But he loved me. He did me honour. And I loved and honoured him. But he couldn't give me what I wanted, and I couldn't take what he had to give me. He knew that. But, Ged, it was a different matter when he saw Therru. The day before he died. You say, and Moss says, that power knows power. I don't know what he saw in her, but he said, "Teach her!" And he said . . .'

Ged waited.

'He said, "They will fear her." And he said, "Teach her *all*! Not Roke." I don't know what he meant. How can I know? If I had stayed here with him I might know, I might be able to teach her. But I thought, Ged will come, he'll know. He'll know what to teach her, what she needs to know, my wronged one.'

'I do not know,' he said, speaking very low. 'I saw – In the child I see only – the wrong done. The evil.'

He drank off his wine.

'I have nothing to give her,' he said.

There was a little scraping knock at the door. He started up instantly with that same helpless turn of the body, looking for a place to hide.

Tenar went to the door, opened it a crack, and smelled Moss before she saw her.

'Men in the village,' the old woman whispered dramatically. 'All kind of fine folk come up from the Port, from the great ship that's in from Havnor City, they say. Come after the Archmage, they say.'

'He doesn't want to see them,' Tenar said weakly. She had no idea what to do.

'I dare say not,' said the witch. And after an expectant pause, 'Where is he, then?'

'Here,' said Sparrowhawk, coming to the door and opening it wider. Moss eyed him and said nothing.

'Do they know where I am?'

'Not from me,' Moss said.

'If they come here,' said Tenar, 'all you have to do is send them away – after all, you are the Archmage –'

Neither he nor Moss was paying attention to her.

'They won't come to *my* house,' Moss said. 'Come on, if you like.'

He followed her, with a glance but no word to Tenar.

'But what am I to tell them?' she demanded.

'Nothing, dearie,' said the witch.

*

Heather and Therru came back from the marshes with seven dead frogs in a net bag, and Tenar busied herself cutting off and skinning the legs for the hunters' supper. She was just finishing when she heard voices outside, and looking up at the open door saw people standing at it – men in hats, a twist of gold, a glitter – 'Mistress Goha?' said a civil voice.

'Come in!' she said.

They came in: five men, seeming twice as many in the low-ceilinged room, and tall, and grand. They looked about them, and she saw what they saw.

They saw a woman standing at a table, holding a long, sharp knife. On the table was a chopping board and on that, to one side, a little heap of naked greenish-white legs; to the other, a heap of fat, bloody, dead frogs. In the shadow behind the door something lurked – a child, but a child deformed, mismade, half-faced, claw-handed. On a bed in an alcove beneath the single window sat a big, bony young woman, staring at them with her mouth wide open. Her hands were bloody and muddy and her dank skirt smelled of marsh-water. When she saw them look at her, she tried to hide her face with her skirt, baring her legs to the thigh.

They looked away from her, and from the child, and there was no one else to look at but the woman with the dead frogs.

'Mistress Goha,' one of them repeated.

'So I'm called,' she said.

'We come from Havnor, from the king,' said the civil voice. She could not see his face clearly against the light. 'We seek the Archmage, Sparrowhawk of Gont. King Lebannen is to be crowned at the turn of autumn, and he seeks to have the Archmage, his lord and friend, with him to make ready for the coronation, and to crown him, if he will.'

The man spoke steadily and formally, as to a lady in a

palace. He wore sober breeches of leather and a linen shirt dusty from the climb up from Gont Port, but it was fine cloth, with embroidery of gold thread at the throat.

'He's not here,' Tenar said.

A couple of little boys from the village peered in at the door and drew back, peered again, fled shouting.

'Maybe you can tell us where he is, Mistress Goha,' said the man.

'I cannot.'

She looked at them all. The fear of them she had felt at first — caught from Sparrowhawk's panic, perhaps, or mere foolish fluster at seeing strangers — was subsiding. Here she stood in Ogion's house; and she knew well enough why Ogion had never been afraid of great people.

'You must be tired after that long road,' she said. 'Will you sit down? There's wine. Here, I must wash the glasses.'

She carried the chopping board over to the sideboard, put the frogs' legs in the larder, scraped the rest into the swill-pail that Heather would carry to Weaver Fan's pigs, washed her hands and arms and the knife at the basin, poured fresh water, and rinsed out the two glasses she and Sparrowhawk had drunk from. There was one other glass in the cabinet, and two clay cups without handles. She set these on the table, and poured wine for the visitors; there was just enough left in the bottle to go round. They had exchanged glances, and had not sat down. The shortage of chairs excused that. The rules of hospitality, however, bound them to accept what she offered. Each man took glass or cup from her with a polite murmur. Saluting her, they drank.

'My word!' said one of them.

'Andrades — the Late Harvest,' said another, with round eyes.

A third shook his head. 'Andrades — the Dragon Year,' he said solemnly.

The fourth nodded and sipped again, reverent.

The fifth, who was the first to have spoken, lifted his clay cup to Tenar again and said, 'You honour us with a king's wine, mistress.'

'It was Ogion's,' she said. 'This was Ogion's house. This is Aihal's house. You knew that, my lords?'

'We did, mistress. The king sent us to this house, believing that the archmage would come here; and, when word of the death of its master came to Roke and Havnor, yet more certain of it. But it was a dragon that bore the archmage from Roke. And no word or sending has come from him since then to Roke or to the king. And it is much in the king's heart, and much in the interest of us all, to know the archmage is here, and is well. Did he come here, mistress?'

'I cannot say,' she said, but it was a poor equivocation, repeated, and she could see that the men thought so. She drew herself up, standing behind the table. 'I mean that I will not say. I think if the archmage wishes to come, he will come. If he wishes not to be found, you will not find him. Surely you will not seek him out against his will.'

The oldest of the men, and the tallest, said, 'The king's will is ours.'

The first speaker said more conciliatingly, 'We are only messengers. What is between the king and the archmage of the Isles is between them. We seek only to bring the message, and the reply.'

'If I can, I will see that your message reaches him.'

'And the reply?' the oldest man demanded.

She said nothing, and the first speaker said, 'We'll be here some few days at the house of the Lord of Re Albi, who, hearing of our ship's arrival, offered us his hospitality.'

She felt a sense of a trap laid or a noose tightening, though she did not know why. Sparrowhawk's vulnerability, his sense of his own weakness, had infected her.

Distraught, she used the defence of her appearance, her seeming to be a mere goodwife, a middle-aged housekeeper – but was it seeming? It was also truth, and these matters were more subtle even than the guises and shape-changes of wizards. – She ducked her head and said, 'That will be more befitting your lordships' comfort. You see we live very plain here, as the old mage did.'

'And drink Andrades wine,' said the one who had identified the vintage, a bright-eyed, handsome man with a winning smile. She, playing her part, kept her head down. But as they took their leave and filed out, she knew that, seem what she might and be what she might, if they did not know now that she was Tenar of the Ring they would know it soon enough; and so would know that she herself knew the archmage and was indeed their way to him, if they were determined to seek him out.

When they were gone, she heaved a great sigh. Heather did so too, and then finally shut her mouth, which had hung open all the time they were there.

'I never,' she said, in a tone of deep, replete satisfaction, and went to see where the goats had got to.

Therru came out from the dark place behind the door, where she had barricaded herself from the strangers with Ogion's staff and Tenar's alder stick and her own hazel switch. She moved in the tight, sidling way she had mostly abandoned since they had been here, not looking up, the ruined half of her face bent down towards the shoulder.

Tenar went to her and knelt to hold her in her arms. 'Therru,' she said, 'they won't hurt you. They mean no harm.'

The child would not look at her. She let Tenar hold her like a block of wood.

'If you say so, I won't let them in the house again.'

After a while the child moved a little and asked in her hoarse, thick voice, 'What will they do to Sparrowhawk?'

'Nothing,' Tenar said. 'No harm! They come – they mean to do him honour.'

But she had begun to see what their attempt to do him honour would do to him – denying his loss, denying him his grief for what he had lost, forcing him to act the part of what he was no longer.

When she let the child go, Therru went to the closet and fetched out Ogion's broom. She laboriously swept the floor where the men from Havnor had stood, sweeping away their footprints, sweeping the dust of their feet out the door, off the doorstep.

Watching her, Tenar made up her mind.

She went to the shelf where Ogion's three great books stood, and rummaged there. She found several goose quills and a half-dried-up bottle of ink, but not a scrap of paper or parchment. She set her jaw, hating to do damage to anything so sacred as a book, and scored and tore out a thin strip of paper from the blank endsheet of the Book of Runes. She sat at the table and dipped the pen and wrote. Neither the ink nor the words came easy. She had scarcely written anything since she had sat at this same table a quarter of a century ago, with Ogion looking over her shoulder, teaching her the runes of Hardic and the Great Runes of Power. She wrote:

> *go oakfarm in midl valy to clerbrook*
> *say goha sent to look to garden & sheep*

It took her nearly as long to read it over as it had to write it. By now Therru had finished her sweeping and was watching her, intent.

She added one word:

> *to-night*

'Where's Heather?' she asked the child, as she folded the paper on itself once and twice. 'I want her to take this to Aunty Moss's house.'

She longed to go herself, to see Sparrowhawk, but dared not be seen going, lest they were watching her to lead them to him.

'I'll go,' Therru whispered.

Tenar looked at her sharply.

'You'll have to go alone, Therru. Past the village.'

The child nodded.

'Give it only to him!'

She nodded again.

Tenar tucked the paper into the child's pocket, held her, kissed her, let her go. Therru went, not crouching and sidling now but running freely, flying, Tenar thought, seeing her vanish in the evening light beyond the dark door-frame, flying like a bird, a dragon, a child, free.

8. Hawks

Therru was back soon with Sparrowhawk's reply: 'He said he'll leave tonight.'

Tenar heard this with satisfaction, relieved that he had accepted her plan, that he would get clear away from these messengers and messages he dreaded. It was not till she had fed Heather and Therru their frog-leg feast, and put Therru to bed and sung to her, and was sitting up alone without lamp or firelight, that her heart began to sink. He was gone. He was not strong, he was bewildered and uncertain, he needed friends; and she had sent him away from those who were and those who wished to be his friends. He was gone, and she must stay, to keep the hounds from his trail, to learn at least whether they stayed in Gont or sailed back to Havnor.

His panic and her obedience to it began to seem so unreasonable to her that she thought it equally unreasonable, improbable, that he would in fact go. He would use his wits and simply hide in Moss's house, which was the last place in all Earthsea that a king would look for an archmage. It would be much better if he stayed there till the king's men left. Then he could come back here to Ogion's house, where he belonged. And it would go on as before, she looking after him until he had his strength back, and he giving her his dear companionship.

A shadow against the stars in the doorway: 'Hsssst! Awake?' Aunty Moss came in. 'Well, he's off,' she said, conspiratorial, jubilant. 'Went the old forest road. Says he'll cut down to the Middle Valley way, along past Oak Springs, tomorrow.'

'Good,' said Tenar.

Bolder than usual, Moss sat down uninvited. 'I gave him a loaf and a bit of cheese for the way.'

'Thank you, Moss. That was kind.'

'Mistress Goha.' Moss's voice in the darkness took on the singsong resonance of her chanting and spellcasting. 'There's a thing I was wanting to say to you, dearie, without going beyond what I can know, for I know you've lived among great folks and been one of 'em yourself, and that seals my mouth when I think of it. And yet there's things I know that you've had no way of knowing, for all the learning of the runes, and the Old Speech, and all you've learned from the wise, and in the foreign lands.'

'That's so, Moss.'

'Aye, well, then. So when we talked about how witch knows witch, and power knows power, and I said – of him who's gone now – that he was no mage now, whatever he had been, and still you would deny it – But I was right, wasn't I?'

'Yes.'

'Aye. I was.'

'He said so himself.'

'O' course he did. He don't lie nor say this is that and that's this till you don't know which end's up, I'll say that for him. He's not one tries to drive the cart without the ox, either. But I'll say flat out I'm glad he's gone, for it wouldn't do, it wouldn't do any longer, being a different matter with him now, and all.'

Tenar had no idea what she was talking about, except for her image of trying to drive the cart without the ox. 'I don't know why he's so afraid,' she said. 'Well, I know in part, but I don't understand it, why he feels such shame. But I know he thinks that he should have died. And I know that all I understand about living is having your work to do, and being able to do it. That's the pleasure, and the glory, and all. And if you can't do the work, or it's taken from you, then what's any good? You have to have something . . .'

Moss listened and nodded as at words of wisdom, but after a slight pause she said, 'It's a queer thing for an old man to be a boy of fifteen, no doubt!'

Tenar almost said, 'What are you talking about, Moss?' – but something prevented her. She realized that she had been listening for Ged to come into the house from his roaming on the mountainside, that she was listening for the sound of his voice, that her body denied his absence. She glanced suddenly over at the witch, a shapeless lump of black perched on Ogion's chair by the empty hearth.

'Ah!' she said, a great many thoughts suddenly coming into her mind all at once.

'*That's* why,' she said. '*That's* why I never –'

After a quite long silence, she said, 'Do they – do wizards – is it a spell?'

'Surely, surely, dearie,' said Moss. 'They witch 'emselves. Some'll tell you they make a trade-off, like a marriage turned backward, with vows and all, and so get their power then. But to me that's got a wrong sound to it, like a dealing with the Old Powers more than what a true witch deals with. And the old mage, he told me they did no such thing. Though I've known some woman witches do it, and come to no great harm by it.'

'The ones who brought me up did that, promising virginity.'

'Oh, aye, no men, you told me, and them yurnix. Terrible!'

'But why, but why – why did I never *think* –'

The witch laughed aloud. 'Because that's the power of 'em, dearie. You don't think! You can't! And nor do they, once they've set their spell. How could they? Given their power? It wouldn't do, would it, it wouldn't do. You don't get without you give as much. That's true for all, surely. So they know that, the witch men, the men of power, they know that better than any. But then, you know, it's an uneasy thing for a man not to be a man, no matter if he can call the sun down from the sky. And so they put it right out of mind, with their spells of binding. And truly so. Even in these bad times we've been having, with the spells going wrong and all, I haven't yet heard of a wizard breaking those spells, seeking to use his power for his body's lust. Even the worst would fear to. O' course, there's those will work illusions, but they only fool 'emselves. And there's witch-men of little account, witch-tinkers and the like, some of them'll try their own spells of beguilement on country women, but for all I can see, those spells don't amount to much. What it is, is the one power's as great as the other, and each goes its own way. That's how I see it.'

Tenar sat thinking, absorbed. At last she said, 'They set themselves apart.'

'Aye. A wizard has to do that.'

'But you don't.'

'Me? I'm only an old witchwoman, dearie.'

'How old?'

After a minute Moss's voice in the darkness said, with a hint of laughter in it, 'Old enough to keep out of trouble.'

'But you said . . . You haven't been celibate.'

'What's that, dearie?'

'Like the wizards.'

'Oh, no. No, no! Never was anything to look at, but there was a way I could look at them . . . not witching, you know, dearie, you know what I mean . . . there's a way to look, and he'd come round, sure as a crow will caw, in a day or two or three he'd come around my place – "I need a cure for my dog's mange," "I need a tea for my sick granny," – but I knew what it was they needed, and if I liked 'em well enough maybe they got it. And for love, for love – I'm not one o' them, you know, though maybe some witches are, but they dishonour the art, I say. I do my art for pay but I take my pleasure for love, that's what I say. Not that it's all pleasure, all that. I was crazy for a man here for a long time, years, a good-looking man he was, but a hard, cold heart. He's long dead. Father to that Townsend who's come back here to live, you know him. Oh, I was so heartset on that man I did use my art, I spent many a charm on him, but 'twas all wasted. All for nothing. No blood in a turnip . . . And I came up here to Re Albi in the first place when I was a girl because I was in trouble with a man in Gont Port. But I can't talk of that, for they were rich, great folks. 'Twas they had the power, not I! They didn't want their son tangled with a common girl like me, foul slut they called me, and they'd have had me put out of the way, like killing a cat, if I hadn't run off up here. But oh, I did like that lad, with his round, smooth arms and legs and his big, dark eyes, I can see him plain as plain after all these years . . .'

They sat a long while silent in the darkness.

'When you had a man, Moss, did you have to give up your power?'

'Not a bit of it,' the witch said, complacent.

'But you said you don't get unless you give. Is it different, then, for men and for women?'

'What isn't, dearie?'

'I don't know,' Tenar said. 'It seems to me we make up most of the differences, and then complain about 'em. I don't see why the Art Magic, why power, should be different for a man witch and a woman witch. Unless the power *itself* is different. Or the art.'

'A man gives out, dearie. A woman takes in.'

Tenar sat silent but unsatisfied.

'Ours is only a little power, seems like, next to theirs,' Moss said. 'But it goes down deep. It's all roots. It's like an old blackberry thicket. And a wizard's power's like a fir tree, maybe, great and tall and grand, but it'll blow right down in a storm. Nothing kills a blackberry bramble.' She gave her hen-chuckle, pleased with her comparison. 'Well, then!' she said briskly. 'So as I said, it's maybe just as well he's on his way and out o' the way, lest people in the town begin to talk.'

'To talk?'

'You're a respectable woman, dearie, and her reputation is a woman's wealth.'

'Her wealth,' Tenar repeated in the same blank way; then she said it again: 'Her wealth. Her treasure. Her hoard. Her value . . .' She stood up, unable to sit still, stretching her back and arms. 'Like the dragons who found caves, who built fortresses for their treasure, for their hoard, to be safe, to sleep on their treasure, to be their treasure. Take in, take in, and never give out!'

'You'll know the value of a good reputation,' Moss said drily, 'when you've lost it. 'Tisn't everything. But it's hard to fill the place of.'

'Would you give up being a witch to be respectable, Moss?'

'I don't know,' Moss said after a while, thoughtfully. 'I don't know as I'd know how. I have the one gift, maybe, but not the other.'

Tenar went to her and took her hands. Surprised at the gesture, Moss got up, drawing away a little; but Tenar drew her forward and kissed her cheek.

The older woman put up one hand and timidly touched Tenar's hair, one caress, as Ogion had used to do. Then she pulled away and muttered about having to go home, and started to leave, and asked at the door, 'Or would you rather I stayed, with them foreigners about?'

'Go on,' Tenar said. 'I'm used to foreigners.'

That night as she lay going to sleep she entered again into the vast gulfs of wind and light, but the light was smoky, red and orange-red and amber, as if the air itself were fire. In this element she was and was not; flying on the wind and being the wind, the blowing of the wind, the force that went free; and no voice called to her.

In the morning she sat on the doorstep brushing out her hair. She was not fair to blondness, like many Kargish people; her skin was pale, but her hair dark. It was still dark, hardly a thread of grey in it. She had washed it, using some of the water that was heating to wash clothes in, for she had decided the laundry would be her day's work, Ged being gone, and her respectability secure. She dried her hair in the sun, brushing it. In the hot, windy morning, sparks followed the brush and crackled from the flying ends of her hair.

Therru came to stand behind her, watching. Tenar turned and saw her so intent she was almost trembling.

'What is it, birdlet?'

'The fire flying out,' the child said, with fear or exultation. 'All over the sky!'

'It's just the sparks from my hair,' Tenar said, a little taken aback. Therru was smiling, and she did not know if she had ever seen the child smile before. Therru reached out both her hands, the whole one and the burned, as if to touch and follow the flight of something around Tenar's loose, floating hair. 'The fires, all flying out,' she repeated, and she laughed.

At that moment Tenar first asked herself how Therru saw her – saw the world – and knew she did not know: that she could not know what one saw with an eye that had been burned away. And Ogion's words, *They will fear her*, returned to her; but she felt no fear of the child. Instead, she brushed her hair again, vigorously, so the sparks would fly, and once again she heard the little husky laugh of delight.

She washed the sheets, the dishcloths, her shifts and spare dress, and Therru's dresses, and laid them out (after making sure the goats were in the fenced pasture) in the meadow to dry on the dry grass, weighting down the things with stones, for the wind was gusty, with a late-summer wildness in it.

Therru had been growing. She was still very small and thin for her age, which must be about eight, but in the last couple of months, with her injuries healed at last and free of pain, she had begun to run about more and to eat more. She was fast outgrowing her clothes, hand-me-downs from Lark's youngest, a girl of five.

Tenar thought she might walk into the village and visit with Weaver Fan and see if he might have an end or two of cloth to give in exchange for the swill she had been sending for his pigs. She would like to sew something for Therru. And she would like to visit with old Fan, too. Ogion's death and Ged's illness had kept her from the village and the people she had known there. They had pulled her away, as ever, from what she knew, what she knew how to do, the world she had chosen to live in – a world not of kings and queens, great powers and dominions, high arts and journeys and adventures (she thought as she made sure Therru was with Heather, and set off into town), but of common people doing common things, such as marrying, and bringing up children, and farming, and sewing, and doing the wash. She thought this with a kind of vengefulness, as if she were thinking it at Ged, now no doubt halfway to Middle Valley. She imagined him on the road, near the dell where she and Therru had slept. She imagined the slight, ashen-haired man going along alone and silently, with half a loaf of the witch's bread in his pocket, and a load of misery in his heart.

'It's time you found out, maybe,' she thought to him. 'Time you learned that you didn't learn everything on Roke!' As she harangued him thus in her mind, another image came into it: she saw near Ged one of the men who had stood waiting for her and Therru on that road. Involuntarily she said, 'Ged, be careful!' – fearing for him, for he did not carry even a stick. It was not the big fellow with hairy lips that she saw, but another of them, a youngish man with a leather cap, the one who had stared hard at Therru.

She looked up to see the little cottage next to Fan's house, where she had lived when she lived here. Between it and her a man was passing. It was the man she had been remembering, imagining, the man with a leather cap. He was going past the cottage, past the weaver's house; he had not seen her. She watched him walk on up the village street without stopping. He was going either to the turning of the hill road or to the mansion house.

Without pausing to think why, Tenar followed him at a distance until she saw which turn he took. He went on up the hill to the domain of the Lord of Re Albi, not down the road that Ged had gone.

She turned back then, and made her visit to old Fan.

Though almost a recluse, like many weavers, Fan had been kind in his shy way to the Kargish girl, and vigilant. How many people, she thought, had protected her respectability! Now nearly blind, Fan had an apprentice who did most of the weaving. He was glad to have a visitor. He sat as if in state in an old carved chair under the object from which his use-name came: a very large painted fan, the treasure of his family – the gift, so the story went, of a generous sea-pirate to his grandfather for some speedy sail-making in time of need. It was displayed open on the wall. The delicately painted men and women in their gorgeous robes of rose and jade and azure, the towers and bridges and banners of Havnor Great Port, were all familiar to Tenar as soon as she saw the fan again. Visitors to Re Albi were often brought to see it. It was the finest thing, all agreed, in the village.

She admired it, knowing it would please the old man, and because it was indeed very beautiful, and he said, 'You've not seen much to equal that, in all your travels, eh?'

'No, no. Nothing like it in Middle Valley at all,' said she.

'When you was here, in my cottage, did I ever show you the other side of it?'

'The other side? No,' she said, and nothing would do then but he must get the fan down; only she had to climb up and do it, carefully untacking it, since he could not see well enough and could not climb up on the chair. He directed her anxiously. She laid it in his hands, and he peered with his dim eyes at it, half closed it to make sure the ribs played freely, then closed it all the way, turned it over, and handed it to her.

'Open it slow,' he said.

She did so. Dragons moved as the folds of the fan moved. Painted faint and fine on the yellowed silk, dragons of pale red, blue, green moved and grouped, as the figures on the other side were grouped, among clouds and mountain peaks.

'Hold it up to the light,' said old Fan.

She did so, and saw the two sides, the two paintings, made one by the light flowing through the silk, so that the clouds and peaks were the towers of the city, and the men and women were winged, and the dragons looked with human eyes.

'You see?'

'I see,' she murmured.

'I can't, now, but it's in my mind's eye. I don't show many that.'

'It is very wonderful.'

'I meant to show it to the old mage,' Fan said, 'but with one thing and another I never did.'

Tenar turned the fan once more before the light, then remounted it as it had been, the dragons hidden in darkness, the men and women walking in the light of day.

Fan took her out next to see his pigs, a fine pair, fattening nicely towards autumn sausages. They discussed Heather's shortcomings as a swill-carrier. Tenar told him that she fancied a scrap of cloth for a child's dress, and he was delighted, pulling out a full width of fine linen sheeting for her, while the young woman who was his apprentice, and who seemed to have taken up his unsociability as well as his craft, clacked away at the broad loom, steady and scowling.

Walking home, Tenar thought of Therru sitting at that loom. It would be a decent living. The bulk of the work was dull, always the same over, but weaving was an honourable trade and in some hands a noble art. And people expected weavers to be a bit shy, often to be unmarried, shut away at their work as they were; yet they were respected. And working indoors at a loom, Therru would not have to show her face. But the claw hand? Could that hand throw the shuttle, warp the loom?

And was she to hide all her life?

But what was she to do? 'Knowing what her life must be . . .'

Tenar set herself to think of something else. Of the dress she would make. Lark's daughter's dresses were coarse homespun, plain as mud. She could dye half this width, yellow maybe, or with red madder from the marsh; and then a full apron or overdress of white, with a ruffle to it. Was the child to be hidden at a loom in the dark and never have a ruffle to her skirt? And that would still leave enough for a shift, and a second apron if she cut out carefully.

'Therru!' she called as she approached the house. Heather and Therru had been in the broom-pasture when she left. She called again, wanting to show Therru the material and tell her about the dress. Heather came gawking around from the springhouse, hauling Sippy on a rope.

'Where's Therru?'

'With you,' Heather replied so serenely that Tenar looked around for the child before she understood that Heather had no idea where she was and had simply stated what she wished to be true.

'Where did you leave her?'

Heather had no idea. She had never let Tenar down

before; she had seemed to understand that Therru had to be kept more or less in sight, like a goat. But maybe it was Therru all along who had understood that, and had kept herself in sight? So Tenar thought, as having no comprehensible guidance from Heather, she began to look and call for the child, receiving no response.

She kept away from the cliff's edge as long as she could. Their first day there, she had explained to Therru that she must never go alone down the steep fields below the house or along the sheer edge north of it, because one-eyed vision cannot judge distance or depth with certainty. The child had obeyed. She always obeyed. But children forget. But she would not forget. But she might get close to the edge without knowing it. But surely she had gone to Moss's house. That was it – having been there alone, last night, she would go again. That was it, of course.

She was not there. Moss had not seen her.

'I'll find her, I'll find her, dearie,' she assured Tenar; but instead of going up the forest path to look for her as Tenar had hoped she would, Moss began to knot up her hair in preparation for casting a spell of finding.

Tenar ran back to Ogion's house, calling again and again. And this time she looked down the steep fields below the house, hoping to see the little figure crouched playing among the boulders. But all she saw was the sea, wrinkled and dark, at the end of those falling fields, and she grew dizzy and sick-hearted.

She went to Ogion's grave and a short way past it up the forest path, calling. As she came back through the meadow, the kestrel was hunting in the same spot where Ged had watched it hunt. This time it stooped, and struck, and rose with some little creature in its talons. It flew fast to the forest. She's feeding her young, Tenar thought. All kinds of thoughts went through her mind very vivid and precise, as she passed the laundry laid out on the grass, dry now, she must take it up before evening. She must search

579

around the house, the springhouse, the milking shed, more carefully. This was her fault. She had caused it to happen by thinking of making Therru into a weaver, shutting her away in the dark to work, to be respectable. When Ogion had said 'Teach her, teach her all, Tenar!' When she knew that a wrong that cannot be repaired must be transcended. When she knew that the child had been given her and she had failed in her charge, failed her trust, lost her, lost the one great gift.

She went into the house, having searched every corner of the other buildings, and looked again in the alcove and round the other bed. She poured herself water, for her mouth was dry as sand.

Behind the door the three sticks of wood, Ogion's staff and the walking sticks, moved in the shadows, and one of them said, 'Here.'

The child was crouched in that dark corner, drawn into her own body so that she seemed no bigger than a little dog, head bent down to the shoulder, arms and legs pulled tight in, the one eye shut.

'Little bird, little sparrow, little flame, what is wrong? What happened? What have they done to you now?'

Tenar held the small body, closed and stiff as stone, rocking it in her arms. 'How could you frighten me so? How could you hide from me? Oh, I was so angry!'

She wept, and her tears fell on the child's face.

'Oh Therru, Therru, Therru, don't hide away from me!'

A shudder went through the knotted limbs, and slowly they loosened. Therru moved, and all at once clung to Tenar, pushing her face into the hollow between Tenar's breast and shoulder, clinging tighter, till she was clutching desperately. She did not weep. She never wept; her tears had been burned out of her, maybe; she had none. But she made a long, moaning, sobbing sound.

Tenar held her, rocking her, rocking her. Very, very slowly the desperate grip relaxed. The head lay pillowed on Tenar's breast.

'Tell me,' the woman murmured, and the child answered in her faint, hoarse whisper, 'He came here.'

Tenar's first thought was of Ged, and her mind, still moving with the quickness of fear, caught that, saw who 'he' was to her, and gave it a wry grin in passing, but passed on, hunting. 'Who came here?'

No answer but a kind of internal shuddering.

'A man,' Tenar said quietly, 'a man in a leather cap.'

Therru nodded once.

'We saw him on the road, coming here.'

No response.

'The four men – the ones I was angry at, do you remember? He was one of them.'

But she recalled how Therru had held her head down, hiding the burned side, not looking up, as she had always done among strangers.

'Do you know him, Therru?'

'Yes.'

'From – from when you lived in the camp by the river?'

One nod.

Tenar's arms tightened around her.

'He came here?' she said, and all the fear she had felt turned as she spoke into anger, a rage that burned in her the length of her body like a rod of fire. She gave a kind of laugh – 'Hah!' – and remembered in that moment Kalessin, how Kalessin had laughed.

But it was not so simple for a human and a woman. The fire must be contained. And the child must be comforted.

'Did he see you?'

'I hid.'

Presently Tenar said, stroking Therru's hair, 'He will never touch you, Therru. Understand me and believe me: he will never touch you again. He'll never see you again unless I'm with you, and then he must deal with me. Do you understand, my dear, my precious, my beautiful? You need not fear him. You must not fear him. He wants you to fear him. He feeds on your fear. We will starve him, Therru. We'll starve him till he eats himself. Till he chokes gnawing on the bones of his own hands ... Ah, ah, ah, don't listen to me now, I'm only angry, only angry ... Am I red? Am I red like a Gontish-woman, now? Like a dragon, am I red?' She tried to joke; and Therru, lifting her head, looked up into her face from her own crumpled, tremulous, fire-eaten face and said, 'Yes. You are a red dragon.'

The idea of the man's coming to the house, being in the house, coming around to look at his handiwork, maybe thinking of improving on it, that idea whenever it recurred to Tenar came less as a thought than as a queasy fit, a need to vomit. But the nausea burned itself out against the anger.

They got up and washed, and Tenar decided that what she felt most of all just now was hunger. 'I am hollow,' she said to Therru, and set them out a substantial meal of bread and cheese, cold beans in oil and herbs, a sliced onion, and dry sausage. Therru ate a good deal, and Tenar ate a great deal.

As they cleared up, she said, 'For the present, Therru, I won't leave you at all, and you won't leave me. Right? And we should both go now to Aunty Moss's house. She was making a spell to find you, and she needn't bother to go on with it, but she might not know that.'

Therru stopped moving. She glanced once at the open doorway, and shrank away from it.

'We need to bring in the laundry, too. On our way back. And when we're back, I'll show you the cloth I got today. For a dress. For a new dress, for you. A red dress.'

The child stood, drawing in to herself.

'If we hide, Therru, we feed him. We will eat. And we will starve him. Come with me.'

The difficulty, the barrier of that doorway to the outside

was tremendous to Therru. She shrank from it, she hid her face, she trembled, stumbled, it was cruel to force her to cross it, cruel to drive her out of hiding, but Tenar was without pity. 'Come!' she said, and the child came.

They walked hand-in-hand across the fields to Moss's house. Once or twice Therru managed to look up.

Moss was not surprised to see them, but she had a queer, wary look about her. She told Therru to run inside her house to see the ringneck hen's new chicks and choose which two might be hers; and Therru disappeared at once into that refuge.

'She was in the house all along,' Tenar said. 'Hiding.'

'Well she might,' said Moss.

'Why?' Tenar asked harshly. She was not in the hiding vein.

'There's – there's beings about,' the witch said, not portentously but uneasily.

'There's scoundrels about!' said Tenar, and Moss looked at her and drew back a little.

'Eh, now,' she said. 'Eh, dearie. You have a fire around you, a shining of fire all about your head. I cast the spell to find the child, but it didn't go right. It went its own way somehow, and I don't know yet if it's ended. I'm bewildered. I saw great beings. I sought the little girl but I saw them, flying in the mountains, flying in the clouds. And now you have that about you, like your hair was afire. What's amiss, what's wrong?'

'A man in a leather cap,' Tenar said. 'A youngish man. Well enough looking. The shoulder seam of his vest's torn. Have you seen him round?'

Moss nodded. 'They took him on for the haying at the mansion house.'

'I told you that she' – Tenar glanced at the house – 'was with a woman and two men? He's one of them.'

'You mean, one of them that –'

'Yes.'

Moss stood like a wood carving of an old woman, rigid, a block. 'I don't know,' she said at last. 'I thought I knew enough. But I don't. What – What would – Would he come to – to *see* her?'

'If he's the father, maybe he's come to claim her.'

'Claim her?'

'She's his property.'

Tenar spoke evenly. She looked up at the heights of Gont Mountain as she spoke.

'But I think it's not the father. I think this is the other one. The one that came and told my friend in the village that the child had "hurt herself".'

Moss was still bewildered, still frightened by her own conjurations and visions, by Tenar's fierceness, by the presence of abominable evil. She shook her head, desolate. 'I don't know,' she said. 'I thought I knew enough. How could he come back?'

'To eat,' Tenar said. 'To eat. I won't be leaving her alone again. But tomorrow, Moss, I might ask you to keep her here an hour or so, early in the day. Would you do that, while I go up to the manor house?'

'Aye, dearie. Of course. I could put a hiding spell on her, if you like. But . . . But they're up there, the great men from the King's City . . .'

'Why, then, they can see how life is among the common folk,' said Tenar, and Moss drew back again as if from a rush of sparks blown her way from a fire in the wind.

9. Finding Words

They were making hay in the lord's long meadow, strung out across the slope in the bright shadows of morning. Three of the mowers were women, and of the two men one was a boy, as Tenar could make out from some distance, and the other was stooped and grizzled. She came up along the mown rows and asked one of the women about the man with the leather cap.

'Him from down by Valmouth, ah,' said the mower. 'Don't know where he's got to.' The others came along the row, glad of a break. None of them knew where the man from Middle Valley was or why he wasn't mowing with them. 'That kind don't stay,' the grizzled man said. 'Shiftless. You know him, miss's?'

'Not by choice,' said Tenar. 'He came lurking about my place – frightened the child. I don't know what he's called, even.'

'Calls himself Handy,' the boy volunteered. The others looked at her or looked away and said nothing. They were beginning to piece out who she must be, the Kargish woman in the old mage's house. They were tenants of the Lord of Re Albi, suspicious of the villagers, leery of anything to do with Ogion. They whetted their scythes, turned away, strung out again, fell to work. Tenar walked down from the hillside field, past a row of walnut trees, to the road.

On it a man stood waiting. Her heart leapt. She strode on to meet him.

It was Aspen, the wizard of the mansion house. He stood gracefully leaning on his tall pine staff in the shade of a roadside tree. As she came out on to the road he said, 'Are you looking for work?'

'No.'

'My lord needs field hands. This hot weather's on the turn, the hay must be got in.'

To Goha, Flint's widow, what he said was appropriate, and Goha answered him politely, 'No doubt your skill can turn the rain from the fields till the hay's in.' But he knew she was the woman to whom Ogion dying had spoken his true name, and, given that knowledge, what he said was so insulting and deliberately false as to serve as a clear warning. She had been about to ask him if he knew where the man Handy was. Instead, she said, 'I came to say to the overseer here that a man he took on for the haymaking left my village as a thief and worse, not one he'd choose to have about the place. But it seems the man's moved on.'

She gazed calmly at Aspen until he answered, with an effort, 'I know nothing about these people.'

She had thought him, on the morning of Ogion's death, to be a young man, a tall, handsome youth with a grey cloak and a silvery staff. He did not look as young as she had thought him, or he was young but somehow dried and withered. His stare and his voice were now openly contemptuous, and she answered him in Goha's voice: 'To be sure. I beg your pardon.' She wanted no trouble with him. She made to go on her way back to the village, but Aspen said, 'Wait!'

She waited.

'"A thief and worse," you say, but slander's cheap, and a woman's tongue worse than any thief. You come up here to make bad blood among the field hands, casting calumny and lies, the dragonseed every witch sows behind her. Did you think I did not know you for a witch? When I saw that foul imp that clings to you, do you think I did not know how it was begotten, and for what purposes? The man did well who tried to destroy that creature, but the job should be completed. You defied me once, across the body of the old wizard, and I forbore to punish you then, for his sake and in the presence of others. But now you've come too far, and I warn you, woman! I will not have you set foot on this domain. And if you cross my will or dare so much as speak to me again, I will have you driven from Re Albi, and off the Overfell, with the dogs at your heels. Have you understood me?'

'No,' Tenar said. 'I have never understood men like you.'

She turned and set off down the road.

Something like a stroking touch went up her spine, and her hair lifted up on her head. She turned sharp round to see the wizard reach out his staff towards her, and the dark lightnings gather round it, and his lips part to speak. She thought in that moment, *Because Ged has lost his magery, I thought all men had, but I was wrong!* – And a civil voice said, 'Well, well. What have we here?'

Two of the men from Havnor had come out on to the road from the cherry orchards on the other side of it. They looked from Aspen to Tenar with bland and courtly expressions, as if regretting the necessity of preventing a wizard from laying a curse on a middle-aged widow, but really, really, it would not do.

'Mistress Goha,' said the man with the gold-embroidered shirt, and bowed to her.

The other, the bright-eyed one, saluted her also, smiling. 'Mistress Goha,' he said, 'is one who, like the king, bears her true name openly, I think, and unafraid. Living in Gont, she may prefer that we use her Gontish name. But knowing her deeds, I ask to do her honour; for she wore the Ring that no woman wore since Elfarran.' He dropped to one knee as if it were the most natural thing in the world, took Tenar's right hand very lightly and quickly, and touched his forehead to her wrist. He released her and stood up, smiling that kind, collusive smile.

'Ah,' said Tenar, flustered and warmed right through – 'there's all kinds of power in the world! – Thank you.'

The wizard stood motionless, staring. He had closed his mouth on the curse and drawn back his staff, but there was still a visible darkness about it and about his eyes.

She did not know whether he had known or had just now learned that she was Tenar of the Ring. It did not matter. He could not hate her more. To be a woman was her fault. Nothing could worsen or amend it, in his eyes; no punishment was enough. He had looked at what had been done to Therru, and approved.

'Sir,' she said now to the older man, 'anything less than honesty and openness seems dishonour to the king, for whom you speak – and act, as now. I'd like to honour the king, and his messengers. But my own honour lies in silence, until my friend releases me. I – I'm sure, my lords, that he'll send some word to you, in time. Only give him time, I pray you.'

'Surely,' said the one, and the other, 'As much time as he wants. And your trust, my lady, honours us above all.'

She went on down the road to Re Albi at last, shaken by the shock and change of things, the wizard's flaying hatred, her own angry contempt, her terror at the sudden knowledge of his will and power to do her harm, the sudden end of that terror in the refuge offered by the envoys of the king – the men who had come in the white-sailed ship from the haven itself, the Tower of the Sword and the Throne, the centre of right and order. Her heart lifted up in gratitude. There was indeed a king upon that throne, and in his crown the chiefest jewel would be the Rune of Peace.

She liked the younger man's face, clever and kindly, and the way he had knelt to her as to a queen, and his smile that had a wink hidden in it. She turned to look back. The two envoys were walking up the road to the mansion house with the wizard Aspen. They seemed to be conversing with him amicably, as if nothing had happened.

That sank her surge of hopeful trust a bit. To be sure,

they were courtiers. It wasn't their business to quarrel, or to judge and disapprove. And he was a wizard, and their host's wizard. Still, she thought, they needn't have walked and talked with him quite so comfortably.

The men from Havnor stayed several days with the Lord of Re Albi, perhaps hoping that the archmage would change his mind and come to them, but they did not seek him, nor press Tenar about where he might be. When they left at last, Tenar told herself that she must make up her mind what to do. There was no real reason for her to stay here, and two strong reasons for leaving: Aspen and Handy, neither of whom could she trust to let her and Therru alone.

Yet she found it hard to make up her mind, because it was hard to think of going. In leaving Re Albi now she left Ogion, lost him, as she had not lost him while she kept his house and weeded his onions. And she thought, 'I will never dream of the sky, down there.' Here, where Kalessin had come, she was Tenar, she thought. Down in Middle Valley she would only be Goha again. She delayed. She said to herself, 'Am I to fear those scoundrels, to run from them? That's what they want me to do. Are they to make me come and go at their will?' She said to herself, 'I'll just finish the cheese-making.' She kept Therru always with her. And the days went by.

Moss came with a tale to tell. Tenar had asked her about the wizard Aspen, not telling her the whole story but saying that he had threatened her – which, in fact, might well be all he had meant to do. Moss usually kept clear of the old lord's domain, but she was curious about what went on there, and not unwilling to find the chance to chat with some acquaintances there, a woman from whom she had learned midwifery and others whom she had attended as healer or finder. She got them talking about the doings at the mansion house. They all hated

Aspen and so were quite ready to talk about him, but their tales must be heard as half spite and fear. Still, there would be facts among the fancies. Moss herself attested that until Aspen came three years ago, the younger lord, the grandson, had been fit and well, though a shy, sullen man, 'scared-like', she said. Then about the time the young lord's mother died, the old lord had sent to Roke for a wizard – 'What for? With Lord Ogion not a mile away? And they're all witchfolk themselves in the mansion.'

But Aspen had come. He had paid his respects and no more to Ogion, and always, Moss said, stayed up at the mansion. Since then, less and less had been seen of the grandson, and it was said now that he lay day and night in bed, 'like a sick baby, all shrivelled up,' said one of the women who had been into the house on some errand. But the old lord, 'a hundred years old, or near, or more,' Moss insisted – she had no fear of numbers and no respect for them – the old lord was flourishing, 'full of juice,' they said. And one of the men, for they would have only men wait on them in the mansion, had told one of the women that the old lord had hired the wizard to make him live for ever, and that the wizard was doing that, feeding him, the man said, off the grandson's life. And the man saw no harm in it, saying, 'Who wouldn't want to live for ever?'

'Well,' Tenar said, taken aback. 'That's an ugly story. Don't they talk about all this in the village?'

Moss shrugged. It was a matter of 'Let be' again. The doings of the powerful were not to be judged by the powerless. And there was the dim, blind loyalty, the rootedness in place: the old man was *their* lord, Lord of Re Albi, nobody else's business what he did . . . Moss evidently felt this herself. 'Risky,' she said, 'bound to go wrong, such a trick,' but she did not say it was wicked.

No sign of the man Handy had been seen up at the mansion. Longing to be sure that he had left the Overfell,

Tenar asked an acquaintance or two in the village if they had seen such a man, but she got unwilling and equivocal replies. They wanted no part of her affairs. 'Let be . . .' Only old Fan treated her as a friend and fellow-villager. And that might be because his eyes were so dim he could not clearly see Therru.

She took the child with her now when she went into the village, or any distance at all from the house.

Therru did not find this bondage wearisome. She stayed close by Tenar as a much younger child would do, working with her or playing. Her play was with cat's cradle, basket making, and with a couple of bone figures that Tenar had found in a little grass bag on one of Ogion's shelves. There was an animal that might be a dog or a sheep, a figure that might be a woman or a man. To Tenar they had no sense of power or danger about them, and Moss said, 'Just toys.' To Therru they were a great magic. She moved them about in the patterns of some silent story for hours at a time; she did not speak as she played. Sometimes she built houses for the person and the animal, stone cairns, huts of mud and straw. They were always in her pocket in their grass bag. She was learning to spin; she could hold the distaff in the burned hand and twist the drop-spindle with the other. They had combed the goats regularly since they had been there, and by now had a good sackful of silky goathair to be spun.

'But I should be teaching her,' Tenar thought, distressed. 'Teach her *all*, Ogion said, and what am I teaching her? Cooking and spinning?' Then another part of her mind said in Goha's voice, 'And are those not true arts, needful and noble? Is wisdom all words?'

Still she worried over the matter, and one afternoon while Therru was pulling the goathair to clean and loosen it and she was carding it, in the shade of the peach tree, she said, 'Therru, maybe it's time you began to learn the true names of things. There is a language in which all things bear their true names, and deed and word are one. By speaking that tongue Segoy raised the islands from the deeps. It is the language dragons speak.'

The child listened, silent.

Tenar laid down her carding combs and picked up a small stone from the ground. 'In that tongue,' she said, 'this is *tolk*.'

Therru watched what she did and repeated the word, *tolk*, but without voice, only forming it with her lips, which were drawn back a little on the right side by the scarring.

The stone lay on Tenar's palm, a stone.

They were both silent.

'Not yet,' Tenar said. 'That's not what I have to teach you now.' She let the stone fall to the ground, and picked up her combs and a handful of cloudy grey wool Therru had prepared for carding. 'Maybe when you have your true name, maybe that will be the time. Not now. Now, listen. Now is the time for stories, for you to begin to learn the stories. I can tell you stories of the Archipelago and of the Kargad Lands. I told you a story I learned from my friend Aihal the Silent. Now I'll tell you one I learned from my friend Lark when she told it to her children and mine. This is the story of Andaur and Avad. As long ago as forever, as far away as Selidor, there lived a man called Andaur, a woodcutter, who went up in the hills alone. One day, deep in the forest, he cut a great oak tree down. As it fell it cried out to him in a human voice . . .'

It was a pleasant afternoon for them both.

But that night as she lay by the sleeping child, Tenar could not sleep. She was restless, concerned with one petty anxiety after another – did I fasten the pasture gate, does my hand ache from carding or is it arthritis beginning, and so on. Then she became very uneasy, thinking she heard noises outside the house. Why haven't I got me a dog? she thought. Stupid, not to have a dog. A woman and child living alone ought to have a dog these days. But this is Ogion's house! Nobody would come here to do evil. But Ogion is dead, dead, buried at the roots of the tree at the forest's edge. And no one will come. Sparrowhawk's gone, run away. Not even Sparrowhawk any more, a shadow man, no good to anyone, a dead man forced to be alive. And I have no strength, there's no good in me. I say the word of the Making and it dies in my mouth, it is meaningless. A stone. I am a woman, an old woman, weak, stupid. All I do is wrong. All I touch turns to ashes, shadow, stone. I am the creature of darkness, swollen with darkness. Only fire can cleanse me. Only fire can eat me, eat me away like –

She sat up and cried out aloud in her own language, 'The curse be turned, and turn!' – and brought her right arm out and down, pointing straight to the closed door. Then leaping out of bed, she went to the door, flung it open, and said into the cloudy night, 'You come too late, Aspen. I was eaten long ago. Go clean your own house!'

There was no answer, no sound, but a faint, sour, vile smell of burning – singed cloth or hair.

She shut the door, set Ogion's staff against it, and looked to see that Therru still slept. She did not sleep herself, that night.

In the morning she took Therru into the village to ask Fan if he would want the yarn they had been spinning. It was an excuse to get away from the house and to be for a little while among people. The old man said he would be glad to weave the yarn, and they talked for a few minutes, under the great painted fan, while the apprentice scowled and clacked away grimly at the loom. As Tenar and Therru left Fan's house, somebody dodged around the corner of the little cottage where she had lived. Something, wasps or bees, were stinging Tenar's neck and head, and there was a patter of rain all round, a thunder-shower, but there were no clouds – Stones. She saw the pebbles strike the ground. Therru had stopped, startled and puzzled, looking around. A couple of boys ran from behind the cottage, half hiding, half showing themselves, calling out to each other, laughing.

'Come along,' Tenar said steadily, and they walked to Ogion's house.

Tenar was shaking, and the shaking got worse as they walked. She tried to conceal it from Therru, who looked troubled but not frightened, not having understood what had happened.

As soon as they entered the house, Tenar knew someone had been there while they were in the village. It smelled of burned meat and hair. The coverlet of their bed had been disarranged.

When she tried to think what to do, she knew there was a spell on her. It had been laid waiting for her. She could not stop shaking, and her mind was confused, slow, unable to decide. She could not think. She had said the word, the true name of the stone, and it had been flung at her, in her face – in the face of evil, the hideous face – She had dared speak – She could not speak –

She thought, in her own language, *I cannot think in Hardic. I must not.*

She could think, in Kargish. Not quickly. It was as if she had to ask the girl Arha, who she had been long ago, to come out of the darkness and think for her. To help her. As she had helped her last night, turning the wizard's curse back on him. Arha had not known a great deal of what Tenar and Goha knew, but she had known how to curse, and how to live in the dark, and how to be silent.

It was hard to do that, to be silent. She wanted to cry out. She wanted to talk – to go to Moss and tell her what had happened, why she must go, to say good-bye at least. She tried to say to Heather, 'The goats are yours now, Heather,' and she managed to say that in Hardic, so that

Heather would understand, but Heather did not understand. She stared and laughed. 'Oh, they're Lord Ogion's goats!' she said.

'Then – you –' Tenar tried to say 'go on keeping them for him,' but a deadly sickness came into her and she heard her voice saying shrilly, 'fool, halfwit, imbecile, woman!' Heather stared and stopped laughing. Tenar covered her own mouth with her hand. She took Heather and turned her to look at the cheeses ripening in the milking shed, and pointed to them and to Heather, back and forth, until Heather nodded vaguely and laughed again because she was acting so queer.

Tenar nodded to Therru – come! – and went into the house, where the foul smell was stronger, making Therru cower.

Tenar fetched out their packs and their travel shoes. In her pack she put her spare dress and shifts, Therru's two old dresses and the half-made new one and the spare cloth; the spindle whorls she had carved for herself and Therru; and a little food and a clay bottle of water for the way. In Therru's pack went Therru's best baskets, the bone person and the bone animal in their grass bag, some feathers, a little maze-mat Moss had given her, and a bag of nuts and raisins.

She wanted to say, 'Go water the peach tree,' but dared not. She took the child out and showed her. Therru watered the tiny shoot carefully.

They swept and straightened up the house, working fast, in silence.

Tenar set a jug back on the shelf and saw on the other end of the shelf the three great books, Ogion's books.

Arha saw them and they were nothing to her, big leather boxes full of paper.

But Tenar stared at them and bit her knuckle, frowning with the effort to decide, to know what to do, and to know how to carry them. She could not carry them. But she must. They could not stay here in the desecrated house, the house where hatred had come in. They were his. Ogion's. Ged's. Hers. The knowledge. Teach her all! She emptied their wool and yarn from the sack she had meant to carry it in and put the books in one atop the other, and tied the neck of the bag with a leather strap with a loop to hold it by. Then she said, 'We must go now, Therru.' She spoke in Kargish, but the child's name was the same, it was a Kargish word, flame, flaming; and she came, asking no questions, carrying her little hoard in the pack on her back.

They took up their walking sticks, the hazel shoot and the alder branch. They left Ogion's staff beside the door in the dark corner. They left the door of the house wide open to the wind from the sea.

An animal sense guided Tenar away from the fields and away from the hill road she had come by. She took a short cut down the steep-falling pastures, holding Therru's hand, to the wagon road that zigzagged down to Gont Port. She knew that if she met Aspen she was lost, and thought he might be waiting for her on the way. But not, maybe, on this way.

After a mile or so of the descent she began to be able to think. What she thought first was that she had taken the right road. For the Hardic words were coming back to her, and after a while, the true words, so that she stooped and picked up a stone and held it in her hand, saying in her mind, *tolk*; and she put that stone in her pocket. She looked out into the vast levels of air and cloud and said in her mind, once, *Kalessin*. And her mind cleared, as that air was clear.

They came into a long cutting shadowed by high, grassy banks and outcrops of rock, where she was a little uneasy. As they came out on to the turn they saw the dark-blue bay below them, and coming into it between the Armed

Cliffs a beautiful ship under full sail. Tenar had feared the last such ship, but not this one. She wanted to run down the road to meet it.

That she could not do. They went at Therru's pace. It was a better pace than it had been two months ago, and going downhill made it easy, too. But the ship ran to meet them. There was a magewind in her sails; she came across the bay like a flying swan. She was in port before Tenar and Therru were halfway down the next long turning of the road.

Towns of any size at all were very strange places to Tenar. She had not lived in them. She had seen the greatest city in Earthsea, Havnor, once, for a while; and she had sailed into Gont Port with Ged, years ago, but they had climbed on up the road to the Overfell without pausing in the streets. The only other town she knew was Valmouth, where her daughter lived, a sleepy, sunny little harbour town where a ship trading from the Andrades was a great event, and most of the conversation of the inhabitants concerned dried fish.

She and the child came into the streets of Gont Port when the sun was still well above the western sea. Therru had walked fifteen miles without complaint and without being worn out, though certainly she was very tired. Tenar was tired too, having not slept the night before, and having been much distressed; and also Ogion's books had been a heavy burden. Halfway down the road she had put them into the backpack, and the food and clothing into the wool-sack, which was better, but not all that much better. So they came trudging among outlying houses to the landgate of the city, where the road, coming between two carved stone dragons, turned into a street. There a man, the guard of the gate, eyed them. Therru bent her burned face down towards the shoulder and hid her burned hand under the apron of her dress.

'Will you be going to a house in town, mistress?' the guard asked, peering at the child.

Tenar did not know what to say. She did not know there were guards at city gates. She had nothing to pay a toll-keeper or an innkeeper. She did not know a soul in Gont Port – except, she thought now, the wizard, the one who had come up to bury Ogion, what was he called? But she did not know what he was called. She stood there with her mouth open, like Heather.

'Go on, go on,' the guard said, bored, and turned away.

She wanted to ask him where she would find the road south across the headlands, the coast road to Valmouth; but she dared not waken his interest again, lest he decide she was after all a vagrant or a witch or whatever he and the stone dragons were supposed to keep out of Gont Port. So they went on between the dragons – Therru looked up, a little, to see them – and tramped along on cobblestones, more and more amazed, bewildered, and abashed. It did not seem to Tenar that anybody or anything in the world had been kept out of Gont Port. It was all here. Tall houses of stone, wagons, drays, carts, cattle, donkeys, market-places, shops, crowds, people, people – the farther they went the more people there were. Therru clung to Tenar's hand, sidling, hiding her face with her hair. Tenar clung to Therru's hand.

She did not see how they could stay here, so the only thing to do was get started south and go till nightfall – all too soon now – hoping to camp in the woods. Tenar picked out a broad woman in a broad white apron who was closing the shutters of a shop, and crossed the street, resolved to ask her for the road south out of the city. The woman's firm, red face looked pleasant enough, but as Tenar was getting up her courage to speak to her, Therru clutched her hard as if trying to hide herself against her, and looking up she saw coming down the street towards her the man with the leather cap. He saw her at the same instant. He stopped.

Tenar seized Therru's arm and half dragged, half swung her round. 'Come!' she said, and strode straight on past the man. Once she had put him behind her she walked faster, going downhill towards the flare and dark of the sunset water and the docks and quays at the foot of the steep street. Therru ran with her, gasping as she had gasped after she was burned.

Tall masts rocked against the red and yellow sky. The ship, sails furled, lay against the stone pier, beyond an oared galley.

Tenar looked back. The man was following them, close behind. He was not hurrying.

She ran out on to the pier, but after a way Therru stumbled and could not go on, unable to get her breath. Tenar picked her up, and the child held to her, hiding her face in Tenar's shoulder. But Tenar could scarcely move, thus laden. Her legs shook under her. She took a step, and another, and another. She came to the little wooden bridge they had laid from the pier to the ship's deck. She laid her hand on its rail.

A sailor on deck, a bald, wiry fellow, looked her over. 'What's wrong, miss's?' he said.

'Is – Is the ship from Havnor?'

'From the King's City, sure.'

'Let me aboard!'

'Well, I can't do that,' the man said, grinning, but his eyes shifted: he was looking at the man who had come to stand beside Tenar.

'You don't have to run away,' Handy said to her. 'I don't mean you any harm. I don't want to hurt you. You don't understand. I was the one got help for her, wasn't I? I was really sorry, what happened. I want to help you with her.' He put out his hand as if drawn irresistibly to touch Therru. Tenar could not move ›he had promised Therru that he would never touch her again. She saw the hand touch the child's bare, flinching arm.

599

'What do you want with her?' said another voice. Another sailor had taken the place of the bald one: a young man. Tenar thought he was her son.

Handy was quick to speak. 'She's got – she took my kid. My niece. It's mine. She witched it, she run off with it, see –'

She could not speak at all. The words were gone from her again, taken from her. The young sailor was not her son. His face was thin and stern, with clear eyes. Looking at him, she found the words: 'Let me come aboard. Please!'

The young man held out his hand. She took it, and he brought her across the gangway on to the deck of the ship.

'Wait there,' he said to Handy, and to her, 'Come with me.'

But her legs would not hold her up. She sank down in a heap on the deck of the ship from Havnor, dropping the heavy sack but clinging to the child. 'Don't let him take her, oh, don't let them have her, not again, not again, not again!'

10. The Dolphin

She would not let go the child, she would not give the child to them. They were all men aboard the ship. Only after a long time did she begin to be able to take into her mind what they said, what had been done, what was happening. When she understood who the young man was, the one she had thought was her son, it seemed as if she had understood it all along, only she had not been able to think it. She had not been able to think anything.

He had come back on to the ship from the docks and now stood talking to a grey-haired man, the ship's master by the look of him, near the gangplank. He glanced over at Tenar, whom they had let stay crouching with Therru in a corner of the deck between the railing and a great windlass. The long day's weariness had won out over Therru's fear; she was fast asleep, close against Tenar, with her little pack for a pillow and her cloak for a blanket.

Tenar got up slowly, and the young man came to her at once. She straightened her skirts and tried to smooth her hair back. 'I am Tenar of Atuan,' she said. He stood still. She said, 'I think you are the king.'

He was very young, younger than her son, Spark. He could hardly be twenty yet. But there was a look to him that was not young at all, something in his eyes that made her think: He has been through the fire.

'My name is Lebannen of Enlad, my lady,' he said, and he was about to bow or even kneel to her. She caught his hands so that they stood there face to face. 'Not to me,' she said, 'nor I to you!'

He laughed in surprise, and held her hands while he

stared at her frankly. 'How did you know I sought you? Were you coming to me, when that man –?'

'No, no. I was running away – from him – from – from ruffians – I was trying to go home, that's all.'

'To Atuan?'

'Oh, no! To my farm. In Middle Valley. On Gont, here.' She laughed too, a laugh with tears in it. The tears could be wept now, and would be wept. She let go the king's hands so that she could wipe her eyes.

'Where is it, Middle Valley?' he asked.

'South and east, around the headlands there. Valmouth is the port.'

'We'll take you there,' he said, with delight in being able to offer it, to do it.

She smiled and wiped her eyes, nodding acceptance.

'A glass of wine. Some food, some rest,' he said, 'and a bed for your child.' The ship's master, listening discreetly, gave orders. The bald sailor she remembered from what seemed a long time ago came forward. He was going to pick up Therru. Tenar stood between him and the child. She could not let him touch her. 'I'll carry her,' she said, her voice strained high.

'There's the stairs there, miss's. I'll do it,' said the sailor, and she knew he was kind, but she could not let him touch Therru.

'Let me,' the young man, the king, said, and with a glance at her for permission, he knelt, gathered up the sleeping child, and carried her to the hatchway and carefully down the ladder-stairs. Tenar followed.

He laid her on a bunk in a tiny cabin, awkwardly, tenderly. He tucked the cloak around her. Tenar let him do so.

In a larger cabin that ran across the stern of the ship, with a long window looking out over the twilit bay, he asked her to sit at the oaken table. He took a tray from the sailor boy that brought it, poured out red wine in goblets of heavy glass, offered her fruit and cakes.

She tasted the wine.

'It's very good, but not the Dragon Year,' she said.

He looked at her in unguarded surprise, like any boy.

'From Enlad, not the Andrades,' he said meekly.

'It's very fine,' she assured him, drinking again. She took a cake. It was shortbread, very rich, not sweet. The green and amber grapes were sweet and tart. The vivid tastes of the food and wine were like the ropes that moored the ship, they moored her to the world, to her mind again.

'I was very frightened,' she said by way of apology. 'I think I'll be myself again soon. Yesterday – no, today, this morning – there was a – a spell –' It was almost impossible to say the word, she stammered at it: 'A c-curse – laid on me. It took my speech, and my wits, I think. And we ran from that, but we ran right to the man, the man who –' She looked up despairingly at the young man listening to her. His grave eyes let her say what must be said. 'He was one of the people who crippled the child. He and her parents. They raped her and beat her and burned her; these things happen, my lord. These things happen to children. And he keeps following her, to get at her. And –'

She stopped herself, and drank wine, making herself taste its flavour.

'And so from him I ran to you. To the haven.' She looked about at the low, carved beams of the cabin, the polished table, the silver tray, the thin, quiet face of the young man. His hair was dark and soft, his skin a clear bronze-red; he was dressed well and plainly, with no chain or ring or outward mark of authority. But he looked the way a king should look, she thought.

'I'm sorry I let the man go,' he said. 'But he can be found again. Who was it laid the spell on you?'

'A wizard.' She would not say the name. She did not want to think about all that. She wanted them all behind her. No retribution, no pursuit. Leave them to their hatreds, put them behind her, forget.

Lebannen did not press, but he asked, 'Will you be safe from these men on your farm?'

'I think so. If I hadn't been so tired, so confused by the – by the – so confused in my mind, so that I couldn't think, I wouldn't have been afraid of Handy. What could he have done? With all the people about, in the street? I shouldn't have run from him. But all I could feel was her fear. She's so little, all she can do is fear him. She'll have to learn not to fear him. I have to teach her that . . .' She was wandering. Thoughts came into her head in Kargish. Had she been talking in Kargish? He would think she was mad, an old mad woman babbling. She glanced up at him furtively. His dark eyes were not on her; he gazed at the flame of the glass lamp that hung low over the table, a little, still, clear flame. His face was too sad for a young man's face.

'You came to find him,' she said. 'The archmage. Sparrowhawk.'

'Ged,' he said, looking at her with a faint smile. 'You, and he, and I go by our true names.'

'You and I, yes. But he, only to you and me.'

He nodded.

'He's in danger from envious men, men of ill will, and he has no – no defence, now. You know that?'

She could not bring herself to be plainer, but Lebannen said, 'He told me that his power as a mage was gone. Spent in the act that saved me, and all of us. But it was hard to believe. I wanted not to believe him.'

'I too. But it is so. And so he –' Again she hesitated. 'He wants to be alone until his hurts are healed,' she said at last, cautiously.

Lebannen said, 'He and I were in the dark land, the dry land, together. We died together. Together we crossed the mountains there. You can come back across the mountains. There is a way. He knew it. But the name of the mountains is Pain. The stones . . . The stones cut, and the cuts are long to heal.'

He looked down at his hands. She thought of Ged's hands, scored and gashed, clenched on their wounds. Holding the cuts close, closed.

Her own hand closed on the small stone in her pocket, the word she had picked up on the steep road.

'Why does he hide from me?' the young man cried in grief. Then, quietly, 'I hoped indeed to see him. But if he doesn't wish it, that's the end of it, of course.' She recognized the courtliness, the civility, the dignity of the messengers from Havnor, and appreciated it; she knew its worth. But she loved him for his grief.

'Surely he'll come to you. Only give him time. He was so badly hurt – everything taken from him – But when he spoke of you, when he said your name, oh, then I saw him for a moment as he was – as he will be again – All pride!'

'Pride?' Lebannen repeated, as if startled.

'Yes. Of course, pride. Who should be proud, if not he?'

'I always thought of him as – He was so patient,' Lebannen said, and then laughed at the inadequacy of his description.

'Now he has no patience,' she said, 'and is hard on himself beyond all reason. There's nothing we can do for him, I think, except let him go his own way and find himself at the end of his tether, as they say on Gont . . .' All at once she was at the end of her own tether, so weary she felt ill. 'I think I must rest now,' she said.

He rose at once. 'Lady Tenar, you say you fled from one enemy and found another; but I came seeking a friend, and found another.' She smiled at his wit and kindness. What a nice boy he is, she thought.

The ship was all astir when she woke: creaking and groaning of timbers, thud of running feet overhead, rattle of canvas, sailors' shouts. Therru was hard to waken and woke dull, perhaps feverish, though she was always so warm that Tenar found it hard to judge her fevers. Remorseful for having dragged the fragile child fifteen miles on foot and for all that had happened yesterday, Tenar tried to cheer her by telling her that they were in a ship, and that there was a real king on the ship, and that the little room they were in was the king's own room; that the ship was taking them home, to the farm, and Aunty Lark would be waiting for them at home, and maybe Sparrowhawk would be there too. Not even that roused Therru's interest. She was blank, inert, mute.

On her small, thin arm Tenar saw a mark – four fingers, red, like a brand, as from a bruising grip. But Handy had not gripped her, he had only touched her. Tenar had told her, had promised her that he would never touch her again. The promise had been broken. Her word meant nothing. What word meant anything, against deaf violence?

She bent down and kissed the marks on Therru's arm.

'I wish I'd had time to finish your red dress,' she said. 'The king would probably like to see it. But then, I suppose people don't wear their best clothes on a ship, even kings.'

Therru sat on the bunk, her head bent down, and did not answer. Tenar brushed her hair. It was growing out thick at last, a silky black curtain over the burned parts of the scalp. 'Are you hungry, birdlet? You didn't have any supper last night. Maybe the king will give us breakfast. He gave me cakes and grapes last night.'

No response.

When Tenar said it was time to leave the room, she obeyed. Up on deck she stood with her head bent to her shoulder. She did not look up at the white sails full of the morning wind, nor at the sparkling water, nor back at Gont Mountain rearing its bulk and majesty of forest, cliff, and peak into the sky. She did not look up when Lebannen spoke to her.

'Therru,' Tenar said softly, kneeling by her, 'when a king speaks to you, you answer.'

She was silent.

The expression of Lebannen's face as he looked at her was unreadable. A mask perhaps, a civil mask for revulsion, shock. But his dark eyes were steady. He touched the child's arm very lightly, saying, 'It must be strange for you, to wake up in the middle of the sea.'

She would eat only a little fruit. When Tenar asked her if she wanted to go back to the cabin, she nodded. Reluctant, Tenar left her curled up in the bunk and went back up on deck.

The ship was passing between the Armed Cliffs, towering grim walls that seemed to lean above the sails. Bowmen on guard in little forts like mud-swallows' nests high on the cliffs looked down at them on deck, and the sailors yelled cheerfully up at them. 'Way for the king!' they shouted, and the reply came down not much louder than the calling of swallows from the heights, 'The king!'

Lebannen stood at the high prow with the ship's master and an elderly, lean, narrow-eyed man in the grey cloak of a mage of Roke Island. Ged had worn such a cloak, a clean, fine one, on the day he and she brought the Ring of Erreth-Akbe to the Tower of the Sword; an old one, stained and dirty and travelworn, had been all his blanket on the cold stone of the Tombs of Atuan, and on the dirt of the desert mountains when they had crossed those mountains together. She was thinking of that as the foam flew by the ship's sides and the high cliffs fell away behind.

When the ship was out past the last reefs and had begun to swing eastward, the three men came to her. Lebannen said, 'My lady, this is the Master Windkey of Roke Island.'

The mage bowed, looking at her with praise in his keen eyes, and curiosity also; a man who liked to know which way the wind blew, she thought.

'Now I needn't hope the fair weather will hold, but can count on it,' she said to him.

'I'm only cargo on a day like this,' said the mage. 'Besides, with a sailor like Master Serrathen handling the ship, who needs a weatherworker?'

We are so polite, she thought, all Ladies and Lords and Masters, all bows and compliments. She glanced at the young king. He was looking at her, smiling but reserved.

She felt as she had felt in Havnor as a girl: a barbarian, uncouth among their smoothnesses. But because she was not a girl now, she was not awed, but only wondered at how men ordered their world into this dance of masks, and how easily a woman might learn to dance it.

It would take them only the day, they told her, to sail to Valmouth. They would make port there by late afternoon, with this fair wind in the sails.

Still very weary from the long distress and strain of the day before, she was content to sit in the seat the bald sailor contrived for her out of a straw mattress and a piece of sailcloth, and watch the waves and the gulls, and see the outline of Gont Mountain, blue and dreamy in the noon light, changing as they skirted its steep shores only a mile or two out from land. She brought Therru up to be in the sunshine, and the child lay beside her, watching and dozing.

A sailor, a very dark man, toothless, came on bare feet with soles like hooves and hideously gnarled toes, and put something down on the canvas near Therru. 'For the little girl,' he said hoarsely, and went off at once, though not far off. He looked around hopefully now and then from his work to see if she liked his gift and then pretended he had not looked around. Therru would not touch the little cloth-wrapped packet. Tenar had to open it. It was an exquisite carving of a dolphin, in bone or ivory, the length of her thumb.

'It can live in your grass bag,' Tenar said, 'with the others, the bone people.'

At that Therru came to life enough to fetch out her

grass bag and put the dolphin in it. But Tenar had to go thank the humble giver. Therru would not look at him or speak. After a while she asked to go back to the cabin, and Tenar left her there with the bone person, the bone animal, and the dolphin for company.

It's so easy, she thought with rage, it's so easy for Handy to take the sunlight from her, take the ship and the king and her childhood from her, and it's so hard to give them back! A year I've spent trying to give them back to her, and with one touch he takes them and throws them away. And what good does it do him – what's his prize, his power? Is power that – an emptiness?

She joined the king and the mage at the ship's railing. The sun was well to the west now, and the ship drove through a glory of light that made her think of her dream of flying with the dragons.

'Lady Tenar,' the king said, 'I give you no message for our friend. It seems to me that to do so is to lay a burden on you, and also to encroach upon his freedom; and I don't want to do either. I am to be crowned within the month. If it were he that held the crown, my reign would begin as my heart desires. But whether he's there or not, he brought me to my kingdom. He made me king. I will not forget it.'

'I know you will not forget it,' she said gently. He was so intense, so serious, armoured in the formality of his rank and yet vulnerable in his honesty, the purity of his will. Her heart yearned to him. He thought he had learned pain, but he would learn it again and again, all his life, and forget none of it.

And therefore he would not, like Handy, do the easy thing to do.

'I'll bear a message willingly,' she said. 'It's no burden. Whether he'd hear it is up to him.'

The Master Windkey grinned. 'It always was,' he said. 'Whatever he did was up to him.'

'You've known him a long time?'

'Even longer than you, my lady. Taught him,' said the mage. 'What I could . . . He came to the School on Roke, you know, as a boy, with a letter from Ogion telling us that he had great power. But the first time I had him out in a boat, to learn to speak to the wind, you know, he raised up a waterspout. I saw then what we were in for. I thought, Either he'll be drowned before he's sixteen, or he'll be archmage before he's forty . . . Or I like to think I thought it.'

'Is he still archmage?' Tenar asked. The question seemed baldly ignorant, and when it was greeted by a silence, she feared it had been worse than ignorant.

The mage said finally, 'There is now no Archmage of Roke.' His tone was exceedingly cautious and precise.

She dared not ask what he meant.

'I think,' said the king, 'that the Healer of the Rune of Peace may be part of any council of this realm; don't you think so, sir?'

After another pause and evidently with a little struggle, the mage said, 'Certainly.'

The king waited, but he said no more.

Lebannen looked out at the bright water and spoke as if he began a tale: 'When he and I came to Roke from the farthest west, borne by the dragon . . .' He paused, and the dragon's name spoke itself in Tenar's mind, *Kalessin*, like a struck gong.

'The dragon left me there, but bore him away. The keeper of the door of the House of Roke said then, "He has done with doing. He goes home." And before that – on the beach of Selidor – he bade me leave his staff, saying he was no mage now. So the Masters of Roke took counsel to choose a new archmage.

'They took me among them, that I might learn what it might be well for a king to know about the Council of the Wise. And also I was one of them to replace one of their number: Thorion, the Summoner, whose art was turned against him by that great evil which my lord Sparrowhawk found and ended. When we were there, in the dry land, between the wall and the mountains, I saw Thorian. My lord spoke to him, telling him the way back to life across the wall. But he did not take it. He did not come back.'

The young man's strong, fine hands held hard to the ship's rail. He still gazed at the sea as he spoke. He was silent for a minute and then took up his story.

'So I made out the number, nine, who meet to choose the new archmage.

'They are . . . they are wise men,' he said, with a glance at Tenar. 'Not only learned in their art, but knowledgeable men. They use their differences, as I had seen before, to make their decision strong. But this time . . .'

'The fact is,' said the Master Windkey, seeing Lebannen unwilling to seem to criticize the Masters of Roke, 'we were all difference and no decision. We could come to no agreement. Because the archmage wasn't dead – was alive, you see, and yet no mage – and yet still a dragonlord, it seemed . . . And because our Changer was still shaken from the turning of his own art on him, and believed that the Summoner would return from death, and begged us to wait for him . . . And because the Master Patterner would not speak at all. He is a Karg, my lady, like yourself; did you know that? He came to us from Karego-At.' His keen eyes watched her: which way does the wind blow? 'So because of all that, we found ourselves at a loss. When the Doorkeeper asked for the names of those from whom we would choose, not a name was spoken. Everybody looked at everybody else . . .'

'I looked at the ground,' Lebannen said.

'So at last we looked to the one who knows the names: the Master Namer. And he was watching the Patterner, who hadn't said a word, but sat there among his trees like a stump. It's in the Grove we meet, you know, among those trees whose roots are deeper than the islands. It was late in the evening by then. Sometimes there's a light among those trees, but not that night. It was dark, no starlight, a cloudy sky above the leaves. And the Patterner stood up and spoke then – but in his own language, not in the Old Speech, nor in Hardic, but in Kargish. Few of us knew it or even knew what tongue it was, and we didn't know what to think. But the Namer told us what the Patterner had said. He said: *A woman on Gont.*'

He stopped. He was no longer looking at her. After a bit she said, 'Nothing more?'

'Not a word more. When we pressed him, he stared at us and couldn't answer; for he'd been in the vision, you see – he'd been seeing the shape of things, the pattern; and it's little of that can ever be put in words, and less into ideas. He knew no more what to think of what he'd said than the rest of us. But it was all we had.'

The Masters of Roke were teachers, after all, and the Windkey was a very good teacher; he couldn't help but make his story clear. Clearer perhaps than he wanted. He glanced once again at Tenar, and away.

'So, you see, it seemed we should come to Gont. But for what? Seeking whom? "A woman" – not much to go on! Evidently this woman is to guide us, show us the way, somehow, to our archmage. And at once, as you may think, my lady, you were spoken of – for what other woman on Gont had we ever heard of? It is no great island, but yours is a great fame. Then one of us said, "She would lead us to Ogion." But we all knew that Ogion had long ago refused to be archmage, and surely would not accept now that he was old and ill. And indeed Ogion was dying as we spoke, I think. Then another said, "But she'd lead us also to Sparrowhawk!" And then we were truly in the dark.'

'Truly,' Lebannen said. 'For it began to rain, there among the trees.' He smiled. 'I had thought I'd never hear rain fall again. It was a great joy to me.'

'Nine of us wet,' said the Windkey, 'and one of us happy.'

Tenar laughed. She could not help but like the man. If he was so wary of her, it behoved her to be wary of him; but to Lebannen, and in Lebannen's presence, only candour would do.

'Your "woman on Gont" can't be me, then, for I will not lead you to Sparrowhawk.'

'It was my opinion,' the mage said with apparent and perhaps real candour of his own, 'that it couldn't be you, my lady. For one thing, he would have said your name, surely, in the vision. Very few are those who bear their true names openly! But I am charged by the Council of Roke to ask you if you know of any woman on this isle who might be the one we seek – sister or mother to a man of power, or even his teacher; for there are witches very wise in their way. Maybe Ogion knew such a woman? They say he knew every soul on this island, for all he lived alone and wandered in the wilderness. I wish he were alive to aid us now!'

She had thought already of the fisherwoman of Ogion's story. But that woman had been old when Ogion knew her, years ago, and must be dead by now. Though dragons, she thought, lived very long lives, it was said.

She said nothing for a while, and then only, 'I know no one of that sort.'

She could feel the mage's controlled impatience with her. What's she holding out for? What is it she wants? he was thinking, no doubt. And she wondered why it was she could not tell him. His deafness silenced her. She could not even tell him he was deaf.

'So,' she said at last, 'there is no archmage of Earthsea. But there is a king.'

'In whom our hope and trust are well founded,' the mage said with a warmth that became him well. Lebannen, watching and listening, smiled.

'In these past years,' Tenar said, hesitant, 'there have been many troubles, many miseries. My – the little girl – Such things have been all too common. And I have heard men and women of power speak of the waning, or the changing, of their power.'

'That one whom the archmage and my lord defeated in the dry land, that Cob, caused untold harm and ruin. We shall be repairing our art, healing our wizards and our wizardry, for a long time yet,' the mage said, decisively.

'I wonder if there might be more to be done than repairing and healing,' she said, 'though that too, of course – But I wonder, could it be that . . . that one such as Cob could have such power because things were already altering . . . and that a change, a great change, has been taking place, has taken place? And that it's because of that change that we have a king again in Earthsea – perhaps a king rather than an archmage?'

The Windkey looked at her as if he saw a very distant storm cloud on the uttermost horizon. He even raised his right hand in the hint, the first sketch, of a windbinding spell, and then lowered it again. He smiled. 'Don't be afraid, my lady,' he said. 'Roke, and the Art Magic, will endure. Our treasure is well guarded!'

'Tell Kalessin that,' she said, suddenly unable to endure the utter unconsciousness of his disrespect. It made him stare, of course. He heard the dragon's name. But it did not make him hear her. How could he, who had never listened to a woman since his mother sang him his last cradle song, hear her?

'Indeed,' said Lebannen, 'Kalessin came to Roke, which is said to be defended utterly from dragons; and not through any spell of my lord's, for he had no magery then . . . But I don't think, Master Windkey, that Lady Tenar was afraid for herself.'

The mage made an earnest effort to amend his offence. 'I'm sorry, my lady,' he said, 'I spoke as to an ordinary woman.'

She almost laughed. She could have shaken him. She said only, indifferently, 'My fears are ordinary fears.' It was no use; he could not hear her.

But the young king was silent, listening.

A sailor boy up in the dizzy, swaying world of the masts and sails and rigging overhead called out clear and sweet, 'Town there round the point!' And in a minute those down on deck saw the little huddle of slate roofs, the spires of blue smoke, a few glass windows catching the westering sun, and the docks and piers of Valmouth on its bay of satiny blue water.

'Shall I take her in or will you talk her in, my lord?' asked the calm ship's-master, and the Windkey replied, 'Sail her in, master. I don't want to have to deal with all that flotsam!' – waving his hand at the dozens of fishing craft that littered the bay. So the king's ship, like a swan among ducklings, came tacking slowly in, hailed by every boat she passed.

Tenar looked along the docks, but there was no other seagoing vessel.

'I have a sailor son,' she said to Lebannen. 'I thought his ship might be in.'

'What is his ship?'

'He was third mate aboard the *Gull of Eskel*, but that was more than two years ago. He may have changed ships. He's a restless man.' She smiled. 'When I first saw you, I thought you were my son. You're nothing alike, only in being tall, and thin, and young. And I was confused, frightened . . . Ordinary fears.'

The mage had gone up on the master's station in the prow, and she and Lebannen stood alone.

'There is too much ordinary fear,' he said.

It was her only chance to speak to him alone, and the words came out hurried and uncertain – 'I wanted to say – but there was no use – but couldn't it be that there's a woman on Gont, I don't know who, I have no idea, but it could be that there is, or will be, or may be, a woman, and that they seek – that they need – her. Is it impossible?'

He listened. He was not deaf. But he frowned, intent, as if trying to understand a foreign language. And he said only, under his breath, 'It may be.'

A fisherwoman in her tiny dinghy bawled up, 'Where from?' and the boy in the rigging called back like a crowing cock, 'From the King's City!'

'What is this ship's name?' Tenar asked. 'My son will ask what ship I sailed on.'

'*Dolphin*,' Lebannen answered, smiling at her. My son, my king, my dear boy, she thought. How I'd like to keep you nearby!

'I must go get my little one,' she said.

'How will you get home?'

'Afoot. It's only a few miles up the valley.' She pointed past the town, inland, where Middle Valley lay broad and sunlit between two arms of the mountain, like a lap. 'That village is on the river, and my farm's a half mile from the village. It's a pretty corner of your kingdom.'

'But will you be safe?'

'Oh, yes. I'll spend tonight with my daughter here in Valmouth. And in the village they're all to be depended on. I won't be alone.'

Their eyes met for a moment, but neither spoke the name they both thought.

'Will they be coming again, from Roke?' she asked. 'Looking for the "woman on Gont" – or for him?'

'Not for him. That, if they propose again, I will forbid,' Lebannen said, not realizing how much he told her in those three words. 'But as for their search for a new archmage, or for the woman of the Patterner's vision, yes, that may bring them here. And perhaps to you.'

'They'll be welcome at Oak Farm,' she said. 'Though not as welcome as you would be.'

'I will come when I can,' he said, a little sternly; and a little wistfully, 'if I can.'

11. *Home*

Most of the people of Valmouth came down to the docks to see the ship from Havnor, when they heard that the king was aboard, the new king, the young king that the new songs were about. They didn't know the new songs yet, but they knew the old ones, and old Relli came with his harp and sang a piece of the *Deed of Morred*, for a king of Earthsea would be the heir of Morred for certain. Presently the king himself came on deck, as young and tall and handsome as could be, and with him a mage of Roke, and a woman and a little girl in old cloaks not much better than beggars, but he treated them as if they were a queen and a princess, so maybe that's what they were. 'Maybe it's his mother,' said Shinny, trying to see over the heads of the men in front of her, and then her friend Apple clutched her arm and said in a kind of whispered shriek, 'It is – it's mother!'

'Whose mother?' said Shinny, and Apple said, 'Mine. And that's Therru.' But she did not push forward in the crowd, even when an officer of the ship came ashore to invite old Relli aboard to play for the king. She waited with the others. She saw the king receive the notables of Valmouth, and heard Relli sing for him. She watched him bid his guests farewell, for the ship was going to stand out to sea again, people said, before night fell, and be on her way home to Havnor. The last to come across the gangplank were Therru and Tenar. To each the king gave the formal embrace, laying cheek to cheek, kneeling to embrace Therru. 'Ah!' said the crowd on the dock. The sun was setting in a mist of gold, laying a great gold track across the bay, as the two came down the railed gangplank.

Tenar lugged a heavy pack and bag; Therru's face was bent down and hidden by her hair. The gangplank was run in, and the sailors leapt to the rigging, and the officers shouted, and the ship *Dolphin* turned on her way. Then Apple made her way through the crowd at last.

'Hello, mother,' she said, and Tenar said, 'Hello, daughter.' They kissed, and Apple picked up Therru and said, 'How you've grown! You're twice the girl you were. Come on, come on home with me.'

But Apple was a little shy with her mother, that evening, in the pleasant house of her young merchant husband. She gazed at her several times with a thoughtful, almost a wary look. 'It never meant a thing to me, you know, mother,' she said at the door of Tenar's bedroom – 'all that – the Rune of Peace – and you bringing the Ring to Havnor. It was just like one of the songs. A thousand years ago! But it really was you, wasn't it?'

'It was a girl from Atuan,' Tenar said. 'A thousand years ago. I think I could sleep for a thousand years, just now.'

'Go to bed, then.' Apple turned away, then turned back, lamp in hand. 'King-kisser,' she said.

'Get along with you,' said Tenar.

Apple and her husband kept Tenar a couple of days, but after that she was determined to go to the farm. So Apple walked with her and Therru up along the placid, silvery Kaheda. Summer was turning to autumn. The sun was still hot, but the wind was cool. The foliage of trees had a weary, dusty look to it, and the fields were cut or in harvest.

Apple spoke of how much stronger Therru was, and how sturdily she walked now.

'I wish you'd seen her at Re Albi,' Tenar said, 'before –' and stopped. She had decided not to worry her daughter with all that.

'What did happen?' Apple asked, so clearly resolved to

know that Tenar gave in and answered in a low voice, 'One of *them*.'

Therru was a few yards ahead of them, long-legged in her outgrown dress, hunting blackberries in the hedgerows as she walked.

'Her father?' Apple asked, sickened at the thought.

'Lark said the one that seems to be the father called himself Hake. This one's younger. He's the one that came to Lark to tell her. He's called Handy. He was . . . hanging around at Re Albi. And then by ill luck we ran into him in Gont Port. But the king sent him off. And now I'm here and he's there, and all that's done with.'

'But Therru was frightened,' Apple said, a bit grimly.

Tenar nodded.

'But why did you go to Gont Port?'

'Oh, well, this man Handy was working for a man . . . a wizard at the lord's house in Re Albi, who took a dislike to me . . .' She tried to think of the wizard's use-name and could not; all she could think of was *Tuaho*, a Kargish word for a kind of tree, she could not remember what tree.

'So?'

'Well, so, it seemed better just to come on home.'

'But what did this wizard dislike you for?'

'For being a woman, mostly.'

'Bah,' said Apple. 'Old cheese rind.'

'Young cheese rind, in this case.'

'Worse yet. Well, nobody around here that I know of has seen the parents, if that's the word for 'em. But if they're still hanging about, I don't like your being alone in the farmhouse.'

It is pleasant to be mothered by a daughter, and to behave as a daughter to one's daughter. Tenar said impatiently, 'I'll be perfectly all right!'

'You could at least get a dog.'

'I've thought of that. Somebody in the village might have a pup. We'll ask Lark when we stop by there.'

620

'Not a puppy, mother. A dog.'

'But a young one – one Therru could play with,' she
pleaded.

'A nice puppy that will come and kiss the burglars,' said
Apple, stepping along buxom and grey-eyed, laughing at
her mother.

They came to the village about midday. Lark welcomed
Tenar and Therru with a festivity of embraces, kisses,
questions, and things to eat. Lark's quiet husband and
other villagers stopped by to greet Tenar. She felt the
happiness of homecoming.

Lark and the two youngest of her seven children, a boy
and a girl, accompanied them out to the farm. The children
had known Therru since Lark first brought her home, of
course, and were used to her, though two months' separa-
tion made them shy at first. With them, even with Lark,
she remained withdrawn, passive, as in the bad old days.

'She's worn out, confused by all this travelling. She'll get
over it. She's come along wonderfully,' Tenar said to Lark,
but Apple would not let her get out of it so easily. 'One of
them turned up and terrified her and mother both,' said
Apple. And little by little, between them, the daughter and
the friend got the story out of Tenar that afternoon, as
they opened up the cold, stuffy, dusty house, put it to
rights, aired the bedding, shook their heads over sprouted
onions, laid in a bit of food in the pantry, and set a large
kettle of soup on for supper. What they got came a word
at a time. Tenar could not seem to tell them what the
wizard had done; a spell, she said vaguely, or maybe it was
that he had sent Handy after her. But when she came to
talk about the king, the words came tumbling out.

'And then there he was – the king! – like a swordblade –
And Handy shrinking and shrivelling back from him –
And I thought he was Spark! I did, I really did for a
moment, I was so – so beside myself –'

'Well,' said Apple, 'that's all right, because Shinny

thought you were his mother. When we were on the docks watching you come sailing in in your glory. She kissed him, you know, Aunty Lark. Kissed the king – just like that. I thought next thing she'd kiss that mage. But she didn't.'

'I should think not, what an idea. What mage?' said Lark, with her head in a cupboard. 'Where's your flour bin, Goha?'

'Your hand's on it. A Roke mage, come looking for a new archmage.'

'Here?'

'Why not?' said Apple. 'The last one was from Gont, wasn't he? But they didn't spend much time looking. They sailed straight back to Havnor, once they'd got rid of mother.'

'How you do talk.'

'He was looking for a woman, he said,' Tenar told them. '"A woman on Gont." But he didn't seem too happy about it.'

'A wizard looking for a woman? Well, that's something new,' said Lark. 'I'd have thought this'd be weevily by now, but it's perfectly good. I'll bake up a bannock or two, shall I? Where's the oil?'

'I'll need to draw some from the crock in the cool-room. Oh, Shandy! There you are! How are you? How's Clearbrook? How's everything been? Did you sell the ram lambs?'

They sat down nine to supper. In the soft yellow light of the evening in the stone-floored kitchen, at the long farm table, Therru began to lift her head a little, and spoke a few times to the other children; but there was still a cowering in her, and as it grew darker outside she sat so that her seeing eye could watch the window.

Not until Lark and her children had gone home in the twilight, and Apple was singing Therru to sleep, and she was washing up the dishes with Shandy, did Tenar ask about Ged. Somehow she had not wanted to while Lark and Apple were listening; there would have been so many explanations. She had forgotten to mention his being at Re Albi at all. And she did not want to talk about Re Albi any more. Her mind seemed to darken when she tried to think of it.

'Did a man come here last month from me – to help out with the work?'

'Oh, I clean forgot!' cried Shandy. 'Hawk, you mean – him with the scars on his face?'

'Yes,' Tenar said, 'Hawk.'

'Oh, aye, well, he'll be away up on Hot Springs Mountain, above Lissu, up there with the sheep, with Serry's sheep, I believe. He come here and says how you sent him, and there wasn't a lick o' work for him here, you know, with Clearbrook and me looking after the sheep and I been dairying and old Tiff and Sis helping me out when needed, and I racked my brains, but Clearbrook he says, "Go ask Serry's man, Farmer Serry's overseer up by Kahedanan, do they need herders in the high pastures," he said, and that Hawk went off and did that, and got took on, and was off next day. "Go ask Serry's man," Clearbrook told him, and that's what he done, and got took right on. So he'll be back down with the flocks come fall, no doubt. Up there on the Long Fells above Lissu, in the high pastures. I think maybe it was goats they wanted him for. Nice-spoken fellow. Sheep or goats, I don't remember which. I hope it's all right with you that we didn't keep him on here, Goha, but it's the truth there wasn't a lick o' work for him what with me and Clearbrook and old Tiff, and Sis got the flax in. And he said he'd been a goatherd over there where he came from, away round the mountain, some place above Armouth he said, though he said he'd never herded sheep. Maybe it'll be goats they've got him with up there.'

'Maybe,' said Tenar. She was much relieved and much disappointed. She had wanted to know him safe and well, but she had wanted also to find him here.

But it was enough, she told herself, simply to be home – and maybe better that he was not here, that none of all that was here, all the griefs and dreams and wizardries and terrors of Re Albi left behind, for good. She was here, now, and this was home, these stone floors and walls, these small-paned windows, outside which the oaks stood dark in starlight, these quiet, orderly rooms. She lay awake awhile that night. Her daughter slept in the next room, the children's room, with Therru, and Tenar lay in her own bed, her husband's bed, alone.

She slept. She woke, remembering no dream.

After a few days at the farm she scarcely gave a thought to the summer passed on the Overfell. It was long ago and far away. Despite Shandy's insistence on there not being a lick o' work to be done about the farm, she found plenty that needed doing: all that had been left undone over the summer and all that had to be done in the season of harvest in the fields and dairy. She worked from daybreak till nightfall, and if by chance she had an hour to sit down, she spun, or sewed for Therru. The red dress was finished at last, and a pretty dress it was, with a white apron for fancy wear and an orangey-brown one for everyday. 'Now, then, you look beautiful!' said Tenar in her seamstress's pride, when Therru first tried it on.

Therru turned her face away.

'You are beautiful,' Tenar said in a different tone. 'Listen to me, Therru. Come here. You have scars, ugly scars, because an ugly, evil thing was done to you. People see the scars. But they see you, too, and you aren't the scars. You aren't ugly. You aren't evil. You are Therru, and beautiful. You are Therru who can work, and walk, and run, and dance, beautifully, in a red dress.'

The child listened, the soft, unhurt side of her face as expressionless as the rigid, scar-masked side.

She looked down at Tenar's hands, and presently

touched them with her small fingers. 'It is a beautiful dress,' she said in her faint, hoarse voice.

When Tenar was alone, folding up the scraps of red material, tears came stinging into her eyes. She felt rebuked. She had done right to make the dress, and she had spoken the truth to the child. But it was not enough, the right and the truth. There was a gap, a void, a gulf, on beyond the right and the truth. Love, her love for Therru and Therru's for her, made a bridge across that gap, a bridge of spider web, but love did not fill or close it. Nothing did that. And the child knew it better than she.

The day of the equinox came, a bright sun of autumn burning through the mist. The first bronze was in the leaves of the oaks. As she scrubbed cream pans in the dairy with the window and door wide open to the sweet air, Tenar thought that her young king was being crowned this day in Havnor. The lords and ladies would walk in their clothes of blue and green and crimson, but he would wear white, she thought. He would climb up the steps to the Tower of the Sword, the steps she and Ged had climbed. The crown of Morred would be placed on his head. He would turn as the trumpets sounded and seat himself on the throne that had been empty so many years, and look at his kingdom with those dark eyes that knew what pain was, what fear was. 'Rule well, rule long,' she thought, 'poor boy!' And she thought, 'It should have been Ged there putting the crown on his head. He should have gone.'

But Ged was herding the rich man's sheep, or maybe goats, up in the high pastures. It was a fair, dry, golden autumn, and they would not be bringing the flocks down till the snow fell up there on the heights.

When she went into the village, Tenar made a point of going by Ivy's cottage at the end of Mill Lane. Getting to know Moss at Re Albi had made her wish to know Ivy better, if she could once get past the witch's suspicion and jealousy. She missed Moss, even though she had Lark here; she had learned from her and had come to love her, and Moss had given both her and Therru something they needed. She hoped to find a replacement of that here. But Ivy, though a great deal cleaner and more reliable than Moss, had no intention of giving up her dislike of Tenar. She treated her overtures of friendship with the contempt that, Tenar admitted, they perhaps deserved. 'You go your way, I go mine,' the witch told her in everything but words; and Tenar obeyed, though she continued to treat Ivy with marked respect when they met. She had, she thought, slighted her too often and too long, and owed her reparation. Evidently agreeing, the witch accepted her due with unbending ire.

In mid-autumn the sorcerer Beech came up the valley, called by a rich farmer to treat his gout. He stayed on awhile in the Middle Valley villages as he usually did, and passed one afternoon at Oak Farm, checking up on Therru and talking with Tenar. He wanted to know anything she would tell him of Ogion's last days. He was the pupil of a pupil of Ogion's and a devout admirer of the mage of Gont. Tenar found it was not so hard to talk about Ogion as about other people of Re Albi, and told him all she could. When she had done he asked a little cautiously, 'And the archmage – did he come?'

'Yes,' Tenar said.

Beech, a smooth-skinned, mild-looking man in his forties, tending a little to fat, with dark half-circles under his eyes that belied the blandness of his face, glanced at her, and asked nothing.

'He came after Ogion's death. And left,' she said. And presently, 'He's not archmage now. You knew that?'

Beech nodded.

'Is there any word of their choosing a new archmage?'

The sorcerer shook his head. 'There was a ship in from the Enlades not long ago, but no word from her crew of anything but the coronation. They were full of that! And it sounds as if all auspices and events were fortunate. If the goodwill of mages is valuable, then this young king of ours is a rich man . . . And an active one, it seems. There's an order come overland from Gont Port just before I left Valmouth, for the nobles and merchants and the mayor and his council to meet together and see to it that the bailiffs of the district be worthy and accountable men, for they're the king's officers now, and are to do his will and enact his law. Well, you can imagine how Lord Heno greeted that!' Heno was a notable patron of pirates, who had long kept most of the bailiffs and sea-sheriffs of South Gont in his pocket. 'But there were men willing to face up to Heno, with the king standing behind them. They dismissed the old lot then and there, and named fifteen new bailiffs, decent men, paid out of the mayor's funds. Heno stormed off swearing destruction. It's a new day! Not all at once, of course, but it's coming. I wish Master Ogion had lived to see it.'

'He did,' Tenar said. 'As he was dying, he smiled, and he said, "All changed . . ."'

Beech took this in his sober way, nodding slowly. 'All changed,' he repeated.

After a while he said, 'The little one's doing very well.'

'Well enough . . . Sometimes I think not well enough.'

'Mistress Goha,' said the sorcerer, 'if I or any sorcerer or witch or I daresay wizard had kept her, and used all the power of healing of the Art Magic for her all these months since she was injured, she wouldn't be better off. Maybe not as well as she is. You have done *all* that can be done, mistress. You have done a wonder.'

She was touched by his earnest praise, and yet it made her sad; and she told him why. 'It isn't enough,' she said. 'I can't heal her. She is . . . What is she to do? What will become of her?' She ran off the thread she had been spinning on to the spindle-shank, and said, 'I am afraid.'

'For her,' Beech said, half querying.

'Afraid because her fear draws to it, to her, the cause of her fear. Afraid because –'

But she could not find the words for it.

'If she lives in fear, she will do harm,' she said at last. 'I'm afraid of that.'

The sorcerer pondered. 'I've thought,' he said at last in his diffident way, 'that maybe, if she has the gift, as I think she does, she might be trained a bit in the Art. And, as a witch, her . . . appearance wouldn't be so much against her – possibly.' He cleared his throat. 'There are witches who do very creditable work,' he said.

Tenar ran a little of the thread she had spun between her fingers, testing it for evenness and strength. 'Ogion told me to teach her. "Teach her all," he said, and then, "Not Roke." I don't know what he meant.'

Beech had no difficulty with it. 'He meant that the learning of Roke – the High Arts – wouldn't be suitable for a girl,' he explained. 'Let alone one so handicapped. But if he said to teach her all but that lore, it would seem that he too saw her way might well be the witches' way.' He pondered again, more cheerfully, having got the weight of Ogion's opinion on his side. 'In a year or two, when she's quite strong, and grown a bit more, you might think of asking Ivy to begin teaching her a bit. Not too much, of course, even of that kind of thing, till she has her true name.'

Tenar felt a strong, immediate resistance to the suggestion. She said nothing, but Beech was a sensitive man. 'Ivy's dour,' he said. 'But what she knows, she does honestly. Which can't be said of all witches. *Weak as women's magic*, you know, and *wicked as women's magic!* But I've known witches with real healing power. Healing befits a woman. It comes natural to her. And the child might be drawn to that – having been so hurt herself.'

His kindness was, Tenar thought, innocent.

She thanked him, saying that she would think carefully about what he had said. And indeed she did so.

Before the month was out, the villages of Middle Valley had met at the Round Barn of Sodeva to appoint their own bailiffs and officers of the peace and to levy a tax upon themselves to pay the bailiffs' wages with. Such were the king's orders, brought to the mayors and elders of the villages, and readily obeyed, for there were as many sturdy beggars and thieves on the roads as ever, and the villagers and farmers were eager to have order and safety. Some ugly rumours went about, such as that Lord Heno had formed a Council of Scoundrels and was enlisting all the blackguards in the countryside to go about in gangs breaking the heads of the king's bailies; but most people said, 'Just let 'em try!' and went home telling each other that now an honest man could sleep safe abed at night, and what went wrong the king was setting right, though the taxes were beyond all reason and they'd all be poor men forever trying to pay them.

Tenar was glad to hear of all this from Lark, but did not pay it much heed. She was working very hard; and since she had got home she had, almost without being aware of it, resolved not to let the thought of Handy or any such ruffian rule her life or Therru's. She could not keep the child with her every moment, renewing her terrors, forever reminding her of what she could not remember and live. The child must be free and know herself to be free, to grow in grace.

She had gradually lost the shrinking, fearful manner, and by now went all about the farm and the byways and even into the village by herself. Tenar said no word of caution to her, even when she had to prevent herself from doing so. Therru was safe on the farm, safe in the village, no one was going to hurt her: that must be taken as unquestionable. And indeed Tenar did not often question it. With herself and Shandy and Clearbrook around the place, and Sis and Tiff down in the lower house, and Lark's family all over the village, in the sweet autumn of the Middle Valley, what harm was going to come to the child?

She'd get a dog, too, when she heard of one she wanted: one of the big grey Gontish sheep-guards, with their wise, curly heads.

Now and then she thought, as she had at Re Albi, 'I must be teaching the child! Ogion said so.' But somehow nothing seemed to get taught to her but farm work, and stories, in the evening, as the nights drew in and they began to sit by the kitchen fire after supper before they went to bed. Maybe Beech was right, and Therru should be sent to a witch to learn what witches knew. It was better than apprenticing her to a weaver, as Tenar had thought of doing. But not all that much better. And she was still not very big; and was very ignorant for her age, for she had been taught nothing before she came to Oak Farm. She had been like a little animal, barely knowing human speech, and no human skills. She learned quickly and was twice as obedient and diligent as Lark's unruly girls and laughing, lazy boys. She could clean and serve and spin, cook a little, sew a little, look after poultry, fetch the cows, and do excellent work in the dairy. A proper farm-lassie, old Tiff called her, fawning a bit. Tenar had also seen him make the sign to avert evil, surreptitiously, when Therru passed him. Like most people, Tiff believed that you are what happens to you. The rich and strong must have virtue; one to whom evil has been done must be bad, and may rightly be punished.

In which case it would not help much if Therru became the properest farm-lassie in Gont. Not even prosperity would diminish the visible brand of what had been done to her. So Beech had thought of her being a witch, accepting, making use, of the brand. Was that what Ogion had meant, when he said 'Not Roke' – when he said 'They will fear her'? Was that all?

One day when a managed chance brought them together in the village street, Tenar said to Ivy, 'There's a question I want to ask you, Mistress Ivy. A matter of your profession.'

The witch eyed her. She had a scathing eye.

'My profession, is it?'

Tenar nodded, steady.

'Come on, then,' Ivy said with a shrug, leading off down Mill Lane to her little house.

It was not a den of infamy and chickens, like Moss's house, but it was a witch-house, the beams hung thick with dried and drying herbs, the fire banked under grey ash with one tiny coal winking like a red eye, a lithe, fat, black cat with one white moustache sleeping up on a shelf, and everywhere a profusion of little boxes, pots, ewers, trays, and stoppered bottles, all aromatic, pungent or sweet or strange.

'What can I do for you, Mistress Goha?' Ivy asked, very dry, when they were inside.

'Tell me, if you will, if you think my ward, Therru, has any gift for your art – any power in her.'

'She? Of course!' said the witch.

Tenar was a bit floored by the prompt and contemptuous answer. 'Well,' she said. 'Beech seemed to think so.'

'A blind bat in a cave could see it,' said Ivy. 'Is that all?'

'No. I want your advice. When I've asked my question, you can tell me the price of the answer. Fair?'

'Fair.'

'Should I prentice Therru for a witch, when she's a bit older?'

Ivy was silent for a minute, deciding on her fee, Tenar thought. Instead, she answered the question. 'I would not take her,' she said.

'Why?'

'I'd be afraid to,' the witch answered, with a sudden fierce stare at Tenar.

'Afraid? Of what?'

'Of her! What is she?'

'A child. An ill-used child!'

'That's not all she is.'

Dark anger came into Tenar and she said, 'Must a prentice witch be a virgin, then?'

Ivy stared. She said after a moment, 'I didn't mean that.'

'What did you mean?'

'I mean I don't know what she is. I mean when she looks at me with that one eye seeing and one eye blind I don't know what she sees. I see you go about with her like she was any child, and I think, What are they? What's the strength of that woman, for she's not a fool, to hold a fire by the hand, to spin thread with the whirlwind? They say, mistress, that you lived as a child yourself with the Old Ones, the Dark Ones, the Ones Underfoot, and that you were queen and servant of those powers. Maybe that's why you're not afraid of this one. What power she is, I don't know, I don't say. But it's beyond my teaching, I know that – or Beech's, or any witch or wizard I ever knew! I'll give you my advice, mistress, free and feeless. It's this: Beware. Beware her, the day she finds her strength! That's all.'

'I thank you, Mistress Ivy,' Tenar said with all the formality of the Priestess of the Tombs of Atuan, and went out of the warm room into the thin, biting wind of the end of autumn.

She was still angry. Nobody would help her, she thought. She knew the job was beyond her, they didn't have to tell her that – but none of them would help her. Ogion had died, and old Moss ranted, and Ivy warned, and Beech kept clear, and Ged – the one who might really have helped – Ged ran away. Ran off like a whipped dog, and never sent sign or word to her, never gave a thought to her or Therru, but only to his own precious shame. That was his child, his nurseling. That was all he cared about. He had never cared or thought about her, only about power – her power, his power, how he could use it, how he could make more power of it. Putting the broken Ring together, making the Rune, putting a king on the throne. And when his power was gone, still it was all he could think about: that it was gone, lost, leaving him only himself, his shame, his emptiness.

You aren't being fair, Goha said to Tenar.

Fair! said Tenar. Did he play fair?

Yes, said Goha. He did. Or tried to.

Well, then, he can play fair with the goats he's herding; it's nothing to me, said Tenar, trudging homeward in the wind and the first, sparse, cold rain.

'Snow tonight, maybe,' said her tenant Tiff, meeting her on the road beside the meadows of the Kaheda.

'Snow so soon? I hope not.'

'Freeze, anyway, for sure.'

And it froze when the sun was down: rain puddles and watering troughs skimming over, then opaqued with ice; the reeds by the Kaheda stilled, bound in ice; the wind itself stilled as if frozen, unable to move.

Beside the fire – a sweeter fire than Ivy's, for the wood was that of an old apple that had been taken down in the orchard last spring – Tenar and Therru sat to spin and talk after supper was cleared away.

'Tell the story about the cat ghosts,' Therru said in her husky voice as she started the wheel to spin a mass of dark, silky goat's-wool into fleecefell yarn.

'That's a summer story.'

Therru cocked her head.

'In winter the stories should be the great stories. In winter you learn the *Creation of Éa*, so that you can sing it at the Long Dance when summer comes. In winter you learn the Winter Carol and the *Deed of the Young King*, and at the Festival of Sunreturn, when the sun turns north to bring the spring, you can sing them.'

'I can't sing,' the girl whispered.

Tenar was winding spun yarn off the distaff into a ball, her hands deft and rhythmic.

'Not only the voice sings,' she said. 'The mind sings. The prettiest voice in the world's no good if the mind doesn't know the songs.' She untied the last bit of yarn, which had been the first spun. 'You have strength, Therru, and strength that is ignorant is dangerous.'

'Like the ones who wouldn't learn,' Therru said. 'The wild ones.' Tenar did not know what she meant, and looked her question. 'The ones that stayed in the west,' Therru said.

'Ah – the dragons – in the song of the Woman of Kemay. Yes. Exactly. So: which will we start with – how the islands were raised from the sea, or how King Morred drove back the Black Ships?'

'The islands,' Therru whispered. Tenar had rather hoped she would choose the *Deed of the Young King*, for she saw Lebannen's face as Morred's; but the child's choice was the right one. 'Very well,' she said. She glanced up at Ogion's great Lore-books on the mantel, encouraging herself that if she forgot, she could find the words there; and drew breath; and began.

By her bedtime Therru knew how Segoy had raised the first of the islands from the depths of Time. Instead of singing to her, Tenar sat on the bed after tucking her in, and they recited together, softly, the first stanza of the song of the Making.

Tenar carried the little oil lamp back to the kitchen, listening to the absolute silence. The frost had bound the world, locked it. No star showed. Blackness pressed at the single window of the kitchen. Cold lay on the stone floors.

She went back to the fire, for she was not sleepy yet.

The great words of the song had stirred her spirit, and there was still anger and unrest in her from her talk with Ivy. She took the poker to rouse up a little flame from the backlog. As she struck the log, there was an echo of the sound in the back of the house.

She straightened up and stood listening.

Again: a soft, dull thump or thud – outside the house – at the dairy window?

The poker still in her hand, Tenar went down the dark hall to the door that gave on the cool-room. Beyond the cool-room was the dairy. The house was built against a low hill, and both those rooms ran back into the hill like cellars, though on a level with the rest of the house. The cool-room had only air-vents; the dairy had a door and a window, low and wide like the kitchen window, in its one outside wall. Standing at the cool-room door, she could hear that window being pried or jimmied, and men's voices whispering.

Flint had been a methodical householder. Every door but one of his house had a bar-bolt on each side of it, a stout length of cast iron set in slides. All were kept clean and oiled; none were ever locked.

She slipped the bolt across the cool-room door. It slid into place without a sound, fitting snug into the heavy iron slot on the doorjamb.

She heard the outer door of the dairy opened. One of them had finally thought to try it, before they broke the window, and found it wasn't locked. She heard the mutter of voices again. Then silence, long enough that she heard her heartbeat drumming in her ears so loud she feared she could not hear any sound over it. She felt her legs trembling and trembling, and felt the cold of the floor creep up under her skirt like a hand.

'It's open,' a man's voice whispered near her, and her heart leapt painfully. She put her hand on the bolt, thinking it was open – she had unlocked not locked it – She had almost slid it back when she heard the door between the cool-room and the dairy creak, opening. She knew that creak of the upper hinge. She knew the voice that had spoken, too, but in a different way of knowing. 'It's a storeroom,' Handy said, and then, as the door she stood against rattled against the bolt, 'This one's locked.' It rattled again. A thin blade of light, like a knife blade, flicked between the door and the jamb. It touched her breast, and she drew back as if it had cut her.

The door rattled again, but not much. It was solid, solidly hinged, and the bolt was firm.

They muttered together on the other side of the door. She knew they were planning to come around and try the front of the house. She found herself at the front door, bolting it, not knowing how she came there. Maybe this was a nightmare. She had had this dream, that they were trying to get into the house, that they drove thin knives through the cracks of the doors. The doors – was there any other door they could get in? The windows – the shutters of the bedroom windows – Her breath came so short she thought she could not get to Therru's room, but she was there, she brought the heavy wooden shutters across the glass. The hinges were stiff, and they came together with a bang. Now they knew. Now they were coming. They would come to the window of the next room, her room. They would be there before she could close the shutters. And they were.

She saw the faces, blurs moving in the darkness outside, as she tried to free the left-hand shutter from its hasp. It was stuck. She could not make it move. A hand touched the glass, flattening white against it.

'There she is.'

'Let us in. We won't hurt you.'

'We just want to talk to you.'

'He just wants to see his little girl.'

She got the shutter free and dragged it across the

window. But if they broke the glass they would be able to push the shutters open from the outside. The fastening was only a hook that would pull out of the wood if forced.

'Let us in and we won't hurt you,' one of the voices said.

She heard their feet on the frozen ground, crackling in the fallen leaves. Was Therru awake? The crash of the shutters closing might have wakened her, but she had made no sound. Tenar stood in the doorway between her room and Therru's. It was pitch-dark, silent. She was afraid to touch the child and waken her. She must stay in the room with her. She must fight for her. She had had the poker in her hand, where had she put it? She had put it down to close the shutters. She could not find it. She groped for it in the blackness of the room that seemed to have no walls.

The front door, which led into the kitchen, rattled, shaken in its frame.

If she could find the poker she would stay in here, she would fight them.

'Here!' one of them called, and she knew what he had found. He was looking up at the kitchen window, broad, unshuttered, easy to reach.

She went, very slowly it seemed, groping, to the door of the room. It was Therru's room now. It had been her children's room. The nursery. That was why there was no lock on the inner side of the door. So the children could not lock themselves in and be frightened if the bolt stuck.

Around back of the hill, through the orchard, Clearbrook and Shandy would be asleep in their cottage. If she called, maybe Shandy would hear. If she opened the bedroom window and called – or if she waked Therru and they climbed out the window and ran through the orchard – but the men were there, right there, waiting.

It was more than she could bear. The frozen terror that had bound her broke, and in rage she ran into the kitchen that was all red light in her eyes, grabbed up the long, sharp butcher knife from the block, flung back the door-bolt, and stood in the doorway. 'Come on, then!' she said.

As she spoke there was a howl and a sucking gasp, and a man yelled, 'Look out!' Another shouted, 'Here! Here!'

Then there was silence.

Light from the open doorway shot across the black ice of puddles, glittered on the black branches of the oaks and on fallen silver leaves, and as her eyes cleared she saw that something was crawling towards her on the path, a dark mass or heap crawling towards her, making a high, sobbing wail. Behind the light a black shape ran and darted, and long blades shone.

'Tenar!'

'Stop there,' she said, raising the knife.

'Tenar! It's me – Hawk, Sparrowhawk!'

'Stay there,' she said.

The darting black shape stood still next to the black mass lying on the path. The light from the doorway shone dim on a body, a face, a long-tined pitchfork held upright, like a wizard's staff, she thought. 'Is that you?' she said.

He was kneeling now by the black thing on the path.

'I killed him, I think,' he said. He looked over his shoulder, stood up. There was no sign or sound of the other men.

'Where are they?'

'Ran. Give me a hand, Tenar.'

She held the knife in one hand. With the other she took hold of the arm of the man that lay huddled up on the path. Ged took him under the shoulder and they dragged him up the step and into the house. He lay on the stone floor of the kitchen, and blood ran out of his chest and belly like water from a pitcher. His upper lip was drawn back from his teeth, and only the whites of his eyes showed.

'Lock the door,' Ged said, and she locked the door.

'Linens in the press,' she said, and he got a sheet and tore it for bandages, which she bound round and round the man's belly and breast, into which three of the four tines of the pitchfork had driven full force, making three ragged springs of blood that dripped and squirted as Ged supported the man's torso so that she could wrap the bandages.

'What are you doing here? Did you come with them?'

'Yes. But they didn't know it. That's about all you can do, Tenar.' He let the man's body sag down, and sat back, breathing hard, wiping his face with the back of his bloody hand. 'I think I killed him,' he said again.

'Maybe you did.' Tenar watched the bright red spots spread slowly on the heavy linen that wrapped the man's thin, hairy chest and belly. She stood up, and swayed, very dizzy. 'Get by the fire,' she said. 'You must be perishing.'

She did not know how she had known him in the dark outside. By his voice, maybe. He wore a bulky shepherd's winter coat of cut fleece with the leather side out, and a shepherd's knitted watch cap pulled down; his face was lined and weathered, his hair long and iron-grey. He smelled like woodsmoke, and frost, and sheep. He was shivering, his whole body shaking. 'Get by the fire,' she said again. 'Put wood on it.'

He did so. Tenar filled the kettle and swung it out on its iron arm over the blaze.

There was blood on her skirt, and she used an end of linen soaked in cold water to clean it. She gave the cloth to Ged to clean the blood off his hands. 'What do you mean,' she said, 'you came with them but they didn't know it?'

'I was coming down. From the mountain. On the road from the springs of the Kaheda.' He spoke in a flat voice as if out of breath, and his shivering made his speech slur. 'Heard men behind me, and I went aside. Into the woods. Didn't feel like talking. I don't know. Something about them. I was afraid of them.'

639

She nodded impatiently and sat down across the hearth from him, leaning forward to listen, her hands clenched tight in her lap. Her damp skirt was cold against her legs.

'I heard one of them say "Oak Farm" as they went by. After that I followed them. One of them kept talking. About the child.'

'What did he say?'

He was silent. He said finally, 'That he was going to get her back. Punish her, he said. And get back at you. For stealing her, he said. He said –' He stopped.

'That he'd punish me, too.'

'They all talked. About, about that.'

'That one isn't Handy.' She nodded towards the man on the floor. 'Is it the . . .'

'He said she was his.' Ged looked at the man too, and back at the fire. 'He's dying. We should get help.'

'He won't die,' Tenar said. 'I'll send for Ivy in the morning. The others are still out there – how many of them?'

'Two.'

'If he dies he dies, if he lives he lives. Neither of us is going out.' She got to her feet, in a spasm of fear. 'Did you bring in the pitchfork, Ged!'

He pointed to it, the four long tines shining as it leaned against the wall beside the door.

She sat down in the hearthseat again, but now she was shaking, trembling from head to foot, as he had done. He reached across the hearth to touch her arm. 'It's all right,' he said.

'What if they're still out there?'

'They ran.'

'They could come back.'

'Two against two? And we've got the pitchfork.'

She lowered her voice to a bare whisper to say, in terror, 'The pruning hook and the scythes are in the barn lean-to.'

He shook his head. 'They ran. They saw – him – and you in the door.'

'What did you do?'

'He came at me. So I came at him.'

'I mean, before. On the road.'

'They got cold, walking. It started to rain, and they got cold, and started talking about coming here. Before that it was only this one, talking about the child and you, about teaching – teaching lessons –' His voice dried up. 'I'm thirsty,' he said.

'So am I. The kettle's not boiling yet. Go on.'

He took breath and tried to tell his story coherently. 'The other two didn't listen to him much. Heard it all before, maybe. They were in a hurry to get on. To get to Valmouth. As if they were running from somebody. Getting away. But it got cold, and he went on about Oak Farm, and the one with the cap said, "Well, why not just go there and spend the night with –"'

'With the widow, yes.'

Ged put his face in his hands. She waited.

He looked into the fire, and went on steadily. 'Then I lost them for a while. The road came out level into the valley, and I couldn't follow along the way I'd been doing, in the woods, just behind them. I had to go aside, through the fields, keeping out of their sight. I don't know the country here, only the road. I was afraid if I cut across the fields I'd get lost, miss the house. And it was getting dark. I thought I'd missed the house, overshot it. I came back to the road, and almost ran into them – at the turn there. They'd seen the old man go by. They decided to wait till it was dark and they were sure nobody else was coming. They waited in the barn. I stayed outside. Just through the wall from them.'

'You must be frozen,' Tenar said dully.

'It was cold.' He held his hands to the fire as if the thought of it had chilled him again. 'I found the pitchfork by the lean-to door. They went around to the back of the house when they came out. I could have come to the front door then to warn you, it's what I should have done, but all I could think of was to take them by surprise – I thought it was my only advantage, chance . . . I thought the house would be locked and they'd have to break in. But then I heard them going in, at the back, there. I went in – into the dairy – after them. I only just got out, when they came to the locked door.' He gave a kind of laugh. 'They went right by me in the dark. I could have tripped them . . . One of them had a flint and steel, he'd burn a little tinder when they wanted to see a lock. They came around front. I heard you putting up the shutters; I knew you'd heard them. They talked about smashing the window they'd seen you at. Then the one with the cap saw the window – that window –' He nodded towards the kitchen window, with its deep, broad inner sill. 'He said, "Get me a rock, I'll smash that right open," and they came to where he was, and they were about to hoist him up to the sill. So I let out a yell, and he dropped down, and one of them – this one – came running right at me.'

'Ah, ah,' gasped the man lying on the floor, as if telling Ged's tale for him. Ged got up and bent over him.

'He's dying, I think.'

'No, he's not,' Tenar said. She could not stop shaking entirely, but it was only an inward tremor now. The kettle was singing. She made a pot of tea, and laid her hands on the thick pottery sides of the teapot while it steeped. She poured out two cups, then a third, into which she put a little cold water. 'It's too hot to drink,' she told Ged, 'hold it a minute first. I'll see if this'll go into him.' She sat down on the floor by the man's head, lifted it on one arm, put the cup of cooled tea to his mouth, pushed the rim between the bared teeth. The warm stuff ran into his mouth; he swallowed. 'He won't die,' she said. 'The floor's like ice. Help me move him nearer the fire.'

Ged started to take the rug from a bench that ran along the wall between the chimney and the hall. 'Don't use that, it's a good piece of weaving,' Tenar said, and she went to the closet and brought out a worn-out felt cloak, which she spread out as a bed for the man. They hauled the inert body on to it, lapped it over him. The soaked red spots on the bandages had grown no larger.

Tenar stood up, and stood motionless.

'Therru,' she said.

Ged looked round, but the child was not there. Tenar went hurriedly out of the room.

The children's room, the child's room, was perfectly dark and quiet. She felt her way to the bed, and laid her hand on the warm curve of the blanket over Therru's shoulder.

'Therru?'

The child's breathing was peaceful. She had not waked. Tenar could feel the heat of her body, like a radiance in the cold room.

As she went out, Tenar ran her hand across the chest of drawers and touched cold metal: the poker she had laid down when she closed the shutters. She brought it back to the kitchen, stepped over the man's body, and hung the poker on its hook on the chimney. She stood looking down at the fire.

'I couldn't do anything,' she said. 'What should I have done? Run out – right away – shouted, and run to Clearbrook and Shandy. They wouldn't have had time to hurt Therru.'

'They would have been in the house with her, and you outside it, with the old man and woman. Or they could have picked her up and gone clear away with her. You did what you could. What you did was right. Timed right. The light from the house, and you coming out with the knife, and me there – they could see the pitchfork then – and him down. So they ran.'

'Those that could,' said Tenar. She turned and stirred the man's leg a little with the toe of her shoe, as if he were an object she was a little curious about, a little repelled by, like a dead viper. 'You did the right thing,' she said.

'I don't think he even saw it. He ran right on to it. It was like —' He did not say what it was like. He said, 'Drink your tea,' and poured himself more from the pot keeping warm on the hearthbricks. 'It's good. Sit down,' he said, and she did so.

'When I was a boy,' he said after a time, 'the Kargs raided my village. They had lances — long, with feathers tied to the shaft —'

She nodded. 'Warriors of the God-Brothers,' she said.

'I made a . . . a fog-spell. To confuse them. But they came on, some of them. I saw one of them run right on to a pitchfork — like him. Only it went clear through him. Below the waist.'

'You hit a rib,' Tenar said.

He nodded.

'It was the only mistake you made,' she said. Her teeth were chattering now. She drank her tea. 'Ged,' she said, 'what if they come back?'

'They won't.'

'They could set fire to the house.'

'This house?' He looked around at the stone walls.

'The haybarn —'

'They won't be back,' he said, doggedly.

'No.'

They held their cups with care, warming their hands on them.

'She slept through it.'

'It's well she did.'

'But she'll see him — here — in the morning —'

They stared at each other.

'If I'd killed him — if he'd die!' Ged said with rage. 'I could drag him out and bury him —'

'Do it.'

He merely shook his head angrily.

'What does it matter, why, why can't we do it!' Tenar demanded.

'I don't know.'

'As soon as it gets light —'

'I'll get him out of the house. Wheelbarrow. The old man can help me.'

'He can't lift anything any more. I'll help you.'

'However I can do it, I'll cart him off to the village. There's a healer of some kind there?'

'A witch, Ivy.'

She felt all at once abysmally, infinitely weary. She could scarcely hold the cup in her hand.

'There's more tea,' she said, thick-tongued.

He poured himself another cupful.

The fire danced in her eyes. The flames swam, flared up, sank away, brightened again against the sooty stone, against the dark sky, against the pale sky, the gulfs of evening, the depths of air and light beyond the world. Flames of yellow, orange, orange-red, red tongues of flame, flame-tongues, the words she could not speak.

'Tenar.'

'We call the star Tehanu,' she said.

'Tenar, my dear. Come on. Come with me.'

They were not at the fire. They were in the dark — in the dark hall. The dark passage. They had been there before, leading each other, following each other, in the darkness underneath the earth.

'This is the way,' she said.

12. Winter

She was waking, not wanting to waken. Faint grey shone at the window in thin slits through the shutters. Why was the window shuttered? She got up hurriedly and went down the hall to the kitchen. No one sat by the fire, no one lay on the floor. There was no sign of anyone, anything. Except the teapot and three cups on the counter.

Therru got up about sunrise, and they breakfasted as usual; clearing up, the girl asked, 'What happened?' She lifted a corner of wet linen from the soaking-tub in the pantry. The water in the tub was veined and clouded with brownish red.

'Oh, my period came on early,' Tenar said, startled at the lie as she spoke it.

Therru stood a moment motionless, her nostrils flared and her head still, like an animal getting a scent. Then she dropped the sheeting back into the water, and went out to feed the chickens.

Tenar felt ill; her bones ached. The weather was still cold, and she stayed indoors as much as she could. She tried to keep Therru in, but when the sun came out with a keen, bright wind, Therru wanted to be out in it.

'Stay with Shandy in the orchard,' Tenar said.

Therru said nothing as she slipped out.

The burned and deformed side of her face was made rigid by the destruction of muscles and the thickness of the scar-surface, but as the scars got older and as Tenar learned by long usage not to look away from it as deformity but to see it as face, it had expressions of its own. When Therru was frightened, the burned and darkened side 'closed in', as Tenar thought, drawing together, hardening.

646

When she was excited or intent, even the blind eye socket seemed to gaze, and the scars reddened and were hot to touch. Now, as she went out, there was a queer look to her, as if her face were not human at all, an animal, some strange horny-skinned wild creature with one bright eye, silent, escaping.

And Tenar knew that as she had lied to her for the first time, Therru for the first time was going to disobey her. The first but not the last time.

She sat down at the fireside with a weary sigh, and did nothing at all for a while.

A rap at the door: Clearbrook and Ged – no, Hawk she must call him – Hawk standing on the doorstep. Old Clearbrook was full of talk and importance, Ged dark and quiet and bulky in his grimy sheepskin coat. 'Come in,' she said. 'Have some tea. What's the news?'

'Tried to get away, down to Valmouth, but the men from Kahedanan, the bailies, come down and 'twas in Cherry's outhouse they found 'em,' Clearbrook announced, waving his fist.

'He escaped?' Horror caught at her.

'The other two,' Ged said. 'Not him.'

'See, they found the body up in the old shambles on Round Hill, all beat to pieces like, up in the old shambles there, by Kahedanan, so ten, twelve of 'em 'pointed theirselves bailies then and there and come after them. And there was a search all through the villages last night, and this morning before 'twas hardly light they found 'em hiding out in Cherry's outhouse. Half-froze they was.'

'He's dead, then?' she asked, bewildered.

Ged had shucked off the heavy coat and was now sitting on the cane-bottom chair by the door to undo his leather gaiters. '*He's* alive,' he said in his quiet voice. 'Ivy has him. I took him in this morning on the muck-cart. There were people out on the road before daylight, hunting for all three of them. They'd killed a woman, up in the hills.'

'What woman?' Tenar whispered.

Her eyes were on Ged's. He nodded slightly.

Clearbrook wanted the story to be his, and took it up loudly: 'I talked with some o' them from up there and they told me they'd all four of 'em been traipsing and camping and vagranting about near Kahedanan, and the woman would come into the village to beg, all beat about and burns and bruises all over her. They'd send her in, the men would, see, like that to beg, and then she'd go back to 'em, and she told people if she went back with nothing they'd beat her more, so they said why go back? But if she didn't they'd come after her, she said, see, and she'd always go with 'em. But then they finally went too far and beat her to death, and they took and left her body in the old shambles there where there's still some o' the stink left, you know, maybe thinking that was hiding what they done. And they came away then, down here, just last night. And why didn't you shout and call last night, Goha? Hawk says they was right here, sneaking about the house, when he come on 'em. I surely would have heard, or Shandy would, her ears might be sharper than mine. Did you tell her yet?'

Tenar shook her head.

'I'll just go tell her,' said the old man, delighted to be first with the news, and he clumped off across the yard. He turned back halfway. 'Never would have picked you as useful with a pitchfork!' he shouted to Ged, and slapped his thigh, laughing, and went on.

Ged slipped off the heavy gaiters, took off his muddy shoes and set them on the doorstep, and came over to the fire in his stocking feet. Trousers and jerkin and shirt of homespun wool: a Gontish goatherd, with a canny face, a hawk nose, and clear, dark eyes.

'There'll be people out soon,' he said. 'To tell you all about it, and hear what happened here again. They've got the two that ran off shut up now in a wine cellar with no wine in it, and fifteen or twenty men guarding them, and twenty or thirty boys trying to get a peek . . .' He yawned, shook his shoulders and arms to loosen them, and with a glance at Tenar asked permission to sit down at the fire.

She gestured to the hearthseat. 'You must be worn out,' she whispered.

'I slept a little, here, last night. Couldn't stay awake.' He yawned again. He looked up at her, gauging, seeing how she was.

'It was Therru's mother,' she said. Her voice would not go above a whisper.

He nodded. He sat leaning forward a bit, his arms on his knees, as Flint had used to sit, gazing into the fire. They were very alike and entirely unlike, as unlike as a buried stone and a soaring bird. Her heart ached, and her bones ached, and her mind was bewildered among foreboding and grief and remembered fear and a troubled lightness.

'The witch has got our man,' he said. 'Tied down in case he feels lively. With the holes in him stuffed full of spiderwebs and blood-stanching spells. She says he'll live to hang.'

'To hang.'

'It's up to the King's Courts of Law, now that they're meeting again. Hanged or set to slave-labour.'

She shook her head, frowning.

'You wouldn't just let him go, Tenar,' he said gently, watching her.

'No.'

'They must be punished,' he said, still watching her.

'"Punished." That's what *he* said. Punish the child. She's bad. She must be punished. Punish me, for taking her. For being –' She struggled to speak. 'I don't want punishment! – It should not have happened. – I wish you'd killed him!'

'I did my best,' Ged said.

649

After a good while she laughed, rather shakily. 'You certainly did.'

'Think how easy it would have been,' he said, looking into the coals again, 'when I was a wizard. I could have set a binding spell on them, up there on the road, before they knew it. I could have marched them right down to Valmouth like a flock of sheep. Or last night, here, think of the fireworks I could have set off! They'd never have known what hit them.'

'They still don't,' she said.

He glanced at her. There was in his eye the faintest, irrepressible gleam of triumph.

'No,' he said. 'They don't.'

'Useful with a pitchfork,' she murmured.

He yawned enormously.

'Why don't you go in and get some sleep? The second room down the hall. Unless you want to entertain company. I see Lark and Daisy coming, and some of the children.' She had got up, hearing voices, to look out the window.

'I'll do that,' he said, and slipped away.

Lark and her husband, Daisy the blacksmith's wife, and other friends from the village came by all day long to tell and be told all, as Ged had said. She found that their company revived her, carried her away from the constant presence of last night's terror, little by little, till she could begin to look back on it as something that had happened, not something that was happening, that must always be happening to her.

That was also what Therru had to learn to do, she thought, but not with one night: with her life.

She said to Lark when the others had gone, 'What makes me rage at myself is how stupid I was.'

'I did tell you you ought to keep the house locked.'

'No – Maybe – That's just it.'

'I know,' said Lark.

'But I meant, when they were here – I could have run out and fetched Shandy and Clearbrook – maybe I could have taken Therru. Or I could have gone to the lean-to and got the pitchfork myself. Or the apple-pruner. It's seven feet long with a blade like a razor; I keep it the way Flint kept it. Why didn't I do that? Why didn't I do something? Why did I just lock myself in – when it wasn't any good trying to? If he – If Hawk hadn't been here – All I did was trap myself and Therru. I did finally go to the door with the butcher knife, and I shouted at them. I was half crazy. But that wouldn't have scared them off.'

'I don't know,' Lark said. 'It was crazy, and maybe . . . I don't know. What could you do but lock the doors? But it's like we're all our lives locking the doors. It's the house we live in.'

They looked around at the stone walls, the stone floors, the stone chimney, the sunny window of the kitchen of Oak Farm, Farmer Flint's house.

'That girl, that woman they murdered,' Lark said, looking shrewdly at Tenar. 'She was the same one.'

Tenar nodded.

'One of them told me she was pregnant. Four, five months along.'

They were both silent.

'Trapped,' Tenar said.

Lark sat back, her hands on the skirt on her heavy thighs, her back straight, her handsome face set. 'Fear,' she said. 'What are we so afraid of? Why do we let 'em tell us we're afraid? What is it *they're* afraid of?' She picked up the stocking she had been darning, turned it in her hands, was silent awhile; finally she said, 'What are they afraid of us for?'

Tenar spun and did not answer.

Therru came running in, and Lark greeted her: 'There's my honey! Come give me a hug, my honey girl!'

Therru hugged her hastily. 'Who are the men they caught?' she demanded in her hoarse, toneless voice, looking from Lark to Tenar.

Tenar stopped her wheel. She spoke slowly.

'One was Handy. One was a man called Shag. The one that was hurt is called Hake.' She kept her eyes on Therru's face; she saw the fire, the scar reddening. 'The woman they killed was called Senny, I think.'

'Senini,' the child whispered.

Tenar nodded.

'Did they kill her dead?'

She nodded again.

'Tadpole says they were *here*.'

She nodded again.

The child looked around the room, as the women had done; but her look was utterly unacceptant, seeing no walls.

'Will you kill them?'

'They may be hanged.'

'Dead?'

'Yes.'

Therru nodded, half indifferently. She went out again, rejoining Lark's children by the well-house.

The two women said nothing. They spun and mended, silent, by the fire, in Flint's house.

After a long time Lark said, 'What's become of the fellow, the shepherd, that followed 'em here? Hawk, you said he's called?'

'He's asleep in there,' said Tenar, nodding to the back of the house.

'Ah,' said Lark.

The wheel purred. 'I knew him before last night.'

'Ah. Up at Re Albi, did you?'

Tenar nodded. The wheel purred.

'To follow those three, and take 'em on in the dark with a pitchfork, that took a bit of courage, now. Not a young man, is he?'

'No.' After a while she went on, 'He'd been ill, and needed work. So I sent him over the mountain to tell Clearbrook to take him on here. But Clearbrook thinks he can still do it all himself, so he sent him up above the Springs for the summer herding. He was coming back from that.'

'Think you'll keep him on here, then?'

'If he likes,' said Tenar.

Another group came out to Oak Farm from the village, wanting to hear Goha's story and tell her their part in the great capture of the murderers, and look at the pitchfork and compare its four long tines to the three bloody spots on the bandages of the man called Hake, and talk it all over again. Tenar was glad to see the evening come, and call Therru in, and shut the door.

She raised her hand to latch it. She lowered her hand and forced herself to turn from it, leaving it unlocked.

'Sparrowhawk's in your room,' Therru informed her, coming back to the kitchen with eggs from the cool-room.

'I meant to tell you he was here – I'm sorry.'

'I know him,' Therru said, washing her face and hands in the pantry. And when Ged came in, heavy-eyed and unkempt, she went straight to him and put up her arms.

'Therru,' he said, and took her up and held her. She clung to him briefly, then broke free.

'I know the beginning part of the *Creation*,' she told him.

'Will you sing it to me?' Again glancing at Tenar for permission, he sat down in his place at the hearth.

'I can only say it.'

He nodded and waited, his face rather stern. The child said:

The making from the unmaking,
The ending from the beginning,

Who shall know surely?
What we know is the doorway between them
that we enter departing.
Among all beings ever returning,
the eldest, the Doorkeeper, Segoy . . .

The child's voice was like a metal brush drawn across metal, like dry leaves, like the hiss of fire burning. She spoke to the end of the first stanza:

Then from the foam bright Éa broke.

Ged nodded brief, firm approval. 'Good,' he said.

'Last night,' Tenar said. 'Last night she learned it. It seems a year ago.'

'I can learn more,' said Therru.

'You will,' Ged told her.

'Now finish cleaning the squash please,' said Tenar, and the child obeyed.

'What shall I do?' Ged asked. Tenar paused, looking at him.

'I need that kettle filled and heated.'

He nodded, and took the kettle to the pump.

They made and ate their supper and cleared it away.

'Say the *Making* again as far as you know it,' Ged said to Therru, at the hearth, 'and we'll go on from there.'

She said the second stanza once with him, once with Tenar, once by herself.

'Bed,' said Tenar.

'You didn't tell Sparrowhawk about the king.'

'You tell him,' Tenar said, amused at this pretext for delay.

Therru turned to Ged. Her face, scarred and whole, seeing and blind, was intent, fiery. 'The king came in a ship. He had a sword. He gave me the bone dolphin. His ship was flying, but I was sick, because Handy touched me. But the king touched me there and the mark went away.' She showed her small, thin arm. Tenar stared. She had forgotten the mark.

'Some day I want to fly to where he lives,' Therru told Ged. He nodded. 'I will do that,' she said. 'Do you know him?'

'Yes. I know him. I went on a long journey with him.'

'Where?'

'To where the sun doesn't rise and the stars don't set. And back from that place.'

'Did you fly?'

He shook his head. 'I can only walk,' he said.

The child pondered, and then as if satisfied said, 'Good night,' and went off to her room. Tenar followed her; but Therru did not want to be sung to sleep. 'I can say the *Making* in the dark,' she said. '*Both* stanzas.'

Tenar came back to the kitchen and sat down again across the hearth from Ged.

'How she's changing!' she said. 'I can't keep up with her. I'm old to be bringing up a child. And she . . . She obeys me, but only because she wants to.'

'It's the only justification for obedience,' Ged observed.

'But when she does take it into her head to disobey me, what can I do? There's a wildness in her. Sometimes she's my Therru, sometimes she's something else, out of reach. I asked Ivy if she'd think of training her. Beech suggested it. Ivy said no. "Why not?" I said. "I'm afraid of her!" she said . . . But you're not afraid of her. Nor she of you. You and Lebannen are the only men she's let touch her. *I* let that — that Handy — I can't talk about it. Oh, I'm tired! I don't understand anything . . .'

Ged laid a knot on the fire to burn small and slow, and they both watched the leap and flutter of the flames.

'I'd like you to stay here, Ged,' she said. 'If you like.' He did not answer at once. She said, 'Maybe you're going on to Havnor —'

'No, no. I have nowhere to go. I was looking for work.'

'Well, there's plenty to be done here. Clearbrook won't admit it, but his arthritis has about finished him for anything but gardening. I've been wanting help ever since I came back. I could have told the old blockhead what I thought of him for sending you off up the mountain that way, but it's no use. He wouldn't listen.'

'It was a good thing for me,' Ged said. 'It was the time I needed.'

'You were herding sheep?'

'Goats. Right up at the top of the grazings. A boy they had took sick, and Serry took me on, sent me up there the first day. They keep 'em up there high and late, so the underwool grows thick. This last month I had the mountain pretty much to myself. Serry sent me up that coat and some supplies, and said to keep the herd up as high as I could as long as I could. So I did. It was fine, up there.'

'Lonely,' she said.

He nodded, half smiling.

'You always have been alone.'

'Yes, I have.'

She said nothing. He looked at her.

'I'd like to work here,' he said.

'That's settled, then,' she said. After a while she added, 'For the winter, anyway.'

The frost was harder tonight. Their world was perfectly silent except for the whisper of the fire. The silence was like a presence between them. She lifted her hand and looked at him.

'Well,' she said, 'which bed shall I sleep in, Ged? The child's, or yours?'

He drew breath. He spoke low. 'Mine, if you will.'

'I will.'

The silence held him. She could see the effort he made to break from it. 'If you'll be patient with me,' he said.

'I have been patient with you for twenty-five years,' she

said. She looked at him and began to laugh. 'Come – come on, my dear – Better late than never! I'm only an old woman . . . Nothing is wasted, nothing is ever wasted. You taught me that.' She stood up, and he stood; she put out her hands, and he took them. They embraced, and their embrace became close. They held each other so fiercely, so dearly, that they stopped knowing anything but each other. It did not matter which bed they meant to sleep in. They lay that night on the hearthstones, and there she taught Ged the mystery that the wisest man could not teach him.

He built up the fire once, and fetched the good weaving off the bench. Tenar made no objection this time. Her cloak and his sheepskin coat were their blankets.

They woke again at dawn. A faint silvery light lay on the dark, half-leafless branches of the oaks outside the window. Tenar stretched out full length to feel his warmth against her. After a while she murmured, 'He was lying here. Hake. Right under us . . .'

Ged made a small noise of protest.

'Now you're a man indeed,' she said. 'Stuck another man full of holes, first, and lain with a woman, second. That's the proper order, I suppose.'

'Hush,' he murmured, turning to her, laying his head on her shoulder. 'Don't.'

'I will, Ged. Poor man! There's no mercy in me, only justice. I wasn't trained to mercy. Love is the only grace I have. Oh, Ged, don't fear me! You were a man when I first saw you! It's not a weapon or a woman can make a man, or magery either, or any power, anything but himself.'

They lay in warmth and sweet silence.

'Tell me something.'

He murmured assent sleepily.

'How did you happen to hear what they were saying? Hake and Handy and the other one. How did you happen to be just there, just then?'

He raised himself up on one elbow so he could look at her face. His own face was so open and vulnerable in its ease and fulfilment and tenderness that she had to reach up and touch his mouth, there where she had kissed it first, months ago, which led to his taking her into his arms again, and the conversation was not continued in words.

There were formalities to be got through. The chief of them was to tell Clearbrook and the other tenants of Oak Farm that she had replaced 'the old master' with a hired hand. She did so promptly and bluntly. They could not do anything about it, nor did it entail any threat to them. A widow's tenure of her husband's property was contingent on there being no male heir or claimant. Flint's son the seaman was the heir, and Flint's widow was merely holding the farm for him. If she died, it would go to Clearbrook to hold for the heir; if Spark never claimed it, it would go to a distant cousin of Flint's in Kahedanan. The two couples who did not own the land but held a life interest in the work and profit of the farming, as was common on Gont, could not be dislodged by any man the widow took up with, even if she married him; but she feared they might resent her lack of fidelity to Flint, whom they had after all known longer than she had. To her relief they made no objections at all. 'Hawk' had won their approval with one jab of a pitchfork. Besides, it was only good sense in a woman to want a man in the house to protect her. If she took him into her bed, well, the appetites of widows were proverbial. And, after all, she was a foreigner.

The attitude of the villagers was much the same. A bit of whispering and sniggering, but little more. It seemed that being respectable was easier than Moss thought; or perhaps it was that used goods had little value.

She felt as soiled and diminished by their acceptance as she would have by their disapproval. Only Lark freed her from shame, by making no judgements at all, and using no words – man, woman, widow, foreigner – in place of what she saw, but simply looking, watching her and Hawk with interest, curiosity, envy, and generosity.

Because Lark did not see Hawk through the words herdsman, hired hand, widow's man, but looked at him himself, she saw a good deal that puzzled her. His dignity and simplicity were not greater than that of other men she had known, but were a little different in quality; there was a size to him, she thought, not height or girth, certainly, but soul and mind. She said to Ivy, 'That man hasn't lived among goats all his life. He knows more about the world than he does about a farm.'

'I'd say he's a sorcerer who's been accused or lost his power some way,' the witch said. 'It happens.'

'Ah,' said Lark.

But the word 'archmage' was too great and grand a word to bring from far-off pomps and palaces and fit to the dark-eyed, grey-haired man at Oak Farm, and she never did that. If she had, she could not have been as comfortable with him as she was. Even the idea of his having been a sorcerer made her a bit uneasy, the work getting in the way of the man, until she actually saw him again. He was up in one of the old apple trees in the orchard pruning out dead wood, and he called out a greeting to her as she came to the farm. His name fit him well, she thought, perched up there, and she waved at him, and smiled as she went on.

Tenar had not forgotten the question she had asked him on the hearthstones under the sheepskin coat. She asked it again, a few days or months later – time went along very sweet and easy for them in the stone house, on the winter-bound farm. 'You never told me,' she said, 'how you came to hear them talking on the road.'

'I told you, I think. I'd gone aside, hidden, when I heard men coming behind me.'

'Why?'

'I was alone, and knew there were some gangs around.'

'Yes, of course – But then just as they passed, Hake was talking about Therru?'

'He said "Oak Farm", I think.'

'It's all perfectly possible. It just seems so convenient.' Knowing she did not disbelieve him, he lay back and waited.

'It's the kind of thing that happens to a wizard,' she said.

'And others.'

'Maybe.'

'My dear, you're not trying to . . . reinstate me?'

'No. No, not at all. Would that be a sensible thing to do? If you were a wizard, would you be here?'

They were in the big oak-framed bed, well covered with sheepskins and feather-coverlets, for the room had no fireplace and the night was one of hard frost on fallen snow.

'But what I want to know is this. Is there something besides what you call power – that comes before it, maybe? Or something that power is just one way of using? Like this. Ogion said of you once that before you'd had any learning or training as a wizard at all, you were a mage. Mage-born, he said. So I imagined that, to have power, one must first have room for the power. An emptiness to fill. And the greater the emptiness the more power can fill it. But if the power never was got, or was taken away, or was given away – still that would be there.'

'That emptiness,' he said.

'Emptiness is one word for it. Maybe not the right word.'

'Potentiality?' he said, and shook his head. 'What is able to be . . . to become.'

'I think you were there on that road, just there just then, because of that – because that is what happens to you. You didn't make it happen. You didn't cause it. It wasn't because of your "power". It happened to you. Because of your – emptiness.'

After a while he said, 'That isn't far from what I was taught as a boy on Roke: that true magery lies in doing only what you must do. But this would go further. Not to do, but to be done to . . .'

'I don't think that's quite it. It's more like what true doing rises from. Didn't you come and save my life – didn't you run a fork into Hake? That was "doing", all right, doing what you must do . . .'

He pondered again, and finally asked her, 'Is this a wisdom taught you when you were Priestess of the Tombs?'

'No.' She stretched a little, gazing into the darkness. 'Arha was taught that to be powerful she must sacrifice. Sacrifice herself and others. A bargain: give, and so get. And I cannot say that that's untrue. But my soul can't live in that narrow place – this for that, tooth for tooth, death for life . . . There is a freedom beyond that. Beyond payment, retribution, redemption – beyond all the bargains and the balances, there is freedom.'

'*The doorway between them*,' he said softly.

That night Tenar dreamed. She dreamed that she saw the doorway of the *Creation of Éa*. It was a little window of gnarled, clouded, heavy glass, set low in the west wall of an old house above the sea. The window was locked. It had been bolted shut. She wanted to open it, but there was a word or a key, something she had forgotten, a word, a key, a name, without which she could not open it. She sought for it in rooms of stone that grew smaller and darker till she found that Ged was holding her, trying to wake her and comfort her, saying, 'It's all right, dear love, it will be all right!'

'I can't get free!' she cried, clinging to him.

He soothed her, stroking her hair; they lay back together, and he whispered, 'Look.'

The old moon had risen. Its white brilliance on the fallen snow was reflected into the room, for cold as it was Tenar would not have the shutters closed. All the air above them was luminous. They lay in shadow, but it seemed as if the ceiling were a mere veil between them and endless, silver, tranquil depths of light.

It was a winter of heavy snows on Gont, and a long winter. The harvest had been a good one. There was food for the animals and people, and not much to do but eat it and stay warm.

Therru knew the *Creation of Éa* all through. She spoke the Winter Carol and the *Deed of the Young King* on the day of Sunreturn. She knew how to handle a piecrust, how to spin on the wheel, and how to make soap. She knew the name and use of every plant that showed above the snow, and a good deal of other lore, herbal and verbal, that Ged had stowed away in his head from his short apprenticeship with Ogion and his long years at the School on Roke. But he had not taken down the Runes or the Lore-books from the mantelpiece, nor had he taught the child any word of the Language of the Making.

He and Tenar spoke of this. She told him how she had taught Therru the one word, *tolk*, and then had stopped, for it had not seemed right, though she did not know why.

'I thought perhaps it was because I'd never truly spoken that language, never used it in magery. I thought perhaps she should learn it from a true speaker of it.'

'No man is that.'

'No woman is half that.'

'I meant that only the dragons speak it as their native tongue.'

'Do they learn it?'

Struck by the question, he was slow to answer, evidently calling to mind all he had been told and knew of the dragons. 'I don't know,' he said at last. 'What do we know about them? Would they teach as we do, mother to child, elder to younger? Or are they like the animals, teaching some things, but born knowing most of what they know? Even that we don't know. But my guess would be that the dragon and the speech of the dragon are one. One being.'

'And they speak no other tongue.'

He nodded. 'They do not learn,' he said. 'They are.'

Therru came through the kitchen. One of her tasks was to keep the kindling box filled, and she was busy at it, bundled up in a cut-down lambskin jacket and cap, trotting back and forth from the woodhouse to the kitchen. She dumped her load in the box by the chimney corner and set off again.

'What is it she sings?' Ged asked.

'Therru?'

'When she's alone.'

'But she never sings. She can't.'

'Her way of singing. "Farther west than west . . ."'

'Ah!' said Tenar. 'That story! Did Ogion never tell you about the Woman of Kemay?'

'No,' he said, 'tell me.'

She told him the tale as she spun, and the purr and hush of the wheel went along with the words of the story. At the end of it she said, 'When the Master Windkey told me how he'd come looking for "a woman on Gont", I thought of her. But she'd be dead by now, no doubt. And how would a fisherwoman who was a dragon be an archmage, anyhow!'

'Well, the Patterner didn't say that a woman on Gont was to be archmage,' said Ged. He was mending a badly torn pair of breeches, sitting up in the window ledge to get what light the dark day afforded. It was a half-month after Sunreturn and the coldest time yet.

'What did he say, then?'

'"A woman on Gont." So you told me.'

'But they were asking who was to be the next archmage.'

'And got no answer to that question.'

'*Infinite are the arguments of mages*,' said Tenar rather dryly.

Ged bit the thread off and rolled the unused length around two fingers.

'I learned to quibble a bit, on Roke,' he admitted. 'But this isn't a quibble, I think. "A woman on Gont" can't become archmage. No woman can be archmage. She'd unmake what she became in becoming it. The Mages of Roke are men – their power is the power of men, their knowledge is the knowledge of men. Both manhood and magery are built on one rock: power belongs to men. If women had power, what would men be but women who can't bear children? And what would women be but men who can?'

'Hah!' went Tenar; and presently, with some cunning, she said, 'Haven't there been queens? Weren't they women of power?'

'A queen's only a she-king,' said Ged.

She snorted.

'I mean, men give her power. They let her use their power. But it isn't hers, is it? It isn't because she's a woman that she's powerful, but despite it.'

She nodded. She stretched, sitting back from the spinning wheel. 'What is a woman's power, then?' she asked.

'I don't think we know.'

'When has a woman power because she's a woman? With her children, I suppose. For a while . . .'

'In her house, maybe.'

She looked around the kitchen. 'But the doors are shut,' she said, 'the doors are locked.'

'Because you're valuable.'

'Oh, yes. We're precious. So long as we're powerless . . . I remember when I first learned that! Kossil threatened me – me, the One Priestess of the Tombs. And I realized that I was helpless. I had the honour; but she had the power, from the God-king, the man. Oh, it made me angry! And frightened me . . . Lark and I talked about this once. She said, "Why are men *afraid* of women?"'

'If your strength is only the other's weakness, you live in fear,' Ged said.

'Yes; but women seem to fear their own strength, to be afraid of themselves.'

'Are they ever taught to trust themselves?' Ged asked, and as he spoke Therru came in on her work again. His eyes and Tenar's met.

'No,' she said. 'Trust is not what we're taught.' She watched the child stack the wood in the box. 'If power were trust,' she said. 'I like that word. If it weren't all these arrangements – one above the other – kings and masters and mages and owners – It all seems so unnecessary. Real power, real freedom, would lie in trust, not force.'

'As children trust their parents,' he said.

They were both silent.

'As things are,' he said, 'even trust corrupts. The men on Roke trust themselves and one another. Their power is pure, nothing taints its purity, and so they take that purity for wisdom. They cannot imagine doing wrong.'

She looked up at him. He had never spoken about Roke thus before, from wholly outside it, free of it.

'Maybe they need some women there to point that possibility out to them,' she said, and he laughed.

She restarted the wheel. 'I still don't see why, if there can be she-kings, there can't be she-archmages.'

Therru was listening.

'*Hot snow, dry water*,' said Ged, a Gontish saying. 'Kings are given power by other men. A mage's power is his own – himself.'

'And it's a male power. Because we don't even know what a woman's power is. All right. I see. But all the same, why can't they find an archmage – a he-archmage?'

Ged studied the tattered inseam of the breeches. 'Well,' he said, 'if the Patterner wasn't answering their question, he was answering one they didn't ask. Maybe what they have to do is ask it.'

'Is it a riddle?' Therru asked.

'Yes,' said Tenar. 'But we don't know the riddle. We only know the answer to it. The answer is: A woman on Gont.'

'There's lots of them,' Therru said after pondering a bit. Apparently satisfied by this, she went out for the next load of kindling.

Ged watched her go. ' "All changed," ' he said. 'All . . . Sometimes I think, Tenar – I wonder if Lebannen's kingship is only a beginning. A doorway . . . And he the doorkeeper. Not to pass through.'

'He seems so young,' Tenar said, tenderly.

'Young as Morred was when he met the Black Ships. Young as I was when I . . .' He stopped, looking out the window at the grey, frozen fields through the leafless trees. 'Or you, Tenar, in that dark place . . . What's youth or age? I don't know. Sometimes I feel as if I'd been alive for a thousand years; sometimes I feel my life's been like a flying swallow seen through the chink of a wall. I have died and been reborn, both in the dry land and here under the sun, more than once. And the *Making* tells us that we have all returned and return forever to the source, and that the source is ceaseless. *Only in dying, life* . . . I thought about that when I was up with the goats on the mountain, and a day went on for ever and yet no time passed before the evening came, and morning again . . . I learned goat wisdom. So I thought, What is this grief of mine for? What man am I mourning? Ged the archmage? Why is Hawk the goatherd sick with grief and shame for him? What have I done that I should be ashamed?'

'Nothing,' Tenar said. 'Nothing, ever!'

'Oh, yes,' said Ged. 'All the greatness of men is founded

on shame, made out of it. So Hawk the goatherd wept for Ged the archmage. And looked after the goats, also, as well as a boy his age could be expected to do . . .'

After a while Tenar smiled. She said, a little shyly, 'Moss said you were about fifteen.'

'That would be about right. Ogion named me in the autumn; and the next summer I was off to Roke . . . Who was that boy? An emptiness . . . A freedom.'

'Who is Therru, Ged?'

He did not answer until she thought he was not going to answer, and then he said, 'So made − what freedom is there for her?'

'We are our freedom, then?'

'I think so.'

'You seemed, in your power, as free as man can be. But at what cost? What made you free? And I . . . I was made, moulded like clay, by the will of the women serving the Old Powers, or serving the men who made all services and ways and places, I no longer know which. Then I went free, with you, for a moment, and with Ogion. But it was not *my* freedom. Only it gave me choice; and I chose. I chose to mould myself like clay to the use of a farm and a farmer and our children. I made myself a vessel. I know its shape. But not the clay. Life danced me. I know the dances. But I don't know who the dancer is.'

'And she,' Ged said after a long silence, 'if she should ever dance −'

'They will fear her,' Tenar whispered. Then the child came back in, and the conversation turned to the bread dough raising in the box by the stove. They talked so, quietly and long, passing from one thing to another and round and back, for half the brief day, often, spinning and sewing their lives together with words, the years and the deeds and the thoughts they had not shared. Then again they would be silent, working and thinking and dreaming, and the silent child was with them.

So the winter passed, till lambing season was on them, and the work got very heavy for a while as the days lengthened and grew bright. Then the swallows came from the isles under the sun, from the South Reach, where the star Gobardon shines in the constellation of Ending; but all the swallows' talk with one another was about beginning.

13. The Master

Like the swallows, the ships began to fly among the islands with the return of spring. In the villages there was talk, second-hand from Valmouth, of the king's ships harrying the harriers, driving well-established pirates to ruin, confiscating their ships and fortunes. Lord Heno himself sent out his three finest, fastest ships, captained by the sorcerer-seawolf Tally, who was feared by every merchantman from Soléa to the Andrades; his fleet was to ambush the king's ships off Oranéa and destroy them. But it was one of the king's ships that came into Valmouth Bay with Tally in chains aboard, and under orders to escort Lord Heno to Gont Port to be tried for piracy and murder. Heno barricaded himself in his stone manor house in the hills behind Valmouth, but neglected to light a fire, it being warm spring weather; so five or six of the king's young soldiers dropped in on him by way of the chimney, and the whole troop walked him chained through the streets of Valmouth and carried him off to justice.

When he heard this, Ged said with love and pride, 'All that a king can do, he will do well.'

Handy and Shag had been taken promptly off on the north road to Gont Port, and when his wounds healed enough Hake was carried there by ship, to be tried for murder at the king's courts of law. The news of their sentence to the galleys caused much satisfaction and self-congratulation in Middle Valley, to which Tenar, and Therru beside her, listened in silence.

There came other ships bearing other men sent by the king, not all of them popular among the townsfolk and villagers of rude Gont: royal sheriffs, sent to report on the

669

system of bailiffs and officers of the peace and to hear complaints and grievances from the common people; tax reporters and tax collectors; noble visitors to the little lords of Gont, inquiring politely as to their fealty to the Crown in Havnor; and wizardly men, who went here and there, seeming to do little and say less.

'I think they're hunting for a new archmage after all,' said Tenar.

'Or looking for abuses of the art,' Ged said – 'sorcery gone wrong.'

Tenar was going to say, 'Then they should look in the manor house of Re Albi!' but her tongue stumbled on the words. What was I going to say? she thought. Did I ever tell Ged about – I'm getting forgetful. What was it I was going to tell Ged? Oh, that we'd better mend the lower pasture gate before the cows get out.

There was always something, a dozen things, in the front of her mind, business of the farm. 'Never one thing, for you,' Ogion had said. Even with Ged to help her, all her thoughts and days went into the business of the farm. He shared the housework with her as Flint had not; but Flint had been a farmer, and Ged was not. He learned fast, but there was a lot to learn. They worked. There was little time for talk, now. At the day's end there was supper together, and sleep, and wake at dawn and back to work, and so round and so round, like the wheel of a water mill, rising full and emptying the days like the bright water falling.

'Hello, mother,' said the thin fellow at the farmyard gate. She thought it was Lark's eldest and said, 'What brings you by, lad?' Then she looked back at him across the clucking chickens and the parading geese.

'Spark!' she cried, and scattered the poultry, running to him.

'Well, well,' he said. 'Don't carry on.'

He let her embrace him and stroke his face. He came in and sat down in the kitchen, at the table.

'Have you eaten? Did you see Apple?'

'I could eat.'

She rummaged in the well-stocked larder. 'What ship are you on? Still the *Gull*?'

'No.' A pause. 'My ship's broke up.'

She turned in horror – 'Wrecked?'

'No.' He smiled without humour. 'Crew's broke up. King's men took her over.'

'But – it wasn't a pirate ship –'

'No.'

'Then why –?'

'Said the captain was running some goods they wanted,' he said, unwillingly. He was as thin as ever, but looked older, tanned dark, lank-haired, with a long, narrow face like Flint's but still narrower, harder.

'Where's dad?' he said.

Tenar stood still.

'You didn't stop by your sister's.'

'No,' he said, indifferent.

'Flint died three years ago,' she said. 'Of a stroke. In the fields – on the path up from the lambing pens. Clearbrook found him. It was three years ago.'

There was a silence. He did not know what to say, or had nothing to say.

She put food before him. He began to eat so hungrily that she set out more at once.

'When did you eat last?'

He shrugged, and ate.

She sat down across the table from him. Late-spring sunshine poured in the low window across the table and shone on the brass fender in the hearth.

He pushed the plate away at last.

'So who's been running the farm?' he asked.

'What's that to you, son?' she asked him, gently but drily.

'It's mine,' he said, in a rather similar tone.

After a minute Tenar got up and cleared his dishes away. 'So it is.'

'You can stay, o' course,' he said, very awkwardly, perhaps attempting to joke; but he was not a joking man. 'Old Clearbrook still around?'

'They're all still here. And a man called Hawk, and a child I keep. Here. In the house. You'll have to sleep in the loft-room. I'll put the ladder up.' She faced him again. 'Are you here for a stay, then?'

'I might be.'

So Flint had answered her questions for twenty years, denying her right to them by never answering yes or no, maintaining a freedom based on her ignorance; a poor, narrow sort of freedom, she thought.

'Poor lad,' she said, 'your crew broken up, and your father dead, and strangers in your house, all in a day. You'll want some time to get used to it all. I'm sorry, my son. But I'm glad you're here. I thought of you often, on the seas, in the storms, in winter.'

He said nothing. He had nothing to offer, and was unable to accept. He pushed back his chair and was about to get up when Therru came in. He stared, half-risen – 'What happened to her?' he said.

'She was burned. Here's my son I told you about, Therru, the sailor, Spark. Therru's your sister, Spark.'

'Sister!'

'By adoption.'

'Sister!' he said again, and looked around the kitchen as if for witness, and stared at his mother.

She stared back.

He went out, going wide of Therru, who stood motionless. He slammed the door behind him.

Tenar started to speak to Therru and could not.

'Don't cry,' said the child who did not cry, coming to her, touching her arm. 'Did he hurt you?'

'Oh Therru! Let me hold you!' She sat down at the table

with Therru on her lap and in her arms, though the girl was getting big to be held, and had never learned how to do it easily. But Tenar held her and wept, and Therru bent her scarred face down against Tenar's, till it was wet with tears.

Ged and Spark came in at dusk from opposite ends of the farm. Spark had evidently talked with Clearbrook and thought the situation over, and Ged was evidently trying to size it up. Very little was said at supper, and that cautiously. Spark made no complaint about not having his own room back, but ran up the ladder to the storage-loft like the sailor he was, and was apparently satisfied with the bed his mother had made him there, for he did not come back down till late in the morning.

He wanted breakfast then, and expected it to be served to him. His father had always been waited on by his mother, wife, daughter. Was he less a man than his father? Was she to prove it to him? She served him his meal and cleared it away for him, and went back to the orchard where she and Therru and Shandy were burning off a plague of tent caterpillars that threatened to destroy the new-set fruit.

Spark went off to join Clearbrook and Tiff. And he stayed mostly with them, as the days passed. The heavy work requiring muscle and the skilled work with the crops and sheep was done by Ged, Shandy, and Tenar, while the two old men who had been there all their lives, his father's men, took him about and told him how they managed it all, and truly believed they were managing it all, and shared their belief with him.

Tenar became miserable in the house. Only outdoors, at the farmwork, did she have relief from the anger, the shame that Spark's presence brought her.

'My turn,' she said to Ged, bitterly, in the starlit darkness of their room. 'My turn to lose what I was proudest of.'

673

'What have you lost?'

'My son. The son I did not bring up to be a man. I failed. I failed him.' She bit her lip, gazing dry-eyed into the dark.

Ged did not try to argue with her or persuade her out of her grief. He asked, 'Do you think he'll stay?'

'Yes. He's afraid to try and go back to sea. He didn't tell me the truth, or not all the truth, about his ship. He was second mate. I suppose he was involved in carrying stolen goods. Second-hand piracy. I don't care. Gontish sailors are all half-pirate. But he lies about it. He lies. He is jealous of you. A dishonest, envious man.'

'Frightened, I think,' Ged said. 'Not wicked. And it is his farm.'

'Then he can have it! And may it be as generous to him as –'

'No, dear love,' Ged said, catching her with both voice and hands – 'don't speak – don't say the evil word!' He was so urgent, so passionately earnest, that her anger turned right about into the love that was its source, and she cried, 'I wouldn't curse him, or this place! I didn't mean it! Only it makes me so sorry, so ashamed! I am so sorry, Ged!'

'No, no, no. My dear, I don't care what the boy thinks of me. But he's very hard on you.'

'And Therru. He treats her like – He said, he said to me, "What did she do, to look like that?" What did *she do* – !'

Ged stroked her hair, as he often did, with a light, slow repeated caress that would make them both sleepy with loving pleasure.

'I could go off goat-herding again,' he said at last. 'It would make things easier for you here. Except for the work . . .'

'I'd rather come with you.'

He stroked her hair, and seemed to be considering. 'I suppose we might,' he said. 'There were a couple of families up there sheep-herding, above Lissu. But then comes the winter . . .'

'Maybe some farmer would take us on. I know the work – and sheep – and you know goats – and you're quick at everything –'

'Useful with pitchforks,' he murmured, and got a little sob of a laugh from her.

The next morning Spark was up early to breakfast with them, for he was going fishing with old Tiff. He got up from the table, saying with a better grace than usual, 'I'll bring a mess of fish for supper.'

Tenar had made resolves overnight. She said. 'Wait; you can clear off the table, Spark. Set the dishes in the sink and put water on 'em. They'll be washed with the supper things.'

He stared a moment and said, 'That's women's work,' putting on his cap.

'It's anybody's work who eats in this kitchen.'

'Not mine,' he said flatly, and went out.

She followed him. She stood on the doorstep. 'Hawk's, but not yours?' she demanded.

He merely nodded, going on across the yard.

'It's too late,' she said, turning back to the kitchen. 'Failed, failed.' She could feel the lines in her face, stiff, beside the mouth, between the eyes. 'You can water a stone,' she said, 'but it won't grow.'

'You have to start when they're young and tender,' Ged said. 'Like me.'

This time she couldn't laugh.

They came back to the house from the day's work and saw a man talking with Spark at the front gate.

'That's the fellow from Re Albi, isn't it?' said Ged, whose eyes were very good.

'Come along, Therru,' Tenar said, for the child had stopped short. 'What fellow?' She was rather nearsighted, and squinted across the yard. 'Oh, it's what's his name, the sheep-dealer. Townsend. What's he back here for, the carrion crow!'

Her mood all day had been fierce, and Ged and Therru wisely said nothing.

She went to the men at the gate.

'Did you come about the ewe lambs, Townsend? You're a year late; but there's some of this year's yet in the fold.'

'So the master's been telling me,' said Townsend.

'Has he,' said Tenar.

Spark's face went darker than ever at her tone.

'I won't interrupt you and the master, then,' said she, and was turning away when Townsend spoke: 'I've got a message for you, Goha.'

'Third time's the charm.'

'The old witch, you know, old Moss, she's in a bad way. She said, since I was coming down to Middle Valley, she said, "Tell Mistress Goha I'd like to see her before I die, if there's a chance of her coming."'

Crow, carrion crow, Tenar thought, looking with hatred at the bearer of bad news.

'She's ill?'

'Sick to death,' Townsend said, with a kind of smirk that might be intended for sympathy. 'Took sick in the winter, and she's failing fast, and so she said to tell you she wants bad to see you, before she dies.'

'Thank you for bringing the message,' Tenar said soberly, and turned to go to the house. Townsend went on with Spark to the sheepfolds.

As they prepared dinner, Tenar said to Ged and Therru, 'I must go.'

'Of course,' Ged said. 'The three of us, if you like.'

'Would you?' For the first time that day her face lightened, the storm cloud lifted. 'Oh,' she said, 'that's – that's good – I didn't want to ask, I thought maybe – Therru, would you like to go back to the little house, Ogion's house, for a while?'

Therru stood still to think. 'I could see my peach tree,' she said.

'Yes, and Heather – and Sippy – and Moss – poor Moss! Oh, I have longed, I have longed to go back up there, but it didn't seem right. There was the farm to run – and all –'

It seemed to her that there was some other reason she had not gone back, had not let herself think of going back, had not even known till now that she yearned to go; but whatever the reason was it slipped away like a shadow, a word forgotten. 'Has anyone looked after Moss, I wonder, did anyone send for a healer. She's the only healer on the Overfell, but there's people down in Gont Port who could help her, surely. Oh, poor Moss! I want to go – It's too late, but tomorrow, tomorrow early. And the master can make his own breakfast!'

'He'll learn,' said Ged.

'No, he won't. He'll find some fool woman to do it for him. Ah!' She looked around the kitchen, her face bright and fierce. 'I have to leave her the twenty years I've scoured that table. I hope she appreciates it!'

Spark brought Townsend in for supper, but the sheep-dealer would not stay the night, though he was of course offered a bed in common hospitality. It would have been one of their beds, and Tenar did not like the thought. She was glad to see him go off to his hosts in the village in the blue twilight of the spring evening.

'We'll be off to Re Albi first thing tomorrow, son,' she said to Spark. 'Hawk and Therru and I.'

He looked a little frightened.

'Just go off like that?'

'So you went; so you came,' said his mother. 'Now look here, Spark: this is your father's money-box. There's seven ivory pieces in it, and those credit counters from old Bridgeman, but he'll never pay, he hasn't got anything to pay with. These four Andradean pieces Flint got from selling sheepskins to the ship's outfitter in Valmouth four years running, back when you were a boy. These three Havnorian ones are what Tholy paid us for the High Creek farm. I had your father buy that farm, and I helped him clear it and sell it. I'll take those three pieces, for I've earned them. The rest, and the farm, is yours. You're the master.'

The tall, thin young man stood there with his gaze on the money-box.

'Take it all. I don't want it,' he said in a low voice.

'I don't need it. But I thank you, my son. Keep the four pieces. When you marry, call them my gift to your wife.'

She put the box away in the place behind the big plate on the top shelf of the dresser, where Flint had always kept it. 'Therru, get your things ready now, because we'll go very early.'

'When are you coming back?' Spark asked, and the tone of his voice made Tenar think of the restless, frail child he had been. But she said only, 'I don't know, my dear. If you need me, I'll come.'

She busied herself getting out their travel shoes and packs. 'Spark,' she said, 'you can do something for me.'

He had sat down in the hearthseat, looking uncertain and morose. 'What?'

'Go down to Valmouth, soon, and see your sister. And tell her that I've gone back to the Overfell. Tell her, if she wants me, just send word.'

He nodded. He watched Ged, who had already packed his few belongings with the neatness and dispatch of one who had travelled much, and was now putting up the dishes to leave the kitchen in good order. That done, he sat down opposite Spark to run a new cord through the eyelets of his pack to close it at the top.

'There's a knot they use for that,' Spark said. 'Sailor's knot.'

Ged silently handed the pack across the hearth, and watched as Spark silently demonstrated the knot.

'Slips up, see,' he said, and Ged nodded.

They left the farm in the dark and cold of the morning. Sunlight comes late to the western side of Gont Mountain, and only walking kept them warm till at last the sun got round the great mass of the south peak and shone on their backs.

Therru was twice the walker she had been the summer before, but it was still a two days' journey for them. Along in the afternoon, Tenar asked, 'Shall we try to get on to Oak Springs today? There's a sort of inn. We had a cup of milk there, remember, Therru?'

Ged was looking up the mountainside with a faraway expression. 'There's a place I know . . .'

'Fine,' said Tenar.

A little before they came to the high corner of the road from which Gont Port could first be seen, Ged turned aside from the road into the forest that covered the steep slopes above it. The westering sun sent slating red-gold rays into the darkness between the trunks and under the branches. They climbed half a mile or so, on no path Tenar could see, and came out on a little step or shelf of the mountainside, a meadow sheltered from the wind by the cliffs behind it and the trees about it. From there one could see the heights of the mountain to the north, and between the tops of great firs there was one clear view of the western sea. It was entirely silent there except when the wind breathed in the firs. One mountain lark sang long and sweet, away up in the sunlight, before dropping to her nest in the untrodden grass.

The three of them ate their bread and cheese. They watched darkness rise up the mountain from the sea. They made their bed of cloaks and slept, Therru next to Tenar next to Ged. In the deep night Tenar woke. An owl was calling nearby, a sweet repeated note like a bell, and far off up the mountain its mate replied like the ghost of a bell. Tenar thought, 'I'll watch the stars set in the sea,' but she fell asleep again at once in peace of heart.

She woke in the grey morning to see Ged sitting up beside her, his cloak pulled round his shoulders, looking out through the gap westward. His dark face was quite still, full of silence, as she had seen it once long ago on the beach of Atuan. His eyes were not downcast, as then; he looked into the illimitable west. Looking with him she saw the day coming, the glory of rose and gold reflected clear across the sky.

He turned to her, and she said to him, 'I have loved you since I first saw you.'

'Life-giver,' he said, and leaned forward, kissing her breast and mouth. She held him a moment. They got up and waked Therru, and went on their way; but as they entered the trees Tenar looked back once at the little meadow as if charging it to keep faith with her happiness there.

The first day of the journey their goal had been journeying. This day they would come to Re Albi. So Tenar's mind was much on Aunty Moss, wondering what had befallen her and whether she was indeed dying. But as the day and the way went on, her mind would not hold to the thought of Moss, or any thought. She was tired. She did not like walking this way again to death. They passed Oak Springs, and went down into the gorge, and started up again. By the last long uphill stretch to the Overfell, her legs were hard to lift, and her mind was stupid and confused, fastening upon one word or image until it became meaningless – the dish-cupboard in Ogion's house, or the words *bone dolphin*, which came into her head from seeing Therru's grass bag of toys, and repeated themselves endlessly.

Ged strode along at his easy traveller's gait, and Therru trudged right beside him, the same Therru who had worn out on this long climb less than a year ago, and had to be carried. But that had been after a longer day of walking. And the child had still been recovering from her punishment.

She was getting old, too old to walk so far so fast. It was so hard going uphill. An old woman should stay home by her fireside. The bone dolphin, the bone dolphin. Bone, bound, the binding spell. The bone man and the bone animal. There they went ahead. They were waiting for her. She was slow. She was tired. She toiled on up the last stretch of the hill and came up to them where the road came out on the level of the Overfell. To the left were the roofs of Re Albi slanting down towards the cliff's edge. To the right the road went up to the manor house. 'This way,' Tenar said.

'No,' the child said, pointing left, to the village.

'This way,' Tenar repeated, and set off on the right-hand way. Ged came with her.

They walked between the walnut orchards and the fields of grass. It was a warm late afternoon of early summer. Birds sang in the orchard trees near and far. He came walking down the road from the great house towards them, the one whose name she could not remember.

'Welcome!' he said, and stopped, smiling at them.

They stopped.

'What great personages have come to honour the house of the Lord of Re Albi,' he said. Tuaho, that was not his name. The bone dolphin, the bone animal, the bone child.

'My Lord Archmage!' He bowed low, and Ged bowed to him.

'And my Lady Tenar of Atuan!' He bowed even lower to her, and she got down on her knees in the road. Her head sank down, till she put her hands in the dirt and crouched until her mouth too was on the dirt of the road.

'Now crawl,' he said, and she began to crawl towards him.

'Stop,' he said, and she stopped.

'Can you talk?' he asked. She said nothing, having no words that would come to her mouth, but Ged replied in his usual quiet voice, 'Yes.'

'Where's the monster?'

'I don't know.'

'I thought the witch would bring her familiar with her. But she brought you instead. The Lord Archmage Sparrow-hawk. What a splendid substitute! All I can do to witches and monsters is cleanse the world of them. But to you, who used at one time to be a man, I can talk; you are capable of rational speech, at least. And capable of understanding punishment. You thought you were safe, I suppose, with your king on the throne, and my master, our master, destroyed. You thought you'd have your will, and destroyed the promise of eternal life, didn't you?'

'No,' said Ged's voice.

She could not see them. She could see only the dirt of the road, and taste it in her mouth. She heard Ged speak. He said, 'In dying is life.'

'Quack, quack, quote the Songs, Master of Roke – schoolmaster! What a funny sight to see, the great arch-mage all got up like a goatherd, and not an ounce of magic in him – not a word of power. Can you say a spell, archmage? Just a little spell – just a tiny charm of illusion? No? Not a word? My master defeated you. Now do you know it? You did not conquer him. His power lives! I might keep you alive here awhile, to see that power – my power. To see the old man I keep from death – and I might use your life for that if I need it – and to see your meddling king make a fool of himself, with his mincing lords and stupid wizards, looking for a woman! A woman to rule us! But the rule is here, the mastery is here, here, in this house. All this year I've been gathering others to me, men who know the true power. From Roke, some of them, from right under the noses of the schoolmasters. And from Havnor, from under the nose of that so-called Son of

Morred, who wants a woman to rule him, your king who thinks he's so safe he can go by his true name. Do you know my name, archmage? Do you remember me, four years ago, when you were the great Master of Masters and I was a lowly student at Roke?'

'You were called Aspen,' said the patient voice.

'And my true name?'

'I don't know your true name.'

'What? You don't know it? Can't you find it? Don't mages know all names?'

'I'm not a mage.'

'Oh, say it again.'

'I'm not a mage.'

'I like to hear you say it. Say it again.'

'I'm not a mage.'

'But I am!'

'Yes.'

'Say it!'

'You are a mage.'

'Ah! This is better than I hoped! I fished for the eel and caught the whale! Come on, then, come meet my friends. You can walk. She can crawl.'

So they went up the road to the manor house of the Lord of Re Albi and went in, Tenar on hands and knees on the road, and on the marble steps up to the door, and on the marble pavements of the halls and rooms.

Inside the house it was dark. With the darkness came a darkness into Tenar's mind, so that she understood less and less of what was said. Only some words and voices came to her clearly. What Ged said she understood, and when he spoke she thought of his name, and clung to it in her mind. But he spoke very seldom, and only to answer the one whose name was not Tuaho. That one spoke to her now and then, calling her Bitch. 'This is my new pet,' he said to other men, several of them that were there in the darkness where candles made shadows. 'See how well trained she is? Roll over, Bitch!' She rolled over, and the men laughed.

'She had a whelp,' he said, 'that I planned to finish punishing, since it was left half-burned. But she brought me a bird she'd caught instead, a sparrowhawk. Tomorrow we'll teach it to fly.'

Other voices said words, but she did not understand words any more.

Something was fastened around her neck and she was made to crawl up more stairs and into a room that smelled of urine and rotting meat and sweet flowers. Voices spoke. A cold hand like a stone struck her head feebly while something laughed, 'Eh, eh, eh,' like an old door creaking back and forth. Then she was kicked and made to crawl down halls. She could not crawl fast enough, and she was kicked in the breasts and in the mouth. Then there was a door that crashed, and silence, and the dark. She heard somebody crying and thought it was the child, her child. She wanted the child not to cry. At last it stopped.

14. *Tehanu*

The child turned left and went some way before she looked back, letting the blossoming hedgerow hide her.

The one called Aspen, whose name was Erisen, and whom she saw as a forked and writhing darkness, had bound her mother and father, with a thong through her tongue and a thong through his heart, and was leading them up towards the place where he hid. The smell of the place was sickening to her, but she followed a little way to see what he did. He led them in and shut the door behind them. It was a stone door. She could not enter there.

She needed to fly, but she could not fly; she was not one of the winged ones.

She ran as fast as she could across the fields, past Aunty Moss's house, past Ogion's house and the goats' house, on to the path along the cliff and to the edge of the cliff, where she was not to go because she could see it only with one eye. She was careful. She looked carefully with that eye. She stood on the edge. The water was far below, and the sun was setting far away. She looked into the west with the other eye, and called with the other voice the name she had heard in her mother's dream.

She did not wait for an answer, but turned round again and went back – first past Ogion's house to see if her peach tree had grown. The old tree stood bearing many small, green peaches, but there was no sign of the seedling. The goats had eaten it. Or it had died because she had not watered it. She stood a little while looking at the ground there, then drew a long breath and went on back across the field to Aunty Moss's house.

Chickens going to roost squawked and fluttered, protesting her entrance. The little hut was dark and very full of smells. 'Aunty Moss?' she said, in the voice she had for these people.

'Who's there?'

The old woman was in her bed, hiding. She was frightened, and tried to make stone around her to keep everyone away, but it didn't work, she was not strong enough.

'Who is it? Who's there? Oh dearie – oh dearie child, my little burned one, my pretty, what are you doing here? Where's she, where's she, your mother, oh, is she here? Did she come? Don't come in, don't come in, dearie, there's a curse on me, he cursed the old woman, don't come near me! Don't come near!'

She wept. The child put out her hand and touched her. 'You're cold,' she said.

'You're like fire, child, your hand burns me. Oh, don't look at me! He made my flesh rot, and shrivel, and rot again, but he won't let me die – he said I'd bring you here. I tried to die, I tried, but he held me, he held me living against my will, he won't let me die, oh, let me die!'

'You shouldn't die,' the child said, frowning.

'Child,' the old woman whispered, 'dearie – call me by my name.'

'Hatha,' the child said.

'Ah, I knew . . . Set me free, dearie!'

'I have to wait,' the child said. 'Till they come.'

The witch lay easier, breathing without pain. 'Till who come, dearie?' she whispered.

'My people.'

The witch's big, cold hand lay like a bundle of sticks in hers. She held it firmly. It was as dark now outside the hut as inside it. Hatha, who was called Moss, slept; and presently the child, sitting on the floor beside her cot, with a hen perched nearby, slept also.

Men came when the light came. He said, 'Up, Bitch!

Up!' She got to her hands and knees. He laughed, saying, 'All the way up! You're a clever bitch, you can walk on your hind legs, can't you? That's it. Pretend to be human! We have a way to go now. Come!' The strap was still around her neck and he jerked it. She followed him.

'Here, you lead her,' he said, and now it was that one, the one she loved, but she did not know his name any more, who held the strap.

They all came out of the dark place. Stone yawned to let them pass and ground together behind them.

He was always close beside her and the one who held the strap. Others came behind, three or four men.

The fields were grey with dew. The mountain was dark against a pale sky. Birds were beginning to sing in the orchards and hedgerows, louder and louder.

They came to the edge of the world and walked along it for a while until they came to where the ground was only rock and the edge was very narrow. There was a line in the rock, and she looked at that.

'He can push her,' he said. 'And then the hawk can fly, all by himself.'

He unfastened the strap from around her neck.

'Go stand at the edge,' he said. She followed the mark in the stone out to the edge. The sea was below her, nothing else. The air was out beyond her.

'Now, Sparrowhawk will give her a push,' he said. 'But first, maybe she wants to say something. She has so much to say. Women always do. Isn't there anything you'd like to say to us, Lady Tenar?'

She could not speak, but she pointed to the sky above the sea.

'Albatross,' he said.

She laughed aloud.

In the gulfs of light, from the doorway of the sky, the dragon flew, fire trailing behind the coiling, mailed body. Tenar spoke then.

'Kalessin!' she cried, and then turned, seizing Ged's arm, pulling him down to the rock, as the roar of fire went over them, the rattle of mail and the hiss of wind in upraised wings, the clash of the talons like scytheblades on the rock.

The wind blew from the sea. A tiny thistle growing in a cleft in the rock near her hand nodded and nodded in the wind from the sea.

Ged was beside her. They were crouched side by side, the sea behind them and the dragon before them.

It looked at them sidelong from one long, yellow eye.

Ged spoke in a hoarse, shaking voice, in the dragon's language. Tenar understood the words which were only, 'Our thanks, Eldest.'

Looking at Tenar, Kalessin spoke in the huge voice like a broom of metal dragged across a gong: '*Aro Tehanu?*'

'The child,' Tenar said – 'Therru!' She got to her feet to run, to seek her child. She saw her coming along the ledge of rock between the mountain and the sea, towards the dragon.

'Don't run, Therru!' she cried, but the child had seen her and was running, running straight to her. They clung to each other.

The dragon turned its enormous, rust-dark head to watch them with both eyes. The nostril pits, big as kettles, were bright with fire, and wisps of smoke curled from them. The heat of the dragon's body beat through the cold sea wind.

'Tehanu,' the dragon said.

The child turned to look at it.

'Kalessin,' she said.

Then Ged, who had remained kneeling, stood up, though shakily, catching Tenar's arm to steady himself. He laughed. 'Now I know who called thee, Eldest!' he said.

'I did,' the child said. 'I did not know what else to do, Segoy.'

688

She still looked at the dragon, and she spoke in the language of the dragons, the words of the Making.

'It was well, child,' the dragon said. 'I have sought thee long.'

'Shall we go there now?' the child asked. 'Where the others are, on the other wind?'

'Would you leave these?'

'No,' said the child. 'Can they not come?'

'They cannot come. Their life is here.'

'I will stay with them,' she said, with a little catch of breath.

Kalessin turned aside to give her that immense furnace-blast of laughter or contempt or delight or anger – 'Hah!' Then, looking again at the child, 'It is well. Thou hast work to do here.'

'I know,' the child said.

'I will come back for thee,' Kalessin said, 'in time.' And to Ged and Tenar, 'I give you my child, as you will give me yours.'

'In time,' Tenar said.

Kalessin's great head bowed very slightly, and the long sword-toothed mouth curled up at the corner.

Ged and Tenar drew aside with Therru as the dragon turned, dragging its armour across the ledge, placing its taloned feet carefully, gathering its black haunches like a cat, till it sprang aloft. The vaned wings shot up crimson in the new light, the spurred tail rang hissing on the rock, and it flew, it was gone – a gull, a swallow, a thought.

Where it had been lay scorched rags of cloth and leather, and other things.

'Come away,' Ged said.

But the woman and the child stood and looked at those things.

'They are bone people,' Therru said. She turned away then and set off. She went ahead of the man and woman along the narrow path.

'Her native tongue,' Ged said. 'Her mother tongue.'

'Tehanu,' said Tenar. 'Her name is Tehanu.'

'She has been given it by the giver of names.'

'She has been Tehanu since the beginning. Always, she has been Tehanu.'

'Come on!' the child said, looking back at them. 'Aunty Moss is sick.'

They were able to move Moss out into the light and air, to wash her sores, and to burn the foul linens of her bed, while Therru brought clean bedding from Ogion's house. She also brought Heather the goatgirl back with her. With Heather's help they got the old woman comfortable in her bed, with her chickens; and Heather promised to come back with something for them to eat.

'Someone must go down to Gont Port,' Ged said, 'for the wizard there. To look after Moss; she can be healed. And to go to the manor house. The old man will die now. The grandson might live, if the house is made clean . . .' He had sat down on the doorstep of Moss's house. He leaned his head back against the doorjamb, in the sunlight, and closed his eyes. 'Why do we do what we do?' he said.

Tenar was washing her face and hands and arms in a basin of clear water she had drawn from the pump. She looked round when she was done. Utterly spent, Ged had fallen asleep, his face a little upturned to the morning light. She sat down beside him on the doorstep and laid her head against his shoulder. Are we spared? she thought. How is it we are spared?

She looked down at Ged's hand, relaxed and open on the earthen step. She thought of the thistle that nodded in the wind and of the taloned foot of the dragon with its scales of red and gold. She was half-asleep when the child sat down beside her.

'Tehanu,' she murmured.

'The little tree died,' the child said.

After a while Tenar's weary, sleepy mind understood, and woke up enough to make a reply. 'Are there peaches on the old tree?'

They spoke low, not to waken the sleeping man.

'Only little green ones.'

'They'll ripen, after the Long Dance. Soon now.'

'Can we plant one?'

'More than one, if you like. Is the house all right?'

'It's empty.'

'Shall we live there?' She roused a little more, and put her arm around the child. 'I have money,' she said, 'enough to buy a herd of goats, and Turby's winter-pasture, if it's still for sale. Ged knows where to take them up the mountain, summers . . . I wonder if the wool we combed is still there?' So saying, she thought, We left the books, Ogion's books! On the mantel at Oak Farm – for Spark, poor boy, he can't read a word of them!

But it did not seem to matter. There were new things to be learned, no doubt. And she could send somebody for the books, if Ged wanted them. And for her spinning wheel. Or she could go down herself, come autumn, and see her son, and visit with Lark, and stay a while with Apple. They would have to replant Ogion's garden right away if they wanted any vegetables of their own this summer. She thought of the rows of beans and the scent of the bean flowers. She thought of the small window that looked west. 'I think we can live there,' she said.

Visit Penguin on the Internet
and browse at your leisure

- ◆ preview sample extracts of our forthcoming books
- ◆ read about your favourite authors
- ◆ investigate over 10,000 titles
- ◆ enter one of our literary quizzes
- ◆ win some fantastic prizes in our competitions
- ◆ e-mail us with your comments and book reviews
- ◆ instantly order any Penguin book

and masses more!

'To be recommended without reservation ... a rich and rewarding on-line experience' – Internet Magazine

www.penguin.co.uk

READ MORE IN PENGUIN

In every corner of the world, on every subject under the sun, Penguin represents quality and variety – the very best in publishing today.

For complete information about books available from Penguin – including Puffins, Penguin Classics and Arkana – and how to order them, write to us at the appropriate address below. Please note that for copyright reasons the selection of books varies from country to country.

In the United Kingdom: Please write to *Dept. EP, Penguin Books Ltd, Bath Road, Harmondsworth, West Drayton, Middlesex UB7 0DA*

In the United States: Please write to *Consumer Sales, Penguin USA, P.O. Box 999, Dept. 17109, Bergenfield, New Jersey 07621-0120.* VISA and MasterCard holders call 1-800-253-6476 to order Penguin titles

In Canada: Please write to *Penguin Books Canada Ltd, 10 Alcorn Avenue, Suite 300, Toronto, Ontario M4V 3B2*

In Australia: Please write to *Penguin Books Australia Ltd, P.O. Box 257, Ringwood, Victoria 3134*

In New Zealand: Please write to *Penguin Books (NZ) Ltd, Private Bag 102902, North Shore Mail Centre, Auckland 10*

In India: Please write to *Penguin Books India Pvt Ltd, 706 Eros Apartments, 56 Nehru Place, New Delhi 110 019*

In the Netherlands: Please write to *Penguin Books Netherlands bv, Postbus 3507, NL-1001 AH Amsterdam*

In Germany: Please write to *Penguin Books Deutschland GmbH, Metzlerstrasse 26, 60594 Frankfurt am Main*

In Spain: Please write to *Penguin Books S. A., Bravo Murillo 19, 1° B, 28015 Madrid*

In Italy: Please write to *Penguin Italia s.r.l., Via Felice Casati 20, I–20124 Milano*

In France: Please write to *Penguin France S. A., 17 rue Lejeune, F–31000 Toulouse*

In Japan: Please write to *Penguin Books Japan, Ishikiribashi Building, 2–5–4, Suido, Bunkyo-ku, Tokyo 112*

In South Africa: Please write to *Longman Penguin Southern Africa (Pty) Ltd, Private Bag X08, Bertsham 2013*

PENGUIN AUDIOBOOKS

A Quality of Writing That Speaks for Itself

Penguin Books has always led the field in quality publishing. Now you can listen at leisure to your favourite books, read to you by familiar voices from radio, stage and screen. Penguin Audiobooks are produced to an excellent standard, and abridgements are always faithful to the original texts. From thrillers to classic literature, biography to humour, with a wealth of titles in between, Penguin Audiobooks offer you quality, entertainment and the chance to rediscover the pleasure of listening.

You can order Penguin Audiobooks through Penguin Direct by telephoning (0181) 899 4036. The lines are open 24 hours every day. Ask for Penguin Direct, quoting your credit card details.

A selection of Penguin Audiobooks, published or forthcoming:

Sense and Sensibility by Jane Austen, read by Joanna David

Cleared for Take-Off by Dirk Bogarde, read by the author

A Period of Adjustment by Dirk Bogarde, read by the author

A Short Walk from Harrods by Dirk Bogarde, read by the author

A Good Man in Africa by William Boyd, read by Timothy Spall

The Road to Wellville by T. Coraghessan Boyle, read by the author

Jane Eyre by Charlotte Brontë, read by Juliet Stevenson

Wuthering Heights by Emily Brontë, read by Juliet Stevenson

The Secret Garden by Frances Hodgson Burnett, read by Helena Bonham Carter

Oscar and Lucinda by Peter Carey, read by John Turnbull

Heart of Darkness by Joseph Conrad, read by David Threlfall

The Winter King by Bernard Cornwell, read by Tim Pigott-Smith

The Naked Civil Servant by Quentin Crisp, read by the author

Great Expectations by Charles Dickens, read by Hugh Laurie

Middlemarch by George Eliot, read by Harriet Walter

Zlata's Diary by Zlata Filipović, read by Dorota Puzio

To the Hilt by Dick Francis, read by Martin Jarvis

The Vulture Fund by Stephen Frey, read by Colin Stinton

PENGUIN AUDIOBOOKS

The Prophet by Kahlil Gibran, read by Renu Setna

Virtual Light by William Gibson, read by Peter Weller

My Name Escapes Me by Alec Guinness, read by the author

Thunderpoint by Jack Higgins, read by Roger Moore

The Iliad by Homer, read by Derek Jacobi

More Please by Barry Humphries, read by the author

Goodbye to Berlin by Christopher Isherwood, read by Alan Cumming

One Flew over the Cuckoo's Nest by Ken Kesey, read by the author

Nightmares and Dreamscapes by Stephen King, read by Whoopi Goldberg, Rob Lowe, Stephen King et al.

Therapy by David Lodge, read by Warren Clarke

An Experiment in Love by Hilary Mantel, read by Billie Whitelaw

Rebecca by Daphne du Maurier, read by Joanna David

Hotel Pastis by Peter Mayle, read by Tim Pigott-Smith

How Stella Got Her Groove Back by Terry McMillan, read by the author

And when did you last see your father? by Blake Morrison, read by the author

Murderers and Other Friends by John Mortimer, read by the author

Nineteen Eighty-Four by George Orwell, read by Timothy West

Guardian Angel by Sara Paretsky, read by Jane Kaczmarek

History: The Home Movie by Craig Raine, read by the author

A Peaceful Retirement by Miss Read, read by June Whitfield

Frankenstein by Mary Shelley, read by Richard Pasco

The Devil's Juggler by Murray Smith, read by Kenneth Cranham

Kidnapped by Robert Louis Stevenson, read by Robbie Coltrane

Perfume by Patrick Süskind, read by Sean Barratt

The Secret History by Donna Tartt, read by Robert Sean Leonard

The Pillars of Hercules by Paul Theroux, read by William Hootkins

The Brimstone Wedding by Barbara Vine, read by Jan Francis

READ MORE IN PENGUIN

A CHOICE OF SCIENCE FICTION

The Forest House Marion Zimmer Bradley

Eilan, daughter of the Druids, is destined to serve the Great Goddess as a virgin priestess; Gaius, son of a Roman father and British mother, serves with the legions. Trapped between forbidden love and duty, their hearts and minds are in turmoil as the waning power of Rome and the rising rebellion of the tribes convulse and clash in the bitter struggle for Britain.

Virtual Light William Gibson

'Studded with crackling insights into the relationship between technology, culture and morality, *Virtual Light* doesn't miss its stride for a nanosecond ... the most influential SF visionary of the past decade' – *Time Out*. 'Cyberpunk doesn't come any more stylish than this' – *Sunday Telegraph*

The Penguin Science Fiction Omnibus Edited by Brian Aldiss

An exciting collection of stories from some of the best-known, best-loved science fiction writers: J. G. Ballard, Harry Harrison, Isaac Asimov, Frederik Pohl, Arthur C. Clarke and dozens more ...

Cat's Cradle Kurt Vonnegut

Vonnegut's relentlessly deadpan humour makes this novel of global destruction chilling and extraordinarily compelling. 'A major novelist and a major novel' – *Sunday Telegraph*

The Chrysalids John Wyndham

A terrifying story of conformity and deformity in a world paralysed by genetic mutation. The narrator of *The Chrysalids* is David, who can communicate with a group of other young people by means of 'thought shapes'. This deviation from a cruelly rigid norm goes unnoticed at first. But sooner or later the secret is bound to be discovered, and the results are violent ... and believable.

READ MORE IN PENGUIN

A CHOICE OF SCIENCE FICTION

The Day of the Triffids John Wyndham

This superbly terrifying novel achieves a razor-edge balance between wry satire and dark tragedy. The story cuts deep into the imagination, leaving the reader shaken by its violent insights and intuitions.

Flatland Edwin A. Abbott

Humour, satire and logic combine in this brilliantly entertaining classic – a capricious mathematical fantasy of life in a sunless, shadowless, two-dimensional country. The narrator is A. Square, whose flat, middle-class life is suddenly given an exciting new shape by his encounter with a sphere, who introduces him to the joys and sorrows of the third dimension.

The Children of Men P. D. James

The year is 2021. For twenty-five years no child has been born. Nor will there be any more children, for infertility has spread like a plague and the human race faces extinction. Under the despotic rule of Xan Lyppiatt, the Warden of England, the young are violent and the old despairing. Only a tiny handful of dissenters can hold out . . .

Son of Soup Rob Grant and Doug Naylor
Second Serving of the Least Worst Scripts

In the beginning there was *Primordial Soup* – a collection of some of the least worst scripts from *Red Dwarf*. Then, the unspeakable happened. It spawned a sequel. *Son of Soup* contains a chunky selection of amusing jokes and drunken ramblings, candid photographs and characters with questionable personal habits.

Body of Glass Marge Piercy

'I have not read a more disturbing or moving novel about artificial intelligence since Mary Shelley's *Frankenstein* . . . it elevates its author to the pantheon of *haute* SF alongside Doris Lessing and Ursula Le Guin' – *Financial Times*

READ MORE IN PENGUIN

A CHOICE OF FICTION

No Night is Too Long Barbara Vine

Tim Cornish, a creative-writing student, sits composing a confession: an admission of a crime committed two years ago that has yet to be discovered. 'A dark, watery masterpiece ... suffused with sexuality, which explores with hypnotic effect the psychological path between passion and murder' – *The Times*

Peerless Flats Esther Freud

Lisa has high hopes for her first year in London. She is sixteen and ambitious to become more like her sister Ruby. For Ruby has cropped hair, a past and a rockabilly boyfriend whose father is in prison. 'Freud sounds out as a clear, attractive voice in the literary hubbub' – *Observer*

One of the Family Monica Dickens

At 72 Chepstow Villas lives the Morley family: Leonard, the Assistant Manager of Whiteley's, his gentle wife Gwen, 'new woman' daughter Madge and son Dicky. Into their comfortable Edwardian world comes a sinister threat of murder and a charismatic stranger who will change their lives for ever. 'It is the contrasts that Dickens depicts so rivetingly ... she captures vividly the gradual blurring of social divisions during the last days of the Empire' – *Daily Mail*

Original Sin P. D. James

The literary world is shaken when a murder takes place at the Peverell Press, an old-established publishing house located in a dramatic mock-Venetian palace on the Thames. 'Superbly plotted ... James is interested in the soul, not just in the mind, of a killer' – *Daily Telegraph*

In Cold Domain Anne Fine

'A streamlined, ruthlessly stripped-down psychological family romance with enough plot twists and character revelations to fuel a book three times as long, as wicked and funny as anything Fay Weldon has written. Anne Fine is brilliant' – *Time Out*

READ MORE IN PENGUIN

A CHOICE OF FICTION

Mothers' Boys Margaret Forster

'Margaret Forster has a remarkable gift for taking huge social issues and welding them into minutely observed human dramas that are perfect portraits of the way we live now . . . The story grips and the heart bleeds for these good mothers who are, like all mothers, never good enough' – *Daily Mail*

Cleopatra's Sister Penelope Lively

'A fluent, funny, ultimately moving romance in which lovers share centre stage with Lively's persuasive meditations on history and fate . . . a book of great charm with a real intellectual resonance at its core' – *The New York Times Book Review*

A Private View Anita Brookner

George Bland had planned to spend his retirement in leisurely travel and modest entertainment with his friend Putnam. When Putnam dies George is left attempting to impose some purpose on the solitary end of his life. 'A beautiful book that one is impelled to read at one sitting and finishes with a deep sense of sadness' – *Evening Standard*

The Constant Mistress Angela Lambert

Laura King is a liberated, intelligent and successful woman. Although she has never married, hers has been an active and emotionally fulfilled life. Suddenly, at the age of forty-four, she learns that she is suffering from a rare liver disease and has only a year or two to live. In typically flamboyant style, Laura invites her ex-lovers to dinner . . .

The Rose Revived Katie Fforde

When May teams up with Sally and Harriet, it is the best day's work she's ever done. Each of them needs money, badly. Which is why they are reduced to working for Quality Cleaners under the watchful eye of 'Slimeball' Slater. When they discover it is *them* being taken to the cleaners, they set up as an independent team – and that is when things really begin to take off.

READ MORE IN PENGUIN

A CHOICE OF FICTION

Felicia's Journey William Trevor
Winner of the 1994 Whitbread Book of the Year Award

Vividly and with heart-aching insight William Trevor traces the desperate plight of a young Irish girl scouring the post-industrial Midlands for her lover. Unable to find Johnny, she is, instead, found by Mr Hilditch, pudgy canteen manager, collecter and befriender of homeless young girls.

The Eye in the Door Pat Barker

'Barker weaves fact and fiction to spellbinding effect, conjuring up the vastness of the First World War through its chilling impact on the minds of the men who endured it ... a startlingly original work of fiction ... it extends the boundaries not only of the anti-war novel, but of fiction generally' – *Sunday Telegraph*

The Heart of It Barry Hines

Cal Rickards, a successful scriptwriter, is forced to return to the Yorkshire mining town of his youth when his father, a leading voice in the 1980s miners' strike, suddenly becomes ill. Gradually, as Cal delves into his family's past and faces unsettling memories, he comes to reassess his own future.

Dr Haggard's Disease Patrick McGrath

'The reader is compellingly drawn into Dr Haggard's life as it begins to unfold through episodic flashbacks ... It is a beautiful story, impressively told, with a restraint and a grasp of technicality that command belief, and a lyricism that gives the description of the love affair the sort of epic quality rarely found these days' – *The Times*

A Place I've Never Been David Leavitt

'Wise, witty and cunningly fuelled by narrative ... another high calibre collection by an unnervingly mature young writer' – *Sunday Times*. 'Leavitt can make a world at a stroke and people it with convincing characters ... humane, touching and beautifully written' – *Observer*

READ MORE IN PENGUIN

A CHOICE OF FICTION

The Ghost Road Pat Barker
Winner of the 1995 Booker Prize

'One of the richest and most rewarding works of fiction of recent times. Intricately plotted, beautifully written, skilfully assembled, tender, horrifying and funny, it lives on in the imagination, like the war it so imaginatively and so intelligently explores' – *The Times Literary Supplement*

None to Accompany Me Nadine Gordimer

In an extraordinary period before the first non-racial elections in South Africa, Vera Stark, a lawyer representing blacks' struggle to reclaim the land, weaves an interpretation of her own past into her participation in the present. 'With great dexterity and force Gordimer combines all these stories – career, colleagues, political struggles, sexual love, identity, family – into a compelling narrative' – *Daily Telegraph*

Of Love and Other Demons Gabriel García Márquez

'García Márquez tells a story of forbidden love, but he demonstrates once again the vigor of his own passion: the daring and irresistible coupling of history and imagination' – *Time*. 'A further marvellous manifestation of the enchantment and the disenchantment that his native Colombia always stirs in García Márquez' – *Sunday Times*

Millroy the Magician Paul Theroux

A magician of baffling talents, a vegetarian and a health fanatic with a mission to change the food habits of America, Millroy has the power to heal, and to hypnotize. 'Fresh and unexpected . . . this very accomplished, confident book is among his best' – *Guardian*

English Music Peter Ackroyd

'Each dream-sequence is a virtuoso performance on Ackroyd's part. In his fiction he has made a speciality of leap-frogging time, so that the past occupies the same plane as the present. Never before, however, has he been so chronologically acrobatic, nor so confident' – *The Times*

READ MORE IN PENGUIN

A CHOICE OF FICTION

Grey Area Will Self

'A demon lover, a model village and office paraphernalia are springboards for Self's bizarre flights of fancy . . . his collection of short stories explores strange worlds which have mutated out of our own – *Financial Times*

A Frolic of His Own William Gaddis

'Everybody is suing somebody in *A Frolic of His Own* . . . Among the suits and counter-suits, judgements and appeals, the central character, Oscar Crease, scion of a distinguished legal family, is even suing himself for personal injury after his aptly named Sosumi car runs over him as he hot-wires the ignition . . . Like all satire this is a very funny but also a very serious book' – *Independent on Sunday*

The Children of Men P. D. James

'As taut, terrifying and ultimately convincing as anything in the dystopian genre. It is at once a piercing satire on our cosseted, faithless and trivially self-indulgent society and a most tender love story' – *Daily Mail*

The Only Problem Muriel Spark

Harvey Gotham had abandoned his beautiful wife Effie on the *autostrada* in Italy. Now, nearly a year later, ensconced in France where he is writing a monograph on the Book of Job, his solitude is interrupted by Effie's sister. Suddenly Harvey finds himself longing for the unpredictable pleasure's of Effie's company. But she has other ideas. 'One of this century's finest creators of the comic-metaphysical entertainment' – *The New York Times*

Small g: a Summer Idyll Patricia Highsmith

At the 'small g', a Zurich bar known for its not exclusively gay clientele, the lives of a small community are played out one summer. 'From the first page it is recognisably authentic Highsmith. Perhaps approaching her lesbian novel *Carol* in tenderness and theme, it has a serenity rarely found in Highsmith's world' – *Guardian*